Whispers of the Heart

by

Jann Rowland

One Good Sonnet Publishing

By Jann Rowland
Published by One Good Sonnet Publishing:

PRIDE AND PREJUDICE VARIATIONS

Acting on Faith
A Life from the Ashes (Sequel to *Acting on Faith*)
Open Your Eyes
Implacable Resentment
An Unlikely Friendship
Bound by Love
Cassandra
Obsession
Shadows Over Longbourn
The Mistress of Longbourn
My Brother's Keeper
Coincidence
The Angel of Longbourn
Chaos Comes to Kent
In the Wilds of Derbyshire
The Companion
Out of Obscurity
What Comes Between Cousins
A Tale of Two Courtships
Murder at Netherfield
Whispers of the Heart

Co-Authored with Lelia Eye

WAITING FOR AN ECHO

Waiting for an Echo Volume One: Words in the Darkness
Waiting for an Echo Volume Two: Echoes at Dawn
Waiting for an Echo Two Volume Set

A Summer in Brighton
A Bevy of Suitors
Love and Laughter: A Pride and Prejudice Short Stories Anthology

WHISPERS OF THE HEART

Copyright © 2018 Jann Rowland

Cover Design by Jann Rowland

Published by One Good Sonnet Publishing

ISBN: 1987929950
ISBN-13: 9781987929959

To my family who have, as always, shown
their unconditional love and encouragement.

PROLOGUE

*N*ewcomers, arriving in a neighborhood which usually sees little change, tend to prompt no little excitement. And so it was in the village of Meryton in Hertfordshire. The grand manor of Netherfield, largest in the district by far, had stood empty for many years, and the word that a young man of fortune had contracted to lease it sent gossip flying through the neighborhood. Nowhere, however, was the talk so outlandish as that which took place at the neighboring estate of Longbourn.

"It is said that our new neighbor is a gentleman by the name of Mr. Bingley," said Lydia, the youngest and silliest of five sisters. "I have also had it from Penelope Long, who has had it from Mrs. Long, who heard from the butcher, that he will bring with him a large party. It could be as many as ten gentlemen!"

"That trail of rumor is far too long," said Elizabeth, the second eldest. "I suspect the truth of the matter has been lost in the transfer from mouth to mouth."

"Well, I am certain the Bennets shall welcome Mr. Bingley," said Mrs. Bennet. "I hope he takes a liking to one of you, though I suspect Jane will be his favorite."

"And what if the gentleman is married?" asked Mr. Bennet. "He could hardly pay his addresses to our Jane if he is already attached."

Mrs. Bennet appeared worried at the suggestion. Though Elizabeth loved her mother—loved all her family—she was confronted by the daily embarrassment of being the daughter of a woman who was not raised a gentlewoman and possessed little knowledge of the social graces. Should the Netherfield party turn out to be a group of married gentlemen with their wives, she had no doubt her mother would make a scene, lamenting the cruel nature of fate and the certainty that they were destined for the hedgerows. Such had been her laments ever since Elizabeth could remember, as an entail on the estate meant that a distant cousin would inherit, leaving her with no home.

"I am sure that *some* of the gentlemen at Netherfield will be unattached," replied Mrs. Bennet after a moment of thought, an airy wave punctuating her words. "We shall simply need to ensure that our Jane is in the best position to take advantage of whatever young man likes her best."

Mr. Bennet caught Elizabeth's eye, and he directed an expressive grin at her, but Elizabeth could only shake her head. She had long known that her mother was eager to marry all her daughters off to whatever man showed the most interest, and it struck her as being much like an auction. Her mother had no care for the feelings and wishes of her daughters—divesting herself of their care and ensuring they were settled in marriage was what was important.

For Elizabeth's part—and that of her elder sister, Jane—she could not but disagree with her mother. As she had daily proof, an unequal marriage could not be agreeable. In fact, Elizabeth thought it akin to a prison from which there was no escape. Mrs. Bennet's self-interest in the matter was also transparent. Should she marry, Elizabeth would be happy to support her mother. But the insistence upon all her daughters marrying whomever was available without thought to temperament, interests, or even love, annoyed Elizabeth. Her mother did not know it, but Elizabeth was determined not to fall in with her schemes. Should she be pushed toward a man she did not love, Elizabeth was ready to refuse any such proposal.

Their talk continued in this fashion, Mrs. Bennet's pronouncements growing ever more outlandish, to the point where Mrs. Bennet might have convinced herself the prince regent himself was in attendance before it was exhausted. And Lydia's own excited comments could only spur her mother to greater heights, not to mention Kitty's dreamier ones. Mary, the middle child, sat and watched them with disapproval, and while Elizabeth might agree with her, she thought

Mary could do with a hefty dose of lightheartedness to go with her overly sober and moral outlook on life.

When the day of the assembly arrived, the Bennet ladies dressed in their finery and descended upon the assembly halls, eager to be introduced to handsome young—single!—gentlemen. The musicians were tuning their instruments when the ladies entered the hall, the discordant sound comforting with the speaking of friends and family and happy times. On a side table, there were bowls of punch and assorted delicacies available for the consumption of the revelers. And the room teemed with people, all eager to do as the Bennet matron had declared—push their female progeny at whatever single young man would pass through the door.

The assembly began with no hint of the Netherfield party's appearance, and when Elizabeth's hand was solicited by her good friend Charlotte Lucas's brother, she willingly stood up with him. For a time, all thoughts of young and eligible gentlemen passed from her mind. She so enjoyed dancing that she completely forgot about any such considerations for her sets with her first two companions.

After her second sets, however, Elizabeth happened to be standing with her mother and elder sister when the noise in the hall suddenly quieted. A quick glance at the doors revealed the presence of a group of people she had never before met. The newcomers had finally graced the neighborhood with their presence.

Elizabeth turned and caught the sight of her friend and beckoned her over. Charlotte came with a will, having long been the best of friends with Elizabeth.

"I dare say you have some knowledge of our new neighbors," said Elizabeth with a wink at her closest friend.

"You know I do, Eliza," said Charlotte.

The two friends laughed together. Charlotte's father, Sir William Lucas, was a jovial and friendly man, whose sense was perhaps a little lacking, but his heart was definitely in the right place. Having been granted a knighthood by the king some years previous, he had used the monies received and purchased a neighboring estate to Longbourn, settling there with his family. As a knight, he had also taken it upon himself to be the town's spokesman, and he could often be found as the unofficial master of ceremonies at these events. He was also excessively attentive to the performance of all his duties, which included visiting all and sundry, and especially those new to the neighborhood.

"Then for heaven's sake, share what you know!" cried Mrs. Bennet.

"I am all anticipation of knowing of these elegant people who have joined us."

Elizabeth and Charlotte shared a look and a minutely shaken head. Charlotte was a young woman of sense, and Elizabeth was excessively fond of her. She was a practical sort of woman, quite different from Elizabeth in essentials, but that practicality often balanced Elizabeth's more romantic outlook. Charlotte was well aware of Mrs. Bennet's character, and she struggled with the same sort of feelings as Elizabeth, as her mother was a bird of the same feather. Fortunately, Charlotte was not averse to sharing what she knew.

"The tallest gentleman there is a Colonel Fitzwilliam," said Charlotte, pointing to a man who was tall and burly, one of the largest men Elizabeth had ever seen. "He is on leave for some months, as I understand, and, furthermore, is said to be the younger son of an earl."

The eyes of all three Bennet ladies widened at such intelligence. But it was Mrs. Bennet who spoke. "Dear me! To have such an august man in our presence! I can scarcely comprehend it."

And you can scarcely comprehend how to behave properly, thought Elizabeth. Though uncharitable, the thought was not without truth.

"The other tall gentleman beside him," continued Charlotte, ignoring Mrs. Bennet's outburst, "is a Mr. Darcy. It is my understanding that he is Colonel Fitzwilliam's cousin."

"He is very handsome," said Jane, and Elizabeth could only agree. She wondered how happy he was to be there, however, for whereas the colonel was watching them all with a smile, Mr. Darcy's countenance was inscrutable. He might as easily have been searching for the most likely lady to partner in a dance as he was to be watching them all with disdain.

"The first couple is a Mr. Hurst and his wife. And by her side is her sister, Miss Bingley."

"Ah, now we come to the infamous Bingleys," said Elizabeth, shooting a laughing smile at her friend. "I do wonder at them, though. Mr. Hurst seems almost bored, and Mrs. Hurst appears ready to drop from ennui."

"I believe Miss Bingley quite considers herself to be above us," added Charlotte.

Elizabeth turned to look at the young woman, and she thought Charlotte might have the right of it. The two ladies were fashionably dressed, though their attire was excessive for a country dance in Elizabeth's estimation. But it was the narrowness of her eyes and the slight rise of her nose in the air which suggested that Miss Bingley might be more than a little supercilious. Her sister by her side was no better, though Elizabeth was less certain of her feelings.

"And what of the final two members of the party?" was Mrs. Bennet's impatient demand.

"Ah yes," said Charlotte, as two others appeared behind their fellow guests, having entered a few moments later. "The gentleman is Mr. Bingley, the man who has leased Netherfield. By his side is his wife, Mrs. Georgiana Bingley. My understanding is that she is the sister of Mr. Darcy."

CHAPTER I

A house party was not Darcy's favorite way to pass the time. Most summers he was tied to Pemberley, though it would be more accurate to say that he was there by choice. At his own estate, Darcy felt the most comfortable, the most at ease. He was a man who was not at all at his best in company, and one such as this was an especial trial on his nerves.

"These people are not objectionable," said his friend, Charles Bingley one day. "Yet your expression suggests you believe we have fallen in with thieves."

Bingley's ability to lighten Darcy's mood was one reason why he had always treasured their friendship. "The company is not so objectionable, Bingley. But they are not all cut from the same cloth. Watson is a good friend, indeed, but I find the attentions of his sister to be fatiguing."

"And yet, she is no Caroline," said Bingley. "You must own that my sister far outstrips her in blatancy and determination. You have withstood my sister most admirably."

"But I have never been trapped in a house with your sister," replied Darcy. "I cannot say she would be any more tolerable under such circumstances."

Bingley laughed. "I suppose I must agree with you there. Then again, should I ever host you, Caroline would likely be my hostess, and in control of the house. At least Miss Watson must give way to her mother."

"I do not believe Mrs. Watson is an enemy to her daughter's designs. In fact, I am certain she is a confederate."

"That may be correct," replied Bingley, a rueful shake of his head indicating his agreement. "I suppose I should thank you, my friend. Your presence frees me from being the object of prey to the misses in attendance."

"I am happy to be of service."

Darcy's reply was dripping with sarcasm, and his friend did not miss that fact. Bingley laughed, as was his wont, and Darcy allowed himself a little levity with his good friend. The cares of an early inheritance of his fortune and the responsibility for a much younger sister weighed down on him, and it felt like he had little joy in his life.

"Now, Darcy," said Bingley, putting his mirth aside and regarding Darcy with a seriousness with which Darcy did not usually expect of his friend, "there seems to me to be something more than simply annoyance over Miss Watson's—or Miss Sandoval's, or Miss Clarke's—blatant interest which is causing your discomfort. You are usually adept at treating them with civility but ignoring their excesses. Is there something particular which is bothering you?"

It was the hazard of having close friends, Darcy thought. When you allowed others to see you in your most private and unguarded times, it must follow that they would know you well enough to understand your moods. There were currently only two such friends in Darcy's circle who could read him so well—Bingley was one, while his cousin, Anthony Fitzwilliam, was the other.

"I am a little . . . disturbed," replied Darcy. At Bingley's questioning glance, Darcy elaborated, saying: "I received a letter from Georgiana."

"A letter from your sister?" asked Bingley, clearly confused. "Why would that be an occasion for disquiet? You usually enjoy receiving her missives."

"So I do," replied Darcy. "But there is . . . something in this one, something . . . elusive. I may simply be reading meaning into her letter that is not there. But it almost seems like she is not telling me something. Or perhaps she wishes to tell me something but is restraining herself."

"You must know your sister well if you can read between the lines to that extent."

"I do," said Darcy. In a fit of nervous energy, he stood and began pacing the small sitting-room in which he and Bingley had sequestered themselves. "It is probable that I am reading meaning into her letter she does not intend. But I find myself worrying. She is . . ."

Darcy swallowed thickly. "She is my only immediate family in the world, as you know, and I am excessively fond of her. I would do anything for her. If there is something wrong, I would wish to protect her from it. But as she is now seventeen, approaching her coming out and becoming a young lady, rather than a girl, I would not wish to appear the overbearing authority figure. I do not wish her to believe I do not trust her."

"I can see that," replied Bingley, regarding Darcy with a thoughtful expression. "But I do not believe a wish to see a beloved sister could be seen as a lack of trust.

"Consider this, my friend," continued Bingley. "We are in East Sussex, no more than a day's journey from Ramsgate. You are not enjoying this house party, and to be frank, I have tired of it. Why do we not join your sister? A change of residence could only benefit us both."

Darcy grinned at his friend, knowing Bingley was completely correct. "Then I shall inform our hosts if you would be so good as to call for the carriage."

A laugh was Bingley's response. "I think we had best inform our hosts and depart on the morrow. Not only will that relieve us from the necessity of finding an inn for the night, but it would be polite to avoid departing within minutes of announcing our intentions."

"Oh, very well," replied Darcy in a tone which suggested longsuffering. As he had intended, Bingley responded with a laugh. Then they left the room to find Watson and inform him of their change of plans.

While Watson himself accepted their change in plans with good cheer and a wish for their safe travels, Miss Watson was not so sanguine. Then again, Watson was familiar with Bingley's impetuosity. Furthermore, a vaguely worded mention of business was enough for him to understand Darcy's need to leave. Miss Watson could only see the escape of the man to whom she meant to attach herself.

"But, Mr. Darcy!" exclaimed she when she discovered their change in plans. "You have only been with us for three weeks. Our invitation was for six, at the very least! We shall become quite dull without your attendance."

Privately, Darcy thought his reticence added to the dullness. "You have my apologies, Miss Watson," said he. "But I find there is a matter of business which has arisen that requires my attention. I thank you and your excellent family for your unstinting hospitality, but I must depart on the morrow. I must also apologize for depriving you of Bingley's absence, for he has chosen to accompany me."

Miss Watson's sharp glance at Bingley was full of disdain and suggested she had little care whether he departed. She continued to plead with him to stay for several moments, her voice gradually descending to whining. Finally, Watson stepped in and curbed her complaints.

"As long as I have known him, Darcy is immovable once his decision has been made. It is fruitless to argue."

Though she subsided, Darcy could easily see that she was not placated. Her injured glances and petulant silences conveyed her annoyance. But Darcy felt that he could easily withstand her sulking, as long as she did not become more demonstrative. In the end, he was quite happy to quit the place the following morning.

"I know not why I even bother," said Bingley after they had been traveling for some few minutes. At Darcy's questioning glance, Bingley elaborated: "This attempt to ascend the heights of society. You know it is Caroline's greatest wish to be looked on with awe, to be a member of the circles you inhabit. For myself, the society of good friends and the love of a good woman is my wish. It is clear to me that among most of those we know, I am tolerated only because of your friendship and not due to any merits I possess."

"It is the way of the world, Bingley," said Darcy. "You are not of any less value as a friend or a man because you were not born to a long line of gentlemen."

"And that is a credit to you, Darcy," said Bingley. "But it has been proven amply to me time and time again that I am considered to be inferior. Miss Watson's incivility was only the latest example."

"The right marriage will ensure your family's acceptance," said Darcy.

"It will. But even should I marry the daughter of a duke I shall still be considered new money. As I said, I wish to have the love of a good woman, one who is gentle, intelligent, and true. I should not care if she is the daughter of a gentleman of the meanest of circumstances, or naught but the daughter of a parson. It is her character which is important."

Darcy could not say his friend was incorrect. While he knew of the duty which beckoned to him, marriage to a woman of society who would increase his wealth and provide him with connections which would further his status, he was loath to enter a society marriage. Darcy by no means thought meanly of all young women of society, but in each to whom he had been introduced, he had found a lack of something he could not quite determine, though some would have been acceptable by every measure on a scale by which most measured success in such matters.

"I cannot say you are wrong, my friend," said Darcy quietly.

They fell silent thereafter, each immersed in his own thoughts. Bingley soon fell asleep, lulled by the rocking of the carriage as they rumbled along the road. Darcy, who had never been able to sleep in a moving conveyance, pulled a book out of his traveling bag and set to reading it. But he was assailed by the thoughts his friend had provoked in him and found himself having read the same page three times, without any recollection of what he had read.

At length, he took to gazing out the window, watching the scenery as it flew by. The Watson estate was located just within the northern border of East Sussex with Kent. Their quickest route lay to the north through Tonbridge, from thence to West Malling, and then straight east to Ramsgate and Margate. It would take them the entire day to travel the distance, and they would only arrive that evening, likely after dinner.

Darcy well knew that if they took the fork toward the northwest, they would go a much shorter distance through Sevenoaks, and could arrive in the vicinity of Westerham and Rosings Park, where his aunt made her home. The journey would take less than half the time than the one to Ramsgate. Moreover, should Lady Catherine discover he had been staying so close to Rosings and had not visited, she would declare her offense in a manner which was destined to annoy. Luckily, Darcy was not in the habit of informing his aunt of his movements, and as he had visited as was his custom in the spring, he had no intention of suffering Lady Catherine again so soon after escaping her.

At length, Bingley awoke from his nap, and Darcy was allowed some respite from the tediousness of the continued clop of the horses' hooves, or from the view which, though fine, soon became monotonous as well. Their discourse, while not concerning matters of much import, was still interesting enough to pass the time. They stopped several times to rest the horses and stretch their legs from being cramped in the carriage. They took a meal in the middle of the day at an inn known to cater to such travelers and were soon on their way yet again.

It was in this manner they passed the time until finally, the carriage rolled into Ramsgate. It was a small, seaside town, situated on the southern end of a small promontory at the mouth of the Thames River. Margate, its opposite, stood at the northern end, at about the eastern edge of the Thames estuary. It was a cozy collection of houses and shops, a popular resort town which catered to the wealthy who could afford to vacation, but who preferred locations which were not so crowded as Brighton or other cities like it.

Initially, when Mrs. Younge, Georgiana's companion, had suggested the holiday, Darcy had been skeptical. But he was soon won over by Georgiana's obvious eagerness for the scheme. She was a young girl in the care of a companion, possessing the same difficulties as Darcy himself possessed in company. She had always been the model charge, never giving them any hint of trouble or rebellion. It had seemed to Darcy that she deserved such a treat as this, and her profuse thanks had been enough to inform him that he had made the correct decision.

When the carriage pulled to a stop in front of the house he had let for her use, Darcy gratefully descended, stretching himself to ease the cramping of the long carriage ride. Even Bingley, who tolerated most discomfort with good humor, appeared happy to have arrived.

"Let us enter, my friend," said Darcy. "Though the housekeeper is not expecting us, we should find warm beds and something for dinner."

"I can hardly wait," said Bingley. "Lead on."

A quick rap on the door soon brought the matronly housekeeper to open it for them. She peered at them for a moment before she started and recognized Darcy.

"Mr. Darcy!" exclaimed she. "We have had no word of your coming."

"I understand, Mrs. Reeves," replied Darcy. "I found that I wished to see my sister and set off with very little thought."

"In that, he behaved much like I would," added Bingley, completely unhelpfully, in Darcy's opinion.

Mrs. Reeves did not seem to know what to make of his comment. Darcy decided it was best to simply move them along and in to where his sister was likely sitting with Mrs. Younge.

"My sister is within?"

"Yes, she is," replied Mrs. Reeves. "She is sitting with Mrs. Younge, along with her gentleman caller."

"Gentleman caller?" echoed Darcy with a frown. "There is someone with them?"

"Yes," replied the housekeeper, oblivious to Darcy's sudden consternation. "The young man has been here often of late. And Miss Darcy seems to like Mr. Wickham's company very well, indeed."

Darcy stiffened at the name of his enemy on the housekeeper's lips, and he heard Bingley's gasp behind him. Finally, Mrs. Reeves seemed to understand that Darcy was not amused, for she peered at him with alarm, though she did not speak.

"He has been coming around frequently, has he? And how long has he been with them this evening?"

"I cannot say, sir," replied Mrs. Reeves. "But it must be above an hour now."

With a nod, Darcy stepped back outside and motioned to his driver and the two footmen who were waiting with him. It was unfortunate Thompson was not here, for Wickham might very well soil himself at the very sight of the burly footman. But he would make do with what he had.

"Follow us inside," Darcy directed the two footmen. "There is a man inside whom I require to be evicted from the premises."

The two men seemed to catch Darcy's mood, for they followed, their countenances a mirror of Darcy's implacable resolve. Once back inside, Darcy motioned to the housekeeper to precede them, and they made their way toward the sitting-room. When they arrived, Darcy caught her attention and motioned her back.

"Please send for tea and see to the disposition of my men."

Mrs. Reeves seemed to be relieved of being excused from the upcoming confrontation, and she fairly scurried away to do his bidding. Darcy made a mental note to inform the owner of the house that his housekeeper was a silly goose. Then, without further ado, he stepped forward and threw the door open, stepping within.

The sight in the room was enough to make Darcy's blood boil with rage. The libertine Wickham was sitting closer to Georgiana than any man ought, and he currently held one of her hands between his own. In an instant of unguarded emotion, Darcy saw the smugness and anticipation on the face of Mrs. Younge. Clearly, Wickham had charmed the woman into allowing this farce.

The countenances of all three turned to shock when confronted by the sight of Darcy. Wickham's jaw fell open, and he stared in sudden fear, while Mrs. Younge responded with utter terror. But it was Georgiana who reacted first to his entrance, rising to her feet and throwing herself into Darcy's arms.

"Oh, Brother!" cried she. "I am so happy that you have come, and at such a propitious moment! I have such news to tell you, for I am engaged to be married!"

The pinched look which came over Wickham's countenance suggested he had hoped to keep the matter secret and make off with her in the night. He glared at her back until Darcy's responding scowl caused him to pale and look away.

"You are?" replied Darcy carefully. "I have heard nothing of such tidings, Georgiana, dearest. In fact, I would wonder why you would wish to give up your freedom in such a manner. You are a young woman not yet out — would you forgo your enjoyment of your first season so easily?"

Clearly, Georgiana had not thought of it in such a manner. She pulled away from him and regarded him askance. Wickham, the lying snake that he was, chose that moment to pull himself from his shock and attempt to salvage the situation.

"When two people are in love as we are, such things become meaningless. Do they not, my dear?"

Georgiana directed a hesitant smile at him. But it was half-hearted at best, for she clearly could sense Darcy's anger. Wickham, however, seemed to think he had the upper hand, for he continued to speak.

"Regardless, I have proposed, and dear Georgiana has accepted. An engagement cannot be broken — you know this, Darcy."

A contemptuous sneer was Darcy's initial response. He glared at Wickham in a manner which was guaranteed to make the scoundrel uneasy. It accomplished its purpose, and it further deepened Georgiana's frown.

"You should still your forked tongue, Wickham," said Darcy at length, "lest it land you in further difficulties. You know Georgiana is underage. No engagement may be solemnized without her guardians' approval. I wonder what Fitzwilliam would think of this situation?"

Wickham paled again, but it appeared he was not willing to surrender. "Her reputation will suffer."

"I would rather she endure the scorn of society for a season than endure marriage to a bounder such as you for the rest of her life."

The two men glared at each other, but the sound of Georgiana's gasp made its way to Darcy's ears. He was heartened by the fact that she had chosen to stand with him, though her choice may have been made without thought.

"William," said she in a small voice, "I thought Mr. Wickham was your friend."

"It appears I erred in not informing you, dearest, but I have not called Wickham friend in many years. He showed his true colors when we were boys, his behavior worsening as we grew older. He is not the kind of man with whom I wish to associate, nor is he a man that a young woman such as yourself should know."

A mournful shake of Wickham's head was followed by his plaintively spoken: "I informed you of this, Georgiana darling. I knew your brother would not accept our marriage unless it were presented as a fait accompli. Perhaps now you see I was correct."

Wickham attempted to step forward, but he was halted in his steps by a clearly irate Bingley. Darcy had never seen his friend in such a state. In stature, Bingley was no larger than Wickham, but the menacing manner in which he regarded Darcy's former friend gave him the appearance of looming over him.

"I would not if you value your life," snarled Bingley. "Miss Darcy is nothing to you."

"On the contrary," said Wickham, eying Bingley warily. "She is to be my future wife."

"Georgiana," said Darcy, turning to look his sister in the eye, now that Bingley had Wickham corralled, "listen to me. I have never lied to you, have I?"

Georgiana shook her head.

"And I do not do so in this instance. I have disassociated with Wickham, which is why you have not seen him at Pemberley these past years."

"He informed me he has been much occupied with studying the law," was Georgiana's slow reply.

"He lied. In fact, he inherited a thousand pounds from our father, and I gave him a further three thousand when he refused the living at Kympton. I have those receipts if you need to see them. Furthermore, I have credible information that he wasted it all on drink and gambling within a year of receiving it."

"Of course, I have not," said Wickham, his tone tinged with just a hint of desperation. "Besides, dearest, we have spoken of our finances. We shall be able to live quite well on your fortune until I secure work in the law."

"Ah, there it comes out," said Darcy, glaring at his former friend. "I am sorry to cause you pain, dearest, but all Wickham has ever wanted is money, an easy life where he may gamble at his leisure and avoid any sort of effort to earn his bread."

"And you do not live in such a way?" said Wickham with a sneer. "A rich man who lives off his estate and looks down his nose at those less fortunate than he."

"But William is not like that," said Georgiana.

Wickham seemed to realize that he had made a tactical error, and he attempted to correct it. "Perhaps not, dearest. But do you not now see that everything I said is the truth?"

"Shall we not ask him to provide proof that he still owns some of the money he was given?" asked Darcy. "I know the approximate cost of schooling in the law. If Wickham is a prudent man, he will have a substantial amount left in a bank account."

"It costs more than you know, Darcy," said Wickham, his tone just short of a snarl.

"Perhaps we should ask Fitzwilliam if you do not trust me," said Darcy. "Do you think he will mislead you?"

"Oh, Brother!" cried Georgiana, melting into his side. "I trust you! You know I do!"

"Then release whatever feelings this man has managed to engender in you. They are just as false as he is."

"Please, Georgiana," said Wickham. "Do not allow your brother to poison our love!"

It seemed Georgiana saw something in Wickham which informed her of his desperation. She looked at him for a long moment before tears filled her eyes, and she shook her head, drawing even closer to Darcy. Darcy shot a triumphant glare at Wickham, to which the man responded with a growl of utter rage.

"I would not have allowed it anyway, Wickham," said Darcy shortly. "You should know that if you attempt to damage my sister's reputation, no glib words will suffice, no hole be deep enough to hide you from Fitzwilliam's rage."

"I think, my dear Darcy," said Wickham, "that you will find that her reputation is already sullied. I have made it quite well known in the town that I have secured her hand. The only way you can protect her reputation is to allow our marriage to go forward."

Georgiana gasped and gaped. It was clear that while she trusted Darcy, she had still held some notion that Wickham actually cared for her. That illusion was being shattered before her eyes.

Carefully, Darcy transferred his precious sister to Bingley and stepped toward Wickham. Though he stood taller by several inches and could loom over the pathetic man, Wickham gave a credible attempt at appearing unaffected. Darcy, who knew him well, was not misled in the slightest.

"As I said before, I would rather my sister suffer the slings and arrows of society for a short season, than marry her to a man such as you. Get out, Wickham, and do not return. It will go ill with you if you do."

It seemed that Wickham understood his implacable will, for he stared at Darcy, a truly ugly expression showing his frustration and rage. Then he turned to Georgiana and said with a sneer: "It is unfortunate you are such a sniveling, wretched little miss, Georgiana. We might have salvaged —"

His diatribe was cut short by the sudden impact of Darcy's fist with the bone of his cheek. Wickham went down in a heap, though his glare at Darcy never wavered. All the hatred which Wickham had held for him over the years was gathered in his eyes at that moment. But he was also a coward, and would not match Darcy's physical violence. It was the first time Darcy had struck the libertine since they had been boys engaged in fisticuffs. Darcy wished he had done it long ago.

"Get this piece of excrement out of here," commanded he to his men. "Do not return, Wickham, or I will see you in debtors' prison."

The footmen sprang to action and soon hauled Wickham from the room. He did not speak again, but his eyes spoke of vengeance to come. Darcy had no care for him. He would protect his sister.

CHAPTER II

*I*n the wake of Wickham's forced departure, Darcy noticed two things in quick succession: the weeping of his sister as she stood, protected in Bingley's arms, and the movement of Mrs. Younge. The woman had sidled toward the door, clearly intent upon escape. Darcy, however, was not about to allow it. He stepped toward her and put himself between her and the door, prompting her to blanch chalk white.

"No, Mrs. Younge. I would appreciate your continued presence. You would not wish to leave your charge at such a time, would you?"

Several emotions passed over her face, but most prominent among them was fear. She looked to Georgiana, who had looked up at Darcy's words. Then Mrs. Younge seemed to sense there was no escape for her. She sat on a nearby chair, and her eyes found the floor. She refused to look up.

"Might I inquire whether Mrs. Younge promoted Wickham's suit?" asked Darcy of Georgiana.

"She . . ." Georgiana paused, seeming taken aback by the question. "She told me that I should follow my heart. She did speak several times about how Mr. Wickham seemed like a good man."

"Mrs. Younge," said Darcy, the quiet menace he felt for this faithless woman not utterly suppressed, "were you known to Wickham before I hired you?"

The woman refused to look up at him. Darcy stepped to her chair, put his hands on the arms, and glared down at her, forcing her to gaze up at him in fear and astonishment. "I asked you if you were known to Mr. Wickham before I hired you."

Sensing there was no escape, Mrs. Younge muttered: "It was at his instigation I applied for the position."

A gasp sounded loudly in the room. Darcy rose from where he had been standing over Mrs. Younge, and Georgiana stepped forward, her eyes ablaze, even as tears streamed down her cheeks. Before Darcy could even think, Georgiana's hand flashed down and struck Mrs. Younge hard on the cheek, causing her head to snap in the opposite direction.

"I trusted you!" screamed Georgiana, then she fled the room, her footsteps echoing down the hall.

"And I trusted you too," said Darcy, looking down on his sister's *former* companion with all the contempt he could muster.

Tears had filled her eyes, and the signs of a red handprint shone already on her cheek. But Darcy had nothing of pity for the woman. She had betrayed the trust for which she had been paid, had conspired with his worst enemy to destroy his sister and steal her fortune. Such treachery was not to be rewarded.

"You will leave this house this instant, Mrs. Younge," ground out Darcy. "You will receive no reference, your final pay is forfeit, and I care not what you do. If I ever hear of you denigrating my sister by word or deed, I shall find you and bring you up on charges. I assure you that I have more than enough influence to see you transported, if not hanged. And if I do not, my uncle, the earl, most certainly does."

The woman's frantic nodding preceded her flight from the room. A moment later, the sound of the outer door opening and closing behind her announced her departure from their lives.

"Come, Darcy," said Bingley, ever the excellent friend, "sit for a time and calm yourself. You are entirely overwrought."

His friend guided him to a nearby chair, and Darcy sank down, hardly aware of where he was or what he was doing. The reality of the situation came crashing down on his head and he moaned at the thought of what his sister must face, should this matter become known to society. For despite his words to Wickham, he knew how savage society could be at any perceived misbehavior.

"I have failed her," said Darcy, resting his face in his hands.

"You have protected her, my friend."

"I should have told her of Wickham. She would have been forewarned of his character."

"Perhaps you should have," said Bingley. "But in a way, it may be fortuitous you did not. Had your sister been wary of him, he may have attempted a more direct approach. Instead, he seemed willing to simply charm her. It will be difficult for her in the short term to recover from her infatuation, but at least he did not openly compromise or seduce her."

"That remains to be seen," said Darcy, shaking his head.

"I doubt any such thing has happened. You forget that I know Wickham too, though I will grant you not as well as you do. He would consider it a victory if he were able to charm her into marriage, and then sully her with the weight of the law on his side thereafter. You must confirm it with Georgiana, of course, but I have no doubt of it."

Though appreciating his friend's words of encouragement, Darcy was unable to see anything but misery in this situation. If Wickham's words were true—and Darcy had little doubt he had told the truth in that, at least—Georgiana faced a hard road until society forgot about her indiscretion or were pulled to some other scandal. But Bingley spoke the truth, and Darcy knew he had best be about seeing to their departure and understanding the true state of the damage to her reputation.

"Thank you for your support, Bingley," said Darcy, grasping his friend's hand in a tight grip. "It has made all the difference."

"You know you have it, regardless of what may come," replied Bingley.

Darcy nodded. Yes, he did know it and also knew he was blessed as a result.

"I shall speak with Georgiana. Can I ask you to investigate the truth of Wickham's words? I would know what we face before I attempt to approach London with my sister."

"Of course," replied Bingley. "I shall be about it directly tomorrow morning. I shall need the services of your footmen to inquire properly."

"You will have whatever you require," replied Darcy.

As it turned out, matters were at once better and worse than Darcy had imagined. A quick word with the housekeeper resulted in a meal being laid out for them, and while they were waiting Bingley went to speak with the footmen and driver, while Darcy took on the unpleasant task of speaking with his sister. Her heartbroken sobs, audible from the hallway outside her room, told him of her feelings concerning the matter. How was he ever to cope with her sorrow?

Steeling himself to the necessity of it, Darcy knocked on the door. The sobs ceased for a moment, and shortly a tremulous voice called out for him to enter. He did so, noting her stretched out on the bed, her dress askew and her hair coming out from its pins. He went to her directly, sitting on the edge of the bed, and accepting her slight form into his arms. For a moment, he was content to simply hold her, providing what comfort he was able.

"You must think me the silliest, stupidest girl in existence," murmured Georgiana, a short time after her tears ceased to fall.

"I think no such thing," replied Darcy. "I should have informed you of my falling out with him, for he is adept at seeming like a gentleman, though not so adept at behaving like one. You could have had no suspicions of his motives."

Georgiana snorted her derision. "I thank you for your absolution, William. But you must allow me to feel how foolish I have been. I knew better than to accept his overtures. But I was so enamored of the notion of being in love, I shunted my intelligence to the side and played the part of the vacuous little girl."

"Then we must agree to share the blame," said Darcy with a mirthless chuckle. "I should have informed you, and you should have behaved better. Bingley has just told me that it is likely for the best that events played out as they did. Hiring Mrs. Younge is entirely on my shoulders, and with a faithless companion, Wickham might have chosen a more direct method of obtaining what he wanted, had you not been charmed."

A gasp escaped Georgiana's lips, and she pulled back at him, regarding him with wild eyes. "Are you suggesting he might have . . . ? That he would . . . ?"

It was clear she could not even say it. Darcy had little desire to voice such a thing himself. "I have never known him to be thus—he has always relied on his wiles and his charm. But your dowry is such an inducement, I cannot predict what he might have done should the situation have turned out otherwise."

Slowly, clearly in thought, Georgiana nodded. "It does not absolve me in any way, but I can see where that might have happened."

"So nothing of that nature occurred between you?" asked Darcy, knowing he had no choice but to ask the question.

"No," said Georgiana firmly, shaking her head to emphasize her denial. "I have not much knowledge about such things, but I believe Mr. Wickham might have alluded to it a time or two. But I am not sure, and I would never allow such liberties before marriage. You have taught me better than that."

"I apologize, dearest," said Darcy. "I hope you understand it was a question I had no choice but to ask."

"I do," replied Georgiana, nodding her agreement.

They sat for some time, not speaking, Georgiana's head again resting against his shoulder. Her tears, at least, seemed to have been spent, for she was quiet and thoughtful. For himself, Darcy felt a weariness settle over him, unlike anything he had felt before. He had not lost his sister to that disgusting excuse for a man. But at what cost?

"I assume Mr. Wickham's words are likely the truth," said Georgiana with a sigh, after a few moments of silence. "I have no doubt I will be the target of scorn for some time to come."

"Were you aware of any whispers in the town?"

"There are a few who do know of Mr. Wickham's presence, but I do not know more than that. I have made a few friends while we have been here, but I do not know any of them well."

"Then let us not concern ourselves for it at present," said Darcy. "I think it would be best if you retired and rested tonight, for you have had a shock. Tomorrow we may consider the matter further."

Georgiana agreed. Her maid was called and prepared her for bed, while Darcy excused himself. He descended again to meet with Bingley and partake of the supper which had been laid out for them. He had no doubt the morrow would bring new challenges. He would need his faculties to withstand them.

The day following their arrival did not bring any good news. As his friend had requested, Bingley absented himself soon after breakfast in the company of the two footmen. They separated soon thereafter to gather what information they could, and when they gathered again, it was with news that Bingley did not wish to be forced to relate to his friend

"It appears Wickham was speaking the truth, inasmuch as he informed you of the town's knowledge of his attempt to woo Miss Darcy."

Bingley smiled at her, attempting to impart a little courage. For her part, he was impressed with her composure, though it was brittle. She was not an assertive woman, and likely never would be, he thought. But she had a core of steel, only uncovered in times of trouble. She would weather the storm, he had no doubt, and perhaps the idea, quickly forming in his head, might speed the healing and provide protection.

"It is true," said Miss Darcy. "Several of the ladies with whom I associated here knew of it."

"The question I have," said Bingley, nodding at her, "is how much of that knowledge has left Ramsgate. It is difficult to know without actually going to London, but I suspect that as the Darcy name is not unknown, anything which makes its way back to London will excite some interest."

"I have no doubt of it," said Miss Darcy. Her mood was morose, as if she fully expected to be led to the executioner. At her side, Darcy was doing a credible job of trying to appear confident for his sister's sake, but Bingley knew his friend well enough to see through the façade.

"It is possible that as it is summer, the matter will not find fertile ground in London," said Darcy.

"That is quite possible," replied Bingley. "I do not think all censure would be avoided in such a circumstance, and the fact that Miss Darcy is not yet out may assist. If she is not present in society to hear the whispers, they can hardly affect her."

"But when she comes out, the matter is almost certain to be raised again."

"That is true," replied Bingley. "That is why I have a potential solution to propose."

The interest of brother and sister was roused by Bingley's words, and he chuckled at the picture they presented. "I have never been struck by such a feeling of similarity between you as now, when you both perked up at my words."

"Please, Bingley," said Darcy, his sister nodding by his side, "if you have a solution to this predicament, then inform us of what you propose."

"What I propose," said Bingley, "is to repair Miss Darcy's reputation. In such circumstances, the means of doing so is for her to marry. As such, I propose that I marry her, thereby restoring whatever respectability she has lost."

The Darcy siblings looked on with astonishment. Again, they were so alike that Bingley was forced to stifle his laughter. A thought caused a little self-consciousness to settle over him, and he spoke hurriedly, aware that he was babbling.

"I realize that I do not have the status to fully rehabilitate that which has been lost. But I think in this instance, whatever censure Miss Darcy will face from being married to *me* is preferable to what might be said about her for desiring a connection to a steward's son. Furthermore, I will promise to treat her well and respect her, and I assure you that I do not suggest this for my own advancement in society."

"Never would I accuse you of it," said Darcy, Miss Darcy nodding vigorously by his side. "But I cannot allow you to make such a sacrifice, my friend."

"I would not have you suffer for my mistake, Mr. Bingley," added Miss Darcy.

"What manner of suffering do you call it?" asked Bingley. "I would not call marrying a beautiful and accomplished girl such as Miss Georgiana Darcy to be a punishment. In fact, I think I may receive the better end of the bargain in the end."

"Think about what you are saying, Bingley," said Darcy. "You would lose all chance you possess of making a marriage with a woman you love."

"Who is to say that love will not develop between us?"

Miss Darcy blushed, but Darcy continued to shake his head. "I know you, my friend. You could never be happy in a marriage of convenience. I am concerned for Georgiana's reputation, but I do not wish to buy her reclamation at such a price."

A sigh escaped Bingley's lips, a gesture he had not meant to make. Darcy regarded him evenly, a question in his gaze. For her part, Miss Darcy was also watching him, but her mien was as inscrutable as Darcy's had ever been.

"Please do not assume I speak this way due to ennui or any ulterior motive. I am truly willing to assist Miss Darcy in whatever way possible, and offer myself as the means by which her reputation may be saved."

Bingley turned his eyes toward Darcy. "My friend, do you remember anything out of the ordinary about our stay at Watson's house?"

Darcy frowned. "Not as such. Of what are you speaking?"

"Come, my friend," said Bingley with a grin. "Surely you must have noticed that I did not fixate on a young woman to the exclusion of all others. We have spoken enough of my habit for the lack of such behavior to have been marked."

"I had not thought of it in that manner," said Darcy slowly. "But now you mention it, I recall wondering if you would fix on one of them."

"The truth is, Darcy," said Bingley, "that I have perhaps grown a bit jaded in the previous months. If you recall, I paid significant attention to Miss Cartwright during the season. But I learned, to my utter relief, that her father is in distressed circumstances, and I was deemed sufficient to assist in rehabilitating their finances. Miss Cartwright cared nothing for me—she cared only for my fortune. At that moment, I felt I understood something of what you feel whenever you are in town."

"I am sorry, my friend," said Darcy. "I never knew you felt that way."

"That is because I wished to consider it myself. I have spent these past months thinking of the matter, and I have realized that I have grown tired of it all. I am well aware of my faults, my friend. I become enamored of a pretty woman, fix on her to the exclusion of all others, but soon lose interest. The reasons of my loss of interest are usually because of something I find objectionable about the woman, the realization that her motivations are not pure, or the understanding that we do not suit as much as I might have thought. In short, I no longer wish to be the man I have been.

"You say I would not wish for a marriage of convenience, a cold union for reasons of prudence or the wish to get gain, such as society would find acceptable. If you will excuse my saying so, Caroline is focused on just such a union, but I have no wish to be the same as she. Having said that, I cannot imagine a marriage with Miss Darcy would ever devolve to such a stale and cold life. You are a beautiful and talented woman, Miss Darcy, and while we do not love each other at present, we get on well, and I have no doubt we would do well together. In time, such ties would grow between us—of this, I have no doubt.

"Furthermore, I simply feel that this is a solution which should be grasped with both hands. We expose Wickham for what he is and put it out that we had a previous arrangement between us. Due to your tender years, we say that we had decided not to marry immediately because you had wished to have a season. With the assistance of his ally, Mr. Wickham attempted to seduce you, but you stood firm. Thus, it appears that you went along with him in order to put him off. Then you become a heroine who fended off a determined fortune hunter while remaining true to your betrothed."

Darcy appeared to be mulling it over in his mind. "I suppose it might work."

"I am certain it would," replied Bingley. "We shall no doubt inspire scrutiny, but as long as we appear the happy couple, I have no doubt the tale will be accepted before long. Those in society will understand the need to accelerate our plans, given Wickham's actions. Furthermore, this will put Miss Darcy firmly beyond Wickham's future ambitions, should he think to make an attempt again.

"For myself, I shall obtain that match which will forge ties that will see me accepted in society. Miss Darcy will receive the protection of a husband who will always treat her well, and if we work at it, we shall find contentment, and more, with each other."

"I thank you for your suggestion, Mr. Bingley," said Miss Darcy, speaking at last, though she spoke quietly, with a diffidence he had long associated with her. "Any woman would be fortunate to receive an offer from a gentleman of your caliber. But I cannot allow you to pay for my mistakes. I must decline your offer."

"Darcy," said Bingley, his eyes never leaving Miss Darcy. "Will you allow me to speak with your sister alone?"

A glance at Miss Darcy was received with a shrug of her shoulders. Seeing his sister had no objection, Darcy agreed.

"Very well, Bingley. I will step into the other room. Please let me state, however, that I will only agree if it is what Georgiana wishes. I will stand beside her against whatever the ton throws at us, regardless of what is decided here. On the other hand," said he, turning a grin on his sister in an attempt to put her at ease, "I would not object to Bingley as a brother. Please, take all the time you require."

With those words, he stepped from the room, leaving them alone. Bingley regarded Miss Darcy for a moment, noting her trepidation, though she gave all the appearance of calm. Had he thought it would not overwhelm her, Bingley would have gone to sit at her side. As it was, he thought it would be best to address her from his current position for the present.

"Miss Darcy," said he after a moment, "I want you to know that I do not make this offer out of duty or pity. I truly believe that you and I would do well together. If I did not think that, I would have contented myself with simply standing by your side, come whatever may.

"But if you do not wish to marry me, for whatever reason, I will cease importuning you. Is there something which prevents you from wishing to be married to me? Do you disagree when I assert that we might do well together?"

"Oh, no!" exclaimed she. "I said any woman would be fortunate, and I mean it. I just . . . I . . . simply never thought I would marry for such reasons."

"Nor did I. But I promise you that if you agree to marry me, I shall spend a lifetime attempting to earn your love."

Miss Darcy regarded him, though her scrutiny did not last long due to her shyness. "I believe you, sir."

"Do you have any other objections?"

A scarlet hue settled over her cheeks. "I . . ." She did not manage to speak, but her eyes darted to him several times, unsure of herself.

"You can tell me anything, Miss Darcy," said Bingley.

"Your sisters," blurted she. "They . . . I am not enamored of them. I especially do not like how they attempt to reach my brother through me."

Bingley could not help but laugh. "Would it surprise you to learn that I find it difficult to tolerate them at times?"

Miss Darcy joined him in mirth. "I am sorry for saying such things, Mr. Bingley. But their society can be a trial."

"That it can. I cannot disagree. I will not promise to throw them off, for they are my sisters."

"I would not ask you to do so!" exclaimed Miss Darcy.

"I know. But I will promise that *you* will be mistress of your own home and that my sisters will have no say. I can also promise that they will not always be with us."

That seemed to mollify her a little. Sensing the critical juncture had arrived, Bingley slid off his seat and knelt by her side. He captured her hand in his, looking into her eyes, noting that she was a pretty girl. He imagined in a few years she would command the attention of the masses when her confidence matched her beauty.

"Georgiana, I offer you my hand in marriage. Will you accept it? Will you marry me, learn to love me as I learn to love you, have children and begin a family with me?"

Her reply came more quickly than Bingley might have expected. "I will. I thank you for the honor of your proposal."

Chapter III

*D*arcy was certain his desire to be anywhere other than where he was at present was hidden to no one. Never the most social or the easiest in company, on that night in Hertfordshire, he was less eager than usual to be in company, particularly with those of a lower level of society who were boisterous and uncouth.

But Bingley had invited him to Hertfordshire, and perform before the masses he must. Now that Bingley and Georgiana were married, it was important that Bingley be seen as a gentleman, rather than a man whose fortune came from trade. It was something of a fiction, but an important one, and it would ease both of their paths in society.

The more pressing reason for Darcy to be here with them — and he was grateful to his friend for recognizing this — was that Darcy could not bear to be parted from his sister at present. It was largely his error, both his choice of Mrs. Younge as a companion and his neglect in failing to inform his sister of Wickham's character, which had led to her current circumstances. He was also entirely transparent to those who knew and loved him best.

"Cousin," greeted Fitzwilliam. Darcy could feel his cousin's look of compassion, though it was mixed with determination. "It seems to me you are not enjoying tonight's festivities."

A snort that Darcy could not quite suppress escaped his lips. "When do I ever enjoy events such as this?"

"That is true."

Fitzwilliam paused and looked out over the company. For once, Darcy could see his cousin was entirely serious, eschewing the teasing which was so often part of his discourse.

"The company is not so bad," said Fitzwilliam, turning back to Darcy. "They are minor gentry, it is true, but I believe there is no harm in them."

"You did not hear whispers of your income the moment you walked into the room." As he spoke, Darcy's eyes found the woman whom he had overheard. She was an attractive matron, perhaps five and forty years of age. She was also utterly silly, mean of understanding, and a notorious gossip, unless Darcy missed his guess.

"No," replied Fitzwilliam, the gleam of irony entering his eyes. "But I heard plenty of whispers about my status as the younger son of an earl. You are not the only one present to be subject to such gossip, old man."

"I suppose I am not," replied Darcy.

"I know why you are out of sorts, Cousin, for your frequent glances in Georgiana's direction give you away."

Without meaning to, Darcy's eyes found his sister once again, as they frequently had that evening. She was standing with Bingley, and they were speaking to two women—a pair of sisters, from what Darcy could see. The elder was willowy and blonde, quite beautiful by society's standards. The other was shorter of stature and brunette, not in possession of her sister's beauty, but still quite pretty, Darcy supposed. The tightness around Darcy's heart eased a little as he noted that Georgiana was speaking to them with composure, though her reticence was easily seen, even from this distance.

"She is well, Darcy," said Fitzwilliam again. "She has Bingley to protect her, and while I might not have credited it even three months ago, he seems quite equal to the task. She is safe, and Wickham will never prey on her again." Fitzwilliam snorted. "I am still unhappy with you about that, Cousin. Though Wickham cannot ply his trade with her again, a little retribution is still in order. A quick flick of my wrist with my cavalry sword and the problem of George Wickham would be solved forever."

The chilling part of Fitzwilliam's speech was that Darcy knew his cousin was not precisely jesting. Fitzwilliam's craft had been honed in the army, and he had obtained a measure of resolve which prompted him to do whatever must be done. If he thought calling Wickham out and emasculating him or running him through was justified and necessary, he would have no compunction in doing so.

"Regardless," continued Fitzwilliam, "I believe it would be best to let go of the past. Perhaps you erred. But if you will think on it, I did too. There is little point in either of us dwelling about what might have been."

"I understand this, Fitzwilliam," replied Darcy at last. "But I hope you will allow me to feel how much I have been to blame. The responsibility for it will ultimately ease, but I will never be free of it. I will grant you that the match has turned out well, thus far. I only hope they continue in this attitude and are happy together."

"How can they not be?" chortled Fitzwilliam. "Bingley is as happy a man as I have seen. Even if Georgiana is more reticent and quiet, I have no doubt he will drag her kicking and screaming, if need be, into that state of bliss he perpetually inhabits!"

Darcy felt the corners of his mouth rise in response. At times Fitzwilliam's jesting was a trial. But he could imagine no firmer friend and supporter than his cousin. They had been close all their lives. Between Fitzwilliam and Bingley, Darcy found his spirits lifting. He needed such support at present.

"I shall be well, Cousin," said Darcy. "I shall not embarrass you, nor shall I lock myself away at Pemberley to indulge in my grief and self-loathing. You simply need to allow me time to become accustomed to this new state of affairs."

"Very well, Darcy. I suggest you ask Georgiana to dance soon, for she will expect it. And it would not hurt you to dance with a few of the ladies present if only to forget your troubles for a time. Perhaps one of the two ladies speaking with Georgiana would suffice?"

With those words Fitzwilliam departed, though contrary to his words, he proceeded to where Georgiana and Bingley were speaking to the local ladies and asked the blonde to dance with him. Darcy chuckled and shook his head. Fitzwilliam was, in his own way, as predictable as Bingley had ever been, and they had much the same taste in women. The woman with whom Fitzwilliam stood up might have been Bingley's infatuation, had he remained unmarried. That he spoke with perfect composure, but no overt admiration, was another form of relief for Darcy. Despite his friend's averred lack of interest in any woman who would have previously attracted his attention, Darcy could not help but wonder over his friend's constancy. Thus far there had been nothing to give him pause.

The thought of making his way toward his sister entered Darcy's thoughts, but an incident occurred which soured his mood yet again. This time, it was from an entirely likely source. As he was contemplating Georgiana and Bingley and resolving to go to them, the grating tones of a woman's voice reached his ears.

"Oh, yes, it is, indeed, the truth."

A quick glance informed Darcy that it was Caroline Bingley speaking, and that she was gathered with a group of local women, preening in her supposed position of prominence among their number.

"I am prodigiously pleased that matters have proceeded in such a happy manner," continued she. "Of course, I knew how it would be all along. My brother always possessed such a tender regard for Georgiana. I was certain they would eventually discover they could not live without each other.

"And do you know her brother is the proprietor of a large estate in Derbyshire?"

The ladies tittered and glanced at him with awe and not a little calculation. Miss Bingley's tone spoke of the assurance of a woman of society, little though she deserved it on her own merits. To be speaking of Georgiana's misfortune leading to Miss Bingley's own perpetual acceptance in society by her connection to the Darcy family was enough to set Darcy to clenching his jaw until it ached.

"A finer man you could not find, even if you scoured the kingdom from Cornwall to John o' Groats. His estate is simply exquisite, and his nobility unquestioned. And the dear colonel too! We are fortunate, indeed, to be connected to such a high family of society as the Fitzwilliam family.

"But dear Georgiana is such a sweet girl too, and so wonderfully suitable for my brother."

It was these last words which forced Darcy to move away from the woman, else he might turn and say something impolitic. Darcy had long known Miss Bingley coveted his estate, his position in society, wishing to be mistress of his estate. To crow about the marriage, knowing the manner in which it had come about, and only mention his sister's person after the fact, was beyond the pale. Miss Bingley might be connected to him by marriage, and he may be required to acknowledge her as such. But Darcy would never allow a closer connection. He would prefer to end a bachelor and allow Georgiana's children to inherit than allow such a mercenary woman to lord her superiority over his beloved estate!

At that moment, Darcy regretted simply removing Wickham from the house in Ramsgate. The final gauntlet had been thrown. It would go ill for Wickham should he ever cross Darcy's path again.

It was soon clear that Mrs. Bingley was as sweet a girl as Elizabeth had ever met. She was shy and discreet, much as Jane, but she accepted their overtures of friendship as if *she* was the one being honored. It was so unlike Miss Bingley, who was everything Elizabeth had always expected of a woman of society. What Elizabeth had heard of Miss Bingley's background gave the lie to her pretensions.

It was also clear that Mrs. Bingley adored her husband. They were little signs, to be sure—the way her hand rested on his arm; the utter happiness with which she regarded him; the way she hung off his every word when he spoke. It was a pretty picture, Elizabeth decided, and one which warmed her heart. Mr. Bingley was the outgoing member of the couple, and he dragged her along with himself by the force of his good cheer. That she was full young and Elizabeth would not have expected so young a girl of society to be married at her age was immaterial. It was clear to her they would be happy together, and even though she had only just made their acquaintance, Elizabeth already felt they were people she could esteem with ease.

But Mr. Darcy, Mrs. Bingley's brother, appeared to be a different sort altogether. It was clear they shared the same sort of reticence, Mrs. Bingley's seeming to be centered on shyness, while Mr. Darcy's focused on . . . superiority? Pride? Haughtiness? Elizabeth could not be precisely certain if her observations were at all correct. He gave the appearance of haughtiness with his stalking along the periphery of the company, with his scowl clear for all to see. But she also thought he might be out of sorts, rather than simply above his company.

After speaking with the Bingleys for a time, Elizabeth found herself on the dance floor with one of the local men, a man she had partnered with several times in the past. As such, their conversation, what there was of it, was banal in nature, allowing her attention to roam. Soon after Elizabeth left the Bingleys, Mr. Darcy approached them. As he stood with them for a time, it seemed that some of his cares were put to rest for the moment. It was clear to Elizabeth's eyes that he held his sister in high esteem, his affection for both her and her husband flowing out in his understated smile and easy conversation.

But Elizabeth also saw the other side of him only moments later when Miss Bingley approached him and began to speak when he was standing alone. While she spoke with great animation, Mr. Darcy's responses seemed monosyllabic. He clearly did not enjoy her company, not that the woman detected it, given the way she continued to chatter in his ear. He stepped away from her at the first opportunity, and the way she watched him, smugness evident in her posture, told Elizabeth *she*, at least, considered their brief moments together a success.

A little more insight was given to Elizabeth soon after, as she was invited to the dance floor by his cousin. In contrast to his relations, Colonel Fitzwilliam seemed much more like Mr. Bingley in character. He was kind and jovial, quick with a quip, and eager to make the acquaintance of them all. He was every inch the gentleman, in his demeanor, manners, upright bearing, and obviously intelligent way of speaking. Elizabeth found that she liked him very well, indeed.

"Well, I must declare that I find Meryton a pleasant place, Miss Elizabeth. The welcome we have received has been everything I might have expected."

"Oh, I assure you, Colonel, that we would never dare give any less welcome to a man of your status in society."

The colonel laughed and fixed her with a stern glare. "Are you attempting to inform me that you are a fortune hunter, intent upon capturing me for my great wealth?"

Elizabeth responded in kind. "Of course not, sir. I will own that there are some whose motives are not entirely altruistic. But I, myself, have nothing more in mind than meeting interesting new people."

"Then I am happy to hear it," replied Colonel Fitzwilliam, still chuckling. "But I feel it incumbent upon myself to warn you, Miss Elizabeth. If you *do* espouse such intentions, you had best put all such thoughts from your mind. I am not Darcy—I am a soldier, though I do possess a small estate that will make me independent, at the very least, when I finally retire."

"That speaks well to your character, sir," said Elizabeth. "Not every man who possesses the means for even a modest independence would put themselves at risk by joining the regulars."

"I only inherited it last year," confided the colonel. "And it was a complete surprise, I assure you."

"Do not spoil my praise!" exclaimed Elizabeth. "I have given you a virtuous character. You should be grateful for it."

"And I shall," said Colonel Fitzwilliam. "I thank you, Miss Elizabeth. You have provided conversation and a hearty welcome, and for that I am grateful. I also saw you speaking to my cousin earlier, and I thank you for that."

"Mrs. Bingley seems to be a sweet girl, indeed," said Elizabeth. "It is no virtue of mine to become friendly with a young woman who is eminently deserving of it."

"She *is* deserving of it. She is my cousin, and I own that my view of her is colored by that near connection. But she is a good girl. She is shy and has often had difficulty in making friends near her age. I think she could use some who are . . . Well, let us say that the female influences near her now, not counting my mother and sisters, of course, are not the best examples."

"Then we will be happy to be a part of her life as long as she is here," said Elizabeth. "Perhaps we can arrange to visit to further our acquaintance."

"That would be very much appreciated."

They fell silent for a time, as they continued in the steps of the dance. As they were thus engaged, Elizabeth thought she saw her partner's attention wandering down the line at various times, to where her elder sister danced with Mr. Bingley. Elizabeth was pleased at the sight—many men found Jane beautiful and wished to cultivate a relationship with them. Elizabeth thought Colonel Fitzwilliam might be a man of enough substance to look past her relative poverty and lack of connections to the jewel Elizabeth knew her sister to be. Only time will tell.

"I have noticed," said Elizabeth, a short time later when they had come together again, "your other cousin does not seem to be enjoying himself as much."

Elizabeth could hardly miss Colonel Fitzwilliam's grimace at the mention of Mr. Darcy. "Aye, Darcy is usually not comfortable in such situations unless he is acquainted with those present. He also has a matter weighing heavily on his mind at present. Moreover, with the constant pretensions of a certain lady with whom we are residing, I am afraid my cousin's mood is unlikely to recover tonight, at least."

Thinking about the man, Elizabeth allowed herself a slow nod. "I guessed as much with respect to Miss Bingley. As for the rest, I suppose that would make anyone wish to be elsewhere."

Colonel Fitzwilliam sighed. "Darcy has a tendency to take matters personally and an unhealthy inclination to blame himself for matters which are not his fault. But a better man you could not find. I would ask you, Miss Elizabeth, not to judge him based on his performance tonight. He is a good man. But he is also a serious one."

"I understand, Colonel Fitzwilliam. I will own that I was curious about Mr. Darcy's behavior. But I had not thought ill of him."

"I am happy to hear it. We shall be in the neighborhood for some weeks, and I am eager to have good relations with you and your neighbors."

"And you shall have it! We are eager to be in your company!"

A few moments later, the dance ended, and Colonel Fitzwilliam escorted her to the side of the room. While Elizabeth thought some of the new company which had arrived in their midst would be a trial to endure, some of them would be a joy to know. This was a most auspicious beginning.

The beginning was promising, but toward the end of the evening, it turned a little sour for Elizabeth. The newcomers were all that was good and friendly, and Elizabeth had even exchanged some words with Miss Bingley and Mrs. Hurst which told her they were intelligent and proper, if a little above their company.

But Mr. Darcy remained an enigma, a man who at once spoke to his sister with great affection and easiness, but who made no attempt whatsoever to come to know anyone not of his party. As the night wore on, he began to resemble a caged lion more than a man, and his companions noticed his temper. When Mr. Bingley approached to speak to him, Elizabeth found herself close enough to hear, though she had not intended it to be so.

"I know you are not in good humor tonight, Darcy," said he as he stepped toward his brother-in-law. "But if you would make some attempt to mingle with those in attendance, you would undoubtedly find relief from your concerns."

"I hardly think that is likely, Bingley," replied Mr. Darcy. "The night is almost at a close, regardless. With the humor I am in, I believe it would be best to simply keep to myself and obtain a good night's rest. Perhaps tomorrow my mood shall be better."

Mr. Bingley regarded his friend, the compassion evident in his scrutiny. "I wish you would allow the matter to rest, Darcy. It is doing no one—least of all you—any good. Georgiana is well, and I have pledged to care for her. Surely you can be content with that."

Mr. Darcy's mien softened, and he directed an understated smile back at his friend. "I know you will, Bingley, and I thank you for it. I suppose I am not an unusual man in my wish that my sister have anything she wants in life."

"And she will receive it. You have my word."

"I know, my friend." Mr. Darcy sighed and turned away slightly. "Please do not take my behavior as a slight against you. You know that

I am grateful beyond the ability of words to describe."

"I do know, Darcy. But I still believe that if you allowed yourself to forget your troubles, you would find relief."

"I pledge I will make the attempt. It may be difficult in a company such as this. These people are not truly the sort with whom I would wish to associate, though I suppose there is no true harm in them."

"Your cousin seems to feel different."

Elizabeth's eyes followed Mr. Bingley's, and she noticed him looking at Colonel Fitzwilliam, who was speaking with Jane. The sight warmed her heart. The colonel was a good man, and while it was still early in their acquaintance, Elizabeth knew he would take care not to break Jane's heart if he did not intend to pursue her.

"Fitzwilliam should take care," replied Mr. Darcy. "It would not do to raise the hopes of the ladies in this neighborhood. He can be an incorrigible flirt when he puts his mind to it."

"The lady is not undeserving, Darcy. In fact, had I not already had your dear sister as my wife, I might have found Miss Bennet to be agreeable myself. She is an angel and would be the making of him, I believe."

"She smiles too much," replied Mr. Darcy. "And given her mother and her mortifying younger sisters, I suspect she will grasp at anything if only to remove herself from her odious family."

Elizabeth felt all the affront of his words. Mr. Bingley, it seemed, also did not care for them.

"I believe you are overly harsh."

"Perhaps I am. Please, Bingley, simply let me be tonight. I will attempt to do better in the future."

It seemed Mr. Bingley understood the wisdom in Mr. Darcy's words, for after giving him a few more words of encouragement, he turned and departed. Mr. Darcy soon moved away as well, not once looking in her direction. Elizabeth was certain he had not even realized she was nearby.

At that moment, her mother's tittering caught Elizabeth's attention, and she noted her standing with several of the local ladies. Words such as "ten thousand a year," "the son of an earl," and "so handsome, indeed" made up a large part of her conversation. Elizabeth grimaced—she was certain Mr. Darcy had been able to hear her mother's words himself before he had walked away.

Elizabeth's eyes once again found his form from across the room. He had taken up station near the door, eager for the evening's festivities to be complete. For some time, Elizabeth stood and considered him, wondering at his troubles.

She supposed she could not fault him for his words, though they had been somewhat incautiously spoken. That his censure of the Bennets had, by a strict interpretation, excluded Jane was something for which she was thankful. Jane was all that was good, and would be a credit to Colonel Fitzwilliam, should the man decide to pursue her. Furthermore, Mr. Darcy had obviously been in ill humor, and she knew that often words were said that should never be spoken when a person was in such a mood.

Consequently, while she felt a little offense, she could also understand him. Thus, she decided to allow him the benefit of the doubt and avoid seeing the worst of his character.

CHAPTER IV

*I*t should not have been a surprise that Miss Bingley would abuse the neighborhood the night of the assembly. Had Darcy given the matter any thought at all, he would have realized it was nigh inevitable.

At her core, Miss Bingley was an insecure woman. She had gained much confidence due to her brother's marriage to Darcy's sister, but her ultimate ambition of marriage to Darcy himself had not been realized—and never would be, though Darcy doubted the woman would acknowledge the fact to herself until he was actually married. Thus, much of what she did was with the purpose of showing him she was a lady of society, not realizing he did not even like most society women.

"How happy I am the night has come to an end," said Miss Bingley the following morning. "I could not have borne a single minute more in company with such uncouth people."

As always, her faithful supporter, Mrs. Hurst, chimed in her own opinion, which was not markedly different from her sister's. Typically, Miss Bingley herself looked to Darcy to see if he was listening and what his reaction might be. But Darcy had no intention of displaying anything she could use to justify her behavior.

"What a quaint neighborhood you have chosen," said she to her brother. Darcy did not miss the slight frown she betrayed at his own lack of response.

"I confess, I saw little difference from the neighborhood in which Snowlock, my father's estate, sits," replied Fitzwilliam.

Trust Fitzwilliam to take up the lead in refuting Miss Bingley's assertions. The dynamic between Miss Bingley and his cousin was actually a curious matter, indeed. Miss Bingley had never cared for Fitzwilliam's flippancy, her distaste for him evident for almost anyone to see. One might have forgotten that he was the son of an earl, considering how she usually viewed him.

But since Georgiana's marriage to Bingley, she seemed to have put such feelings aside in favor of the need to assert her connection to the Fitzwilliam family. Darcy was forced to acknowledge her opportunistic qualities if nothing else.

"It is also close to town," said Bingley, his tone slightly injured. He had already been forced to defend his choice to his sister on more than one occasion. "That was a condition we put to the agent who investigated the viability of estates on the market."

"Just because it is close to town does not make it any less a backwater county," said Miss Bingley. "Though it is no more than half a day's journey, the residents here are countrified and provincial."

"I do not intend to settle here, Caroline," admonished Bingley. "Netherfield is convenient for the ability it gives us to travel to and from town." Bingley turned an affectionate smile on his wife, one which heartened Darcy every time he saw it. "I am certain Mrs. Bingley would much rather settle much closer to her ancestral home. Thus, I will search for an estate closer to Derbyshire when the time comes."

"Thank you, Charles," said Georgiana, true appreciation in her tone.

At the same time, Miss Bingley exclaimed: "Derbyshire, of course! There are few locales in the kingdom which can boast the sophistication and elegance of your neighborhood, Mr. Darcy. And the location is all that is beautiful! I cannot imagine my brother ever wishing to leave it, should he be so fortunate to find a home there."

It did not escape Darcy's attention that Miss Bingley was speaking of her own desire to be installed as the mistress of Pemberley, using her brother's future home as a proxy. But he was accustomed to her ways by now, and it allowed him to ignore them and reply in an indifferent manner.

"I truly doubt Bingley will be able to purchase an estate in

Pemberley's neighborhood. There are no families of which I am aware that I can see selling for any reason."

"It does not need to be in Lambton's neighborhood," said Bingley, speaking before his sister could. "If we can find something in Derbyshire or the nearby counties, I think I shall be very well pleased."

"Of course, you will have my support, when the time comes."

"I *am* curious about your characterization of the people in this neighborhood, Miss Bingley," said Fitzwilliam. The gleam in his eye told Darcy that the lady would likely not like the result of this conversation. But Darcy refrained from involving himself. "Have you seen anything in particular which gives you pause?"

"You did not?" asked Miss Bingley, seeming astonished. "You did not see the behavior or hear the noise we all endured at that cacophony which passed for an assembly last night?"

"I am not certain to what cacophony you refer," replied Fitzwilliam. "Was it something in particular which offended you?"

Miss Bingley snorted. "Shall I direct your attention to the uncouth screeching of those in attendance or the younger members of the company running amok among their betters? Or perhaps the musicians, none of whom seemed to possess more than a passing familiarity with their instruments?"

"The best musicians can be found in the larger centers, Miss Bingley," said Fitzwilliam. "That is true wherever you go. One would not expect the standards of music here to equal what you would find in my mother's ballroom in London."

"Of course not!" exclaimed Miss Bingley. "How I long to meet your mother! I understand she throws a grand ball every year."

It was an attempt to turn the conversation, for Miss Bingley sensed that Fitzwilliam had no intention of allowing her opinions to go unopposed. It was also doomed to failure, for Darcy's cousin was not a man to be diverted so easily.

"She does," replied Fitzwilliam. "And I am certain she will be happy to invite you, based on your connection with Bingley here.

"I am happy you have allowed that country assemblies will not have the truly skilled musicians in attendance, Miss Bingley," continued Fitzwilliam, dashing her hopes of moving away from the subject. "I will say, however, that I thought the musicians were quite fine last night. They seemed to play as well as one might expect."

"You have my agreement, Fitzwilliam," said Bingley. "I could find nothing lacking in them."

Fitzwilliam nodded at Bingley before turning his attention back to

Miss Bingley. "Regarding the members of society, they seemed friendly and open to me, perhaps not polished, but not unlike those I might meet near Snowlock or Pemberley, or even Thorndell, my own estate. I will grant you, however, that certain of the younger members of the party seemed to behave with less than perfect decorum."

"There," said Miss Bingley, triumph emanating from her like the light of a candle. "Though I know you are not capable of behaving with such lack of restraint, my dearest sister," Miss Bingley never lost a chance to refer to Georgiana as her sister, "I would also not recommend that you allow such ladies who behave in such a way to become close friends. You do have a reputation to uphold, after all."

"The ladies to whom you refer were all rather young," said Fitzwilliam. "Why, Miss Lydia Bennet is not more than fifteen, if I am not mistaken. Our Georgiana is seventeen, and possesses two more years of experience."

"What of Miss Kitty Bennet? She is Georgiana's age unless I am mistaken."

"No, you are correct there."

Miss Bingley seemed to think she had won a significant point.

"But not all ladies mature at the same pace," continued Fitzwilliam much to Miss Bingley's annoyance. "They will improve, I dare say. Now, as for their elder sisters, I believe there is nothing which can be said in reproach."

"Oh, Miss Jane Bennet is a sweet girl," said Mrs. Hurst, apparently eager to assist her sister. "I found her manners to be lovely."

"I cannot disagree," said Fitzwilliam. "Miss Elizabeth, too, is a pleasant girl, though perhaps much more outspoken than her sister."

"She gave the impression that she is laughing at the company, which I found distasteful," said Miss Bingley.

Fitzwilliam laughed. "I suppose she does at that. But her observations are delivered with such an artless and droll air that I cannot imagine anyone would take offense. I suspect she is quite clever. I am anticipating knowing more of her, for I suspect she will make an interesting acquaintance."

"I found I rather liked Miss Bennet and Miss Elizabeth," said Georgiana quietly.

"My dear sister," said Miss Bingley, speaking in that condescending tone Darcy knew his sister found annoying, "you would do best not to emulate such ladies as Miss Elizabeth Bennet. Her manners are not at all fashionable and would not be received well in London. In fact, I believe it would be best if we kept ourselves separate from the rest of the neighborhood. We will not be in this district long anyway."

"They are my neighbors, Caroline," said Bingley. "We can hardly avoid them."

"Bingley speaks the truth," said Fitzwilliam. "And I will say this: my care of my niece has passed to another, and as such, I will not attempt to direct her or her husband." Fitzwilliam grinned at Georgiana, which she returned. "But were I still her guardian, I would not oppose her coming to know such estimable ladies as we find here. Miss Bennet is, I believe, much like Georgiana in essentials. And you could do with a bit of Miss Elizabeth's confidence in company."

"I believe you may be correct, Cousin," said Georgiana.

"I suppose we must associate with them," said Miss Bingley, conceding defeat. "The eldest Bennets are, I believe, the best of the lot."

Darcy thought he understood. With Georgiana already Bingley's wife, Miss Bingley had nothing to fear of her brother making an imprudent match, something he knew had weighed on her mind. Darcy himself had shown little interest in society, and nothing of admiration for any female in the district. This allowed Miss Bingley to remain secure in her position as the only woman he would consider, allowing her to feel like she had a captive audience. She was incorrect in that, for Darcy did not consider her a prospective bride. But he would never inform her of that.

Thereafter, the topic of the previous evening seemed to be dropped by unspoken accord. It was just as well, for Darcy did not wish to speak of such matters, and Miss Bingley's vitriol, though understated in this instance, was always tiresome.

In fact, Darcy found the situation at Netherfield to be rather amusing. Due to her position as the wife of the man leasing the estate, Georgiana was the mistress of Netherfield, and she had had instruction from their aunt concerning the proper manner of running a house. Miss Bingley was nominally assisting her, but it was clear on many occasions that she was forced to restrain herself. It was also clear that she wished she was the mistress in fact, for it would have been the perfect opportunity, in her mind, to show her skills.

Though they had been at the assembly until the late hours, they had come to Netherfield during the prime hunting season, and as few other things brought Hurst pleasure, the gentlemen were all chivvied from the house after breakfast to thin the flocks of birds on the estate. Darcy was not a great hunter himself, but he did not dislike the activity and went along without complaint. If nothing else, it took him from Miss Bingley's company for a time, which was always an occasion for celebration.

"Bingley truly has given us an interesting new relation," said Fitzwilliam as they were walking back to the estate after a successful hunt. "Miss Bingley's pretentions are amusing in the extreme."

"So I have always thought," replied Darcy, though he looked about, making certain Bingley and Hurst were not close enough to overhear them.

"They are some distance ahead of us, so you need not fear," said Fitzwilliam. "Even if they were privy to our conversation, you know they would agree with it."

"Perhaps. But I would not wish to censure Bingley's sister in his hearing."

Fitzwilliam's snort told Darcy everything he needed to know about his cousin's opinion. "In truth, I wonder if she shall not be disappointed when she finally makes my parents' acquaintance. We Fitzwilliams have never been known to push our noses into the clouds as is Miss Bingley's custom. She might wish her brother had married into a more supercilious family so she might fit in better."

Darcy could not stifle his laughter, though he attempted to glare at his cousin. It was not at all efficacious in silencing him.

"You did not speak much this morning, Darcy. Dare I say you agree with Miss Bingley's opinions? Would Georgiana, had she still been under your care, been forbidden from associating with the young ladies we met last night?"

"I noticed nothing more than what you noticed yourself," replied Darcy. "There are a few who could use a little decorum. I did find Mrs. Bennet to be a trial, and I expect she will not improve upon acquaintance. Her youngest daughters were little better."

"I cannot say you are incorrect." Fitzwilliam eyed him. "I do think you should have kept silent instead of saying what you did about Miss Bennet's family. It might be true, but it is impolitic to say it in a ballroom where anyone might overhear."

Knowing his cousin was correct, Darcy only grunted. His mood was better this morning, and he could acknowledge Fitzwilliam's rebuke. But he had no desire to continue to speak on the subject. No one had overheard, so there was little reason to dwell on it.

Fitzwilliam seemed to take his response as agreement. "Besides," said he, "I believe that Miss Bennet and Miss Elizabeth—and perhaps to a certain extent, Miss Mary—make up for their relations' ridiculousness."

"What do you mean?" asked Darcy, looking at his cousin askance.

"Only that I find them to be exemplary ladies," replied Fitzwilliam. "It is odd, I suppose, considering how closely they are related to girls who have not a lick of sense. But Miss Bennet is perhaps the sweetest woman I have ever met, and Miss Elizabeth, the most intelligent. I will be happy to come to know them better."

Something in his tone suggested to Darcy that Fitzwilliam's statement might tend to something more than friendly intentions. The look with which his cousin regarded him did nothing to dispel Darcy's suppositions. Thus, Darcy felt it incumbent upon himself to further the conversation.

"Miss Bennet *was* sweet," conceded he, "but many a time a placid countenance can hide other, less impressive character traits."

"I will ask you not to judge the woman without having actually made her acquaintance," admonished Fitzwilliam. "Correct me if I am wrong, but I believe you did not exchange two words with her last night."

It was nothing less than the truth, and Darcy did not attempt to refute it. His cousin nodded when Darcy did not speak.

"Please allow me the power of discernment, Darcy. I danced with her and spoke with her several times, and I can confidently state that Miss Bennet is no more and no less than she appears. She is gentle and decorous, and she possesses an almost naïve propensity to attribute the best intentions to all she meets. She even spoke of her confidence in Miss Bingley's friendship, if you can believe that."

Darcy snorted, and Fitzwilliam grinned. "Miss Elizabeth, on the other hand, saw through Miss Bingley in an instant, and while she would not speak openly of her distrust of our new relation, her opinion was clear."

"That is shrewd, indeed," said Darcy, "though I will point out that Miss Bingley does not hide her prejudices nearly so well as she thinks."

"I will agree with you there."

"I am curious, Cousin," said Darcy, steering the conversation back to the topic of Miss Bennet and Fitzwilliam's intentions. "You speak of Miss Bennet and Miss Elizabeth, and while I would not injure you by suggesting you are infatuated, it seems to me that your words presage a certain level of interest beyond that of simply coming to know a new acquaintance."

"How observant of you to have noticed," said Fitzwilliam, his tone mocking.

With a frown, Darcy said: "You cannot be serious."

"Why can I not be?" asked Fitzwilliam, eyebrow arched.

"Because they are entirely unsuitable."

"How can you call them unsuitable?" asked Fitzwilliam. "They *are* gentlewomen, are they not?"

"They are. But they have no connections, and you cannot think they possess dowries of any worth. Their family has been buried in this backwater neighborhood since time immemorial, their mother is a silly woman who openly schemes to entrap gentlemen into marrying her daughters, and their younger sisters ought to be locked in the schoolroom until they are thirty years of age."

Fitzwilliam laughed and shook his head. Darcy was beginning to feel cross with his cousin. "Perhaps what you say is true. Regarding the mother or the sisters, I would not be marrying *them*, so it is of little consequence."

"If the father dies, you may be responsible for them."

"Ah, but then I may demand better behavior from a position of authority. Besides, I am content to leave the family honor in yours and James's hands. I wish for a woman who will be a credit to me, but who will be one I can love and who is not tainted by society."

"You know I wish for the same."

"You do. But you have confined your searching to the simpering debutants of society. I have no desire to cast my hook into those waters. I wish for a genuine woman. My income is much smaller than yours or James's will ever be. Yes, I am the younger son of an earl, but upholding the honor of the family will be James's responsibility, not mine."

A little surprise flashed through Darcy's mind. He had known of his cousin's opinions—they mirrored Darcy's closely, and they had discussed it many times over the years. But he had not been aware that Fitzwilliam had become so jaded, so resolved to avoid a society lady as a wife.

"Have you not informed me many times over the years that you need to marry a woman with money so you may keep your lifestyle?"

"Thorndell changed all that, Darcy," replied Fitzwilliam. "Though my income will be less than four thousand, I am more than content with that. If I married a woman with fifty thousand, our income would be half of that. The independence I gain from the possession of the estate allows me the power of choice.

"And before you say it, my father and mother will be nothing but happy with my choice. I am convinced they will have nothing but praise for her, should I choose Miss Bennet."

Darcy looked at his cousin with interest. "I had thought it possible you might favor Miss Elizabeth."

"She *is* a jewel of the first order," replied Fitzwilliam with a grin. "But I think we are too similar for a closer relationship to work between us. Were we to marry, we would become cynical and bitter before two years had passed.

"Miss Bennet is the one I think better suits me. Her quiet calmness will compliment my more outgoing manners."

"It seems you have this all planned out," said Darcy with some asperity.

"I have planned nothing," replied Fitzwilliam, unperturbed by Darcy's displeasure. "I have merely recognized the possibility of having found a woman who will match me. But I have only just met her. I will not rush to the altar, I assure you."

"What will you do about your commission?" asked Darcy. "With all this talk of being independent, I might have thought you eager to leave the army behind."

"Eager, yes," said Fitzwilliam. "But the war against Napoleon is worsening, and a part of me says that to resign now would be a betrayal."

"You have more than served England, Fitzwilliam."

"I believe I have." Fitzwilliam paused. "I *have* considered it, Darcy. I have not come to any conclusions, but as I have several weeks' leave before me, I may take my time and decide what is best. Miss Bennet is a lovely and amiable girl, and I would like to know her better. Right now I do not know we are compatible. But I wish to know."

Darcy shook his head. "Consider the matter carefully before you make so rash a decision as to marry the girl. I doubt she will fit into the world we inhabit."

"That, my dear Darcy, is a point in her favor. As I said, I do not wish for a society wife. I am happy with a beautiful, intelligent, loving, kind country miss."

The look in Fitzwilliam's eyes was far away, and it was clear he was thinking of Miss Bennet. Darcy did not think his cousin had lost his heart to the woman. With any luck, in the end, he would remember the disadvantages of marrying her and refrain from making a colossal mistake.

CHAPTER V

As the month of October wore on, it became clear to all who cared to see that Colonel Fitzwilliam admired Miss Jane Bennet. When they were in company, the colonel would seek her out, standing with her the majority of the evening speaking, dancing as the opportunity presented itself, and generally showing himself to be a man who was interested in a woman. What was less evident, in Elizabeth's opinion, was Jane's returning level of interest in the colonel.

Anyone who lived in Meryton or its environs knew Jane Bennet was a reticent young woman. Since her coming out, many men had paid attention to her, but none had gone further than light flirtation, though one young man, when she had been visiting their uncle and aunt in London, had written some poetry for her. He had been no Byron, unfortunately, for his verses had been some of the worst drivel, given Jane's account of it.

Elizabeth, who knew her sister better than anyone else in the world did, was intimately familiar with Jane's character, her dreams and her hopes and fears. And yet, with all these advantages, Elizabeth could not determine Jane's feelings for Colonel Fitzwilliam. If she could not, how was the man himself to detect them? It worried Elizabeth. She knew that a man could carry on charmingly if he possessed enough interest. But could he take that next step if he was not given *some* encouragement from the lady? Elizabeth was not at all certain. But as it was still early in their acquaintance, Elizabeth was content to allow them the opportunity to determine their own wishes for the future without her speaking to Jane on the matter.

To anyone who knew her mother, however, it would come as no surprise that Mrs. Bennet did not see matters quite the same as Elizabeth. Nor was she shy about sharing her expectations for her daughter's future felicity. This was amply demonstrated at an event only two weeks after Colonel Fitzwilliam's appearance in the neighborhood.

It was also well known that Mrs. Bennet was one of the foremost gossips in Meryton. In this, she was joined by her sister, Mrs. Phillips, by Lady Lucas, and by several of the other ladies. At the party in question, she was joined by Lady Lucas and Mrs. Goulding, another of the matrons with more ability to chatter than sense. Elizabeth might not have minded her mother's love of gossip, had she ever learned to speak in a quieter voice than was her wont.

"I dare say, Lady Lucas," said she to the group of clucking hens, "Colonel Fitzwilliam carries along charmingly with my Jane. And she is happy to receive him."

"Why, anyone could see that," said Lady Lucas, though her glance in Jane's direction suggested she was attempting to puzzle Jane's feelings out for herself.

"Should she not give him some encouragement?" asked Mrs. Goulding.

"She shows him enough," said Mrs. Bennet, brushing her friend's comment off as if she was brushing lint off her dress. "You must understand my Jane. She is demure and quiet, and I dare say this is as demonstrative as she can manage. She is such a good, proper girl. She has been taught all her life to be a good wife to a man of consequence, and I have no doubt the dear colonel will find her irresistible!"

For all that Elizabeth agreed with some of what her mother said—Jane likely *was* being as demonstrative as she could be—other parts of her mother's speech were patently absurd. There was a level of self-congratulation in her words which had Elizabeth rolling her eyes. The suggestion that Mrs. Bennet had taught her daughter how to behave was laughable.

"What an excellent match it will be!" exclaimed she at that moment. "And what a wonderful thing it will be for our family to be connected to an earl."

"You are fortunate, indeed," said Lady Lucas. Her tone, however, was more envious than congratulatory.

Elizabeth knew Lady Lucas wished to marry off her own daughters as soon as possible, but while Maria was still young, Charlotte was seven and twenty and on the edge of being considered to be on the shelf. The fact that Elizabeth thought Charlotte one of the dearest persons in the world, eminently suitable to be an excellent wife to any man, carried little weight with young men looking for a woman of fortune and fine face.

But Mrs. Bennet noticed none of this—*all* her friends must necessarily be as happy as she was, and the fact that she was boasting had likely never entered her head. In her mind, she was simply speaking of her hopes for the future.

"I dare say, you will also have the opportunity to marry your other daughters to men of society," said Mrs. Goulding. While Lady Lucas's tone had indicated some envy, Mrs. Goulding's was positively dripping with it.

"Of course," replied Mrs. Bennet. "Being the son of an earl, Colonel Fitzwilliam must know many men of society. I have no doubt that my other girls will be put in the paths of other wealthy men. My Lydia, especially, will be so popular, for she is so lively!"

At that moment, Lydia strode by with Kitty and Maria Lucas, all three giggling loudly, seeming to punctuate Mrs. Bennet's words. Elizabeth, however, saw Mr. Darcy watching the scene, and she noted his carefully bland expression. Had Elizabeth worried for the colonel's resolve, she might have wondered if he might be in danger of being swayed by Mr. Darcy's disapproval. As it was, she decided the colonel would persevere, as long as Jane possessed his heart.

Another member of the party to quickly grow close to the eldest Bennet sisters was Mrs. Georgiana Bingley. The girl was young— Kitty's age, in fact—but she was much different from either of Elizabeth's youngest sisters in character. She was shy and mild, for one thing, though Elizabeth noted she had little difficulty speaking when she became acquainted with others. She was also eager to have friends, as she told them herself on that same night.

"I have often experienced difficulty in coming to know other young ladies my age," said she, her blush attesting to her shyness. "I tend to be bashful when meeting new people, and it is often left to others to make the first steps."

"If it means gaining a wonderful lady such as yourself for a friend," said Elizabeth, "then it is well worth it."

Mrs. Bingley started and looked up at Elizabeth, eyes searching Elizabeth's face. She must have found something in Elizabeth's countenance which pleased her, for a slow smile curved her lips.

"I thank you both," said she in a voice which was almost inaudible. "It means much to me to meet such genuine ladies as yourselves. When I went to school, it was always difficult to know if a young lady truly wished to be my friend. To many, I was merely a means to become acquainted with my brother."

A shocked gasp escaped Jane's lips. "Young ladies would behave in such a manner?"

"Of course, they would, Jane," said Elizabeth, though she did not say it in a censuring tone.

Mrs. Bingley nodded. "William is quite prominent, for our family is old and respected. We also have the more recent connection to the earls of Matlock, as well as other, older connections to other nobility. Though my brother is not titled, I have often heard it said that his situation is as good as if he possessed a title."

Both Elizabeth and Jane were impressed. Elizabeth had not known that about Mr. Darcy, though she had known he was of some standing in society. Mrs. Bingley, however, kept speaking, not noticing their reaction.

"I can sense you both are more interested in learning to know me for myself, and it is good to feel valued in such a way. It has not always been that way in the past."

"Well, I will not promise you will not find such behavior in Meryton at all," said Elizabeth. "But in speaking for myself and Jane, we are happy to be your friends for no other reason than our esteem for you."

"I am happy to hear it," said Mrs. Bingley. "I find far too much of that *other* behavior at Netherfield."

Her significant look at the Bingley sisters, who were sitting on the other side of the room whispering quietly to each other, was missed by neither Jane nor Elizabeth. Jane appeared to be struck with more than a little disbelief, but Elizabeth was well aware of the Bingley sisters' natures.

"Then we are happy to provide a buffer whenever required," said Elizabeth, steering the girl away from such topics. "But I am curious. I understand that Mr. Bingley is your brother's friend, but I had not thought that would translate easily to love and marriage, especially in one so young."

Though she made a valiant attempt to avoid blushing, Elizabeth could still see the embarrassment in Mrs. Bingley's reaction to her words. Though she had meant to inquire as a point of interest, it appeared to Elizabeth that she had managed to raise a sensitive point with Mrs. Bingley. For the first time, Elizabeth wondered if there was some other reason why she had married at such a young age.

"Oh, I apologize, Mrs. Bingley," said Elizabeth, eager to correct her mistake. "I realize now how my question might have sounded, and I assure you I meant nothing of the sort. It is clear to anyone who cares to look how much affection you hold for each other."

"Mr. Bingley *is* very good," said Mrs. Bingley. "I do not deserve him."

"Mrs. Bingley," said Elizabeth, pulling her eyes back from her contemplation of her new friend's husband, "I am assured that you do, indeed, deserve him. It is clear from Mr. Bingley's actions that *he* believes you do. I dare say his is the only opinion which matters."

"That is true," said Mrs. Bingley. From thence the sisters were little able to induce her to speak, for she continued in earnest observation of her husband for the rest of the evening.

In keeping with his self-appointed role as the host of all Meryton society, Sir William Lucas often hosted gatherings at his home. His penchant for company was legendary amongst local society. And so it was that soon after the previous evening in company, the Bennets were invited, along with the rest of the neighborhood, to dinner at Lucas Lodge.

There, for the first time, the members of a militia company, which had recently arrived in Meryton to their winter quarters, were seen in Meryton society. Sir William, eager as he was to be civil to all and sundry, could hardly be expected to include such a new and varied addition to their society. The company was therefore graced with the commander of the regiment—a Colonel Forster—and a selection of his senior officers.

For herself, Elizabeth was always willing to meet newcomers, and she welcomed the officers with witty conversation and an eagerness to take their measure. For the most part, Elizabeth was not disappointed, for they seemed to be a likable lot. Lydia and Kitty were excited to see them, so much so that Elizabeth thought several months of the regiment's presence in Meryton would leave them lucky to escape with their reputations intact. But she ignored them as best she could and was heartened when her father spoke a few words to them on occasion.

"You find a man in a red coat striking, do you?" asked Colonel Fitzwilliam at one point later in the evening when Lydia made some comment in his hearing. Jane and Elizabeth both had been speaking with him at the time and were privy to everything he said.

"I think a man is nothing if he is not in regimentals," said Lydia in that fearless voice of hers, which suggested she believed everything she was saying.

"What of a man who usually wears regimentals but is dressed in a gentleman's suit?"

Lydia eyed him, surely aware of his reference to himself. They all knew him to be a colonel. But the girls had not paid him much attention, likely because he did not appear to be a colonel or because he had concentrated on their eldest sister.

"I believe I should like it much better should that man deign to wear the scarlet on occasion."

Colonel Fitzwilliam laughed. "I am sure you would, Miss Lydia. Perhaps sometime I shall oblige you and wear it. But before you become too enamored with these fellows here—who seem like good men in general, I think there are one or two things you ought to remember."

"And what would that be?" said Kitty.

"The first is that it is not the uniform which makes the man, Miss Kitty. It is the man that makes the uniform."

Both girls frowned. "I do not understand," said Lydia.

"It is simple," said Colonel Fitzwilliam. "A man may distinguish the uniform by his behavior, his valor, and his very character. But the uniform in and of itself is nothing more than a piece of brightly colored fabric. It does not grant the wearer nobility of character—the man wearing it is of a noble character, or he is not.

"Furthermore, you would do well to remember that there are plenty of men of questionable character in the army, the same as anywhere else. A handsome man is not always a good one, nor is an ill-favored man necessarily bad."

"I think I see what you mean," said Kitty, frowning. By her side, Lydia was as introspective as her sister.

Colonel Fitzwilliam turned back to Jane and Elizabeth, to continue their conversation with them, when Lydia demanded: "You said there was another thing we should know."

"Of course, Miss Lydia," said Colonel Fitzwilliam. Elizabeth was hard pressed to refrain from laughing, for she understood his tactic as forcing the girls to come to him with their curiosity, thereby making the lesson of much greater impact.

"The second thing you should know is that while the officers are *usually* good men, they have little to their names other than their commissions. Only men in Colonel Forster's position are able to take a wife, and even then, he is not a wealthy man and may not give his wife the life that the daughter of a gentleman enjoys.

"I know you are both full young to consider marriage." The colonel smiled softly at them, and Elizabeth thought he looked on them both with amused affection. "But you should remember that you should not be so eager that you forget propriety, lest you be forced to marry one. They cannot afford to have you. Therefore, enjoy their company and admire them if you wish. But take care to do it from afar."

With thoughtful expressions, the two girls moved away, Colonel Fitzwilliam's advice ringing in their ears. Elizabeth looked on him with wonder, for he had managed in a few moments what Elizabeth and Jane had been struggling to impart for months. When she pointed this out to him, Colonel Fitzwilliam laughed.

"Your sisters are much like many other young girls I have had occasion to know," said he. "They are neither the worst nor the most determined. Most girls, when the reality of the life and prospects of a militia officer are explained to them, will temper their interest quickly."

Elizabeth laughed, and as Colonel Fitzwilliam began to speak with Jane, she excused herself, feeling she was superfluous. Soon, she found herself with Charlotte, who, it seemed, had much to say concerning Jane's good fortune.

"It seems Jane has captured the interest of a prominent man," said she.

"Yes, and I am happy for her, Charlotte. Jane deserves everything life could possibly give her. Colonel Fitzwilliam is a good man, and I am certain he shall make her very happy, should he decide to offer for her."

"Oh?" asked Charlotte, turning a questioning glance on Elizabeth. "Are you certain of this?"

For a moment, Elizabeth was confused, not having expected Charlotte to challenge her in such a manner. Charlotte used Elizabeth's momentary silence to continue speaking.

"For myself, I am unable to understand Jane's feelings on the matter. Oh, it is clear that she enjoys speaking to him, but then again, so do I, and I cannot say that I am in love with him. In fact, I suspect that Jane may not really have much feeling for him, though I suppose she would not refuse him should he ask.

"Nor should she! We are, none of us, in a position where we may refuse *any* offer of marriage, no matter our opinion concerning the offer or the gentleman who extends it."

"You make it sound so dispassionate!" exclaimed Elizabeth. "Should a woman not search for a man with whom she shares compatible interests and temper? Should she not wish for something more?"

"Not if she wishes to avoid poverty," said Charlotte. "We cannot afford to be fastidious, Lizzy."

"Then I shall advise her to induce him to fall in love with her quickly," said Elizabeth in jest. "With such arguments as you put forward, how can one dissent?"

"You know I am correct, Lizzy," said Charlotte.

Elizabeth shook her head, but she did not reply. Charlotte's feelings regarding marriage had never been precisely hidden, though she had rarely spoken with such candor. Elizabeth herself would never behave in such a way. But there was no sense in provoking an argument.

While Miss Elizabeth and Miss Lucas spoke in their sportive way, they were not aware that Darcy was near enough to them to hear every word. And it should not be a surprise he was not amused by what he was hearing.

This neighborhood was truly an oddity in that no one lived here who could claim to be more than a country squire. Rarely had he seen so many small estates all clustered together. And where such people congregated, he knew there must be many among them who would wish to improve their lot, to climb the ladder of society to a higher rung. It appeared the Bennets and Lucases, at the very least, were among that number. Darcy had never doubted it when it came to the mothers. But he had hoped in Miss Elizabeth's case, at least, that she was above such machinations.

With an unfriendly eye, Darcy watched his cousin's continued attention to Miss Jane Bennet. The girl was all that was proper—Darcy had no choice but to allow her that much. But the more he watched her, the more he came to Miss Lucas's opinion. She accepted Fitzwilliam's overtures with pleasure, but there was a lack of particular regard he would hope to see in the woman his cousin was pursuing.

Was Fitzwilliam pursuing her? If it were Bingley, Darcy would say that it was his typical proclivity for falling in love with the prettiest girl present. At least until he lost interest in her. Fitzwilliam, by contrast, had always spread his notice out to any woman who interested him, his friendliness not indicative of particular regard. Miss Bennet was a departure from that, to be certain, for while he was pleasant with them all, most of his regard was reserved for her.

Darcy was resolved to watch the entire family and, if necessary, dissuade his cousin from making a disastrous mistake. He did not think the younger women themselves would stoop to something as underhanded as to effect a compromise, but he could not trust Mrs. Bennet. And if she would, it was possible her progeny would fall in with her plans out of duty to their mother.

A short time later, Miss Lucas opened the pianoforte, and Darcy was privy to another conversation between the two young women. This one, at least, was not so improper as the last had been.

"I have opened the instrument, Lizzy," said Miss Lucas. "You know that means I wish you to perform to the company."

Miss Elizabeth laughed. "I wonder why you do not simply learn to play yourself, so you may amaze the company with your own playing. I have, as you know, little desire to display my lack of talent to all."

"Why would I learn to play myself," teased Miss Lucas, "when you are so close at hand?"

"Why, indeed?" asked Miss Elizabeth, attempting a fierce glare, but failing miserably. "Truly, Charlotte, I am not inclined to play. Mary, as you can see, is eager to go to the instrument in my place."

Darcy followed Miss Elizabeth's glance to where her younger sister was standing, and he noted that she was, indeed, eagerly watching them. She almost reminded him of Georgiana, though she liked to play, not exhibit.

"Mary may have her turn once you have finished," said Miss Lucas. Miss Mary appeared crestfallen.

"Then perhaps Miss Bingley, Mrs. Hurst, or Mrs. Bingley will oblige us. Truly Charlotte, I have little inclination for it tonight."

"Please, Lizzy. A song or two for me. Then you may dispense with it for the rest of the evening."

An exaggerated sigh met her friend's pleading. "Very well, Charlotte. I will play a little. But I will not stay at the instrument long."

When Miss Elizabeth took her place at the pianoforte, Darcy moved closer, though careful to stay on the fringes of the company, eager to avoid her notice. The company — at least those nearby — quieted a little, and as a result, Darcy was able to hear her playing quite well.

She was not a capital performer — Darcy realized that immediately.

Her claims had not been made due to false modesty or any other stratagem a young woman might use, and for that Darcy was grateful. But where she lacked technical proficiency, she more than made up for it in her obvious joy in the music and the feeling with which she played. Darcy enjoyed himself very much, both in the song and in looking on the countenance of a pretty woman as she sang to the room.

When Miss Elizabeth finished playing, she relinquished the pianoforte to her younger sister, whose playing was more proficient, but not quite so pleasing. And Darcy was left considering all he had heard tonight, from their imprudent words to Miss Elizabeth's surprisingly agreeable performance.

She was, he decided, the most impressive woman in Meryton, not that that was saying much. She was pretty and interesting. But that was the extent of it, for her predatory nature rendered her pleasing attributes less enticing because of them. Thus, Darcy was able to say with absolute honesty that she was no danger whatsoever to him.

However, he sensed his cousin *was* in danger, as strange as that may sound. But Fitzwilliam was also independent and did not appreciate attempts to interfere in his life. Darcy resolved to speak with him only if necessary.

CHAPTER VI

*O*ne of the things which quickly became apparent to Elizabeth was that their friendship with Georgiana Bingley allowed the colonel greater opportunity to be in Jane's company. This was true, not only in the course of typical societal amusement but was also made plain when the mistress of Netherfield invited the eldest Bennets to dinner one evening.

The invitation came that morning as they were eating breakfast, and Elizabeth thought it might have ended very differently but for her inclusion in the scheme. When the letter was delivered and its contents disseminated to the family—and the appropriate exclamations given on the part of her mother—the inevitable scheming began. It would not do for Longbourn's most beautiful and eligible daughter to go to Netherfield without the hope of seeing Colonel Fitzwilliam, who was to dine, along with the other gentlemen, with the officers that evening.

"I think, Jane," said Mrs. Bennet, "you must go to Netherfield on horseback."

"On horseback?" echoed Jane, unable to understand what her mother was saying. To Elizabeth, it was all too clear.

"Of course, my dear," said Mrs. Bennet. "If you will but glance out the window, you will see it is about to rain, and if it does, you will be required to stay the night."

"Unless Miss Bingley simply offers her brother's carriage to convey her home," said Mr. Bennet.

As usual, Mrs. Bennet ignored anything which did not fit in with her machinations. "And if you stay the night, you will have the opportunity to see Colonel Fitzwilliam before you return. For why would you go to Netherfield and *not* see Colonel Fitzwilliam? It is unfathomable in every way."

"Except that I have been invited as well," said Elizabeth, smiling in true amusement at her mother's sudden confusion. "Or perhaps you mean for us both to sit on the back of our poor Nelly."

"Why would Mrs. Bingley invite *you*?" screeched Mrs. Bennet.

"Perhaps because I am her friend too?" said Elizabeth, arching an eyebrow at her mother.

"Of course, you may have the carriage," said Mr. Bennet, forestalling his wife's anticipated objection to Elizabeth's inclusion in the invitation. "We would not wish you to be seen to any less advantage by the appearance of not being able to use our family carriage."

Elizabeth watched her mother, anticipating her protests. But it seemed Mr. Bennet's final comments had won her over, though she clearly did not appreciate being forced to abandon her stratagem. She continued to glare at Elizabeth as if she was somehow at fault for being invited by Mrs. Bingley. It was no trouble for Elizabeth to ignore her mother's injured glares. In fact, she attended to it with a will.

They were greeted in front of Netherfield by an obviously eager Mrs. Bingley and shown into the room where her two sisters by marriage were waiting. The greetings were exchanged cordially, and they sat down to visit before dinner. Their conversation covered a variety of topics and was pleasing and interesting, both to Elizabeth and to Jane. But while Mrs. Bingley was enthusiastic for their company, Mrs. Hurst was quiet, and Miss Bingley seemingly exasperated at times, though Elizabeth thought she hid it for the most part in a creditable manner.

"Oh, yes," said Miss Bingley, in a tone which suggested superiority, but only a hint of arrogance, "we are very happy to have our dear Georgiana as a sister." The subject of the girl's recent marriage to Mr. Bingley had been raised, and Miss Bingley was only too happy to speak of it. "I had known for some time that my brother admired Georgiana, and it was no surprise to me that he moved to secure her hand in an expeditious manner."

"You had been acquainted long before your marriage?" asked Elizabeth.

"Some years at least," said Mrs. Bingley. "My brother, you see, made Mr. Bingley's acquaintance at university, and I was introduced to him when I was, perhaps, fifteen."

"And an instant connection it was!" exclaimed Miss Bingley.

Mrs. Bingley rolled her eyes at the other woman's enthusiasm and confined herself to a simply spoken: "I knew immediately that Mr. Bingley is a good man. When he turned his interest on me, I was happy to accept."

"Louisa and I were pleased for them both," said Miss Bingley. "My brother, you see, possesses an unguarded temper and the ability to make himself agreeable to all. To see him make a true match of affection was a relief, for he drew the attention of many ladies who were unworthy and would have forced his hand, had the opportunity presented itself."

Elizabeth thought she understood Miss Bingley's words, and she wondered how she might have behaved had Mr. Bingley come to Netherfield still single. Would she have considered a lady of this neighborhood unworthy, had Mr. Bingley shown an interest in one of them? Elizabeth did not doubt she would have, for the simple fact that a lady of this neighborhood could not have been considered high enough in society.

It seemed that Mrs. Bingley was not at all comfortable with this line of conversation, so Elizabeth obliged her by changing it, observing that they had a beautiful instrument in the room. It was an inspired choice, for Mrs. Bingley, she discovered, was fond of music.

"It is a wedding present," said she, glancing lovingly at the instrument. "My brother informed me that he had meant to replace our pianoforte at Pemberley next summer, but when I became engaged, he decided to gift me with it instead."

"It is, indeed, a handsome gift," observed Jane.

"But that is how it is with Mr. Darcy," said Miss Bingley. "Anything which can be done for his sister's enjoyment is done without hesitation."

"William is an excellent brother," said Mrs. Bingley. "I do not deserve him."

"Mrs. Bingley," said Elizabeth, her tone slightly admonishing, belied by her wink at the girl, "as I informed you before, it is clear you *do* deserve whatever blessings you have in your life, including your brother and your husband."

"Thank you, Miss Elizabeth," said Mrs. Bingley, beaming in pleasure.

"Miss Elizabeth, is completely correct," added Miss Bingley. "We could not be happier to have you as a sister."

The response given by Mrs. Bingley was less enthusiastic, which fascinated Elizabeth. The only reason she could think of why Mrs. Bingley would accept the compliment from her with greater pleasure than from Miss Bingley was that the woman was not entirely sincere. Could Miss Bingley have an ulterior motive in mind? If so, it was not difficult to imagine what it could be.

Two gentlemen in residence could be considered an excellent match for Miss Bingley. The fact that she did not seem to resent Jane suggested Miss Bingley was focused on Mr. Darcy, rather than Colonel Fitzwilliam. Furthermore, Mr. Darcy's lack of interest in either Bennet sister explained the reason for Miss Bingley's willingness to exchange friendly relations with them, though her arrogance did not allow her to be *too* friendly.

Having solved the puzzler, Elizabeth put her hand to her face to hide a smile. The movement attracted Miss Bingley's notice, but she did nothing more than glance at Elizabeth. Elizabeth could not help but wonder what might have ensued had the situation been different. Would she have behaved worse had her brother been attracted to one of them or had Mr. Darcy been inflicted by a similar fascination? The thought amused her and removed her from the conversation for several moments.

The discussion turned to a general discourse of music with them all participating to a certain extent. Even Jane, who did not play an instrument, possessed a fine singing voice and a decided opinion about what she liked and did not like. When Elizabeth once again participated in the conversation, she found herself once more provoking Miss Bingley's dislike.

"I do not often attempt Beethoven," said Elizabeth when Mrs. Bingley commented about the German composer's piece as one of her favorites. "I find his music is so intricate that even if one can play it technically, one must be truly proficient to capture the essence of it."

"I heard you play at Lucas Lodge, Miss Elizabeth," said Mrs. Bingley. "I did not find anything wanting."

"I am sorry to contradict you, Georgiana," said Miss Bingley, "but I think I understand what Miss Elizabeth is attempting to say." Miss Bingley turned to Elizabeth and, in a supercilious tone, said: "It is to your credit that you understand your limitations. There is nothing worse than one who does not possess enough talent attempting to play pieces she should not."

"It seems we agree on this point," said Elizabeth, even though she knew by now that Miss Bingley did not think much of her. "I could, perhaps, be more proficient than I am. I do enjoy playing, but I find there are so many things I enjoy that I do not take the time to practice as I should."

"That is a failing, though it is a common one." Miss Bingley did not even seem to realize she was directing a superior sneer at Elizabeth. "In society, one must be proficient in many things to be considered truly accomplished."

"I have no pretensions, Miss Bingley," said Elizabeth. "I am quite happy to leave it to others who care for such things. While I do attempt to improve myself in a variety of ways, it bothers me little what others think of me."

Miss Bingley directed an eloquent look at Elizabeth before she turned her attention away. Elizabeth was certain Miss Bingley thought she had gotten the better of the exchange. Perhaps she had. She had shown herself to be a condescending woman, and Elizabeth could not bother herself to care for her opinion.

While this, and other instances, showed Miss Bingley to be an arrogant woman who considered herself better than any daughter of a tradesman ought, the evening passed without incident. The conversation flowed effortlessly, and while it was often carried by the Bennet sisters and Mrs. Bingley, Miss Bingley said enough to acquit herself well. Mrs. Hurst was largely silent, but Elizabeth suspected that was because she was naturally reticent, though it was possible she did not care to be friends with the Bennet sisters.

In all, Elizabeth could not consider it anything other than a successful evening. Mrs. Bingley was the important one, for she was the relation to the man who was paying Jane attention at present. And as her good opinion was assured, Elizabeth was certain she would be no impediment to Colonel Fitzwilliam's continued interest in Jane. And later that evening, she had occasion to see his ever-increasing ardency toward Jane.

Elizabeth thought the gentlemen were surprised to see the eldest Bennet ladies dining at Netherfield. It was also clear that at least to some of the party, the surprise was not an unwelcome one.

"Miss Bennet, Miss Elizabeth," said Mr. Bingley when he entered the room, finding them there. "How good it is to see you here."

"Thank you, Mr. Bingley," said Elizabeth. "We have been enjoying the company of your wife and sisters." She directed an arch look at him. "But I might have expected that you would not be home yet for some time. I had thought you gentlemen would stay up half the night, indulging in stories of your prowess."

Colonel Fitzwilliam laughed, but Elizabeth could tell it was half-hearted, for his attention immediately returned to Jane. Mr. Darcy's expression was unreadable, and Mr. Hurst was already helping himself to some libations. Mr. Bingley, however, grinned and was not at all hesitant in answering.

"Such gatherings are not nearly as interesting as you might think, Miss Elizabeth. It is possible that Fitzwilliam might have sat with Colonel Forster half the night exchanging increasingly unlikely stories, but the rest of us have not been soldiers and did not have so much interest in such things."

"I will have you know that my stories are nothing but the absolute truth," said Colonel Fitzwilliam, affecting affront.

Even Mr. Darcy smiled at the jesting between them. "I highly doubt a third of what you say is the truth, Fitzwilliam."

"Perhaps you are correct," replied Colonel Fitzwilliam, eyes twinkling merrily. "The trick is to decipher *which* third it is."

They all laughed again, though Elizabeth thought Miss Bingley was merely humoring them. Then Mr. Bingley delivered news which was not at all welcome. Elizabeth knew her mother would be ecstatic when she heard it.

"I am afraid the reason we returned early is due to the heavy rain which has descended upon us."

Elizabeth's gaze darted to the windows in surprise. "I was not aware it had begun to rain."

"I must attribute that to your interest in my beautiful wife," said Mr. Bingley. Mrs. Bingley blushed, though she clearly appreciated his praise. "Be that as it may, we determined to return before the roads became too sodden for the carriage to transport us home. I think it would be best if you ladies stayed here the night, for conditions have undoubtedly become that much worse since we came inside."

"Oh, of course, you must stay!" exclaimed Mrs. Bingley. "I would not have my newest and dearest friends put themselves in danger unnecessarily."

"We would not wish to impose," said Elizabeth quickly. She had noted that Miss Bingley did not seem sanguine about the idea of their staying. Elizabeth was not enthusiastic about it at all."

"Nonsense!" cried Mr. Bingley. "It is no imposition."

"No, indeed," said Mrs. Bingley. "Please say you will stay with us."

There was nothing to do but accept the invitation, which Jane did, speaking for them both. Thus, their mother would be happy she had received her wish. Jane had not only been fortunate enough to meet Colonel Fitzwilliam at Netherfield, but she had also been invited to stay the night.

While the ladies spoke and laughed, and the gentlemen attended them, neither were aware they had become a subject of particular interest to at least one of the gentlemen. Besides the obvious one, of course — Fitzwilliam was as blatant in his admiration of Miss Bennet as Bingley himself used to be.

They were estimable ladies, Bingley decided. Miss Bennet was beautiful and kind, but also intelligent and interesting. And Miss Elizabeth was like a breath of fresh air, a vibrant magnet of a girl Bingley imagined could not help but draw interest.

Miss Bennet was, Bingley noted to himself, a woman he might have fallen in love with himself, had he remained unmarried. She was exactly the type he might have pursued previously, being blonde, beautiful, and willowy. In fact, even now, as he sat and watched Fitzwilliam making love to her, he felt a stirring in the bottom of his heart, an echo, he thought, of what might have been.

But then he looked at his dear Georgiana, and he realized that marriage to her had been the best decision he had ever made. She was his beautiful bride, and no other woman could take her place. He could not count her brush with misery as a good thing, but in a certain way, he was grateful it had happened. He might never have considered her otherwise, and he could not imagine missing the wonderful presence in his life that was his wife. He truly was blessed.

"Did you know Georgiana was to invite the Bennet sisters tonight?"

Bingley turned to Darcy, who had spoken, and denied any knowledge, saying: "It was as much of a surprise to me as it was to you, Darcy."

An absent nod was Darcy's immediate reply. He did not appear inclined to say anything else, which prompted Bingley to speak again.

"I am glad she invited them. They are estimable young ladies, and as Georgiana has often had difficulty making friends, I can only count their presence in her life a boon."

Darcy turned to Bingley sharply, and Bingley thought that at one point he might have been cowed by such a look. In this instance, he was nothing more than amused.

"I am not so sure," said Darcy. "In a neighborhood such as this, with naught but small estates and lesser gentry, gentlewomen such as these may hide other tendencies. I would not wish her to be hurt by false friends."

"I hardly think these ladies are anything but genuine, Darcy," said Bingley. "My wife is happier than she has been in months. Happier, I dare say," Bingley lowered his voice, "than when she is in company with only Caroline and Louisa, who, I will point out, are exactly as you described."

"I hope they will prove true, Bingley," said Darcy. "But I very much fear they will not."

"Not every woman is a fortune hunter. I know you have felt hunted from the time you entered society, but it is unfair to paint all young ladies by the same brush. And inaccurate too."

A shake of Darcy's head was the only answer Bingley was to receive. Well aware of his friend's tendency toward such thoughts, Bingley turned his attention away. He would not view the world through a cynical perspective as his friend. Bingley much preferred his own sunnier outlook.

As the evening lengthened, the company broke up to retire. Elizabeth suspected that Miss Bingley and Mrs. Hurst had little intention of loaning their own nightgowns to the Bennet sisters, but as Mrs. Bingley was eager, Elizabeth thought little of the sisters' behavior. After rooms were assigned and wishes of a good night were offered, they all went to their own rooms.

The bedroom was large and handsome, and Elizabeth settled into it with gratitude. She changed, with Jane's assistance, rendering the same assistance to her sister in turn, before the sisters bid each other good night and retired. And given the fatigue Elizabeth felt at the end of a long day, she thought she would fall asleep with little trouble.

But that did not happen. It is odd, Elizabeth thought as she lay there, her eyes wide open, sleep far away, that the occasions when the most fatigue was felt were often the times when sleep was the furthest distant. It was not any one thing, she thought. Memories of the night, the strange room and bed, the unfamiliar surroundings—all these things likely contributed to her insomnia.

She lay there for perhaps a half hour, and when sleep did not seem any closer, she decided it would be best to find some other way to find her rest. At Longbourn, she would sit up with a book for some time, allowing the words on the page to lull her into a more receptive state. She had no such volumes at hand at Netherfield, but the library was downstairs, and that deficiency could be easily rectified.

Thus, Elizabeth rose from the bed, donned the robe which had been provided to her, and made her way down the stairs. It was fortunate the library was near the entrance hall, for it did not require her to traipse through the house in her bedclothes. She entered therein, candle in hand, and began to peruse the shelves which lay before her, disapproving when she noted that there was little in the way of selection. Then the clearing of a throat informed her she was not alone.

Heart thumping painfully in her surprise, Elizabeth jumped around, a hand rising to her mouth. She almost dropped the candle in her shock. There, situated in the far corner of the room, sitting in a chair with a book in hand, a candle on a nearby table, sat Mr. Darcy.

He rose and approached her, his countenance severe and almost accusing. He was still dressed, Elizabeth noted, meaning he had not yet visited his bedchamber. He stood tall and forbidding, and in the faint light of her candle, his disapproving mien seemed almost demonic. She shivered at the sight of his unfriendly eyes cast upon her in judgment.

"What are you doing here, Miss Elizabeth?" said he, his tone not at all friendly.

His tone pricked Elizabeth's indignation, and her courage surged to the fore, as it did whenever any attempt was made to intimidate her. Elizabeth stood taller, though she could not hope to match this man's great height, and she regarded him with some asperity.

"I should think it is quite obvious why I am here, Mr. Darcy. I was not able to sleep and thought to help myself along by borrowing a book from Mr. Bingley's library. I will make certain to put it back tomorrow morning before I depart."

Her explanation produced no immediate response. Mr. Darcy continued to look at her, impassive and threatening at the same time. He was a maddening man, and Elizabeth could not quite make him out. She thought he did not like her and could not determine why he would regard her with such asperity. After all, it had not been *she* who had spoken of *his* family in such a disparaging way.

"Do not concern yourself for me, Mr. Darcy," said Elizabeth when he did not respond. "I shall gather a book and be gone. You may have the library to yourself again."

With those words, Elizabeth turned and began to look at the shelves again, though she was aware that Mr. Darcy did not move from his position. The problem, of course, was that there was a paucity of tomes for her to choose from, the selection so small and largely uninteresting that Elizabeth could not believe it from an educated man such as Mr. Bingley.

"One would think the man would have a larger selection," muttered Elizabeth as she pulled one volume from the shelf, thinking it might be enough to bore her to sleep if nothing else.

She heard a snort from behind her and turned to regard Mr. Darcy once again. "Bingley, as you may have noticed, is not a great reader."

"I would never have guessed, Mr. Darcy. But I have something now, so I shall leave you. Good night, sir."

Darcy watched as Miss Elizabeth gave the barest hint of a curtsey and fled, her book clutched to her breast. It was only because of his ingrained good manners that he remembered to bow in response, not that she took any notice.

She was as interesting a creature as he had met in this backwater neighborhood—Darcy could confess that much to himself. The fact that she was interested in books said much about her character, and Darcy suspected that if he allowed himself to come to know her, he might be impressed by her wit and intelligence. There were so few women who intrigued him in such a way that meeting one here, of all places, was interesting by itself.

For several minutes after she left, Darcy stood rooted to the spot, watching where she had disappeared through the door. She had looked quite fetching in her nightgown and dressing gown, which revealed more of her ankles than propriety might allow. For a moment, he had almost thought there was a connection there, something in their shared amusement over Bingley's pitifully small collection of books.

But reality then set in. Miss Elizabeth Bennet was a fortune hunter, had come from a family of fortune hunters who were pretty and interesting enough to snare the unwary. It would not do to give even a hint of interest in her any sway over his actions. He had no wish to be drawn in by such as she.

Thus, putting any thoughts of Miss Elizabeth aside, Darcy returned to his seat and his book.

CHAPTER VII

*The problem of the Bennet ladies stayed with Darcy through the night, and he had still not come to a resolution by the following morning. He only knew he wished to have them out of the house, to return them to their home before they could further work their wiles on those he wished to protect. That moment did not come soon enough for Darcy's taste.

He would not have sent them away without breakfast to sustain them; that would be the height of rudeness. But as breakfast progressed, he wished they could do just that.

"Miss Bennet," greeted Fitzwilliam as the Bennet sisters entered the room that morning. "I hope you both slept well and are prepared for the day?"

"Of course, sir," replied Miss Bennet, her eyes lowering in demure pleasure. Though Darcy had long determined the entire family was motivated by nothing but avarice, he might have thought the woman was sincere. "Everything was lovely."

"I am happy to hear it. Might I fix a plate for you and your sister?"

It was difficult, but Darcy stifled a groan. Fitzwilliam truly was laying it on a little thick. They both agreed and gave him their preferences, seating themselves while he played the chivalrous knight.

When they were served, Fitzwilliam sat beside Miss Bennet and proceeded to give all his attention to her.

They looked rather cozy together, and had Darcy not already had confirmation to the contrary, he might have thought the woman's affections engaged. The way Miss Elizabeth sat, however, watching with an entirely inappropriate level of smugness, as if she had managed a great coup, suggested that the woman was congratulating herself with every word which was spoken between them, every glance or laugh. It made him more determined than ever to save his cousin by whatever means available to him. Miss Bingley's determined chatter did not make his mood any better.

"Where do you intend to spend the Christmas season this year, Mr. Darcy?" said she, interrupting Darcy's vigilance over his cousin. "Are you for Pemberley, or do you intend to spend it with your cousin's family?"

"I do not believe I have decided, Miss Bingley," replied Darcy with an absence of thought. "Perhaps it will be both—I cannot say at present."

"That would be delightful," said the woman around a bite of her breakfast. "I have always thought Pemberley in the winter must be a delight to see."

"I find I prefer it, no matter the season."

"I can understand why. With the greater amount of snow which falls in the north, I suppose there are times when you are quite snowed in."

"Yes, that is not unusual," replied Darcy. Then, with more politeness than interest, he said: "Do you expect to stay at Netherfield the entire winter?"

Miss Bingley gave a credible effort at not rolling her eyes, but Darcy could see the inclination was clearly there. "I suspect Charles is settled here for the time being." She paused and then added in a grudging voice. "Dear Georgiana, too, seems to be quite pleased with the neighborhood."

The reminder was not at all welcome, and he looked back to where Georgiana was now engaged in speaking with Miss Elizabeth. Georgiana, however, could not necessarily be expected to recognize ladies of baser characters, for she had not the experience in society. Fitzwilliam should know better, and yet he was allowing himself to be drawn in.

"There is, of course, one possible location I did not mention?" said Miss Bingley, drawing Darcy's attention back to her. "You could stay here at Netherfield with your beloved sister."

"Perhaps," replied Darcy, noncommittally. "But I do not imagine I shall stay at Netherfield for three or four months complete, though I am always happy to be in my sister's company."

"You have responsibilities," was Miss Bingley's sage observation.

"Indeed, I do," said Darcy.

"There are times," said Fitzwilliam, proving he had not been unaware of their conversation, "that I believe Darcy takes his duty to entirely excessive levels."

Darcy frowned, wondering if his cousin's words were meant to criticize. "I only do what I must, Cousin."

"I am not suggesting anything less, old boy," replied Fitzwilliam. "I only suggest that there are times when it is possible to still fulfill your duties while living life to its fullest."

"I have no complaints concerning my life."

"That is the trick, I suppose. It is not possible for anyone to go through life without regrets. But I do believe that as much as we are able, we should do what we can to live our lives, not only in a virtuous manner but also in a manner which will provoke the least amount of regrets."

"I believe it is best to leave the past where it belongs," said Miss Elizabeth. "Think of the past only as it brings you pleasure. That is the creed by which I attempt to live my life."

"But if you forget the past or do not understand its lessons, are you not then doomed to repeat your mistakes?"

"I do not believe that is what Miss Elizabeth was saying, Darcy," said Fitzwilliam, throwing him a reproving look.

"Not at all, Colonel," said Miss Elizabeth, smiling at him. Then she turned her attention back to Darcy. "I do not say we should not remember the past or refuse to learn from it, for that would be foolish, indeed. I merely suggest we do not allow ourselves to be so caught up in the mistakes we make that we forget to live in the present. Learn your lessons and move forward with determination and hope. Forever allowing our past to rule us is not healthy."

"*That* is my Lizzy," said Miss Bennet, affection shining through in every word.

For a moment, Darcy almost saw something in Miss Elizabeth he had not seen before, and he looked at her with interest. Her philosophy, when she put it in such a way, was one of which Darcy thought he could approve, though he could readily own that he would have difficulty living it himself.

The sparkle of her eyes, moreover, struck Darcy, informing him of her appeal, for which he had hitherto given her little credit. She was, he decided, quite pretty, her light figure complemented by all the right curves in the right places. Her obvious intelligence shone in those eyes, which seemed to look into a man's very soul. But then he remembered what she was, and her attractions, though he could confess they were substantial, lost all ability to move him.

"What say you, Darcy?" said Fitzwilliam, his mien amused, but his tone more than a little challenging.

"It is a sensible notion, Miss Elizabeth," said Darcy, nodding at her, but ignoring his cousin. "I will note that there are those who are not adept at forgiving themselves easily. Furthermore, I think there are times when we must give a certain level of thought to events of the past. But I cannot argue against your philosophy."

Miss Elizabeth watched him closely, and Darcy wondered if he might have said too much. When she finally spoke, he could hear the compassion in her voice.

"I am happy to hear it, sir. It is, indeed, unfortunate when one cannot move past the mistakes of the past. But I do understand and sympathize with it."

As Miss Elizabeth turned back to her breakfast, Darcy felt resentment well up within him. It seemed to him like Miss Elizabeth was judging him. Who was she to do so? She had never faced the trials he had. As a young woman, daughter to an insignificant man whose claim to the title of a gentleman was tenuous at best, she could not understand the pressures of the world in which he lived. Her sympathy was false and her words condescending, just as her philosophy.

Breakfast passed, though not swiftly enough for Darcy, and the Bennet sisters soon departed in their carriage. Sullenly, Darcy watched as Fitzwilliam handed first Miss Elizabeth into the carriage, and then Miss Bennet. His hand lingered on hers as she climbed up into the carriage and took her seat. Fitzwilliam leaned toward her and said something which prompted the laughter of both sisters. Then he closed the door, allowing the coach to lurch into motion. Darcy determined then and there to have words with his cousin.

It seemed Fitzwilliam anticipated him. "What is wrong, Darcy? You appear as angry as a hornet."

"I am not angry." Darcy had not intended to be short with his cousin, but his words came out in such a manner regardless.

"Oh?" said Fitzwilliam, clearly skeptical.

"No. I am merely wondering what you are about."

"What I am about? I am not certain to what you refer, Cousin. In fact, I am about many things, and you may be speaking of any one of them."

Darcy had often despaired of his cousin's flippant nature. At present, he was on the verge of being utterly infuriated by it. But he summoned all of his considerable well of patience and attempted to speak in a manner which would prompt his cousin to seriousness.

"I am speaking of Miss Bennet, Fitzwilliam. I am speaking of the preference you are showing her, the hopes you may be raising in her. What do you mean by this behavior?"

"At present," said Fitzwilliam, "I mean nothing by it."

"Nothing?" Darcy was openly skeptical. "It certainly does not appear to be nothing to me. In fact, if I did not know you better, I might think you are about to lose your head, something I would never have expected to see."

"Let us be clear then, Darcy," said Fitzwilliam. All trace of jesting was now absent from his cousin's demeanor. "At this moment I am engaged in nothing more than enjoying the company of a beautiful woman. I enjoy the company of both Miss Bennet and her younger sister, and even, to a certain extent, the rest of the family."

"You do?"

"Yes, Darcy, I do. Miss Bennet is probably the best young woman I have ever known. As for her sister, she is unpretentious, lively, and witty. Perhaps you should attempt to come to know her better. I believe you would esteem her as much as I do if you only gave her a chance."

"I believe I have already taken her measure," replied Darcy. "And that of her entire family. Knowing them better is not required."

Fitzwilliam shook his head, prompting Darcy's annoyance again. But his cousin spoke again before he could.

"As I said, Darcy, I am merely enjoying their company at present. That is all I am about."

"You are not concerned about raising her hopes, or possibly raising the neighborhood's expectations?"

"If I raise her hopes, that is my business, is it not?" Fitzwilliam apparently saw Darcy's temper rising, for he chuckled and grasped his shoulder. "Do not worry, Darcy. I have no intention of raising hopes I cannot fulfill. I am completely aware of my actions and the possible consequences. I am not Bingley that you must hover over me and ensure I know what I am about."

Then Fitzwilliam squeezed his shoulder and turned to walk away, leaving Darcy entirely unsatisfied as to the conclusion of their conversation.

There was another who was soon frustrated, though for an entirely different reason. Elizabeth and Jane's homecoming to Longbourn was met with welcome from their father and sisters, as well as lamentation from their mother that they had not managed to extend their stay. That Colonel Fitzwilliam continued to visit regularly, sometimes in the company of certain members of the Netherfield party, was a balm to their mother's eager heart, and as such, she became ever so slightly less irritable.

But several days after the return, an event occurred which was to cause Elizabeth much exasperation. There was no word of it until Mr. Bennet raised the matter at the dinner table, and the reactions to his news were not precisely surprising.

"Mr. Collins is to visit us?" cried his wife. It was very nearly a shriek, causing more than one of the diners to tap at their ears, trying to quell the ringing within.

"I am glad you are as excited as I find myself, Mrs. Bennet," said Mr. Bennet, completely unperturbed concerning his wife's horrified reaction to his statement. "In fact, he shall be here tonight, and I believe he is eager to meet us all."

"Of that, I have no doubt," replied Mrs. Bennet. She sniffed, a disdainful action which informed them all of her opinion of Mr. Collins. "No doubt he wishes to know those he will be dispossessing in an intimate matter, and to count the silver so we do not leave with a single piece of it."

"As I recall, Mrs. Bennet," said Mr. Bennet, "that silver was your mother's and, as such, is not part of the entail."

"And Mr. Collins had best remember it," was Mrs. Bennet's sulky reply.

Elizabeth did not know the genesis of it, but she knew her father and Mr. Collins's father had fallen out many years before, perhaps before her birth, and had not spoken since. Mr. Collins's stated purpose was to heal the breach, as her father informed them. Mrs. Bennet, Elizabeth thought, held out the hope that the peacemaking gentleman meant to offer to house them in the event of her husband's early death. He *was* a clergyman, so Elizabeth supposed it was possible. Unfortunately, his purpose was not that benign.

When he came that evening, they were all introduced to a tall and portly man, with thinning lank hair on his head. He possessed the grave air of one who considered every pronouncement before speaking, and when he did speak, saying something which could not be expected. And it was not that he was artful or profound. Unfortunately, it was only that he was servile and stupid, speaking of his patroness excessively, spouting nonsensical nothings and showing them all that within moments of his inheriting the estate, it would no doubt be bankrupt.

"It seems you are blessed with several amiable daughters, Mrs. Bennet," said Mr. Collins when they sat down to dinner. When Mrs. Bennet allowed it to be so, the man said: "I had heard of their charms, but thought I would journey here to admire them myself. I find that I am utterly delighted, especially to find them all yet single."

At that moment, Elizabeth thought her mother would mention Jane's recent interactions with the colonel. But while she opened her mouth to speak, she looked at all of them, an expression of fear came over her, and she remained silent. Elizabeth sighed — it was clear her mother was not so secure in Colonel Fitzwilliam's ardency as she liked to suggest, and would offer up any of them — even Jane — on the altar to Mr. Collins in exchange for security.

Considering one's viewpoint, it might be termed either fortuitous or entirely disastrous when Mr. Collins's choice was made known to them the next day. While it was a relief that he had not fixed on either Kitty or Mary — both of whom eyed him with distaste — Elizabeth was not eager about being forced to fend the dullard off. But that was exactly what she was required to do.

"Cousin Elizabeth," said he as soon as they sat down in the sitting-room after breakfast the following morning. "I noticed that you appear to be a devotee of the written word. Might I ask what you are reading?"

"This is only a book of Shakespeare's sonnets, Mr. Collins," said Elizabeth, showing him the volume in her hand. "I have read it many times before, but on occasion, I enjoy returning to those texts I have read before."

"Ah, yes," replied Mr. Collins, a sage nod, which was utterly hilarious from such a silly man, his response to her information. "I am quite partial to Shakespeare myself. Do you have a favorite play?"

"I believe I am rather partial to *A Midsummer Night's Dream*, Mr. Collins. I usually prefer the comedies, for I dearly love to laugh."

"Comedies," said Mr. Collins, his lip curling in distaste. "Laughter is, indeed, a healthy part of life. But too much laughter can lead to frivolity."

"A life without laughter is dreary, indeed, Mr. Collins," said Elizabeth.

"Perhaps it is. My preference is the histories. They are much more serious, provoking us to great thought and consideration."

"That they are," replied Elizabeth. "I did not say I do not like the histories—or the tragedies, for that matter. I only stated I prefer the comedies as a general rule." Elizabeth eyed the man, wondering how much knowledge he actually possessed. "Tell me, sir, which of the histories do you prefer? Is Edward III to your taste, or do you prefer King John? Or perhaps you prefer the epic saga of the tetralogy, the history of the War of the Roses, including the three Henry VI plays followed by Richard III. Would you like to discuss your impressions of them with me?"

Mr. Collins gazed at her, apparently dumbfounded that she would know so much of the bard's works. Elizabeth patiently waited, her estimation of Mr. Collins's slowness of thought suggesting he might take some time to respond. It turned out to be longer than she might have expected, as he was silent for a full minute complete.

"You have read them?" was his eventual question.

"I have already stated that I enjoy Shakespeare, sir. While some of his plays I prefer to others, ones that I return to frequently, I have read all of the bard's works. Indeed, it is the re-reading of such masterpieces which gives further insight into tone and message he attempts to impart, is it not? What is *your* favorite history?"

Mr. Collins's mouth worked for a moment before he finally gathered himself and said in a patronizing tone: "I expect my observations will be difficult for you to grasp, my dear cousin. Perhaps we should speak of the sonnets instead?"

The answer informed Elizabeth that her cousin had not actually read any of the works she had mentioned, and likely had not even heard of all the names. A snort from her father and the raising of his paper suggested he had seen the same thing. But Elizabeth decided against being rude and turned back to Mr. Collins.

"I am happy to turn to the sonnets if you prefer. Of what did you wish to speak?"

"*Shall I compare thee to a summer's day?*" quoted Mr. Collins. "*Thou art more lovely and more tempting.*"

Once again her father's newspaper shook with his mirth, and he rose and excused himself, though he winked at Elizabeth as he left. Elizabeth watched him, branding him a traitor as he left the room. Mr. Collins, however, was waiting for a response, as he regarded her, clearly expecting her to declare her everlasting love for him. Elizabeth was not about to allow a piece of misquoted poetry to move her heart, especially when delivered by such an unappealing man.

"I believe, Mr. Collins, the word is actually 'temperate,' not 'tempting.'"

"My knowledge of Shakespeare is obviously more extensive than your own, my dear cousin," said Mr. Collins. "I am more concerned about what you think of my declaration."

Elizabeth ignored his question, flipped to sonnet eighteen in the book she held in her hand and held it open for him. But Mr. Collins refused to look at it, instead continuing to make doe eyes at Elizabeth.

"Fine," said Elizabeth with a sigh. "I do not think anything of your declaration for you did not, in fact, make one."

"Of course, I did!" exclaimed Mr. Collins, sputtering in denial.

"Mr. Collins," said Elizabeth. "You did nothing more than quote poetry to me, and incorrectly at that."

"But poetry is the food of love!" protested he.

"Perhaps of a hearty, stout sort of love, it may be." Elizabeth shrugged and turned away, turning to the first page of her book. "But quoting sonnets to a woman of your acquaintance without knowledge of them, or any prior feeling existing between you would kill any inclination stone dead before you completed the first line."

As Elizabeth turned her attention away from Mr. Collins, she was still sensitive to everything the man did. For the moment, he sat and considered her, seeming to be attempting to understand her. But she ignored him. It would not do to give him any hope that his suit might be acceptable.

"Ah, I think I see," said he at length, at a time when Elizabeth had become absorbed in what she was reading and had shunted him to the back of her mind.

"How happy for you, sir," muttered Elizabeth.

"Indeed, I must consider myself fortunate. In fact, I understand your reticence better now, for I have some understanding of young ladies. You do not mean to make it easy for me, as I had originally anticipated. In fact, it appears to me, you wish to force me to earn your regard. Bravo, my dear cousin!"

A sigh escaped Elizabeth's lips. True to form, the man had added two and two and come up with some absurd number such as seven and thirty.

"I assure you that I am equal to the task. By the end of my time here in Hertfordshire, I am convinced you will be begging for my proposal."

It was all Elizabeth could stand, and she soon fled, Mr. Collins's scrutiny following her as she went. Once she was in the hall, Elizabeth thought to go to her room, but she soon decided to turn, instead, toward her father's room. A knock on her father's door was followed by a command to enter, which Elizabeth did, instantly fixing her father with a displeased grimace. She might not have bothered.

"Ah, Lizzy," said he, lazily waving her to a chair. "I had wondered how quickly you might join me. I must acknowledge that you have exceeded my expectations. I might have thought you would endure another fifteen minutes."

"Apparently, I shall be begging Mr. Collins for a proposal by the end of the week," replied Elizabeth, unable to help the wry note in her voice despite her displeasure.

Mr. Bennet chortled. "What a fine fellow my cousin is. I think I shall keep up the acquaintance, at least from a distance. He is far too diverting to give it up but much too annoying to endure him nearby."

"Papa," said Elizabeth, her tone reproving. "You know I will not accept his offer, should he choose to make one."

"I would never expect anything different."

"Then will you not inform him that I am not available?" Elizabeth gave an exasperated huff. "For that matter, if I am not available, you know he will turn to Mary, and she does not favor him."

"She does not?" asked Mr. Bennet, seeming bemused. "I had thought she might, for you know she is always going on about Fordyce and other such subjects. It seems to me Mary would make an excellent parson's wife."

"I am certain she would," replied Elizabeth. "But while she would be a good parson's wife, she would not be a good wife to a fool."

"I suppose you must be correct."

Elizabeth, however, was not about to allow herself to be put off by her father. She continued to watch him, waiting for his answer while her annoyance mounted. At first, her father attempted to ignore her, but after a time, he finally seemed to understand she would not be put off.

"What would you have me do, Elizabeth?" asked he. "I cannot forbid *every* man from developing an interest in my daughters. And what do you think your mother's reaction would be if I told her I will not allow him to pay his civilities to you?"

Feeling the rictus of a grimace coming over her face, Elizabeth nevertheless was not willing to give up. "Mama will be disappointed anyway."

"You do not know that, Elizabeth. Mr. Collins might not ever come to the point. Perhaps you only need to put him off until he returns to Kent. I would prefer to avoid provoking your mother's hysteria until we absolutely must. But I promise I will support you. I would not see you married to a man you cannot respect."

With that, Elizabeth was forced to be content. It seemed her father was intent upon protecting his privacy and avoiding provoking her mother, and while Elizabeth understood, she thought he was motivated more by selfishness than concern for her. But there was little choice, so she decided to simply let the matter rest.

Chapter VIII

*M*rs. Margaret Bennet was not a sensible woman. It had been her good fortune to come to the attention of a gentleman as a young girl, which had, of course, led to her assuming a position she might never have expected to take. Moreover, as an insensible woman, she was in no position to even understand her husband.

But she *was* a woman who could sense an interest in her daughters from miles away, an ability which had been honed by years of fear that her ultimate destination was the hedgerows so common in that part of the country. Mr. Collins presented a unique opportunity for Mrs. Bennet. While she had possessed this impression of Longbourn's heir as a hard, unfeeling man, one who would personally see to her removal minutes after her husband's death, it was a shock to discover Mr. Collins to be a silly, ineffectual man. Mrs. Bennet could see this, even if she did not possess great understanding herself. Mr. Collins, she felt, would be easily led, perfect for a woman in Mrs. Bennet's position. Why, with one of her daughters installed as the man's wife, Mrs. Bennet might even hold her position as mistress, for surely her daughter would not wish to supplant a mother!

Elizabeth knew all this of her mother. Had she cared to watch the woman, she fancied she might have understood the exact moment when each successive thought had entered her mind. But Elizabeth did not concern herself with such matters. She was much more concerned about avoiding Mr. Collins.

It was not always possible. A young woman could not be walking at all times, though Elizabeth spent as much time away from the house as she could. When at home, she confined herself to her room with a book whenever possible. But there were many times when her mother would chivvy her out of her room and instruct her to accept the inept pursuit of the silly parson.

"Come, Lizzy," Mrs. Bennet would say. "You have remained in your room in the company of your books quite long enough. Mr. Collins has been asking after you, and you will attend him."

Knowing not to sigh, Elizabeth would allow her mother to pull her from her room and down into the sitting-room. And then the pattern would play out again, with Mr. Collins's exclaimed: "Cousin Elizabeth! How charming it is to see you! Come, sit with me, so we may further discuss the appointments at my parsonage."

It was not long before Elizabeth grew to hate the sight of Mr. Collins's vacuous smile, and she grew desperate to escape from him. It came to a head when Mr. Collins announced his attention to accompany Elizabeth when she was about to depart on her morning constitutional.

"I am, I assure you, Miss Elizabeth, not unacquainted with walking for exercise." Mr. Collins fixed her with that silly smile he often wore when he thought he was making love to her. The very thought made Elizabeth want to gag. "Indeed, you are much to be praised. Walking for exercise is, of course, beneficial, though I am convinced that when you come to the parsonage, you will have other things with which to occupy your time. A parson's wife must be actively engaged in the neighborhood for good, after all."

"Mr. Collins," said Elizabeth, her temper fraying, "I walk alone, sir. I am fond of solitude when I walk, and the presence of another person would quite defeat the purpose."

"Do not concern yourself, my dear cousin. I shall be as unobtrusive as a mouse. I shall return directly when I have prepared."

The man darted into the hall, and his footsteps could soon be heard to be pounding up the stairs. Privately Elizabeth thought Mr. Collins could be no more unobtrusive than a mountain. The sight of her mother, however, finally snapped Elizabeth's patience. The woman stood at the edge of the vestibule nodding her satisfaction before she turned and entered the sitting-room again.

Unable to support the thought of having Mr. Collins *again* intruding himself upon her senses with his inept attempts to woo her, Elizabeth slipped out the door and fairly ran down the drive, taking the nearest path away from Longbourn. It was clear after a few moments of exertion that she had managed to escape him—he did not know the neighborhood and would not know where she had gone. She might face her mother's displeasure when she returned—she was certain to face Mr. Collins's—but that paled with the blessed relief she felt at having eluded him.

Elizabeth wandered the paths she knew so well for many minutes, the chill in the air invigorating her, allowing her to walk further and faster than a hot day would allow. And as she walked, she turned the problem of Mr. Collins over in her head, trying to find some way of doing away with his attentions. But nothing came to mind. At this point, she was certain he would laugh and call her charming if she suggested she had no interest in his suit, and while her mother would likely take her more seriously, she would likely insist on Elizabeth's compliance, at least until that moment when she actually rejected a proposal.

For a moment Elizabeth toyed with the idea of provoking him to make his addresses, but she knew that would not work either. For one, she had no idea how to go about it, and she would not give him even a hint of hope which did not originate in his imagination. For another, a part of her still hoped he would eventually be required to depart without achieving his design and without a miserable proposal and the aftermath.

Such were Elizabeth's thoughts that morning, and she was caught up in them to the extent that she lost all track of time. The grumbling in her stomach which signaled the arrival of the lunch hour informed her of her oversight, and though reluctantly, she began to think of turning her steps back toward her home. That was when she was confronted with a group of riders.

"Ho, Miss Bennet!" hailed the lead rider, whom Elizabeth noticed was Colonel Fitzwilliam. She waved her hand at him, thinking he would continue to ride on, but he turned his mount toward her, cantering easily in her direction, his companions following behind. When they drew near, Elizabeth discovered it was Mr. and Mrs. Bingley, followed by Mr. Darcy.

"You are far from home, Miss Bennet," said Colonel Fitzwilliam when he reined his mount to a walk near where she stood. "Are you lost?"

Elizabeth laughed and shook her head. "I know you have heard of my prowess as a walker, Colonel. I cannot be lost so near to my home, as I have walked these paths so many times I know them as well as I know the lines on my face."

"I can see no lines," said the colonel, his gallantry accompanied by a wink. "You are as pretty as ever."

"Now you are engaged in flattery, sir," responded Elizabeth with another laugh.

"Perhaps. But I also speak as I find."

The others soon pulled up to them and joined them, Mrs. Bingley dismounting and curtseying to her, while Mr. Bingley and Mr. Darcy bowed. When the greetings had been completed, Elizabeth turned back to the colonel.

"The true question is whether *you* are lost."

"I believe I have a good sense of where we are," said he, Mr. Bingley nodding with enthusiasm. "If I am not mistaken, we are near the boundary between Bingley's estate and your father's, perhaps a mile and a half from Netherfield."

"That is correct," replied Elizabeth. "You do seem to have room to carry a map in your head."

"It is a skill which benefits a soldier, Miss Bennet. Especially one who must lead other men. It can be disastrous to become lost in a battle, and the cost to men and strategy alike, if a company arrives in the wrong location, can be substantial."

"I can see sense in that, sir."

"We have been taking in some of the beauties of Hertfordshire, Miss Elizabeth," said Mrs. Bingley. "This county is a pretty sort of place, and while I do not think we will eventually settle here, I should like to see some of it before we must depart."

"It *is* pretty," said Elizabeth. "I could describe a few places you could visit of which you might not be aware. Perhaps the best and easiest to find is Oakham Mount, which lies at the northern edge of Netherfield where its border with Longbourn diverges. The northern side of the hill is forested, but there is a fine view toward the south, where both Netherfield and Longbourn—and beyond—can be seen."

"That sounds lovely, Miss Elizabeth," said Mr. Bingley.

"Indeed, it does," replied Mrs. Bingley. "My home in Derbyshire lies near the peaks." Mrs. Bingley suddenly colored, and she said in a whisper: "My former home. I suppose I cannot call Pemberley my home any longer."

"My dear Georgiana," the deep tones of Mr. Darcy's voice washed over them, "Pemberley will *always* be your home, no matter how long you are away. You know that you and Bingley are welcome whenever you wish to come."

Mrs. Bingley fairly beamed at her brother. "Thank you, William."

Elizabeth watched with interest. The Mr. Darcy she had often seen was severe and unapproachable, but he had shown a different side in assuring his sister of her welcome in his home. Not everyone could be cold and distant all the time, Elizabeth supposed, and it was very easy to love the shy and kind Mrs. Bingley.

"There are many places in Pemberley's vicinity which are absolutely lovely, Miss Elizabeth. If you are ever presented with the opportunity, I encourage you to visit and partake of the delights to be seen there."

"I have not traveled much," said Elizabeth, charmed by the girl's earnest entreaty. "But should the opportunity present itself, I shall be happy to do so. I have heard something of Derbyshire, you know."

"You have?" asked Mrs. Bingley. "Do you know someone who lives there?"

"I know someone who *lived* there," replied Elizabeth. "My aunt lived there for some years, among those which she counts the best of her life. She often speaks of her love of the county."

"Do you know where she lived?" asked Colonel Fitzwilliam.

"I am afraid I do not remember the name," replied Elizabeth. "If you are in residence long enough, you will have the opportunity to ask her yourself. My aunt and uncle usually join us for some days during the Christmas season."

"Then we shall anticipate making their acquaintance," said Mrs. Bingley. Then she seemed to realize something and continued: "I apologize if we are interrupting your solitude, Miss Elizabeth."

"I am always pleased to meet with dear friends," said Elizabeth. "Besides, I should have turned back in a moment. I had just begun to think I have been walking long enough."

"That is fortunate," replied Colonel Fitzwilliam. "I believe I should like to call at Longbourn. Shall we escort you the rest of the way to your home?"

Elizabeth agreed, taking his proffered arm and turning in the direction of Longbourn. Colonel Fitzwilliam's horse trailed along behind them obediently, while the others arranged themselves behind, following them and leading their own mounts. It was not long before Elizabeth made some reference to the fact that there was a houseguest at Longbourn, which prompted an interesting discussion.

"Your cousin is a parson from Kent, you say?"

"Yes, that is what he informed us."

"Do you know where?"

"I believe he said the name of his parish is Hunsford, though I do not remember the name of his patroness's estate."

"Rosings Park."

Astonished, Elizabeth turned to her companion, noting his suppressed mirth. She could not account for his knowledge of Mr. Collins's home, not to mention his sudden amusement.

"I apologize, Miss Elizabeth," said Colonel Fitzwilliam, "but it appears I have confused you. I am familiar with Hunsford because Rosings Park is the home of my aunt, Lady Catherine de Bourgh."

"Oh!" exclaimed Elizabeth. "I am quite familiar with that name, though I heard it for the first time only two days ago. My cousin speaks of his patroness incessantly."

It occurred to Elizabeth after she spoke that it might have given Colonel Fitzwilliam the impression that her cousin was ridiculous. But then she realized that as an intelligent man, he would understand that within moments of making Mr. Collins's acquaintance.

"I have no doubt of it," replied the colonel. He grinned at her. "You see, Miss Bennet, my aunt is a woman of decided opinions, a forceful personality, and a dislike for being contradicted, no matter the situation. If she has followed her usual pattern, her new parson must be a man who will venerate her from morning until night and never dare to question or disobey."

Elizabeth could not help the giggle which escaped her lips. "You have taken Mr. Collins's likeness with exactness, sir. And without meeting him!"

"There is no difficulty in doing so, Miss Elizabeth. Mr. Collins cannot be any more ridiculous than the last man who inhabited the parsonage. My aunt, you see, would not stand for it!"

They laughed together yet again. "I dare say she would not, Colonel. Mr. Collins has given us such an image of Lady Catherine that I can only assume she is an . . . interesting patroness, to say the least."

"That she is, Miss Elizabeth. You do not need to speak in a circumspect fashion with me." Colonel Fitzwilliam shot her a grin. "The truth is that she is nothing less than a meddling, intolerant, forceful woman who is intent upon having her own way about many things. In the family, she is barely tolerated. Darcy and I visit her every year to look at her books and deal with matters of the estate, but we do so only because my father has requested it."

"I understand. But I would not speak in a derogatory manner about a woman I have never met."

"Then you are nothing like *she,* for she would have no compunction whatsoever. In fact, she would inform all and sundry she knows everything there is to know about you due to nothing more than your situation in life."

Elizabeth shook her head. There was little reason to continue this conversation, she decided, for she did not base her own behavior on that of others. If she did, she would carry on about their need to marry as her mother, laugh and behave as a silly flirt like her youngest sisters, or glare at all and sundry as if she considered them beneath her like Miss Bingley!

"I am curious, Miss Elizabeth," said the colonel, seeming to sense that the previous line of conversation had run its course. "Given what you have said of him, it seems you have not known your cousin previously. If that is the case, what has prompted his visit now?"

Elizabeth shook her head, reminded of her own trials concerning Mr. Collins. "First, he is my father's heir due to an entail on the estate."

"Then he wishes to learn of it."

"If only it were simply that," muttered Elizabeth. "Perhaps that plays a part in it, though I believe it a small part. We had never met him before because his father had a longstanding disagreement with mine. It appears your aunt caught wind of this and instructed him to bridge the distance between us. She also took the opportunity to direct him to procure a wife from among my father's daughters."

The sour manner in which Elizabeth made this comment informed Colonel Fitzwilliam of the identity of the sister on whom he had fixed his attention, and he laughed gaily. Elizabeth, though she was, in fact, a little annoyed by his mirth, could not help but see the humor in it. She chuckled along with him, though she could not enjoy it nearly so much.

"I think I understand why you are walking, Miss Elizabeth."

"I have informed you that I am fond of walking."

"And I do not doubt it. But you seem to have stayed out late for a morning walk."

Elizabeth sighed. "That is the truth." Then the manner of her departure returned, and she could not help but laugh. "Mr. Collins was intent upon accompanying me this morning. But I managed to slip away before he could join me."

Colonel Fitzwilliam's eyes twinkled in merriment at her confession.

"I have no doubt he will be less than happy when you return."

"Perhaps. But better that than I be forced to endure him at all hours of the day and night."

A nod was Colonel Fitzwilliam's response. "I suppose that is true." Colonel Fitzwilliam paused and regarded her, as if not sure he should speak. At length, however, he did so, saying: "If you will excuse my impertinence, Miss Elizabeth, might I inquire as to your father's thoughts about his cousin's actions?"

"My *mother* is quite happy to allow Mr. Collins's imaginary admiration," said Elizabeth, deliberately switching to her other parent.

"You call it imaginary?" asked a bemused Colonel Fitzwilliam. "I rather think you are entirely estimable."

"I do when he has only been in residence for three days," said Elizabeth. "A man may admire a woman for being beautiful, but even were I the most beautiful woman in existence, he still does not *know* me."

"I suppose you must be correct. And what of your father?"

"Papa is amused by Mr. Collins's antics and does not wish to provoke my mother's nerves. He has, however, assured me that I have his support should I be required to refuse his cousin's proposal."

Colonel Fitzwilliam nodded, though he appeared distracted. Though she could not be certain, Elizabeth thought he was not approving of Mr. Bennet's way of handling the situation. Elizabeth did not approve of it, so she could well understand the sentiment. But he knew enough not to trod on another man's toes.

"If you require assistance avoiding Mr. Collins, you need only ask," was the only thing he said on the subject.

The walls of Longbourn soon rose in the distance and Elizabeth braced herself for what she knew would ensue when she arrived. She was not disappointed—or rather, she *was* disappointed, but not surprised.

When she led her friends into the vestibule, the servants on hand to take their outerwear, her mother bustled into the room, stopping short when she caught sight of the guests. Elizabeth thought for a moment that her mother would actually behave with circumspection, but it was not to be.

"Colonel Fitzwilliam!" exclaimed she, then turning and greeting the others as well. Then she fixed her attention on Elizabeth. "Lizzy!" hissed she. "Mr. Collins was *not* happy when you abandoned him here. He was so anticipating walking with you, and you have ruined it!"

"I have no apology to offer Mr. Collins, Mama," said Elizabeth, her tone icy. "I prefer to walk in solitude. Mr. Collins's presence was neither requested nor welcome."

Mrs. Bennet's eyes narrowed, her gaze suggesting this was not the end of the conversation. But she did not speak again to Elizabeth, instead directing her next words to Colonel Fitzwilliam, who had come to stand beside her.

"I thank you for escorting my daughter home, Colonel. There are times when she is far too headstrong for her own good."

"I find your daughter no less than charming, Mrs. Bennet," said Colonel Fitzwilliam. "It was no trouble to walk back to Longbourn with her. We had meant to call regardless."

"That is very kind of you, I am sure," said Mrs. Bennet. The matron moved back toward the sitting-room, muttering to herself as she went. "I am sure she was traipsing all over the countryside without any care for her petticoats or what she left at Longbourn. What shall become of us all I do not know."

The problem with her mother's incessant commentary was that she had never learned to moderate her voice, and thus, everything she said was audible to not only Colonel Fitzwilliam, but likely to the rest of the company too. Elizabeth felt her cheeks heating in mortification, even as she steeled herself for what she knew would be Mr. Collins's equally imprudent comments the moment they entered the sitting-room.

"Courage, Miss Elizabeth," said Colonel Fitzwilliam as they walked. He caught her eye and favored her with a smile. Elizabeth felt a hint of her unease lessen because of his support.

When they entered the room, Elizabeth could see Mr. Collins sitting nearby, but more than him, Elizabeth noted Jane and Mary's apprehension. She felt ashamed for having left them to deal with the parson and her mother, though Jane also directed a smile at her, one which informed her that all was forgiven.

"Cousin Elizabeth!" cried Mr. Collins, shooting to his feet as soon as he caught sight of her.

"Miss Elizabeth," said Colonel Fitzwilliam at the same time, "will you do me the honor of introducing me to your friend?"

Neatly cut off, Mr. Collins could only gape at the colonel. Elizabeth could see his stratagem at once, and she nodded to him in her gratitude. But she did not delay further, as it seemed Mr. Collins was drawing in air to deliver his interrupted harangue.

"Of course. Please allow me to introduce my father's cousin, Mr. William Collins to your acquaintance. Mr. Collins, this is Colonel

Fitzwilliam, his cousin, Mr. Darcy, and our new neighbors at Netherfield Park, Mr. and Mrs. Bingley."

Mr. Collins utterly started when she mentioned the first two names. But when he attempted to speak, he could voice no more than a stammer, so great was his stupefaction.

"It is a pleasure to meet you, Mr. Collins," said Colonel Fitzwilliam. But while he expressed pleasure, Elizabeth thought she detected a hint of hardness in his tone which belied his words.

"You are *the* Colonel Fitzwilliam?" squeaked Mr. Collins at last.

"I am the only one of which *I* am aware," replied Colonel Fitzwilliam. His eyes twinkled in suppressed mirth, even while he continued to all but glare at the parson.

Seeming to realize he had spoken nonsense—which was odd, considering all the other times he had spoken so and *not* realized—Mr. Collins shook his head. "You have my apologies, Colonel Fitzwilliam, for my astonishment has overwhelmed my sense."

"You must possess sense first," muttered Elizabeth, to Colonel Fitzwilliam's delight.

"What I meant to say," said Mr. Collins, likely not even hearing Elizabeth's words, "is that I had not expected to meet such an exalted personage as you and your companions. You *are* the Colonel Fitzwilliam who is nephew to Lady Catherine de Bourgh of Rosings Park?"

"I am, Mr. Collins."

"Oh, how wonderful!" cried Mr. Collins. "I am enraptured at the chance which has led me to make your acquaintance!"

"I have no need for you to attempt to make love to me, Mr. Collins," said Colonel Fitzwilliam.

Mr. Collins, however, did not hear, though Elizabeth thought she might swallow her tongue in her attempt not to laugh. "It appears I am in the happy position to inform you that your aunt and cousin are very well. In fact, Mr. Darcy," said he in his most obsequious tone, "your dear cousin, I dare say, is anticipating your coming nuptials keenly. As the rector of Hunsford parish, I will have the honor of performing the ceremony, and I can assure you that I am ready to officiate in a manner which will honor you and your fair bride."

It was evident Mr. Darcy was not amused, for he glared at the parson. "Mr. Collins," said Mr. Darcy, his words infused with steel, "I am afraid you will not officiate at my marriage, for I am not engaged to my cousin."

"But I am certain you are!" exclaimed Mr. Collins. "Lady Catherine herself has assured me that it is so."

"Not another word, Mr. Collins," said Mr. Darcy. "I am not bound to my cousin. If you do not wish to provoke my anger, you will be silent.

"Now, Mr. Collins!" barked Mr. Darcy when Mr. Collins tried to speak again. Clearly hearing the command in Mr. Darcy's voice, Mr. Collins fell all over himself attempting to refrain from speaking. Then he seemed to notice something else.

"Did you say Mr. and Mrs. Bingley?"

"Yes," said Colonel Fitzwilliam, seemingly enjoying the show. "Mrs. Georgiana Bingley is Darcy's sister and my cousin. She is lately married to our good friend."

Though Elizabeth might not have been able to credit it, Mr. Collins looked down at his nose at Georgiana. She could not account for his apparent disdain. Of course, he lost no time in explaining himself.

"I have heard of you too, Mrs. Bingley," said he. "My patroness herself informed me of you and your marriage to a most unsuitable man. Quite married down and stained the family name it appears. Lady Catherine is ashamed of you!"

"Mr. Collins!" spat Mr. Bingley, a fire in his eyes that Elizabeth had never seen from the genial gentleman. "If I hear one more word from your mouth concerning *my wife*, I shall call you out!"

"And I second the sentiment," said Colonel Fitzwilliam in a tone touched with ice. Mr. Darcy, though he appeared as incensed as the others, contented himself with glaring at the parson. Mr. Collins seemed to understand his mistake, for he wilted under their combined displeasure, bobbing up and down in hasty bows.

All the while he said in a high-pitched and panicked voice: "Of course, of course. I meant no offense."

It was clear to Elizabeth the visitors did not believe him. But rather than continue to berate him, they ignored him. Colonel Fitzwilliam guided Elizabeth past the pasty Mr. Collins and toward the rest of the family, who were watching with some surprise—though Mr. Bennet's expression was gleeful. Colonel Fitzwilliam made certain to keep Elizabeth with him as he approached Jane and sat by her. And when they were seated, he turned to Elizabeth.

"I take back my words, Miss Elizabeth. Somehow my aunt has managed to find a specimen which quite outstrips her last parson in terms of ridiculousness. I would not have credited it if I had not seen it."

Mr. Bennet snorted, and Elizabeth stifled a laugh. Jane looked at them both wide-eyed but did not reply.

"Well done, Mr. Collins," said Mr. Bennet in a soft tone, which was nevertheless audible to everyone in the room. "You have managed to offend all our guests who are close relations to your patroness. It is a feat, indeed."

Mr. Collins seemed to take his faux pas seriously, for he did not speak again, and attempted to keep out of the way of all the visitors. For Elizabeth, it was a blessed bit of time away from the ineffectual dolt. Would that it would last. She knew that as soon as their visitors departed the man would recover, forgetting his mistake had ever happened.

CHAPTER IX

One consequence of Elizabeth's decision to walk without Mr. Collins was a brief cessation of his intrusion into her life. In truth, Elizabeth had not thought the parson capable of self-reflection — he was much too assured for such a thing. But regardless of his reasons, Elizabeth found herself blessedly free of him for the rest of the day, though she knew it would not last.

Thus freed from the necessity of guarding against Mr. Collins's inept lovemaking, Elizabeth turned her thoughts to the continuing attentions of Colonel Fitzwilliam to her sister. Jane Bennet was a woman known to be more than usually reticent. Even though Elizabeth was her sister and the closest person to her in the world, she often had difficulty in understanding her sister's feelings, though often she could guess.

As Colonel Fitzwilliam's courting grew ever more ardent and obvious, Elizabeth watched her sister more closely. She thought Jane was welcoming. She thought Jane was rapidly coming to esteem the gentleman. Elizabeth knew that Jane would not accept a proposal if she did not love Colonel Fitzwilliam. But she also knew Colonel Fitzwilliam could not know that. Elizabeth's primary worry was that Jane was not showing enough interest in the colonel to give him the resolution to eventually come to the point.

Thus, Elizabeth decided to speak to Jane about just that, hoping to encourage her sister to be as demonstrative as she was able. It was not in Jane's nature to be as open as Lydia. But she did not need to be.

"Jane, may I come in?' asked Elizabeth, opening the door and sticking her head into Jane's room.

It was late, the family having retired for the night. Jane, who had been staring into the fire, apparently deep in thought, turned and smiled at Elizabeth, beckoning her to enter.

"Of what are you thinking, Sister?' asked Elizabeth as she stepped forward and rested a hand on Jane's shoulder.

Jane's response was her typical gentle smile, followed by a softly spoken: "Nothing, really. I suppose I was considering all that has happened these past weeks."

Elizabeth could not have asked for a more perfect opening. "And might I inquire as to your conclusions? It has been an eventful time, has it not?"

"It has. I never would have thought a new group of people joining our society would provoke such changes."

"You would not?" asked Elizabeth, eyebrow arched.

"No."

"That is the difference between us, Jane," said Elizabeth. "I expect a gentleman to come into the district and immediately fall in love with you. But you are so self-effacing that you cannot see how you affect everyone you meet."

Jane turned a slightly censorious look on Elizabeth. "Oh, Lizzy. Must you always speak in such a manner?"

"I believe I must," replied Elizabeth. She sat in the chair next to Jane's and fixed her sister with a smile. "You are far too modest, so it falls to me.

"Now, Jane, I wish to know your thoughts of Colonel Fitzwilliam. Are you in love with him?"

It was a long moment before Jane responded, and Elizabeth thought for a time she would not. As an intensely private person, it was difficult for Jane to articulate her feelings, and she found it still more difficult to share them, even with her closest sister. But Jane, in the end, did not leave Elizabeth in suspense.

"You know, when they first arrived, it was Mr. Bingley to whom I was drawn." Elizabeth felt her eyes bulging from her sockets. But Jane laughed and said: "I know he is married, Lizzy, and I have no desire to attempt to gain the notice of a married man. He has not spoken much to me, and I have not wished for more of his notice.

"But he did strike me as a wonderful husband to his wife. I would be lying if I did not confess to imagining what it might be like if his love was *mine*."

"And now?" asked Elizabeth, wondering what her sister was saying.

"I am not pining for a married man, Lizzy," said Jane, her tone faintly admonishing.

"I would never have expected it of you," replied Elizabeth, though with a pointed look. "But your words make me wonder what you *are* saying, Jane."

"Only that I thought I might have esteemed Mr. Bingley very much had he come here unmarried. In a way, I believe that has helped me understand my feelings for Colonel Fitzwilliam."

"It has?" prompted Elizabeth.

"Watching how Mr. Bingley treats his wife has informed me what I should search for in a husband." Jane paused and directed a hint of a wry smile at Elizabeth. "We do not have many examples of felicity in marriage, Lizzy. Our parents cannot be held as an example, and most of the couples of this district seem to have made similar matches."

"What of Aunt and Uncle Gardiner?" asked Elizabeth.

"Yes, they are a good example, indeed," replied Jane. "But they have been married for some time. Mr. and Mrs. Bingley are newly married. They display a pleasing affection for each other which I want to emulate in my own marriage. And I think I might have found it with Colonel Fitzwilliam."

The sudden way in which Jane came to the point caught Elizabeth off guard, and she could not speak for a moment. Then the import of what Jane said began to filter its way into Elizabeth's consciousness, and she smiled widely at her sister.

"You *do* love him."

"I think I do, Lizzy. He is a good man. He treats me with such care and devotion, and yet he is interested in my opinions and solicits them. He is considerate and kind, he is happy and at times garrulous, and I feel like I can speak of anything at all. He is quite the most amiable man of my acquaintance, one to whom I could see tying my life. I . . . I long for his declaration, Lizzy. I hope he feels enough for me to offer it."

Though delighted for her sister, they had come to the point of Elizabeth's reason for approaching Jane. As such, she tempered her exuberance and contented herself with putting an arm around Jane's shoulders, or as close as she could manage on separate chairs

"That is wonderful, Jane. I hope he does. The question I have, however, is whether he has seen enough of your feelings to be assured of them."

Jane instantly understood the thrust of Elizabeth's words. "You feel I am too reticent?"

"I do not know, dearest," replied Elizabeth fondly. "I cannot say, as I have not spent so much time in Colonel Fitzwilliam's company as you have. But you are a reticent creature, and while your manners are above reproach, I wonder if boldness is what is required in this instance. If you truly wish for his declaration, you would be best served to ensure *he* is aware of it."

"You speak sense, Lizzy," replied Jane, returning to her contemplation of the fireplace. "I am not Lydia, but allowing him to see more of my regard would not make me like our youngest sister."

"Exactly," replied Elizabeth. "Colonel Fitzwilliam is observant enough to see what you wish him to see, even if you do not bludgeon him over the head with it." Jane giggled and swatted at Elizabeth, who drew playfully out of reach. "He is also firm enough in his convictions to take the required step, as long as he has some indication of your regard. I implore you, Jane, for your own happiness—do not leave him in suspense. Do not leave him in doubt of your feelings."

"I shall do my best, Lizzy."

"Then I am certain that will be enough."

Elizabeth rose and kissed her sister's forehead. Then she bid her good night and let herself from the room. There was no doubt in Elizabeth's mind that Jane would have her happiness. She could hardly wait.

Elizabeth could not be happier for Jane, for she saw some deepening of her relationship with Colonel Fitzwilliam in the days following their conversation. It seemed to Elizabeth that her sister's efforts, modest though the change in her behavior might be, had altered their connection. While Colonel Fitzwilliam did not say anything to Elizabeth, she thought he understood her role, and the way he smiled at her in appreciation told her he was grateful.

At the same time, however, Mr. Collins returned to his own brand of wooing. If anything, he redoubled his efforts. Elizabeth did not know where his conclusions concerning her abandonment of him had led him. But wherever it was, it had not resulted in the cessation of his pursuit. Quite the contrary, in fact.

Concerned the man was working himself up to a proposal, and knowing she could not spend all her days above stairs, nor could she walk at all hours, Elizabeth began spending much more time in her father's study. Mr. Bennet, though he did not wish to upset her mother unless required, enjoyed her company, as they had spent many hours in this attitude in the past. He looked on her new interest in being with him with some amusement, waving her to a seat when she invaded his sanctity for the first time.

"Of course, you are welcome, Lizzy," said he. "Perhaps we could resume our discussions of *Paradise Found*."

"I would like that, Papa."

Her mother, on the other hand, was not amused at Elizabeth's new tactic, and she lost no opportunity to voice her frustration. What she did not do was force Elizabeth from the room and back into Mr. Collins's company. For that, Elizabeth had her father to thank.

"Come, Lizzy," said Mrs. Bennet the first time Elizabeth found refuge in the study, bustling into the room without knocking or a by your leave. "Mr. Collins wishes to speak with you. You have been sequestered in this room long enough."

'Mrs. Bennet," said Mr. Bennet, glaring at his wife. "If you recall, this room is my own, and entrance into it is only gained if one knocks *and* waits for permission to enter to be granted. You did neither."

"I shall depart at once, Mr. Bennet," said Mrs. Bennet, unconcerned with her husband's rebuke. "I have need of Lizzy at present."

"Whether you have need I care not. Your daughter is sitting with me. Mr. Collins may wait to say whatever he needs to say. Perhaps you should direct him to Longbourn's parson—I do not believe he has visited yet."

Mrs. Bennet pursed her lips. She was well aware that pressing her husband usually did not end well, but she was also unaccustomed to having her daughters ignore her instructions.

"Surely she has been in this room long enough."

"That is not for you to decide, Mrs. Bennet. Lizzy and I were in a discussion of Milton, which you have interrupted. I will thank you for the use of my study."

Though Mrs. Bennet huffed, she did not protest further. She departed, throwing an exasperated look at Elizabeth, one which promised she had not yet won the war. For Elizabeth's part, she knew the war was already won, though there were undoubtedly battles yet to be fought.

"There, Lizzy," said Mr. Bennet. "It seems you have a refuge from which even your mother cannot prevail in removing you. In all honesty, however, I wonder that you have not encouraged Mr. Collins to propose so you may have done with it altogether."

"I do not wish to provoke Mama to further anger, Papa," said Elizabeth. "If I can keep Mr. Collins from proposing, he will eventually be forced to return to Kent. Then, in time, this whole business will be forgotten."

Mr. Bennet chuckled and shook his head. "I think you attribute too much sense to both your mother and my cousin, but I commend you for grasping onto any hope. Perhaps you will even be proven correct."

Unfortunately, Mr. Collins did not take the hint, though she did not truly expect he would. When he was required to return to Kent at the end of the week, his words to her confirmed that he had by no means surrendered.

"As you know, my dear cousin," said he in his usually ponderous tone the night before he departed, "I am required to return to Kent tomorrow. It is, indeed, to be a bittersweet parting, for I know your feelings, tender as they are, will be bruised by my going, as much as mine will be at the necessity of leaving you. Take heart, for it is for but a little season, I assure you. I will return before long."

Elizabeth, who had been wondering how she could tell him his going would provoke nothing but celebration, heard his intention to return with nothing less than apprehension.

"Surely you cannot be absent from your parish for so long!" said she with more feeling than tact. "Your lady patroness cannot be happy with your frequent absences."

"My patroness is charity itself!" said Mr. Collins. "She understands the workings of young hearts, and in her condescension, she will know the reason for my return."

'There is no reason for you to return," said Elizabeth, frustrated with the man's abject stupidity. "It is not required. Do not concern yourself for me, for I am quite well and not eager for your company."

Elizabeth heard the gasp of outrage from her mother, who was listening to the conversation, though with much less pleasure now. Mr. Collins, however, favored her with a leer that she had often seen from him, an expression she had taken for the man's attempt at a seductive smile.

"Oh, I perfectly understand, my dear cousin. I have often had occasion to ponder the minds of young ladies, and I know you are all accustomed to protesting, even as you are flattered by a man's notice.

I have no doubt you will accept my assurances with gratitude when I am ready to offer them. Thus, I shall go tomorrow, with hope for better days when I return. Until then, I bid you adieu."

Mr. Collins departed early the next morning without saying anything further to Elizabeth. He bowed low to her when he was off, her mother forcing her to be there for his departure, though she would have wished to be anywhere else instead. Though Elizabeth had never wished harm on another being, she found herself wishing the man would meet with an unfortunate accident; nothing fatal, of course—just enough to perhaps sprain an ankle or break his leg. If he were so immobilized, he would not be able to return as he promised, which was Elizabeth's most fervent wish.

"Come into the sitting-room, Lizzy," said her mother, her firm hand on Elizabeth's arm. "I believe I must speak with you."

While Elizabeth might have preferred to avoid her mother as much as she would Mr. Collins, she allowed herself to be led away, knowing Mrs. Bennet would become even more difficult if denied. Though Kitty and Lydia were in the sitting-room laughing, they were soon sent away by a sharp command. Lydia, in particular, looked at Mrs. Bennet as if affronted, but she and Kitty soon departed, leaving the Bennet matron with Elizabeth.

"It seems to me that you are avoiding Mr. Collins," said Mrs. Bennet without preamble. "I do not know what you are thinking, Lizzy, and I can only consider it fortunate that he has not noticed. But I will not stand for it!"

Mrs. Bennet started to pace, her agitation evident in her short, clipped motions and swift pace. "You girls have little enough to recommend you, and the entail means you cannot afford to turn your nose up at a potential suitor."

The look Mrs. Bennet turned on Elizabeth did not bode well, and when Mrs. Bennet spoke to disparage her, Elizabeth was not surprised. "I have always found you particularly difficult to understand, Lizzy, what with your carrying on, your books, and your walks. I love all my girls, but I have always thought you and Mary would be particularly difficult to marry, even though you are among the prettiest of my daughters."

Elizabeth was actually a little flattered by her mother's words—she had not thought her mother considered her in such a way. "But the fact remains, we shall be homeless unless at least one of you marries. If you marry Mr. Collins, we can stay at Longbourn should the worst happen."

"Mama," said Elizabeth quietly when her mother paused. "Do you not think that Jane is on the cusp of becoming engaged?"

"Dear Jane!" exclaimed her mother, fluttering and fanning herself, proving she had not completely been replaced by a stranger. "He is as good as a lord, for he is intimately connected to one!

"But we cannot rely on it, Lizzy, especially as the colonel is not a wealthy man. It would be much better to have you both married, for then our support would be ensured, even if the rest of your sisters do not find husbands."

"I am afraid, Mama," said Elizabeth, "that I do not agree with your idea of felicity in marriage. Why, I should be miserable with a man such as William Collins for my husband."

For a moment Elizabeth thought her mother would agree with her, even to the point of backing down. She regarded Elizabeth, compassion written upon her brow, a truly regretful sigh issuing forth from her lips. Then Elizabeth noted the exact moment when her mother hardened her resolve, for she looked Elizabeth in the eye and made her position abundantly clear.

"It *is* unfortunate your father's cousin is not a more impressive man, for you are too good for him. But he is what has been presented to us, Lizzy, and the opportunity is too good to allow it to pass. You had best reconcile yourself, for when Mr. Collins proposes, you will have no choice but to accept."

Mrs. Bennet then rose, patted Elizabeth's knee, and departed from the room. Elizabeth watched her go, amused that she had misunderstood her husband enough to assume he would insist on Elizabeth's engagement. That her mother had spoken to her in such rational tones gave Elizabeth pause, for she had expected her to rant and rave and insist, not that Elizabeth had ever expected to listen, let alone agree, to her mother's demands.

It was truly unfortunate for Mrs. Bennet, though Elizabeth thought she would get over it in a tolerable enough fashion. But even if her mother should speak to her softly, maintaining her temper and presenting every reason why Elizabeth should accept Mr. Collins, Elizabeth would not yield. The man was an odious sycophant, and Elizabeth wanted nothing to do with his patroness, his parsonage, or the man himself.

"Lizzy," a voice called her from her reverie and, looking up, Elizabeth could see Mary entering the room. Elizabeth could not say she had ever been close to her next youngest sister, but she could easily see that Mary was troubled, given the way she regarded

Elizabeth.

"Come in, Mary," said Elizabeth, attempting to push her thoughts to the side. But Mary was having none of it.

"Did you have words with Mama, Lizzy?"

"It is nothing, Mary," replied Elizabeth, not wishing to speak of the discussion with her mother.

"It did not seem like nothing to me, Lizzy," was Mary's slightly frosty reply. "I was about to enter when I heard voices."

Elizabeth sighed. "Yes, Mary, Mama felt it necessary to speak of Mr. Collins with me."

Mary regarded her, seeming troubled. "I know what Mama wishes for you, Lizzy. Mr. Collins has not exactly been circumspect."

"I think Mr. Collins does not even know the meaning of the word circumspect," muttered Elizabeth.

Frowning, Mary regarded Elizabeth. "Is it not your duty to marry Mr. Collins, should he propose?"

The roll of Elizabeth's eyes was avoided with the greatest difficulty. "Would *you* wish to marry Mr. Collins?" asked Elizabeth, spearing her sister with a pointed look.

"He is not focused on me, Lizzy," said Mary.

"You are evading the question," replied Elizabeth. "I know we do not agree on matters of love and marriage, and I respect your opinion. For myself, I would be nothing less than miserable with Mr. Collins for a husband."

Mary did not speak, which was all Elizabeth required to continue. "Can you imagine *me* with Mr. Collins? I love to read, love to walk, I wish for love in a marriage. Do you think Mr. Collins would allow me the things which would bring fulfillment in life? He would not."

"But should not a woman honor her parents and bow to their wishes?"

"Some think so," replied Elizabeth. "I understand our position, Mary. I understand that we will be left with very little should Papa pass away. I am not insensible to Mama's fears. But it is my opinion that there are more important things than simply being married at all costs. One of those things is happiness in marriage."

"I suppose that is so," replied Mary, apparently deep in thought. "But what about Mama's insistence?"

Elizabeth smiled at her younger sister, reaching out to squeeze her hand. "There is nothing about which I need to be concerned, Mary. For it is Papa who must approve or reject any offer of marriage for any of us."

With those final words, Elizabeth let herself from the room. She was certain Mary had understood the thrust of her words and, therefore, nothing more needed to be said.

CHAPTER X

$\mathcal{A}$fter that day, the situation seemed to settle at Longbourn. Mrs. Bennet, confident she had made her point, turned her attention to other matters, most notably Colonel Fitzwilliam's continuing visits to see Jane and the militia's presence for Kitty and Lydia's sake. Elizabeth could confess that her mother had made her point, but she knew — even if her mother did not — that her ambitions concerning Mr. Collins would not be realized. According to her father, Mr. Collins meant to return in a week or two, and while Elizabeth hoped he would be prevented, she thought it unlikely. Still, she would not provoke a heated argument with her mother until the time came that it was unavoidable.

In all other matters, little changed. The Netherfield party were constant visitors to Longbourn, though Miss Bingley, in particular, and Mr. Darcy were seen less often, and the Bennets returned their visits promptly. Colonel Fitzwilliam continued to prefer Jane's company to anyone else, Jane and Elizabeth continued to grow closer to Mrs. Bingley, Kitty and Lydia still frequently embarrassed them with their antics in company with the officers, and nothing Elizabeth or Jane did or said had any effect on them.

One day almost a week after Mr. Collins's departure, a note came from Netherfield, in which was enclosed an invitation to a ball to be held the following Tuesday. Needless to say, the raptures this provoked were loud and long-lasting.

"This must be a credit to you, Jane," said Mrs. Bennet amid her crowing of the family's good fortune.

"Is it?" asked Mr. Bennet. "I must own that I am having difficulty following your logic, Mrs. Bennet. This is clearly a ball given by Mr. and Mrs. Bingley. The last I saw, our Jane had the colonel hanging off her every word."

Jane blushed at her father's characterization, but Mrs. Bennet cried: "Of course, it is a compliment to Jane! For Colonel Fitzwilliam is Mrs. Bingley's cousin, and as he is all but engaged to our Jane, I am certain she wishes to show her approval. Thus, Mrs. Bingley has obliged him by holding a ball."

"I have heard nothing from Colonel Fitzwilliam concerning this ball," said Jane in a quiet voice.

"That is only because he wished to surprise you, dear," said Mrs. Bennet, patting Jane's hand. "Mark my words—Colonel Fitzwilliam will visit before the date of the ball to request your hand for the first sets. When he does, I shall be proven correct."

This last was the most sensible part of Mrs. Bennet's assertions, in Elizabeth's opinion. In fact, she thought it likely that Colonel Fitzwilliam would like nothing better than to open the ball with Jane as his partner. But she was not able to work out why this would constitute proof of the ball being planned as a special compliment to Jane. For his part, Mr. Bennet seemed to lack understanding as well, but he only exchanged a look with Elizabeth, rolled his eyes, and returned to his paper.

In fact, it was the very next day when Colonel Fitzwilliam's horse came trotting up the drive, the sound of its hooves crunching against the gravel beneath. The sound had alerted Kitty and Lydia, who were at home that morning, rather than in Meryton chasing officers. They could not allow such an opportunity to pass in good conscience.

"Colonel Fitzwilliam is here to see you, Jane," said Lydia in a singsong voice, Kitty giggling by her side. "Shall today be the day you receive a proposal?"

"Today is likely nothing more than a request for the first dance," said Kitty. "But I should not be surprised if a proposal was forthcoming tomorrow."

The girls collapsed against each other, giggling in response to their own feeble witticisms. Jane, quite able to withstand the teasing of her youngest sisters, called them to order and silenced them. Their mother was, that morning, above stairs, suffering from an indisposition, and Elizabeth thought Jane was grateful she was not here. When Colonel Fitzwilliam was announced by the butler, the Bennet sisters were all sitting demurely, though the youngest ruined the effect by their continued tittering.

"Is this not a lovely scene?" said Colonel Fitzwilliam after the greetings had been completed. "Is your mother or father at home?"

"Mama is above stairs and not at liberty to descend," said Jane.

"And Papa is out on the estate this morning," added Elizabeth.

"Very well," said Colonel Fitzwilliam. "I dare say my errand may be completed whether your parents are present or not."

"And what errand would that be, Colonel?" asked Elizabeth, her tone daring him to respond.

He laughed and waggled his finger at her. "I think not, Miss Elizabeth, for I believe I should like to keep you in suspense." Then he turned to Jane. "Miss Bennet, today is a fine day. I have often heard it said — and have experienced it myself — that your sister is an excellent walker. I understand we all have different strengths, but might you oblige me in walking with me out in the back gardens?"

"Of course, Colonel," said Jane. "Will you accompany us, Lizzy?"

"I would be delighted, for I have not had my constitutional yet."

"That is a very serious matter," said the colonel, as he regarded her with a mock frown. "I understand no day has truly started until Miss Elizabeth has her walk."

"You would think that to be the truth," said Lydia. "There are times when Elizabeth disappears, and we do not see her again until after luncheon."

"Lydia," said Elizabeth, her tone warning.

"I do not know why you reprimand me. It is nothing less than the truth."

"And it does not show you to disadvantage, Miss Elizabeth. Quite the opposite, in fact."

"Thank you, Colonel. But I hardly think we need to speak of such subjects."

Colonel Fitzwilliam bowed, and the three made their way to the vestibule where Elizabeth and Jane gathered their coats and made their way out of doors. The air was, as the colonel suggested, warm, though there was a bit of an autumn chill in the wind. As soon as they stepped out, they made their way around the side of the house to the back lawn. And once there, Elizabeth held back, allowing the couple courting in all but name to concentrate on each other.

They walked in this manner for some time. Elizabeth was far enough away that she could not hear what they were saying, though she could hear the rumble of the colonel's voice, accompanied by the higher pitch of Jane's response. From what she could see, it seemed like their conversation was effortless, that of two people wholly devoted to each other, not needing great events and deep subjects to exchange meaningful communication.

At one point, they stopped and stood together in earnest conversation for several moments before continuing to meander along the paths at the back of Longbourn's gardens. Elizabeth was certain that the invitation to dance the first had just been offered and accepted, a glimpse of Jane's shining countenance confirming Elizabeth's supposition.

Jane was, Elizabeth noted, more demonstrative than she had ever seen her sister before. It seemed like she was taking Elizabeth's advice, a matter of much satisfaction. It seemed the colonel appreciated it also if his smiles for Jane were any indication. This was another matter which was soon confirmed for Elizabeth.

"Miss Elizabeth," said Colonel Fitzwilliam after some moments, turning and directing Jane back to where Elizabeth was following them. "Your sister has informed me that I have you to thank."

"Oh?" asked Elizabeth. "For what am I being thanked?"

"Miss Bennet informs me it is on your recommendation that Miss Bennet has been more open these past few days."

Colonel Fitzwilliam directed a truly tender look at Jane, who shyly smiled back. Elizabeth watched with interest—had a man bestowed such a look on her, she might have been tempted to order her wedding clothes forthwith!

"I was not in doubt of her feelings," continued Colonel Fitzwilliam, "but had she continued to be so reticent, I might have hesitated."

"Hesitated in what?" asked Elizabeth, unable to believe that the colonel had proposed.

"Never you mind," was the colonel's jovial response. "Be that as it may, I think you should have some reward for your assistance. Thus, as I have already secured the hand of your sister for the first dance at the ball at Netherfield, I should like to request your hand for the second."

Elizabeth burst out laughing. "It appears, my dear colonel, that you possess a hint of narcissism. A dance with you is a reward, is it?"

"I *could* ask Darcy to dance the first with you as a reward," was his sly tease.

"Mr. Darcy?" echoed Elizabeth.

"No, I suspect that would be a punishment, rather than a reward," said the colonel, his eyes still twinkling with mirth. "And he never dances the first, regardless — something about not wishing to raise the hopes of any young lady."

Elizabeth nodded, though slowly. "For a man as averse to society as Mr. Darcy is, that is likely for the best."

"He is at that," agreed Colonel Fitzwilliam. "Now, in all seriousness, Miss Elizabeth. I should like to stand up for the second with you."

Very well," said Elizabeth. "But I warn you — after my angelic sister, standing up with me will be nothing less than a disappointment. Perhaps you should dance the first with me and the second with Jane? Then you will save the better dance for after."

The colonel guffawed while Jane admonished with a sharply spoken: "Lizzy!"

But Elizabeth was not affected in the slightest. She grinned impudently at him, to which the man was more than willing to respond in like kind. And they spent the rest of the colonel's time at Longbourn in this merry fashion, though Elizabeth noticed that more often than not, they fell back into the same habit of speaking to each other while Elizabeth remained silent. But she was by no means offended. In fact, she appreciated how everything was proceeding in an expeditious manner. Though Elizabeth knew her mother would proclaim her sure knowledge when she became aware of Colonel Fitzwilliam's visit later that evening, Elizabeth could well endure it, knowing her sister would be happy.

Darcy had taken himself to the library that morning, having received some correspondence from Pemberley which required his attention. There had been no plans for visits that day that Darcy knew of, which suited him well, indeed.

The announcement of the ball Darcy had received with more resignation than anything else. While he personally might not wish for such society, he could understand why Bingley and Georgiana would, notwithstanding their intention to find a permanent home in another neighborhood.

Thus, when he emerged from the library about the time for luncheon, he was surprised to see his cousin, dressed in his riding clothes, whistling as he strode down Netherfield's halls. The fact that his cousin was not at all musical, and thus his whistling was particularly tuneless, did not interest Darcy. The fact that he appeared so happy did.

"Why did you not inform me you intended to ride, Fitzwilliam?" asked Darcy. "I would have welcomed the opportunity to escape Netherfield."

"Has Miss Bingley been that difficult?" asked Fitzwilliam with a laugh.

A sheepish Darcy could only shake his head. "No more than any other time. I know she considers herself to be a perfect future Mrs. Darcy, but she is too intent upon maintaining her sophisticated persona to behave with anything other than restraint."

"You should be grateful, I think," said Fitzwilliam. When Darcy tilted his head a little to the side, wondering as to Fitzwilliam's meaning, the man grinned. "Since Bingley is married, Georgiana is the mistress of Netherfield. Had Miss Bingley maintained that position in Bingley's house, I think you might have been presented with a more aggressive Miss Bingley."

Darcy shook his head, ruefully considering such a scenario. "I had considered that possibility. I believe you might be correct.

"She is not without her attractions as a potential bride, you know," continued Darcy, eliciting a shrug from Fitzwilliam. "She *is* an excellent hostess, and her assistance to Georgiana in preparing for the ball has helped her gain confidence. I dare say that she will eventually find a man who will be happy to have her as a wife, though I suspect she may need to adjust her sights a little."

"That much is without a doubt," agreed Fitzwilliam pleasantly. "If you will excuse me, Darcy, I believe I should change."

When his cousin turned and began to start walking away, Darcy called out: "Tomorrow, should you ride, I hope you will include me."

"Perhaps. I might have invited you today, but I believed you would not appreciate my destination."

Darcy frowned as Fitzwilliam turned to regard him. "Destination? You did not simply ride the estate?"

"No, Darcy. In fact, I called at Longbourn this morning and spent most of my time there walking the gardens with the enchanting Miss Jane Bennet and her sister."

"You did?" blurted Darcy, his frown deepening. "Have you not been paying a little too much attention to Miss Bennet, Fitzwilliam? You should not raise expectations you cannot fulfill—it would not be fair to Miss Bennet."

"I am surprised you have not seen the fallacy in your own statement, Darcy," said Fitzwilliam. When Darcy looked at him, demanding he explain, Fitzwilliam chuckled and shook his head. "No, I should not raise unwarranted expectations. But those expectations which I *do* intend to follow to their conclusion? Those, I may raise as much as I choose."

Then with a jaunty salute, Fitzwilliam turned and began walking again, his atonal whistling fading away, accompanied by the tapping of his footsteps on the stairs. Then he was gone, leaving a speechless Darcy standing in the entrance hall, looking up toward where his cousin had just disappeared.

"Was that Colonel Fitzwilliam?" asked a voice, as Miss Bingley stepped into the room.

Darcy turned and acknowledged it was. "He has apparently been to Longbourn this morning."

Miss Bingley's glance skyward told him of *her* opinion. "If you will forgive me, Mr. Darcy, I am grateful that Charles is already married to your sister and not prey to every young woman in the neighborhood. I do not mean to suggest that I think your cousin should be caught by one of the Bennet sisters. But though Jane would have made an acceptable sister and Miss Elizabeth is tolerable, I find I am not sorry to know I shall never be anything more than friends with them."

"I am happy to have Bingley as a brother," said Darcy, finding it incumbent upon himself to respond. Though the circumstances of their marriage had not been ideal, it was nothing less than the truth. And while Miss Bingley had likely heard some of the rumors which had spread through London after the fact, it was a subject they had never canvassed. He knew she never would, for her objective—gaining a closer connection to an old family such as the Darcys—had been accomplished, regardless of the manner in which it had come about.

"We are grateful, sir," said Miss Bingley. "Not everyone of your station would befriend my brother and welcome him into his family."

Darcy nodded, having no desire to continue to speak of this matter. "Am I correct in deducing it is almost time for luncheon?"

"I believe so," said Miss Bingley, a slight look of distaste about her, though she nodded. Having risen late, in accordance with her preference of keeping town hours, she had likely breakfasted not long before. But Bingley and Georgiana were more like Darcy in that they arose earlier and thus served breakfast early and then a light luncheon.

"Then let me escort you to the dining room," said Darcy, offering his arm.

Miss Bingley accepted and they proceeded there. In the back of his mind, Darcy kept thinking of his cousin and what he said about Miss Bennet. It was time he paid more attention to Fitzwilliam, for it appeared that Darcy had miscalculated the extent of the danger.

As the day progressed, Darcy thought about what might be done to curb Fitzwilliam's interest in Miss Bennet. It appeared as if his cousin was truly interested in the woman, a circumstance that Darcy had not foreseen. Fitzwilliam had always maintained the necessity of marrying a woman of means, for he had little himself. His unexpected inheritance of Thorndell had changed matters to a certain extent, it was true, but the estate would yield less than four thousand a year, to say nothing of any improvements it might need. Jane Bennet was a woman with no fortune—it would be a struggle to provide dowries for daughters, should Fitzwilliam actually be induced to marry her.

Then there was always the conversation Darcy had overheard between Miss Elizabeth and Miss Lucas hovering in the back of his mind. Surely Fitzwilliam would listen if Darcy proved to him they were a family full of fortune hunters, would he not? But Darcy was reluctant to use such a tactic, for he had no desire to speak poorly of others, even if they deserved it. So he would watch and wait.

After dinner that evening, the discussion turned to the upcoming ball. It was primarily carried by the ladies, as Georgiana spoke of the preparations with Mrs. Hurst and Miss Bingley. But the gentlemen also added their own thoughts on occasion, particularly Bingley and Fitzwilliam, who were both fond of society. Hurst was indifferent as usual, though Darcy knew he would stand up with his wife for one obligatory set. As for Darcy himself, he had little to say on the matter.

"I am certain your arrangements will charm the neighborhood," said Fitzwilliam at one point when Georgiana spoke of her concerns for her preparations.

"Oh, indeed," said Miss Bingley. "For no one here knows much of higher society. They will assume that you are the consummate hostess, Georgiana, and so they should. The arrangements we have made are exquisite."

Fitzwilliam laughed, drawing Miss Bingley's attention. "I am happy to hear that you are so confident, Miss Bingley. The first part of your statement suggested Georgiana would impress the neighborhood only by virtue of their ignorance."

Her eyes widened, and then Miss Bingley colored a little as she understood the implications of Fitzwilliam's words. Darcy, for his part, was amused, for her statement *had* seemed to say the opposite of her obvious meaning.

"I can assure you I meant nothing of the kind," said Miss Bingley after a moment of stammering. "As I have said, the preparations are excellent. It is only that there cannot be many in this neighborhood who have any notion as to the proper way to host a ball."

"Do not worry, Caroline," said Georgiana. "I am not offended, and I know what you were trying to say. I think the only reason for your declaration is the fact that most of the estates in the area are too small to host a true ball. But the assembly we attended was everything lovely, so I do believe there is some skill among them."

It was clear to Darcy that Miss Bingley did not agree with Georgiana's assessment, but she was intelligent enough to avoid speaking on the matter any further. The conversation then turned to dances and partners, and as it would be the first true ball Georgiana had ever attended, it would be her first opportunity to dance the first with Bingley. From the way she glanced at him with fondness as they spoke, Darcy knew she was anticipating it.

"I suppose Mr. Darcy must dance the second with Georgiana then," said Miss Bingley, "since Charles is to have the first. Unless Colonel Fitzwilliam wishes to dance that set with her."

"For my part, Darcy may have Georgiana's second dance," said Fitzwilliam. "I will, however, reserve the third with my cousin."

"Of course, Anthony," said Georgiana, smiling warmly at him.

"It is good of you to cede that dance to your cousin," said Miss Bingley, "though I suppose, as Georgiana's brother, Mr. Darcy has more right to it. Of course, that will leave Mr. Darcy's first dance open."

It escaped no one's attention that Miss Bingley meant to have that first dance, despite knowing that Darcy never danced it. But Darcy was saved the trouble of responding to—or ignoring—her comment when Fitzwilliam spoke.

"You are correct in that I would likely have stepped aside for Darcy," said Fitzwilliam. "But that is not why I have ceded it to him. You see, my second dance is already taken."

"It is?" asked Georgiana, eyes wide. "I had expected you would dance the first with Miss Bennet, but I had not thought of your second sets."

"I *have* asked Miss Bennet for the first sets," said Fitzwilliam, winking at Georgiana. She clapped with eager glee, even as Darcy looked on with dismay. "But knowing that Darcy would likely dance the second with you, I asked her sister, Miss Elizabeth, for her second sets."

"I am happy to hear it, Cousin!" exclaimed Georgiana. "Miss Bennet and Miss Elizabeth are wonderful ladies, and I am thankful I have made their acquaintance."

"As am I, Georgiana," said Fitzwilliam. "I consider them among the finest ladies of my acquaintance."

"Well, who would have thought as much?" said Miss Bingley, throwing an expressive look at Fitzwilliam. "I had no notion that you would be attracted to one such as Miss Bennet, though I will own she is a sweet girl."

"She is the best of women," said Fitzwilliam. "I am absolutely certain of it."

"Good show, Fitzwilliam!" exclaimed Bingley. "She is everything a woman ought to be."

"A damn fine woman, indeed," echoed Hurst. Darcy was surprised, as he had not thought Hurst had even been listening.

"Thank you all," replied Fitzwilliam, leaning back on the sofa and draping one arm across the back. "But I will remind you that nothing has been decided yet, and it all may come to nothing."

"Your protests lack conviction, Fitzwilliam," said Bingley. "I, for one, would be quite surprised if you do not marry the girl."

"It does seem very much like love is in the air," said Miss Bingley. No one missed her glance at Darcy as she spoke. But while a few amused glances passed between the rest of the company, no one said anything.

Darcy, for his part, ignored Miss Bingley, as he did her less than subtle suggestion that he should ask her for the first sets. Darcy was too engaged in regarding his cousin, wondering at what he had said. It seemed he was inching closer to a decision to offer for Miss Bennet, and Darcy could not approve in any way. The time was swiftly coming where he would be required to act to prevent his cousin from making an egregious error. Darcy only hoped he could convince Fitzwilliam of the folly of his designs.

CHAPTER XI

$\mathcal{E}$ lizabeth Bennet was a social creature as much as she was a solitary one. While she loved her walks and the ability they afforded her to think, to consider her life and the events which shaped her, she was just as happy in company with the society of those she loved and respected. In this respect, the ball to be held at Netherfield was no different from any other society event. But it was also so much more.

The ballroom at Netherfield was decorated in a tasteful, but understated manner. The lighting was a little more subdued than one would find at most such events, a nod to the more romantic tone of the evening. Add to that the flowers which made up a large part of the décor with the low music, enhancing the atmosphere further, and Elizabeth was certain Georgiana had made the arrangements with her cousin in mind.

"Thank you, Elizabeth," said Georgiana when Elizabeth complimented her on her arrangements. Elizabeth had refrained from making any allusion to her suspicions, but Georgiana's glance at her cousin and Jane informed Elizabeth of the truth of the matter regardless.

"I presume this is your first opportunity to plan an event as its hostess?" said Elizabeth.

"It is," replied Georgiana, some embarrassment coloring her features. "I had never thought it would be required so soon after my marriage."

"You have done wonderfully. I know our society is not grand or intimidating, but I cannot think your designs would have been found wanting had you been in London."

"Caroline and Louisa assisted me. Their taste is exquisite—I could not have done it without them."

Elizabeth regarded her new friend and gave her a gentle smile. "I am certain they helped, Georgiana. But I know the mistress must have a greater share of the responsibility. Despite what assistance you received, it is clear you have exceeded all expectations, regardless. Please accept my compliment in the spirit in which it was intended. You have done very well."

While she did not say anything further, it was clear Georgiana was pleased. When she excused herself only moments later, Elizabeth fancied she could see an extra spring in her step, a hint of newfound confidence.

Though Elizabeth was to dance the second with Colonel Fitzwilliam, her first sets were unclaimed before she arrived. She had always been in such demand as a partner that it was not a surprise when she was approached by a gentleman of the neighborhood a few minutes before the dancing was to start. Thus, she had all the pleasure of an activity she enjoyed, combined with the obvious pleasure Jane evinced when the colonel led her to the floor not far away.

"Jane has taken my advice to heart," murmured Elizabeth to herself after a few moments of contemplation of her sister.

"Excuse me, Miss Elizabeth," asked her partner, for she had not spoken quite softly enough. Elizabeth assured him it was nothing and endeavored to give him as much of her attention as she could spare for the rest of the set.

But try as she might, her notice was often caught by her sister's smiles and the colonel's obvious enjoyment of her company. Jane was, Elizabeth thought, no less than radiant that evening. Her smile when she looked at Colonel Fitzwilliam was as soft as was her wont, but she could see an additional level of attention she paid to him, an interest in his opinion and enjoyment of his company that Elizabeth could not see how he would misinterpret her feelings. From his manners with her, Elizabeth was certain he did not. Thus contented, she allowed her eyes to leave them, assured in her sister's future happiness.

That was when she was arrested by the sight of another who was not so friendly to the colonel's interest in Jane as Elizabeth was herself. The way Mr. Darcy stood by the side of the dance floor and glared at them, his disapproval plain for all to see, Elizabeth could not understand how anyone could not see *his* feelings concerning the matter.

For a further moment, Elizabeth looked between the aforementioned couple, who seemed lost in their own world, and the man watching them with unfriendly eyes. She thought to go to him and call him on his behavior which bordered on rude. But then she contemplated Colonel Fitzwilliam, thought of his character and his ability to direct his own life and decided it was unnecessary. Colonel Fitzwilliam was by no means the sort of man who would allow his cousin to sway him from his purpose, and as he showed all the signs of a man who loved a woman, Elizabeth thought it unlikely that anything Mr. Darcy said would have any effect on him.

When the time came to dance the second with Colonel Fitzwilliam, Elizabeth could not help but notice the difference between his behavior toward Jane as compared to herself. Though he clearly appreciated her company, they were more kindred spirits, those who would likely have been nothing more than friends, even if Jane had not been at liberty to accept his overtures.

"I am disappointed, Colonel," said Elizabeth in a teasing tone after they had been dancing for some moments.

"Oh?" asked the colonel, his eyes alive with mischief in response to her tone. "I am not aware of anything I have done which merits your censure."

"It is your attire, sir," said Elizabeth, gesturing to his perfectly tailored suit. "I should like to have seen my youngest sisters' reaction to seeing you in your full uniform."

Their attention was caught by a loud bark of laughter from Elizabeth's youngest sister. She was dancing with Lieutenant Denny, flirting outrageously with him as was her custom. Though Elizabeth was usually ashamed of such behavior by her youngest sisters, she knew the colonel had likely seen worse. "I dare say the sight of a full colonel would have had them hanging off your every word."

"They do not hang off Colonel Forster's every word," observed Colonel Fitzwilliam.

"No, they do not," replied Elizabeth. "But *he* is a mere militia colonel and a married man, at that. Besides," continued Elizabeth, leaning forward and speaking in a soft tone as if imparting a secret,

"Colonel Forster is perhaps ten years your senior, which Lydia and Kitty consider to be positively ancient."

Then Elizabeth winked and allowed the steps of the dance to guide her away from him, though she could not escape the sound of his laughter. To Elizabeth, he appeared to be formulating his reply the entire time they were apart. Elizabeth was not disappointed when he was close enough to speak to her again.

"To young women of your sisters' age, a man of forty must have one foot in the grave, to be sure. But I have never considered myself handsome enough to have every young lady of fifteen smitten with me."

"I assure you, Colonel," said Elizabeth, "you are not lacking in any quality which is of any importance. I am not the only one who thinks so."

Colonel Fitzwilliam's glance in Jane's direction, where she was dancing with another neighborhood man, highly gratified Elizabeth. The colonel seemed to understand the thrust of Elizabeth's words, for he looked back at her, one eyebrow raised.

"That seems to me to be a subtle way of informing me that a certain young lady of your acquaintance does not find my presence onerous."

"You could certainly take it in such a way, Colonel Fitzwilliam," replied Elizabeth. "I would not attempt to dissuade you from it."

A nod was Colonel Fitzwilliam's response, though he did not immediately speak. Elizabeth allowed him his thoughts, for she was certain she knew to where they tended. There could be no greater joy than to see Jane achieve her heart's desire; if she could help in any small way, Elizabeth was happy to act on Jane's behalf.

"You seem to be intent upon making me aware of your sister's feelings," said Colonel Fitzwilliam, when he had returned to Elizabeth's side by the steps of the dance. "While I am already certain of them, I thank you nonetheless."

Before Elizabeth could respond, they were arrested by the voice of Sir William Lucas, who had accosted them as they danced at the end of the line. "Such elegant dancing is rarely to be seen, sir," said he, a note of enthusiasm Elizabeth had often heard staining his voice. "Then again, I suppose you must be accustomed to company much superior to this, in which the ladies have been taught to dance while still in leading strings and the men, by the most renowned dance instructors."

"Society is much the same wherever one goes," said Colonel Fitzwilliam to Sir William, his voice infused with good humor. "I am quite as comfortable here as I might be during the season in London."

"Oh, aye," said Sir William. "We have good people and beauties aplenty."

He winked at Elizabeth, who felt her cheeks heating at his words. But there was no harm in Sir William, and Elizabeth had long been accustomed to his ways.

"But I hope you find your partner everything you expected she would be and not inferior due to her residence in our little neighborhood."

"I assure you, no," said Colonel Fitzwilliam. "Miss Elizabeth is everything charming. I suspect I would have been no more in her power had I met her at the height of the season in London and she, the daughter of a duke."

Sir William laughed. "Yes, she does have that effect, I must agree."

"Stop it, both of you!" exclaimed Elizabeth, her cheeks flaming. "I am sure I am no more estimable than any other lady in attendance."

"I dare say you are among the jewels of our neighborhood," said Sir William. "You and your elder sister." Sir William turned a sly glance on Colonel Fitzwilliam. "But I am assured that you are as well aware of the charms of the eldest Bennet daughter as you are of the second."

"Had you not noticed it," replied the colonel, amusement dripping from his tone, "I might have thought you witless."

"Bravo!" exclaimed Sir William, clapping his hands. "I congratulate you then, good sir. "I will not speak of it overtly, for I know it is not proper. Let me just say that the entire neighborhood waits with bated breath."

It was all Elizabeth could do not to shake her head. Despite his stated intention of not speaking of the matter openly, Elizabeth hardly doubted anyone who had spent even an instant in company the past few weeks could have misunderstood his words. Fortunately, it appeared that Colonel Fitzwilliam was not offended.

"I am perfectly willing to fulfill my obligations, Sir William," said he. "Though I will not speak of the matter openly either, I can confirm that I feel nothing but admiration and respect, and the next steps will be taken at the appropriate time."

"Excellent, sir!" cried Sir William. "I knew you were a man of honor, and I salute you for your excellent taste. I shall not detain you a moment longer."

Sir William bowed and stepped away, allowing Elizabeth and Colonel Fitzwilliam to resume their places in the line of the dance. Elizabeth was still feeling the hint of mortification for her neighbor's words, but on the other hand, she could not help the satisfaction which welled up within her. Had she thought Jane remained ignorant of the colonel's growing feelings, she might have gone to her sister that moment and informed him of the conversation she had just participated in.

"Well, Miss Elizabeth, do events meet your approval?" asked Colonel Fitzwilliam when the opportunity presented itself. "I have Sir William's sanction—now I only need to obtain yours, and I will be quite pleased, indeed."

"You most certainly do have it," replied Elizabeth. "I do wonder, however . . . ."

A raised eyebrow met Elizabeth's words, and she was quick to continue. "Surely the good opinion of others besides myself and Sir William would be welcome, at the very least."

"I assume you speak of my cousin?" asked Colonel Fitzwilliam, instantly understanding the thrust of her question.

Elizabeth's gaze darted to where Mr. Darcy was standing on the side of the dance floor, but now he was watching Jane, as if attempting to understand her. His look was not precisely unfriendly. But Elizabeth thought she noted a hint of displeasure inherent in it, as if he could not quite approve of her.

"I have not misunderstood Darcy's unhappiness tonight, Miss Elizabeth."

"You once told me that Mr. Darcy was not at his best in company," said Elizabeth, a challenging tone entering her voice. "You also asserted that he was pressed down by some heavy matters weighing on his mind. I hope those matters are not still weighing upon him."

Colonel Fitzwilliam shook his head, though he regarded her wryly. "I suspect there are entirely new matters weighing down on Darcy's shoulders tonight, Miss Elizabeth. However, I would ask you to acquit him of pride, for he is an estimable man, regardless of how he has shown himself in Hertfordshire. I would also ask you to allow me to handle the matter in my own way. You shall not be disappointed with the outcome."

While Elizabeth considered it for a moment, she readily assented to his request. It was nothing to her what Mr. Darcy thought, after all. Her opinion that Colonel Fitzwilliam would not be moved from his course by anything his cousin said had been firmed during their dance. Colonel Fitzwilliam could deal with Mr. Darcy—Elizabeth wished to have little to do with him.

* * *

"Darcy!" hissed Fitzwilliam, the annoyance he was feeling with his cousin making him short tempered. Darcy, who had been regarding Miss Bennet, turned to him with surprise. "I would ask you to soften your scowl, for you are becoming quite the spectacle."

Darcy's frown deepened. "I am not aware of your meaning. I believe I am behaving no different now than at any other ball I have ever attended."

"And that speaks well to your behavior, I am sure."

It was apparent that Darcy understood his meaning quite well, for his eyes fairly impaled Fitzwilliam where he stood. It was fortunate he did not say anything, for Fitzwilliam did not trust himself at present where his cousin was concerned.

"I do not wish to argue with you, Darcy," said Fitzwilliam, cutting off whatever Darcy was about to say. "We shall discuss this matter at a more appropriate time. For now, I would ask you to adopt a more congenial countenance and try to allow yourself not to be so fearsomely disapproving of these people."

"I have nothing against them," replied Darcy. "But on the other hand, I do not know why I should concern myself with what they think of me."

"Because they are your sister's neighbors," replied Fitzwilliam in a pointed fashion. "And do not give me that tired line of how they will not be for long. For all you know, Bingley and Georgiana may decide the neighborhood suits them and purchase Netherfield."

Darcy's jaw tightened. Fitzwilliam was certain he knew what his cousin was about, and wondered how Darcy had thought to remove him from the neighborhood and from Miss Bennet's side. Though he had all the respect in the world for Charles Bingley, Fitzwilliam was well aware of the fact that he was not a man blessed with much firmness of purpose, though he could readily own that Bingley had stiffened in recent months. But Fitzwilliam was not the same sort of man as Bingley, and the same arguments would not have worked with him.

"Very well, Cousin," said Darcy. "I will not press the matter, nor will I force your confidence. But I do expect to speak with you in the near future. For the present, I will attempt to present a more agreeable countenance to these people."

"Thank you, Darcy," replied Fitzwilliam. "And it would not hurt for you to request the hands of a few of the ladies to dance. It would be better for you to have some occupation, rather than stalking the outskirts of the dance floor as is your custom."

The scowl which returned to his cousin's countenance suggested that Fitzwilliam should not expect his final instructions to be heeded, but Darcy did not respond. While Fitzwilliam could not count it a victory when Darcy subsequently danced with Miss Bingley and Mrs. Hurst, at least he was not brooding by the side of the dance floor, leading everyone in the room to believe he held them in contempt.

Fitzwilliam watched him as the night wore on, searching for signs of his cousin's distemper. But it seemed that Darcy had taken his words to heart, and while he danced with no young ladies of the neighborhood, his behavior was acceptable. He was even to be seen speaking with Sir William Lucas, which Fitzwilliam knew could not be agreeable to his cousin.

That all changed when the time for the supper sets arrived. By previous arrangement, Fitzwilliam collected Miss Bennet and led her to the dance floor, eager to once again have the excuse to touch her, if only her hand, and look into her beautiful face to the exclusion of all others. She truly was an exquisite creature, gentle and beautiful of form and character. Fitzwilliam felt fortunate to have made her acquaintance, and doubly so that she was not the kind of woman who would have been more interested in his cousin for Darcy's worldly possessions.

"Is that your cousin dancing with my sister?" asked Miss Bennet suddenly, pulling Fitzwilliam's attention away from her person.

Turning, Fitzwilliam followed her gesture, discovering that she was entirely correct. Far distant down the line, Darcy and Miss Elizabeth were dancing together, exciting the interest of those nearby. Fitzwilliam could hardly believe it himself, given how he had despaired of his cousin ever giving these people any hint of his respect.

"It appears to be so."

"And do you know what his intentions are?"

Surprised, Fitzwilliam turned and regarded his partner, wondering at her suddenly hard countenance and intense interest. She was so mild, so kind, that one would be forgiven for assuming she was always this way. But it was clear she was in possession of a measure of determination which Fitzwilliam found quite pleasing.

"I doubt his intention is anything other than to enjoy a dance with a handsome young woman," replied Fitzwilliam.

Miss Bennet eyed him, clearly skeptical of his assertion. Fitzwilliam's admiration for this woman was growing in leaps and bounds.

"You will forgive me if I am suspicious, Colonel Fitzwilliam," said

Miss Bennet. "Your cousin has done little to make himself agreeable since he came, and his expression when you and I were dancing the first was decidedly unfriendly."

"I noticed it. But let me inform you at once, Miss Bennet—my cousin is a good man, for all he gives himself the appearance of pride and conceit. I hope you do not suspect him of nefarious purposes concerning your sister."

Though she had the grace to color a little, Miss Bennet did not back down. "You are such a good man, I cannot think you would be so close to a man who is not your equal in goodness. But while Mr. Darcy *may* be a good man, he has rarely spoken to Lizzy, let alone given her any of his attention. You will forgive me for wishing to protect my sister."

"There is nothing to forgive, Miss Bennet," replied Fitzwilliam warmly. "You show a protective instinct toward your sister which is pleasing, indeed. I suppose my words to Darcy were more efficacious than I had thought."

At Miss Bennet's questioning glance, Fitzwilliam said: "I suggested to Darcy that he should consider dancing with some of the local ladies. Until this moment, I had not thought he would listen to me. It seems he has seen the sense in my instruction."

Miss Bennet considered this for a moment. "Then he shows some discernment in seeking out my sister. Lizzy is exceptional. She is my closest sister, and I would do anything for her."

"That much is evident, Miss Bennet," replied Fitzwilliam, smiling at her. "I have the same impression of her, though I obviously do not know her nearly as well as you do."

Seeming satisfied, Miss Bennet allowed the subject to drop. They continued to dance, speaking of less consequential subjects, which though of little importance, served the purpose of allowing them to understand each other better. Fitzwilliam was thrilled at her eagerness to know more of him, and he wished to know everything he could about her. Darcy and Miss Elizabeth were shunted to the side, for Fitzwilliam focused all his attention on the woman before him.

It was later in the evening, at the end of dinner, when Fitzwilliam was treated to the sight of Miss Lydia Bennet making a fool of herself. She was giggling in a loud voice, twirling around a man of the militia, a bright yellow ribbon which she had taken from her hair fluttering in the air behind her. The soldier was laughing and watching her, a gleam in his eyes which Fitzwilliam had seen far too many times in other soldiers, men with whom he would never willingly associate.

"Oh, Lydia," said Miss Bennet, shaking her head in her

exasperation.

"If you will excuse my saying so," said Colonel Fitzwilliam, "it seems to me your younger sisters were brought out before they were prepared. Miss Lydia would not even be allowed to be out for another two years, had she been born to a higher level of society."

"Well do I know it," replied Miss Bennet. "We were all brought out early, as our mother is deathly afraid we will not make marriages if we are not given the time to do it."

Fitzwilliam wanted to reassure her that she had no need to worry for her future, but he knew now was not the time to give her such assurances. Instead, he posed a question he had been wondering for some time.

"But you and Miss Elizabeth — and to a certain extent Miss Mary — are acquainted with how to behave. I find it difficult to credit how your sisters are so different."

"You are not aware of all our history," replied Miss Bennet. "My father cannot take the trouble to correct any of us, and my mother sees Lydia's behavior as high spirits. Lizzy and I were the recipient of our aunt and uncle's tutelage, and as Mary is of a more governable temper, she listened to our instruction more than our sisters ever have. But when aunt and uncle began to have their own family, they were not at liberty to continue to devote so much time to us."

"I understand." Fitzwilliam favored her with a bright smile. "Your aunt and uncle sound like wonderful people. I should like to make their acquaintance when the opportunity presents itself."

Miss Bennet flushed, for she understood his meaning. "I hope you are at liberty to make their acquaintance. If you stay until Christmastide, I am sure you shall, for they visit Longbourn every Christmas."

A new burst of raucous laughter caught Fitzwilliam's attention, and he turned to see that Miss Lydia was still dancing around the soldier, evading his attempts to grasp the ribbon. Fitzwilliam frowned — he did not know this officer, but he was certain if matters continued on as they were, her reputation could be in jeopardy.

"I hope you do not mind, Miss Bennet, but I think something should be done about your sister."

"Please," said Miss Bennet, her eyes shining as she regarded him. "Do not concern yourself for my father, for he will consider it a joke, no doubt."

Fitzwilliam nodded and rose. The officer with whom Miss Lydia was flirting caught sight of him first, and he frowned, which did not deter Fitzwilliam in the slightest. When he approached, he put himself in the girl's path, halting her progress as she regarded him with astonishment. Fitzwilliam summoned a smile for her and offered her his arm.

"Miss Lydia, I believe your sister would appreciate your company. And yours too, Miss Kitty," he added with a smile at the other girl, who was watching him with surprise.

"But Colonel Fitzwilliam—"

"*Now*, Miss Lydia," said Fitzwilliam, his tone allowing for no objection. "I am sorry, but your actions are not appropriate, and I believe you need to settle a little before supper ends. Please come with me."

The girl saw something in his countenance which informed her of his determination, and though she huffed, she allowed herself to be led away. Fitzwilliam saw the two girls seated with their elder sister and returned to the soldier who was watching them with exasperation.

"I suggest you steer clear of the Bennet sisters," said Fitzwilliam without preamble. "They are under *my* protection."

"And who are you?"

"Colonel Anthony Fitzwilliam of the First Dragoons," said Fitzwilliam. "Do not let my mode of dress fool you. Now, who are you?"

Though the man was reluctant to reply, he finally said: "Lieutenant Gregory Sanderson."

"Well, Lieutenant Sanderson," replied Fitzwilliam, "I do not know your colonel well, but I am assured he would not approve of your behavior with Miss Lydia Bennet."

"I have done nothing wrong," said Sanderson, though his tone was sullen. "Perhaps you should speak with Miss Lydia. She is a known flirt with naught more than a bit of fluff in her head."

"I am acquainted with Miss Lydia, Lieutenant. Furthermore, I am acquainted enough with officers and men, in general, to know when a man looks at a young girl with a predatory eye. I suggest you turn your attention to some other 'bit of muslin.' I will not appreciate any attempt to dishonor her."

It appeared the lieutenant knew when he was overmatched, for he bowed and departed with haste. Fitzwilliam watched him go, hoping the man would take his threat seriously. Perhaps it would be best to be on his guard.

"Why did you have to scare him away?" asked Miss Lydia, her petulance evident in her pout and tone. "We were just having a bit of fun."

"Perhaps you were," said Fitzwilliam. "But there are proper ways to have fun, and you were not adhering to them. I know officers, Miss Lydia, and that young man had little in mind which was proper."

Miss Lydia sighed and pouted, but she did not speak. Knowing these girls would be his relations someday, Fitzwilliam began the patient task, with Miss Bennet's support, of educating them of the proper way to behave in society. He was not foolish enough to believe they would change overnight. But perhaps, with patience, they would one day be well enough behaved to be admitted to society.

CHAPTER XII

*P*lerhaps it was to be expected. Had Darcy taken the time to think about such matters, he might have predicted it himself. He had known Miss Bingley long enough to have a sense of her character, and he knew she was most comfortable in society, ingratiating herself to those of a higher station, the cynical would say. While she was an annoyance to Darcy because of her expressed opinions, the way she always expected him to support them, and her clear ambition to become the mistress of his estate, he knew she would never be content to be stuck in a small neighborhood without anyone of consequence, such as that where her brother's estate was located.

The complaints began the day after the ball, and it was no surprise to Darcy that she looked to him as an ally to persuade her brother from Netherfield. It was also no surprise that her arguments had little effect on Bingley.

"What a tedious place this is," said she one morning, two days after the ball. "There is little for us to do here. How I long to be back in London!"

While she had been making noises these past days, this was the first time she had made such a blatant statement. Mrs. Hurst, her confederate in all things, only sighed and looked away from her sister.

"I fear we are stuck here for the winter, Caroline."

"But why should that be?" demanded she. Her eyes swung to her brother. "Charles, do you not think we should go to London for the winter?"

"What is there for us in London?" asked Bingley. "The little season is all but over, and there is little society to be had anyway. You know that anyone who is anyone will be returning to their estates. If we go to London now, it will be no different than had we stayed here."

"At least in London we will have Bond Street, Hyde Park, the tower and the menagerie, and many other attractions besides."

"Most of which have become too cold to visit."

"But there is *something*." Miss Bingley's tone was petulant, which Darcy found amusing for a woman he knew thought herself sophisticated.

"I am afraid you will need to become accustomed to this kind of life," said Bingley. "I have it on good authority that most gentlemen spend the winters at their estates, and only go to town for the season. When you marry, Caroline, I am sure your husband will follow a similar custom."

Darcy did not misunderstand Miss Bingley's glance in his direction, nor did he think anyone else in the room did. Fortunately, she did not speak to him directly, though she knew he wished for his contribution to the conversation. It would not be long before she beseeched him for his assistance.

"Surely Hurst does not intend to stay here for the entire winter."

"Actually, I have spoken with Hurst on this very subject," said Bingley, "and he has assured me he considers himself quite fixed here."

Miss Bingley scowled at the news, but Darcy wondered that she had not thought of it herself. Hurst's father was a miserly man, difficult and tight with the purse strings, and Darcy knew that Hurst's allowance was constrained. He did not get along with the old man, which meant he preferred to be away from the family estate. Should they go to London, they would stay in the family townhouse with few funds to seek amusement. Hurst would not abandon the home of his brother, who provided him with all the brandy, food, and sofas on which to sleep that he desired.

"What of you, Darcy?" asked Bingley. Miss Bingley also turned to Darcy with keen interest, pleased her brother had brought him into the conversation. "Georgiana and I have enjoyed your company with us these past months. Do you plan to stay in the neighborhood, or will we be bidding you goodbye in the near future?"

"I should probably return to Pemberley before long," said Darcy. "There are matters which require my attention."

"Oh, yes!" cried Miss Bingley. "Spending Christmastide at Pemberley would be so lovely!"

"I do not believe I will spend all of Christmas at Pemberley, Miss Bingley," contradicted Darcy. "Only that there are some matters I must see to. My Christmas plans are not yet fixed."

"You should stay here," said Bingley, ignoring his sister's crestfallen expression. "Your uncle, from what I understand, is in Ireland at a family estate, and will not return until the spring. I was going to invite both you and Fitzwilliam to remain here."

Darcy frowned. "While I do not know the extent of Fitzwilliam's leave, it has already spanned many weeks. I would think he must return to his regiment before long."

"Then I will ask him about it, for he has made no mention of being required to leave."

In truth, Darcy was thinking about Fitzwilliam's recent interest in Miss Jane Bennet. Perhaps that was the key to removing his cousin from the situation—surely his leave would expire before too much more time had passed. Should that happen, Darcy could join him in London—assuming he was not assigned to some other location—and work on him there, urging him to forget Miss Bennet. He would need to speak to Fitzwilliam on the matter and discover his future plans.

Bingley, however, was speaking to his sister again. "I am aware Netherfield is not your preference, Caroline. I understand it is not to your taste. But I see no reason to return to town. Georgiana gets on well with several ladies in the neighborhood, and I should take some thought to the management of the estate. Though the lease only runs one year, it will be important to make sure the next year is a success so we may begin the process of finding a permanent home."

"You do not mean to settle here?" asked Miss Bingley.

Bingley turned a fond look on Georgiana, which heartened Darcy. "I believe my wife prefers to be closer to her family on a permanent basis. We have made no firm plans. But it is my thought to ask Darcy and Lord Matlock for their assistance in finding an estate closer to Derbyshire."

"That would be lovely," said Georgiana.

"You know you have only to ask," replied Darcy. "I would be quite happy to assist you."

"Thank you, Darcy," said Bingley, beaming.

Miss Bingley watched them and listened to their conversation, and she seemed to weigh what was said. In the end, she took the only option available to her, no doubt encouraged by the thought that her brother would soon reside in what she considered a more appropriate neighborhood.

"Very well, Charles. But I hope you plan to go to London for the season."

"Of course," replied Bingley. "We have every intention of attending the season, though it is possible we will return to Netherfield early for the spring planting. We also must go to York to introduce Georgiana to our family there."

"There is also the annual visit to Kent at Easter," added Darcy. "Usually only Fitzwilliam accompanies me when I go, but I suspect Aunt Catherine will summon you and Georgiana to Rosings."

Bingley grimaced, and Darcy could commiserate with him. Lady Catherine's response to the marriage between Bingley and Georgiana had not been positive, and she had said some highly uncomplimentary things through letters to both Darcy and the earl about Bingley. But she was a relation, and it was only good manners to introduce a new member of the family to her acquaintance. She would wish to know if Bingley was acceptable, and if he was not—in her mind—what she must do to make him so.

"Yes, that is a matter we must consider," said Bingley, though his reluctance was clear. He turned back to Miss Bingley. "There you have it, Caroline. We will definitely attend at least part of the season, but we will likely be required to go into Kent at Easter. After that, I am uncertain at present."

"Very well, Charles," said Miss Bingley. "I hope, Mr. Darcy, that you will consent to stay with us. With your dear sister here and your family across the Irish Sea, it would make the most sense."

"I shall consider it, Miss Bingley," said Darcy. "As I said, I am required to go to Pemberley soon, but it is possible I might return before Christmas."

When he left the room soon after, Darcy's mind was occupied by plans and stratagems, thoughts of how he should approach his cousin. That he needed to go to Derbyshire was the absolute truth. But he thought his business there could be completed in a short time, leaving him free to return to the south after only a few days. It all depended on Fitzwilliam's plans, and for those, he would need to speak to his cousin himself. Thus, he determined to do so as soon as may be.

The problem was that Fitzwilliam was in little evidence that day.

Darcy had heard nothing of his cousin's plans, but he was not to be found in his usual haunts in the house. While he might have decided to go riding, Darcy would have thought Fitzwilliam would have returned long before he began looking for him. It was decidedly unusual behavior in a time when his behavior had been becoming more unusual by the day.

It was early afternoon when Darcy finally came across his cousin, walking the halls of Netherfield away from his rooms. Fitzwilliam was so rarely tied to them during the day that Darcy had not thought to look there, but as he was not dressed in riding clothes and showed no signs of having been away from the house, Darcy suspected that was where he had been. He was also whistling again, his toneless melody completely unrecognizable. Darcy could not account for his ebullience, which was uncommon, even for his jovial cousin.

"You appear to be quite happy, Cousin," said Darcy as he approached. "It seems your time at Netherfield away from your regiment has done you good."

"Without a doubt it has," said Fitzwilliam. "Come to the library, Darcy, for I have some news to share with you."

For a moment, Darcy was panicked, his mind filled with thoughts that his cousin had taken a drastic step and already proposed to Miss Bennet. But then the rational side of him reasserted itself. Though he was not aware of what his cousin had been doing that day, Darcy knew he had not left the estate.

When they reached the library, Fitzwilliam turned and fixed Darcy with a grin. "You should congratulate me, Cousins, for I have now joined the ranks of the gentlemen."

Darcy was nonplused. "You have been a gentleman for some time, Fitzwilliam. Ever since you inherited Thorndell."

"Ah, that is so. But now, I am *naught* but a gentleman. You see, I have just received confirmation of the sale of my commission from my former commanding officer. You see before you a man who is at leisure to take up residence at his estate and not concern himself with the defense of king and country." Fitzwilliam grinned. "Though I have no respect for the ability of your average French soldier to hit anything at which he aims, one of them may eventually become lucky. I am thankful I shall no longer be a target."

"That is good news, indeed!" exclaimed Darcy, capturing his cousin's hand and pumping it vigorously. "I had no notion you were considering such a step."

"My mother has been pressing me for many years now," reminded

Fitzwilliam.

"She has. But you have always resisted." Darcy grinned, slapping his cousin on the shoulder. "I wonder how you shall do at it. You have never been much for the sedentary lifestyle of a gentleman. Will you miss the excitement of the army?"

"I am convinced I shall have ample matters to keep me busy, Cousin," replied Fitzwilliam. "And considering how often you are in the saddle when you are at Pemberley, I do not think I would call the life of a gentleman precisely sedentary."

"I suppose it is not for those who are actively engaged in the management of their estates. I believe you will have some work ahead of you. Thorndell has not had anyone in residence for many years."

"Father tells me the house is sound. Changes will need to be made, and it will need the touch of a woman's hand. But it will provide me with a good life and a good life for my children."

The reminder of Fitzwilliam's recent amorous attentions was akin to a bucket of cold water being thrown over Darcy's head. Fitzwilliam was grinning without seeming to realize he was doing so, no doubt anticipating his future life. As a younger man, he had been resigned to the army, though his mother had wished him for the church. Fitzwilliam, however, was in no way suited for such a life. His father had provided for him, but as the family estates were tied up in the earldom, his prospects had always been limited by the amount his father had provided him. That amount, though substantial, would not allow for the purchase of an estate unless his wife also possessed a substantial dowry.

Now that he was essentially independent, the thought of that state might lead him to make a poor choice of wife. Thorndell was not large, being somewhat less than half in size to Pemberley. With a large dowry a society wife would bring, he would have the ability to expand it, to raise his income to levels which, while it may not rival Darcy's or Lord Matlock's, would still be substantial. A woman of little fortune—such as Miss Bennet—would leave Fitzwilliam struggling to provide dowries for any daughters he might sire.

"I am happy for you, Cousin," said Darcy, his mind still consumed with the need to extract Fitzwilliam from the neighborhood. "I believe the timing is auspicious too. I seem to remember some mention of your regiment being destined for Spain next spring."

"That did have some influence on my decision," confessed Fitzwilliam. "But I believe the deciding factor has been my good fortune to obtain the love of a good woman."

That last bit shocked Darcy. But he was given no time to make a response, for his cousin was apparently caught up in his thoughts for the future.

"You should try falling in love, Darcy," said Fitzwilliam, a grin upon his face. "It is entirely invigorating. I anticipate the woman I choose will make my estate into a home for us both. I expect it will require a lot of work to make Thorndell profitable again. I know I cannot give her as much wealth as I might wish, but I think, in the end, she will have no cause to repine."

"No, indeed," said Darcy.

His cousin shot him a glance, apparently surprised at Darcy's comment, which he had not meant to make out loud, and then shrugged. "We will be happy, I think. I cannot thank my good fortune enough, Cousin, for my inheritance has given me the power of choice. I will be forever grateful for it."

"The power of choice is a boon, indeed," said Darcy, thinking furiously about what he should say. "Having that power, however, means you have a duty to choose wisely. I had not thought you were so close to making such an important decision."

"Then I must think you are blind, Darcy. I have hardly hidden my admiration."

"Your admiration has not been hidden. But admiring a woman and proposing marriage to her are two separate matters entirely."

"I have no notion of why you would think they are separate," said Fitzwilliam. The way he looked at Darcy suggested he knew exactly what Darcy was thinking and was amused by it. "It seems to me that you search for a woman who will complement you, whose goals in life are similar, one you can love and who can make you happy, one you can make happy in turn. Then when you have found that woman, you do not lose any time in making her your own, lest someone else realize her worth and snap her up before you do."

Darcy scowled at his cousin. "Compatibility in marriage is desirable — yes, I would agree. But you must give some consideration to fortune, connections, breeding, and even, as Miss Bingley is so fond of pointing out, a woman's accomplishments."

"I do not disagree. But where complementary characters exist and a true meeting of the minds has been forged, all these other considerations must give way."

"But how do you know that what you have found is true and abiding?" asked Darcy. He was becoming more frustrated by the moment. "A man's head may be turned by a pretty face, an infatuation may be mistaken for a deeper feeling."

The snort which Fitzwilliam released was sardonic in nature and told Darcy he was not amused by Darcy's words. "Such a high opinion you have of me, Cousin. I am not some callow youth, a man who falls in love with every pretty face he sees. I am a man full grown, one who has given of himself in the service of king and country. I do not claim to be nobler than the next, but I have experienced much. Breeding, such as you call it, is overstated by many in our society, and nobility is largely a function of character, and not of lineage."

"You have not answered my question."

"Perhaps you should be explicit, Darcy," said Fitzwilliam. "If you have something to say about my choices in life, by all means, do not beat around the bush. I can withstand your contempt, I am certain."

"Cousin," said Darcy, reining in his pique as much as he was able, "you are well aware that I have the highest opinion of you. I possess neither contempt for you, nor do I suggest you are incapable of understanding your own mind. But I have serious reservations about this course you seem to be set upon."

"Then it is fortunate for you that the decision is *mine* to make."

Darcy glared at his cousin, which Fitzwilliam returned in full measure. "Proposing to Miss Bennet is a mistake. She is penniless, and she comes from a family of fortune hunters. If you propose to her, not only will you be gaining a wife who will do you no credit in society, but you will be gaining her family in the bargain, who will be no more than a millstone around your neck!"

"I thank you for speaking in a plain fashion," said Fitzwilliam, his tone laced with irony. "I do wonder, however, how you may have gained the impression that the Bennets are fortune hunters.

"And before you mention Mrs. Bennet," said Fitzwilliam, forestalling Darcy from doing just that, "I suggest you attempt to understand her. She is a woman of little education, one who was not born to the position she now holds, and who is in desperate fear of genteel poverty. She is inelegant and does not express herself well, but though she wishes her daughters to make good marriages, she does not stoop to anything underhanded to achieve her ends. She *speaks* a great deal, but in the end, there is little harm in her."

"What of her daughters?" demanded Darcy. "Do you think any of them would be allowed to refuse a proposal? I have no doubt Miss Bennet would be obligated to accept you, should you propose. And what of her feelings for you?"

"What of them?"

"Has she any?" Fitzwilliam raised an eyebrow, but Darcy continued on relentlessly. "She behaves no differently with you from the manner she does with me or any other man of her acquaintance. She smiles and accepts their attentions, but she does nothing more. I suspect her heart will not be easily touched."

"I will thank you for allowing me the greater knowledge of Miss Bennet's feelings," replied Fitzwilliam, a stubborn shake of his head further angering Darcy. "You have rarely spoken with her, while I have been in company with her many times, speaking with her and focusing all my energies upon her. Though at first, I will own that I was not certain, these past weeks she has taken care to show me her growing regard."

"It is easy for a woman to feign more than she feels."

"Not when a woman is as genuine as Miss Bennet. I doubt she could feign a cough and be believed."

The cousins stared at each other, Darcy becoming frustrated with Fitzwilliam's intransigence, while Fitzwilliam watched him, sardonic amusement alive in his countenance. Why his cousin could not take matters seriously, Darcy did not know. So upset was Darcy that thoughts of relating the conversation he had overheard fled, and he was left grasping at straws.

"You should trust my judgment!" cried Darcy. "Why are you set upon this destructive course?"

"In this instance, I think it is *you* who should trust *my* judgment," replied Fitzwilliam, ignoring Darcy's second statement. "I *know* Miss Bennet, and I know her sister nearly as well. Neither would ever behave in the manner you suggest. They are not Miss Bingley."

"And what of your family?" asked Darcy, desperate to deflect Fitzwilliam from this path. "You know the earl hopes for better for you in a marriage partner."

"But he understands it is my choice. In fact, I have written to my mother of Miss Bennet, and she has informed me that she is eager to make her acquaintance."

Darcy glared at his cousin stonily. "Are you set on this madness?"

"I am only intent upon securing my own happiness. You may not agree with me, Darcy. But you will allow me to make my own choices. I will have your respect for the woman I mean to have as my wife. Your approval is not required."

"I hope very much you do not regret this, Fitzwilliam. But I fear it is inevitable."

Then Darcy turned and walked away. Fitzwilliam was right about one thing—though Darcy wished to save his cousin from an imprudent match, there was nothing he could do on the matter. Fitzwilliam would make his own choice. But Darcy was not required to watch as his cousin did so.

CHAPTER XIII

$\mathcal{B}$ingley was disappointed when Darcy announced his intention to depart the very next morning. In fact, one could say that was a large understatement. But Bingley was not in the habit of questioning Darcy's motives. That did not, however, prevent him from attempting to convince Darcy to stay.

"We were hoping you would stay until the New Year, Darcy. There cannot be much to do at your estate at this time of year. Can you not remain here with us for the present and return at a later date?"

"I am sorry, Bingley," said Darcy. "There are some matters which have arisen, and there is little I can do at a distance. I have put off my departure for too long as it is."

"Georgiana will not be happy to see you leave."

Darcy's countenance softened, a relief, as it happened, for he had felt like the stoniness of his countenance was beginning to make his jaw ache. "I know she will, Bingley. But she is now mistress of your home. I could not have asked for a better husband for her."

It seemed Bingley was pleased by Darcy's praise, though it was not the first time he had offered it. While Darcy had not been convinced of the wisdom of Bingley's impulsive proposal, he had come to appreciate the fact that his sister would, indeed, be happy with his friend. There was nothing more for which he could hope. In part, it was best that he left, for it was time for his sister and her husband to stand on their own.

"I will not be gone forever, Bingley. You will see me again, in London during the season, if not before."

Bingley frowned. "Surely your business will not keep you in Derbyshire for long. There is still time for you to travel there, handle matters, and then return before Christmas."

"I do not know, Bingley," said Darcy, unwilling to make any commitments. "It will depend on how much I am able to finish quickly. If I am able to return, I shall."

For a moment, Darcy thought Bingley would call him on his lie, for in truth, he had no intention of returning before Christmas. But in the end, he only sighed and shook his head, bowing to the inevitable.

"Then I shall wish you a safe journey, my friend. I hope to see you again sooner than you suggest."

Darcy clasped his friend's hand and departed from the room. The next morning, he left Netherfield without any intention of returning.

His cousin's departure, Fitzwilliam watched without giving any hint of his feelings on the matter. Darcy would, of course, do as he wished, though Fitzwilliam had hoped he would not quit the place simply because he did not agree with Fitzwilliam's choice of a wife. The proof of his correct choice would be in the life he meant to forge with Miss Bennet, so Fitzwilliam did not concern himself with his cousin's anger. Soon Darcy would understand his mistake.

Not everyone at Netherfield was sanguine about his going, however, as Fitzwilliam might have predicted in advance. Georgiana was distressed and pleaded with him many times to reconsider, though she was resigned in the end. Miss Bingley, however, was positively distraught at the news, not that Darcy would allow himself to be swayed from his purpose by the likes of his new brother's sister.

"Now we are positively stuck in the desolation of this neighborhood," said Miss Bingley the night after Darcy left. "How shall we endure the months before the season starts?"

"I am sorry you do not find me an adequate substitute for my cousin, Miss Bingley," said Fitzwilliam, fighting the urge to laugh openly.

"Oh, it is nothing against you, Colonel," said the woman, shaking her head. "You are all that is gentlemanly. But the diminution of our party lessens us, and in such a neighborhood as this. I can hardly fathom what we shall do with ourselves until the spring."

"For one," said Bingley, "we shall be going to the north in the New Year, as long as the weather allows it." Bingley directed a grin at Georgiana. "I must introduce my new wife to our family, after all."

"Returning to York is not my idea of an improvement on our current situation, Charles," said Miss Bingley.

"But it will be a change," said Georgiana. "I am anticipating meeting your family, for I have heard so much of them, and I am relying on your support."

"Of course, dear Georgiana," said Miss Bingley, perking up. "For a short time, it will be agreeable to be in their company again." Then Miss Bingley turned to Bingley. "But you have promised we shall be in town for the season."

"So I have, and I have no intention of reneging on that promise. Perhaps, on the way south, we may even stop at Pemberley to visit with Darcy again."

There was nothing he could have said which could be better calculated to ensure Miss Bingley's favor. The woman's countenance positively glowed at the thought of once again being at Pemberley, and he could almost see her plans to ingratiate herself to Darcy forming before her very eyes. If it had not been so very pathetic, Fitzwilliam might have found it amusing.

As it was, Fitzwilliam wondered if his cousin had not done this woman a disservice. Miss Bingley was attractive enough, he supposed, though she was not his idea of a beautiful woman. Though Georgiana had assumed her role as the mistress of Bingley's house, Fitzwilliam had heard that Miss Bingley was a good hostess, and he knew she possessed the usual accomplishments expected of young women of her age. Unfortunately, she had also fixed her attention on Darcy to the exclusion of all others. Fitzwilliam knew that Darcy would not marry her, and as she was beginning to approach the age where she would be considered on the shelf, it would be best if her delusion was ended, and she widened her search for a husband to a man who might find her acceptable.

Perhaps he could take it upon himself to open her eyes to the reality of the situation. Fitzwilliam was loath to clean Darcy's messes for him, but it would be kinder if she knew, rather than continuing to hope that Darcy could be induced to offer for her. He would need to think on it.

While he was considering the problem of Miss Bingley, Bingley turned his attention to Fitzwilliam, saying: "I am not certain why your cousin felt it necessary to return to Pemberley with such haste, but I hope you are not required to leave us."

"No, indeed," replied Fitzwilliam. He had already informed them of his resignation from the army, a matter over which Georgiana had actually shed tears of happiness and relief. "I find myself quite at my leisure, Bingley, and have no need to depart. Unless, of course, you find yourself wishing me gone."

"Of course not!" cried Bingley, as Fitzwilliam had known he would. "I am certain Georgiana will join me in inviting you to stay as long as you wish it."

"I do," said Georgiana in her usually quiet voice. "Furthermore, considering the presence of a certain young lady in this district, I cannot imagine you will wish to depart anytime soon."

Hurst snorted and Bingley grinned while the man's sisters nodded their understanding. While they were quite obviously not happy with the neighborhood and wished to leave as soon as could be arranged, Fitzwilliam had noted their acceptance of the eldest Bennet sisters as friends. Though he did not care for their opinions, Fitzwilliam supposed it was better for them all to get along, as the Bennets were becoming Georgiana's particular friends. Fitzwilliam intended that the connection would become a more intimate one.

"With such a warm welcome," said Fitzwilliam, "I could not imagine refusing. If you feel you can withstand my flippant nature, as Darcy often calls it, I would be pleased to accept."

"Excellent!" exclaimed Bingley. "You must stay over Christmas. Then you will be quite at your leisure to accomplish your designs at any time convenient."

While Fitzwilliam knew he was being teased, he was too busy indulging in thoughts of exactly what his designs consisted. And he was intent upon seeing them realized long before any of the present company could imagine.

When it came to missing family members, some were more missed than others, Elizabeth decided. When Colonel Fitzwilliam came the day after his cousin's departure from the neighborhood, Elizabeth knew from his words that he would miss his cousin, though there was a subtle undercurrent of feeling which suggested he was happy Mr. Darcy had decided to leave. Elizabeth could not imagine the reason why, for she had often observed them to be very close. Regardless of the reason, she could not find herself missing the man, though she had no reason to wish him gone. Even the dance they had shared had largely been silent, leaving Elizabeth wondering why Mr. Darcy had bothered to ask her at all.

On the other side of the equation was their own cousin, Mr. Collins. He had left, promising to return, though with no firm plans of when that dreaded event would occur. Elizabeth knew that of the family, her mother was the only one who could tolerate the dullard, and only then because she wished to marry Elizabeth off to him. Thus the news that he was to return was not welcome by most of the family.

"I have a letter," said Mr. Bennet at the dinner table, holding it up to show them all, "which informs me that my cousin intends to return to us tomorrow."

"Mr. Collins!" exclaimed Mrs. Bennet with an excited glance at Elizabeth. "I had no notion he would return so soon, but I am happy nonetheless. I shall have Hill make up the guest room tomorrow."

Elizabeth directed an appealing look at her father, but Mr. Bennet chuckled and shook his head. There would be no help from that quarter. Fortunately for Elizabeth, not all of her family were so hard of heart.

"Stay close to me, Lizzy," said Jane that evening when they had retired to Jane's room. "Mr. Collins can hardly make his addresses in the company of myself, Colonel Fitzwilliam when he is here, or any of the rest of the family."

"I would not be so certain of that," replied Elizabeth with a mirthless laugh. "I suspect he would simply speak to Mama and request a moment of privacy with me. You know Mama too well to think she would do anything other than lock me in a room with the odious man."

While it was not in Jane's nature to criticize her mother, she well knew the truth of Elizabeth's assertion and did not reply. A hysterical laugh escaped Elizabeth's lips.

"I think I might almost be obliged to Mr. Collins if he would come to the point in an expeditious fashion. If he does, then I may refuse him and free myself from his vacuous attentions."

"I am not sure that would provide relief," said Jane. "You know our mother will not be pleased with such an outcome."

"No, she would not," replied Elizabeth. "But I have Papa's assurance of support, so there is little she can do. I would rather be the subject of Mama's anger than of the objectionable attempts of an inept lover. Mama's injured silences would at least be a respite, though I am not foolish enough to believe they would comprise her entire reaction."

"They would not," agreed Jane.

In the end, the matter was resolved in a much more expeditious manner than Elizabeth might have expected, though her expectations of her mother's response were wildly inaccurate. Mr. Collins did come the following day, entering the house with all the self-confidence of a man with much more reason to be so than William Collins. As he told them, at length, of his happiness at being there, he learned of some of the doings of the neighborhood the previous week. Mrs. Bennet was sure to inform him of the ball he had missed, and his regret was expressed to Elizabeth in particular.

"It was such a fine evening," said Mrs. Bennet, waxing poetic on the subject, which her family had heard already on several occasions. "The Bingleys are truly excellent people, you know, and we were so happy to have been invited."

"Oh, I can imagine the splendid scene in detail!" exclaimed Mr. Collins, not to be outdone by his cousin's wife. "For Mrs. Bingley is my patroness's niece, and while her ladyship is not happy with her niece's marriage, I cannot imagine that Mrs. Bingley could host anything but the most elegant celebration. Of course, her celebrations would be nothing to what Lady Catherine herself would prepare. But I am certain it must have been fine, indeed."

"Is that so, Cousin?" asked Elizabeth, feeling cross and impish all at the same time. "You should regale us with tales of the balls your patroness has thrown, for I am certain we shall all be enraptured by such elegance and fineness as you have seen."

Mr. Collins regarded Elizabeth with wide eyes for a moment, after which he endeavored to cover his error. "In actuality, my dear cousin, I have not attended a ball given at Rosings."

"No?" asked Elizabeth, feigning astonishment. "By the enthusiasm with which you discuss the subject, I might have thought Lady Catherine invited the neighborhood on a monthly basis if only to show her neighbors the elegance of her arrangements."

"I am afraid you have misunderstood, my dear cousin," said Mr. Collins, his tone all superiority. "Rosings is, indeed, as fine and elegant a house as any I have ever seen, but Lady Catherine is very discerning in choosing her friends. Naturally, *if* she did host a ball, I am certain it would be as fine as any ever seen in the neighborhood, if not in the entire county. Lady Catherine is a woman in possession of exquisite taste and the most comprehensive understanding of what is to be done."

"Then she has not hosted a ball," said Elizabeth. "What of dinners, parties, picnics, or even a simple gathering of friends. Surely you have witnessed some of these."

It was clear to Elizabeth that Mr. Collins thought she was asking because of her interest in his situation. He could not be more wrong. But he puffed up in his self-importance and said:

"I have often been invited to dine, and among Lady Catherine's friends there several of the neighborhood, including Lady Metcalfe, who is, of course, a fine woman herself, though not the equal of Lady Catherine. I commend you for your interest, my dear cousin, and hope that you may experience such fine company yourself one day."

"Your hope is a vain one," replied Elizabeth.

Mr. Collins looked at her askance, and her mother fairly scowled at her, but Elizabeth did not care for either of their opinions. Mrs. Bennet did not say anything, and Mr. Collins ignored what he did not like, which was fine with Elizabeth.

The next day, Colonel Fitzwilliam visited again. His reception of Mr. Collins was cool, though the man in question certainly understood none of it. His wooing of Jane continued apace, and Elizabeth decided that was enough to make her happy at present, regardless of Mr. Collins's continued attempts of his own.

"Stay close to your sister and me," said Colonel Fitzwilliam to Elizabeth on an occasion in which they were to walk the back gardens. "We will do what we can to assist you in escaping him."

Elizabeth was grateful for the colonel's assistance, but she knew he was close to coming to the point with Jane and did not wish to keep him from it. The first day, they were able to escape when Mr. Collins was distracted by a question of the Bible posed by her sister Mary. That did not mean he did not find them in the garden soon after, though Elizabeth found she was able to ignore him completely when out of doors.

They continued to do what they could for her, though their attention was more often focused on each other. That, unfortunately, seemed to spur Mr. Collins on, for seeing Colonel Fitzwilliam's ardent pursuit of Jane inspired him to emulate the colonel, often saying the same things, though in his own words, which typically rendered them nonsensical. On several occasions, when she was not completely ignoring him, Elizabeth pondered the relative benefit of breaking a tree branch over his thick head. Unfortunately, she was forced to discard the idea, as she did not doubt the branch would receive the worst in the exchange.

This all came to a head on the First of December. It seemed that Colonel Fitzwilliam was not of a mind to wait any longer to achieve his heart's desire, for on that morning, though Elizabeth had accompanied them out of doors before Mr. Collins had descended, she soon found herself alone, as Colonel Fitzwilliam and Jane had ducked into a dense copse of trees. Though she knew where they were, Elizabeth waited for them, certain she knew what they were about. She was not disappointed.

Jane emerged a few moments later, with Colonel Fitzwilliam following, the happy tears on her face telling the story of what had just happened. Elizabeth did not wait for them to make an announcement; she flew into her sister's arms, crying her congratulations, excited for the good fortune of the best person in the world.

"It seems we have your approval, Miss Elizabeth," came the dry voice of Colonel Fitzwilliam as he witnessed their tearful celebration. "Do you think I am spared the requirement of asking your father's permission?"

Elizabeth could not help but laugh. She turned and fixed him with a firm glare and a pointed finger, saying: "I think not, sir. With five daughters, you cannot think my father has not anticipated the days that he could intimidate his daughters' suitors when they come to ask for their hands."

A laugh comprised the colonel's response, followed by a jovially spoken: "I can well imagine it! But I shall persist and take courage, for I am skilled with both sword and pistol, should he descend to violence."

"My father? Violent?" Elizabeth shook her head. "I *am* certain you have met the man. I believe he is more likely to chase you from his bookroom, foil in hand, for no more reason than your interruption!"

"Lizzy!" admonished Jane.

But Colonel Fitzwilliam laughed. "I think he is hardly as you make him out to be. But be that as it may, I am more than happy to allow him his fun, if only he approves."

"I am sure he shall," said Elizabeth with a warm smile.

"Then I am off. I hope you shall both wait for me in the sitting-room."

The sisters repaired inside while the colonel braved their father in his room, whispering as they went. Elizabeth's sincere congratulations were met with a wish that Elizabeth would stand up with her for their wedding, which assent Elizabeth did not hesitate to give. Then Mr. Collins came.

"There is something different about you this morning, Cousins," said Mr. Collins when he had observed them for several moments.

Then his ugly face lit up in an unctuous smile. "Of course, I knew how it would be all along. For a period, I had almost thought you were attempting to avoid me. But it is clear such could not be the case, and your current happiness proves my supposition."

As it was, Elizabeth did not care for his assumption, nor did she wish to speak to him. As such, she directed a look skyward and turned her attention back to her sister. But she did not miss the speculative looks from Mary, Kitty and Lydia's giggles, which she thought were directed at the parson's foolishness, and her mother's severe look, which suggested she knew Elizabeth had not changed her opinion of Mr. Collins. Then the gentlemen entered the room.

"Mrs. Bennet," said Mr. Bennet, "it seems to me that you are finally to achieve your heart's desire today."

"Lizzy?" said Mrs. Bennet, turning wide eyes on Elizabeth. For a woman who had always known of any hint of interest in her daughters long before it was manifest and who had witnessed Colonel Fitzwilliam's increasing ardency toward Jane these past days, Elizabeth could only shake her head at her mother's arriving at the wrong conclusion.

"No," replied Mr. Bennet. "Not Lizzy. In fact, this young man by my side, who I am told is *not* a colonel in the regulars any longer, has accosted me in my bookroom this morning, demanding he be allowed to marry your eldest daughter. After performing my duty as a father to a young woman and making him sweat for fifteen minutes, I granted my consent."

"Oh, Jane!" shrieked Mrs. Bennet. She threw herself from her chair and caught Jane up into a fierce embrace, while her daughters crowded around them, speaking their congratulations all at once. For a few moments, a cacophony raged in the sitting-room, a mixture of laughter, crying, and one voice trying to make itself heard over the tumult. When the furor died down, that voice rose above the rest.

"Colonel Fitzwilliam!" exclaimed Mr. Collins, his countenance all astonishment. "Am I to understand you have proposed to my eldest cousin?"

Grinning, Colonel Fitzwilliam shook his head. "No, Mr. Collins. I would never presume to propose to Mr. Bennet." Mr. Bennet guffawed at the colonel's outrageous statement, but Colonel Fitzwilliam continued to speak, saying: "However, it is correct that I have proposed to his eldest daughter."

Mr. Collins appeared like a fish out of water. But all too soon he gathered whatever existed of his wits. "Oh, no, Colonel, that cannot be. Surely you recall my informing you all of how my patroness was unhappy with your cousin's marriage to a man of trade? I cannot think she will be made any happier by this. You have clearly made a mistake, and must now retract your proposal."

Several gasps split the air at once, most in shock at the parson's audacity. One, however, was due to utter outrage.

"Mr. Collins!" cried Mrs. Bennet. "Are you suggesting that my daughter is not good enough for Colonel Fitzwilliam?"

"They come from entirely different spheres, Mrs. Bennet," said Mr. Collins with a haughty sniff. "Your daughters are everything lovely, but they cannot match Colonel Fitzwilliam's family for their position in society, wealth, and sheer nobility of character. No, my patroness will not be happy with this, and she must be obeyed. I am certain the colonel will wish to reconsider, now that I have brought it to his attention."

"You presume much, Mr. Collins," said Colonel Fitzwilliam.

Mrs. Bennet appeared on the verge of speaking again, but the colonel stepped forward and laid a hand on her arm. "Please, Mrs. Bennet—allow me the right of response."

While it went against her very nature, Mrs. Bennet subsided, though not without a hateful glare at the parson. It seemed for the first time that Mr. Collins understood he was not in friendly territory. While Mr. Bennet looked on, hilarity in his mien, the colonel, Mrs. Bennet, and Elizabeth all regarded him as if he was naught but a particularly disgusting rodent. Mr. Collins attempted bravado at this near-universal show of disgust, but the way his eyes darted about suggested he had been made uncomfortable. It was just as well, Elizabeth thought, for he had made them all uncomfortable with his very presence.

"In fact, Mr. Collins," said Colonel Fitzwilliam, "I am well aware of my aunt's disapproval of my cousin's marriage. Unfortunately for her ladyship, I care no more than my cousin did—or her brother. Darcy was not swayed by Lady Catherine's arguments, nor was Georgiana. I do not know why you believe I would give heed to *your* arguments, a man who is completely unconnected with us."

"I am your aunt's parson—"

"Irrelevant," snapped Colonel Fitzwilliam, cutting the parson off. "You may advise my aunt in whatever manner you wish. I neither need nor want your advice. I will not retract my proposal, nor could I, in good conscience. I am a man of integrity, a man of my word. I will not disappoint Miss Bennet now that I have offered for her."

For a moment, it seemed Mr. Collins might object further. But then paused in a contemplative fashion, and he nodded his head slowly.

"You have my apologies, Colonel Fitzwilliam," said he, bowing low. "I never would have accused you of being a dishonorable man. Though I am certain my patroness will consider your engagement to Miss Bennet to be a most unfortunate alliance, I agree you cannot escape it now. As such, I wish you the best."

"Thank you, Mr. Collins," said Colonel Fitzwilliam. Though his tone was laced with irony, the steel inherent in it warned the parson he had best cease speaking.

Unfortunately, as one of the dullest of his species, Mr. Collins could not be counted on to act in a logical manner. But his response took them all down a path Elizabeth could not have expected.

"My dear cousin," said he to Elizabeth, in a tone extravagant and smug, "it seems to me this is a propitious opportunity, indeed. For, having witnessed your dearest sister obtain her happiness, I must assume you are eager to reach out and grasp your own. I am not reluctant to be the means of that happiness, I assure you.

"My patroness, Lady Catherine de Bourgh, sent me here with the express purpose of finding a wife to grace my parsonage, for she thinks it a right thing for the parson in her employ to set the example of matrimony in the parish. And as my courting of you these past weeks cannot have been misunderstood, I am certain you must have been expecting my proposal. Thus, I offer my hand to you now, and propose marriage, confident in your eagerness to accept."

Elizabeth gaped at Mr. Collins, more shocked than she had ever been in her life. The witless parson had just proposed to her, in front of her entire family, in spite of everything she had done to dissuade him.

"Expecting your proposal, yes," said Elizabeth at last. "Welcoming it, no. I have no notion of how you have misunderstood me, Mr. Collins, but I have no desire to accept you. Thank you for the honor, but I am afraid I must decline."

Mr. Collins's manner went from arrogant confidence to disbelief in the blink of an eye. But he was by no means cast down, as he was quick to point out himself.

"Oh, you are charming!" exclaimed he. He turned his eyes to Jane and leered at her. "I must assume you refused your proposal at first to increase Colonel Fitzwilliam's love by suspense. And now your sister wishes to follow in your footsteps. How could I expect anything less?"

"Of course, I did not," said Jane, seeming bewildered. "Why would

I risk my happiness by refusing the man I love?"

Now appearing less sure of himself, Mr. Collins turned back to Elizabeth. "You have no other prospects before you. Thus you cannot be serious."

"Are you completely witless?"

The screeched question came from the most unlikely of sources. Mrs. Bennet stood, arms akimbo, glaring at the parson, while he returned her gaze with confusion and shock.

"My Jane was not good enough for Colonel Fitzwilliam, and you think to propose to my Lizzy? I begin to think *you* are not good enough for *her*!"

"Madam!" sputtered Mr. Collins. "I was only protecting the interests of my patroness."

"What do we care for your patroness?" snapped Mrs. Bennet. She seemed to realize what she said and turned to Colonel Fitzwilliam with an apologetic smile. "I do not mean to speak ill of your aunt, Colonel Fitzwilliam. But she is not connected to us."

"Yet," replied Colonel Fitzwilliam. "I have taken no offense, Mrs. Bennet."

"The situations are completely different," said Mr. Collins, his temper rising. "Your eldest daughter is, indeed, attempting to climb the heights of society by accepting Colonel Fitzwilliam's proposal. I am not as high as he, but I am in every way a suitable match for your second daughter."

"Except that her second daughter cannot stand the sight of you," said Elizabeth.

"Will you allow her to speak to me this way, Mr. Bennet?" demanded Mr. Collins. "I assure you that when she is my wife, I will not tolerate such insubordination."

"You will never be her husband," spat Mrs. Bennet. "Lizzy is much too good for the likes of you."

"Well, Mr. Bennet?"

Though his mirth had caused tears to roll from Mr. Bennet's eyes, he shook his head and gathered himself. "I am afraid you shall not have Lizzy for a wife. It seems *my* wife has already spoken on the subject."

Mr. Collins's eyes bulged out in shock. "You will allow your wife to rule you?"

"I am not surprised that you have not understood the fallacy of your thinking, sir," said Mr. Bennet. "My daughters are all precious to me, Lizzy no less than any of the others. Your fate was sealed when she refused you. I would never force her to marry against her will. It appears you must look elsewhere for your bride."

With increasing shock and consternation Mr. Collins watched Mr. Bennet. His eyes searched the Bennet patriarch for any hint that he was jesting or that the situation might be salvaged. It was apparent he saw nothing, for an ugly sneer soon came over his features.

"Very well! It seems I have made a fortunate escape this morning, for which I will be forever grateful. I hope you have made provisions for your family, sir, for they will find no succor from me when you are dead."

"My aunt will be interested to hear you say that, Mr. Collins," said Colonel Fitzwilliam, all amusement erased from his countenance. "Whatever else she is, Lady Catherine is not without generosity, and she will not be pleased to hear you have renounced all interest in charity."

But Mr. Collins was too angry to heed the censure in Colonel Fitzwilliam's words. "I shall depart forthwith. I have never been more insulted in my life. I will not stay here another minute!"

So saying, he exited the room, closing the door behind him with excessive force. No one regretted his going.

CHAPTER XIV

*T*he days after Mr. Collins's departure from Longbourn brought welcome relief, and Elizabeth was pleased to discover she had not had to fight her mother to obtain it. Mrs. Bennet had railed against the man long before she had made his acquaintance, solely as he was the means, in her estimation, of the ultimate loss of her home. Now, however, she continued to rail against him, but with much more reason.

"My first instinct was correct," said she, on more than one occasion. "His father was an odious man, and Mr. Collins has been brought up at his father's knee. I should have expected nothing further from him, so I am now free to dislike him at my leisure."

While Elizabeth could not disagree with that statement, she also remembered that her mother had expected her to marry the man to save the family until he had committed the unforgivable sin of insulting her eldest daughter. Elizabeth was grateful Mr. Collins had managed to turn her mother against him. But despite her gratitude in that respect, she could not forget how Mrs. Bennet had sought to force her to accept the man.

"I hope you see now, Mama," said Elizabeth on one occasion in which the subject had been raised, "how I would have been miserable with him."

"Yes, I suppose you would have," said Mrs. Bennet, the lack of apology for her actions evident. "But we cannot pick and choose, Lizzy. You girls do not have much between you when your father dies. Jane has made an advantageous match, but her future husband is not wealthy enough to keep you all should your father pass."

"I am sure my future husband would consent to support *all* my sisters, should the worst happen," said Jane.

"That is not the point, Jane," said Mrs. Bennet, patting her eldest on the knee. "He is a good man and would, no doubt, assist. But it would be best if your sisters were protected in their own marriages."

"Perhaps that is so," said Elizabeth, becoming crosser with her mother by the moment. "But please allow me to understand my own mind, Mama. I do not wish you to attempt to force me on the next man to enter the neighborhood. I will choose my own husband, even if that choice is to have no husband at all. The matter of my own support shall be *mine* to make."

Mrs. Bennet eyed Elizabeth, disapproval radiating from her in waves. "Your father has always indulged you too much, Lizzy. These fanciful notions of yours will result in your remaining an old maid."

"That is my decision to make, Mama."

"You must do what is best for the family!" shrilled Mrs. Bennet, becoming agitated.

"I must also do what is best for *me*," said Elizabeth. "Jane has found her happiness, and with it, your future is secure. I would ask you to leave me to fend for myself, and I warn you — even had you not soured on Mr. Collins's suit, I still would have refused you and my father would have supported me."

"He would have made you do your duty!"

"Mama, can you truly think that? My father will not force me, regardless of what you say. Let us not argue about it. If an opportunity for a good marriage comes along, I shall not dismiss it out of hand. But as it is *I* who will be forced to live with the consequences of my decision, please allow me the power of choice."

Whether it was Elizabeth's assertion of her father's support or her assurance she would not reject an eligible match out of hand which stayed Mrs. Bennet's objections, Elizabeth was not certain. Her mother regarded her, her gaze searching, for several moments, before she turned away with a shrug.

"Very well. You always were headstrong and intent upon having your own way. But I warn you, Lizzy — if you do not shake the fanciful notions from your head, you will never marry. You are looking for a perfect man. He does not exist."

"I am well aware of that, Mama," replied Elizabeth.

"Furthermore, do not expect the Fitzwilliams to support you, should Mr. Collins take control of Longbourn. They will have enough to do to support their children, without being required to support a spinster sister."

The way Mrs. Bennet spoke, Elizabeth could hear the contempt in her voice at the word "spinster." Having made a better marriage than she had a right to expect in marrying a gentleman, Elizabeth was well aware of what Mrs. Bennet thought of women who failed to marry. It was that, as much as her fear of being forced from her home with nowhere to go, which drove her manic insistence upon her daughters marrying. In the end, it appeared her mother was willing to allow the matter to drop, and Elizabeth was eager to do so as well.

Time passed and the month of December passed with it. Those at Longbourn were becoming ever more intimate with the residents of Netherfield. Mrs. Georgiana Bingley had nothing but praise for her cousin's choice, welcoming Jane to her extended family with true pleasure and excitement. And while not all those at Netherfield were the friendliest, at least they were all civil, for which Elizabeth was grateful. Mr. Darcy, though Mr. Bingley had expressed the hope that he would return from the Christmas season, sent them word that he would be kept in Derbyshire. His absence was regretted only by his family, and Elizabeth, in particular, suspected there was more at work than simply estate business. But it was none of her concern, so she pushed it from her mind.

A few days before Christmas, the Gardiners arrived at Longbourn for their annual Christmas visit. The night after their coming, the entire party had been invited to the traditional Christmas party at Lucas Lodge, and it was there they were introduced to Jane's fiancé. It was clear both parties liked what they saw in the other.

"What is your line of business, Mr. Gardiner?" asked Colonel Fitzwilliam as they stood talking together in one of the rooms at Lucas Lodge.

"I am an importer," said Mr. Gardiner. Elizabeth, who had always held the Gardiners as especial favorites, was pleased with her uncle's comportment, how he showed himself to be a gentleman at heart, if not profession. "I import goods from the Orient, primarily, though part of my custom is from the continent as well. The dresses which adorn my sisters and the Bennet girls typically use fabrics from my warehouse."

Mr. Gardiner turned a mock frown on Elizabeth, who stood close by. "In fact, they use so much of my fabrics that I have often wondered if I will be made a pauper because of it."

"Do not listen to him, Colonel Fitzwilliam," said Mrs. Gardiner, jabbing at her husband with an elbow. "He always declares himself happy to do it, and I know for a fact that Lizzy's father has been compensating him for his daughters' dresses for years."

"But not nearly what I would make should my stock be sold to London's modistes," grumbled Mr. Gardiner. His wink at Elizabeth belied any censure in his words.

"Do you supply many?" asked the colonel.

"I have not yet made contacts with several of the most exclusive modistes," replied Mr. Gardiner. "But, yes, I do supply several."

"Then perhaps our meeting is fortuitous. I have heard my cousin, Georgiana, speak of her admiration for the fabrics the Bennet ladies have used. Should she be allowed to purchase fabric from you, it is possible the dressmakers might be interested in learning from whence she obtained it."

Mr. Gardiner raised his glass. "I am always looking for more ways to market my materials, sir. I have the ability to obtain greater quantities, should the demand increase."

The two gentlemen continued to discuss Mr. Gardiner's business at length, and while Elizabeth did not find the subject to be to her taste, she was grateful they were getting on so well. Before she left them, they had turned to a conversation of various ventures Mr. Gardiner was following, as he explained the art of speculating in various endeavors which, if successful, would pay a handsome profit. The gleam in Colonel Fitzwilliam's eyes suggested he was considering investing himself.

As always, the Lucas Christmas party was well attended, with most members of the neighborhood gathering at Lucas Lodge that evening. Sir William, fond as he was of company, greeted all and sundry with good humor and an invitation to make themselves at home. As a result, the party was a press, considering the men of the militia had also been invited, and liberally dotted the gathering with their red coats shining like beacons. The younger members of the party—Kitty and Lydia among them—were enjoying themselves with so much giggling that Elizabeth thought they could not have said anything of substance. And she also expected it would likely devolve to impromptu dancing later that evening, as was often the case at these gatherings.

As Elizabeth and Charlotte Lucas had been friends for some years, it was natural they would find themselves speaking that evening. And the topic of their conversation was, unsurprisingly, the matter of Mr. Collins, of which Elizabeth had informed Charlotte at great length and in terms which were now humorous to her.

"I see your mother is speaking of Mr. Collins again," observed Charlotte.

Considering her mother rarely spoke in a voice which could not be overheard by everyone in the room, Elizabeth was well aware of her words. The trouble, in Elizabeth's mind, was how her mother was not only speaking of what an odious man Mr. Collins had turned out to be. She was also speaking of her disappointment with Elizabeth and of her expectations that her second daughter would never marry.

"She actually told me she did not wish to marry," said Mrs. Bennet to Mrs. Goulding, another silly woman of the neighborhood. "Can you imagine such a thing? I have tried speaking with her, but it seems she will go her own way. I suppose I have no choice but to allow her to shift for herself."

Elizabeth grimaced, as annoyed with her mother for speaking about such a subject as she was about Mrs. Bennet's ability to be completely wrong in everything she said. She knew her mother was not truly distressed about the business. But her tendency toward theatrics meant that whenever she spoke of something, it was the most distressing thing in the world.

"I assume you did not inform your mother you would not marry," said Charlotte.

It was not a question, and Elizabeth did not treat it as one. "I did not. I only informed her that *I* would choose my husband — I will not allow my mother to force me into a marriage I do not want."

Charlotte nodded. "I would not have expected anything less. Unfortunately, I suspect that, in the end, you may discover you have done a very foolish thing."

"And what is that?" asked Elizabeth with more testiness than tact. She had no wish to allow Charlotte to lecture her on the precarious nature of their situations.

"Lizzy, I know you did not like Mr. Collins," said she, her tone conciliatory.

"That is a heavy understatement," Elizabeth replied shortly. "To be completely honest, I cannot imagine how anyone could feel anything other than contempt for him."

"Perhaps that is so. But Mr. Collins is respectable. He has a good living and an enviable situation. And one day, he will be master of Longbourn. Had you accepted him, you would be mistress one day, and considering how Mr. Collins is not . . . gifted intellectually, I dare say in everything but name, *you* would have been master of the estate."

"You are correct," replied Elizabeth. "But I could not have been happy in such a situation, even were Longbourn an estate of twenty thousand a year. You say it was foolish to refuse the only offer of marriage I may ever receive. I say it would have been infinitely more foolish to marry a fool, a man for whom I feel nothing but contempt. You may have been happy in such a situation. I cannot imagine I would be anything but miserable."

Charlotte regarded Elizabeth evenly, and Elizabeth returned it with stony resolve. In the end, Charlotte realized it was fruitless to continue to speak in such a manner, and she subsided.

"I suppose you must be correct, Lizzy," said she. "You *would* be miserable in such a marriage."

Elizabeth did not respond. She contented herself with a tight nod and allowed the subject to drop. Charlotte too understood that was best, for she introduced the subject of Jane's engagement. For the rest of the time they stood together, they spoke of Jane's happiness and what a good man Colonel Fitzwilliam was. When Charlotte was beckoned away by her mother, Elizabeth allowed her to leave, feeling much happier about their ending conversation than she had earlier in their talk.

Still later that evening, Elizabeth was given an opportunity to escape from the madhouse that Longbourn often was. But it was one which she was not certain she should take.

It was a rare occasion that Jane was separated from Colonel Fitzwilliam at any gathering, but as he was speaking with Colonel Forster about some matter or another, Jane quickly found Elizabeth. The pianoforte had been opened, and Elizabeth had taken a turn, at Charlotte's insistence, before she had ceded the instrument to the other young ladies of the neighborhood, chief among them, of course, being their sister Mary.

"Lizzy," said Jane in greeting, "I have been speaking with Anthony tonight about our wedding tour."

"And where do you mean to go?" asked Elizabeth, pleased for her sister. "I have always wished to visit the lakes or the Peak District. It is not the season for it, however, for if you go right after your wedding in January, I cannot imagine the weather would be warm enough to enjoy your time there."

"No, we do not mean to go immediately," replied Jane. "Thorndell is not far from the peaks, it seems, and Anthony has promised me we shall go there when the opportunity presents itself. Instead, we shall go to Brighton."

"Oh, that will be lovely too!" exclaimed Elizabeth.

"I believe it will be. And I wish you to join us when we go."

That surprised Elizabeth. She knew of the custom for the newlywed couple to travel with a member of the family, usually a sister of the new bride. But Elizabeth had not truly thought of the matter in such terms, though she knew she would be the logical choice, considering their closeness and her position as the next eldest.

"But would you not prefer to be alone with your husband?" asked Elizabeth. "I would not wish to intrude upon your new felicity."

"What intrusion do you call it!" exclaimed Jane. "How could I not wish to have my dearest friend and sister with me?"

"Well, my dearest Jane," said another voice, as the colonel himself stepped up to them, "shall you not congratulate me? I knew what your sister's response would be."

"As did I," said Jane, smiling at her future husband. "I believe this is when my sister begins to stubbornly assert her point of view."

The colonel laughed, even as Elizabeth directed a harsh look at her sister. Jane only rolled her eyes, not intimidated in the slightest by Elizabeth's displeasure.

"Since my sister seems intent upon teasing," said Elizabeth, turning to Colonel Fitzwilliam, "I will direct my comments to you. Although I would be happy to accompany you wherever you go and would be relieved to avoid being separated from my dear sister, I do not wish for you to invite me based on custom. I know I shall see Jane again in the future and do not wish to impose."

"And I join my future wife in informing you that there is no imposition. In fact, Jane wishes to have you, and as I would do anything for her, it is no concession for me to agree. In fact, I believe your presence would be welcome to us both."

"Please, Lizzy," said Jane. "We shall be in London at the earl's house after our wedding, and soon after the earl and countess will join us."

Elizabeth did not miss the trepidation which had made an appearance in Jane's voice. Neither, it seemed, did Colonel Fitzwilliam.

"Do not worry for my parents, Jane. They will love you as much as I do."

Smiling happily at the picture they presented, Elizabeth waited patiently until they recalled they were not alone. It happened sooner than she might have expected, though she was still amused that they had forgotten themselves in such a manner at all.

"Regardless," said Colonel Fitzwilliam, turning his attention back to Elizabeth, "my parents will join us about two weeks after we arrive in London. We will then journey to Brighton, where we will stay for some weeks. We would like you to join us in London about the time my parents arrive, after which we will go to Brighton."

"If you truly do wish to have me with you, then I will accept."

"Excellent!" said the colonel. Jane only wrapped her into an embrace and murmured her thanks. Elizabeth, however, was having none of it.

"The thanks are all mine to make. I shall be happy to be in your company, though I suspect I shall be forced to see to my own amusement. A mere sister cannot hold a candle to the allure a husband must present."

They both laughed at Elizabeth's joke, though it was the colonel who spoke. "Then it is all settled. I will speak with your father and confirm the details with him.

"There is only one more thing." The colonel glared at her, though his severity was ruined with an outrageous wink. "Since I am to be your brother, I should like it if you would call me Anthony, as your sister does."

"Then I shall do so," replied Elizabeth happily. "You may call me Elizabeth, or any of the other monikers my sisters often use to refer to me."

It should not be a surprise to the reader, considering her character and the words which passed between Elizabeth and her mother, that Mrs. Bennet was not generally pleased with the thought Elizabeth would accompany her sister to Brighton. Elizabeth could not imagine what form her mother's protests would have taken had she not become violently opposed to Mr. Collins after his unfortunate proposal. The reality of her protests as it was, were bad enough.

"Take Lizzy to Brighton?" demanded she when the plans were made known to her. "No, indeed! Why should Lizzy have all the amusement? She will profit nothing from it anyway since she has refused to consider the possibility of marriage."

"That is *not* what I said, Mama," said Elizabeth quietly, though she knew her mother would ignore her. In that she was correct.

"It would be better to take my dear Lydia with you," continued

Mrs. Bennet. "She is so lively and easy in company, and I have heard that Brighton is positively teeming with officers. Why, she might come home with a beau or even an engagement!"

Kitty predictably protested such an amusement for Lydia which excluded herself, while Lydia exclaimed at the thought of so many officers. Colonel Fitzwilliam, however, was not amused.

"You should not be so eager to put your daughters in the way of officers, Mrs. Bennet," said he. "Though there are many good men in the army, there are inevitably those who are not of good character. Furthermore, Miss Lydia has been raised to expect more from marriage than a poor officer, most of whom cannot afford a wife."

"Then I must simply attract a colonel," said Lydia with a superior sniff, which reminded Elizabeth of Miss Bingley at times.

"Even if she is not to marry an officer," said Mrs. Bennet, "I am certain there will be society aplenty. With Lydia's disposition, I am certain she cannot fail to capture the interest of a man of consequence."

While Elizabeth thought it unlikely Lydia would attract any man with any more intelligence than she possessed herself, she knew that to speak could be to invite her mother's further protests. As such, she stayed silent and allowed Colonel Fitzwilliam and Jane to make the argument in her stead.

"Mother," said Jane, her tone uncharacteristically firm, "I do not wish for Lydia's presence. You know Lizzy and I have always been close. I want Lizzy nearby when I embark upon my marriage."

Mrs. Bennet sucked in a breath, no doubt to further protest, when she was cut off by her husband's voice. "It seems, Mrs. Bennet, that Jane cannot do without Lizzy. Though I am loath to part with my most sensible daughter for many more weeks than I care to imagine, I believe you shall not carry your point. Let Jane have her way, my dear, for she has asked for it few enough times in the past."

It was clear that Mrs. Bennet was not happy in the slightest, but she seemed to understand the truth of her husband's words. And thus it was settled. Elizabeth would accompany her sister on her wedding trip. Longbourn was her home, but Elizabeth could not look upon the opportunity to leave it for a while with anything other than relief.

CHAPTER XV

$\mathcal{M}$rs. Bennet preparing for a wedding celebration was a revelation to everyone at Longbourn. But it did not follow that the revelation was a good one. Having realized her lifelong dream of seeing the first of her daughters married, Mrs. Bennet went into a frenzy of preparations for the wedding breakfast thereafter, informing them all there was much to do to organize a celebration for no less than the marriage of the son of an earl.

"We must ensure Colonel Fitzwilliam's father and mother find nothing wanting in our celebrations," said she, while instructing Jane on some matter or another which she seemed to think the most important thing in the world. "People of such high society expect the very best, and we must give it to them, else we will not be able to hold our heads up high."

"But, Mama," said Jane, "Georgiana informed me that she had a small wedding celebration. I am certain they do not expect us to go to any trouble."

"Yes, yes, they do!" declared Mrs. Bennet. "I will not be spoken of in town as a woman who cannot plan a fête for the younger son of an earl which was worthy of him."

"I apologize, Mrs. Bennet," said Colonel Fitzwilliam when Jane pleaded with him to speak to her mother. "But my parents will not be able to attend the wedding."

"Not attend the wedding of their son?" gasped Mrs. Bennet. Elizabeth was certain her mother was seeing visions of the earl, stern-faced and disapproving of his son's choice of bride.

"They are in Ireland at present. Though they are happy for me and have declared their eagerness to meet Jane, their business cannot be put off and travel at this time of year is difficult. They will meet Jane in London when they come for the season."

Though it was clear for anyone to see that Mrs. Bennet still fretted, she accepted his explanation. But that did not make any difference in her planning for the event, and nothing anyone of them said made her change her mind. Her eldest daughter was to be married, and the celebration of the occasion would be as grand as anything the town had ever seen.

"I truly do admire you, Jane," said Elizabeth on one occasion when they were ensconced in Jane's room after a long day in which they—or, more particularly, Jane—had been pulled into their mother's plans for hours on end.

"What for?" said Jane, and from her voice, Elizabeth thought her sister was bone weary from her mother's indefatigable planning.

"For withstanding our mother. I doubt I could possibly be so patient with her. I might have run off screaming long before now had *I* been the focus of her scheming."

Jane's slight smile lit up the room. "Just remember, Lizzy: one day it will be you who is to be married. Then you *will* be in my position."

With a shudder, Elizabeth said: "Then I shall request my betrothed make for Scotland at the first opportunity."

Their giggles started quietly, but soon both sisters were laughing openly, tears streaming down their faces. It was well that Elizabeth so loved to laugh, for it was cathartic and strangely freeing, especially when she knew that tomorrow would be another trial on their sensibilities.

As the days grew closer, the sisters took to spending every spare moment together, knowing they would soon be parted. Mrs. Bennet's schedule usually only allowed them the evenings, as the only other escape was when Colonel Fitzwilliam came and insisted he be allowed time with his fiancée. But they made good use of what time they had.

"Are you nervous?" asked Elizabeth one night as they were preparing to retire.

"Of being married?" asked Jane in turn.

Elizabeth shrugged. "Of being married, of tying your life to a man, of the actual ceremony itself. All of it, I suppose."

Though she considered it for a moment, Jane shook her head. "I am not nervous." Then she paused and smiled. "Well, perhaps I am a *little* nervous. One is always anxious when facing something new and, after all, I have never been married."

A laugh escaped Elizabeth's lips. "No, I suppose you have not."

"But I am not truly worried at all," said Jane, sitting on her bed and leaning back against the headboard. "I am marrying a good man whom I love and whom I trust with my very life. I suppose I would not be marrying him if I did not feel this way about him."

A sober Elizabeth could only nod. "That is one reason why I wish to marry only for love. A woman literally entrusts her life and wellbeing into the hands of her husband. She must be certain he is a good man who will treat her well."

"Then I have no worries whatsoever. I know exactly how Anthony will treat me. I have no doubt of his love or of his character."

Elizabeth sat on the edge of the bed and leaned toward her sister, resting her head on Jane's shoulder. "I am glad, Jane. He is the best of men and will surely make you happy. My only regret is that we shall be separated."

"What separation do you call it?" asked Jane with a laugh. "We shall only be separated for two weeks, after which you shall join us in London."

"That is true," replied Elizabeth. "But you will be married, and nothing will be the same between us."

"But life is change, is it not?" said Jane. "We will be well, I think. In the future, when you marry, you must choose a man who is a good friend of my future husband and lives nearby. That way we shall always be in each other's company."

"That would be marvelous, Jane," said Elizabeth. "*If* I marry."

"I can hardly think you will not. There will be a man out there who sees what a prize he would gain by marrying you."

"I hope so, Jane."

Fitzwilliam was much more sanguine than those residing at the house at Longbourn in those days. While he witnessed the Bennet matron's frenzy of planning, he was able to escape it by simply returning to his place of residence. That did not spare Jane, of course, but he did what he could when he was there to give her a respite.

At Netherfield, matters continued to be the same as they ever were.

Their days, when he was not at Longbourn, consisted of Hurst becoming soused at all hours of the day and night, Miss Bingley complaining about how she wished to be in London, echoed by her sister, and the truly welcome society of Bingley and Georgiana. The more of the last item he could get, the more pleased he was, though he spent as much time as he could at Longbourn.

But the longer they remained in residence, the more the problem of Miss Bingley intruded on his senses, and the more he realized that the woman had no notion of Darcy's true feelings for her. Fitzwilliam did not wish to be unkind to her and to be fair, he knew Darcy did not *dislike* her. Though Fitzwilliam knew Darcy was aware of Miss Bingley's ambitions, he simply did not think of the woman often, as he had no interest in her as a prospective bride.

While he also knew Darcy did not intend to be unkind, the fact remained that the woman hoped and schemed, and it was all in vain. Though Fitzwilliam had no interest in cleaning Darcy's messes, a conversation he overheard between Miss Bingley and Georgiana only days before his wedding made up his mind on the subject.

"Georgiana, dearest, have you had any word from your brother of late?"

"Not since the last letter I received from him, Miss Bingley," said Georgiana, displaying no hint of annoyance for the woman's fixation.

"I have had a letter from him," said Fitzwilliam. "He confirmed his intention to be present for my marriage to Miss Bennet and to stand up with me."

"That is excellent news, indeed," said Miss Bingley in her usually calm manner. Underneath, however, Fitzwilliam was certain he detected a frisson of excitement in the woman's voice. "I am certain that must be welcome news to you all. We are all made better by his presence."

"I am happy my brother shall come," said Georgiana quietly. "It would not be right if he did not stand up with Anthony."

"Oh, I am certain he would not think of disappointing you." Miss Bingley smiled at him. "I have often observed that you are as close as brothers."

"That is very true," said Fitzwilliam. "We were playmates as boys and have been companions all our adult lives. Though I wish my family were to be present, I can be contented, as long as I have Darcy's well wishes."

"I cannot imagine anything better," said Miss Bingley.

Fitzwilliam was forced to stifle a laugh—it was at times like this when she was praising Darcy to the skies, that she resembled, in some small way, the absent Mr. Collins and his veneration of Lady Catherine.

"There is something of nobility in Mr. Darcy's bearing and character which are quite out of the common way. I see it in all of your family, of course," said Miss Bingley with a nod at Fitzwilliam. "But in Mr. Darcy there is something in the way he carries himself which suggests a man uncompromising, yet of a special character, upright, good, and everything anyone knowing him must not only acknowledge, but feel edified for the simple fact of knowing him."

Miss Bingley smiled at Georgiana, which she hesitantly returned. "I cannot wait to see him again, dear Georgiana. I cannot be happier that we have become family. I hope we shall continue in our association, and that our ties will grow ever stronger."

It was a trial to avoid rolling his eyes, but somehow Fitzwilliam managed it. There was no mystery concerning Miss Bingley's meaning, and no one present could have any doubt of it. Georgiana, who usually became uncomfortable when Miss Bingley spoke in such a manner, turned to her husband and began speaking to him. The only one who truly responded was Hurst, and he only grinned at his sister, seemingly amused that she could not see Darcy's disinterest in her. Though Fitzwilliam did not think it proper for the man to be so gleeful in his amusement toward his sister, he could understand it.

The problem was finding a moment alone in Miss Bingley's company, as he did not wish to embarrass her in front of anyone else. She could usually be found with Georgiana or her sister, speaking in the same sycophantic way to the former or scheming with the latter. But Fitzwilliam persevered and was gratified to find her alone the very next day.

"Miss Bingley," said he when he came across her in the music room. "I am happy to have found you here, for I wished to speak with you."

Surprise flickered across the woman's normally stoic features. Fitzwilliam had never sought her out before. In fact, he did not care for the kind of woman she was, one who constantly strove to increase her own consequence with cold calculation. Fitzwilliam much preferred his dear Jane, else he might have considered Miss Bingley and her twenty thousand pounds.

"Of course, Colonel Fitzwilliam," said Miss Bingley, indicating he should sit with her. "How may I help you?"

Fitzwilliam sat in the designated chair and said: "It is not that you can help me. Rather, I thought I could assist you."

This time the surprise was more pronounced, but she quickly gathered herself. "I am intrigued. Of what are you speaking?"

"I speak of Darcy, Miss Bingley, and of your attempts to attract Darcy's attention."

This time her surprise was well hidden, though as Fitzwilliam was looking for it, he spotted it easily. Miss Bingley was silent, considering him, and Fitzwilliam allowed her to respond before speaking again. It was some moments before she did so.

"Mr. Darcy is my brother's dear friend," said she, attempting to obfuscate. "I also consider him a friend myself. I am certain he feels the same."

Fitzwilliam sat back in his chair, regarding her. "Miss Bingley, let us dispense with any attempts to demur, shall we? I am well aware of your interest in my cousin. In fact, it is well known not only to myself, but also to Georgiana and to Darcy himself, and I would be shocked if your brothers do not know of it also.'

With pursed lips, Miss Bingley watched him, her gaze turning quite frosty. "So what if I am? I consider myself an excellent candidate to become Mrs. Darcy. I have not done anything improper."

"I do not dispute you would make a fine mistress, and I do not accuse you of anything wrong. I am merely saying that Darcy does not favor you."

"You have asked him?" asked Miss Bingley, her eyes boring through him.

"I have not."

"Then you do not know. In fact, I am convinced that Mr. Darcy has come to appreciate the benefits of having me as a wife. I neither control him nor have I attempted anything to provoke his response. But should I refuse him should he offer for me?"

"I suggest no such thing, Miss Bingley. But I know my cousin, Miss Bingley. He will not offer for you. You are wasting your time in focusing your attention on him."

"I will not sit and listen to this," said Miss Bingley, rising to her feet. "You have made your position very clear, Colonel Fitzwilliam. I perfectly comprehend it. But I am no less suitable to be Mr. Darcy's wife than Miss Bennet is to be yours. I will ask you to mind your own concerns. Mr. Darcy and I can find our way without your interference."

Miss Bingley turned to leave the room.

"Then watch him."

Fitzwilliam rose to his feet, as Miss Bingley came to a halt. When he saw she was not about to flee from him and had stopped to give his words consideration, he approached her, walking around her until they were face to face. She was angry—that much was evident from her heightened color, furrowed brows, and pinched lips. But she was watching him, waiting for him to speak again.

"Darcy is to come and stand up with me at my wedding to Miss Bennet. When he is here, watch him, consider his actions, attempt to take his measure. I apologize if you took offense, Miss Bingley, for it was not my intention. I mean only to give you a friendly warning. If Darcy *does* decide on you as a wife, neither I nor anyone else may gainsay him, and I will give him my heartiest congratulations. But he will not marry you for material gain or for any other reason. His example of marriage was his parents, and they were devoted to each other. He will accept nothing less."

With those final words, Fitzwilliam bowed and excused himself, leaving Miss Bingley rooted to the place where she stood. Fitzwilliam hoped she would take his words in the spirit he had intended them. But the choice, of course, was hers.

It was obligation which drew Darcy back to Hertfordshire and to his cousin's wedding. Or, perhaps, he reflected, it was not entirely obligation.

Certainly the affection he felt for his cousin never waned, and any number of poor choices—for he was convinced that marrying Jane Bennet was, indeed, a mistake—would never diminish it. Fitzwilliam deserved his support. And that was the major reason why he, alone of the family, had agreed to stand up with his cousin. Thus, duty was a minor consideration.

Once Darcy had worked that out in his mind, he felt easier, though it took him half the distance back to Hertfordshire to come to that conclusion. When he arrived at Netherfield, the bride and her younger sister were visiting, and once he refreshed himself, Darcy made his way to the sitting-room. There, he was forced to confess that the sisters carried themselves without a hint of any behavior which would prompt censure. Miss Bennet *was* a beautiful woman, and her sister, scarcely less pretty. But marrying a woman of physical attraction was not the only consideration. He was not certain how Fitzwilliam had managed to lose himself to this woman's charms, but Darcy was determined it would not happen to him.

"Good afternoon, Miss Bennet, Miss Elizabeth," said Darcy, greeting the sisters along with his family. "Please allow me, Miss

Bennet, to offer my congratulations." A thought struck him, and he felt his lips rise at the corners if only slightly. "I believe I must caution you, however. Any woman who takes on my ne'er-do-well cousin must be brave indeed, for I have often thought him to be more trouble than he is worth."

It seemed that Miss Bennet caught the tone of his jest, for she smiled. Miss Elizabeth, for her part, fairly goggled at him, though he was not quite certain why she should be so surprised.

"I believe I can manage him," came Miss Bennet's serene reply.

Fitzwilliam laughed, along with several others, among whom was Georgiana. "I have tried to tell her that myself, William," said she, grinning at Fitzwilliam. "But it seems she has been hoodwinked into some depth of feeling for our cousin, and nothing I say will deter her."

"I should hope not," said Fitzwilliam, his posture suggesting he was finding much amusement, but no offense, in their teasing. "As long as I have my future wife's affections, I promise that I will behave myself."

"Of course, you have it," replied Miss Bennet.

"It *is* fortunate, indeed," said Miss Elizabeth, "that two of such like minds have come together. I would wish you luck in managing my sister, Anthony, but I know very well she is so complying, you will never argue."

They all laughed at Miss Elizabeth's witticism, though Darcy could see Miss Bennet's mock glare at her sister. "You know very well I am not *that* agreeable, Lizzy. I am able to stand up for my beliefs when the situation demands it."

"I know you are, dearest. But the picture you present to the world is quite different."

Darcy looked on them with some interest. He had not been in their company for close to two months, and he had not witnessed their engagement or interactions in all that time. But from what he remembered of Miss Bennet, she had always been serene, and she treated all with the same quiet interest. As he watched her speak with the company, and with Fitzwilliam in particular, Darcy could detect nothing in her manners which indicated she felt anything special for him.

But there was nothing to be done. Fitzwilliam had proposed, and she had accepted, and the engagement, nearly two months old. Even if Darcy wished to argue with his cousin again, there was no honorable way to withdraw. He hoped that Fitzwilliam would not live to regret his choice. Darcy thought it likely he would.

"Thank you for coming, Cousin," said Fitzwilliam later when they had a moment together. "I know you do not approve."

"You do not require my approval, Fitzwilliam," said Darcy.

"No, I do not. But I should like to know that I have it all the same. I would never wish to be at odds with you."

"We are not at odds, Cousin. Miss Bennet is not the choice *I* would have made, but I respect your right to choose her. I wish you every happiness."

It seemed he had said what Fitzwilliam wished to hear, for his cousin seemed to relax a tension Darcy had not even noticed. "I thank you, Cousin. I am happy to hear it."

And so a few days later it was done. The ceremony was short, but in the end, Anthony Fitzwilliam and Jane Bennet were married. The wedding breakfast was a little taxing on Darcy's sensibilities, for while he could acknowledge Miss Bennet and Miss Elizabeth's good behavior, the same was not true for their family. Mrs. Bennet was as loud and obnoxious as he had remembered, and her youngest daughters, as wild.

But while Darcy stood with his cousin, signed the register as required, and then endured everything which followed, none of that stood out in his memories. While he might have thought such matters would remain foremost in his mind, it was actually the sight of Miss Elizabeth which remained with him thereafter. She stood, watching her sister, obviously ecstatically happy, a single tear rolling down her cheek, attesting to her joy. And as the light of the sun fell on her through the window of the church, Darcy had never seen her looking so beautiful. It was at that moment he was forced to confess that he had been quite mistaken. She was, in fact, one of the handsomest women of his acquaintance.

CHAPTER XVI

*H*ad Elizabeth known what would ensue after her sister's departure, she might have begged them to take her with them rather than waiting for two weeks. The wedding breakfast, in Mrs. Bennet's estimation, proceeded in a manner which would establish her as one of the foremost hostesses in the neighborhood. That she had already been considered as one never crossed her mind.

For a day or so after the newlyweds' departure, matters calmed at Longbourn, and they settled once again into their routines. Or they did not, for to Elizabeth, nothing was the same anymore. For Jane was gone, her dearest sister and closest friend in the world had left her father's house for her own, and she would not return. And Elizabeth missed her sister more than she ever thought she would. They had been separated before—at times for months, as one or the other of them would visit the Gardiners in London. But this separation seemed final. It felt permanent.

Elizabeth knew it was not, and she scolded herself for feeling the way she did. But she could not help it. There was little of amusement to be had, society was dull and sporadic, and even the Bingley family had departed from Netherfield to visit Mr. Bingley's relations in the North. The days before her removal to London passed so slowly that

Elizabeth might have thought time had stopped in its tracks.

Adding to this feeling was Mrs. Bennet. For no more than a day had passed when she roused herself, summoned Elizabeth, and set about "educating" her daughter for her time away with her newly married eldest sister. And this after Mrs. Bennet had declared that Elizabeth must "shift for herself."

"Lizzy," said Mrs. Bennet, the first time she had been cornered in the sitting-room, "I believe we must speak. I know you have always been close to Jane and that your elder sister wants you to be with her. As you know, I favored Lydia's going instead. But since you are what I have to work with, I suppose there is no help for it."

"To work with?" echoed Elizabeth. "I have no notion of what you speak, Mama."

"That is why I am concerned," said Mrs. Bennet. "You must understand that going to London to be with your sister will give you a perfect opportunity to find a husband of your own."

"That is not what I am going to London for, Mama," protested Elizabeth.

"Of course, you are," replied Mrs. Bennet. "And there are certain behaviors which must stop if you are to find a husband. Come, Lizzy — let us sit, so I may instruct you."

What followed was a litany of instructions which were, in turn, silly, offensive, and even improper. And this was not the only time her mother took it upon herself to instruct Elizabeth. No, her instructions were repeated many times over. Elizabeth did not even wish to think of what her mother was telling her, let alone speak of it. Thus, she took to avoiding Mrs. Bennet whenever possible.

On one such occasion, Elizabeth received a visit from Charlotte. Eager as she was to escape her mother, she pulled Charlotte away to a smaller, lesser used parlor so they could speak privately. Charlotte followed along behind Elizabeth's lead, and a glance back at her friend informed Elizabeth that she knew exactly what was taking place. Her friend's words when they had gained the sanctuary of the parlor confirmed it.

"Your mother has been a trial since Jane left?"

It was impossible for Elizabeth to resist rolling her eyes, and she did not even make the attempt. "That is an understatement, Charlotte. She has it in her mind that I shall be put into the path of Colonel Fitzwilliam's friends while I am in London, and she has taken it into her head to instruct me on the proper way of catching a husband."

Charlotte's grimace was affected and caused Elizabeth to laugh. "I cannot imagine it would be any different from what *my* mother might have to say on such an occasion."

They shook their heads together. Neither of their mothers had been born as gentlewomen—Elizabeth's mother had been raised to that estate when she had married Mr. Bennet, and Lady Lucas when her husband had received his knighthood.

"She has even taken it into her head to forget how objectionable Mr. Collins was," said Elizabeth, shaking her head in her frustration. "Though I suppose she has not carried on about that to any great length. But she does bemoan the lost opportunity to keep Longbourn in the family by marriage. I am at my wit's end!"

"At least you shall soon escape," replied Charlotte. "And perhaps you *will* attract the attention of one of the colonel's friends."

"That is not the reason for my going," said Elizabeth. "I go to be with my sister, not to throw myself at every man I meet."

"I know you do not, Eliza. But you must recognize the possibility that you might meet someone."

Elizabeth grudgingly allowed this to be so and thought to change the subject. But Charlotte changed it before Elizabeth could.

"As for Mr. Collins, I know you would have been miserable with him, even if he had not been intolerable. But you know I am not as choosy about a potential marriage partner as you are. I . . ." Charlotte paused for a moment, flushing in embarrassment. "I had thought to try to attach myself to Mr. Collins."

The words were spoken in a rush as if Charlotte had forced them out before she lost her nerve. Initially, Elizabeth was surprised that Charlotte would do such a thing. Then she remembered that Charlotte had on several occasions suggested that her desire was for the marriage state, rather than for any particular wishes concerning her eventual companion. And Elizabeth was forced to own it may have been a desirable situation for Charlotte, though Elizabeth could not even stand the thought of it.

"I knew you would reject him, regardless," said Charlotte, seeming to see that Elizabeth had not become upset or censured her for her confession. "When you rejected him, I thought to become a substitute for you in his eyes. But he went away too quickly, and my plans ended before they ever began."

Elizabeth smiled at her friend and caught Charlotte's hands in her own. "You are too good for Mr. Collins, Charlotte. Even knowing your wishes in a marriage partner, I still cannot help but think that an alliance with Mr. Collins would not be desirable. He truly is as odious a man as I have ever met."

"I understand what you are saying, Lizzy," said Charlotte with a sigh. "I suppose we shall never know. But I would much prefer to be married to anyone rather than remain an old maid at home, becoming a burden on my parents and then on my brother."

There was such a sense of melancholy about Charlotte that Elizabeth decided to eschew replying. Soon Charlotte went away, leaving Elizabeth to think. Perhaps Charlotte was not completely incorrect about the matter—surely marrying a good man, one who would care for her and respect her, would be preferable to remaining a spinster, even if she did not love him. It was something Elizabeth would need to think on in the future.

Only days before her departure, Elizabeth once again found herself in her father's bookroom, using that sanctuary as an escape from her mother. On this particular occasion, Elizabeth found him lost in introspection. Mr. Henry Bennet was not an introspective man. He tended toward laughter, even at himself at times, in lieu of considering the past with an eye toward what had been done, as opposed to what might have been done differently. Thus, on this occasion, it was quite strange to Elizabeth, who had never seen him like this.

"Your mother is still speaking of your stay with your sister?" asked Mr. Bennet.

"She will not cease," replied Elizabeth with a shaken head. "If I was to follow her advice, I would disgrace Colonel Fitzwilliam and Jane and would likely need to be shipped to a convent, as I would be completely unmarriageable!"

Mr. Bennet chuckled and shook his head, turning to look out the window. His ever-present book was sitting on his desk, open to the page he had been reading when he put it down. The glass of port wine he favored sat on the desk, and every so often he took it and sipped from it. For a time, Elizabeth thought he had forgotten of her presence.

"While I would never suggest your mother's way of expressing herself is precisely proper," said he at length, "there may be some sense in what she says."

"Papa!" gasped a shocked Elizabeth. "Surely you do not think I should throw myself at every man I meet as Mama is suggesting!"

"No," replied her father. "And I have no notion you would ever behave in such a manner. But now that your sister is married, it *is* true you shall be part of a wider society, indeed, one which is of a higher level than anything we can boast here. I cannot but think you will have an opportunity."

"That is not why I am going to Jane, Papa."

Mr. Bennet turned and regarded her, an eyebrow raised. Elizabeth resisted the instinct to hang her head and apologize, as she might have done when she was a child. What her father was suggesting was not sensible, and she was not about to confess otherwise.

"It has been long since you were cowed by my looks," said Mr. Bennet, shaking his head in amusement. Then he became completely sober yet again. "But you should think on this matter carefully, Lizzy."

A sigh escaped his lips and he leaned back in his chair. "I shall not sport with your intelligence, Lizzy. I know you are aware of what happens in this house. To a large extent, I have abrogated my responsibilities as a husband and father. I have not checked your mother and your youngest sisters, and I doubt I ever will, knowing the tumult which must ensue should I make the attempt." He paused and chuckled. "I shall simply send Lydia to Colonel Fitzwilliam. He can be a stern man when the situation demands it—I have no doubt she would listen to him more than she ever listens to me."

"Oh, Papa! I would not wish their marriage to have such tension enter it so soon after the ceremony."

"I would not send her now," replied Mr. Bennet. He winked at her to let her know he was jesting. "I would wait at least a month.

"But either way, I doubt I have the fortitude to effect a change in any of them. Furthermore, I have not put aside any money, so that you and your sisters may support yourselves in case of my early demise. I should have, but I was short-sighted in my youth, expecting to sire a son who would protect you all. By the time Lydia was born, I was set in my ways and little disposed to saving money for you. More importantly, the thought of trying to induce your mother to economize was daunting."

"There is no reason to dwell on it," replied Elizabeth. "It does no good."

A shaken head was Mr. Bennet's response. "Do not concern yourself for me, Lizzy. I am certain that by tomorrow I shall be myself again, and this will all be pushed into the back of my mind. I am not concerned about being overwhelmed by my feelings of failure.

"But the point remains that despite your mother's inelegant manner of stating it, the protection of marriage is your best chance for fulfillment and happiness in life. Since it is obvious you will not find such a marriage *here*, it follows that your best chance will be when you are with your sister and her husband."

"I should like something of what Jane has," replied Elizabeth quietly. "I wish to be married to a man I respect and love."

"And so you shall," Mr. Bennet regarded her with a fond smile. "You are the best of my daughters, Lizzy, and I do not think even Jane, who is closest to you in excellence, would dispute my assertion. You are intelligent and quick, independent and strong, and I dare say you are pleasing to look upon as a young woman. I must think there is some man in the world who can see your worth despite the disadvantages of fortune and some very silly relations.

"I do not ask you to marry the first man who comes along. All I ask is to keep an open mind and show yourself to advantage wherever you are, though I hardly think you can do otherwise. Do your best, Lizzy, for, with your elder sister forever removed from this house, I cannot think it will be as comfortable for you as it has been."

Having spoken, Mr. Bennet turned back to his window and contemplated the scene outside. Knowing it as a dismissal, Elizabeth stood and left the room without speaking.

It was a surprise, she decided, to hear her father speak so. But Elizabeth was forced to acknowledge that there was some sense in his words. And had she not determined not long before that she *could* settle for a man who respected and esteemed her, even if love was not part of the equation? Elizabeth had no desire to put herself forward, attempt to gain the interest of a man, as Miss Bingley did with Mr. Darcy when they had been in Hertfordshire. But she thought she could keep an open mind. And she decided she would do so, little though she thought she would find a marriage partner in either London or Brighton.

Two days before Elizabeth's departure for London, a letter came with an announcement Elizabeth might have found amusing, had it not contained information which was certain to cause a ruckus at Longbourn. That her father found it amusing was no surprise at all.

"Lizzy, come into my bookroom," said her father, as Elizabeth was walking toward the stairs, intent on returning to her room to continue her packing. She hesitated for a moment and followed him, hoping she would be at liberty to return to her room quickly.

"I have received a letter this morning which must be of some interest to you."

Frowning, Elizabeth asked: "From whom?"

"Mr. Collins," replied Mr. Bennet. The hilarity was on the edge of release, a matter for which Elizabeth had some understanding.

"What can he have to say? And why would it concern me?"

"Because you refused an offer of marriage from him. For you see, he has written to me to inform me of his engagement to a young woman of the neighborhood. Furthermore, the self-congratulatory tone of his missive, combined with his stated relief that he was not successful in 'obtaining the hand of a certain young woman' is the most absurd thing I have ever read."

By this time, Mr. Bennet was in stitches. And while Elizabeth did find it diverting, she thought of the reaction of her mother to this news, and she could only shake her head. Her departure could not come soon enough!

"Come now, Lizzy," said Mr. Bennet, wiping his eyes. "Surely you must enjoy the dimwitted words of my cousin. Or are you perhaps regretting your missed opportunity? Mayhap I should allow you to read his words so you may bask in the glory of Mr. Collins's ridiculousness."

"No, Papa, I have no need to read his words," said Elizabeth. "Nor am I in any way sorry I did not take his offer. But I know the news of Mr. Collins's upcoming nuptials will affect Mama, and I am not looking forward to it."

Mr. Bennet shook his head. "I suspect you are correct, though I know not why. After he departed the house, it was clear none of you would be marrying him. Why his marrying another should be a matter of any interest to us, I cannot even begin to fathom."

Though she nodded, Elizabeth knew he was correct. "Will you return his letter?"

"Of course, I shall," replied Mr. Bennet. "I would not lose Mr. Collins's correspondence for the world. But now, Lizzy, you must make an excellent match, for Mr. Collins has thrown down the gauntlet. Nothing would please me more than to return the favor by informing him of the stupendous match you have made!"

There was nothing to be said to such a statement, and Elizabeth did not even attempt it. She listened to her father's exclamations for a few more moments before excusing herself to return to her packing.

As Elizabeth had expected, the response to her father's announcement that evening at the dinner table was loud and full of howls of outrage and recrimination. Mrs. Bennet's daughters all seemed to take the news in stride, but the matron could not contain her distress. Naturally, that distress was soon turned toward Elizabeth.

"This is all *your* fault, Lizzy! You should have accepted Mr. Collins's proposal. If you had, we would not be facing the prospect of losing our home! You have sabotaged our future."

Though Elizabeth could do naught but roll her eyes at her mother's hysterics, it seemed her father was by no means afflicted similarly. "It seems you have forgotten, Mrs. Bennet," said he, amusement flowing off him in waves, "but did you not object to Mr. Collins in the end? As I recall, you all but declared that Lizzy could not marry him."

That brought her mother up short. But Mrs. Bennet had never been one to allow sense to invade her mind. She shook her head at her husband and began bemoaning their fate again in a loud voice. In time, Mr. Bennet, rather than enjoying the spectacle, began to weary of her display.

"I will remind you, Mrs. Bennet," said he, his voice cutting over her continued lamentations, "that you already have a daughter married to a man of some means. Furthermore, as said daughter is closest to the daughter you are currently castigating for not doing her duty—after *you* objected to the man yourself—you might remember that should Elizabeth live with Jane in the future, Jane might not be inclined to have a woman in her house who would create such tumult as this, while belittling her favorite sister."

With those words, Mr. Bennet rose and departed, leaving blessed silence in his wake. Mrs. Bennet blinked once, and then twice, and then with a darting glance at Elizabeth, rose herself and departed from the dining room. She made not a sound as she went to her room, only the closing of her door reaching their ears.

"I cannot understand Mama," said Lydia into the silence. "Mr. Collins turned out to be as odious a man as ever lived. Why would she wish you married to him?"

"Because Mama has always been so fearful of the entail," replied Elizabeth. "She has feared it for so many years, she forgets Jane is now married and can take us in should the worst happen."

"Do you think Jane will refuse to help Mama?" asked Kitty tentatively.

"Jane will do her duty," said Mary, confidence brimming in her tone. "'Honor thy father and thy mother, that thy days may be long in the land.' Jane is a dutiful daughter. She would not allow her mother to be homeless."

Though Elizabeth was not entirely certain that Mary's quote from the Bible applied in this situation, she agreed with her younger sister. Jane was kind-hearted to a fault. She would not do as her father had suggested. When Elizabeth voiced her agreement with Mary's assessment, the younger girls nodded. It was no surprise when Lydia changed the subject.

"I know you and Jane are close, Lizzy, but you appear to have all the luck. You shall be going to Brighton, where the regiment is to go this spring. You will have the company of all the officers while we shall be stuck in Hertfordshire where it shall be ever so dull."

"I doubt we will be in the company of the officers much, Lydia," said Elizabeth. "You forget that Jane's husband is no longer a colonel."

"But still, he must know many who still are officers." Lydia sighed. "How I wish I could go with you. I would cut a swath right through all the officers, make them all fall in love with me."

To Elizabeth, this was a good reason why Lydia should not go. But she would not provoke an argument when there was so little reason to do so. She only smiled at her sister and reminded her that Jane was now married to a man who was a member of the highest circles of society.

"But London is different from Meryton," admonished Elizabeth when Lydia's eyes lit up at the thought.

"How so, Lizzy?" asked Kitty.

"It is much more formal. What you can do in Meryton without censure would see you shunned in London. You are too young at present—young women do not come out into London society until they are eighteen. But if you wish to prove yourself to earn an invitation, I suggest you begin to behave better now."

It was clear that her suggestion held no interest for either girl. But Elizabeth was certain that as they approached the age where they could reasonably attend events in London that would change. She had no notion as to whether they would change enough to make them acceptable. But at least the regiment would depart, taking away the worst provocation of their bad behavior.

CHAPTER XVII

$\mathcal{A}$s eager as Elizabeth had been to join her sister in London, she was equally eager for the journey to be over, though it had been a short one. Colonel Fitzwilliam's coach arrived the evening before she was to go, much to the exclamations of her mother and commentary of her sisters. Her father only displayed his amusement.

"I suppose they do not require it much," said Mr. Bennet, a knowing smile on his face. "Sparing it for a day is no trouble. They *are* newlyweds, after all."

Elizabeth chose not to respond to this. She certainly knew he was speaking of the desire of young couples for each other. Exactly what that entailed she had little knowledge, being a proper young lady. But her father's words seemed to invite her response, and she had no desire to speak on the matter.

"It *is* a fine carriage," said Mrs. Bennet when she had inspected it as Elizabeth's trunks were loaded for departure the following morning. "Of course, one could not expect less. He *is* the son of an earl, regardless of his own income."

She stopped and considered the matter for several moments, looking back and forth between Elizabeth and the carriage. Elizabeth was preparing for a renewal of her mother's instructions. In the end, however, Mrs. Bennet simply leaned in close.

"Remember what I have told you. I am sure you will attend some events which are very fine, indeed. With all these advantages, I expect you to return to Longbourn an engaged woman."

Then her mother returned to the house, leaving Elizabeth alone with her father and sisters. When the carriage was prepared, she farewelled them and stepped aboard, and they were off.

Traveling in winter was never pleasant. Heated bricks were thoughtfully provided and replenished throughout her journey, and it *was* only four hours as the roads were generally good. But it was a cold day, and Elizabeth was certain that the bricks began to cool within minutes of their departure. While she had several blankets to keep herself warm, a persistent chill pervaded the air, leaving her fingers cold and brittle where she was holding her book and the air around her, heavy and dank from her breathing. It was, she supposed, better than what the driver and footmen endured, sitting outside on the box, but she was still relieved when they entered the city, the clops of the horses' hooves and carriage wheels echoing between the buildings, and even happier when the carriage pulled to a stop in front of her destination.

The first thing Elizabeth noticed when she looked out the window to the house which was to be her residence until they departed for Brighton was the sheer size of the edifice. It was a large, brick building, towering over the tree-lined road, three stories tall and taking up the corner of a pleasant street. Having heard Mr. Collins drone on about the windows in his patroness's home, Elizabeth could not imagine there were any more there than what she saw before her now. There was even a hint of a little park, fenced in, around the side and perhaps the back of the house.

The second thing she saw was, of course, the large hand of Colonel Fitzwilliam reaching in to assist her from the carriage. And the third was Jane, standing on the front step, looking every inch the highborn lady she had now, Elizabeth supposed, become.

"Welcome, Elizabeth," said Anthony as she stepped down. "Jane and I are pleased to have you join us."

Elizabeth managed some return of his greeting, though she knew not what, and then she was in Jane's arms, her tears mixed with Jane's as they laughed like a pair of giddy children. Though Elizabeth had recognized how she had missed Jane, she had not realized until that moment how very much she had wanted her elder sister.

"I am so glad you have come, Lizzy," whispered Jane.

"I am happy to be here, Jane. How I have wanted you since you went away."

"Can I suppose," came the voice of Colonel Fitzwilliam, "that I have now become superfluous? Since you have your dearest sister, it seems you shall be content with her company to the extent that I should simply spend my days at the club."

"Perhaps we shall be intent upon each other for a time," said Jane, her heart in her eyes as she regarded her husband.

Elizabeth, however, was not about to allow his witticism to go unchallenged. "Did you not know? You men are always superfluous. Jane and I shall allow you to supervise the disposition of my trunks. After that, you may find something for yourself to do, as we shall be busy."

"Lizzy!" cried a shocked Jane.

But Anthony just laughed. "I believe I have missed you as much as my beloved wife has, Elizabeth. Go, reacquaint yourselves, and I shall do exactly as you command. We can reconvene after you have satisfied yourselves of your mutual wellbeing."

"Thank you, dear husband," said Jane, stepping forward and kissing Anthony on the cheek, a very public display of affection for the reticent Jane. "I shall see my sister settled and rejoin you, say, in an hour? I think Lizzy would be happy to partake of a light lunch."

"Take your time, dearest," replied Anthony. "I shall be waiting for you."

The room to which Jane escorted her was a spacious and handsome room, decorated in muted greens and yellows. It was clearly a room intended for a woman's occupation, though Elizabeth thought a man might be comfortable there too. Two sisters as close as they must have much to say, even after being separated for only two weeks. Elizabeth related news of Meryton, while Jane reciprocated with her doings in London, the locations she had seen, and the visit they had paid to their aunt and uncle. But while Elizabeth was interested to hear of her beloved relations, she was more interested to hear her sister's account of how she was getting on with her new husband.

"It is wonderful, Lizzy," said Jane, speaking in her soft voice, a reverence about her which delighted Elizabeth. "My husband is everything for which I could ever wish. I have been blessed."

"I am happy to hear it, Jane," said Elizabeth, not wishing to press her private sister for details. "So very happy."

When they descended for luncheon, Anthony extended a measure of good-natured surprise. "I had thought you would shunt me to the side for days if not weeks. And yet you have condescended to join me."

"It must be so very dull in town by yourself," said Elizabeth, regarding him with barely suppressed mirth. "We shall delay our shunting you to the side until we are in Brighton."

Anthony guffawed. "We are so happy to have you, Elizabeth. You shall brighten our time together."

They sat down to a light luncheon as Jane had promised. Soon, Elizabeth was relating her two weeks at home and especially her mother's instructions and her reaction to the letter Mr. Collins had sent them. While Jane was distressed at her mother's behavior, she was not surprised. Anthony, however, was thoughtful.

"I *can* introduce you to my friends if you would like," said he with a wink. "I dare say there are some among them who may find you irresistible."

Elizabeth turned and scowled at him. "I assure you, I have no desire to turn your wedding tour into a husband search. I am simply happy to be with you both. I have no intention of following my mother's instructions, I assure you."

"Mary is correct, of course," said Jane. "I would not refuse to support my mother, see her living in poverty when it was in our power to assist her."

"No, we would do no such thing," said Anthony. "On the other hand, all this nonsense about Mr. Collins and Elizabeth is no less than astonishing."

Elizabeth exchanged a wry look with her sister. "But it is so very like Mama. She only sees what she wishes and forgets what she does not wish to remember. Though she can recall how odious she found Mr. Collins and how she wished him gone from her house, she still believes her daughters need to be married at all costs. It is one of the reasons, I think, that I have always been her least favorite daughter, though Mary could make that claim as well."

"Your mother has always favored Jane," observed Anthony.

"And Lydia," said Jane. Elizabeth appreciated that her sister had not even attempted to deny it. "Lydia is the nearest to her in character."

"And she is the youngest," added Elizabeth. "Jane was relied on to save the family. But she has always doted on Lydia."

"But as you are the next eldest, she has turned her matchmaking attentions upon you."

"I cannot deny that," said Elizabeth. She directed a melancholy smile at her sister. "I might have to throw myself on your mercy, even after we return from Brighton. Longbourn may very well become unbearable."

"You will always be welcome," said Jane.

"Of course, you will," echoed Anthony. "Jane is correct—we would never deny your mother our assistance. But should it become necessary that both you and Mrs. Bennet live with us, I would insist upon her good behavior. I expect that she will comply, if only because she wishes to keep a roof overhead."

"There is no need to fret," said Elizabeth, now wishing to bring this conversation to a close. "I will be well. And perhaps even should I not marry, one of my sisters might, and you can simply send Mama off to live with one of them."

"I believe your mother would be difficult to remove, should she live with us," said Anthony in a dry tone. "Be that as it may, let us deal with that situation when we must. For now, I think there is no need to discuss such subjects."

Jane and Elizabeth both agreed with him, and they turned their attention to other matters. "You expect we will depart for Brighton in the next week?" asked Elizabeth.

"My family will be returning to London in about a week," replied Anthony. "Assuming they are not plagued by bad weather. I would like to wait until they arrive so I may introduce you both to their acquaintance before we go. Thus, I believe we shall be in London for a little longer than a week."

Anthony turned to Elizabeth and flashed her a grin. "In fact, I am interested to see how you will get on with my mother. She will like you very well, I think. And your mother could have no better ally than she. She has often taken young ladies under her wing, guiding them in society and assisting them in making good matches."

Though she gaped at him for a moment, Elizabeth could see the twinkle in his eye and thought he was not serious. Or perhaps not completely serious.

"I think, my dear brother," said Elizabeth, affecting a stern tone, "I have had as much as I can stomach of matchmakers in my own family. I pray you would not encourage *your* mother to fill such a role when she comes."

Both Anthony and Jane laughed at Elizabeth's words, though she did not find them especially amusing herself. "Do not concern yourself, dearest Sister," replied Anthony, responding in the same way Elizabeth had spoken. "We will only be in town for a few days after they come, and you shall escape her soon enough. Of course, I can make no guarantees after we have returned from Brighton."

Once again, her relations were overcome by mirth. But Elizabeth decided to ignore them and attend to her luncheon. Anthony was an overly teasing man, and it seemed like he had affected Jane, though teasing had never been unknown between the sisters. She would bide her time, for surely there would be an opportunity to turn their bantering back on them.

For the next week, they occupied themselves much as Anthony had suggested. The season had not yet begun, so events were sparse, but that did not bother Elizabeth, for she found she was not much interested in society. They made up for that lack in other activities, visiting the theater and the museum, walks in nearby Hyde Park, and even a shopping expedition.

"Jane has told me you are not fond of shopping," said Anthony when Elizabeth was informed of their plans. "But I am afraid on this occasion I must insist. I know for a fact that my mother is planning to hold one dinner before we depart, and while your clothing is lovely, those of society expect a certain level of sophistication in their dress." Anthony paused and winked. "That is a kind way of saying we will be surrounded by the pompous and proud who will judge based on trivial matters such as the amount of lace on your gown."

"If it is lace," replied Elizabeth, "then I hope you will not insist, for I have no love of it. That is the reason I usually do not like to shop— my mother and I have had some infamous arguments over the years, for I do not favor the styles she does."

"That is true," added Jane. "Lizzy and I both began to shop in London several years ago with our aunt's assistance. She not only allows us our preferences, but Mother cannot complain about the dresses if they are made by a London modiste, even if she does not like the styles we choose."

"And the fabric always comes from Uncle's warehouse, which helps reduce the cost."

Anthony grinned at them. "As Jane already knows, I have not much knowledge of ladies' fashion. I am certain our modiste will know what will suit and what will be acceptable to ladies of society. Your father has ensured you have generous funds to purchase clothing, and I have pledged for the rest myself."

"I am certain we will enjoy ourselves, Lizzy."

Elizabeth was certain they would, though she was uncertain of the cost. Their plans sounded expensive. But Anthony was much more knowledgeable of society than they could hope to be, so she bowed to his superior knowledge.

As it happened, Elizabeth did enjoy their stop at the modiste, though she wondered if so many new dresses were completely necessary. It seemed that Jane had already done some shopping with her husband, and it was the sight of her sister and her sister's new husband which stilled any protests she might have thought to make. Clearly, Anthony doted on his new wife and wished to see her have the finest, and that wish included Elizabeth herself. She could not be so churlish as to refuse such generosity.

During those days they were also introduced to Anthony's friends. They were an eclectic group, those who were on hand to meet them, and Elizabeth thought they were equally likely to be younger sons, military men such as he had been, as they were to be titled as his brother. Elizabeth, who was interested in meeting new people, found most to be perfectly unassuming. She thought there might be some interest in her from certain quarters, but she knew those in the army could not afford to marry her, while those of higher station would not be tempted by her meager dowry. As she did not wish to think about marriage at this time, she contented herself with making new acquaintances.

It was early the next week when the Fitzwilliam family arrived at their London home. Anthony, who had received word the previous day of their coming, informed them and led them to the front door when the wheels of their carriage were heard upon the street below. Though Elizabeth herself felt little more than curiosity, it was clear that Jane, who was more intimately connected to them now, was nervous. Elizabeth held her hand as the family exited the carriage, providing what support to her sister she could.

"This must be your new wife, Anthony," said a woman of perhaps ten years their mother's elder.

She stepped forward and embraced Jane without even waiting for an introduction, startling her elder sister. Elizabeth, who knew what the countess was about, grinned at the sight, drawing her ladyship's attention. The elder woman winked at Elizabeth and turned her attention back to Jane.

"Will you not do me the honor of introducing me to these lovely ladies, Anthony? Or must I ignore you and introduce myself?"

"Of course, Mother," said Anthony, grinning at his mother's act of deliberately setting Jane at ease. "This is my wife, Jane Fitzwilliam, and her sister Elizabeth Bennet, who has agreed to accompany us to Brighton.

"Jane, Elizabeth, these are my parents, Lord Henry and Lady Susan Fitzwilliam, Earl and Countess of Matlock. With them is my brother, James Fitzwilliam, Viscount Banbridge, and my sister, Lady Charity

Fitzwilliam."

The newly acquainted bowed and curtseyed to one another. Then the countess took charge and directed them all into the house and out of the chill of the day, claiming Jane's company for herself, while Elizabeth was claimed by Lady Charity. The men grumbled with good cheer about the ladies not accepting their escort but were not paid any attention.

They spent some few moments together before the newly arrived retired to their rooms to refresh themselves from their journey, after which they met again in the house's main sitting-room, Jane having called for some refreshments. Elizabeth watched her sister, noting that while Jane carried herself well, she was still apprehensive about making a mistake. She would be grateful to relinquish the position of mistress of the house to its true mistress, Elizabeth thought.

As the countess had made a good initial impression, so too did Elizabeth soon discover that the rest of her family was unpretentious and kind. The earl and the viscount were men much like Anthony, though neither was as jovial as he. The viscount, in particular, was a man of a more serious nature than his younger brother, while the earl would often joke, saying things as outrageous as Anthony did himself. As for the other member of the party, Lady Charity was quite similar to Elizabeth in essentials. Anthony teased her in a good-natured fashion, to which she responded, clearly a custom of longstanding between them.

"Oh, no, this will not do," said Charity the first time Elizabeth referred to her by her honorific title. "We are almost-sisters, and I will not have you calling me 'Lady' all the time. Please call me Charity, if I might have the honor of it also." She turned to Jane. "You too, if you please. We are sisters by marriage, after all."

Jane and Elizabeth both agreed, and there was a chorus of agreement from the rest of the party, the earl and countess requesting mother and father to be used, while the viscount preferred the simple use of his title. With that settled, they fell into closer conversation.

"We must have some friends join us for dinner before you go, of course," said Lady Susan, confirming Anthony's assertion. "It is unfortunate you mean to depart for Brighton so soon, for Jane must have her curtsey before the queen." Lady Susan's eyes found Elizabeth and she nodded. "And Elizabeth, too, I believe."

"I am afraid her Majesty must wait for another year," said Fitzwilliam, "for our plans are already set. I am certain she will not miss the absence of two ladies this year."

Though Jane seemed shocked at his referring to the queen in such terms, the rest of the family grinned. "There is not enough time to plan for it anyway," said Lady Susan. "Next year, however, you must ensure it is a priority. It is an important step in a lady's acceptance into society."

With a smile and a nod, Anthony acknowledged his mother's point, and the subject was dropped.

While they were only to stay in London for a few more days, Elizabeth soon found herself coming to know the Fitzwilliam family. They were, as she had noted, good people. Any fear she might have of their looking down on them because of their lower birth was disproven immediately, which allowed Elizabeth to relax and enjoy their company.

While she enjoyed the company of them all, and Lady Susan more particularly took an interest in them, insisting on shopping with them to ensure they possessed the necessities and guiding them to a better understanding of the society they had now entered, it was to Charity Elizabeth soon became closest. Charity reminded Elizabeth of herself, only she was of a more volatile, fiery personality. But she was also intelligent, possessed of a quick and ready wit, and seemed to instinctually understand the motives of others. On their shopping trip, when she had come to the attention of others she knew, she had been ready and willing to introduce her new sisters, as she called them, and eager to defend them against any perceived slights.

On one occasion, not long before they were to depart for Brighton, Elizabeth found herself with Charity, speaking of various matters of relatively little consequence. Charity, Elizabeth found, was rather curious, possessing a desire to know everything about Elizabeth, who found herself speaking of her family, sharing stories of when she had been a child. So eager was she to hear Elizabeth's accounts that she was not as diligent in returning the favor, though she did not hesitate when reminded of that fact. She also had a particular interest in hearing of Jane's courtship with her brother.

"That is a droll way in which you portray my brother," said Charity, after Elizabeth had related some anecdote of his attentions to Jane. "I always suspected when he found a woman he would pursue her with his whole heart."

"And so he did," replied Elizabeth. "Nothing would deter him, and for his constancy, I could only be grateful. He was also quite perspicacious in heeding my advice about my sister."

"Oh, so you congratulate yourself in the part you played to bring them together?" Charity's eyes were sparkling with amusement.

"I do not so much congratulate myself," said Elizabeth, aware by now her new friend would not think her actions officious or deceitful. "I merely pointed out to Jane that she should not leave your brother guessing as to the extent of her feelings. Knowing Jane, I understood how difficult it is for her to be open with anyone—even me, who has known her all my life. As for your brother, I only told him Jane's feelings were not lacking."

Charity nodded. "Good for you, Elizabeth. It is clear they belong together. Had I been there, I would have said the same."

Though she had known Charity supported her brother's marriage to Jane, Elizabeth felt more than a little relief she had taken Elizabeth's words in the spirit in which they had been intended.

"Of course, they did not come together without opposition," said Elizabeth.

"Opposition? To what do you refer?"

Elizabeth paused, suddenly wishing she had not said anything. Her recitation would not put one of Charity's cousins in a good light, after all. But she could hardly refuse to answer now that she had spoken.

"Your cousin, Mr. Darcy, did not seem to me to be a friend of the match."

A laugh was Charity's response. "When does Darcy approve of *anything*? For a moment, I had wondered if you meant to censure Georgiana."

"No, indeed!" cried Elizabeth. "She is the sweetest woman I have ever known. I doubt she would disapprove of anything her brother or cousin said or did, for she quite reveres them."

"You are correct," said Charity. "But come—what did Darcy do to suggest he did not approve?"

"He did not do or say anything overt," said Elizabeth, frowning as she thought back to what she had witnessed. "He was not precisely friendly with anyone in Meryton, though I would not say he was rude. There were times when I thought he was disapproving, but the greatest evidence was that he departed from the neighborhood immediately before your brother became engaged to my sister."

Elizabeth paused and was forced to offer one more observation: "He *did* return to Hertfordshire for the wedding and stood up with your brother, so I suppose, in the end, he chose not to cling to his disapprobation."

"But that is just how Darcy is," said Charity. "He is much like his father was—quiet and reticent, though Darcy's reticence is often mistaken for haughtiness or displeasure." Charity winked at her. "His stern and unyielding demeanor has kept him safe from some of the more predatory females of society. One of these I am certain you have already met—Miss Bingley."

"I have, indeed," said Elizabeth with a laugh. "I will own that I know little true harm of her. She was a little supercilious and proud, I thought, and there were times when she seemed to wish she was anywhere other than Hertfordshire. But she always behaved scrupulously proper."

"Oh, aye, she is *always* proper," said Charity. "But she has long set her cap for Darcy, and she means to be his wife. I know for a fact that Darcy considers her to be nothing more than a sister to his good friend, now his brother, of course. But Miss Bingley is clearly determined to have him, little chance though she has of succeeding."

"Perhaps they would be a good match," said Elizabeth slyly. "He is reticent and haughty, where she thinks far too well of herself. No doubt they would cut a swath through society."

Charity laughed again and grasped Elizabeth's hand in a tight grip. "I do enjoy your society, Elizabeth. I am happy your sister married my brother and brought you here to us.

"With respect to Darcy, I will only caution you thus: he is, in essentials, a good man. Some might even say the best of men. He is not perfect, to be certain. He *can* be proud and haughty, and he is taciturn and unapproachable at times. But there is no better man or master of his estate. His tenants and servants are fiercely loyal and will give him a flaming character, and those who know him well count him among their staunchest friends."

"With all this praise, I wonder that *you* do not set your cap at him," said Elizabeth. "If he is such a paragon of virtue, he would make an excellent husband, indeed."

Then Elizabeth winked at her friend and continued: "But of course, you would not wish to provoke strife in your family!"

"Do you speak of something particular?" asked Charity, though Elizabeth had the impression she knew exactly of what Elizabeth spoke.

"Why, his cradle engagement to your other cousin—a Miss de Bourgh, I believe?"

"Where did you hear of that?" asked Charity.

Elizabeth could not help laughing at the thought of Mr. Collins, though he had made her wish to cry more than once when he had refused to turn his focus on a more willing female. Charity would no doubt find his antics amusing, and Elizabeth could own they were, now that time and distance had softened the vexation.

"I can well imagine this cousin of yours," said Charity, laughing at Elizabeth's recitation. "Aunt Catherine has long been a source of amusement and exasperation in the family, and those she installs in positions of authority are legendary for their unwillingness to do *anything* against her will."

"That describes Mr. Collins to a tee!" exclaimed Elizabeth.

"And to think he was dull enough to consider you, a woman of wit and vivacity to be an appropriate match. And then to propose after only a few days, doing so immediately after my brother proposed to your sister!" Charity shook her head, her laughter causing tears to roll down her cheeks. "What a diverting scene it must have been!"

"In retrospect it was. But I will own I was tempted to break my mother's finest china over his stupid head!"

They laughed together, falling into each other's arms. For a moment they could not speak due to their mirth, the hilarity which was renewed on several occasions when they did nothing more than look at each other or some quip was spoken to return them to that state.

"Ah, Elizabeth, I am quite undone," said Charity once they had gained control of their mirth. "I have not laughed this much in an age. The 'engagement' between Darcy and Anne is nothing more than my aunt's overactive imagination. And while Anne is as taciturn as Darcy, I believe she has some expectations in that quarter herself, little likely though it is they will ever be gratified.

"As for Darcy and myself—let us just say that I do not think we suit." Charity looked at Elizabeth with a critical eye. "In fact, I rather suspect *you* would be good for Darcy."

Elizabeth was shocked, and she regarded her friend through wide eyes. "I think you have laughed so much that something has come unhinged, Charity."

Far from being offended, Charity grinned, amused, at Elizabeth. "I only say that Darcy requires a lively wife to pull him from his reticence, and I think you might be the woman who could do it."

"Would *your* liveliness not suffice?"

Charity shook her head, clearly diverted by Elizabeth's protests. "No, I do not believe so. I am the younger cousin whom he has seen grow from a girl in leading strings. My relationship with Darcy is decidedly companionable, and I do not believe either of us could ever see the other as a marriage partner."

Charity did not allow her to respond. She rose to her feet and patted Elizabeth's shoulder, her countenance still alight with mirth. "Every spring Darcy goes to Aunt Catherine's estate, and Anthony usually accompanies him. I imagine your steps will eventually take you there, Elizabeth. Though I usually avoid Rosings, perhaps I shall go this year, for it seems to me it will be far livelier than it has ever been before.

And with those final words, Charity left Elizabeth to her thoughts.

CHAPTER XVIII

*P*emberley in Derbyshire was a great estate. Near enough to the Peak District to see those lofty spires on a clear day, Pemberley was situated in a long valley, the fertile ground in its center producing the bulk of her prosperity and wealth. Many a traveler had remarked on the lovely picture the manor made, sitting as it did beside a small lake, with verdant trees and golden fields of grain rising in the background. It was steady, solid, a physical demonstration of the family which had held sway over their lands for hundreds of years.

Fitzwilliam Darcy was proud of his home. He well knew that improper pride was not a laudable trait, but pride in one's lands, pride in the work of one's hands, the work of countless generations of Darcy forebears—there was nothing to censure in that sort of pride, especially when it made up a great deal of the master's determination to follow in the footsteps of those who had gone before. Unlike many of his station, Darcy was a conscientious manager of his lands, overseeing it all, yet allowing those who worked the land the autonomy to use their experience and make decisions based on their own determination to see their small portion of the estate thrive. It was not a utopia by any means. Pemberley had its share of strife, and the valley in which it sat could also be a curse when the rains produced flooding. But its inhabitants had always endured, had always brought back the former glory and increased it whenever anything untoward occurred.

It was his home, the one place in the world he was the most comfortable. It was his refuge against the world, his place of solace when society became too much for his sensibilities. It was to Pemberley he had retreated when informed of what he was certain would be Fitzwilliam's mistake in choosing an unsuitable woman for his bride. It was a place he was able to gain perspective, to examine his opinions, discard those made in haste or misunderstanding, to once again be at peace with himself, his family, and the world.

The situation with his cousin and his new wife dominated Darcy's thoughts in the days following his return from Fitzwilliam's wedding. While Darcy remained opposed to the marriage on the grounds of what he had learned of the Bennets, he had been obliged to consider the matter further in light of what he had witnessed.

The fact was that Darcy was not certain at all of what he had witnessed. He had been against Fitzwilliam's interest to Miss Bennet from the start, knew she and her family were nothing more than fortune hunters. The conversation he had overheard had proved his point. Or so he had thought. The banter he had heard upon his arrival at Netherfield, and thereafter, had painted a slightly different picture from that he had thought to see.

It was clear, or it seemed to be so, that Miss Elizabeth's opinion was that her sister loved Fitzwilliam—it was clear from her teasing, the way she smiled at them, satisfaction shining in her eyes. Furthermore, Darcy thought he had seen some of it in Miss Bennet's demeanor, in the way she had looked at her future—now present—husband, something he could see beyond her general reticence. It was possible they had both been playing to their audience, to show a greater affection and happiness than they felt to secure the marriage which had, at that time, not yet been solemnized. But the thought kept niggling at the back of Darcy's mind that they had not needed to do so. Fitzwilliam had already proposed, been accepted, the engagement announced. A man could not withdraw from an engagement in any way and not be completely ruined.

And Georgiana was convinced of Mrs. Fitzwilliam's affection for her husband. Darcy knew that Georgiana could be tricked, for it had happened with Wickham. But she had also grown and learned. She knew the Bennet ladies much better than Darcy did, after all. Could they have continued to dupe her, even after coming to such a close friendship?

Darcy was not certain, was, in fact, less certain than he had ever been before. In the end, he decided it did not truly matter. Fitzwilliam was married to the young woman, for good or for ill, and that would not change. It was for that reason Darcy had gone to Hertfordshire to stand up with his cousin. If Darcy persisted in voicing his beliefs, he risked driving a wedge between himself and his cousin, and if there was any man in the world whose good opinion he desired, it was Fitzwilliam's. Thus, it was imperative he allow the matter to rest.

It was not solely on this matter that Darcy's thoughts rested in those days. Indeed, after making the resolution to allow the matter to rest, he was quite successful in pushing it from his mind. The longer he remained in solitude at Pemberley, the more he was struck by how quiet the estate had become. It had been quiet for many years, with his mother's death, his father's continuous, but quiet grieving and subsequent death. Now it was even more solemn due to the absence of his sister, married and gone to her own home.

Fitzwilliam Darcy was the last of the Darcys at his home, and while there were others who bore the Darcy name, they were several generations distant and not at all close to him. Darcy had always known it would be his duty to marry and sire an heir—or more, given the small size to which his family had dwindled. But he had thought it a matter to consider in the future, one which was not in any way urgent. Perhaps it was now urgent. Regardless of his distaste for society, he knew he should use the upcoming season to finally choose a wife.

But Darcy was not the only one to be affected by the quiet of his home, as he discovered soon after his return from Hertfordshire. There was one at the estate who had known him long, and who could speak to him without fear of overstepping her bounds or inviting censure. And she was not the kind of woman to remain silent when she thought something needed to be said.

"There you are, Mr. Darcy," said Mrs. Reynolds one day when Darcy was sitting in the music room, looking through some correspondence. He had often come to this room of late, for though his study was preferable for the bulk of his work, he often imagined himself closer to Georgiana in this room, where she had often sat at the pianoforte, the exquisite sounds of her playing spilling out into the hallways, lifting the spirits of all within reach. For many years, the pianoforte was the only loud noise the estate had seen, and Darcy found himself missing it.

"Yes, Mrs. Reynolds?" asked Darcy, looking up from the letter he had been reading.

"I wished to inquire, sir, whether you had planned to go to London this year." She paused and gave him a look which seemed faintly apologetic. "As you know, there are changes which must be made should you decide to decamp for the spring."

"Yes, that is true," said Darcy, though he did not give her an answer immediately.

When he did not immediately speak, Mrs. Reynolds filled the silence herself. "It is tranquil without Miss Darcy—Mrs. Bingley—in residence."

"It is," replied Darcy. "Though I will assert it was quiet even when she was here. She has always been quiet."

"That is true, though that was not always the case." Mrs. Reynolds favored him with a smile. "I remember some of her energy when she was a child. Then she was as active as any young child would be."

"I suppose she was," mused Darcy. He had not thought of Georgiana as a child for some time. She had possessed a piercing shriek of a laugh, especially when he played with her, catching her and swinging her in the air as she loved.

"If you excuse my saying, sir," said his housekeeper, bringing Darcy's attention back to the present, "it has been too long since the laughter of children rang through the halls of this estate. Pemberley is a home, beloved to many generations of the Darcy family. It is not, and should not, be a mausoleum."

"No, I do not suppose it is," said Darcy softly.

"Then perhaps you will return from the season and introduce changes here. I am sure we would all welcome a change. Just remember, young master Darcy." Mrs. Reynolds directed a severe look at him. "Your mother and your father married for love, and despite the heartache your father suffered when your mother passed on, I do not believe he would have had it any other way. He was happy with your mother."

"I have no doubt of it," said Darcy.

"Then I hope you will take his example to heart, sir," said Mrs. Reynolds. "You deserve a young lady to dote over and children of your own. I hope in my heart that you will find her."

At last, Darcy thought to remind her that she should not speak in such a manner, but when she mentioned a young lady to dote over, in his mind's eye a picture of a laughing Miss Elizabeth Bennet rose, clear as if she were standing before him. Darcy shook his head and looked up at his housekeeper, then made a sudden decision.

"My sister, her husband, and Miss Bingley will be visiting next week."

"Aye, sir, I recall you informing me of it."

"Then you may plan for my departure when they leave, for I shall accompany them."

Mrs. Reynolds smiled and curtseyed. "Very well, Mr. Darcy. And thank you for indulging the impertinent remarks of an old woman who would love to see Pemberley become a happy home again before I retire. You may be assured that the house will be protected as it is whenever you are not in residence."

And with those words, she turned and departed. Darcy watched her as she left, bemused by the words they had just exchanged.

When the image of Miss Elizabeth entered Darcy's mind, he had not counted on its refusing to be dispelled. Many times Darcy told himself that he did not intend to be captured by Miss Elizabeth, did not wish to tie himself to an unsuitable woman as his cousin had done. But he was betrayed by his heart and head, for the thought of her rarely left him, even when he pushed it to the back of his mind.

She would come to him in the oddest moments. When he worked in his study, her laughter, an echo of what he had heard so often in Hertfordshire, would echo through his mind, as if he could hear it. A problem between two tenants' wives arose, and Darcy found himself wondering how Miss Elizabeth would handle it, were she mistress of the estate. He found himself daydreaming of her, seeing her mouth turn up in response to something her ridiculous cousin said, her eyes sparkling as she made some jest, or the way one errant curl which always seemed to escape her coiffeur bobbed along the soft line of one cheek. She even haunted his dreams, her siren call beckoning him as a mariner is called to his death upon the rocks.

The most annoying part of it was that he did not find the recollection unpleasant. Far from it, in fact. Miss Elizabeth Bennet was not the most beautiful woman, by any means — her sister possessed a far greater claim to beauty than she could boast herself. But there were several advantages in her favor. She was light and well-formed, her chestnut hair shone with a healthy glow, she was intelligent and witty, and her eyes, though he had not noticed until he began seeing her in his mind's eye, were perhaps the most beautiful he had ever seen. And they were even more beautiful when her mood was high, equally fine in the flashing of anger or the glow of happiness.

Why Darcy could not put her from his mind, he could not quite say. He had not thought of her since coming away from Hertfordshire, had not truly thought much of her when he had been in Hertfordshire. He had never admired her before. Why would she grow on his thoughts so much now when he was several days' journey from her?

When the Bingley party arrived as scheduled, Darcy was grateful for the distraction — any distraction which would shake the hold Miss Elizabeth seemed to have gained over his mind. Darcy was happy to see his sister and his friend, regardless of who they brought with them. Had Miss Bingley stayed with her sister, he would have been very well pleased. But of course, she would not — not when the opportunity to come to Pemberley presented itself.

The travelers alit from the carriage, and Darcy greeted them, but he was unprepared for his sister's actions. Georgiana, clearly ecstatic at the prospect of seeing him again, fairly skipped to him, throwing herself into his arms. Even Darcy, stoic as he usually was, felt his tears mingling with hers.

"Welcome home, Sister," said he in her ear. "Welcome home."

Georgiana pulled back, and he noted the expression of astonishment with which she regarded him. "But William — Pemberley is not my home any longer."

"You are a Darcy, dearest," reminded Darcy. "Whatever name you have taken on due to your marriage, you will always be a Darcy. Pemberley will always be a home to you."

Tears streaming from her eyes, Georgiana nodded and stepped away a little. But Darcy thought he saw a new life shining from within, a confidence and purpose he had not seen from her in some time. The girl who had been confused enough by Wickham to plot to run away with him had been replaced with a woman who was coming into her own. Perhaps there had been some residual fear, some deep concern she carried, that her brother had not forgiven her for her mistake. Darcy's words had dispelled those, never to return.

After his guests had refreshed themselves from their travels, Darcy met them in the music room again, grateful there was once again conversation and laughter in his home. Georgiana was, he insisted, to take up the reins of the house as long as she was there, and she eagerly agreed, pleased to once again be where she had been raised. Soon after tea had been served, their conversation turned to matters of interest to them all. Darcy had little to share, having lived a quiet life since his return. But the Bingleys had experienced a much more interesting time in the months of their separation.

"Hurst thought his father would never release his grip on life," Bingley was telling them in his usual lively way. "But they received word only two weeks ago of the old man's passing, and they immediately made their way to Norfolk."

Though Darcy's bond with his own father had been so close that he could not understand how losing one's father could be a relief, he was prompted to say: "Then I assume the Hursts will not be joining you in London."

"Not at first," said Miss Bingley. "They will be in mourning for three months. Hurst has said that they will not venture into society until it is complete."

"I suspect," added Bingley, "his decision is in no small part due to the timing of his father's death. Their half mourning will not be finished until April. I am sure he feels there is little to be gained by going to London when the season is half finished, and they are still restricted due to the remainder for half mourning."

"That is a sensible decision," said Darcy, thinking it was one he would have made and with considerably more eagerness than he imagined Hurst had.

"Louisa is, of course, relieved to finally be mistress of her own home," said Miss Bingley. "I believe she also suspects herself of being with child, so I suppose the lack of society this year cannot be considered much of a loss."

Darcy thought it was rather tactless of her to say it, an opinion it seemed Bingley shared if his glare at his sister was any indication. "And how was your visit with your relations?" asked Darcy as a means to change the subject. He smiled at his sister. "Can I assume Bingley's myriad relations were eager to accept you into their midst."

"Oh, yes!" cried Georgiana, even as Bingley grinned and his sister, though seeming somewhat annoyed, kept her countenance carefully blank. "Everyone was so kind and welcoming that I felt I had known them forever. It is nothing like our family, William. Charles's family is so large, I could hardly keep track of them all."

"*I* can hardly keep track of them, Georgiana," said Bingley with a laugh. "But you have the right of it. They were all pleased with my wife. We had an agreeable visit, indeed."

"I suppose it could not be helped," said Miss Bingley. She shot a glance at Darcy and shrugged. "I know you are aware of my feelings, Mr. Darcy. I appreciate my family and am happy to see them. But York is not to my taste."

"That is understandable," said Darcy, though he knew the lady well enough to know *exactly* what she would say was to her taste. Fortunately, though her meaning was clear, she was not so gauche as to state it outright.

"How long do you mean to stay?" asked Darcy, once again changing the subject.

"Only four or five days," replied Bingley. "As I am certain you are aware, your uncle will return to London soon. We have been summoned to meet your family. And Fitzwilliam and his new bride will be there as well."

Darcy was well aware of it, for his uncle had sent him the same summons. "Then I shall journey to London with you, as my uncle has requested my attendance as well."

"Excellent!" said Bingley. "We can travel together, and perhaps attend the same events of the season. I hope you will enjoy your time there more than you have in past seasons."

"Perhaps," said Darcy, preferring to remain noncommittal. He had decided he needed to seek for a wife. But he was a private person and preferred not to speak of the matter openly, especially with Miss Bingley in attendance.

Of the aforementioned Miss Bingley, Darcy soon became aware that something had changed. While Darcy had known from almost the first moment of their acquaintance that she meant to be his wife, he was forced to acknowledge that the woman did not behave improperly. She agreed with every word which proceeded forth from his mouth, had attempted to praise Georgiana whenever possible to broker a marriage between his sister and her brother, and had endeavored to put herself in his company whenever possible. But she did not openly stalk him as he had seen other women do, and was generally well behaved. Darcy had acknowledged to himself that she would make a fine wife to some man. But that man was not him.

In the days leading to their departure to London, however, Miss Bingley was much more reserved than he had ever seen her. She seemed to watch him, an expression of utmost concentration furrowing her brow. She did not even agree with his opinions as much as had previously been the case. Darcy was not certain what to make of her.

The matter became clear the day before they were to depart. Darcy, knowing he was not to return until the summer, had spent the morning closeted with his steward, speaking of the upcoming spring, dealing with the last few items to ensure a successful planting season. When his steward had exited the room, Darcy sat for a time, looking out the window, lost in thought. He was surprised when a knock sounded on his door.

When he called out permission to enter, he was even more surprised when Miss Bingley opened the door and let herself into the room. For a split second, Darcy thought her purpose was to try to effect a compromise. But his intention to rise was arrested when she left the door ajar and approached his desk. On her countenance was a look of determination, mixed with trepidation, and Darcy was struck by the thought that he had never seen her in such a state. She was always supremely confident, even when she had no right to be so.

"I apologize for intruding, Mr. Darcy," said she. "But I wished to know if I might have a moment of your time."

"Of course, Miss Bingley," said Darcy, rising and gesturing to one of the chairs before his desk. Darcy had always thought the woman dressed with more formality and elaboration than required. As soon as the thought struck him, an image of Miss Elizabeth Bennet, her dress simpler, but at the same time handsomer, entered his mind, and he thought he caught the scent of the lavender water he had often detected on her person, a stark contrast to Miss Bingley's preferred rose water. They were both lovely scents, but though Darcy had grown up loving his mother's rose garden, at that moment he preferred the lavender.

"What can I do for you, Miss Bingley?" asked Darcy, shaking off such thoughts.

Miss Bingley was silent for a moment, seemingly lost for what to say. Her eyes were upon him, and he thought she was trying to see through him, to understand what made Darcy the man at his very core. This lasted only a moment, though it seemed longer when he was the focus of her attention. A moment later, however, she sighed and shook her head.

"I apologize, sir, for I have not known until this very moment what I wished to say."

"It is no trouble, Miss Bingley. Please take your time."

She favored him with a slight smile and then spoke: "I suppose I wished to ask after your intentions."

Darcy frowned. Was the woman truly asking him if he meant to propose to her? There could be little other interpretation for her question.

"I know my question may be impertinent, sir," said Miss Bingley, her voice hurried as if wishing to prevent him from speaking. "But I wish to understand you so that I do not waste my time. I have attempted to show you I would make a good mistress of your estate. I do not need to enumerate the qualities I possess, for I am certain, as an intelligent man, you already understand them. I believe we would do well together.

"But it has recently . . . come to my attention that you may not be of the same opinion. Though I did not wish to believe it, further reflection induced me to consider the possibility, leading to my presence here today. If you do not mean to pursue me as a marriage partner, I ask you to inform me so I can turn my attention to finding a man who is interested in me. I do not wish to end an old maid."

Though he listened with growing astonishment, Darcy grasped hold of the notion that someone had interfered and spoken to her. For a moment he was put out — he did not appreciate interference in his affairs!

"Did someone speak to you, Miss Bingley?"

"Does it matter?" asked she.

Darcy gaped at her for a moment. Then he realized she was correct. "I suppose it does not, though I would not wish for others to involve themselves in matters which do not concern them."

"If you answer in the negative," said Miss Bingley, "I will owe a debt of gratitude to that person. Will you not answer my question?"

While he was still a little annoyed over the interference, and though he knew who it was, Darcy could not refuse to answer. "I am sorry, Miss Bingley. Whoever spoke to you was correct — I have no intention of making an offer for you."

Miss Bingley nodded her head slowly. He might have thought her response to be bitter recriminations or a plea to reconsider, but she did none of these things. She remained silent a moment, considering before she fashioned a reply.

"I see. And I thank you for speaking openly. Might I ask what deficiency there is in me which prevents you from seeing me as a possible wife?"

"There is nothing in you specifically, Miss Bingley," said Darcy. "I believe you will make the right man an excellent wife. But I wish for something more in marriage than simply a wife to satisfy my duty as a gentleman, I wish for a woman with whom I can share affection, one who will share my life and my home, and equally important, my values. You and I are not similar in any way. I am more comfortable at Pemberley than anywhere else in the world and would stay here always if I could. Would you be happy living a retiring life in the country, only going to town when necessary?"

A slow shake of her head met Darcy's question. "No, I suppose you are correct. I love society and would find Pemberley, as fine as it is, to be dull, should we stay here for months on end."

"Exactly. You are a fine woman, Miss Bingley—I have never doubted that. But I believe it would be best for you to search elsewhere for a partner who can give you what you wish in life. I do not believe that person is me."

"Thank you, Mr. Darcy. I appreciate your candor."

Then Miss Bingley stood and excused herself, leaving Darcy bemusedly watching her as she left. Whatever else he might have expected, it certainly was not what had happened. He supposed that Fitzwilliam—if, indeed, it was he who had informed her—had the right of it. She would now focus her attention on the season and other gentlemen looking for a wife. Darcy was certain she would be required to lower her expectations. But he now had some hope that she would find that for which she was searching.

CHAPTER XIX

*J*ourneying from Derbyshire to London was never pleasant, being a long and tedious affair, exacerbated by Darcy's aversion to long periods of time cramped in his carriage. Even the best carriage money could buy could do nothing to make the three-day trek any more pleasant than it was, and the late winter roads did not help either. All in all, they made good time, and the often fickle weather of February remained fair, which was all they could ask for. But Darcy was still relieved as their journey came to a close.

It was made more comfortable than it might have been. Always in the past, Miss Bingley could be counted on to have far more than her share of the conversation when she had a captive audience in him while in the confines of a carriage. On this occasion, however, while she did participate in the conversation when it arose between them, she preferred either to look out the window at the passing scenery or rest her head against the side of the carriage, lightly dozing. There was more of the former than the latter, and Darcy could not help but conjecture that she was considering the coming season, making plans to finally capture a husband. Darcy was more than relieved that he had been removed from consideration.

Darcy discovered the woman was actually tolerable when every word which issued from her mouth did not have an ulterior motive. He had always known she was intelligent, and while her interests were not similar to his own, she could speak on most subjects with intelligence, her opinions interesting, and surprising at times. It did not cause him to regret how he declined to pursue her. But it did influence him to alter his sometimes poor opinion of her.

Soon they had arrived in London, and after the carriage stopped at the Bingley townhouse where his three companions disembarked, Darcy traveled the final few streets to his own house. There, he was happy to note that his valet, Snell, had already arrived, requested a light repast for his master, and arranged for his bath. It was not long after that Darcy retired to his chambers with a good book, feeling clean, his hunger sated, where he whiled away the rest of the evening with his book until he blew out the candle for an early night.

The next morning was devoted to a few matters of business, after which he went to his club for a short time. That evening, he was to dine with his Fitzwilliam relations—including the Bingleys--at his uncle's house. As the season had not truly started yet, Darcy did not meet many with whom he was acquainted and no close friends, and he was content with that for his first day back in London. Then his equilibrium was shattered, like the effect of a stone passing through a pane of glass.

Darcy could see nothing untoward when he arrived at his uncle's house that evening—everything seemed to be in order. He was shown to the sitting-room, noting the Bingleys had already arrived. When he stepped into the room, he was immediately greeted by his cousin, who stepped toward him with a wide smile.

"Darcy!" exclaimed Fitzwilliam, thumping him on the back as he drew Darcy in for a manly embrace. "I am glad to see you made it, man!"

"Hello, Cousin," said Darcy, grinning back at him. "I see married life agrees with you." Then he caught sight of Mrs. Fitzwilliam, who was standing nearby and smiled, going to her and bowing over her hand. "Mrs. Fitzwilliam. I extend to you my congratulations once again. But I am curious—have you managed to tame this reprobate?"

Mrs. Fitzwilliam smiled at him, and she sent a look at Fitzwilliam which was affectionate and seeming stern. "I doubt I am able to tame him, Mr. Darcy. But I shall not repine that inability, for I like him the way he is."

Looking on with interest, Darcy was at least a little heartened. For it seemed that no matter what her reasons were for marrying his cousin, Mrs. Fitzwilliam did possess some affection for Fitzwilliam. He had never seen her bantering before. Perhaps it was an ease in company she had gained while in London, coming to know his relations.

Darcy greeted the rest of his family, and for a few moments, they engaged in idle conversation. Darcy asked after their Irish holdings while the earl asked after Pemberley, the recent weather, and what Darcy thought of the coming growing season, Banbridge adding his own comments to this discussion. To Charity and the countess, Darcy said nothing more than a greeting, and they were engaged in conversation with the Bingleys, while Miss Bingley stepped back to speak to Fitzwilliam and his wife. Then it happened.

"Ah, Elizabeth!" exclaimed Charity, rising and walking toward the door. "I had wondered when we could expect you."

As she walked toward the door, Darcy followed her movement, and he almost gasped when he saw Miss Bennet standing just inside the door. The time and distance between them had been kind, for she was more handsome than he remembered, and far more than his daydreams could boast. She was wearing a light yellow muslin that evening, embroidered white flowers running up the sides and across the bodice. Her fine, mahogany hair was done up in an elegant knot with several combs set within, glittering in the light. Her eyes, as she looked out over those assembled, seemed impossibly deep and beautiful, and as she walked toward them, she seemed to glide several feet above the ground. Darcy did not know what he saw when he looked at her before in Hertfordshire, but he was seeing an angel, exquisite and fine like expensive china. He had never seen anything so lovely.

"I apologize," said Miss Elizabeth to the company as Charity drew her forward. "The hem on my dress had come loose and needed to be mended."

"None of that now, Lizzy," said Charity. "Our relations have arrived."

"Yes, I can see that." Elizabeth turned to greet his Bingley relations, and Darcy noted absently that his sister was excessively happy to see her. Then she turned to Darcy himself. "Mr. Darcy. How do you do?"

"I do very well, indeed," said Darcy, gathering his wits together to make a coherent reply. "I was not aware you were in London, Miss Bennet."

The smile with which she favored him seemed to suggest she thought his statement quite obvious. "It seems my sister cannot do without me, Mr. Darcy. I am to travel to Brighton in their company."

"Yes, we are quite happy to have her," said Fitzwilliam, while Charity grinned as she looked on. "Jane and Elizabeth are very close, you know."

"We are," said Miss Bennet, her tone light and slightly teasing. "Of course, given your performance these past days since I have arrived, I have no doubt I shall be forced to fend for myself much of the time we are there, for I suspect you will be far too interested in each other to spare any attention for me."

Her words produced general laughter, though they might be construed as impertinent or even mildly improper. Miss Bingley seemed to think so, for she rolled her eyes. Darcy regarded her for a moment, realizing that Miss Bingley did not think much of Miss Bennet.

"Then it is good you are able to amuse yourself," said Charity. She threw a wink at her brother and added: "If Mother were not so insistent upon my finding a husband this season, I would go to Brighton with you. It would be much more interesting than fending off hordes of admirers, all intent upon securing my dowry."

"Half of my children are now married," said Lady Susan. "And yet I have no grandchildren. James seems to be a lost cause, so I must now focus on you, Charity."

As expected, Banbridge protested while the earl looked on with affection at his progeny. In truth, his cousin was only three years older than Darcy, and at thirty, it was not uncommon for a man of his level of society to remain unmarried. Such thoughts flittered across the edge of Darcy's consciousness, but his attention kept wandering back to Miss Bennet. She had been pulled to sit with Charity and Georgiana, Lady Susan also sitting nearby. And while Darcy stood in a group with his uncle, his cousins, and Bingley, he found his eyes drawn to her frequently.

It was fortunate his family was so open and friendly, Darcy decided. Bingley, who was by far the lowest standing in society, regardless of his marriage to Georgiana, might have been made to feel uncomfortable otherwise. But he was not at all, for he fit in with the Fitzwilliam men well, bantering with Anthony, speaking of various matters with Banbridge, and talking of estates with his uncle.

"I understand you are leasing an estate at present, Bingley," said his Uncle Matlock. "How much longer is remaining on the lease?"

"It expires at Michaelmas," replied Bingley. "Darcy was a great help to me in the autumn, sharing his knowledge and expertise. We shall return after we visit your sister in Kent, for I wish to oversee the estate in the late spring and summer months."

"And you expect to purchase thereafter?"

"Yes, I do. I hope to find something closer to Pemberley, for Georgiana wishes to be close to her ancestral home."

Lord Matlock considered this for a moment before saying: "I believe there may be something nearby Snowlock which may suit. I shall contact my man of business and have him inquire after it."

"Is it located in Derbyshire?" asked Bingley.

"Yes. As I recall, it is some miles to the north of the border with Staffordshire, perhaps halfway between Snowlock and Thorndell, which would put it within twenty miles of Pemberley. The estate was owned by a Mr. Sutton who has passed. I believe his heir possesses an estate in Wiltshire and does not care to manage an estate at such distance from his own."

"I would be interested in learning more," replied Bingley. He turned a grin on Darcy. "I was going to ask Darcy if he knew of any in the area which would suit, but this sounds like a good opportunity."

"I will also have my men investigate the area nearer to Pemberley," said Darcy. "I do not know of anything which might be available for purchase, but there may be something."

"Excellent!" enthused his friend.

The conversation devolved into more mundane topics after that, and Darcy found that to be as much a curse as a blessing. With less to occupy his mind, he was much more at liberty to watch Miss Elizabeth Bennet. She was effortless, he noted, speaking to Lady Susan and Charity with as much ease and animation as he had ever seen. They were clearly already fond of her—and of Mrs. Fitzwilliam too—and between Charity and Miss Bennet there seemed to be a close friendship. Knowing what he did about the Bennets, Darcy was not certain he could approve, and none of the rest of the family would fit with them, as their manners were not at all fashionable. But he could not precisely tell his family to avoid women who were now connected to them.

Back and forth Darcy's thoughts went that evening, alternately watching Miss Bennet, and attempting to do anything else which might distract him. But despite his avoidance, he could not help but note her effervescence, her *joie de vivre*, the bright light which was at her very heart. He wondered how he could have missed it in Hertfordshire. While he knew he could never offer for her, never request a closer connection than they possessed now, he could not help but be drawn into her orbit.

It was not a surprise then, as the evening progressed, that others should note his preoccupation. Fitzwilliam, of course, knew him as well as any other. Likewise, he was the subject of interest from both his aunt and uncle. But when he was called on his behavior that evening, it came from an entirely unexpected source.

"It seems to me, Mr. Darcy," said a voice when he was standing by the fire, contemplating the situation, "you have some interest in Miss Elizabeth Bennet this evening."

Darcy turned and noted that Miss Bingley had approached him. While she was as composed as ever, Darcy thought he detected a slight tightness about her mouth and eyes, her brow furrowed ever so slightly. She was not a woman to give much away, but Darcy thought her displeased.

"Nothing out of the common sort," replied Darcy, shrugging to effect a lack of interest in the subject. "I was merely surprised to see her tonight."

"As was I. I had no notion she had attached herself to your cousin's coattails in such a manner."

It was with interest that Darcy turned to regard his companion. She had never seemed to look down on Miss Bennet—or rather she had not done so any more than anyone else she would normally find beneath her.

"I hardly think it is as you say, Miss Bingley. My cousin *is* married to her sister, after all, and it is not uncommon for a younger unmarried sister to accompany a newly married one on her wedding tour."

Miss Bingley grunted. "I suppose that is so. No doubt she means to use the connection to your cousin to find herself a wealthy man. I should not be surprised to see them return for the season. Surely Colonel Fitzwilliam will wish to dispense of her impertinence before long."

The woman tittered at her own jest, but Darcy did naught but offer a slight smile. In fact, Fitzwilliam seemed to have a high regard for Miss Bennet. But Darcy could not disagree with the first part of Miss Bingley's assertion. He had no doubt that Miss Bennet meant to make the most of her sister's fortuitous alliance.

"A word of advice, Mr. Darcy." Darcy's eyes swung back to his companion, and she seemed to take the curiosity inherent therein as permission to speak. "While I quite adore dear Jane and congratulate your cousin for securing her, I do not think her sister is possessed of the same character. She means to have a man of wealth and society, and I have no doubt she will use her impertinent manners and beguiling ways to ensnare one as soon as may be. I have no doubt you are her primary target, as you are cousin to her sister's husband, and she is already acquainted with you. I suggest you take care."

Then Miss Bingley curtseyed and walked away, joining the small group which included Lady Susan and Georgiana. Lady Susan looked to Darcy, and Darcy only gave her a slight shrug. She rolled her eyes and turned her attention back to her companions.

As for Darcy, there was much on which to think. Miss Bingley's assertions were a study in contrasts. But Darcy had long had the measure of the woman, and he was certain he knew what she was about. She had invested almost three years in trying to elicit a proposal from him, and while she had withdrawn with grace, she was also a proud woman. She would no doubt consider it an insult should a woman like Miss Bennet succeed where she had failed. Thus, Miss Bennet, who had been acceptable to Miss Bingley before, was now the recipient of her dislike.

Fortunately for Miss Bingley, Darcy had no intention of being caught by the likes of Miss Elizabeth Bennet, no matter how fine her eyes or magnetic her personality. While Darcy could see nothing of Miss Bingley's assertion that Miss Bennet meant to have him—she had not approached him at all that evening, other than their initial greeting—prudence was the order of the day. He knew she was a fortune hunter, but he did not think she would focus on him with the intense ferocity Miss Bingley had displayed. He would not raise her expectations by paying undue attention to her.

Elizabeth could not quite understand Mr. Darcy. The man was as aloof as ever, seeming reticent even among his family, though she could sense more openness than he showed in Hertfordshire. But at the same time, he seemed to watch her far more than he ever had before, and she was not certain what this new attention portended. Perhaps he meant to amuse himself at the evidence of her inferiority and that of her sister.

She did not know. Mr. Darcy was as lively as he ever was when in the company of Mr. Bingley or his cousins. But still, he watched. At times, Elizabeth felt like she was a horse up for auction, inspected for any flaws or faults. After a time she began to feel quite annoyed with him.

The season was not yet underway, and there were few events for them to attend. Since they were to stay only a few days after that initial night when Mr. Darcy and the Bingleys had come for dinner, Elizabeth did not repine the loss. But the countess had planned a dinner for the night before they were to depart for Brighton, and the events of the evening left Elizabeth even more confused than before.

The dinner was not a crush. There were perhaps only twenty guests, all close friends or relations of the Fitzwilliams. The event was held for the purpose of introducing Mr. Bingley and Jane to all their friends. As a consequence, Elizabeth was also introduced to them, and she found some interesting characters amongst them. There was also a young man who seemed to show her more interest than she might have expected. Which led to Elizabeth's confusion.

Mr. Farnsworth Mortimer, the eldest son of Baron Longfellow, was a tall, gangly man of perhaps a few years Elizabeth's senior. He was also possessed of a pair of dark, beady eyes, a countenance which was fair and not handsome, with an unfortunate predilection for pimples. On his head was a shock of messy brown hair, and Elizabeth thought she might be able to find shade under his protruding nose on a hot summer day. He was not at all handsome, though Elizabeth found that he was kind, if a little excitable.

They spoke for several minutes, and Elizabeth was the recipient of all the admiration the young man could muster on the strength of an acquaintance of only thirty minutes. He seemed to possess a passing familiarity with current events, and he was not deficient on the subject of literature, which was one of Elizabeth's favorite subjects. In all, she found herself enjoying his company, though she could not say that she was overly interested in him. He was at least superior to Mr. Collins, though that was not saying much.

"Are you to stay for the season, Miss Bennet?" asked he in his nasally voice when they had spoken for some minutes. "I hope you are, for I have rarely met a woman as enchanting as you."

At that moment, Elizabeth was more than a little bemused. It seemed that Mr. Mortimer was capable of falling in love with as little provocation or acquaintance as Mr. Collins.

"No, I am not," replied Elizabeth, seeing his countenance fall at her response. "I am to accompany my sister and her husband, Colonel Fitzwilliam, on their wedding tour."

"I see," replied Mr. Mortimer. "And do you know how long you shall be away? Surely the colonel wishes to return for at least part of the season to introduce his new wife to society."

"Perhaps," replied Elizabeth noncommittally. "I do not know the schedule he means to keep, though I have heard some mention of perhaps visiting his aunt in Kent. Whether that visit would be made before or after the season, I cannot say."

"Lady Catherine de Bourgh, I would assume," said Mr. Mortimer, apparently deep in thought.

"Yes, I believe that is her name. Are you at all acquainted with her ladyship?"

Mr. Mortimer grimaced. "Not at all well. You see, my mother and Lady Catherine share a mutual dislike, and as Lady Catherine has rarely come to London, we have not seen her, even in passing, for many years."

"Ah, that is unfortunate," said Elizabeth. She favored him with a mischievous smile and said in a tone intended to impart a secret: "I understand her ladyship is very free with her advice. I know not how you have managed to cope without it all these years."

The laughter with which he responded was not feigned, but she thought he regarded her with a greater intensity than he had before. Elizabeth bit back a sigh—she truly did not need this puppy to fall in love with her, for she did not wish to be forced to reject *another* offer of marriage. Then Mr. Darcy intervened.

"Mortimer," said he in greeting. Then he turned to Elizabeth and with a soft smile for her, which she had rarely seen from the gentleman, said: "Miss Bennet. I hope you are enjoying the gathering this evening."

"Yes," replied Elizabeth, taken aback by his sudden appearance. "Are you acquainted with everyone here?"

Though she almost winced at the inanity of her question, Mr. Darcy seemed to take no notice. "Yes, I am. Mortimer and I are not truly related, but we are connected through the Fitzwilliam family, as his father and my uncle are cousins."

"Ah, I had not known of that connection," said Elizabeth.

They stood speaking together for several moments, though the conversation was truly banal in nature. There seemed to be some measure of tension between her two companions, though Elizabeth could not quite detect the reason for it. Before long, something unspoken seemed to have passed between them, and Mr. Mortimer excused himself from their company. But Elizabeth noticed he did not go far, and it seemed he remained vigilant in watching them.

After his departure, Elizabeth stood awkwardly with Mr. Darcy for several moments, only a few words passing between them. There seemed little to say to a man she had seen much of, but of whom she knew little. Elizabeth thought to extricate herself from this uncomfortable situation when Mr. Darcy spoke.

"I see Georgiana has been coaxed to the pianoforte." Mr. Darcy nodded toward the instrument where Mrs. Bingley had, indeed, begun to play, the company quieting to listen. "She has always been shy, you see. There was a time when she would never have played in front of so many people."

"She is talented, Mr. Darcy," said Elizabeth. "Her marriage to your friend seems to have given her courage."

While this beginning was innocuous, they continued to speak of music and his sister's talents and soon progressed to a discussion of a recent book Elizabeth had read, with which Mr. Darcy was also familiar. And while Elizabeth initially wondered at the man's behavior, soon she began to simply enjoy their conversation. Who knew that Mr. Darcy could be so easy in company, especially with one whom he looked down on, such as Elizabeth Bennet?

CHAPTER XX

$\mathscr{S}$oon the time had come to depart for Brighton, and Elizabeth prepared to go, eager to see the place of which she had heard so much. While she knew it was too early in the season to expect to go sea bathing, Elizabeth was eager to walk the beaches, to explore the streets of the city. Brighton had long been spoken of in glowing terms, and it had seemed to her that it was a place where the sun shone at all times, and where winter would never dare to intrude. Furthermore, she learned Georgiana had summered in Kent last year, and she was eager to learn more of what her friend had thought of the place she was to go.

"Charles and I did not go to Brighton, you understand," said she when Elizabeth raised the subject. "We spent the time after our wedding in the Lake Country."

"Oh!" said Elizabeth, wondering at the mistake in her assumption. "I have long wished to go to the lakes—my aunt and uncle may travel there this summer, and should they do so, I am to accompany them."

"It is a lovely country," said Georgiana. "But it is not the first time I have gone. My family has a lodge there."

"I can see how it would be a special place for you, Georgiana," said Elizabeth kindly. "I apologize, but I thought I had heard that you spent some time on the southern coast last summer."

"I was in Kent for some weeks," said Georgiana. "But it was not in Brighton. In fact, I was in Ramsgate with my companion."

There was something in Georgiana's voice, some hitch in the way she spoke which suggested that there was some story behind her time there, something more than she had said. Elizabeth did not wish to pry, nor did she wish to unearth unpleasant memories, if that is what they were. But she had long thought it unusual that a girl of Georgiana's level of society should be married at such a young age. And it was this that prompted Elizabeth to probe gently, wondering what Georgiana might say in response.

"I have heard that Ramsgate is a quaint town. How did you find it?"

"Oh, it is quaint, indeed," said Georgiana. "As I said, we stayed some weeks. While Ramsgate does not have the open beaches and sand of Brighton, it was still quite pleasant."

"I should like to visit," said Elizabeth. "I have not had much opportunity for travel, you understand. Every new location must be an occasion for new experiences."

"Perhaps you shall go there, then. I am certain Anthony would be happy to tour Kent. Ramsgate will always hold certain . . . memories for me." The girl blushed and averted her eyes, and when she spoke again, it was more softly than she had before. "Soon after I left Ramsgate, I became engaged to my dear Charles. It was the last place I stayed in which I was still a single woman."

Elizabeth regarded her, wondering at Georgiana's turn of phrase. Now, more than ever, Elizabeth was convinced that something had occurred, likely in Ramsgate, which had affected her friend. But while she suspected something, she did not know what, nor did she know whether it was good or ill.

But the way Georgiana spoke of Mr. Bingley suggested that regardless of what it was, she was happy now. It was clear they shared a close and loving relationship. Whatever had happened before no longer had the power to affect her. And Elizabeth decided that it was none of her concern, and she would not pry for the sake of her curiosity.

"Then perhaps I shall mention it to Anthony," said Elizabeth, her tone deliberately light and playful. "Perhaps *I* shall also find my companion in life in Ramsgate. Since it worked so well for you, you should share your secrets with me."

As she had intended, Georgiana laughed. "I hardly think that would be the case. But if you return for the season, I am certain you will come to the attention of some of Anthony and William's friends, if you wish to marry."

"While I will not deny that I *do* wish to marry eventually," replied Elizabeth, "I am quite content as I am for the present. I shall, however, attempt to use your cousin's inability to deny my sister anything to induce him to take us to Ramsgate. Then, when I return, we shall compare notes."

"I would like that, Elizabeth. I hope you have a wonderful journey."

Elizabeth's farewell with Charity was equally pleasant, though much more lively. The two teased each other throughout the course of the final day, and Elizabeth hoped she would meet with her new friend again very soon.

"We might meet before you expect," said Charity. "As I suggested before, I suspect Anthony will be summoned to Rosings. If you are all to go, then perhaps I shall attend as well. I should like to see your impression of Aunt Catherine."

"She sounds like a truly fearsome lady," replied Elizabeth. "If we are to go, I hope you will join us."

The strangest farewell, however, was with Mr. Darcy. On the morning they were to depart, the travelers' trunks were being carried out to the carriage to be loaded, while Elizabeth shared a final breakfast with the earl and countess. It was while they were thus engaged that Mr. Darcy arrived.

"Ho, cousin!" said Anthony, greeting Mr. Darcy with his usual cheer. "What do you do here?"

"To see you off, Cousin."

"That is neighborly of you, Darcy," said Anthony with a wide grin. "I cannot think of any other time you have done so, except perhaps when I was bound for the continent. What can you mean by it?"

Mr. Darcy shrugged. "If I do not point you in the correct direction, you may not find your way there at all."

The earl and the viscount laughed, though Lady Susan contented herself with shaking her head. Anthony, however, attempted to feign injury.

"Must you still bring that up? I was nine years of age!"

"Oh, this sounds like a story," said Elizabeth, shooting a delighted grin at Anthony. "Do tell, Mr. Darcy."

Though Anthony glared at his cousin, Mr. Darcy was not intimidated in the slightest. "We had an argument as lads, you see. I cannot remember the gist of it—"

"Yes, you most certainly do." Anthony turned to Elizabeth and said: "Darcy, here, had pranked one of the boys of the estate—his father's steward's son—and then had the temerity to put the blame on me."

"You were shoulders deep in the planning yourself, Cousin," said Mr. Darcy, his tone remaining even, if amused. "Regardless, Fitzwilliam thought to avoid punishment, so he mounted his horse and set out to the north to return home to Snowlock."

Elizabeth could not help but giggle. "Pardon me, Mr. Darcy, but I understood that Snowlock is to the south of Pemberley."

"Yes, well it is possible he thought to take the long way, though I suppose he might have been stymied at John O'Groats."

They all laughed at that, even Anthony, though he still eyed his cousin with a look that suggested vengeance. For Elizabeth's part, she was surprised, though she supposed she should not be. Mr. Darcy had shown another side of himself these few days. She never could have imagined him joking with his cousin when they had been in Hertfordshire.

"Since then," continued Mr. Darcy, "I have taken it upon myself to ensure my cousin is at least *pointed* in the correct direction. I would not wish him to wake up one morning and realize he has reached the Indies."

They all laughed again and laughed harder when Elizabeth turned an arch look on Anthony, saying: "Now I wonder if we shall make it to Brighton unscathed. Would it not be best to hire a guide?"

Then while the others were laughing, Elizabeth exclaimed: "I suppose if your carriage driver is not afflicted by your lack of direction, we shall be well. *If* you simply allow him to do his work."

Anthony glared at Elizabeth, but she only favored him with a cheeky smile. None of the others restrained their laughter, and even Jane was hiding her mouth behind her hand, her eyes brimming with amusement.

"Perhaps we should depart, my dear," said he to Jane. His eyes then raked over Elizabeth. "And perhaps your sister should stay here. She is far too teasing for my tastes."

"Oh, Anthony!" exclaimed his mother. "You are only receiving a taste of your own medicine."

"Aye, that is the truth," added the viscount.

"Just wait until I have my revenge," said Anthony, smirking at Mr. Darcy. "But I do fear it is time for us to depart. Shall we?"

Jane and Elizabeth assented, and they rose to take their leave of their hosts. They walked out to the front door as a group, and Elizabeth was the recipient of many wishes for good travels and hopes that she would return some day. So welcome was she made to feel that Elizabeth thought she would be happy to return, should the occasion present itself.

As they neared the door, Elizabeth found herself walking next to Mr. Darcy, and rather than stay silent like she might have expected, he turned to her and said: "I hope you enjoy yourself in Brighton, Miss Bennet. It is a lovely city, quite unlike London in many ways."

"I suppose the society is much smaller and the city, less crowded," observed Elizabeth.

"Yes, that is true. Those who partake in the local society are much less pretentious than those you might find in London, and I have often found it is much easier to enjoy oneself."

"Have you spent much time there?" asked Elizabeth, curious in spite of herself.

"On one or two occasions. I think you will find it to your taste."

"Thank you, Mr. Darcy," replied Elizabeth.

Soon they had stepped up into the carriage and, with one final farewell, the carriage lurched into motion. As it drove away, Elizabeth happened to look back, and she noted that the occupants had returned to the house. All except for Mr. Darcy—he stood and watched the carriage until it rolled out of sight around a corner. Elizabeth was confused, for there was something in Mr. Darcy's behavior which did not match her impression of the man. She could not quite make him out.

When Lady Susan invited Darcy back into the house for tea, Darcy agreed without much thought. His mind was much more agreeably engaged, and his thoughts were focused upon the carriage which was even now making its way through the streets of London. He knew he had no business thinking of Miss Bennet in such a fashion, especially given his decision that he would not be caught, as his cousin had been. But much of the time he was not even aware of how his thoughts had fixed upon her—it was beyond his ability to control.

"You are very thoughtful today, Darcy," said Lady Susan, interrupting his reverie.

"There are merely some matters of business on my mind," replied Darcy, raising his previously forgotten teacup to his lips.

"Is there anything I can do to help?" asked his uncle.

"No, I have everything in order, though I thank you for your concern." Darcy paused—he truly did not like to employ disguise, but he also could not speak of his thoughts to his relations. "They are important matters, but nothing excessively complicated."

His uncle nodded but did not speak. A glance at his cousin Charity revealed a hint of amusement, as though he had not deceived her in the slightest. Lady Susan appeared to be thinking of something else, while the viscount was immersed in his paper.

"I must say," said Lady Susan, "that I adore my new daughter. She is everything lovely and kind. I do not think Anthony could have found a better woman to be his wife."

Darcy looked at his aunt with interest. "She is a most genteel woman. But I cannot think you would not wish for something better for your son?"

Without a word, Lady Susan's eyes found Darcy's, a question inherent in them. Darcy was willing to oblige.

"Mrs. Fitzwilliam *is* a lovely woman. But she does not possess most of the benefits a man of his station would expect in a bride. In particular, her father is a minor country gentleman, she possesses no connections other than a country parson, a man of business, and an attorney, and she brought little dowry to the marriage, as far as I am aware. By society's standards, she is not acceptable. Had Fitzwilliam not inherited Thorndell, he would have been quite unable to take her as his wife."

"I am sure you must be quite correct, Darcy," said Lady Susan. "But surely you do not consider us so concerned with what society deems correct that you would think we would disapprove of her for such reasons."

"I know you are quite liberal in your thinking, and I applaud you for it," replied Darcy. "But were you not the daughter of an earl yourself? Has Rachel not married a duke? For that matter, I do not see Banbridge scouring the countryside for a country miss to make his bride."

"Perhaps I should," said Banbridge, winking at Darcy. "It has worked for Anthony quite well, and I have not found anyone I like in town. If I could secure a woman as beautiful and angelic as Anthony's wife, I should be very well pleased, indeed."

"Do not jest, Banbridge," said Darcy shortly. "You know of what I speak."

"You suppose I am not serious," was Banbridge's reply. "Perhaps I am. The wife of a future earl will face a much more difficult road to acceptance if she does not have the right connections. But I would not hesitate, should I find a woman who would meet *my* requirements."

Darcy frowned at his cousin, wondering how much to take as completely serious. But before he could think on it any further, his aunt spoke up.

"We understand what you are saying, Darcy. But there are very good reasons to accept Anthony's choice."

"I well understand them," replied Darcy, putting his hand up in a gesture of surrender. "Family unity is important, and even if the family respectability is damaged in the eyes of others by Anthony's marriage, it would be much worse if he and his wife were shunned for it."

"That is, indeed, a consideration," replied Lady Susan. "But of more importance is the fact that as a grown man, Anthony has the right to choose for himself. We respect and support that as his family. And what I said before is true: Jane is a lovely woman, and there is no falseness about her. As long as my son is loved by his wife, it matters not what society thinks, nor does the size of their fortune matter. He will always be my son. And Jane is now my daughter, and I think very highly of her."

"And Elizabeth is an excellent woman as well," said Charity. "I have grown close to her in our short time together. She will be an excellent addition to our family."

Darcy frowned at what he thought was Charity's deliberate mention of Elizabeth. Lady Susan, however, smiled at her daughter and nodded.

"Yes, she is. In fact, she reminds me of my youngest child."

Charity laughed. "I suppose that is true. But I do not like her merely because of her similarity to my character. There is something estimable about Miss Elizabeth Bennet—I cannot imagine anyone would disapprove of her. Should we sponsor her in society, I have no doubt she would cut a swath through the puffed-up peacocks, leaving broken hearts in her wake."

The ladies laughed together knowingly, while the men chuckled and shook their heads, no doubt agreeing with them. Given how much Darcy had struggled with his attraction to her in recent weeks, he was more than a little annoyed at their praise of the woman. It would be much easier had they spoken at least some words of disapproval!

"I am only afraid they are fortune hunters," said he. "Their mother was not precisely circumspect in stating her desire for all her daughters to make wealthy matches."

A round of protestations met Darcy's words, but it was Lady Susan who responded for them all. "I do not know Mrs. Bennet, of course, but I saw nothing of any fortune hunting tendencies in either Bennet sister."

Darcy thought to reveal what he had overheard, but he suspected they would still protest, given how much they were defending the two ladies. Thus, instead of replying, he contented himself with watching them. He did not think he was sullen, but it may have been a near thing.

"Oh, Darcy," said Lady Susan. "I believe this business of Anthony's marriage has got you out of sorts."

"It is your father's doing," rumbled the earl.

"You criticize my father?" asked Darcy, offended at the earl's suggestion.

"No, Darcy," said the earl. "I merely suggest that your father was quite traditional concerning such matters as this." The earl paused and chuckled. "It is odd, I suppose. As a member of the peerage, I am expected to be steeped in tradition. But your father was much more rigid about these things. The Darcys are an old family, well respected and even revered, though never of the peerage themselves. As a member of such an august family, he felt he deserved the daughter of an earl for his wife—and he obtained one."

Surprised did not even begin to describe what Darcy was feeling. "B-but," stammered he, attempting to find the words. "He and my mother made a love match!"

"They did," said Lady Susan. "But that came a little later. Your father knew what he wanted in a woman's standing in society, but he was also interested in a woman who was compatible with him. They were good friends when they married. They were in love by the time you were born."

Darcy nodded, though his mind was far away. His parents *had* been in love—of that he was certain. His memories of his childhood, how they had interacted, the three of them as close as a family could be, confirmed that fact. His father's slow decline, steeped in depression and sorrow at his wife's passing also testified to it. Darcy had known of his father's rather rigid beliefs, but he had not known this.

"In fact," said Aunt Susan, her tone of voice pulling Darcy from his thoughts and leaving him to believe she was attempting to suppress amusement, "I *have* had the impression in the past few days that Miss Elizabeth would be a good match for you."

It was all Darcy could do not to gape at his aunt. Had he been so transparent as to plant the suspicion in his aunt's mind as to his attraction for her?

"We have already established that your father likely would not have approved," said Lady Susan.

"But he would not have stood in your way," said Lord Matlock. "Any more than we would consider standing in Anthony's way."

"Your mother, however, would have adored Miss Bennet," said Lady Susan. "And she would not have cared for her status. The Darcy family is old and respected, and your connections are such that the lack of connections in a wife would not hurt you."

"I have no interest in Miss Bennet," managed Darcy, though he wondered if his relations could hear the lack of conviction in his voice.

"I never said you did, Darcy," said Lady Susan. "I only said she would suit you. But then again, I must assume many others would suit you as well. The choice of bride is yours. I would urge you to avoid assuming a woman is unsuitable for the reasons we have discussed today. Marry a woman who will make you happy. No one can gainsay you, and we will stand with you."

The earl nodded and returned to some letters he had before him. It was not long after that, Darcy excused himself and departed. But while he had some business of his own to see to, he knew his heart would not be in it.

CHAPTER XXI

$\mathcal{B}$ righton was everything Elizabeth had expected it to be. It was a city of wide avenues, parks, and beautiful scenery, and possessed the benefit of being situated next to the ocean. It was cleaner than London, as the buildings were generally well maintained, and there was not the miasma which often hung over the larger city like a cloud, especially during the summer months. Though she was a country miss at heart, Elizabeth could easily imagine falling in love with Brighton.

Their journey was an easy one, taken at an average pace, for as Anthony had said: "We have no particular reason to hurry." They stayed the night in an inn two-thirds of the way there and set out early enough in the morning that it was just after noon when they arrived in the city. From thence the carriage took them directly to the house which had been let for their use.

It was not a large house, but it was clean and comfortable. It also boasted a parlor which contained a small pianoforte, a dining room large enough to seat eight, and was situated on a street near a shopping district. It was also only five streets from the edge of one of Brighton's famous beaches.

"We are on the west side of town," said Anthony as they met in the parlor after refreshing themselves from their journey. "Most of the militia presence is encamped to the west of the city, though the number of companies is much diminished now due to the season. In the late spring and summer months, their numbers will swell a great deal, as the militia companies are ordered to their summer camps."

"Then it is unfortunate, indeed, that Lydia has not accompanied you," said Elizabeth. "She would be beside herself at the thought of so many officers nearby to pay court to her."

"Lizzy!" admonished Jane. "Lydia is not so bad as that."

"Far be it for me to contradict you, my dear," said Anthony, "but I believe she is. Fortunately, she is confined for the time being with those currently encamped at Meryton. Or she will be until they are ordered away, which will come in another two months or so. And equally important, the men of *that* regiment are good sort of men and have been warned against trifling with her."

The two sisters turned interested looks on the former colonel. He saw the questions in their eyes and was not hesitant to respond.

"I am well aware of what kind of girl your sister is, for I have seen her like many times. I took the liberty of speaking with the colonel and some of his senior officers, warning them against any of the men attempting anything improper with Kitty or Lydia. As I was still a colonel at the time, I believe they understood how disastrous it would be for them if they set a foot out of line."

Elizabeth felt her heart lighten, and she grinned. "I knew there was a reason I always wished to have a brother! I believe you will do."

They all laughed at her sally and then began to plan to explore the city. Anthony, who was already familiar with it, interjected his thoughts of what they would find interesting, but he was quick to agree with anything they suggested. He was a new husband, eager to please his blushing bride, and while Elizabeth knew he was happy to accede to her requests as well, she knew she was not foremost in his mind. It was as it should be, thought she with a grin.

The next day after they had rested from their travels the previous day, they set out in search of amusement and delight. The shopping district they found to contain some delightful shops, including a bookshop, a milliner's—where Elizabeth thought she could purchase some items for Kitty and Lydia which would hopefully reduce the sting of being left at Longbourn—as well as a curio shop, among others. Elizabeth thought she would spend a significant amount of time here, especially the bookshop, which she already longed to peruse.

"Oh, no you shall not!" said Jane in a laughing tone when Elizabeth expressed her desire for the written word. "I am well aware of how long you can spend in a bookshop, Lizzy. You can do that later—for now we are merely exploring."

"You remind me of Darcy, Sister dearest," said Anthony. "I have never seen anyone who could spend so much time browsing for books. From what Jane says, he may just have met his match."

Though she replied with a good-natured grumble about being prevented, Elizabeth was more than willing to be guided by them. After visiting the shops, they walked the few blocks and soon found themselves on one of Brighton's sandy beaches. Her first sight of the sea impressed Elizabeth so much that she found herself speechless. The sand sparkled in the light of the sun, the edge of it relentlessly pounded by frothing waves of water.

And there was so much of it! Elizabeth had pored over her father's maps and atlases enough to have a notion of how large the world was. But this was so vast that she could not even see the other side and so alive! What would it be like to actually travel on those waves, to see new and strange lands? In that moment, Elizabeth envied those who had, wishing they were bound for Italy, Greece, or even further, to the Indies or the Orient! What an adventure such journeys must be!

"Rare is the occasion in which my sister is struck speechless. We must relish this time, Anthony, for it may be long before it is repeated."

Pulled from her thoughts by her sister's teasing remarks, Elizabeth turned a glare on her. Jane just laughed and pulled Elizabeth into an affectionate embrace. "It is wonderful, is it not, Lizzy?"

"As amazing a sight as I have ever seen," replied Elizabeth. "Thank you both for inviting me. Though there are many reasons to be thankful to be included in your travels, this view alone would have been worth the journey."

"We are happy to have you, Elizabeth," said Anthony. "Come, let us walk to the beach, so we can see it even closer."

And so they did, spending an agreeable afternoon walking along the beaches, looking out at the sea. Many times as they walked, Elizabeth noted when Anthony and Jane's attention wandered to each other, and at those times Elizabeth would fall back to follow at a discrete distance, allowing their privacy. At others, Anthony would tell them of his previous opportunities to stay in Brighton.

"If you go down the beach a little further," said he, pointing to the east, "you will come upon the men's beach. This section is reserved for women."

"Then why are you allowed to walk here now?" asked Elizabeth.

"Because it is winter," replied Anthony with a wink. "The beaches are separated in the summer for the purpose of privacy during sea bathing." He turned and gestured the length of the beaches, adding: "If you come here in the summer, the beaches will be lined with bathing machines and their dippers. But we cannot have men and women bathing together, so they are segregated with strict rules against appearing on the wrong beach."

"It is unfortunate we are too early in the season to partake in it," said Elizabeth, looking about wistfully. "I should have liked to have experienced it. Besides, it would make Lydia wild with envy."

This last she said with a wink at Jane, who giggled and nodded her agreement. Lydia had not been best pleased that Elizabeth had been invited, regardless of whatever custom said on the matter. Even now, Elizabeth expected a letter at any time from her sister, berating her for usurping Lydia's place.

In the end, they spent most of the afternoon walking along the beaches. When they returned to the house, Elizabeth was satisfied with the day as it had gone. There would be many diversions in Brighton while they were in residence. She could hardly wait to savor the delights she knew awaited her.

The weather in Brighton was notably warmer than it would have been to the north, even though Hertfordshire was not very far away. Elizabeth was not certain whether that was due to the presence of its location by the sea, but she was grateful for it nonetheless. She had always been a young woman who enjoyed nature, especially since it was her refuge from a house which was almost always boisterous. Winter denied her that escape,

The weather was not perfect by any means. There were still cooler days, and the wind was often a factor, cutting through clothes with the ease of an arrow through a target. There was also as much rain as she might have expected for the season, which often curtailed her outings as well. But the days of fair weather often found Elizabeth out in the city, and whenever possible she was eager to walk with the sun on her face, even if she had no destination in mind other than to simply enjoy the sights.

Much of this solitary activity came about because of her companions. Elizabeth would never have suspected Anthony and Jane of excluding her of a purpose. But they were a newly married couple, caught up in the throes of new and wondrous love, their focus was very much on each other. Many were the times when they would be sitting together when her companions' attention would gradually be drawn to each other, and Elizabeth's presence would be largely forgotten.

Elizabeth had expected this behavior, had known there would be times when she would be required to fend for herself. The frequency of those times did not bother her; rather it amused her and filled her heart with warmth for them both, especially a most beloved sister who deserved such happiness more than anyone else in the world. Thus, Elizabeth went her own way, allowing them their privacy while she enjoyed herself in her new surroundings.

"You wish to walk out?" asked Anthony the first time Elizabeth announced her intention to go out alone.

"I am certain you have been informed that I am an excellent walker," said Elizabeth, shooting him an arch grin. "There is nothing I love better than to feel the sun and wind on my face and revel in the beauty of nature. Since there is not much of that in a city, I thought I would visit that park we saw the first day we came. One must take what one can get."

"I would have expected nothing less," said Jane, as she fixed Elizabeth with a fond look. "There are times we might not see her for hours, Anthony."

"Yes, I am aware of it," replied Anthony, his manner sterner than was his wont. "But this is not Hertfordshire, Elizabeth. You cannot simply walk the city without an escort. Not only would it be improper, but it is also dangerous."

"In a city such as Brighton?" asked Elizabeth mildly. She was not averse to having an escort, but she was curious of what she might expect.

"Brighton *is* a great deal safer than London, especially certain areas," replied Anthony. "But it is not without its own dangers. I am responsible for your safety while you are with us, and I have no wish to face your father should something happen to you."

Elizabeth laughed. "I am happy to hear that you take your duties so seriously, though I am not certain I should be grateful to be considered no more than that."

When Anthony made to reply, Elizabeth stepped forward and laid a hand on his arm. "Dearest Brother, pay no attention to my teasing. I am quite happy to submit to an escort when I walk out, for I see sense in your words."

The grin which her new brother favored her was slightly relieved, she thought. "Then I shall speak with one of the footmen, for I have just the man in mind. If you wait a few moments, you should be able to depart before long."

The man Anthony assigned to her escort was named Jackson. He was a tall man, though not quite so tall as Anthony himself, and while he was not burly like her new brother, he was lean and hard and quick, and Elizabeth was certain he would demonstrate a surprising amount of strength should he be required to use it. When they were out, the man walked some distance behind her, allowing her as much privacy as possible, while keeping her in sight at all times. After the first time, Elizabeth noted with amusement that Anthony questioned the man and seemed to be more at ease when he had the report of her outing in hand.

Not all Elizabeth's time in Brighton was spent alone, as Jane and Anthony did not always abandon her to her own devices. There was also a certain amount of society to be had, and while they were not acquainted with many people, there were events they could attend which did not require an invitation. In particular, they attended a local assembly about a week after arriving.

"There are more militia here than I might have expected," observed Elizabeth to her companions when they had entered into the room.

As they looked out over the assembled, they could see the gathering was liberally dotted with the red coats of the officers, gathered in groups or sprinkled among the others. They seemed to be in great demand as partners, and many a young girl's eye was filled with adoring looks.

"You have not seen them during your daily walks?" asked Jane.

"I have," replied Elizabeth. "But not in such quantities."

"During the day, the officers are often about their tasks," said Anthony. "There will be some in the city, but you will need to go to the camp to see them in any great numbers."

Elizabeth shook her head and grinned. "I was not pining for their attention. I am not my youngest sister." Then Elizabeth turned and looked out over the assembly, saying: "I can only be glad Lydia is not here. Can you imagine our youngest sisters among so many officers? They would constantly be badgering us to visit the camp, and their behavior in this room would leave us embarrassed within minutes."

"They are not that bad," said Jane.

Though Elizabeth did not reply, she noted that Anthony did not disagree with her. "It is well, then, that they are not here," said he. "I believe they need more maturity before they are acceptable in a society such as this."

Elizabeth nodded, eager to drop the subject. Anthony and Jane soon left to dance, Anthony promising Elizabeth he would partner her next. Anthony had introduced her to a man of his acquaintance, who saw to it that she was introduced to his friends. Thus, before long she knew several young men of the militia and a few young ladies, and knowing the first man was a friend of Anthony's, she was confident the others would be of good character.

It could never be said that Elizabeth Bennet was without partners at an assembly, and after her dance with Anthony—in which she noted that Jane stood up with Colonel Dwyer, the man to whom Anthony was known—she had a stream of partners. It was an enjoyable evening, meeting new people, speaking, laughing, and moving about the floor in the patterns she knew so well.

"It seems to me you have become quite popular tonight, Lizzy," said Jane on a rare occasion in which she was not dancing. Anthony was at that moment engaged in a dance with a lady with whom it seemed he had a prior acquaintance, leaving Elizabeth and Jane by the side of the floor.

"And you have not been?" asked Elizabeth, regarding her sister with an arch of her brow. "It seems to me you have been as popular as I."

"But I am already married," replied Jane. "These men cannot have designs on me."

Though Elizabeth would not have accused any of the pleasant gentlemen to whom they had been introduced of ulterior motives, she also knew the way of the world. Jane would never consider such actions, but she knew some men would not concern themselves over her married status.

"Surely you do not think any of them look on *me* with any designs," said Elizabeth playfully.

Jane shrugged. "There are several who *have* been quite attentive."

"Then perhaps I should run off with one of them tonight. Do you think there is any chance of making Gretna Green before your husband descends upon us like an avenging angel?"

"It depends how much of a head start you obtain."

The sisters shared a glance and burst into laughter. "Then you will need to distract him so that I can make my escape. I am certain you are up to the task, dearest Sister, for it *is* my happiness which is at stake."

"What a lovely picture you both present," said Anthony as he approached, the dance having ended. "Perhaps you would explain the joke so that I may share your mirth?"

Elizabeth grinned at him. "We were merely speaking of my future elopement. But do not worry—I shall protect you from my father's wrath."

As Elizabeth had intended, Anthony laughed at her sally. "Perhaps you should simply wait until July. You turn of age at your next birthday, do you not?"

"I am impressed you know my birthday," exclaimed Elizabeth. "Or at least my birth month. But while you are correct, it would not produce nearly the excitement if I should do such a dull thing as that. No, I think Gretna is in my future."

"A little dullness, my dear Elizabeth, is much to be preferred, though the alternative often seems to be everything one would ever want."

Their banter continued until the next dance, which was to be the last of the evening. Anthony would partner it with Jane, of course, and as Elizabeth's hand had been solicited by a new acquaintance, she would also stand up for it. Soon they were situated on the dance floor, the two couples side by side, when the music began.

The first part of the dance passed as it normally would, but as she was dancing, Elizabeth caught sight of a man who appeared to be watching her. He was tall and dark-haired, though the light in the room and the distance rendered her unable to make any other details. He was dressed like a gentleman—not a member of the militia. And his attention seemed to be fixed upon her.

Several passes of the dance proceeded, and every time Elizabeth looked in the man's direction, she noted his attention had not wavered. She had no notion of what he was about and why she would command such attention from him. But before the dance finished, and while she had her back turned to him, he suddenly disappeared, and she did not see him for the rest of the evening.

When she told Anthony and Jane of this as they were leaving the hall, they listened, but there did not seem to be anything to be done on the matter. "Perhaps he was simply watching the dancers," said Anthony. "It may only have seemed like he was watching you in particular."

"That is possible," replied Elizabeth, though she felt this explanation was incorrect.

"Mayhap you have found the companion of your future life," teased Jane.

"That would be wonderful, except that I have not, in fact, *found* him," said Elizabeth. "Then again, maybe he will return at some unexpected time, sweep me from my feet and carry me off to Gretna."

Her family laughed at her sally, and Elizabeth grinned in return. "I have no doubt there is no man alive who could resist you, Elizabeth," said Anthony. "I only request you learn something of the man who spirits you away, for I would not wish you to be unhappy in life."

"I am certain I shall be quite well, Anthony," said Elizabeth in a lofty tone. "For as you have said: what man could resist me? I shall have him deliriously in love with me and eating from the palm of my hand in no time."

And so, with laughing banter, the subject was dropped. It was not the first time Elizabeth had felt the interested eyes of a man on her, and she assumed it would not be the last.

CHAPTER XXII

$\mathcal{S}$o the pattern was established during their time in Brighton. Though they were often together in their activities, Elizabeth was also required to fend for and amuse herself. In a city such as Brighton, however, there was no lack of sources of amusement, and Elizabeth was quite contented with her situation and the newness of everything she was seeing. And so the days and weeks passed away in this pleasant fashion.

When they had been in Brighton for perhaps a month, Elizabeth received a letter from home, one which amused and exasperated her at the same time. Letters from Longbourn had not been plentiful, and for that Elizabeth was not surprised. Her father could rarely be bothered to take up his pen, and her sisters, to varying degrees, were involved in their own concerns and not of a temperament which lent itself to letter writing. Mary was the most diligent correspondent of them all, but her letters were often dry and offered little of interest.

The missive in question came from Lydia, and Elizabeth was not at all surprised at what it contained. And her temptation to speak ill of a sister who was, after all, poorly behaved, was once again roused. Elizabeth tried to rein in her criticism, but she would share it with Jane, at the very least.

"You seem annoyed Elizabeth," said Jane, speaking before Elizabeth felt she was ready.

"It is from Lydia," replied Elizabeth with a shake of her head. "When are her letters anything other than exasperating?"

Though Jane shot Elizabeth a quelling look, she did not censure her, merely saying: "What does she have to say?"

"It seems it has now been confirmed that the militia will depart from Meryton. They are to join us in Brighton."

Jane nodded. "We always knew that was likely. Militia companies rarely stay in place for long."

"You and I both know that," replied Elizabeth. "But Lydia is rarely able to keep such a thought in her head for long, especially when there is amusement to be had. Furthermore, as I am now—in her mind unworthily—living in Brighton with you, she believes it is her turn to travel and insists upon taking my place."

"May I?" asked Jane, reaching out for the letter. Elizabeth was not at all reluctant to allow her sister to read Lydia's words and handed it over immediately.

It was a rarity to see her sister show much emotion. But it was soon clear that she was not happy with what her sister had written. But true to Jane's custom, she only folded the missive when she was finished reading it, handing it back to Elizabeth, but remaining pensive and thoughtful.

"We have long spoken of Lydia's behavior," said Jane at length. "But I have never been as convinced of the folly of allowing her to run on in this matter as I am now. She is a child and should be treated as one, not allowed in society where she may ruin us all."

Elizabeth was surprised by Jane's speech but decided to avoid voicing it in favor of discussing the subject. "I cannot but agree. But I am certain she has been speaking with Mama. I suspect another letter will come from our mother before long, commanding me back to Longbourn so Lydia may take my place."

"I will not agree to that," said Jane, shaking her head. "I rather like having my dearest sister here with me."

"And I am happy with your company and that of Anthony," said Elizabeth, squeezing her sister's hand in affection. "But you know how Mama can be."

"I shall speak with Anthony when he returns," said Jane of her husband, who was presently out with some acquaintances. It was one of the few times he had left the house without Jane. "I know he does not wish Lydia to join us any more than I do."

Elizabeth nodded, deciding it would be best not to speak, lest she speak in censure. When Anthony returned later that afternoon, it was clear he was not amused. He requested permission to read the letter also, which Elizabeth readily granted, and his countenance darkened as his eyes scanned the pages.

"Can I assume you have no wish for your youngest sister's company, Jane?" asked he when he had finished reading.

"Not when I can have Lizzy's," replied Jane. She sighed and shook her head. "I love all my sisters. But Lydia can be trying. I strive to avoid complaining of her behavior, but I am not unaware of it. I would not wish to be embarrassed here as a new bride, and I would not wish to bring shame upon my husband."

"No man could be shamed with *you* as a wife," said Anthony, grasping her hand and raising it to his lips. Elizabeth looked away, her lips curved up in a smile. It was these little utterances, the little gestures which he constantly made which spoke of his love for her. Elizabeth's heart was full—she had never wished for anything more for her sister.

"But I understand what you are saying," continued Anthony. "And I must agree with it. The question is, what should we do to handle this?"

"I doubt this is the extent of it," said Elizabeth. "I have no doubt Mama is her confederate, and I suspect we shall receive a letter from her before long."

Anthony considered the matter for a few moments before nodding his head slowly. "Yes, I can see where that might happen. Then I shall write to your father, asking him to intervene."

Elizabeth shared a look with her sister, each knowing what the other was thinking. Anthony did not miss the look, nor did he misunderstand it.

"If necessary, I shall also write to your mother." He paused and grinned. "I have no doubt she will release her designs should I—her favorite son-in-law—request it."

A laugh bubbled up from Elizabeth's breast. "You are her *only* son-in-law."

"Exactly," replied Anthony with a grin which was more than a little smug. "She will not wish to annoy the man who is the means of her family's salvation. Or at least she will not until Elizabeth marries a man of much higher consequence—then I shall be relegated to a lower standing in her eyes."

"Never!" exclaimed Elizabeth. "You are her favorite daughter's husband. You will always be her favorite."

They laughed together, and when they fell silent, Anthony's expression grew pensive again. "It may be necessary to attend to Lydia's education, Jane." He paused and appeared apologetic. "While I do not wish to cast aspersions, your mother is not equipped to teach the girl, and your father is not likely to take the trouble."

"No apology is necessary," said Jane. "Elizabeth and I both understand, though we love our father."

Elizabeth looked at her sister with interest; Jane had grown because of her marriage. The old Jane would have looked for some way to excuse her family's behavior, as she wished to attribute the best in others. Jane caught her look and rolled her eyes.

"I am not blind, Lizzy. I *do* understand."

"I never thought you were, Jane." Elizabeth turned back to Anthony. "While I applaud your resolve, you are newly married and not yet even settled into your home. It should not be your task to see to my sister's improvement."

"Perhaps it should not," replied Anthony. "But the situation is what it is regardless. And there is some self-interest in my designs."

When Elizabeth and Jane looked at him askance, he obliged their curiosity by saying: "You have both met my parents, and I am pleased they were open and welcoming with you. But they also guard our family's reputation and position in society jealously. My father will not take kindly to being embarrassed by my new relations and will expect me to take steps to ensure it does not happen."

"I cannot fault him for that," said Elizabeth, and Jane murmured her agreement.

"Perhaps a governess could be hired to assist?" asked Anthony. "She could stay with us for a time, but a stern woman to oversee her education would be best."

"If one could be found who could handle her."

Anthony smiled at Elizabeth. "Some ladies specialize in turning wild young girls into respectable ones. My mother knows of some. We shall speak to her about it when the time comes."

By tacit agreement, the subject was dropped and not raised again. As he had promised, Anthony wrote a letter to Mr. Bennet, informing him of his youngest daughter's actions and requesting he put a stop to it. As Elizabeth had expected, a letter arrived from her mother only days after Lydia's missive, almost certainly sent before Anthony's arrived at Longbourn. Mrs. Bennet's missive contained nearly a demand that Elizabeth return home and make way for Lydia to join her. Then a letter from Kitty, complaining about Lydia's supposed good fortune was also not a surprise.

Not long after, a short missive from Mr. Bennet arrived with the information that he had not only informed Lydia she would not be going to Brighton, but that she was forbidden to write Elizabeth with any repeat of her entreaties. Elizabeth did not know that it would stop the girl, but she was grateful her father had spoken to her anyway.

"Perhaps Lydia will actually listen to him," said Elizabeth upon reading the letter. "She *has* always been intimidated by our father's anger. Would that he had shown it more often, for she might not be the way she is if he had."

Her companions agreed with her, and they again dropped the subject. Other than one more letter from Mrs. Bennet, accusing Elizabeth of selfishness and ruining her favorite daughter's fun, all correspondence from them both soon ceased altogether. Needless to say, Elizabeth was well able to bear the deprivation.

The very next day, Elizabeth found herself once again alone—Jane and Anthony had not come down that morning for breakfast. After breaking her own fast, Elizabeth decided it was a perfect day to go out and replenish her supply of books, of which she had read almost all. Thus, she informed Jackson of her intention to go out, left a message for Jane, informing her of her destination, dressed, and was soon walking down the street, swinging her arms as she went, humming a song under her breath.

It was now the middle of March, and as such, the weather had warmed considerably, even from that she had experienced when they had arrived. Birds were chirping all manner of songs, flying overhead and chasing one another in their joy of life and warmth. The bookstore to which she was bound was situated in the shopping district they had visited on their first day in Brighton. It was not a large shop—rather it reminded her of the bookstore in Meryton. It was small and cozy—some might say cramped—with shelves lining the walls and standing in the middle of the shop, leaving narrow aisles between. It also smelled of paper and ink, comforting scents which reminded her of her father's study and of the happy hours she had spent there since her youth.

As she had visited a few times, she was known to the proprietor, a kindly man of middling years, spectacles, and unruly greying hair, named Mr. Hunter. He greeted her with a pleasant wave and a word of welcome before he returned to the notebook in which he had been writing. Elizabeth was amused to note he had a smudge of ink staining the side of his nose, a situation Elizabeth had seen more than once. She returned his greeting and began walking through the aisles, looking for books which interested her.

It happened as Elizabeth was perusing the books that she bumped one she had put down on the shelf so that it fell to the floor. As she reached down to pick it up, she noticed a slender hand grasp it. Elizabeth recoiled in surprise, not having known she was not alone in the shop.

"I apologize for startling you, madam," said a male voice.

Elizabeth's eyes followed his arm up to his face, noting that it was, in fact, a man—a gentleman by the look of him. He was tall, possessing wavy brown hair and soft blue eyes. He was also a very handsome man, one she thought ladies would swoon over, should he pay them even a hint of attention. A shiver of excitement passed through her, as Elizabeth was well aware of the effect this man could have on her.

"I believe you dropped this," said he, cutting through Elizabeth's thoughts.

"Thank you, sir," managed Elizabeth. "It was clumsy of me."

She almost winced at the inanity of her words, but her companion did not seem to notice. "I hardly think a graceful woman such as you could be termed clumsy. It happens to the best of us, does it not?"

"I suppose it does," said Elizabeth. She was beginning to realize the impropriety of the situation. She had not been introduced to this man, after all, and she was alone with him, though in a shop. Furthermore, the way he was looking at her was doing strange things to her insides, and she wondered if this was how silly Lydia felt whenever a man paid her attention.

"Pardon me, Miss," said the man before Elizabeth could excuse herself. "I know it is not precisely proper, but I should introduce myself. Robert Chandler at your service."

"Elizabeth Bennet," replied Elizabeth, curtseying to his bow.

"A lovely name for a lovely lady," said he in a smooth and matter of fact voice, as if he was commenting on nothing more than the weather. "I am pleased to make your acquaintance, Miss Bennet."

Elizabeth voiced her own pleasure, though she was not certain she should. Then feeling incumbent upon her to say something to further the conversation, she said: "Are you visiting Brighton, sir?"

"After a fashion. My estate, you see, is situated to the north of the city. I can often be found here, but I do not live here." Then he looked on her with interest. "And you, Miss Bennet? Do you live in Brighton?"

"I do not. My sister has recently married, and I have accompanied them here for their honeymoon."

"Ah," replied he with a knowing grin. "Do you know if you mean to stay here long?"

"I do not know," replied Elizabeth, wary of revealing too much, though she had been given no indication this man was anything but what he appeared. "I believe we are settled here for at least another week or two, but I do not know the particulars."

"That is excellent news, Miss Bennet, for I hope we may come to know each other better while you are in residence."

"But now," said he, before Elizabeth had time to process what he said, "I think we have stretched propriety as much as we ought. I shall bid you a good day and hope to see you again before long."

With a bow, Mr. Chandler excused himself and left the shop, Elizabeth looking after him with astonishment. She was not certain what to make of the incident. He had been everything friendly and charming, but he had not pushed the bounds of propriety, except, perhaps, in introducing himself. Perhaps she would see him again. In spite of herself, she could not help but anticipate the eventuality.

When Elizabeth left a short time later with a package of books in her hand, she looked about the district to see if the gentleman was still present. But she could not see him—he seemed to have departed. Elizabeth could not help but wonder why he had chosen to approach her, or if it had been a spur of the moment decision. It was not often a man introduced himself to a woman without another to perform the task.

"Are you well, Miss Bennet?"

Elizabeth started at the sound of another voice so close. But it was only Jackson, and she realized that she had been standing in the door to the bookshop for some moments. Embarrassed at her behavior, Elizabeth shook her head.

"I was merely woolgathering, Mr. Jackson."

The footman nodded and stepped away from Elizabeth, allowing her to move on her way. Elizabeth visited some of the other shops, doing nothing more than browsing. But her heart was not in it, for she kept thinking of her encounter with Mr. Chandler in the bookshop. In the end, she visited a café for tea and cakes and then made her way back to the house. There, she found Anthony and Jane looking a little embarrassed.

"Do you not already have enough books, Lizzy?" asked Jane, Elizabeth thought in an attempt to hide her discomfiture.

"One can never have enough books, Jane," said Elizabeth, winking at her sister.

Anthony laughed and said: "Now *that* is a point of view to which I could see my cousin ascribing."

Having little desire to speak of Mr. Darcy, Elizabeth shook her head. "I have exhausted the books I brought with me and thought to purchase a few more. I believe I shall be satisfied now for some weeks."

Much to Elizabeth's amusement, Jane and Anthony shared a look again. It was Anthony who spoke. "We would like to apologize to you, Elizabeth for neglecting you, which I believe we have been doing of late."

"You have nothing for which to apologize," replied Elizabeth, gazing warmly on them. "I was fully aware of the fact that I would often be required to amuse myself when I accepted your invitation to accompany you. I am not offended."

"That is good of you, Lizzy," said Jane. "But we both feel we have not paid as much attention to you of late as we ought."

"Our time here is coming to a close," added Anthony. "As such, we believe we should spend some time in some activities together before we depart."

The brief conversation with Mr. Chandler returned to Elizabeth's mind, but she forced it away, deciding not to speak to them about it. Nothing had happened, and she did not wish to excite Anthony's protective instinct.

"We are to depart soon?" asked Elizabeth. "I had thought we were settled here for some time yet."

"Our plans were never set in stone," replied Anthony. "My aunt, who, as you know, is a demanding woman, has insisted we visit her estate by Easter. We have decided to oblige her, as Darcy, Charity, and the Bingleys are also to attend." Anthony winked at her. "We cannot leave my cousin and her husband to Lady Catherine's attention alone."

"Oh?" asked Elizabeth. "I thought your aunt would primarily be focused on Mr. Darcy. She *does* wish him for a son-in-law, does she not?"

"She does, indeed," replied Anthony with a grin. "But her attention may be diverted for a time, and Georgiana's marriage to an 'obviously unsuitable man' will draw Lady Catherine's attention like a moth to a flame.

"So you wish my sister to be the focus of your aunt's displeasure?" asked Elizabeth, trying to suppress her laughter to show a suitable level of outrage.

"I am not afraid of Lady Catherine, Lizzy," said Jane.

"Nor should you be, dearest," said Anthony. "I believe you know me well enough to know that I would not allow my aunt — or anyone — to behave unfairly toward my wife." He smiled at Elizabeth. "Or my new sister, for that matter. But showing a united front before my aunt will blunt her displeasure. And I believe she will, in the end, accept both my wife and my cousin's husband."

"That may be because she has little choice," observed Elizabeth with a wry smile.

"I have no doubt that will be a large part of it," agreed Anthony. "But whatever the reason, she will accept it in the end, if for nothing more than to preserve family unity."

"Then when will we depart?" asked Elizabeth. "And are we to go directly to Rosings Park?"

"We thought we would remain for another week or so," replied Anthony. "We will take in some other sights of the city, and after that, I thought we could spend some days touring other locations in Kent before we finally turn our steps toward Rosings."

"Georgiana suggested we visit Ramsgate," said Elizabeth. "I understand she spent some time there last summer."

Had Elizabeth not been watching him, she might not have noticed the shadow passing over his countenance. Now she was certain there was something that happened the previous summer which had affected these people profoundly. But Elizabeth was not one to pry into such matters, and when Anthony responded, she was happy to put it from her mind.

"We could certainly go there. I believe there is more than enough to occupy ourselves for a week. It is not Derbyshire, and I would share Darcy and Georgiana's assertion that nothing can compare to the beauty of that county. But I think we shall be quite content."

"My Aunt and Uncle Gardiner have spoken of touring the lakes in the summer," said Elizabeth. "It is possible I might have an opportunity to go then."

"If you do not, I would like you to join us at Thorndell," said Jane.

"Are you certain you wish me to be constantly in your way?"

"I am," replied Jane, ignoring Elizabeth's attempt at humor. "I would like you to live with us as long as you remain unmarried."

"I believe you shall have to speak with Papa," replied Elizabeth.

"Leave that to me."

Anthony, grinning at them, turned the conversation back to the previous subject, and they spent some time discussing their plans. In the end, Elizabeth was satisfied with what they decided. She was sad that their time in Brighton was coming to an end. But the new adventures on the horizon would keep her interest for some time.

CHAPTER XXIII

*I*ntrospection was a state with which Fitzwilliam Darcy was intimately familiar. But questioning himself, re-examining his opinions once they had become firmly set in his mind — that was not something in which he had engaged often.

Perhaps it could be called overconfidence, he mused. Or hubris, or pride, or any number of other adjectives could be used to describe him. Darcy did not know, and to a large extent, he had never concerned himself with others' opinions. But he had always been taught to consider matters carefully and come to a decision, and he felt that had served him well. He was not any more perfect than the next man. But a careful consideration of the facts before coming to a conclusion tended to lead a man to the correct opinion, more often than not, and he had rarely been required to second guess himself.

The matter of the Bennet family — Elizabeth Bennet in particular if he examined his motives deeply, loath though he was to do so — was one which troubled him. He knew what he had heard Miss Elizabeth say, and couple that with her mother's behavior, what he had observed of her sister, the family's circumstances, and other observations too numerous to mention, he thought he was justified in labeling them fortune hunters. But his aunt and uncle, two of the people he most respected in the world, disagreed. Furthermore, Fitzwilliam's belief in them was also telling, as he had always been as adept as Darcy at spotting those who were not as they appear. Yet he defended the Bennets as vigorously as Darcy had ever seen.

So Darcy thought about the matter until he was not certain he considered anything else, so fixed on it was he. Darcy could not state for certain why this might be—their connection to him was slight, after all, as they were nothing more than his cousin's family by marriage. But still, Darcy's mind refused to leave the subject, at times leaving him feeling more than a little cross.

But Darcy knew that at least some of his motive for continually fixing on the subject was due to Miss Bennet herself. By now Darcy had acknowledged his attraction for her, even as he disapproved of her. She was lovely, he thought, and she had an intelligence and archness about her which was pleasing, indeed. It was unfortunate she was from such a family!

"You told me you thought Miss Bennet was an excellent woman," said Darcy to Charity one day when they were attending the same event. "How can you possibly know?"

"How can one *not* know?" asked Charity. When Darcy glared at her, Charity shook her head. "Anyone admitted to the pleasure of Miss Bennet's company must confess that she is an excellent woman. In my mind, she can almost be too open, for often she says *exactly* what she means without any concealment." Charity grinned at him. "In that way, she is much as *you* are, Darcy."

Darcy frowned at the implication. "I am in no way like Miss Bennet."

"No, I did not say you were. In essentials, you are very different. But she is honest and open and free with her opinion. She loves her family and promotes their welfare, though it is clear she often does not approve of their behavior. And she considers Jane to be the dearest person in the world, and I must own that I cannot gainsay her."

For a moment, Darcy hesitated, not certain if he should bring up what he had overheard in Hertfordshire. In the end, the second-guessing had taken its toll on him, and he was eager for someone to share his opinion. And so he told her the story of what he had overheard at Lucas Lodge, and when he was finished, he waited, hoping she would see the matter his way. He was destined to be disappointed.

"It sounds to me, Darcy, that Elizabeth was making a jest."

"You were not there, Charity," replied Darcy, his annoyance rising in direct response to her intractability.

"No, I was not. Nor do I know this friend of Elizabeth's, though she has mentioned Miss Lucas in passing. I know neither the circumstance, nor was I present to overhear it. But it does seem like something she would say when bantering."

Darcy nodded, but he did not speak. Charity shook her head.

"I do not know why you seem determined to disapprove of the Bennets, Darcy. It is not like they can be anything to you, though I would wonder if you are trying to convince yourself of their unworthiness. Could it have something to do with the eldest unmarried daughter?"

"Certainly not!" exclaimed Darcy, though a little voice whispered in his head, telling him he was lying. He ignored it—he had already confessed his attraction. There was nothing else to it. "When I take a wife, she will be a woman of society, not a forgettable country miss with nothing to recommend her."

"Miss Elizabeth Bennet is anything but forgettable," was Charity's reply. "And though she has neither fortune nor connections, I would not say she has nothing to recommend her. One simply must dig deeper to discover the gem she is."

When Darcy made no response, Charity sighed. "I will not persuade you, it seems. I shall not even attempt to do so. I would ask you, however, for Anthony's sake, to keep your opinions to yourself. Anthony clearly adores his wife, and he thinks highly of Elizabeth. He will not welcome your continual questioning of their motives."

That much was true, and Darcy knew it. Fortunately, he had already determined to avoid saying anything in Anthony's presence which could be construed as critical of his wife. It was that thought which finally allowed Darcy to put his thoughts in the back of his mind and focus on where he was.

Fitzwilliam Darcy had never been one to engage in an excess of society. His taciturn nature and disinclination for the company of those with whom he was not well acquainted was legendary, and while many a young lady had attempted to capture him for her own, Darcy was adept at avoiding them.

It was unusual for him to participate as much as he did that season. Whispers began to circulate, some of which he heard himself, that he was exerting himself to find a wife, and they were correct. What the gossips did not know was that he was forcing himself to do so, for he had no real desire at present. He knew he was lonely at Pemberley, knew he needed to produce an heir. But for some reason, the thought of marrying any one of these ladies was abhorrent to him.

But he had determined to do it, and he pushed himself as much as he was able. He still did not dance the first, supper, or last sets of the evening, not wishing to elevate any one of these young women above the others. But he danced more than his wont, tried to become more open, to show interest in those with whom he met. He attempted to act more like Bingley or Fitzwilliam, though it was not in his character to be as open as they. And in general, he simply tried to come to know young ladies with whom he would not even have deigned to speak before.

And it was all a miserable failure. They were as insipid and boring as he had ever thought, he grew to detest dancing more every time he found himself on the dance floor, and the whispers of his consequence and innuendos concerning his connections grew ever more grating. It was with a sense akin to relief that Easter approached, as he would have the opportunity to escape for a time, even if his haven against society was the company of an irascible old woman determined to see him married to her colorless daughter.

Not long before he was to depart for Kent, he was invited to dinner with Bingley and Georgiana. Eager to be out of society for even one night, he accepted, not that the prospect of visiting with his dearest sister would have caused him to hesitate for even an instant. It was there he finally found someone to agree with him about Miss Bennet, once again bringing the matter of the young woman—which had been simmering in the back of his mind—to the forefront of his consciousness.

"I understand you have been much more engaged with society, Mr. Darcy," said Miss Bingley as they waited to be called to dinner.

"Perhaps a little," said Darcy. It was easier to converse with the woman now she knew he had no intention of offering for her, even if she did appear more eager than at any time since their conversation at Pemberley. "I am not truly fond of society, but I do have obligations."

"Oh, of course, sir," said she, her smirk telling Darcy she had deciphered his meaning. "I am happy to hear it, of course, for there was a time when I wondered if you were on the verge of making a terrible mistake."

"What mistake would that be?"

"Why, to follow your cousin's mistake and connect yourself with the Bennet family," said Miss Bingley.

Darcy should have known. He had thought previously that Miss Bingley, though she would reluctantly relinquish her own designs on becoming his wife, would never wish for what she considered an unsuitable woman to succeed where she had failed. But Miss Bingley spoke again before Darcy could muster a response.

"While I have all the respect in the world for your cousin, I cannot but think he has made an unfortunate alliance. Jane Bennet is a sweet girl to be sure, but I am not certain her feelings are the equal of his."

Though Darcy knew he should stay silent, weeks of such thoughts, coupled with his exasperation with his relations, caused his tongue to be loosened. "I cannot disagree. I have always thought the Bennets were grasping social climbers."

The irony of his words was not lost on Darcy, though he ignored it for the present. Miss Bingley, after all, was one of the worst examples of a social climber he had ever met.

"It is so, Mr. Darcy," said Miss Bingley. She leaned closer to him and in a low voice, added: "I am convinced Jane married your cousin for no other reasons than his possession of an income exceeding that of her father and for protection against the entail on Longbourn. It is unfortunate, but in the end, your cousin will be responsible for Mrs. Bennet's support, and likely Miss Elizabeth and Miss Mary, at the very least. Neither is likely to ever catch a husband."

Darcy frowned—though his opinion of their grasping nature was firm, he could not imagine that Miss Elizabeth would go through life without attracting the attention of *some* man. But Miss Bingley did not see his reaction.

"If he is *very* lucky, perhaps the youngest two girls will run off with officers, and he can declaim all connection to them. Else, he will likely be forced to support them as well."

Again Darcy did not say anything. He remembered that Mrs. Bennet had a brother, and though he did not know much of the man, he was, it seemed, in trade, well thought of, and likely possessing an income greater than Fitzwilliam's. Should the worst happen, should Mr. Bennet die and Mr. Collins inherit Longbourn, Darcy suspected the uncle would also offer his assistance.

"Either way, I commend you for seeing through Miss Bennet. She is in every way unsuitable for life in the circles we inhabit, and it is unfortunate your cousin is connected to her. Perhaps he can marry her off to a tenant so that he may be rid of her." Miss Bingley paused and she chuckled darkly to herself. "I find the thought of Miss Eliza Bennet sequestered in a cottage, bearing seven or eight of the tenant farmer's children, to be more than satisfying. It is no more than she deserves."

While Darcy agreed with Miss Bingley concerning Miss Bennet's nature, he did not like this picture she drew of the woman, and he knew there was not the smallest chance of it coming to fruition. Fortunately, he was saved from having to respond to Miss Bingley's spite when they were called in to dinner.

As he sat next to Georgiana partaking of the excellent dinner she had ordered, he was allowed to think on Miss Bingley's words, as the aforementioned ladies were speaking of some event they had recently attended. Miss Bingley, Darcy decided, was not a difficult creature to understand. She had obviously detected Darcy's attraction to Miss Bennet and decided to speak in a disparaging manner to convince him of the folly of connecting himself to her.

In this, however, her efforts were wasted, as Darcy had never had any notion of offering for Miss Bennet, admiration or no. The fact that he agreed with the first part of Miss Bingley's assertions was of no consequence. Yes, Miss Bennet was a social climber and fortune hunter, but Darcy would not wish the fate Miss Bingley had spoken of in her diatribe on such a bright creature. Thus, he decided to once again put the matter out of his mind.

As they were speaking, a subject arose which piqued Darcy's interest, and he said: "You have a gentleman caller, Miss Bingley?"

Miss Bingley blushed and turned to look at him. Her manner told him that she held out a shred of hope that he might decide he did not wish to lose her to another man, now that the possibility existed. She batted her eyes in a coquettish fashion and said:

"I do."

"And who might this man be?" asked Darcy, determined to end her pretentions once and for all.

"It is Powell," said Bingley, answering for his sister. "He has been calling these past two weeks and shows a promising interest in Caroline."

"I am not well acquainted with Mr. Powell," said Darcy. "But what I have seen of him suggests he is an excellent man. I offer you my congratulations, Miss Bingley. I hope everything is resolved to your satisfaction when the proper time arrives."

To say that Miss Bingley was disappointed would have been a large understatement. She regarded him for a moment, seemingly attempting to determine if he was quite serious in his congratulations. When Darcy did not recant or make any other such declaration, Miss Bingley clearly held in a sigh and replied:

"I thank you, Mr. Darcy. I am hopeful too."

They continued on with the meal thereafter, though Miss Bingley was largely silent. At the end of the meal, Bingley decided to follow custom and separate the sexes after dinner, something he usually eschewed, even in larger parties than were present that evening.

Once the ladies had left and the brandy was delivered, Bingley raised his and grinned. "I must own that I am quite amused, Darcy. It seems like Caroline has finally given up her dream of being settled at Pemberley. I *am* curious, however; before our visit last month, I would not have thought she would have allowed a gentleman caller who was not *you* to pass through the door. But then again, she has been subdued, and she has mentioned you but little. Did something happen?"

While Darcy had not thought Miss Bingley would keep the matter from her brother, he knew, as her guardian, Bingley deserved to know the gist of it. Thus, his only recourse was to reply.

"I spoke to her before we left Derbyshire."

"Oh?" asked Bingley, curiosity written on his brow. "I will own I am surprised. You have always put up with her airs, rather than correcting her. This change is rather sudden."

"It was not I who raised the subject," replied Darcy. When Bingley's eyes widened, Darcy quickly said: "It seems like my cousin spoke with her and informed her that I would not offer for her. She wished to confirm his words so she would not waste her time with me."

Bingley shook his head. "Fitzwilliam overstepped his bounds. But I cannot say I am displeased, for it is not as if I have ever had any success in convincing her." Bingley paused and a slow grin settled over his countenance. "Then the reason she suggested we invite you this evening was to give you one final opportunity to change your mind. How like my sister."

"I had come to that conclusion too." Darcy chuckled. "I hope she has her answer. I doubt Powell is one to continue to call if he feels she is not fully committed to receiving him."

"I do not doubt it," replied Bingley.

They sat in silence for some moments, each considering the woman of whom they had been speaking. Though Darcy did not say so, he was even more relieved now that he would be free of her cloying attentions. At least he was now reasonably certain she would not bring the matter up again.

"What do you mean to do with Caroline when you go into Kent?" asked Darcy. "I understand you are to accompany me this year?"

"Your aunt is a formidable woman, Darcy," was Bingley's amused reply. "She has all but commanded us to attend her. As for Caroline, I believe Hurst intends to be in London by the time we must go. They will still be in full mourning and will not be able to attend events, but Caroline will be able to receive callers."

"I assume staying in Norfolk was far too tame for them?"

Bingley rolled his eyes. "Hurst can be happy anywhere there is food and drink. But it seems Louisa's complaints about missing the season were grating on his nerves. Apparently, she sees little reason to mourn a man who despised her, one who Hurst did not care for either."

"One's level of affection for the deceased is of little importance in mourning rituals."

"Very true, my friend. Hurst gave in to her complaints, but he has made it clear she will not be allowed to attend anything until they are in half mourning. Once they are, he will relax the restrictions a little, enough to allow them dinner parties, the theater, and the like. No balls, from what I understand.

Darcy considered the matter. "That is likely for the best. Miss Bingley will be required to receive Powell at Hurst's home, but I seem to recall he is not enamored of balls anyway."

Bingley only shrugged, and the subject was dropped in favor of another. "I understand your cousin is also to be at Rosings?"

"If you mean Fitzwilliam, then yes. He will arrive the week of Easter, with his wife and new sister in tow. Charity also plans to go, though I believe that is largely because she wishes to see Miss Bennet again."

"From what little we saw, it did seem like she was well pleased with Miss Bennet."

A grunt was Darcy's only response, eager as he was to avoid thinking about Miss Bennet again. Unfortunately, the subject was to be obtruded upon his attention once more. Long had he known that the new Mrs. Fitzwilliam and Miss Bennet were Georgiana's friends, and he was not surprised she thought highly of them.

"I long to see them again," said she. "I am certain Elizabeth will have many stories to tell of her time in Brighton, and she has a most interesting manner of speaking. And I am eager to hear how Jane is accustoming herself to married life with Anthony."

Georgiana did not see Miss Bingley's rolled eyes at the mention of the sisters, but she did not say anything. It seemed that Darcy's insistence that he would never marry Miss Elizabeth had placated the woman for a time. Hopefully, she would stem the tide of her venom now.

"Given the way Fitzwilliam acted with her," said Bingley, "I have no doubt he has been wrapped about Mrs. Fitzwilliam's little finger. It will be most amusing to see such an independent and self-possessed man in such straits."

"Oh, and are you not in such straits yourself?" teased Darcy.

Bingley laughed and gave Georgiana an affectionate smile. "Of course, I am, Darcy. And there is nowhere else I would like to be, I assure you. A man who has the privilege of marriage to an excellent young woman cannot complain of such things. I am quite content where I am."

With those words, Darcy was allowed to think on much more pleasant matters. Though he had been concerned initially when Bingley had proposed his solution to Georgiana's problems, Darcy's worries had been eased. It seemed they had settled into a happy and affectionate partnership. Darcy was not certain that his sister loved Bingley, or vice versa, but he was pleased they had found a measure of happiness. A quick question to his sister a little later revealed that the other matter was equally promising.

"There has been nothing said in my hearing since we have been in London, William.
It is nothing like it was during the little season after Charles and I married, and even then, there was little said but sympathy. It seems our ruse, suggesting that Charles and I had a previous understanding, was successful."

Georgiana paused and blushed, but then she added bravely: "I have heard some comments that I have made an unfortunate match, but even those have been largely muted. Uncle and Aunt's support has been instrumental in ensuring our acceptance."

"I am glad to hear it," replied Darcy. "Now, are you ready for Aunt Catherine?"

The giggle which escaped Georgiana's lips could not have been fathomed only a year ago. Lady Catherine had always terrified Georgiana, not the least because the lady had spoken several times of taking Georgiana's care from Darcy and Fitzwilliam and raising her at Rosings. Neither Darcy nor his cousin had ever had any intention of yielding, but that had never quelled her fear of it. Now, however, she was actually laughing at the mention of braving the dragon in its den.

"I do not know that anyone is ever *ready* for Aunt Catherine. But I think Charles and I shall do quite well."

"And you will have Fitzwilliam there with his new bride," said Darcy.

"Exactly," replied Georgiana. "I am sure we will succeed in

deflecting her if we are all there to see to it."

Darcy agreed, and they turned to other subjects with Bingley and his sister joining into their conversation. When Darcy left later that evening, it was to a sense of relief. The night had allowed him to concentrate on other matters, and for that, he was profoundly grateful. Perhaps this visit to Rosings, with Miss Bennet in residence as well, would not be so difficult as Darcy had originally been led to believe.

CHAPTER XXIV

*T*rue to their promise, Jane and Anthony took pains to ensure that Elizabeth was given much of their attention. Her laughing assurances that she understood and it was unnecessary were heard, but they would not give in.

"No, Lizzy," Jane would say. "We appreciate your understanding, but we are determined that we shall spend more time together."

"And I welcome it," replied Elizabeth more than once. "But you do not need to feel as if you must see to my amusement. This is your honeymoon—of course, you wish to be in your husband's company."

"I will have all the time in the world for that." Jane would squeeze Elizabeth's hand. "But my time with my sister will be limited as we each build our own lives. Let us treasure this time together, Lizzy."

And so Elizabeth acceded, though not with any true reluctance. The fact of the matter was that her companions were excellent company, and while she was content to amuse herself, she was as aware as Jane that the necessity of living in different houses with their own families would lessen their intimacy. Elizabeth had no notion of marrying any time soon, but she knew it was a possibility, especially given the wider circle of which she was now a part.

The one thing which bothered Elizabeth was the continued absence of Mr. Chandler. She had met him only once in the bookshop and had exchanged only a few words. But contrary to his words of promise that they should meet again, Elizabeth caught not a glimpse of him, though she often looked about as she walked. It *was* silly, she supposed. She was by no means in love with the gentleman and knew nothing of him, but the thought of such a handsome man fixing his attention on her was a fine thought, indeed.

They continued in those days being active in society. While there were no assemblies and they were not well enough acquainted with anyone to be invited to a private ball, there were other diversions aplenty. There was a fine theater in Brighton, and they went out one night, attending a performance of *A Midsummer Night's Dream*. Elizabeth, who preferred Shakespeare's comedies and especially loved the whimsical work they had seen that evening, enjoyed herself immensely.

"Did it meet your standards, Elizabeth?" asked Anthony when they were making their way back to the house.

"I did enjoy it," replied Elizabeth. "I have seen plays at Covent Gardens before, and I noticed that it was perhaps not so polished, the settings not so fine as might be seen there. But its charm is not in the props on stage but in the story. I thought the troupe was quite skilled, indeed."

"Very true," replied Anthony. "Perhaps there will be another opportunity to see it in London at some point, so we can compare."

Elizabeth grinned, saying: "Unfortunately, our memories of tonight will fade with time. The only true way to make a comparison would be to return to London and see it at once."

"I believe Covent Gardens is performing *King Lear* this season, and *Much Ado About Nothing* a little later."

"Then we shall have to allow the matter to rest," replied Elizabeth. "But all is well, for I am quite content with our activity this evening, whether it was the equal of London or not."

Her companions smiled fondly. "That is the truly wonderful thing about you, Lizzy. You are content with whatever you have in life, never wishing for more, though there are few who *deserve* more."

"Here, here," said Anthony, to Elizabeth's utter embarrassment.

"It is nothing praiseworthy," said Elizabeth, feeling her cheeks blooming. "Should not we all strive to be content with our lot?"

"Aye, we should," was Jane's fond reply. "But few do it so well as you."

There was no reply to be made, and Elizabeth did not even attempt it. She was a woman who had never concerned herself much with what others thought of her. But to have those she cared about most state their love in a manner which could not be misunderstood brought a wealth of feelings from her heart. Jane had always been nigh unto perfect to Elizabeth. To be the focus of such sweet words from her dearest sister was enough to cause tears to well up in her eyes.

The theater was only the beginning. They resumed their walks along the beach, listening to Anthony's tales of sea bathing or of some of the more humorous incidents on the continent or other times during his service. The beaches still were not segregated — Anthony informed them that would happen sometime in late April or early May. But Elizabeth could imagine the sight of bathing machines on the beach, with the welcoming gaze of the dippers standing nearby, eyes twinkling with mirth for the silly members of upper society who put stock in such things.

On other occasions, they attended dinners, including one given by a colonel with whom Anthony was acquainted. It was an event which Elizabeth took much relish in describing for her younger sisters, for while some might call it teasing, Elizabeth took care to assert there had been nothing special about it.

And through it all, she kept her eyes open, trying to catch a glimpse of Mr. Chandler, wondering if he would once again appear. But he remained absent, and Elizabeth wondered if he had been obliged to return to his estate sooner than he had intimated.

Only two days before they were to depart, Anthony and Jane informed her that they had decided to leave the city for a short time for a picnic. "It is an opportunity to once again be among nature, Lizzy," said Jane as they were speaking of it. "I know you prefer the country, though you have been good enough to be happy with Brighton."

Elizabeth laughed. "Come, Jane — you should not attempt to make a virtue of *everything* I do. Brighton has been interesting, and I have been happy to be here. Besides, if you meant to allow me to store up time in the country to better withstand the city, we should have gone some time ago, rather than waiting until only two days before our departure."

"I suppose that is true," said Jane, as her husband chuckled at Elizabeth's words. "But I believe you will be happy to go out for a time, regardless."

"I cannot deny it. Do you have a particular location in mind?"

"To the north of the city," said Anthony. "As you know, to the south is the sea and to the west lies the militia encampments. To the north are some locations with which I am familiar, which will allow us to eat our lunch in peace and enjoy the countryside."

"Then I am eager to be away," said Elizabeth.

In the morning, an hour or so before noon, the three companions boarded the carriage for the short journey to the outskirts of town. Elizabeth gazed out the window with interest, for there had been little opportunity to go in this direction during her frequent walks about the city. And it had one more claim on her interest, albeit a small one—Mr. Chandler had indicated his estate lay to the north, though he did not say where it was or anything of its proximity to the city. Elizabeth did not have any notion that she would see him during their outing, but she remained watchful nonetheless.

The area to which they were taken was, indeed, beyond the edge of the city, the cobblestones of Brighton's thoroughfares giving way to the gravel roads of the country beyond. For some minutes they drove through scenes of tall trees waving in the wind and farmers' fields, though there were no crops to be seen this early in the season. A short time later, however, they entered a wood and a small valley, within which wandered a bubbling brook and a small waterfall. There the coach stopped, and they stepped out, stretching their legs and looking around with interest.

"How fortunate that you know of such a delightful place!" exclaimed Elizabeth when she had examined her surroundings. "What a lovely place this is."

"It is actually quite well known to the locals," replied Anthony. "It is a popular destination for those who wish to retreat from the city for a time, and as it is heavily wooded and the ground undulating, it is at a convergence of several estates without being within the borders of any one."

"Are there many walks? I suspect the edge of the stream will lead to many beauties."

"There are," said Anthony, while at the same time Jane laughed and turned a mock glare on Elizabeth. "Lunch first, Lizzy. I should not wish to be required to wait for two hours while you satisfy your curiosity."

"Of course, dearest. I find that I am famished myself."

They made their way from the coach, finding a delightful spot a little inside the trees, not far from the stream and shaded by several large old oaks, and there they stopped. Jane and Elizabeth took out the old blanket they had brought for the purpose and spread it on the ground. Next, they opened the basket Anthony had carried, spreading their lunch on the blanket, careful to keep it away from the curious denizens of the location who now found much to attract their interest.

"Be gone with you!" exclaimed Elizabeth, swatting at a reddish squirrel who had run down the tree to obtain a closer look.

The squirrel, which Elizabeth noted was a rather plump and fine fellow, scampered away, racing up the tree and stopping on a branch overhead. It chittered at her for a moment, scolding her for refusing to share the bounty, before it disappeared into the canopy of the trees.

"You appear to have made an enemy, Elizabeth," said Anthony. He flashed her a grin and sat himself down on the edge of the blanket. "I hope he does not get it into his head to throw nuts at us."

"I hardly think he would waste perfectly good nuts on us," said Elizabeth. "His store for the winter cannot be so extensive as to allow him to spend them so frivolously."

The cook at the house had provided them with an excellent repast. The food was simple but tasty, consisting of meats and cheeses, several lovely cucumber and tomato sandwiches, a carafe of light wine, and fruits of various varieties. They each served themselves according to their tastes, and they sat partaking of their lunch, bantering in a light and affectionate fashion.

"Is your aunt's estate much like this?" asked Elizabeth, gesturing to the woods about them.

"In some respects, yes," replied Anthony. "Rosings is quite large, and the wooded park is quite beautiful, especially at this time of the year when the leaves have just sprouted. But nearer the house, you will find formal gardens done in the French style. My aunt, you see, does not approve of nature, and takes every opportunity to tame it. The gardens at Rosings are beautiful, with a hedge maze, topiaries and flower gardens aplenty. Not that Lady Catherine enjoys them much— she usually prefers the comforts of the house."

Elizabeth made a face, which did not go unnoticed, given Anthony's amused chuckle. "I much prefer nature as it was intended to be. While gardens have their charms, there is nothing to compare with the tangle of trees, lovely paths under their branches, and wildflowers growing without any hint of human interference."

"You may wish to keep such observations to yourself. My aunt will think you are positively medieval if you espouse such views."

"She is your father's sister?" asked Elizabeth.

"That she is, though my father often laments the connection. Darcy's mother was kind and gentle, quiet, yet possessing a rare fortitude. Lady Catherine has never been kind or gentle in her entire life, and I dare say she can be heard all the way to London when her dander is up. The only similarity between them was a slight resemblance and their determination."

"I wish I could have met her," said Jane, a wistful sort of smile settling over her face. "A woman who gave birth to such excellent people as Mr. Darcy and Mrs. Bingley must have been a joy to know."

"She was," agreed Anthony. "She was beloved by all. I often thought Lady Catherine was a little jealous of her sister, though I would never say that to her. Lady Anne Darcy was a woman who inspired love in all she met. Lady Catherine only inspires them to flee."

Jane and Elizabeth laughed, and Jane swatted at her husband. "You will teach us to believe your aunt is an ogre, and long before we have even made her acquaintance!"

"An ogre she is not, though ogres might fear her," replied Anthony with a wink. The two ladies protested again, but he shook his head and laughed. "I will not speak any more of Lady Catherine but to say that she is a singular woman. You will know of what I speak when you make her acquaintance."

The conversation exhausted, they turned to other matters. "Rosings itself is a handsome house. It is situated on a bit of rising land, and it is a modern house with all the current amenities. It is decorated in a style which is too ornate and pretentious for my taste, but it is not gaudy. I dare say we shall all be quite comfortable there. Lady Catherine is a good manager of the estate, despite her other flaws of character, though some might consider her officious."

"You said that you and Mr. Darcy have always visited at Easter?" asked Elizabeth.

"That is a tradition which extends back to when we were all much younger. When Lady Anne and Robert Darcy were alive, the family would gather together each summer, at Rosings, Pemberley—Darcy's estate—or Snowlock, which is my family's home. After Lady Anne and Sir Lewis de Bourgh passed—they died within months of each other—Lady Catherine became much more insular, unwilling to leave Rosings for any length of time. Robert Darcy, though he was dealing with his own sorrow, began visiting every Easter to assist Lady Catherine with anything that required a man's touch. Darcy and I have kept up the practice, though I have been absent due to other duties on occasion."

"Mr. Darcy is quite diligent in the performance of his duties," observed Elizabeth.

Anthony's eyes swung to her, and he studied her, seeming to be attempting to make her out. There was nothing in Elizabeth's question but what she had stated, which allowed her to meet his gaze without any hint of embarrassment. It was not as if she was in any way interested in Mr. Darcy!

"He is," was Anthony's reply at length. "You will not find a more industrious man or firmer friend than Fitzwilliam Darcy. As you can imagine, Darcy is made uncomfortable by Lady Catherine's insistence that he will marry her daughter. But he does not shirk his responsibility."

"There is no foundation to Lady Catherine's assertions?" asked Jane.

"None whatsoever," replied Anthony, his tone firm and sure. "I do not know of what my two aunts spoke when their children were babes, but nothing has been formalized, which is, you know, the salient point. After Lady Anne passed away, Lady Catherine attempted to induce Robert Darcy to agree to a contract, but he flatly refused to oblige her, even going so far as to inform her that he would cease to assist her if she persisted. Darcy has always been free to marry according to his own conscience."

The sisters nodded and the subject was dropped. Their lunch was, by this time, consumed, or as much as they wished to eat, for there would be a large amount left. Soon Elizabeth noted that Jane and Anthony had begun to focus on each other and were taking turns feeding luscious red grapes to the other. Hiding a smile, Elizabeth decided it was time to explore the area, and rose, stating her intention.

"Oh, Lizzy," said Jane, her cheeks stained a little red, "we did not mean to exclude you."

"Dearest Jane," said Elizabeth, smiling at the couple, "I would be concerned if you did *not* wish to spend time alone. You know I love to walk, and here, a place I have never before seen, is a perfect opportunity to indulge in my favorite pastime. There is no need to fret."

"Very well, Elizabeth," said Anthony. He winked at her, where she was certain Jane could not see, and Elizabeth was obliged to once again attempt to stifle a smile. "But please do not range far. You are *not* familiar with the area, and I would not wish for you to become lost."

"I should be offended at your lack of faith in my sense of direction," teased Elizabeth with a grin. "But I shall forebear and agree to your excellent advice."

Then with a final grin, Elizabeth turned and walked away, leaving the lovers to themselves for a time. Her first destination was the stream which lay only a stone's throw away from their picnic site. The bubbling of the narrow stream had just reached Elizabeth's ears as she had sat with her relations, becoming louder as she approached. When she arrived, she noted that it was, indeed, a small waterfall, though it was more a series of rapids, water flowing around moss-covered rocks and over a bed of small, multicolored stones. The water was clear and cool, and Elizabeth stooped to take a drink, enjoying the cool refreshing taste on her tongue.

She spent some little time beside the little brook, a rough stick held in one hand, tracing lazy patterns in the water where it had gathered into a small pool. Inside that pool, a few small fish swam, darting this way and that in response to the movements of her stick. Then after a time of this, Elizabeth turned away and made her way down the stream, pausing every so often to decapitate some unfortunate dandelion seed heads with her sword-stick.

The brook, she found, ran in the general direction of the city, though she thought it might skirt Brighton to the west, rather than joining one of the larger rivers which flowed through the city. She used the stream as a reference point to find her way back to their picnic site and remained mindful of Anthony's instructions to avoid ranging too far.

But it was a delightful walk. The trees were a mixture of alder, ash, oak, and elm, many of the same varieties she would find on her father's estate. Though they were still in the process of gaining their summer greenery, there was enough of it to be seen that when the soft breeze blew, they rustled delightfully. The fields were a riot of colors, though the most predominant of the flowers she saw appeared to be bluebells, their scent rising heavenward, prompting Elizabeth to breathe their fragrance deeply. The setting was utterly charming, and Elizabeth wished she had more time to explore it.

There were other companies scattered here and there, though Elizabeth avoided them as much as she was able. The thought of Mr. Chandler and whether he would appear was now a matter of indifference to Elizabeth. She had been silly to even wish to see him — what did she know of him, after all? Elizabeth Bennet was not a silly flirt like Kitty and Lydia, not one to lose her head over a man she had met once.

After a time of exploring, Elizabeth made her way back to where she had left Anthony and Jane, striding into the clearing with purpose. She was charmed by the sight of Anthony leaning against a tree, cradling a dozing Jane in his arms. The way he looked down at her, the tenderness in his countenance reaffirmed what Elizabeth had always known: that her sister was deeply loved. And she was happy at the sight, for no one deserved it more than Jane.

But at the same time, Elizabeth felt a pang for herself, for the lack of a man to share such a connection in her own life. Looking at them, thinking of her uncle and aunt and the love they shared, contrasted with the lack of any such feelings between her parents, firmed Elizabeth's resolve to find a love of her own. Perhaps it would not be found immediately, but she was yet a young woman. There was still time.

"Thank you for returning so quickly," said Anthony, speaking softly to avoid waking his slumbering wife.

"I would not wish for you to worry for me," said Elizabeth. "But this is a lovely locale. I can see why you favor it."

Anthony's eyelashes fluttered, and his gaze dropped to the crown of Jane's head. "It is. But it is somehow different visiting here with you and Jane, rather than with a company of my friends in the army or a group of local ladies."

"I am certain it is," replied Elizabeth with a warm smile. "I do not believe I have told you before, but please allow me to thank you. Not only have you seen my sister for the gem she is, but you also acted to secure her hand and heart. It is everything I could have wished for her."

"On the contrary, Elizabeth," said Anthony, "I believe *I* am the one who should be thanking you and your family. My Jane was formed in part due to the influence of your family, especially due to *your* influence. She is everything I have ever wanted in a wife."

Though Anthony could not see, Elizabeth saw Jane's lips curl up into a smile and knew her sister was awake. But she did not betray her sister's state. Let Jane do that later when they were alone and could express their love more freely.

"I am very happy for you, Anthony—and for Jane. My heart is so full I can hardly express myself. I can only hope that I will find something akin to what you have found some day."

Anthony grinned. "It may be closer than you think, Elizabeth. Jane and I will be happy to play whatever role is required to ensure you also find your happiness."

Elizabeth shook her head. She was in no rush.

CHAPTER XXV

*T*wo days later they departed as Anthony had designed. From Brighton, they made their way toward Dover, and from thence around the coast, finding their way through Canterbury and to Ramsgate. Elizabeth found herself interested, noting that Ramsgate was exactly as Georgiana had suggested. She preferred Brighton, in general, though the smaller communities on the mouth of the Thames possessed a charm all their own. They did not stay in any of these locations long, for their footsteps were to take them to the fabled Rosings Park by the end of the week.

Their travels also took them to a number of large and handsome estates dotting the Kent countryside. Anthony shared what he knew, informing them that most of the truly impressive estates were to the north of London. They toured some few and marveled at what they saw, but Elizabeth did not enjoy that part of the journey nearly as much. Her thoughts were turned to Rosings and what awaited them there, finding herself impatient to be there.

At length the road they traveled finally turned toward the estate of Lady Catherine de Bourgh, and the great house was sighted on the horizon. And Elizabeth found herself impressed.

"It *is* a handsome building," said Elizabeth as they approached from the west. "It is larger and finer than Netherfield, which is the largest house in my father's neighborhood."

"Yes, it is," replied Anthony, "and Lady Catherine is very proud of it. The de Bourghs are an old and respected family, though they have dwindled to the point where Anne is the only scion remaining."

"Then I wonder that Lady Catherine does not search for a second son, a man who would be willing to change his name to ensure the de Bourgh name survives."

Anthony grinned. "Perhaps she should. But Lady Catherine has always been a Fitzwilliam, first and foremost. In her mind, the benefits of uniting Pemberley and Rosings are far greater than saving the de Bourgh family name."

"Do they still have any relations remaining in France?" asked Jane, noting the French name.

"I do not know," replied Anthony with a shake of his head. "There may have been, but with the revolution and Napoleon's subsequence reign, it is uncertain whether they have retained whatever property they possessed if they existed."

By this time there were approaching the lane which led to the front drive of the manor house. As they were passing, Anthony drew their attention to another house, much more humble, yet pretty, situated in a grove of trees as it was. In the distance beyond it, a small town stood, and Elizabeth could see the spire of a church rising like a sentry above the jumble of trees.

"That is Hunsford, of which I am certain you must have heard."

Elizabeth could not help but make a face, and Anthony laughed. Jane smiled, knowing how Elizabeth had been obliged to fend off the overly amorous master of that particular house.

"Does Mr. Collins have much congress with Lady Catherine?" asked Elizabeth, though she already knew the answer.

"I believe you can answer that question yourself," replied Anthony, apparently diverted by her question. "Do you think Lady Catherine would install anyone who would not consult her about every minute detail of the parish?"

Though not certain she approved of the level of interference Anthony suggested, she shook her head mournfully. "I suppose not. Then my best option is to simply avoid his company as much as possible. I cannot think he will be pleased to see me here."

"It is not for him to approve," replied Anthony, his words firm, though his grin never wavered. "You will be a guest at Rosings, not the parsonage. Should he step out of line, I will be more than happy to put him in his place."

No doubt he would, thought Elizabeth. For the moment, the coach turned onto the drive and the parsonage was left behind. Elizabeth put it—and its odious master—from her mind for the present. Something told her she would require all her wits to withstand the mistress of Rosings. Despite her eagerness to arrive, she felt a shiver of apprehension pass through her.

When they arrived, they were met by the butler and housekeeper, their trunks were removed from the carriage, and they were shown into the house. Everything was handled with the ease and efficiency the lady would no doubt demand. The house was decorated much as Anthony had stated, and while Elizabeth found it was not to her taste, it was still a fine and handsome home.

"Please follow me to your rooms," said Mrs. Broadhead, the housekeeper. "I have been instructed to inform you that Lady Catherine expects your attendance within half an hour of your arrival."

Though Elizabeth was startled at the assertion, which she immediately sensed was nothing less than a command, she said nothing. Instead, she followed and noted the locations of the various rooms.

The room to which Elizabeth was assigned was a handsome room, comfortable and bright, with a large four poster bed and light pastel wallpaper. The room overlooked the front drive and was situated across the hall from the suite which had been given to Anthony and Jane. Elizabeth suspected she was not considered as important as Lady Catherine's nephew, even if he now had an unfortunate wife. Their rooms looked out over the gardens, which must be more desirable, though the view of the trees across the lane more than made up for the lack of formal gardens, in Elizabeth's opinion.

Mindful of making a good impression on the great lady, Elizabeth hurried to wash away the dust of the road and don a new gown before meeting Anthony and Jane in the hallway outside their rooms. Then they made their way downstairs, the housekeeper once again meeting them, and guiding them to the sitting-room where Lady Catherine awaited them.

Elizabeth's first impression of Lady Catherine de Bourgh was that of a lady larger than life. She was tall when she stood from the high-backed chair, one which appeared suspiciously like a throne. She was dressed in costly fabrics which Elizabeth suspected would be far too warm if she wore them in the middle of summer's heat. Lady

Catherine was a woman possessing a strong jaw, piercing eyes, and a long and pointed nose, and while time had robbed her of what beauty she might have possessed, Elizabeth thought she would have been of striking looks, rather than a true beauty. By her side, standing from a sofa, was a young woman, perhaps two or three years Jane's elder, slight and dark of coloring, appearing cross at their entrance. She possessed no resemblance to Lady Catherine whatsoever, though Elizabeth was certain she knew of the woman's identity.

"You have arrived at last," said Lady Catherine, her voice high and piercing. "I expected you more than two hours gone."

"I am on my honeymoon, Lady Catherine," was Anthony's mild reply. "We traveled with no set plans, nothing which required our attendance or attention."

While it was clear she did not appreciate being contradicted, Lady Catherine only gave him a tight nod. Her attention was turned on Jane and Elizabeth, and she looked on them with a calculating gleam in her eye which spoke to her disapproval.

"I suppose this must be your new *wife* and her sister," said the lady shortly. It was not at all difficult to hear her emphasis on the word "wife," but Anthony, who had clearly known what form this introduction was to take, refrained from taking offense. Jane only stood stoically, while Elizabeth, who had expected much the same as Anthony, fought to hide a grin.

"You will introduce us, Anthony," said a testy Lady Catherine when Anthony did not immediately speak again.

"Of course, Aunt," replied Anthony. Taking Jane's hand and smiling at Elizabeth, motioning her forward, he said: "This is my wife, Jane Fitzwilliam. And traveling with us is her sister, Miss Elizabeth Bennet. Jane, Elizabeth, this is my aunt, Lady Catherine de Bourgh, and her daughter, Miss Anne de Bourgh."

The Bennet sisters curtseyed to their hostess, though Lady Catherine did nothing more than nod in response. Miss de Bourgh did nothing, choosing to remain silent and look on them with something akin to contempt.

"Let us sit together for a time," said Lady Catherine, indicating a sofa across from the one on which her daughter had again settled herself. "I shall call for tea. I wish to know more of you ladies, as we are now to be relations."

As good as her word, a tea service and some cakes were soon delivered, and the great lady began her interrogation. While Elizabeth might have laughed at an introduction being referred to in such terms, in this case, it was the best description.

Nothing was beneath Lady Catherine's notice, for she expertly drew the smallest details from the sisters, learning more about them than Elizabeth might have wished to disclose. Elizabeth could not help but consider the woman obnoxious and prying, though she bore it for Jane's sake. It was fortunate that her attention was more particularly focused on Jane, who was blessed with enough patience for ten young ladies. But Elizabeth was not to be ignored—not when the lady was determined to learn everything she could about them.

"You are still unattached," said Lady Catherine when she turned to Elizabeth.

"If you refer to the presence of a suitor or a gentleman caller, you are correct, your ladyship."

Lady Catherine looked Elizabeth up and down, her lips pursed, though whether it was with disapproval or deep thought, she could not say. "It would not be wise for you to remain in that state for long. What I know of your circumstances suggests you have not much with which to support yourself, should the worst happen, and I have it on good authority that the next master of your father's estate does not favor you."

"Mr. Collins has spoken of me?" asked Elizabeth, feeling a spike of annoyance for the odious parson.

"Yes, yes, he has," said Lady Catherine, waving Elizabeth's comment away. "That is neither here nor there, though I will own that you would not suit him. The important matter is your current state. Some young men of the neighborhood would find you irresistible, I should think, and for whom your lack of dowry would be no impediment. I should be happy to introduce you."

While Elizabeth was inclined to decline, she knew the lady would not be denied. It was better, then, to simply thank her ladyship.

"As for you, Mrs. Fitzwilliam," said Lady Catherine, turning back to Jane, "it is clear to me that you are a well-behaved, rational sort of woman, regardless of your unfortunate upbringing. When I originally heard of your marriage to my nephew, I worried lest your common origins stain the family name. I am relieved to discover that you are well able to conduct yourself in a manner befitting a Fitzwilliam."

Elizabeth did not know if she would have been able to withstand such an insulting speech as this. But then again, she was not Jane. Her sister, angel that she was, smiled at Lady Catherine and thanked her.

"I am happy I meet your approval, Lady Catherine," said Jane. "I would also be grateful for any advice you believe would assist me. I am not accustomed to the world my husband inhabits and am eager to be a credit to him."

There could be no response which could have done more to ensure Lady Catherine's approval. When Jane had finished speaking, the lady looked on her with a softer countenance, seeming to have come to favor Jane in the short time they had been in the room.

"You also show a willingness to learn, when I suspect many young women in your position would find my interest in you officious. I wish for nothing more than my nephew to be happy in his life, Mrs. Fitzwilliam, and it seems his happiness is bound up in you. I will not sport with your intelligence and try to convince you that I approved of this marriage. I did not.

"But it is clear to me that he has chosen as well as may be expected. Should you have questions or concerns about the society you will inhabit or your place within, I should be happy to assist. Now, do you play pianoforte Mrs. Fitzwilliam?"

"No, not at all," replied Jane, "for I found I had little aptitude for instruments. Lizzy plays, however, and we have often sung duets together."

Lady Catherine's sharp-eyed gaze fell upon Elizabeth, who wished her sister would not offer so much information. "Perhaps you may perform for us this evening, then. It is unfortunate you do not play, Mrs. Fitzwilliam, for it falls to a wife to entertain her husband's guests. But I suppose you must make do with what talents you have."

"We should be happy to," replied Jane.

Soon after, the sisters were released from the inquisition much to Elizabeth's relief. They returned to their rooms to rest for a time, and Elizabeth, not inclined to sleep, used the freedom from Lady Catherine to consider what she had seen and heard. The lady was much as she would have expected, given Anthony's account, though the reality was much larger than she might have thought. Fortunately, however, Elizabeth thought the lady's meddling questions would cease, for no one could continue on in such a manner for long.

Miss de Bourgh, however, was a quandary, and Elizabeth did not know what to make of her. The woman had been quiet throughout their stay in the sitting-room, though Elizabeth was certain she had heard everything which had been said. She seemed to affect a haughty demeanor, though Elizabeth did not know if it was because she disapproved of the sisters or if it was simply her character. In the end, she felt it did not matter — there was no reason to worry about Miss de Bourgh's opinion, after all.

When they were called for dinner, they were shown into Rosings' opulent dining room, and a large meal was served to them. While Elizabeth wondered if the three courses were a compliment to their arrival, she rather thought they dined like this at all times. Perhaps it could be considered wasteful, but she supposed the very rich could afford to be extravagant, and their servants would eat very well, indeed.

The after-dinner entertainment was provided as demanded, and while the pianoforte at which Elizabeth sat did not seem to have much use—the A directly below middle C was out of tune and clashed with the rest of the keys—it seemed like a fine instrument. There was, fortunately, a piece with which she and Jane were familiar, and they performed it as well as they ever had, in Elizabeth's opinion. While her playing was, as ever, indifferent, Jane's rich soprano rose over the room as if a veritable choir of angels sang, and blended with Elizabeth's contralto seamlessly. Lady Catherine listened without much reaction, but it was clear from Anthony's gleaming eyes that he was not insensible to his wife's performance.

When they had finished, Lady Catherine reserved the first right of response, as expected. "It seems you have some talent, Mrs. Fitzwilliam. Your voices blend beautifully, and I can hear you have sung together before."

"Indeed, we have, Lady Catherine," said Jane. "It is one of our favorite pastimes."

Lady Catherine nodded regally and turned to Elizabeth. "I do see some deficiency in your playing, Miss Bennet."

"And I own to it without disguise," replied Elizabeth cheerfully. Anthony's soft snort into his teacup spoke to his amusement, though Jane contented herself with a minute shake of her head. "But I have so many interests that I rarely take the time to practice."

"Practice, indeed, is what I suspect you require," said Lady Catherine thoughtfully. "Though I am sure hiring a master would not have gone amiss." Privately, Elizabeth agreed with her ladyship's assessment, though masters had been scarce in Hertfordshire, and the expense would not have allowed it for long. "Perhaps you should engage one for your sister while you are here and in town."

"I would be happy to do so if you know of one," replied Anthony.

"I would not wish you to go to such trouble on my account," protested Elizabeth.

"Nonsense," was Lady Catherine's dismissive reply. "It is clear you have some talent, and such talent should be nurtured. Even given your age, it should not be too late for you to improve. I should be happy to assist whenever you would like."

"Your ladyship also plays?"

"I do not," was Lady Catherine's short reply. "Though if I had ever learned, I should have stopped at nothing to become a true proficient. But I have an ear for music such as few possess and a taste which can only be of benefit to you."

While Elizabeth was ready to put this bit of boasting down to nothing more than hubris, she was surprised when the lady frowned at the instrument. "I suppose I must engage a man to tune my pianoforte, for I noticed the A was flat. I shall send to London on the morrow."

With that bit of surprising perception, she moved on to other topics. Elizabeth followed the conversation, so she would not look foolish and responded when spoken to, though she spent more of her time in thought. It seemed, at the very least, that Lady Catherine could read music, or she possessed, as she had claimed, a good ear for it. Perhaps the lady was not so very foolish after all. Elizabeth resolved to remain on her toes, as it would not do to insult the lady through carelessness.

The park in which Rosings sat was, Elizabeth was obliged to confess, as beautiful as Anthony had said. Early the next morning, Elizabeth broke her fast and determined to sample it, deprived of walking as she had been these past weeks. And she was not to be disappointed. These trees were unknown to her, unlike her old friends in Hertfordshire, but she felt as if she could come to know and love them as well as those in the vicinity of her home.

Furthermore, there was a delightful stream or two, as well as a hidden pond not far from the edge of the formal gardens. Elizabeth amused herself for a time, skipping stones on the water of the still mere, wondering what Lady Catherine would say if she knew Elizabeth possessed this particular accomplishment. No doubt she would rail at the unladylike pursuit and command Elizabeth to refrain.

A sense of peace fell over Elizabeth as she left the water and wandered the paths in the midst of the trees. She could imagine herself far from any civilization, at one with nature and all the glory and majesty it possessed. At ease, more than she could ever feel in the middle of a bustling city, Elizabeth wandered to her heart's content, perhaps staying out longer than she should and certainly longer than was her custom.

It was not to last, however, for in her wanderings she came across a person she had no desire to meet, though she supposed it was inevitable sooner or later. Not having any clear sense of direction yet, her footsteps took her through a tangle of woods on what she thought was the western edge of the estate, and when she emerged from the trees, she found herself far closer to the parsonage than she had expected. And it was just her luck that the house's master was nearby at that very moment.

"Miss Elizabeth Bennet!" cried he, his voice akin to the bleating of a sheep. "What are you doing here?"

Mindful of her manners, Elizabeth curtseyed, though Mr. Collins made no returning bow. "I am simply walking about the park, Mr. Collins. How do you do?"

The parson's gaze raked over her form with contemptuous dislike. "I know not how you have managed to impose yourself on Lady Catherine, but I will put it to rights. Or are you staying in some wretched hovel nearby in the hopes of ingratiating yourself on the great lady's notice?"

"Neither, I am sure," replied Elizabeth. "In fact, we are staying at Rosings   itself."

His jaw working in his anger, Mr. Collins said: "And by what right do you claim an acquaintance with Lady Catherine de Bourgh?"

"I am sure you must remember my sister's marriage, Mr. Collins," replied Elizabeth, already weary of the stupid man.

"Yes, I do remember the proposal very well." The sneer with which he regarded her might have been offensive if the man was not so very ineffectual. "I counseled Lady Catherine to intervene, but it seems Colonel Fitzwilliam was determined to connect himself to your family, despite your low origins. I suppose you must congratulate yourselves on your ability to capture a man as illustrious as he."

"I congratulate myself on nothing more than my sister's happiness," snapped Elizabeth.

"I know exactly what you are," hissed Mr. Collins, looming over her in an attempt to intimidate. "I understand your purpose here. It shall never be gratified. You may have taken advantage of Colonel Fitzwilliam and induced him to forget himself, but you shall not prey upon my patroness!"

"Excuse me, Mr. Collins," said Elizabeth with a curtsey. "I believe it is time I returned to the house."

Elizabeth's purpose was to be out of the vile parson's sight as soon as may be, for she knew she might speak words in anger that she might later regret. But it was all for naught, for Mr. Collins was not of a mind to allow the matter to rest. He followed her as she walked, his voice a continual buzz, threatening to overwhelm her composure. But Elizabeth bore it as best she could, knowing Mr. Collins was nothing more than an annoying gnat with much less influence than he thought.

Still, Elizabeth was grateful when the house, tall and sturdy, rose up before her, for she knew she would find refuge from this man, in her room if nothing else. Waiting for her on the steps, however, stood Anthony. He watched them approach, something of tightness about his eyes which Elizabeth knew was not for her. Mr. Collins had not noticed his presence and continued to berate her as she endeavored to escape.

"Do not think you can hide in your room," exclaimed he as they came close enough for Anthony to hear his words. "For I shall see to it that you are thrown from it in disgrace. Lady Catherine will not suffer you to pollute the very stones of Rosings when she hears what I have to say!"

"Mr. Collins!" Anthony's voice cracked like a whip, startling the parson to silence, blessed and golden. "What do you mean by accosting *my sister* in this manner? Have you no sense whatsoever?"

But Mr. Collins was not to be deterred from his self-righteous anger. "Colonel Fitzwilliam, your humble servant," said he with a low bow. "I assure you, sir, that you do not need to concern yourself for my unfortunate cousin. I have no notion of how she came to be here, but I shall speak with Lady Catherine and ensure she is returned to her home without delay."

"Are you witless, man?" demanded Anthony, causing Mr. Collins's jaw to fall wide open in his shock. "Can you not fathom that she has come to Rosings in *my* company?"

"In *your* company?" squeaked Mr. Collins.

"Of course, she has! If you were not so foolish, you might have realized that I am on my wedding tour and that Elizabeth has accompanied my wife and me. Do you think she came here on her own to impose upon my aunt?"

Rational response was apparently beyond Mr. Collins. "I will not tolerate you accosting my *sister*, Mr. Collins. From this point forward, I suggest you avoid her if you cannot act properly."

Mr. Collins could not bow low or quickly enough, though his sidelong glances at Elizabeth were still hateful. "Of course, of course. But how could I have known? I consider my cousin capable of anything which would improve her lot."

"You could have used whatever wit you possessed," said Anthony.

"Regardless, I believe we are done here. You may return to the parsonage now."

"I beg your pardon, Colonel," said Mr. Collins, "but I have come for my daily meeting with your lady aunt. I shall repair to the parlor directly."

With a final bow, Mr. Collins sidled away, fairly rushing up the stairs in his haste to escape them. Anthony did not miss a final glare at Elizabeth, which prompted him to scowl at the parson. That served the purpose of hastening him along. When Mr. Collins was gone, Anthony turned back to her.

"I assume he did nothing more than bore you to death with his stupid jabbering?"

"You are correct, Anthony. That was enough for me to wish for his absence, I assure you."

Anthony grunted. "If he should so much as lay a finger on you, I wish to know. I shall beat him within an inch of his life if he does."

"Thank you, Anthony," replied Elizabeth. "But I suspect that will not be necessary. He is stupid and apparently resentful, but I do not believe he is violent." Elizabeth paused and regarded the door through which the parson had just disappeared. "You know he will be spouting his poison in your aunt's ears."

"I do not doubt it," replied Anthony with a snort. "I will sort Lady Catherine if need be. I do not believe she will give credence to anything he says. Regardless of my aunt's seeming foolishness, she is a keen judge of character. She chose Mr. Collins for his willingness to do her bidding, but I do not believe she is insensible to his shortcomings."

Elizabeth hoped this to be so. She had no wish to defend herself before a woman as officious as Lady Catherine de Bourgh.

CHAPTER XXVI

$\mathcal{E}$ xpected though the call for her attendance might have been, Elizabeth was annoyed all the same. She had retreated to her room after arriving back at Rosings, even eschewing any kind of luncheon, not wishing to go to the dining room, nor to even test Lady Catherine's hospitality by requesting a tray to her room. At first, Elizabeth attempted to amuse herself with a book, but it was a fruitless exercise. Instead, she passed the time by exasperating herself against the stupidity of the parson.

For a moment after the summons arrived, Elizabeth considered the merits of refusing it. It was not Lady Catherine's business, and Elizabeth still had no more interest in discussing it with her ladyship than she had before. A moment's thought, however, induced her to reconsider. The lady would undoubtedly be unwilling to leave the matter be and would not be above seeking Elizabeth out in her room if necessary. Though she had done nothing wrong, Elizabeth was not certain how Lady Catherine would act. If she decided Elizabeth could not stay, she would be happy to return home, though she would miss Jane. With that thought in mind, Elizabeth splashed some cool water on her face, assured her hair and dress were presentable, and descended the stairs.

The servant had directed her toward the sitting-room in which Lady Catherine always held court, and it was to that room she repaired. As she drew close, the door opened and Mr. Collins stepped out. He favored her with a sneer, one which bespoke his smugness, and strode past her, forcing her to step adroitly to the side to avoid him. Elizabeth did not know they had an audience until Anthony's voice drew Mr. Collins up short.

"That is enough, Collins!" said he, his voice low and dangerous. "You may not appreciate my new sister, but I will not have you treating her with contempt."

"It is all she deserves," was Mr. Collins's reply, though the mopping of his forehead with the handkerchief produced from his pocket belied his seeming confident tone.

"Heed me well," said Anthony, his tone nothing less than a snarl. "If you touch her in any way, push her aside, or simply brush her in passing, I will take it out on your hide."

"I did nothing."

"No, but I can see the aggression inherent in your movements."

"Mr. Collins," the sound of Lady Catherine's voice rose from the sitting-room. "I will not have you accosting guests in my house. Our meeting is over—you may leave now."

"Yes, yes, of course, Lady Catherine," groveled Mr. Collins. He stepped back into the doorway to make his obeisance, but he must have been waved from the house, for he stood and walked down the hall, his stride clipped and angry. This time, however, he gave Elizabeth a wide berth.

"Miss Bennet," called Lady Catherine. "I require your attendance."

Though she shared a look with Anthony, Elizabeth did not hesitate to enter therein. Lady Catherine was sitting in her throne-like chair, watching her with gimlet eyes. But while Elizabeth had often thought the lady was silly, she had not the advantage of knowing her moods. Lady Catherine might have been equally likely to throw Elizabeth from the house as praise her for standing up to such an odious creature as William Collins.

"Your presence is not necessary, Anthony," said Lady Catherine, turning to her nephew. "I will speak with Miss Bennet alone."

"On the contrary, Aunt Catherine," said Anthony, "Elizabeth is under my protection while she is with me. There is no reason why I cannot be present."

"Do you think I mean to berate the girl?" demanded Lady Catherine. "I am not so foolish as to accept the words of my parson without reserve. I merely wish to speak with her and ascertain how much of what I was told was correct, and how much was the silliness of Mr. Collins. I cannot do so with you looming over us."

The way Lady Catherine spoke heartened Elizabeth. Thus, when Anthony turned a questioning glance on her, Elizabeth was able to agree to his aunt's request. Though he hesitated, Anthony eventually bowed to his aunt's wishes.

"Very well. But know this, Lady Catherine: if Elizabeth must leave because of the bitter ramblings of your vicious parson, we shall all depart."

Then without another word, Anthony turned and walked from the room. Lady Catherine, who was not accustomed to others having the last word, huffed as the door closed behind him. Then her gaze found Elizabeth.

"Sit beside me, Miss Bennet," said she, indicating the sofa on which they had sat the previous evening. "This is not an interrogation, nor are you a girl in school standing before the headmistress. I wish to speak with you, not obtain a pain in my neck."

Though saying nothing, Elizabeth sat as indicated. Then, straight-backed and attentive, Elizabeth looked to Lady Catherine to make her case.

"I will repeat what I said a moment ago: I do not mean to interrogate you nor do I accept Mr. Collins's words without verifying for myself that they are the truth. Mr. Collins has leveled some serious accusations against you, and while I am certain I know the reason for them, I would hear you speak of your history with him. If you will oblige me."

"Of course, Lady Catherine," replied Elizabeth. "What would you like to know?"

"I wish to know what happened in Hertfordshire between you, for Mr. Collins has not been forthcoming, other than the fact that you refused his proposal."

"If you can call it that," muttered Elizabeth.

Lady Catherine's keen gaze made Elizabeth uncomfortable. "That is exactly my point. According to Mr. Collins, he made you an offer in good faith, and you spurned him most cruelly. Furthermore, he suggests you are a temptress, luring men into your clutches with your wiles. I know his silliness is without bounds. Therefore, would you be so good as to relate the matter to me in full?"

In truth, Elizabeth would have preferred to do almost anything else, but she was again reminded that Lady Catherine was not about to allow the matter to rest. As such, she obliged, informing her ladyship of the entire affair, from Mr. Collins's arrival and subsequent departure, and then his return and what happened the day of Anthony's proposal to Jane. She did not stint in relating the whole of the matter, including the disagreement which led to even Mrs. Bennet declaring him an unfit candidate to marry her daughter. Through it all, Lady Catherine listened carefully, interjecting a question or two to clarify certain points, but mostly refrained from commenting.

When Elizabeth had finished speaking, Lady Catherine was quiet for a few moments. Then she sighed and shook her head, looking on Elizabeth with a softer expression than Elizabeth had hitherto seen from her.

"I suppose I must give you the benefit of sagacity, Miss Bennet. It is clear Mr. Collins would not have suited you, though I will assert that *you* would have been the making of *him*."

Elizabeth did not deign to respond to that statement. She could not have been the making of him if she had strangled him in his sleep before they were even past the honeymoon!

"You cannot fail to understand that I would have wished for more than your sister for my nephew." When Elizabeth steeled herself to respond, Lady Catherine continued, saying: "But I have already informed you that I approve of your sister, after a fashion. In every particular, except connections and fortune, she is the perfect wife for Fitzwilliam, and I cannot blame him for acting to secure his happiness.

"While I encourage my subordinates to defend my interests, Mr. Collins has proven himself to be . . . Well, he is overzealous, to say the least. It was not his place to question my nephew, and I can see why your mother and father became offended."

"Then you do not blame me for refusing him?" asked Elizabeth, feeling relieved at the manner in which this interview was proceeding.

"It was, perhaps, imprudent of you," said Lady Catherine, seeming to lack the ability to let anything go without some sort of criticism. "If your father should pass on, you would find yourself in unenviable circumstances, and you must know that Fitzwilliam's wealth is not extensive, despite his possession of an estate."

Elizabeth allowed it to be so, but she did not speak further. She sensed Lady Catherine wished to have her say and would not take kindly to overt interruption.

"Yes, he can support you, but to take on the support of a mother-in-law and four sisters would be burdensome. But I can see how you would find Mr. Collins's company irksome. I possess a greater well of patience than most, and yet I cannot but agree."

With a sigh, Lady Catherine sat back in her chair, giving all the appearance of brooding. "When I sent Mr. Collins to your father's house, I had hoped he would find in one of you a woman who was clever, and who would endure his silliness for the sake of a home of her own. I know not of your sisters, but it is clear you do not possess the temperament to long endure him as a husband. It is unfortunate, indeed, for left to his own devices, Mr. Collins is a disaster waiting to happen. There is a reason I direct him in everything he does, Miss Bennet, for he would make a mess of everything if I did not. I had hoped I could hand that responsibility to his wife."

"I understand he has married," ventured Elizabeth. This conversation was not proceeding in a manner which she might have expected, and she almost wanted to pinch herself to ensure she was awake.

"That is not a welcome development," was Lady Catherine's caustic reply. "The woman he married was the one from whom I was hoping to detach him. Mrs. Althea Collins is not a sensible woman, and a marriage in which neither partner possesses the sense God gave a sow cannot but be a disaster for all involved.

"They appear to be happy together," said Lady Catherine, waving Elizabeth's grin away. "I suppose that is something, for I doubt Mr. Collins would have been happy with you, once he realized how much more intelligent you are. But the new Mrs. Collins is as foolish as my parson. She did possess some little dowry and is the daughter of a gentleman, which gives him connections to the gentry outside of your father. But I have had to take twice as much care with him."

"I apologize, Lady Catherine," said Elizabeth, unable to keep a hint of irony from her tone. "I had no idea I was causing you so much trouble by refusing my witless cousin. Next time, I shall consider the matter with greater care."

Lady Catherine actually laughed at Elizabeth's words, though she turned a stern eye on her thereafter. "You are possessed of an acerbic sense of humor, Miss Bennet, and you are not intimidated. That will serve you well when you join your sister in London. But you do not need to be that way with me, though I am happy to see you are not one of those simpering females who agrees with everything I say."

"I would not dream of it, Lady Catherine," said Elizabeth, saying nothing more than the truth.

"Very well, then. You may go and inform Fitzwilliam that you are entirely unscathed by our tête-à-tête. If Mr. Collins should give you any difficulty, refer him to me. I shall set him straight."

Thanking Lady Catherine, Elizabeth rose and curtseyed, departing from the room. She had not gone more than five steps from it, however, when she was waylaid by Anthony.

"Well?" asked he. "Are you to meet Lady Catherine on the field at dawn?"

Elizabeth could not help but laugh, especially as the tension of the morning with Mr. Collins, followed by Lady Catherine's inquiry, demanded a release. Pleased as she was by Anthony's protectiveness, Elizabeth smiled and laid a hand on his arm.

"No, indeed. I explained exactly what happened at Longbourn, and your aunt took my side in the matter. She is not insensible to his foolishness."

"To be insensible of it, one would have to be as foolish as he," replied Anthony. "But I am grateful nonetheless. You will inform me if he becomes bothersome?"

"I think I shall instead inform your aunt. Her method of dealing with him is likely to be less painful."

Anthony barked a laugh. "Very well. I shall leave it to you."

"We are to go into Kent by Friday," said Bingley. "I must own, my friend, that I am anticipating the form your aunt's welcome will take."

Darcy grimaced and sipped from his glass and looked about the room. The club that day was sparsely inhabited; few with whom Darcy could claim an acquaintance were present, and no close friends. It was better that way, for he was not in a sociable mood.

"I am not certain I would anticipate if I were you, Bingley. Lady Catherine has never been known for her tact, and she is not shy about sharing her opinions. I cannot think she will be any different in this instance."

"What can she do?" asked Bingley rhetorically. "My marriage to your sister has been solemnized and is more than half a year of existence. She can bluster and complain, but she cannot separate us. And I am not afraid of Lady Catherine's displeasure."

"No, it is not something to be feared," replied Darcy. "Avoided, yes." At Bingley's look, Darcy shook his head. "Yes, I understand that you must be introduced to her at some time or another. But if I were you, I would wish for the pleasure to be postponed as long as possible."

Bingley laughed, an infectious sound which brought Darcy along with a few amused chuckles of his own. "Then I shall count on you and Fitzwilliam to protect me from the sharp edge of her scorn. I am assured she will be too intent upon seeing you married to her daughter to devote too much attention to me."

His glass raised to his lips once again hid Darcy's grimace. In fact, he had every intention of begging off going to Rosings this year. Lady Catherine would be upset, he knew. But better she was upset by his absence than his refusal to marry Anne.

It was unfortunate that Bingley chose that moment to be observant. "You *will* go to Rosings, correct?"

"Actually," replied Darcy, knowing he had best speak of it openly now, "I had considered sending my regrets and staying here this year."

"Because you are so fond of society?" asked Bingley, a sardonic edge in his voice. "Are you so set upon finding a mistress for your estate this year that you would willingly put up with the attention of the masses of young ladies?

"Of course, you are not," said Bingley, answering his own question. "For I am quite familiar with your ways, my friend, and I know you have all but abandoned hope of finding a wife this year."

Darcy pulled a face at Bingley's description, but he knew it was no less than the truth. His participation at the beginning of the season, while more than his usual custom, had waned in recent weeks, and now he attended the various soirees infrequently and danced even less. The rumors which had sprung up upon his unusual engagement in the season had tapered off as well, and he had caught many a matchmaking mother regarding him with sad discouragement.

"Come, my friend," said Bingley, drawing Darcy's attention back from his morose thoughts. "Your aunt cannot be all that bad, especially when compared with the masses of insipid young debutantes, all eager to become the next mistress of Pemberley. Do say you will go to Rosings with us. I would appreciate your support, and I know Georgiana would as well."

A grunt was Darcy's response, for he was annoyed with Bingley for not fighting fair. Bringing his sister into the conversation, knowing that Darcy would do anything for his dearest sister, was unfair to say the least. Bingley knew when to refrain from pushing him, thankfully, for he did not press Darcy on the matter again.

Soon, their time together had elapsed, and Bingley rose, stating his intention of returning to his home, inviting Darcy to go with him. "I am sure Georgiana would love to see you, for it has been several days."

Though it was against his better judgment, Darcy agreed, though he knew it would be best to return to his house and his own sour mood.

But being among those he loved most was a powerful lure. It would not ease the sense of ennui and restlessness under which he had existed all spring. But it would not do him any harm either.

The state of affairs in which he existed was to be laid at Miss Elizabeth Bennet's feet, thought Darcy as they boarded Darcy's carriage for the ride to Bingley's townhouse. Bingley spoke as was his custom, making observances concerning the state of the roads, or of some people they passed with whom he was acquainted. Darcy paid him little heed, outside of a periodic response to give the impression he was attending Bingley's words.

The blasted woman had rarely left his mind since her departure from London, and Darcy was heartily tired of it. The matter of whether she and her family were nothing but fortune hunters was pushed to the side, and now all Darcy thought about was having her in his life. She attracted him far more now when he had not seen her in more than a month than she ever had when she had been before him. It was unfathomable how this had happened. But it had, and Darcy had not been able to remove her from his thoughts.

"Why this sudden desire to avoid your aunt?"

Surprised by Bingley's change in subject, Darcy could only gape at him for a moment. Then he shook his head, annoyed all over again by Bingley's inability to allow the matter to rest.

"As you know, my aunt has been insistent about my supposed betrothal to my cousin Anne, and every year she becomes more strident. I have no desire to withstand her constant comments on the subject."

"I can understand why that would be difficult to ignore," replied Bingley. "I apologize for jesting about it before."

Darcy waved his apology away. "It is nothing, Bingley. Do not concern yourself."

"Then I shall not importune you on the subject again. I hope you reconsider, but I understand if you do not."

It was a relief to hear his friend speak in such a manner, and Darcy thanked him. Soon they arrived at Bingley's house. They went inside and doffed their coats, handing them to the butler. Mrs. Bingley was in the sitting-room with Miss Bingley and her suitor, Mr. Powell. The gentlemen entered and greeted them, receiving a warm welcome in response.

Powell seemed like a good man in essentials, though Darcy was not at all well acquainted with him. He was quiet and thoughtful, possessed of a handsome estate in Bedfordshire, and was not encumbered in any way, being his own master. In this matter, he was much like Darcy himself. Why a man such as he would wish to pay his addresses to a woman like Miss Bingley was beyond Darcy's understanding.

For Miss Bingley's part, she only nodded at Darcy and turned away, which was likely for the better. The woman had learned through experience that her suitor did not appreciate her deference to another man. For Miss Bingley, it was likely nothing more than the force of habit. But it was best for her to refrain from paying him any attention at all when Powell was present.

"William!" exclaimed Georgiana. "I am happy you have come! I had hoped Charles would invite you around for dinner tonight, for we have seen little of you of late."

"Bingley did not mention anything about dinner," said Darcy. When his sister appeared a little crestfallen, he hastened to add: "But I have no plans for this evening, and would be happy to stay."

"I am happy to hear it," was Georgiana's warm reply. "Now, there was another matter of which I wished to speak. For, as you know, we are to go to Rosings by Friday, and we must make the arrangements. Charity is also to accompany us."

Surprised, Darcy looked to Bingley, noting his friend's slightly smug expression. And in that instant, he knew what Bingley had been planning. Since he was unable to persuade Darcy to go to Rosings, he had, indeed, left it up to his wife. Georgiana, not knowing Darcy had thought to demur, treated it as if it was an established fact, and if he wished to stay behind, Darcy was forced to speak to his sister and disappoint her.

Far from being annoyed, however, Darcy was amused. And in that moment he decided that Rosings would not be terrible this year, not with so many in residence to distract Lady Catherine away from him. Perhaps it would do him some good to get out of the city and spend time in the country.

"Brother," said Miss Bingley, "can I assume Louisa and Hurst will arrive before you are to depart?"

"According to his last letter, he should be here by Wednesday. That should give you enough time to be settled in his house before we leave for Kent."

Miss Bingley nodded, but her attention was on Darcy. He could almost see the way her mind worked, as she thought for a moment on whether she should speak. In the end, she did so, not that Darcy was shocked that her sense of prudence had not prevailed.

"You seem reluctant to go into Kent, sir. If you prefer, I am certain we would be happy for your continued presence in town."

The woman was nothing if not predictable. Darcy was certain Miss Bingley still clung to her opinion about Darcy's vulnerability to the charms of Miss Bennet. That she would attempt to keep him here and away from Miss Bennet spoke to her pride.

"On the contrary, Miss Bingley," said Darcy, speaking before his sister or brother could, "I go into Kent every year. This year is no different from any other. I shall accompany you on Friday, Bingley."

"Excellent!" exclaimed Bingley. "I am sure we shall be a merry party, indeed!"

"I am sure we shall," added Georgiana. "Not only will Charity accompany us, but Miss Bennet and Mrs. Fitzwilliam will also be present. I cannot wait to see them again!"

While Miss Bingley grimaced at the mention of the Bennet ladies and regarded him, a half frown adorning her face, in the end, she did not speak. It was a wise choice, as Darcy would have no compunction in reminding her to mind her own concerns if she did.

However, she did not refrain from shooting him a meaningful glance, which Darcy felt himself at liberty to ignore. It was of no concern to Miss Bingley whom he married, even if he chose so unsuitable a bride as Miss Bennet. Let Miss Bingley feel insulted at the thought of him choosing what she considered to be an inferior woman. Though he had been unable to shake her from his thoughts, Darcy knew he was in no danger from the likes of Miss Elizabeth Bennet.

CHAPTER XXVII

*I*t came as no surprise that Mr. Collins was heartily displeased with the result of his complaint to Lady Catherine. Though Elizabeth had not set out to observe him the following day when he came for what she now knew was a daily meeting, fate sometimes intervenes. Thus, she happened to be walking toward the library at Rosings the following morning when the man departed.

The sight of her caused his lip to curl in a sneer, and his stance to become more rigid. But he said not a word, instead marching past her with nary a second glance, his shoes echoing on the tiles until the sound of the door closing behind him reached her ears.

"It seems Mr. Collins has been put in his place."

Elizabeth turned to the sight of her sister watching the departure of the parson, a frown like Elizabeth had rarely seen following Mr. Collins's retreat. A moment later, Jane turned her attention back to Elizabeth.

"He did not brush past you like he attempted to do yesterday, did he?"

The only thing Elizabeth could do was laugh, though she also captured Jane's hand in her own and gave it an affectionate squeeze. "Indeed, he did not. If I did not know better, I might have suspected he thinks I carry the plague."

"If there is anyone who is plague-ridden, it is Mr. Collins," muttered Jane.

Utterly surprised at her sister's words, Elizabeth gaped at her. Jane's response was to shake her head and glare at Elizabeth.

"I know I attempt to see the best in others, Lizzy, but that does not extend to loathsome parsons who attack my dearest sister."

"Thank you for your care, Jane," said Elizabeth, brushing her lips against her sister's cheek. "With a sister like you, I shall not fear anything he can do. I dare say Lady Catherine has put him in his place, and he shall not trouble me again."

"I sincerely hope not, Lizzy. I shall speak to my husband if he does, and I have no doubt Mr. Collins will regret it should Anthony become involved."

With a chuckle, Elizabeth squeezed her sister's hand again. "Then I shall not concern myself."

The sisters went their separate ways then, Elizabeth to the library, while she suspected Jane went in search of her husband. Though Lady Catherine said nothing, Elizabeth knew enough of the lady by now to understand her feelings on the matter. Mr. Collins did not come the next day, and Elizabeth could only assume it was in punishment for his behavior. When he did arrive at the estate the following day, his servility was beyond even what Elizabeth had witnessed from him before. That he ignored Elizabeth completely was a matter of supreme indifference and maybe even a hint of relief.

Being, as she was, once more in the country, Elizabeth once again took up her habit of walking almost daily. While Rosings was not her beloved home, Elizabeth was well able to confess the beauty of the grounds. While much of the estate was, of course, devoted to the fields which provided its wealth, there was a slightly hilly section behind the manor which had been left to nature's sway. Within, Elizabeth found many pleasures, including a wide avenue perfect for walking or riding, trees of many varieties, a beautiful meadow teeming with wildflowers, and the pond she had discovered the day after her arrival. The last became her favorite place, for she would often take a book and sit there reading in the tranquility of the scene.

"I see you have discovered our hidden retreat," said Anthony in greeting only a day or two after the confrontation with Mr. Collins. He was walking with Jane on his arm, his voice having pulled Elizabeth from her book. Jane stepped forward and embraced Elizabeth while Anthony looked on with pleasure.

"Hidden retreat?" asked Elizabeth. "Though it is not easily seen through the woods, it was not at all difficult to find."

Anthony chuckled and shook his head. "No, I suppose it is not. But the casual walker would pass by and not even note its existence."

"I am not a casual walker."

"No, you are not, Lizzy," said Jane.

With a grin, Anthony sat his wife on the bench next to Elizabeth. "When Darcy and I were children, we would often play near — or in — this pond. At times, we imagined we were pirates and this our secret island where we would hide our gold from rival pirates."

"Is there still treasure buried hereabouts?" asked Elizabeth, looking about with interest. "Or has a rival crew carried it all off in your absence?"

"I suspect there is little left," replied Anthony. "We hid some things of value to only a child in certain places, but most of that was dug up when we returned home. I do recall that we were never able to find one of Darcy's soldiers, so if you wish to have a turn trying to discover it, by all means."

"No, Anthony," said Elizabeth, shooting him a grin. "It is best to leave a buried treasure strictly alone. One never knows how it may be cursed."

"Aye," replied Anthony. "It would be a shame, indeed, if one ran afoul of the protections we cast over our treasures."

At times, Elizabeth did see Jane and Anthony on the paths of Rosings, but Jane was not the walker Elizabeth was, and they often did not range far from the house. And while Elizabeth knew Anthony was a consummate horseman, he rarely rode out, apparently preferring to be with his wife. Elizabeth was pleased with his obvious devotion.

But there was another who did not seem to appreciate Elizabeth's predilection for walking. She was also not shy about sharing her opinion.

"You walk out daily, do you?" asked Lady Catherine one morning when Elizabeth returned to the estate.

"Whenever I can manage it, Lady Catherine," replied Elizabeth. "It is a favorite activity of mine, and it is very beneficial exercise."

"I prefer to obtain my exercise in driving my phaeton," said Miss de Bourgh. It was one of the few times the woman had spoken, and it took no greatness of mind to discern that she felt all the superiority of her position and her elevated manner of obtaining her freedom. Anthony's snort suggested he had much the same opinion as Elizabeth of Miss de Bourgh's manner of *exercising*, but he did not say anything.

"Yes, it is beneficial exercise," said Lady Catherine, ignoring her daughter. "I have often informed Mr. Collins that to walk more often would be beneficial for him as well."

Elizabeth could well imagine it, as she could see him taking his patroness's advice as a command, which he had been likely doing when he had met her that first day. And it would almost certainly do him good, considering his portly frame.

"But for a young lady, it borders on unseemly. There may be unsavory characters about, and you would be entirely unprotected."

Restraining a laugh which threatened to break forth, Elizabeth said: "But this is a highly civilized part of the country, is it not? I have walked about my father's estate for many years and never experienced difficulty. And I do so enjoy it."

It appeared Elizabeth's words had done enough to mollify Lady Catherine, though it was equally clear she still did not like it. At least her primary concern was for Elizabeth's safety.

"I shall inform the groundskeepers to look out for you," said Lady Catherine at length. "Should you require it, simply ask the butler for a footman to accompany you, and one will be made available."

"Thank you, Lady Catherine," said Elizabeth with more warmth than she would have thought she could ever possess for this woman. "Should the need arise, I will be certain to do so."

The longer Elizabeth remained at Rosings, the more she began to feel she had managed to create something of a rapport with Lady Catherine. The woman was as overbearing as ever, prying into matters which were not her concern and dispensing advice when it was least likely to be wanted. But she was solicitous of their comfort, to Elizabeth's surprise, and it soon became clear that she was not without sense, as Elizabeth had initially thought. For chasing Mr. Collins away alone, she would have Elizabeth's gratitude.

The same could not be said of Miss Anne de Bourgh. The woman was not precisely unkind, but it was clear she felt high and mighty, for she had little to say to the Bennet sisters and Elizabeth in particular. As she had averred, she was often to be found upon her phaeton, driving the paths nearby Rosings, to Hunsford (though she never called at the parsonage that Elizabeth had heard) and along the paths of the estate which could support her conveyance. The few times she had seen Elizabeth, she had barely deigned to nod her head in greeting, let alone stop and speak. That suited Elizabeth well, for she had no real wish to speak to the haughty woman.

One day while Elizabeth was walking—which was, incidentally, the day before the Bingleys were to arrive at the estate—Elizabeth saw a curious thing. For she noted Miss de Bourgh in the distance, but it seemed she had stopped to speak to someone. Though too far away to make out who it was, Elizabeth knew it was a gentleman, for he doffed his hat and they spoke for several moments. Then the man bowed and departed, allowing Miss de Bourgh to continue on her way. On this occasion, however, Miss de Bourgh stopped when she came near and looked down in her usually superior manner.

"Miss Bennet," said she, a slightly sneering quality in her greeting. "I see you are once again out *walking*."

"Indeed, I am," replied Elizabeth without any hint of rancor. There was little point in it, after all. "I see you met someone you know. I understand we are to receive visitors today. Perhaps he will be among the company?"

"No, I dare say he will not. I often meet in passing those who live nearby and claim an acquaintance with the de Bourghs. But there are those who are particular about those with whom they associate."

Elizabeth stifled a grin, for it took little insight to discern to whom Anne was referring. The conversation ended there, for Anne inclined her head slightly—an action which Elizabeth returned—and drove off. Elizabeth did not even watch her go, so indifferent was she.

The expected visitors came to tea that afternoon, and as it was the first of Lady Catherine's neighbors whom she was to meet, Elizabeth was interested to see what kind of friends she could boast. The first was a brother and sister from a neighboring estate called Stauneton Hall, James and Elia Baker. James was tall and handsome, not to mention a bit of a rake, while Elia was kind and intelligent, yet a little quiet. She was also engaged to a Mr. Norland who was part of the second family who came to visit. They consisted of the aforementioned Mr. Norland, his parents, and two younger sisters—Abigail, who was Elizabeth's age, and Alexandra, who was two years younger. It was around Elizabeth and Jane the young ladies congregated, though again Miss de Bourgh remained aloof.

"You are from Hertfordshire?" asked Miss Baker, a kindly smile on her face.

"Yes," replied Elizabeth. "Jane is recently married to Colonel Fitzwilliam."

"Ah, so you are the one who swooped in and broke my sister's heart," said Miss Alexandra, with a sly smile at her sister. "Abigail has been smitten by him for quite some time, you know."

The intended tease had little effect, for Miss Norland only smirked at her sister. "I am entirely uninjured by the colonel's defection, Alexandra, though I will own that he is a handsome man. But there is another handsome man who usually comes to Rosings at this time of year, and I am sure my sister would give anything to be mistress of *his* estate."

With a shocked gasp, Miss Alexandra swatted at her sister, who laughed at her expense. Miss Baker gazed fondly at them, saying: "Though I will own I am quite biased toward your dear brother, even I can own Mr. Darcy is as handsome a man as I have ever seen."

"But he is to marry Miss de Bourgh," said Miss Alexandra, lowering her voice for only their small group to hear. "Lady Catherine can be ever so stern—I would never presume to try to capture Mr. Darcy, though I would not refuse him should he pay his addresses to me."

"Yes, that is probably best," said her sister. "But he has had many years to come to the point, and yet he has not seen fit to propose. That must give a woman a bit of hope, must it not?"

They all laughed together. Then Miss Norland turned her teasing on Elizabeth. "What of you, Miss Bennet? You would seem to have as great a chance as anyone, given your sister's marriage to Colonel Fitzwilliam."

Elizabeth shook her head, amused that she should be pulled into this debate. "I do not think Mr. Darcy and I suit, Miss Norland. It shall not be I who stands in the way of you or your sister."

The blush which spread over Miss Norland's face told Elizabeth she had guessed correctly, though the elder sister was a little more prepossessed than the younger. Miss Norland proved this by not protesting—instead she changed the subject.

"I hope we shall see much of you here, Miss Bennet, Mrs. Fitzwilliam. It has become rather dull of late."

"Do you usually go to town for the season?" asked Elizabeth.

"We do, and we have been there until recently," replied Miss Alexandra. "But our time was cut short this year because my mother wished to return home to help prepare for the wedding." She turned and smiled at Miss Baker. "Since Miss Baker's parents have passed on, Mama will be hosting the wedding breakfast."

"And when are your nuptials?"

"We will marry in July," replied Miss Baker.

"Then I offer my congratulations. You are fortunate, indeed, to find the one man to whom you wish to bind your life. I can only hope the rest of us are so fortunate."

They continued to banter in this friendly manner, and by the time the visitors departed, Elizabeth was referring to the young ladies with their Christian names. Mr. Baker, however, was another matter. He did not approach and speak with Elizabeth, but she often caught his attention on her, and she wondered at his purpose. In the end, she decided she did not need to concern herself, for he went away without opening his mouth.

As had been their design, the Bingleys, with Mr. Darcy and Charity, arrived the following day. They were greeted with Lady Catherine's brand of demanding welcome that she displayed the day Elizabeth had arrived with the Fitzwilliams. In particular, Elizabeth was pleased to be reunited with Charity and Georgiana. The newly arrived were assigned their rooms and retired there to refresh themselves. But Lady Catherine, of course, required their attendance as soon as they were settled, which was far sooner than Elizabeth suspected any of the travelers would have preferred. But the initial visit did not proceed like Elizabeth might have imagined.

"Darcy!" exclaimed Lady Catherine when her nephew entered the room. "Come and sit with me, next to Anne, for we have missed your presence these past months."

It seemed to Elizabeth that Mr. Darcy had expected this, though he also appeared to wish he was anywhere else. Still, he did his duty and sat in the indicated position, after which Lady Catherine looked up and directed the rest of the company to sit. Mr. Bingley, who had been introduced when they had entered, was not treated to the same interrogations she had leveled at Jane and Elizabeth. Rather, she focused all her energies on Mr. Darcy.

"It was well that you have come, Darcy, for there are a few matters of the estate which require your attention."

"As always, I am happy to assist," was Mr. Darcy's rather unenthusiastic reply.

"Of course, you are, Darcy. I know of your attachment to Rosings and to Anne and me, in particular. We so anticipate your coming."

Lady Catherine's significant glance at her daughter was missed by no one. Mr. Darcy did not say anything and Miss de Bourgh appeared as caught in the grips of ennui as usual. But Anthony grinned behind his teacup, as did Charity, while Georgiana only gave her head a minute shake in her exasperation.

"Does Anne not look exquisite this year, Darcy?" asked Lady Catherine. Then, not waiting for a response, she said: "Of course, she does, for I know how you dote upon her. While she will never be robust, I dare say her health this year is as good as it has ever been. I declare that she is ready to be mistress of her own home, for I have taught her everything she will need to know to be a credit to any man."

"I am certain you have," muttered Mr. Darcy.

But Lady Catherine appeared to take no notice. "A spring wedding is a lovely affair, is it not? Mr. Norland will wait until the heat of July to take Miss Baker to wife, an inconvenient time for a wedding, to say the least. I tried to inform Mrs. Norland of this fact, but she paid no notice to me. I suppose there is nothing to be done. But to be married in the spring would be exquisite. Do you not agree?"

"I suppose it would depend on the principals involved," replied Mr. Darcy. "If the affianced favor a spring wedding, I dare say it is the best season to be married."

The snickers which sounded throughout the room were a testament to the humor inherent in Mr. Darcy's dry reply. Lady Catherine eyed him, as if not quite certain what he was trying to say. It was at this time, of course, that she dropped all pretense.

"I believe this is the year you must finally put aside your procrastination and propose to Anne, Darcy. As you know, it was the favorite wish of myself and your dear departed mother. We planned the union while you were in your cradles. And while she is not here to see the fruition of our dream, I am determined to see it done in her stead."

While Elizabeth would have thought such a brazen statement would prompt a response from Mr. Darcy, he did nothing more than shake his head minutely, his mouth set in a grim line. Fortunately, Lady Catherine did not seem to require a response. She continued to speak on the subject for some time, expounding with some detail about the plans she and Mrs. Darcy had made, how they had planned it should come about, and even some of the details of the wedding breakfast, which she would plan herself, of course.

Mr. Darcy seemed to understand that protestation was futile. Elizabeth wondered about it, however, for she knew that such constant harping must soon break the man's composure. But Mr. Darcy stayed quiet, stoically enduring that which he could not change. She was not even certain he listened at all, for he seemed to be considering some other matter deeply.

"Elizabeth," said Charity quietly from her side. When Elizabeth turned to her, she grinned. "I seem to remember you suggesting that some members of your family possessed a flair for the ridiculous. Behold the absurdity in the Fitzwilliam family!"

While attempting to stifle a giggle, Elizabeth managed to say: "She *is* quite determined, is she not?"

"Oh, yes. Not that it will do her any good at all. Darcy is as immovable as a mountain and stubborn as the day is long. Nothing is more guaranteed to provoke that state than Lady Catherine's insistence that he marry Anne."

"Do you know how much of Lady Catherine's assertions are grounded in truth?"

Charity grinned. "Are you accusing my aunt of telling falsehoods?"

At Elizabeth's protests, Charity laughed and told her: "It is a fair question. The truth is that nobody knows. Lady Catherine insists on it, but neither of Darcy's parents ever spoke to him about it. The most likely explanation seems to be that Lady Catherine spoke of it and Lady Anne, not accustomed to standing up to her strong-willed sister, agreed for the sake of harmony."

"I do not blame Mr. Darcy for not wishing to fall in with his aunt's designs," replied Elizabeth. "I should not wish to have my husband chosen for me."

"Then it is fortunate you were born into the situation you were. The Fitzwilliam family have generally been unfashionable in allowing their scions to marry where they please, but few other families do likewise."

"I suppose I *am* fortunate, though if I had been born to such a family, I might have taken the simple expedient of running away."

Charity laughed. "I might have suspected you of it.

"As for the present subject," said Charity, nodding in Lady Catherine's direction, "she will speak of little else all evening. But on the morrow, the subject will be largely forgotten, as she will have had her say. Then, as we approach the time of our departure, it will become a subject of discussion again."

The rest of the evening was punctuated by Lady Catherine's continual speaking, for while she pronounced and instructed as was her wont, she also spent a considerable amount of time pontificating on the subject of Mr. Darcy and Miss de Bourgh. Miss de Bourgh, for her part, remained unmoved and seemingly bored. Mr. Darcy, gave the appearance of listening, though it was clear to Elizabeth that his thoughts were in actuality miles away.

All of this might have remained an unremarkable bit of family intrigue had she not happened to witness Lady Catherine's brief moment of annoyance. As she was pontificating, she made some observation, one which required a response. The unfortunate part was that she did not receive one from Mr. Darcy, who may as easily have been considering the price of grain as his aunt's comments. Lady Catherine, who was forced to repeat herself, looked on him with annoyance when she restated her observation. And then when Mr. Darcy replied, she watched him for a moment before shrugging and picking up where she left off after he finished speaking.

Perhaps Lady Catherine was not as oblivious as she often appeared. Elizabeth was not certain. But the thought entered her mind that Lady Catherine was speaking out of the hope of inducing them to fall in with her plans, but not the expectation. It was a habit and nothing more.

But she decided she would not make this observation to anyone of the lady's family. She could not be certain of it, and she thought Anthony and Charity would see it as some particularly diverting joke. By now Elizabeth was, in an odd sort of way, fond of the older lady, and she did not wish to open her to ridicule.

CHAPTER XXVIII

Once Lady Catherine had satisfied herself in speaking of the supposed betrothal, she turned her attention to the Bingleys. Or at least that was how it seemed. The next morning they breakfasted, went their sundry ways according to their own respective interests, and nothing was said on the matter. That all changed when they gathered together that afternoon in Lady Catherine's sitting-room.

"Now, then, Georgiana my dear," said she, beckoning her young niece to her. "Come and sit with me, and your husband too, for we have not yet become acquainted."

Georgiana, it appeared, considered the invitation to sit nearby her aunt to be tantamount to a date at the gallows. Mr. Bingley, however, was cheerful as ever, directing her there without hesitation or any hint of concern. It seemed to garner Lady Catherine's approval, for she gave him a tight nod before beginning to speak. And one thing Elizabeth had learned about her hostess was that she possessed very little tact and seemed to consider it a quality much to be despised.

"I wish to learn more of you and your situation, Mr. Bingley. As I informed Fitzwilliam and his wife, she was not what the family might have wished for my nephew, though it appears he has made a good choice outside the considerations of fortune and connections. But at least *she* is the daughter of a gentleman. I understand your background is very different."

Elizabeth doubted many men could withstand such an opening without becoming offended. And while many of the family looked on with shaken heads and sighs of exasperation, Mr. Darcy appeared to be the one who seemed ready to burst. But Mr. Bingley was not one of those men, and his response diffused much of the tension Lady Catherine's one statement had produced.

"I dare say Mrs. Fitzwilliam *is* the daughter of a gentleman and a fine woman she is. I cannot imagine anyone would disapprove of her.

"As for myself, you are correct, Lady Catherine, for I am not the son of a gentleman, though I aspire to that state. Darcy and your brother have been assisting me, and I hope I shall purchase an estate before long."

The slow nod with which Lady Catherine favored him suggested she was at least a little mollified by his words. That did not stop the questions, however. "It is well that you are conscious about such things, for the credit of my niece, our very respectability will be put into question by your status. Of course, being connected to the families Fitzwilliam, Darcy, and de Bourgh will assist in raising your status. But come, tell me of yourself."

"My father was the head of our family shipping concerns," said Mr. Bingley. "His business was inherited from his father, back to the time of my great-grandfather, who established it. My father had long wished to purchase an estate of his own, but he found his fortune was not yet sufficient to do so. Thus, the task fell to me."

"Do you have any relations who are already members of the gentry?"

"Only Darcy," replied Mr. Bingley, his smile never wavering.

"And are you still involved in this family business?"

"I still possess interests in it," replied Mr. Bingley. "In the late stages of his life, my father sold a portion of his interest to my uncle, who now owns the majority of it. I receive some income from the venture, and on occasion, I have discussed matters of mutual concern with him. But I am not involved with the management of it."

"That is something, at least," was her ladyship's response. "I take it, then, you are able to support my niece in a style somewhat resembling that to which she is accustomed as a daughter of the Darcy family."

"I think few men could claim to be as wealthy as Darcy," said Mr.

Bingley, grinning at his friend. For his part, Mr. Darcy seemed only a little affected by it, for his exasperation with his aunt was readily apparent. "But, yes, I am wealthy enough that she will not want for anything. Once I am able to purchase an estate, I hope to continue to raise our fortune."

"It is, indeed, fortunate that our family has been enlivened by our new relations," interjected Charity. "We all like Mr. Bingley very much, and Jane's quiet confidence perfectly complements Anthony's temperament. And Elizabeth has become like a sister to me. My mother and father also like them very much."

While Charity grasped Elizabeth's hand in a show of solidarity, her interference was met with a raised eyebrow. Lady Catherine glared, her expression suggesting her niece ought to be silent until her ladyship addressed her.

"I have observed you since your arrival, and I have noticed your closeness with Miss Bennet. It is astonishing, though hardly pertinent, that you have taken to her so quickly. But I wish to know more of Mr. Bingley."

She turned with an expectant air toward her niece's husband, and Bingley was seemingly eager to oblige. "I have two sisters, your ladyship. The eldest is married to a Mr. Hurst, who has inherited his estate in Norfolk from his recently deceased father. My younger sister is being courted by a man possessing an estate in Bedfordshire. And there are a whole host of aunts, uncles, and cousins still living in the vicinity of York."

"Oh, you have a large family do you?"

"There are so many of us that I sometimes forget names!"

"The Fitzwilliam family has never been large," said Lady Catherine, her tone slightly introspective. "The Darcy and de Bourgh families less so. In fact, you can find the last scions of both families in this very room!"

"That may be true for the de Bourghs," said Mr. Darcy. "But Georgiana and I have some cousins several generations removed."

"Nothing more than minor gentry, hardly worth the name, and a selection of parsons and attorneys."

Mr. Darcy bristled at the characterization, but Lady Catherine had already turned back to Mr. Bingley. The examination continued from there. Much the same as she had when Jane and Elizabeth arrived, the lady inquired into every detail of Mr. Bingley's life, his family, and his past, and everything else she could think of. And while his comments often provoked frowns, Elizabeth had become familiar enough with her ladyship that she thought Lady Catherine had gained a grudging respect and approval for the gentleman.

"Well, it seems you may be good for my niece, after all," said Lady Catherine when her questioning had finally wound to its conclusion. "If nothing else, you appear to have little difficulty in company. Georgiana, as you must already know, is quite reticent. I think a little of your openness can only do her good."

"Thank you, Lady Catherine," replied Mr. Bingley with a graciousness Elizabeth doubted many could have possessed. "I assure you that not only will I protect your niece to the best of my abilities, but she will never want for anything if I have a say in it."

"That is good to hear, Mr. Bingley," said Lady Catherine. "Now, you mentioned that you were seeking out an estate. I believe there are one or two not far from here which might suit, should you wish to investigate them."

"I would, of course, be happy to look at them," replied Mr. Bingley. "But I think my dear wife has her heart set on Derbyshire as the place she wishes to settle." Mr. Bingley grinned. "She is quite attached to Pemberley and devoted to her brother, you understand."

"Yes, I do know of it," said Lady Catherine, who looked on Georgiana with something almost approaching tenderness. "You resemble my dearly departed sister, Niece. I can see the shade of her countenance in yours, see the spark of her life in the depths of your eyes." Lady Catherine paused and seemingly considered her words, before saying: "I am happy you are settled with a good man. It is all your mother would have wished for you."

"Thank you, Aunt," replied Georgiana. She rose from her chair and kissed Lady Catherine's cheek. Elizabeth noted the mistiness in the elderly lady's eyes and knew she was not nearly so hard and imperious as she liked to pretend.

"Now," said Lady Catherine, "I would suggest you do not delay in your intention to purchase an estate, Mr. Bingley. The credit of the family must be upheld, after all. Darcy and my brother will assist you in whatever you require."

"Of course, Lady Catherine," replied Mr. Bingley. "Now that I have obtained my heart's desire in marrying your niece, there is nothing I want more than to be settled."

Lady Catherine's tight nod ended the conversation, to the relief of more than one. It had gone much better than she might have expected, mused Elizabeth. But then again, so had her own inquisition with the lady. Had she come here as a visitor with no connection to the family,

Elizabeth was not certain she would ever have seen this side of her ladyship.

"Well, Bingley," said Fitzwilliam. "I must hand it to you. Few could successfully put our aunt off in such a manner as you did. Few would have the fortitude to even make the attempt."

Though Darcy did not care for his cousin's overly jesting manner, he was forced to agree with the sentiment. With an expert flick of the reins, Darcy motioned his horse forward through the trees, followed by his cousin and brother, taking great solace in the beauty of the estate which surrounded them. They had managed to escape any further questioning on Lady Catherine's part that morning, departing the house as soon as they could after luncheon. But Darcy still brooded about his aunt's behavior. Had it been anyone other than Bingley, he almost certainly would have been offended.

"It was nothing," Bingley's response pushed through Darcy's introspection. "It was actually less than I was expecting."

Fitzwilliam snorted. "*Less?* Her methods would have done the clerics of the Spanish Inquisition proud. I thought Darcy here would expire with mortification when she said, in a voice as forceful as ever, mind you, that at least my wife was the daughter of a gentleman."

The two men chortled together as if Lady Catherine had not been egregiously rude in saying such a thing. For his part, Darcy did not think it was amusing in the slightest.

"I will own that bit tested my fortitude," said Bingley in between his laughter. "It is fortunate, indeed, that I am well aware of my own background and have no reason to feel shame for it. I will be a gentleman soon enough, and if I am still new money, it will not concern me a jot. With your parents' support, I have no doubt we will be accepted. If someone wishes to whisper behind my back, that is their concern."

"I could not have advised you any better," replied Fitzwilliam. "We do not need to care for the opinions of others."

"No, indeed." Then Bingley changed the subject. "So how was your honeymoon, old man? Was it everything you might have hoped for?"

"Very pleasant," replied Fitzwilliam. "And Elizabeth's presence was welcome, too, though I am afraid she was forced to fend for herself more than she might have expected."

Bingley laughed. "Yes, I can imagine you were quite focused on your wife. I hope Elizabeth was not too put out."

"She was not," replied Fitzwilliam. "My new sister is an excellent woman, and I am very fond of her. In fact, she attempted to tell us that we had no need to see to her amusement when we realized she had been left to her own devices longer than we had intended. She was eager to allow us our time together."

"I cannot imagine *my* sister behaving in such a way," said Bingley with a shaken head. "Caroline would almost certainly require the attention of both, else she would consider herself quite ill-used."

"I shall take your word for it, Bingley. You know your sister better than I. But I will say that I am very pleased with my new sister. Someday she shall make a fine wife, though I am not certain I know any man who is deserving of her."

Though Fitzwilliam did not say it outright, the glance he directed at Darcy suggested he thought Darcy might have some interest. Nothing could be further from the truth, Darcy stubbornly told himself. He had thought much of Miss Bennet, it was true, but she was in no way suitable to become his wife. And he would not be caught by the same fortune hunting family as his cousin.

In truth, it was becoming more difficult to maintain his opinion of the Bennets as fortune hunters, and Darcy clung to the memory of Mrs. Bennet's open scheming. Mrs. Fitzwilliam had never been anything other than gracious and poised, and even Miss Bennet showed no signs of behaving as if she wished to garner his attention. But Darcy had heard what he had heard, and his experiences in society had jaded him, making him sensitive to the machinations of young ladies. The effort of hanging onto his opinion was becoming a strain. Thus, it was, perhaps, not a surprise when the dam burst.

Darcy did not even know of how the conversation had progressed, immersed, as he was, in his own thoughts. Bingley and Fitzwilliam continued to banter, their laughter ringing through the woods in which they rode. It was an innocuous sort of jest which led to Darcy's sudden loss of his temper.

"Then again, perhaps we should not speak so openly." The voice was Fitzwilliam's, and it pulled Darcy from his thoughts. "After all, we are both old married men now, while Darcy is still a bachelor. It would not do to bruise tender ears by speaking of such subjects."

It was as much the laughter the two men shared as the tease which burst through the dam of his restraint. For Darcy instantly passed the threshold of fury and reined in his horse, turning a baleful eye on his cousin.

"Yes, you are correct, Fitzwilliam, for I would not wish to hear of your marriage. I have no wish to hear further of the fall of a man I have long respected to the clutches of a fortune hunting woman."

"Are you still on about that tired old argument?" asked Fitzwilliam with a shake of his head. His lack of anger in response to Darcy's comment had the reverse effect of angering Darcy even more.

"It is the truth, is it not?" snapped Darcy.

His cousin eyed him, while Bingley could be seen shaking his head at his side. The attitude of the two men, side by side facing him, suggested their common stance against him. And so it should, thought Darcy viciously, for he knew he was in the right.

"It is *not* the truth," was Fitzwilliam's reply at length. "I am surprised at you, Darcy, for you have never been overly concerned with standing in society. You despise society. I might have expected you to behave in a rational manner and judge without your pride getting in the way."

"My pride has nothing to do with this. I *heard* them, Fitzwilliam."

Fitzwilliam regarded him as if he had sprouted a second head. "You heard my Jane speaking?"

"No," cried Darcy, his frustration stilling his tongue, such that he was forced to pause for a moment to gather his wits. "I heard Miss Bennet—Elizabeth—speaking with Miss Lucas. They spoke of their plans, how Miss Bennet was planning to encourage your wife to show more than she felt to secure you. I have always known your new family is not what they seem. But you were determined, and you allowed yourself to be caught, though you should know better. And while Lady Catherine seems to have taken to your new wife, *I* know the truth."

"You know nothing, Darcy," said Fitzwilliam, his own voice finally rising in response. "I married my wife for nothing more than pure inclination, and I know she feels the same."

Darcy shook his head. "Your willful blindness is astonishing."

"I have daily proof of my wife's regard." Fitzwilliam's eyes bored into him, and though his cousin had never before intimidated Darcy, he found himself looking away. "And even if I did not have proof of it, what concern is it of yours? May I not live my own life as I see fit?"

"No, I see that I cannot." Fitzwilliam's tone had become hard with anger. "For you believe you know best, and you are quick to let everyone else know how discerning you are.

"If you are so infallible, perhaps you should answer this question: *if* the Bennet family is so intent upon improving their fortune and entrapping men, why was Elizabeth allowed to reject a proposal of marriage?"

That caught Darcy's attention, and he directed a questioning glance at his cousin. "She refused a proposal?"

"She did."

"And when was this?"

"The day that I proposed to her sister."

Darcy was confused. He had left only a short time before Fitzwilliam had proposed, and he had not known of anyone courting her. Unless . . .

"Do you refer to that cousin of hers?" asked Darcy.

"Yes, it was Mr. Collins," replied Fitzwilliam, his smirk suggesting he thought he had made a point.

Whatever else Miss Bennet was, she was an intelligent woman. The thought of her bound in life to a dullard on the order of Mr. Collins was unthinkable. The hubris of such a man to think himself able to attract a woman on the order of Miss Bennet was beyond belief.

"I hardly think that is in any way proof of Miss Bennet's integrity," said Darcy. "A woman should be celebrated for refusing such a man as Mr. Collins."

"Do not question her integrity, Darcy," said Fitzwilliam, his voice low and dangerous.

"Come now," said Bingley, interjecting between Darcy and his cousin. "Let us speak calmly and rationally. I never thought I would see the day when you would be arguing."

"On the contrary, Bingley," said Fitzwilliam, though he never looked away from Darcy, "Darcy and I have had some prodigious arguments."

"Perhaps, but this is no mere argument. Cooler heads must prevail."

Fitzwilliam nodded. "Then let me inform you of what happened, Darcy, so that you may judge for yourself. Mr. Collins, as you must know, is Mr. Bennet's heir, and as such, marriage to him would secure the future for his wife and other daughters, independent of my marriage to Jane.

"But Elizabeth never had any interest in Mr. Collins. In fact, his manners irk her, his admiration was nothing more than a fantasy, and furthermore, she wishes for something more than to marry a man for the sake of her own comfort. If I had not been so captivated by her sister, I might have found myself more than a little interested in Elizabeth herself."

"I, too, have nothing but praise for Miss Bennet," said Bingley. "And your sister likes the Bennet ladies very well, indeed."

"And this proposal of which you speak?" asked Darcy in spite of himself.

Fitzwilliam smiled thinly. "Mr. Collins returned to Kent, as you know, but he once again came to Longbourn only days after the ball. I had already decided upon paying my addresses to Jane and proposed the day after Mr. Collins's arrival. He was not pleased that I had offered for Miss Bennet."

What a mess it must have been, and Darcy could only shake his head at the man's foolishness. "I will assume you do not mean that he fancied Miss Bennet for himself. It was none of his business what you do. He is not family."

"No, he was not. But he was eager to defend Lady Catherine's interests in this matter, whatever those may be. Our aunt was forced to speak to him quite firmly after he discovered Elizabeth here with us, for he had some highly uncomplimentary things to say about her."

"That simply proves my point," said Darcy. "No woman possessing even a shred of self-respect could ever consider accepting Mr. Collins."

"I cannot agree with you more. Then, would it be a surprise that Mrs. Bennet herself was against Mr. Collins by that time?" Fitzwilliam took Darcy's surprise for confirmation. "Indeed, she was. Mr. Collins made such a fuss about *my* proposal that she was quite offended for her daughters. She declared he was the last man Elizabeth should ever accept."

"I agree with her. But that does nothing to prove your point."

"Think, Darcy! Mrs. Bennet is a woman long accustomed to her own home in Hertfordshire. Do you not think a truly mercenary woman would not overlook such insults for the sake of capturing a man for her daughter?"

"Well . . ." said Darcy, realizing Fitzwilliam had made a very good point.

"Listen, Darcy, I do not wish to be at odds with you. I understand your feelings. But I wish you would give me the benefit of understanding the woman I married. I am happy with her and she with me, and I like Elizabeth so much that I am determined that she will stay with us for as long as she pleases.

"But I cannot allow criticisms of her character. Not only are they baseless, but they are unkind to the woman I married. I will protect her against all naysayers—even those among my own family if I must. Mother and Father already love her and Elizabeth, Georgiana is enamored of them, and Charity, though she has only known Elizabeth a short time, considers her a sister. Even Lady Catherine has accepted them, and I have it on good authority that Elizabeth has begun to make her way past Lady Catherine's prickly exterior. Can you not at least give my wife and her sister your kindness and refrain from nasty comments?"

"Perhaps I have been harsh," muttered Darcy.

Fitzwilliam nodded and grasped the reins tighter. "I hope you truly realize that. Please, Darcy, for my sake — do not say anything further in my hearing. I do not wish to be forced to defend my wife again."

And Fitzwilliam heeled his horse and cantered away. Bingley directed a sympathetic glance at Darcy and followed suit, leaving Darcy alone with his thoughts. His mind heavy with thought, Darcy soon kicked his horse into motion, though nothing faster than a walk. His mind was occupied with the conversation for the rest of the morning.

CHAPTER XXIX

"*H*e is right, you know."

Bingley's voice cut through the fabric of Darcy's thoughts, and he looked up in surprise. His friend was watching him, his air one of mixed amusement and exasperation. Darcy frowned — he had never seen Bingley look on him the way he was now.

"I apologize, Bingley, but what did you say?"

It seemed Bingley understood that Darcy had heard him, but he repeated himself regardless. "Your cousin. He is correct in what he said to you."

"How so?" asked Darcy.

"Do not give me your infamous Master of Pemberley stare, Darcy, for it does not affect me any longer." Bingley grinned at his own jest and sat on a nearby chair. "You have been against the Bennet sisters from almost the first day you met them, and unless I miss my guess, it was partially due to your mood when we first went to Netherfield. You tend to be quite dour when you are out of sorts, Darcy, and at that time you were still blaming yourself for Georgiana and Wickham."

Darcy sighed and sat back in his chair. "There is some responsibility to be laid at my door, Bingley. It was I who hired Mrs. Younge and entrusted Georgiana's care in her hands."

"You are not a perfect man, Darcy," said Bingley, leaning forward, as earnest as Darcy had ever seen him. "At the time, you did what you felt best. There was no reason to suspect the woman, as I understand. Fitzwilliam informed me that he had no suspicions himself.

"But I do not wish to speak of that. What is more pertinent at the present time is how your mood affected you. Yes, I understand you considered Jane Bennet to be a poor match for your cousin, and I can sympathize with your opinion, as it is one many of your circle would espouse. I will assert, however, that your experience with Wickham's grasping attempts at Georgiana's dowry jaded you, made you see fortune hunters behind every potted plant."

"I have always been wary of fortune hunters," said Darcy in a weak attempt to defend himself. "Would that I had been more vigilant with respect to Georgiana."

"If you will excuse my saying so," said Bingley, "I believe I must give thanks to your former friend for his attempt." Darcy looked up at Bingley, confused by his words. "Do you remember the conversation we had when I proposed to Georgiana?"

A slow nod was Darcy's response. "I do. You had grown tired of focusing on the next pretty woman and wished for more out of life."

"That is correct. I believe marrying your sister has been the making of me. I might have continued on as I was then, regardless of my intention and desire to change. I believe I have finally grown into the man my father knew I could be."

"I always knew what you could be, Bingley," said Darcy. "It may have seemed like I was intent upon directing you, but I have never wished to be anything more than your friend."

"Thank you, Darcy," said Bingley, extending his hand and gripping Darcy's firmly. "Your friendship has meant the world to me, and your support even more. This summer I will purchase an estate, give your sister a home, and begin producing that family of which we spoke that day." An entirely Bingley-like grin shone on his friend's face. "And I believe I may happily inform you that the past year has done much for us. I love your sister, Darcy, and had Wickham not importuned her, I might never have seen her as anything more than your little sister. So while his actions were contemptible, in a peculiar way, I believe I am indebted to him."

Darcy could not help the laughter the bubbled forth from his breast. "That *is* peculiar, indeed. I will not thank the man, but I am glad you are happy with my sister."

"There is no other way I could have been. She is sweetness itself, angelic in every way. How could I have ended anything other than incandescently happy?"

"How, indeed?" replied Darcy, once again filled with quiet introspection.

"Thus, you may release your burden of guilt for Georgiana," said Bingley. "She is happy, and the past need not trouble you again.

"But let us bring this back to the topic at hand. At the time you were still weighed down by guilt and, if you will excuse my saying so, were wary of any and all. You saw the Bennets as grasping, artful people. I do not know the whole of what you overheard Miss Bennet say to her friend, but on what little you shared, I must tell you that it sounds suspiciously like a young woman jesting with a friend. And you know that Miss Bennet is fond of a laugh."

"I suppose you must be correct," replied Darcy, his mind flitting, as it had so often, to an image of her laughing countenance. It was one of the things that attracted him to her so much.

"She is not unserious," continued Bingley. "She speaks intelligently, is serious and even more at the appropriate times. But if you observe her, you can see that she always returns to that lightness of character which I believe is her defining trait. I can see her joking with a friend about a dear sister.

"Face it, Darcy. Early in our acquaintance, you branded the Bennet sisters — the whole family, actually — as nothing but a bunch of fortune hunters. You have never truly given them a chance to prove themselves. When you look at Mrs. Fitzwilliam, it is clear to see that she adores your cousin, and Miss Bennet has become a good friend to Charity and my own dear wife. In fact, I credit Miss Bennet with helping Georgiana develop a new level of confidence. She has been good for us all."

Darcy nodded slowly. "I suppose she has."

"Then I suggest you let go of your prejudice, Darcy." Bingley rose and favored him with a smile. "You have been so often correct in the past that I know it will be difficult to confess your error. But the good man I have always known you are will accept nothing less."

How quickly the roles were reversed. Bingley, being a younger man and, more importantly, finding his way in the world and society, and being of a modest disposition, had always looked to Darcy for guidance. And Darcy had been happy to provide it while guiding his friend to obtain greater confidence and independence. But Bingley had never spoken to him in this manner, and Darcy was grateful he had.

After the argument with Fitzwilliam the previous day, Darcy had taken to watching Miss Bennet even more closely than was his custom. The conversation with Bingley further clarified matters for him. Bingley was correct—it had never been easy for Darcy to own his errors in such matters. On the other hand, it was far too easy for him to accept guilt in other matters, such as what had happened with Georgiana and Wickham. It was an interesting dichotomy.

And with this new understanding, Darcy continued to watch the woman over the next several days. He did not like what he observed when it reflected back on his own behavior. Bingley and Fitzwilliam were absolutely correct—Miss Bennet was not a fortune hunter. If she was, she would have paid more attention to Darcy himself, much in the manner of Miss Bingley. But Miss Bennet, though she was happy to speak with anyone, did not attempt to intrude upon his senses. She was perfectly demure and well behaved, if lively.

As Darcy watched her, he began to realize that this liveliness was, indeed, what had attracted him to her. That attraction he had acknowledged some time ago had never diminished. But it was his jealously held opinion which had prevented it from becoming more.

The truth was that Darcy did not know if he wished his fascination with her to lead to a closer connection. But he was beginning to understand that he wanted to learn the answer to that question. He wished it very much.

Silliness was not something Elizabeth had ever thought to associate with the stately and imposing home of Lady Catherine de Bourgh. Indeed, it had sometimes seemed that the very stones of the manor conspired to ensure whatever laughter there was remained muted, that the dignity of the family living within should always be protected. That was until Mr. Collins and his wife were finally summoned for dinner.

While he had come to Rosings every day for his meeting with Lady Catherine, Mr. Collins had recently had little contact with Elizabeth herself. This suited Elizabeth very well, and she thought he actually agreed with her in this matter, unlikely though the thought of agreeing with *any* opinion Mr. Collins possessed seemed. What little she had seen of him had given her the impression that he felt his current disfavor with Lady Catherine keenly. Elizabeth assumed he considered this invitation to be evidence of his return to favor and was not anticipating it in the slightest.

As she left her room, Elizabeth paused to fortify herself. She did not expect him to continue to accost her—in fact, she thought he intended to leave her strictly alone. But what she had heard of his wife told Elizabeth that she was also a silly woman, and while the pair of them would likely provide amusement aplenty, of Mr. Collins's brand of the ridiculous, a little went a long way. At least the rest of the company would not prove objectionable.

"Miss Bennet, may I escort you to dinner?"

Turning, Elizabeth noted the approach of Mr. Darcy, her thought of objectionable and not seeming ironic at present. Elizabeth had not quite been able to determine in which group Mr. Darcy belonged. At times he was pleasant and even friendly, while at others he was forbidding, taciturn, and even seemed disapproving. At least the former had appeared before her at that moment.

"Thank you, sir," said she, placing her hand lightly on his arm.

"I apologize if I interrupted you, Miss Bennet," said Mr. Darcy as they began walking toward the stairs, "but it seemed to me as if you were attempting to gather your strength. Does the coming of Mr. Collins provoke such distress?"

"It could not be described as distress, exactly," replied Elizabeth, surprised at his words. "But you are correct in that I do not anticipate his company."

"That is understandable." Elizabeth looked at him askance. "My cousin has told me of what has passed between you, so I understand your apprehension."

Mortification flooded through Elizabeth, and she looked away from his keen gaze. "I had not known that such stories were of such interest that men of your station would be willing to trade them."

"When it concerns one's family, it is," replied Mr. Darcy. Once again, Elizabeth turned to him, curious about his meaning. "You are sister to my cousin's wife. Though that does not technically make us family, there is a connection between us. Fitzwilliam was merely attempting to inform me of the possible behavior of the man so I would be on my guard."

Something was missing, something Mr. Darcy was not telling her. But Elizabeth supposed it did not matter. That she would have another man to curb Mr. Collins's stupidity and any criticism he might decide to level at her was welcome, though she did not require a protector.

"In all honesty, I doubt Mr. Collins will make a scene tonight," said Mr. Darcy. "Especially since I understand Lady Catherine commanded him to cease his harassment of you. He strikes me as a man held in thrall, unwilling to tempt her displeasure."

"Perhaps you are correct, Mr. Darcy. But that does not mean he will obtain any measure of sense, and I am far from expecting it in his wife, considering what your aunt has said of the woman. As my father has said on other occasions, we are unlikely to hear two words of sense from the pair of them throughout the entire evening."

"I quite agree with you, considering what I remember of Mr. Collins." He turned a grin on her. "But fortunately, Mr. Collins's attention will likely be fixed on Lady Catherine, and his wife will likely be the same. If you stay near your sister and Charity, Bingley and my sister, or even myself, I doubt you will suffer much."

Elizabeth smiled at him, though her heart was not in it. "Yes, there are many sensible members of our company. But I suspect he will come prepared with at least a few barbs aimed at me, though he will no doubt consider them subtle." Elizabeth huffed. "Mr. Collins is about as subtle as a cannon blast, and I suspect his head is about the same consistency as a cannonball."

Though he seemed surprised at Elizabeth's caustic remark, Mr. Darcy was soon laughing heartily. Elizabeth joined in, feeling sheepish at what she had said, knowing she had just spoken quite improperly but unable to muster the will to regret it.

"You do have a gift for speaking, Miss Bennet," said Mr. Darcy, his icy blue eyes seeming filled with warmth at that moment. "I have rarely been so entertained."

"I should not speak so," replied Elizabeth. "He will be a guest in your aunt's home this evening."

"Yes, he will. But I cannot disagree with your assessment. Do your best to ignore him, Miss Bennet. The rest of us will provide a respite from him if you require it."

By this time they had reached the sitting-room where she expected Mr. Collins was already present. The footman opened the door and allowed them entrance, and Elizabeth noted, as expected, that Mr. Collins was already there. He looked up to see her enter, narrowed his eyes at the sight of her, his gaze rested on Mr. Darcy for the briefest instant, and then he turned his attention back to Lady Catherine, completely ignoring Elizabeth.

Elizabeth noted the presence of the rest of the company and went to sit with Jane, Mr. Darcy following behind her. But before she could sit, Lady Catherine spoke to Mr. Collins.

"Now that we are all gathered, perhaps you would introduce your wife to the company. I believe she is unknown to most of those here."

"Of course, Lady Catherine," said Mr. Collins, his glance once again at Elizabeth clearly intended to show his superiority for finding a wife he considered above Elizabeth.

The company all stood, and Mr. Collins began the introductions. Even in that, he was inept as he was about everything else he did.

"My dear, please step this way, for I have the great pleasure in introducing to your acquaintance Colonel Fitzwilliam and Mr. Darcy, Lady Catherine's nephews, Lady Charity Fitzwilliam, her niece, my cousin Jane, wife to Colonel Fitzwilliam, and Mr. Bingley and his wife, Mrs. Georgiana Bingley, who is also niece to our patroness. Ladies, gentlemen, may I present my beloved wife, Mrs. Althea Collins. Mrs. Collins and I were married in February, to my great joy and advantage."

Not only had he gotten the order of the introductions wrong, but he had neglected to mention Elizabeth as well, though Elizabeth was certain her omission had been entirely intentional. Anthony and Darcy both frowned at the parson, while Mr. Bingley shook his head along with the rest of the family. But before anyone could say anything, Lady Catherine cleared her throat in a significant manner.

"Oh, of course," said Mr. Collins. "My cousin, Elizabeth Bennet."

It seemed the rest of the company was affronted for Elizabeth's sake, but for her own part, Elizabeth felt like laughing in the silly man's face. Thus, she was provoked to respond to his silliness by focusing on his wife and stepping forward to greet her.

"Mrs. Collins," said she, curtseying to the woman. Mrs. Collins, though Elizabeth thought her completely aware of why he had omitted Elizabeth, possessed the sense to curtsey in response. "How lovely it is to make your acquaintance. And may I congratulate you on your recent marriage?"

The woman's momentary silence spoke to her surprise, but then she seemed to gather herself to respond. And in so doing, she proved herself a perfect match for Mr. Collins.

"Thank you, Miss Bennet." Mrs. Collins's tone was lofty, and the way she looked down her nose reminded Elizabeth of a bird in a tree, looking down on the ground-bound creatures below with contempt. "I have heard of you from my husband, and I can only say that I am indebted to you for your actions. But I should not speak with you, for I am wary of being contaminated by those of a baser nature.

Mr. Collins beamed at his wife as if she had just made a statement likely to be remembered a thousand years in the future. But while Elizabeth was barely holding in a smile at this evidence of the woman's silliness, very few of her family were of a similar mind. Anthony, in particular, seemed ready to pick both Collinses up by the scruffs of their necks and forcefully deposit them on the front steps. It was fortunate Lady Catherine once again intervened.

"Mr. and Mrs. Collins! You will both attend me, *at once!*"

The couple was truly a curious entity, for while Mrs. Collins seemed to have no knowledge of proper behavior at times, at others, Mr. Collins took the lead in their headlong flight into silliness. Mrs. Collins turned and dutifully made her way to her patroness's side with nary a hint of trepidation. Mr. Collins, perhaps, had more experience with Lady Catherine and knew when she was displeased, for he winced and followed his wife. But he did not go without shooting a glare at Elizabeth, as if the dressing down he and his wife were about to receive from Lady Catherine was *her* fault.

"If that man, or his stupid wife, say another word to you throughout the evening, I shall not be responsible for my actions." Anthony was actually shaking with fury, and at his side, Mr. Darcy seemed to be caught in the grips of similar emotions.

"I hardly think they will venture to say another word to *any* of us," said Mr. Bingley. "Lady Catherine gives all the appearance of immense displeasure with them both."

Mr. Bingley's observation was clearly accurate, for Lady Catherine had gathered the pair before her and left them standing as if they were supplicants to the throne. While they did not speak, she provided a continual stream of instructions. Lady Catherine, in the time Elizabeth had known her, had rarely moderated her voice, and as such, much of what she said was audible to the rest of the company.

". . . atrocious behavior."

". . . guest in my home, and one who is above you both by every measurement!"

". . . sister to my own nephew's wife, and cousin to you, Mr. Collins!"

". . . I will not repeat myself . . ."

And finally, she fixed them with a stern glare, saying: "Do I make myself quite clear?"

Again, Mrs. Collins seemed almost bewildered. But Mr. Collins was busy demeaning himself, bowing even lower than he had when first making Mr. Bennet's acquaintance. And from his mouth issued a constant stream of apologies and assurances, all of which were some variation of: "I humbly beg your forgiveness for my oversight and my wife's unfortunate words. They shall not be repeated."

Elizabeth did note that he did not apologize for the content of the words, but then again Elizabeth had not expected him to. Lady

Catherine eyed him, and her gaze met Elizabeth's for a moment, a question clearly contained within. Elizabeth, however, had no interest in hearing Mr. Collins's apologies, for she knew they would be perfunctory and insincere. Thus, she contented herself with shaking her head slightly. Lady Catherine, it seemed, understood her perfectly, for she grimaced and allowed the matter to rest.

For the Collins's part, it seemed they were eager to ignore Elizabeth's existence for the rest of the evening. Would that Elizabeth could ignore them as well! But that was nigh impossible, for the parson's words were plentiful and his wife's never-ending.

They went into dinner soon after, and Lady Catherine directed Mr. and Mrs. Collins to sit near her—which Elizabeth supposed was only a small breach of proper dining etiquette. While she was seated near the other end of the table near Anthony and Mr. Darcy, she could not help but hear the continual stream of compliments, sycophantic statements, and words of self-congratulation which he felt obliged to make. Even though Lady Catherine had made her own bed in hiring the ridiculous twit, Elizabeth still felt sorry for her after a time, for Lady Catherine appeared quite fatigued before long.

"I hope this is not an invitation which will be repeated much while we are here," said Anthony, looking down the table at the pair with distaste.

"Look to Lady Catherine, Fitzwilliam," said Mr. Darcy. "I expect she only invited them because she felt it was necessary to introduce them to us. She will not be repeating it any time soon, though I suppose she must be a gracious host to her parson."

Anthony's eyes swiveled to meet Mr. Darcy's. "You appear to be taking their incivility rather easily Darcy."

There was something of a challenge in Anthony's words, the meaning of which Elizabeth could not quite make out. Whatever it was, Mr. Darcy diffused it with his reply.

"I was on the verge of planting a facer on the stupid man, I assure you. And Mrs. Collins has all the sense of a sheep."

A curt nod was Anthony's reply. Then Charity spoke.

"Perhaps the responsibility of responding to the man's odious wife should have been mine. After all, I may strike another woman where you men cannot do so and remain gentlemen."

"You are all far more insulted by this than I am," interjected Elizabeth into the conversation. "All their paltry attacks provoked in me was the desire to laugh at them. Indeed, they deserved nothing else."

A movement down the table caught Elizabeth's eye, and she noted Mr. Collins sitting stiffly, as if in the grips of some great offense. It seemed he had heard her, though he did not even deign to look at her.

"I assure you, Lizzy," said Jane, "any one of us would have responded to them with much more than laughter."

Elizabeth directed a fond look at her sister, but she shook her head. "I know you would, and I am grateful to you all for it. But I think it would be a much pleasanter evening if we discussed something else."

The suggestion was agreed to by all, and they spent the rest of the dinner bantering about other subjects. The only ones who were not part of their conversation were Lady Catherine and the Collinses, and Miss de Bourgh, who watched them all with little seeming interest.

After dinner, they returned to the sitting-room and the unpleasant evening continued. The gentlemen abjured the separation of the sexes, and the reason for it was readily apparent. When Mr. Collins moved about the room, attempting to ingratiate himself with the gentlemen, he was given the short shrift and was soon seated by Lady Catherine, plying her with his sycophancy. Mrs. Collins had a little more success with Miss de Bourgh, though she was as taciturn as ever, but none with any of the other ladies. She, too, ended by Lady Catherine's side.

When the evening had progressed a little later, Lady Catherine asked the ladies to perform on the pianoforte. Georgiana seemed to lack confidence, though Elizabeth knew she was talented, and while Lady Catherine seemed unamused by her niece's reticence, she was allowed to demur.

"As a married woman, you will be required to play for your guests at times. But tonight we can dispense with it if you prefer."

Thus, first Charity, and then Elizabeth, being the only ones who played, made their way in turns to the pianoforte. Charity, as Elizabeth had already known, was as talented as Georgiana, and as such, Elizabeth felt a little self-conscious following her performance. But those present — aside from the Collinses, of course — clapped heartily when she finished, so she was at least mollified by their kindness.

"As I have said before, Miss Bennet," said Lady Catherine when she had finished playing, "I believe you require more practice, though I will say your performance is quite pleasing. Please feel free to use this pianoforte, or the one in the west parlor, to practice at any time convenient."

"Thank you, Lady Catherine," said Elizabeth. "I believe I will accept your offer, for extra practice will do me no harm."

The lady nodded regally and turned back to Mr. and Mrs. Collins, after asking Elizabeth if she would stay at the instrument. As it happened, Elizabeth had no objection and chose another piece to play quietly while the other members of the party spoke together. It seemed, however, that Mr. Collins was not capable of allowing this praise to go unanswered, for he spoke up in his self-congratulatory fashion.

"Mrs. Collins plays, Lady Catherine. Perhaps she could also amuse us this evening?"

Lady Catherine turned a speculative eye on the parson's wife. "I did not know that of you, Mrs. Collins."

"I do not publish it much," said Mrs. Collins, the picture of modesty. "But my mother has often said my playing is very fine, indeed."

A slow nod was the lady's answer. "Then perhaps next time. I believe our evening will come to a close before long."

"I would be happy to play the next time we are together."

For a time, Elizabeth was not able to hear them, for Lady Catherine had drawn them close, and seemed to be imparting instructions to them. Elizabeth played for some few moments before she saw Mr. Darcy approaching her. When he drew near, he stopped for several moments to listen before he finally spoke.

"There seems to be something more in your playing than I remember when we were in Hertfordshire."

"Oh?" asked Elizabeth, arching an eyebrow at him. "And you specifically remember my playing in Hertfordshire?"

"The night we were all at Lucas Lodge, Miss Bennet. I remember Miss Lucas insisting you favor us all with your talents that evening."

"I do remember that evening," said Elizabeth. "But I was not aware that you had paid so much attention."

Mr. Darcy shrugged. "I am not what you might call a connoisseur of music, but I do enjoy it. And your playing is fine and pleasing to hear."

"Thank you, sir," replied Elizabeth, "though your words prove you to be lacking an expert knowledge of music. My playing is, sadly deficient, for as your aunt has informed us all, I do not practice as much as I should."

"And yet, you do well enough that those listening are uplifted by your   efforts."

"Thank you again, Mr. Darcy," said Elizabeth, feeling a sudden shyness come over her.

It was at this moment that the dullard in their midst decided to show his silliness yet again. For Mr. Collins approached, his eyes hard and fixed on Elizabeth. He stooped low to her around the pianoforte and hissed:

"I see your purpose here, Cousin. Do not attempt to distract Mr. Darcy away from his duty, for you will only find censure if you persist on such a path."

"Mr. Collins!" said Mr. Darcy, his voice like the crack of a whip, for all he spoke quietly. "What has my aunt already told you this evening?"

Mr. Collins made some attempt to respond, but Mr. Darcy did not allow it. "I have no need to hear your excuses. It is time for you and your wife to depart. Do not approach Miss Bennet again."

Once again Mr. Collins's angry and accusing eyes found Elizabeth, but he bowed hurriedly and stalked away. Elizabeth was not sad to see him go. He was as odious a man as Elizabeth had ever met, and she was struck by the thought that she had been correct in her assessment. A little of Mr. Collins's silliness went a very long way.

CHAPTER XXX

$\mathcal{G}$iven the behavior of the Collinses the previous evening, Anthony Fitzwilliam possessed half a mind to pay the silly man a visit and put the fear of God into him. A number of factors stayed his hand, among them the fact that Lady Catherine had not put up with Mr. Collins's stupidity and Elizabeth's own resilience when confronted by her detractor. The knowledge that Darcy had also played an advocate for Elizabeth was also a serious factor, and one which Fitzwilliam found himself considering the following morning, so much so, in fact, that he brought the matter up with his wife.

"What do you think of Darcy, Jane dearest?" asked Fitzwilliam before they departed their chambers for the breakfast room.

"In what way?" asked Jane.

She turned and faced him from the vanity before which she sat, and Fitzwilliam was once again struck by the fact that she was very beautiful. He was a lucky man, indeed.

"I assume you do not ask me without reason," continued she when Fitzwilliam was distracted.

"Perhaps not," said Fitzwilliam, forcing his thoughts back to the matter at hand. "It has occurred to me that Elizabeth is a very good match for Darcy, and I wondered as to your thoughts on the matter."

"Mr. Darcy and Lizzy?" asked Jane with a frown. "Excuse me, but I was not aware that Mr. Darcy saw anything in my dearest sister. He has always struck me as a man who thought very well of himself."

Fitzwilliam chuckled and shook his head, though at the same time he was considering how to placate his wife. Jane was, everyone assumed, meek and mild and incapable of thinking of anyone else with anything other than approbation. But where Elizabeth was concerned, Jane was a mother hen. She was protective, and as Darcy had not shown himself in the best light, she was uncertain of him.

"In some respects you are correct," replied Fitzwilliam. He stepped close to his wife and put a hand on her shoulder, catching hold of the hand she raised to rest on his own. "But Darcy is also a good and loyal man, an excellent master, and when you have him as a friend, there are none firmer. What he needs in his life is a good woman, one who will not bend to his moods, one who will stimulate his interest and balance his tendency toward gravity."

"And you think Lizzy is such a one?"

"I do not suggest anything, Jane, nor do I think we should intervene. For Elizabeth to be happy, I believe she must decide on her own future."

"You are correct," replied Jane. "But I do wonder as to your reason for speaking. What do you propose?"

Fitzwilliam paused and thought for a moment. When he spoke, his words were slow and careful, for he was not quite certain himself. "I believe Darcy is attracted to your sister, and I believe Elizabeth would respond, given the right inducement."

"I do not wish to push my sister," replied Jane.

"No, you are correct," replied Fitzwilliam. Then he chuckled. "I rather suspect Elizabeth would dig in her heels should she think she was being pushed."

Jane looked up and fixed him with a gentle smile. "I cannot say you have not taken the measure of my dearest sister."

"Then I suppose we shall simply be required to offer our assistance if the occasion demands it. They are both stubborn—perhaps they can be stubborn enough to find each other together."

There was no reply to his comment. A moment later, Fitzwilliam assisted his wife to rise, and they made their way below stairs to break their fast. Darcy and Elizabeth both joined them, being early risers, as was Lady Catherine. But while the conversation went on around him, Fitzwilliam did not partake in it much, instead focusing his attention on his cousin.

Evidence of Darcy's growing partiality had been present the previous evening—of that Fitzwilliam was certain. But Darcy was a man whose adherence to duty was legendary. Fitzwilliam thought it likely he would never move to show his interest in Elizabeth unless he was prompted to do so. In the end, Fitzwilliam decided that although he had all but promised his wife not to push *Elizabeth*, he had made no promise with respect to *Darcy*. And thus, he sought his cousin out after they had finished their morning meal.

"Good morning, Cousin," said Fitzwilliam upon entering the study where Darcy was looking over the estate books.

Darcy looked up and acknowledged Fitzwilliam's presence, but then he returned to his task. Fitzwilliam, however, was not about to be put off in such a manner.

"It seems to me you have finally confessed I was correct about Jane and her sister."

This time Darcy regarded him with a frown. "Are you speaking of something in particular?"

"Last night at the pianoforte?" asked Fitzwilliam. In truth, he was feeling rather complacent. He sat on one of the chairs in front of the desk and lifted his feet to rest on the sturdy oak. Darcy hated it when Fitzwilliam did this at Pemberley or the house in town, but at Lady Catherine's estate, he usually did not bat an eyelash.

"Again, is there something specific to which you refer?"

"Please answer the question, Darcy. Do you concede that my wife and her sister are everything I have always claimed them to be?"

With pursed lips, indicating growing annoyance, Darcy said: "It is possible I might have misjudged them."

Fitzwilliam snorted. "This would be so much easier if you would simply own to your error and be done with it."

"Very well, then," said Darcy with an exaggerated and put-upon sigh. "I spoke with Miss Bennet last night when I escorted her to the sitting-room, and she seemed quite genuine. Sagacious as well."

The way Fitzwilliam raised his eyebrow seemed invitation enough for Darcy to elaborate. "She predicted quite exactly Mr. Collins's behavior, though it was perhaps even beyond what she expected. I had thought the presence of Lady Catherine and the fact that she was staying at Rosings would curb his tongue."

A bark of laughter escaped Fitzwilliam. "Yes, Mr. Collins was quite beyond anything I had expected. He attempted to turn Lady Catherine against Elizabeth with stories which were heavily embellished."

Darcy shook his head. "Caper witted fool," muttered Darcy with no little contempt. "I know he is naught but her cousin, but continuing to speak against her so could harm his own reputation as much as hers."

"There is little chance of that," replied Fitzwilliam. "Anyone who meets him must understand that Collins possesses not a lick of sense."

"Perhaps not. But the fact remains that his actions are short-sighted, indeed."

"I cannot but agree," replied Fitzwilliam. "Which is why I thank you for dealing with him last night when he accosted her at the pianoforte." Darcy looked up and Fitzwilliam responded with a thin smile. "I was at a distance such that I could not hear what he said, though I can guess. Lady Catherine did not notice it at all, for she was busy instructing the man's silly wife."

Darcy grimaced. "He thought to protect Anne's interest with respect to me."

"Loyal to the last, I suppose. It shall, indeed, be his last, if he does not moderate his behavior. Though I am certain he does not know one end of a pistol or a sword from the other, I might call him out, if only to cut his tongue from his mouth."

"That would be an improvement," replied Darcy. "Rendering him incapable of speaking would be worthy of a medal."

They laughed together, and Fitzwilliam reveled in it. Darcy's unreasoning and implacable opposition to Jane and Elizabeth had driven a wedge between them which Fitzwilliam had not truly noticed until it had come to a head. Their laughter together had been in short supply of late.

"Then I am sure Mr. Collins thanks you as well," said Fitzwilliam. "It is by your intervention that the man still possesses a tongue." Fitzwilliam paused, considered his next move, and said: "What do you mean to do?"

Darcy blinked, then his eyebrows furrowed in confusion. "About what?"

"His intention to protect your virtue for Anne."

"There is nothing I need to do," said Darcy with a shrug. "I shall continue on as I have. Should the man make a nuisance of himself, I will deal with him as the situation demands."

"I am happy to hear it," said Fitzwilliam. He stood to depart, but before he left the room, he turned back. "I commend you, Darcy. It is high time you realized what a treasure Elizabeth is. Perhaps you should act quickly to snap her up before some other man beats you to it."

Then, disregarding the surprise on Darcy's countenance, Fitzwilliam turned and left the room. Darcy did not follow him, not that Fitzwilliam had expected him to do so. He knew Darcy would almost certainly have little attention for Lady Catherine's ledgers now, but Fitzwilliam could not find it in himself to be sorry. Hopefully, Darcy would do something about his attraction. If he proved obstinate, Fitzwilliam would act at that time.

The arrival of the newcomers to Rosings meant Elizabeth had been reunited with her dearest friends, and for that she was grateful. Anthony had become dear to her and Jane was Jane, and even Lady Catherine had proven to be a woman Elizabeth could tolerate with equanimity. But Georgiana and Charity had become almost like sisters, certainly closer than her younger sisters were. And Elizabeth was happy to once again be in their company.

The four ladies had taken to spending their afternoons together, as that was the time when the gentlemen were usually involved in some business of the estate. From what Elizabeth could see, Mr. Darcy seemed to take the lead in looking over the books, though he could often be found among the tenants. Anthony was out more often than not, while Mr. Bingley seemed to assist wherever needed as if he was being tutored in the proper management in preparation for his own purchase.

"Charles is competent," confided Georgiana one day when they were together on the terrace at the back of the house. "What he lacks is confidence and experience."

"I am certain he is receiving it now," replied Elizabeth, smiling warmly at her friend. She sipped her glass of cool lemonade provided by Rosings' servants and continued, saying: "Your brother appears to understand what needs to be done—I am certain both your husband and Jane's are learning much from him."

"You are correct," replied Georgiana, her voice lowering in contemplation. "William is very knowledgeable, for he was taught by our father from a young age to manage an estate." Georgiana's eyes once again found Elizabeth. "But he claims that when he inherited Pemberley, he was perpetually one step away from ruin. It was a difficult transition."

Elizabeth was interested to hear of this side of Mr. Darcy, not having had any knowledge of it before. "It is understandable. After all, managing even a portion of a great estate under the direction of your father must be quite different from having the full responsibility of it."

"Yes, that is exactly what he said." Georgiana paused and smiled. "And yet it is difficult for me to imagine that my excellent elder brother could struggle to do *anything*. He is quite perfect in my eyes."

Joining her in laughter, Elizabeth said: "In my eyes, Jane is much the same way. But there, you see? Your husband is in excellent hands. In no time, I am sure when you have found your home, your husband will have all the experience and confidence necessary to do what is needed."

"I am sure he will."

The two women looked to the side where Jane and Charity were deep in conversation, a sight that warmed Elizabeth's heart. Elizabeth herself had become so close to Charity in such a short time, she wondered if she was intruding on her sister's ability to form a close friendship with the woman who was, after all, *her* sister. Of late, they seemed to get on well, though Elizabeth suspected they might not ever be so close as she was to Charity.

"Come, Elizabeth," said Charity, catching sight of Elizabeth's scrutiny. "We have sat in this attitude long enough. I wish to stretch my legs in the garden."

They all agreed though they could not depart without teasing. "I have it on good authority that Lizzy has already walked far today," said Jane. "Perhaps she does not wish to concern herself with such tame surroundings as a formal garden."

"I am not against them," replied Elizabeth. "But I will own that I am much more interested in nature as it was intended to be."

"Enough speaking!" cried Charity. "And more walking!"

The laughter followed them as they made their way down the stone stairs and into the gardens. Their surroundings, Elizabeth could readily confess, were rather fine. Flowers of many varieties had been planted in rows, giving a riot of contrasting color to the greenery, while paths meandered in exact patterns throughout. There were a number of topiaries situated at regular intervals, and while Elizabeth found she did not enjoy them as much as Lady Catherine obviously did, she could respect the skill which went into creating them. The gravel path crunching beneath their feet, the wind caressing their sun-kissed cheeks and the calls of birds all added to the beauty of the scene. It was a lovely, calm sort of place and one which Elizabeth could easily become attached to.

"Should we not invite Miss de Bourgh to join us?" asked Jane before they had gone far from the house.

The rest of the ladies followed Jane's gaze, noting the swish of the curtains in one of the windows, as a dark head of hair disappeared from their view. None of the other windows showed any scrutiny of their activity.

"I am quite happy to invite our cousin," said Charity. "But it is difficult to induce Cousin Anne to associate with anyone, even those in the family."

Jane appeared shocked, but Georgiana nodded in agreement with her cousin. "My brother is often called taciturn. But it is Anne who truly deserves the appellation. I cannot remember hearing her speak ten words to me in the entirety of my life!"

"Surely you exaggerate," said Jane with a frown of confusion.

"It is not much of one," said Charity. "The only one among us to whom Anne ever speaks is her mother. "Even Darcy, to whom she is *supposedly* engaged, rarely can induce her into conversation."

Georgiana laughed. "Not that he wishes to. Whenever William attempts to speak to her, Lady Catherine appears as if she is planning their wedding breakfast!"

The ladies joined in laughter at this, though Jane's was a little forced. Elizabeth, however, was troubled, for she was remembering what she saw of Anne only a few days before. A moment later she noted that Jane and Georgiana had walked on ahead and were speaking in animated tones, while Charity held back.

"What is it, Elizabeth?"

"I was just thinking. I saw Anne speaking with a man while she was driving her phaeton only a few days ago."

Charity frowned. "That does not sound like Anne at all. Did they speak long?"

"I do not know," said Elizabeth. "Perhaps I overstated. I did see them exchange a few words, but I do not know how long she stopped. When she drove past me later, she informed me that he was a man of the area with whom she was acquainted. Then she reminded me, in no uncertain terms, that it was none of my concern."

"That sounds like my cousin," said Charity, chuckling under her breath. "It seems you have heard more words together from Anne than any of the rest of us. I am sure you feel the privilege keenly."

The stifled laugh Charity's words provoked almost set Elizabeth to coughing. She glared at her friend, but Charity only grinned and stepped forward, forcing Elizabeth to hurry to catch her. Elizabeth was not certain Charity should be speaking in such a way concerning her cousin, but there was little she could do.

The four ladies continued to walk for some time, talking and laughing as they went. They reached the outer edge of the formal gardens, looking out at the park beyond, and the woods in the distance. The afternoon sun warmed them just enough that it was not cold, though it was still spring. Elizabeth inspected some of the nearby flower beds, noting the new blooms bursting out in the new warmth the season had brought. It was such a relief that winter, with all its misery, was now firmly in the past.

"Does Lady Catherine have a rose garden?" asked Jane, looking about with interest. "Lizzy and I always tended the roses at Longbourn. I would imagine an estate such as this has a much larger garden than our few small bushes."

The look which passed between Georgiana and Charity was telling, though Jane, looking about as she was, did not notice. It appeared that between them, Georgiana had become a little somber and was not capable of answering. Thus, it fell to Charity.

"There are no roses at Rosings, ironic though it is."

"No?" asked Jane, turning to look at Charity, curiosity alive in her countenance.

"Once, there were many," continued Charity. She turned back toward the house and pointed toward the western edge. "There were substantial rose gardens near the edge of the house, down two avenues and ending in a circle at the end. It was my aunts' favorite place in the gardens—both of my aunts: Lady Catherine, and Lady Anne Darcy."

"They are not there any longer?" asked Jane, frowning.

Charity favored Jane with a wan smile. "Unfortunately, no. Lady Catherine had them all removed and replaced with other blooms, and while they are not nearly so beautiful as the roses had been, no one could gainsay her.

"For you see, roses were the favorite flowers of Georgiana's mother." Charity paused and smiled softly at the younger woman. "You remind me so much of her, Georgiana. She was quiet, patient, kind, and beautiful." Then Charity laughed. "But she was not a woman to be trifled with. You might think that Lady Catherine dominated their relationship. But in reality, Lady Anne held her own against her more forceful sister. They were very close."

"I wish I could have known my mother," whispered Georgiana.

"I know you do, dearest," replied Charity. "I was only a child when she passed, and my memories of her are those of a child. But some things I do remember, and one of my clearest memories was coming to Rosings the year after Lady Anne's passing to find that the rose gardens were no more."

Charity showed them all a sad smile. "Lady Anne tended to the rose gardens at Pemberley herself, and whenever she visited here, she loved to sit among them, shape them with a tender hand. The sisters were often to be found there when Lady Anne visited. After she passed, Lady Catherine could not bear the sight of them. So she had them removed."

"Oh, that is a sad story," said Jane, a single tear flowing from her eye. Jane's tender heart could not withstand the sorrowful tale they had heard.

"It is," replied Charity. "The pain of her loss has, of course, dulled with time. But even when she visits Pemberley, Lady Catherine will not go into the rose garden. She claims it still brings her unbearable pain."

"I love Pemberley's rose gardens," said Georgiana. "It is the one place on earth where I feel I am close to my mother."

"Have you tended to them yourself?" asked Elizabeth.

Georgiana gave a little laugh, though tinged with sadness. "I have not the talent my mother possessed. Should I tend to them, I have no doubt they will all perish quickly."

The laughter once again restored their spirits. Elizabeth suggested they walk the paths which once led through the rose gardens, and they all agreed. Soon they were ambling along, taking in the sights, imagining what it might have been like. Elizabeth thought she could almost see the scene as it would have been twenty years before when Lady Anne Darcy had still been alive. She wondered at the pain which would have resulted in the complete removal of what must have been an integral part of the formal gardens. Then her eyes found Jane, and she thought she felt an echo of what Lady Catherine must have felt.

"Well, is this not a pretty sight?"

The sound of the voice caused the four ladies to turn at once. Approaching them from the veranda were the three gentlemen in residence at Rosings. Anthony and Mr. Bingley, though they greeted them all, were quick to secure the arms of their wives. Mr. Darcy, who was not attached to either of the two remaining women, offered them both his arms. They accepted, but Elizabeth noted that Charity was grinning at her, not that she knew what had amused her friend.

"I suppose I should have known," said Mr. Darcy as they walked. "Where Miss Bennet is, nature must follow, though I might have expected to find her on some far-flung path near the edge of Rosings."

"I have not ventured nearly so far," replied Elizabeth, a hint of primness in her voice. Then she grinned. "But once I am more familiar with the lay of the land, I may see how far I can go."

"Oh, it is much too far to go, Lizzy," said Charity. "There are a few places which are worth seeing, but they are a little too far to walk. Perhaps we could ride out some day."

"I am not a horsewoman," protested Elizabeth. "Jane is the one who rides."

"But surely you *have* ridden before."

"On occasion. But I am not at all accomplished at it."

"There should be a docile mare which will serve," said Mr. Darcy. "Should the chance arise, I should be happy to accompany you."

Charity snickered, not that Elizabeth understood her mirth. But then Mr. Darcy began speaking of some of the sights to be seen in the more remote regions of the estate, and Elizabeth found herself interested in what he had to say. And they passed a pleasant time together, though Elizabeth was vexed at the significant grins her friend kept throwing in her direction.

CHAPTER XXXI

*I*t was, indeed, strange, Elizabeth decided only a few days later. No, it was more than strange, for it could not be coincidence, though initially she attempted to ascribe that most innocuous of explanations. But it happened far too often to be nothing more than fortunate happenstance. There was a guiding hand involved, though she could not quite determine the reason.

The matter to which Elizabeth was bending her thought was the sudden appearance of Mr. Darcy in her life. Or perhaps it was more correct to say the appearance of Mr. Darcy at certain times or occasions in which she had not thought to see him, nor had she come across him in the past. The first of these events happened the very day after their walk in the gardens of Rosings.

It was a beautiful spring day, and as was her custom, Elizabeth had left soon after breaking her fast to walk among the woods of Rosings. It was not a leisurely stroll, such as she might have indulged in with Jane and Charity in the gardens. No, this was a fast-paced walk, where Elizabeth swung her arms and lengthened her stride, determined to take her exercise while breathing deeply of the country air, listening to birdsong and the buzzing of bees about their spring tasks. And while she slowed at times to watch a deer in the distance or examine a particularly bright patch of wildflowers, she mostly continued on her way, covering the ground quickly and with purpose.

Thus, the appearance of a tall man from a side path where she had not expected to see anyone caught her by surprise and halted her progress in a manner akin to running headlong into a wall. "Mr. Darcy!" exclaimed she.

"Miss Bennet," said Mr. Darcy, showing her a proper bow. "How delightful it is to see you this morning. I had not thought to see you so far from the house."

"It is not a far distance at all," replied Elizabeth. She turned and pointed to where the roof of Rosings could just be discerned in the distance above a small break in the trees. "Rosings, as you can see, is just on the other side of this wood."

Mr. Darcy smiled at her, amused, it seemed. "I am quite familiar with Rosings Park, Miss Bennet. Enough so that I know exactly where I am at all times. I was referring to the fact that most young ladies do not walk so far."

"I believe we had this discussion yesterday, Mr. Darcy," said Elizabeth. "I am not like most young ladies when it comes to walking."

"No, I suppose you are not. Now that we have arrived at the same location, however, shall we continue on together?"

In some respects, Elizabeth was vexed to have her walk interrupted. It would not do, however, to castigate a man for nothing more than happenstance. He would, of course, offer to accompany her, as any gentleman would. And Elizabeth, though she would have preferred to continue on her own, could not be so rude as to refuse his company.

If it had only happened once, or perhaps once more, she might not have thought of the matter at all. But it seemed that Mr. Darcy sought her out, though she was not successful in divining his purpose. Every day for four days straight she happened upon him while walking, and the locations in which he came upon her were disparate enough that she thought it unlikely he could have done so without carefully observing her departure, determining her likely path based on his knowledge of the estate. On the fourth day, Elizabeth even altered her course once she was out of sight of the house, only to feel the annoyance when he found her, though a little later than usual.

"The coincidence of the last few days is astonishing, Mr. Darcy," said Elizabeth when he joined her that last day.

"How so?" asked Mr. Darcy. His eyes swung to her, and Elizabeth realized he must have been in the midst of some introspection.

"Why, you have come upon me while walking every day this

week," said Elizabeth, deliberately keeping her words noncommittal, wondering if he would reveal something. "I had not realized Rosings was such a small estate that two people walking it must come upon each other with such frequency."

It was all Elizabeth could do not to laugh at his shocked consternation. Whatever his purpose, it seemed as if he had not given any thought to how his actions might appear to her.

"I apologize, Miss Bennet. I had not considered that my presence might not be welcome."

It was as near to an admission as she thought she was likely to receive from him. However, while she understood that her solitude might be restored — and ensured in the future — with the correct response, she could not find it in her to speak in such a fashion.

"I *do* walk for exercise, sir, and there are times when I value my solitude. But it does not follow that I do not also welcome company on occasion. It is just that we have been meeting so often lately, I cannot but wonder if there is some guiding hand involved."

"It is possible there has," said Mr. Darcy with a straight face. "I will own that I have been walking out more of late. If you wish my absence, I am quite willing to follow a different path. You have only to say so."

"I am quite comfortable, sir. What shall we discuss today?"

The beaming smile with which he regarded her became him well, and he began to speak of matters of very little consequence — some anecdote of his cousin, of which Elizabeth was always interested to hear. It was, she decided, no hardship to walk with him. Though he was often reticent in company, it seemed he lost a little of that reserve when there were none but the two of them present.

It was an interesting progression, her feelings for this man at her side. He had seemed little interested in society when he had first arrived in Meryton, and while Elizabeth had never shared an antagonistic relationship with him, they had never been friends either. She had never had much interest in furthering an acquaintance with him, even after Jane had married his cousin. But little by little, she found that she liked him better the longer she was in his company. He had progressed from taciturn in Hertfordshire, to slightly more open in London, to interesting and talkative here in Kent. Elizabeth wondered at this change, and the only thing she could account for it was the fact that he was now among those with whom he was comfortable.

This seemed to become a little more as time passed, and especially when Lady Catherine invited the families nearby to dinner at Rosings the next day. Elizabeth and the ladies at Rosings had seen the Miss Norlands and Miss Baker again in the intervening days, but the gentlemen had not been included. On the evening in question, the two families were invited together.

"I must say," said Elizabeth to Charity while they were awaiting the arrival of their guests, "I find tonight's company much more welcome than the last visitors who were invited to dine."

Nearby, Elizabeth could see Anthony grinning at her, and by his side, Mr. Darcy let loose a chuckle. Even Lady Catherine appeared to overhear, and she allowed herself a brief smirk in response. Charity was delighted with Elizabeth's jest, for she laughed aloud, drawing the attention of all those who had not overheard the remark.

"I think I might prefer even the company of the little tyrant himself!" said she. "At least the conversation would be a great deal more intelligent."

"It is not as if he would have a high standard to surpass," was Elizabeth's dry reply.

At that moment, the Norlands were announced, and right after them, the Bakers. The reunion between the ladies was, as always, affectionate and even approaching boisterous. Mr. and Mrs. Norland were both genial, well-spoken people, he a gentleman of moderate means, tall and handsome like his son, she a plump, ruddy-cheeked woman who seemed more akin to a farmwife than the wife of a gentleman.

"How happy we both are to see you all!" exclaimed Abigail when they entered.

"At Cloverwood, all we have is wedding talk," added Alexandra.

"We must prepare for your brother's wedding," said their mother, smiling in an indulgent fashion at her daughters. "You wish to celebrate your brother's happiness, do you not?"

"Of course, Mama," said Abigail, while Alexandra rolled her eyes where her mother could not see. "It is just that we rarely speak of much else of late."

"Perhaps we *have* been busy of late," replied her mother. "Soon, they shall be married, and we will be able to leave such talk behind. Unless, of course, one of you girls finds a young man to whom you may attach yourselves."

Mrs. Norland's significant look at Mr. Darcy left no one in any doubt as to whom her words had been directed. Mr. Darcy, who had overheard their conversation in its entirety, stoically refused to react to the matron's words. Surely he had heard worse, Elizabeth was certain. Abigail kept her countenance as well, though Elizabeth knew she was not unaffected by the gentleman. Alexandra, on the other hand, blushed and looked away, and might have been quite embarrassed had Charity not begun speaking at that moment, diffusing what might have been an awkward moment.

Elizabeth's attention, however, was captured by another of the newcomers. For Mr. Baker approached her and bowed to her hasty curtsey, capturing her hand in one of his, and bowing over it. It was a near thing, she thought, for she was certain he had been about to kiss it.

"Miss Bennet," said he, "please allow me to tell you how positively enchanting you appear tonight."

Unsure what to say, for this man had not spoken two words together to her before that evening, Elizabeth thanked him and was about to turn away. But it seemed Mr. Baker was not yet done with her.

"I am curious, Miss Bennet. Though Stauneton Hall, my estate, is on the other side of Hunsford from Rosings, I believe I have seen you walking at times through the lanes. Do you walk often?"

"Ah, yes," said Charity, coming to stand by Elizabeth, fixing her with a gentle grin. "Our Lizzy is quite the walker, you see.   Rarely does the day go by when she is not found amongst the trees. I wonder at times if she does not feel more comfortable among them than among the company at Rosings."

"Indeed?" asked Mr. Baker. His gaze lingered on Charity for a moment, but soon he turned back to Elizabeth. She could not quite make him out. "Perhaps you should walk the paths of my estate. I dare say that Rosings does not lay claim to *all* the beauty of Kent."

"I believe I should be happy to walk anywhere there is peace and tranquility," replied Elizabeth. "But Stauneton is a little distant, is it not?"

"If one insists on walking," agreed Mr. Baker. "But should you ride, you could come there in no time. Or perhaps if you visit my sister, she might be happy to show you the best paths?"

"Of course, Miss Bennet would be welcome," said Elia Baker, who was standing nearby. The look she shot her brother seemed full of some meaning Elizabeth could not quite understand. "I do not believe I am the walker she is, but I would be happy to take those paths near the house with a dear friend."

"Perhaps we should host an event at Stauneton," said Mr. Baker. "The meadow by the stream, for example, would be the perfect place for a picnic. And then perhaps we could have games for the ladies and sports for the men."

Again Elia regarded her brother for a few moments before nodding slowly. "I believe I would be happy to host such an event." She turned back to Elizabeth. "We shall send out some invitations when we decide on a date."

Elizabeth thanked her, but at that moment they were called in to dinner, and a curious thing happened. Facing Mr. Baker as she was, Elizabeth noted his movement and thought he was about to offer her his arm to escort her. But suddenly Mr. Darcy appeared by Elizabeth's side and secured her arm for himself. And so she sat by the gentleman throughout dinner, though she noted the eyes of the other on her frequently.

There was one other event that evening, and it was one which was a little disturbing for Elizabeth. After dinner, they adhered to the traditional separation of the sexes, the gentlemen remaining behind in the dining room while the ladies repaired to the sitting-room. It was there that Elizabeth was approached by Elia, and she thought from the gravity in the other woman's manner that she had something, in particular, she wished to say.

"Miss Bennet," said Elia proving Elizabeth's conjecture correct, "I thought I should speak with you and inform you of something of which you may not be aware. Though I am aware it may suggest ill of one to whom I am close, I could not allow you to remain in ignorance."

"Yes?" asked Elizabeth, curious as to the other woman's meaning.

"You have marked my brother's interest in you tonight, I assume?"

"If you can call it that," said Elizabeth, surprised by her new friend's words. "He did not speak to me at all before tonight. I was surprised at his invitation to walk your estate, but I did not notice anything untoward in his actions."

"He lacked time and opportunity," replied Elia with a shaken head. "I do not speak in this way lightly, Elizabeth, but my brother, on occasion, is known to be a bit of a rake and unserious in his manner of conducting himself."

Elizabeth frowned. "Surely you do not think me in danger of him?"

"For yourself, no," replied Elia. "I have known you for only a short time, and already I am impressed with your intelligence. But James is . . . Well, let us say he can be very charming. I do not say he will attempt anything underhanded—I do not think he would behave that way with a gentlewoman. But it is possible he will flirt and woo, without any true intention. I merely wished you to be on your guard, though he is my brother."

"Thank you, Elia," replied Elizabeth, pressing her hand to Elia's. "I shall be wary of him."

With a smile, Elia changed the subject, and they spoke of other matters. Abigail and Alexandra, being nearby, also joined their discussion. When the gentlemen returned, Elizabeth did not see anything in James Baker's manners which suggested any particular interest. But then that changed when he spied her without another in attendance.

While Elizabeth did not know if there was anything about which to be concerned, she held herself back a little. At the very least, she would not allow herself to feel anything for this man unless he first showed her feelings of substance of his own.

One matter of which Elizabeth could not help but be aware was the effect of Mr. Darcy's attention toward her on his relations. Though she could not be certain if Georgiana had seen anything, and she knew Charity would likely cheer, should Mr. Darcy declare himself to her, the same was not true of the de Bourghs.

Miss de Bourgh, for her part, seemed to care little. She gave Mr. Darcy as little of her attention as she did anyone else in the family, and if he was more attentive to Elizabeth, her demeanor did not change in the slightest. But Lady Catherine was a different matter entirely. Elizabeth was certain that Lady Catherine was preternaturally aware of everything Mr. Darcy did, particularly when it concerned the likelihood of his proposing to her daughter. The existence of an impediment would surely not be received with any equanimity on the part of the lady.

Elizabeth felt fortunate, therefore, when Lady Catherine did not say anything on the subject, for she felt she had forged an understanding of sorts with the lady. Whether this would continue, should Mr. Darcy's attentions grow more pointed, she could not say. But at present, she was grateful the peace was kept. In the back of her mind, however, she wondered how long it would take Lady Catherine to demand her attendance so as to determine the truth of the matter.

Two days after the dinner party, the gentlemen suggested they go into Westerham for a day. "It cannot be agreeable to young ladies to be confined to an estate, even one as fine as Rosings, for days on end," said Anthony with a teasing grin. "Westerham is not large, though perhaps it is a little larger than Meryton. Still, there are some shops we could visit, and perhaps an inn would be available where we could take luncheon."

The plan was agreed on by most of the company, and they prepared to depart. Lady Catherine, unsurprisingly, waved them off, admonishing them to take care while traveling, while Miss de Bourgh declined to go for reasons of her own.

"Shall you not go as well, Anne?" asked Lady Catherine, frowning at her only daughter. "Though I would not wish you to tax your strength by wandering about Westerham the entire day, I should think a little amusement would do you good."

The significant glance in Mr. Darcy's direction informed them all as to her meaning. But Miss de Bourgh was not to be persuaded. "I have little desire to be in such a dingy little town. It is dusty and small, and I am sure I would much rather drive my phaeton."

It may have been that in the past Lady Catherine might have simply commanded her daughter. But Miss de Bourgh was an adult, and it seemed she was accustomed to making such choices as these for herself. Lady Catherine regarded her for a few moments before she sighed and allowed the matter to rest. Elizabeth's conjectures about Lady Catherine were borne out when the subject arose in the carriage.

"Did that seem odd to you, Darcy?" asked Charity.

Mr. Darcy, who had been looking out the window, said: "Anne and Lady Catherine?"

"Yes. Lady Catherine has rarely *asked*, in my experience. She is more likely to command and expect to be obeyed."

"It seems Anne has developed more than a hint of determination about her," said Mr. Darcy with a shrug. "It is past due, in my opinion. Anne *is* four and twenty, after all. It is unseemly for her mother to command her in all things when she is of age."

Charity nodded and the subject was dropped. For the rest of the short journey to the town, the two ladies continued to speak, while Mr. Darcy contented himself to listening, occasionally interjecting with his own comment. They arrived at Westerham and disembarked, reunited with the Bingleys and the Fitzwilliams, who had come in another carriage, and set off in search of amusement.

It was, as Miss de Bourgh had averred, a small town, much on the same level as Meryton, and not lacking in dust. There were all the usual sorts of shops one might find in such a town, and Elizabeth was pleased to find there was a small bookstore where she might replenish her stock of books. It was no surprise to her that she was not alone in this desire.

"My cousin informed me of your predilection for books, Miss

Bennet," said Mr. Darcy. He extended his arm. "Shall we browse the selection together?"

"You like books, do you, Mr. Darcy?"

"Indeed, I am quite fond of the written word. My family library at Pemberley is quite extensive, the collection being the work of several generations of Darcys." He grinned as he opened the door and ushered her inside. "Given what I know of you, I suspect I might not see you again, should you be shown the library there."

"But then I would have no time for walking," said Elizabeth. "I *do* have other interests."

"I am sure you do," replied Mr. Darcy, apparently enjoying the conversation.

They browsed the bookstore for some half hour, continuing a running conversation as they did so. At times, each pointed out a work they had read or heard of, and it would further the discussion of their likes and dislikes. Elizabeth found several books she thought she might enjoy which came of his suggestions, while she thought she was able to return the favor.

They met with the other members of the party and made their way toward the inn. Elizabeth was not unaware of the significant looks and muted laughter they had attracted, but she decided to simply ignore her companions. The inn was clean and the food was good. They sat around rough tables, eating their fill of the fare offered there. As chance had it, she was once again seated by Mr. Darcy, and the conversation in which they engaged was somehow more personal than anything of which they had spoken before.

"No, I have no close family other than Georgiana," said Mr. Darcy in response to a query of Elizabeth's. "I think you might have heard me speak of some cousins, but they are distant, though we do see them on occasion. My father had no siblings, and while my grandfather had both a brother and a sister, neither survived to adulthood."

"It must have been difficult," said Elizabeth. "I understand your father passed when you were yet a young man. To take responsibility for an estate and a much younger sister must have been overwhelming."

"At times it certainly seemed so," replied Mr. Darcy. She could see his eyes moving down the table until they alighted on his only sister, who was speaking with Elizabeth's favorite. "But Georgiana has always been a quiet girl, never giving a hint of trouble. There . . . She is the best sister a man could have. I would do anything to keep her safe, no matter who it was who endangered her wellbeing."

Mr. Darcy seemed to gather himself, and he turned back to Elizabeth. "She was close to my father, as he was the only parent she ever knew. But he . . . he was never the same after my mother's death."

"Your parents were close."

"They were," replied Mr. Darcy. "Theirs was a love match. I might have scorned the poets who write of the devastation of a broken heart had I not witnessed it myself. In the end, I think my father was eager to be reunited with his beloved wife. As difficult as it was to lose him, the thought that they were once again together made it possible to bear."

Elizabeth thought on his words, considered what they might mean for her. There seemed to be drawbacks to marrying for love, though she had long wished for it herself.

"Would it be worth it?"

"Marrying for love?" asked Mr. Darcy.

Embarrassed, as she had not meant to speak out loud, Elizabeth could do nothing more than nod. Mr. Darcy thought for a moment, his focus on something beyond sight and sound. But when he spoke, she was touched deep in her heart.

"I think it must be. I know that the fashion is to marry for other reasons, but I do not think a marriage can be full unless the partners possess an affection for each other which goes beyond their interest in wealth and position."

"Hearing of your family makes me a little jealous, Mr. Darcy."

Mr. Darcy turned to her, and the way his interest was aroused reminded Elizabeth of a dog perking up at a sound only it could hear. The image almost prompted Elizabeth to laughter, though she was able to rein it in.

"In what way?"

"Surely you must have seen that my parents do not share an equal felicity," replied Elizabeth. "They have little affection for each other. My mother does not understand my father, and my father has little respect for her. It was this, in part, which has always driven my desire to avoid such a union myself."

The expression with which Mr. Darcy regarded her was unreadable, though she thought she saw him nod to himself ever so slightly. When he spoke, she thought there was a warmth in his tone even beyond that which had been present before.

"You wish for love in marriage, then."

"I do," replied Elizabeth. "Any union in which respect and love are not present cannot be agreeable." Elizabeth paused and sighed. "It has not been difficult to see the discord between my mother and father, Mr. Darcy. In some way, I suppose I have contributed to it."

A frown settled over his face. "What do you mean?"

"I am my father's favorite child," replied Elizabeth. "I am most like him in temperament, sharing the interest of books and a love of debate. Having a daughter who enjoys such things, who behaves in what my mother considers a manner so unlikely to ever attract a husband, is difficult for her. It is also difficult for me, as there have been times when I thought I could not ever please her."

"And do you still feel that way?"

"I have long become accustomed to my mother's opinions. I think she has greater hope for me now, though I was admonished to return to Longbourn with a suitor in tow." Elizabeth shot him a grin, in part because she was eager to leave the subject behind. "Do you know of any possibilities, Mr. Darcy?"

His gravity was entirely feigned she thought, and he made a great show of considering the matter for several moments. "At present, I do not," said he at length. "But perhaps a little thought on the matter will bring someone to mind.

"Now, Miss Bennet," said he, gesturing to the package of books on the table beside her, "I believe you have some books there which I have read. Perhaps when you have also read them, we may compare our opinions?"

"I should like that, Mr. Darcy," said Elizabeth. "Very much."

CHAPTER XXXII

$\mathcal{T}$he preparations had been completed for the event to be held at Stauneton Hall, and while Elia Baker was enjoying her last few weeks as mistress of her brother's home, she looked forward to marrying and moving into her own home. Now, she only had to keep her brother from inserting himself into a mess of his own making. And for that purpose, she sought him out the morning of the event.

"James," said she when she found him in his study. It was not a location he could often be found. Estate business was, as James was fond of saying, a tedious business. He could be termed an indifferent master at times, though he did enough to maintain the profitability of the estate. But he did nothing more.

"Yes, Elia?" said James, his smirk informing Elia that he was likely aware of what she wished to speak. "Has everything been arranged?"

"Of course," was Elia's simple reply.

"Excellent!" said he, clapping and rubbing his hands together. "I am anticipating this afternoon's diversion keenly."

Elia regarded him for a moment before raising the subject. "I was not unaware of your interest in Miss Bennet the last time we saw her."

"She *is* a fine woman, is she not?" mused James. "Such spirit, such vivacity! Taming it will be a pleasure, indeed."

"I doubt she wishes to be tamed, James."

"Oh, you know what I mean." James waved his hand and chuckled to himself. "Her spirit is the most appealing thing about her, though she is quite pretty. It was merely an expression—nothing more."

"It would be best, James, if you practice circumspection in this instance."

"Oh?" was James's lazy reply. "In what way?"

"I am aware of your usual manner with young ladies, Brother—do not attempt to deny it. I urge you to avoid trifling with Miss Bennet."

"And you think I mean to trifle with her?"

Elia avoided looking skyward in exasperation, though it was a near thing. "I cannot say. You have done it many times in the past, you must own." His mouth opened to protest, but Elia shook her head and silenced him. "Yes, I know you do not set out to play with their emotions. But you flirt far too much, and your manner of lovemaking is altogether unserious. Not only will Miss Bennet see through your efforts, but she has powerful protectors who will not appreciate your manners."

"Protectors?" asked James, once again infuriating her with his lack of seriousness. "It seems to me there is only Fitzwilliam."

"What of Mr. Darcy?" asked Elia. "He is connected to her now through marriage. And do not discount Lady Catherine's interest in the matter. Furthermore," continued she, fixing him with a sly look, looking to provoke a response, "I do not think Mr. Darcy is indifferent to her. Quite the opposite, in fact."

"Perhaps he is not," was James's scornful reply. "But I have every confidence that Darcy will behave in his usual manner, and it is not one likely to incite a woman's good opinion. The man is as stiff as a board and about half as interesting. I do not fear his interference."

"James," said Elia, a warning note in the voice.

"Do not worry, Sister. I have nothing in mind but to pay Miss Bennet the attention of a true suitor. I shall not act in a manner which will set off her 'protectors,' nor will I attempt to trifle with her feelings. I am interested in her—that is all."

It was clear the subject was closed, in James's opinion, and with that Elia was forced to be content. If he did provoke Colonel Fitzwilliam's anger, Elia did not think the colonel would be too harsh with him. At least she hoped so. If Mr. Darcy had an interest in Miss Bennet as Elia suspected, his would be the greater anger. Hopefully, James would be as good as his word.

*   *   *

As Mr. Baker had promised, the invitation to the picnic was received and accepted, and the Rosings party made their way to Stauneton Hall in two carriages. Lady Catherine was, unsurprisingly, not of a mind to grace the youngsters with her presence. Miss de Bourgh, however, actually consented to go.

"I shall drive my phaeton there," said she, her tone suggesting none of them were invited to accompany her.

Elizabeth did not think anyone was offended by her words, and when the time came to depart, she noted the phaeton being prepared by the stable hands. As it was, it took her a little longer to arrive than the carriages, a fact which Elizabeth attributed to her tendency to drive slowly, as per Lady Catherine's repeated instructions. It seemed there were still some things about which the lady still held sway over her daughter.

The scene which greeted them when they arrived was picturesque, one which Elizabeth found charming. The meadow sat some little distance to the east of the manor, and Elizabeth could immediately see why it had been chosen. It was wide and flat, allowing plenty of space for sports for the gentlemen, and games had been set up to one side. On the edge of the meadow furthest from the house, a small brook bubbled and bustled along on its way to the sea, wide enough that it could only be crossed by stepping on a series of stones which might have seemed like they had been put there for that purpose. But it was not deep at all, and Elizabeth knew that should she slip from the rocks, nothing more than her shoes and the bottom of her petticoats would be wet, as long as she kept her feet.

Upon their arrival, it seemed evident to Elizabeth that the whole party had yet to gather. Not only were there still carriages pulling up to the house, but those guests already in attendance were milling about, some speaking together in small clusters, while others seemed engaged in exploring the area in which they found themselves. Elizabeth felt the pull of new vistas to discover and indicated her intention to her companions, who, it seemed, were equally eager to have a little time to themselves among the bustle.

"Of course, you wish to walk down to the stream," said Anthony, giving her a knowing grin. "I trust you will not go far?"

"There appears to be a little time before the festivities truly begin," replied Elizabeth in kind. "But not so much time as to allow me to walk to Rosings and back. I promise I shall not go far."

"Then go to it."

"I would be happy to escort Miss Bennet," said Mr. Darcy from where he was standing nearby. "That is if you would not find my presence an inhibiting factor in your need to wander."

Though initially hesitant, Elizabeth found she was not opposed to Mr. Darcy's presence. Anthony and Jane exchanged a look, but Elizabeth decided to ignore them. If they had seen the same thing she had, there was no reason to reply or to give them any fuel for their mirth. Instead, she fixed Mr. Darcy with a smile and agreed to his escort. A moment later they were off.

"I would offer you my arm," said Mr. Darcy as they set out. "But I suspect part of your enjoyment of the exercise is the freedom to move in whatever way you choose."

Elizabeth turned a smile on him. "While your offer would be appreciated, I cannot say you are incorrect." Turning, she continued on her way, leading him toward the stream while she swung her arms in an exaggerated fashion. "Are you familiar at all with the area, Mr. Darcy?"

"Not at all," replied Mr. Darcy. "While I have visited Stauneton Hall on occasion, I have never been on the estate other than the manor. The last time I was here, it would not have been wise, and James Baker is not a man with whom I associate."

There were all sorts of intriguing inferences in Mr. Darcy's statement, but Elizabeth was mindful of not prying. As such, she contented herself with a softly spoken "Oh?" inviting explanation, but not requiring it. Mr. Darcy seemed little concerned with her curiosity, and he readily replied.

"Miss Baker, you see, at one time held . . . Well, to be honest, I am not sure what it was. I think it was not infatuation, as it seemed quite more calculated than that."

Elizabeth turned with some surprise. "Elia Baker? I should not have thought it of her. She is perfectly amiable and seems to regard her betrothed with all the affection one would hope to find in one affianced to another."

"I believe theirs *is* a love match," agreed Mr. Darcy. "But it was not always thus. You must understand this was several years ago when she was yet young and her father yet lived. Mr. Baker was a man who always seemed to me to be grasping for more than he had, and a connection to the Darcy family — and by extension, the de Bourghs and Fitzwilliams — would have been a feather in his cap."

"You suspect he was guiding his daughter?"

"It is possible," said Mr. Darcy with a shrug. "The change in her seeming ambitions did come about some time after her father's death, and she was further changed by the attentions paid to her by Mr. Norland. Whether her father was the true force behind her actions I cannot say, nor do I wish to inquire. It is enough that she is now diverted, and I have every reason to believe she will be happy in her future life."

"That does seem to be in her future," replied Elizabeth.

By this time they had reached the stream, and Elizabeth took to examining every inch of it she could. It was a happy brook, and she reveled in the picturesque scene, stopping every few moments to inhale the scent of the wildflowers which grew on its banks. She even picked one or two of the blooms, noting that Mr. Darcy appeared bemused at her actions. He stooped and plucked a bluebell of his own, handing it to her with a bow.

"I believe, Miss Bennet, that this bloom would look beautiful set in your hair. It complements the blue of your dress quite perfectly."

With a shy smile, Elizabeth took the bloom and situated it in her hair, poking out above one ear, such that she could only just see it out of the corner of her eye. Then she looked at Mr. Darcy and posed a little for him, before bursting into laughter. Then, feeling entirely free and uninhibited, she hopped lightly to a large flat rock which lay some little distance from the edge of the bank.

"It is as lovely as I thought, Miss Bennet," said Mr. Darcy, looking at her intently. "But perhaps traversing these stones would not be the best course of action? I promised Fitzwilliam I would keep you safe."

"I shall not go further," said Elizabeth. "But you must own they are entirely inviting. Do you know what lies beyond this river?"

"I believe the land belonging to Stauneton Hall extends some distance further. Unless I am mistaken, Briar Ridge lies beyond."

"The home of Lady Metcalfe?"

"You have met her."

"No, I have not yet made her acquaintance," replied Elizabeth. Then she grinned before springing to the next rock. "But Lady Metcalfe is a great friend of your aunt's, I believe. One could hardly be at Rosings long and not hear of her."

"Indeed," replied Mr. Darcy, returning her smile. "In fact, I understand Lady Catherine congratulates herself on recently placing a young woman with Lady Metcalfe's young niece as a companion."

Elizabeth laughed. "Yes, we heard of the matter at great length after we arrived. It seems that Miss Pope is a veritable treasure, to hear Lady Catherine speak of her."

In this manner, they continued for some time, though Elizabeth, noting Mr. Darcy's concern for her jumping from rock to rock soon returned to the edge of the stream. They amused themselves with further banter, though nothing of much depth was said between them, interspersed with pauses to stop and survey the scene or look back at the meadow where the guests were gathering.

While Elizabeth was speaking with Mr. Darcy, she was struck by the easiness with which they conversed, the old silent and cold Mr. Darcy having given way to this new man who did not appear in the slightest uncomfortable. Elizabeth wondered at the change in him. The interest with which he viewed her, she had acknowledged, though a part of her mind hurried to remind Elizabeth that she still did not know what his interest presaged. Either way, a man did not suddenly change, become a completely different man. Something must have happened to suppress this man, to make him uncommunicative and surly in company. But Elizabeth could not understand what.

Their interesting tête-à-tête was not destined to continue, however, for not only was the party gathered together before long, but another intruded on their walk together. Elizabeth espied his approach first, drawing Mr. Darcy's attention thither. And soon James Baker stood before them.

"Darcy," said he, his tone distant. Then he turned to Elizabeth, and the warmth was unmistakable, even had no contrast existed. "Miss Bennet. I believe everyone has now assembled. May I escort you back to the tables?"

It was impossible not to glance back at Mr. Darcy. She did not know what to make of Mr. Baker approaching and claiming her in this manner, but Elizabeth was heartened when Mr. Darcy nodded and smiled at her.

"Of course, Mr. Baker," said Elizabeth. "I would be happy to return with you."

"I hope you are enjoying the views of my home," said Baker as he escorted Miss Bennet back to the rest of the company.

"It is very lovely, sir," replied Miss Bennet.

Baker beamed as if she had just paid him the highest compliment. Darcy, who was walking to Miss Bennet's other side, could see her bemusement. He expected the other man was too blind to notice.

"Kent *is* a lovely county," replied Mr. Baker. "I am fortunate my home is situated within. It is not called the garden of England for no reason."

"Yes, Kent is lovely," said Darcy, drawing Miss Bennet's attention back to him. "But though the north is certainly more rugged and untamed, the wildness has a beauty all its own. Have you ever visited the north, Miss Bennet?"

"I have not had that pleasure, Mr. Darcy," replied Miss Bennet.

By her side, Baker only sniffed with disdain. "I suppose there is a sort of wild prettiness about the peaks. But the southern counties are where true people of culture live, where society thrives and grows ever more sophisticated. And Kent is at its heart."

"I believe I should like to see the peaks someday, Mr. Darcy," said Miss Bennet, turning to him. "I understand your cousin's estate is not far distant from them?"

"Not far at all," replied Darcy. "But from Pemberley—my estate—you can actually see them on a clear day, from certain locations. If you should come to Thorndell with your sister, you would likely have the opportunity to come to Pemberley as well. I would be happy to show you, and I am sure Fitzwilliam would be happy to go there as well."

"Yes, yes, we all know how proud of your estate you are, Darcy," said Baker, waving his hand in a mixture of annoyance and dismissal. "Perhaps you should speak of it another time." Baker turned to Miss Bennet as they were walking, and he gave her a flirtatious smile. "I would be happy to show you the woods of my estate. Should we go there in a curricle? I am an expert driver, you understand."

"Perhaps," said Miss Bennet. "Are they much different from those I have found in Rosings?"

Baker seemed a little disappointed. "The varieties are likely the same. But I have often found the pattern of the woods of Stauneton is superior to those at Rosings."

"Is it?" asked Miss Bennet, while at the same time she stifled a laugh. "Has nature somehow designed a more pleasing formation of your woods? How fortunate."

At first, Baker watched her, a hesitation in his manner suggesting he thought Miss Bennet was making sport with him. For Darcy himself, he was well aware Miss Bennet was mocking him ever so slightly. It was difficult for Darcy to contain his own laughter—to suggest that Stauneton had somehow received the benefit of the trees growing in exactly the proper locations, superior to those of Rosings, was more than a little silly. Darcy might have imagined the estimable Mr. Collins saying something similar!

"Ah, here we are!" said Baker, using their proximity to the tables to change the subject. "Shall I fix you a plate, Miss Bennet?"

For an instant, Darcy felt annoyance well up within his breast, for he had thought to offer Miss Bennet that service himself. But then Darcy realized that vying with this man for her attention must necessarily lessen her pleasure in the activity of the day. Thus, he decided to simply stay near to her, ready to assist, should Baker show his true nature and become too familiar with her. It was a determination made easier by the fact that she seemed little impressed with his flattery and not at all affected by his artificial manners.

Having given her consent, Miss Bennet turned her footsteps to where Fitzwilliam and Jane had taken a blanket beneath a tree which offered a bit of shade. Bingley and Georgiana were also there, as was Anne, though she did not appear any more likely to interact with those present than at any other time. As Darcy watched, he noted Elia Baker's approach, watched as she spoke with Miss Bennet for a few moments, after which she continued on to see to the comfort of some other guests. Then Darcy turned his attention to acquiring a plate for himself, unintentionally drawing himself back near Baker. It appeared the man could not keep from speaking, though Darcy might have wished he kept his own counsel.

"A marvelous woman, is she not, Darcy?" Baker shot a sly look at him and turned back to the table. "It *is* a pity her portion is so small, though she herself is enough to overcome such a deficiency."

"I think very highly of Miss Bennet," replied Darcy, careful not to insinuate anything. "She is my cousin's sister now, and family."

"That she is," replied Baker. "I suppose that must make her much more attractive to a potential suitor. A connection to Matlock is not a trifling matter."

Darcy observed as Baker heaped a generous portion of cheese, meats, and bread on Miss Bennet's plate—or at least he assumed it was for her. He shook his head ever so minutely. Watching her as he had these past months, Darcy thought her tastes were a little lighter than what Baker was providing, and Darcy specifically remembered her asking for more fruits and less of the cakes that Baker was now adding to her plate. It appeared the man had not been listening as she had made her requests.

Though knowing it might be difficult to allow her to take them from his plate with any hint of propriety, Darcy ensured he had some berries which were just in season for her to consume. Then he turned and made his way back toward where Miss Bennet was waiting for their return.

"I think I may try my luck with her," said Baker, hurrying to join Darcy as he walked. "Stauneton is a prosperous estate. I can weather the lack of a dowry from a prospective bride, as long as she is the right woman for me. What say you, Darcy? Is a woman worth more than the sum of money she brings into a marriage?"

"The right woman is worth her weight in gold," replied Darcy, again refusing to rise to Baker's bait.

Baker was unable to respond, for they had come too close to the group awaiting them. Miss Bennet was sitting beside her sister, daintily chewing on several berries she had obtained, no doubt from her sister's plate. Darcy was given all the pleasure of seeing her receive her plate with a hint of exasperation, though it was clear that Baker did not notice anything.

And so they sat to partake of their meal. True to Darcy's concern, Baker began to be very forward with her, attempting to sit close and tempt her with little delicacies from his own plate. Fitzwilliam noticed it too, for he watched Baker as a hawk watches a fat mouse scurrying through the grass below. But Miss Bennet proved entirely capable of fending Baker off herself.

"Come, Miss Bennet," said he, holding a small tart before her. "I neglected to add one of these custard tarts to your plate, but I assure you they are our cook's specialty, and quite delicious."

"I thank you, sir," was Miss Bennet's determined reply, "but I find you have provided me with quite enough of this sort of fare. Perhaps another time."

Baker frowned in disappointment, but when he pressed her further, she only said: "No thank you, sir."

Even Fitzwilliam seemed to relax when he noted Miss Bennet's adeptness in putting Baker off. Darcy chuckled and shook his head. He surreptitiously passed a few berries from his plate to Fitzwilliam's, who grinned and gave them to his wife. Then Mrs. Fitzwilliam, apparently catching on to their game, smiled and offered them to Miss Bennet.

"Would you like some blueberries, Lizzy?"

"Yes, thank you, Jane," replied Miss Bennet. The way her eyes found Darcy's, however, suggested she had seen exactly what had happened.

"Ah, yes!" exclaimed Baker. "Those are from our hothouse. I would be happy to show it to you, Miss Bennet, for there are many varieties of fruits growing therein. We have been able to coax many of the trees and bushes to give of their bounty quite out of their usual seasons."

"I am sure there will be ample opportunity to do so another day, Mr. Baker," said Miss Bennet. "At present, I am enjoying the picnic far too much."

And so it continued. It was fortunate, Darcy decided, that Baker did not try some of the more forward tactics he had seen from many others—Wickham among them. But that was no doubt due to Miss Bennet having Fitzwilliam, Bingley, and Darcy himself nearby as her protectors. When forced to resort to more proper methods of wooing a woman, it seemed Baker was in unfamiliar territory, for his attempts were ineffectual and often ended making him look silly.

When the meal was finished, the guests were encouraged to partake in the games, and Baker was quick to solicit Miss Bennet's participation in croquet. Darcy, not interested in playing the lawn games they had assembled, contented himself with watching her pleasing form as she played. She was quite good at it, he decided—no doubt she had played often with her sisters or other friends.

"If Baker was not being quite so much of a fool," said Fitzwilliam, standing by his side as he watched, "I might decide I do not like his familiarity with Elizabeth. As it stands, I fear Elizabeth's wrath should I interfere, much more than the thought he might succeed in anything underhanded."

"She does appear well capable of handling him," agreed Darcy.

Fitzwilliam turned and eyed Darcy for a moment. "You seem to be rather sanguine about it. It appeared to me that you and Elizabeth were rather comfortable together before he inserted himself between you."

"It was quite enjoyable," replied Darcy. "But I do not wish to come between her and her pleasure today. Vying for her attention would vex her and understandably so."

"Wise choice," said Fitzwilliam. "Then I suppose I shall content myself with watching him closely. But should he step out of line, I will take great pleasure in informing him it would not be wise to trifle with her."

"I entirely agree, Cousin."

After a time of this, the gentlemen gathered together in a game of cricket. It seemed Baker was attempting to induce her to provide a favor for his efforts, but Miss Bennet appeared to be quite obtuse as to his meaning. Darcy took great pleasure in noting how much more athletically inclined he was than Baker. In fact, on Baker's first bowl, Darcy hit it so far over the fielders' heads, he thought they would have some difficulty finding the ball thereafter. The scowl Baker directed at him did nothing to dampen Darcy's mood either.

CHAPTER XXXIII

*I*t seemed to Elizabeth that the picnic at Stauneton Hall was the final removal of all restraint, at least when it came to the attentions of one James Baker. While she could not accuse him of *improper* behavior, his wooing was an odd mix of awkward entreaties, grandiose declarations, and even, occasionally, entirely forward behavior. It was as if the man did not quite know how to recommend himself to a woman or was holding himself back in some way.

While Elizabeth was required to fend off his ardency in those moments when he became too eager, she found him to be rather endearing, though at times she was annoyed by his persistence. She had no notion that he was insincere or had ulterior motives in mind. He seemed entirely serious, and though she did not find herself falling madly in love with him, she also did not wish to unduly hurt him. Thus, she allowed herself to enjoy those times when he behaved like a suitor, rather than a man who wished something from her that no respectable lady would give.

"I can warn him off if you like," said Anthony one day about a week after the picnic. "He has a certain reputation in the neighborhood which I cannot like, and there are times when his behavior makes me wish to call him out."

"And ruin our Elizabeth's fun?" demanded Charity with a laugh. "Heaven forbid, Anthony. What does a woman like more than a man at her beck and call?"

Elizabeth glared at her friend, but Charity only winked and laughed. Charity had grown increasingly amused at the situation and was not shy about giving her opinion, which was usually in the form of a jest. While Elizabeth appreciated her high spirits, which helped raise her own, at times they became a little much.

"Do you suspect him of anything improper?" asked Elizabeth, turning her eyes back toward Anthony.

He paused while he scratched his chin, and then he shook his head. "There are occasions when he is a little forward. But overall he seems to be behaving himself better than I might have expected."

"Then there is nothing which needs to be done. Warn him on those occasions, but I can handle him otherwise."

"Surely you are not falling in love with him, Lizzy," said Jane.

"No, Jane," replied Elizabeth with a fond smile at her sister. "He *can* be charming at times. But most often he seems more like a lost puppy. I will not lose my heart to him."

Anthony guffawed at Elizabeth's characterization, and she had to warn him most sternly to refrain from telling Mr. Baker what she said. The rest of her companions all seemed amused, though Georgiana's amusement appeared a little strained. Mr. Darcy just sat and watched it all, and once the discussion had ended, he changed the subject and turned her attention to other matters.

He was, of course, the other player in this drama. The interest Elizabeth had marked on Mr. Darcy's part had not waned, but he seemed willing to move slowly, to come to know her better, and to allow her to know him. When Mr. Baker came, he did not attempt to insert himself between them, instead content to watch and wait. This behavior was a matter of some smugness for Mr. Baker, a fact which *did* cause Elizabeth some annoyance. But she was also grateful to Mr. Darcy for his forbearance, for whatever his intentions comprised, she did not wish to become the prize to be won between two warring factions. And while there were no hostilities in Lady Catherine's sitting-room, Elizabeth knew her ladyship watched all with a keen eye. Elizabeth knew it was only a matter of time before Lady Catherine began demanding some answers. She would wish to protect her daughter's interests.

So this continued until the days spent at Rosings began to lengthen into weeks. All of April had passed away and May arrived, and with it a letter from Mr. Bennet.

"You have a letter from Papa?" asked Jane when the missive was delivered to her on a silver salver.

Elizabeth nodded with distraction, turning it over, noting it was only one sheet of paper, as was her father's wont. "This is only the second time since we have left Longbourn," said Elizabeth with an absence of mind. "The first was before we left Brighton."

"You have written regularly, I assume," inquired Jane.

"Yes, I have. But you know Papa. It seems I am destined to be continually writing letters to him without the hope of a reply, especially when I leave his home forever."

Opening it, Elizabeth read through the short missive and could not help but laugh. Seated by her side, Jane waited patiently, obviously noting from Elizabeth's laughter that there was nothing untoward contained within. After a short time, Elizabeth passed the letter to her sister and allowed her to read it herself.

"What do you do here, ladies?" asked a voice. They looked up as one to see Anthony standing there watching them, with Mr. Darcy at his side.

"I have received a letter from my father," replied Elizabeth. "It seems he is being driven to distraction at Longbourn by our youngest sisters."

The gentlemen took seats nearby, and Mr. Darcy fixed them with a grin. "Knowing your sisters, might I hazard a guess that the militia is to depart?"

"They are to summer in Brighton." Elizabeth shook her head. "Apparently my mother and my two youngest sisters have joined forces in pleading with my father to take them all to Brighton this summer. After all, we cannot allow Lizzy to have all the amusement."

"And will your father yield, do you think?" asked Anthony.

"It is unlikely," said Jane, passing the letter back to Elizabeth.

"Papa hates to travel," added Elizabeth. "He will endure their complaints by locking himself in his study, and while the noise will increase to a crescendo after the militia left, eventually they will subside into a sullen silence." Elizabeth paused and then in a quiet voice said: "He also asks when he might expect my return."

At that, Elizabeth could see Mr. Darcy's eyebrows rise with interest, though he allowed his cousin to make the response. "Do you wish to return home, Elizabeth?"

"At present, I do not wish it. If you feel you can continue to endure my presence."

The warm smile with which he regarded her filled Elizabeth's breast with pleasure. "You know we are happy to have you with us, for as long as you wish."

"I believe the company would be much diminished should you leave us," added Mr. Darcy.

It was strange, but Mr. Darcy's words evoked that much more delight, and the thought passed through Elizabeth's mind, wondering if she were coming to feel more for him than she was aware. The demands of the moment must be met, however, and she endeavored to reply to their still open question.

"Then I shall stay for the present." She paused and laughed. "But I am still underage, you know. He can order me home at any time he pleases."

"Oh, Lizzy," said Jane with a fond shake of her head. "You know that Papa will not deny you anything you want."

"And in another two months I shall be of age," replied Elizabeth. "Then he shall not have the power to order me anywhere."

"Freedom shall then be yours," said Anthony, rather expansively.

Elizabeth directed a fond smile at him. "Perhaps I shall redirect him, then. Mary is a good girl, though she does pay too much attention to Fordyce, and other such works. I think if Papa took the trouble to speak to her, he would find in her an acceptable substitute in my absence."

"Then you should write to him," said Anthony. "For we are not willing to forgo your company just yet."

So Elizabeth did just that. When she went to post the letter sometime later, she placed her missive on the platter near the entrance for posting and turned to go back to the veranda where she had just been sitting with her sister. But when she arrived there, she noted that only Mr. Darcy was still present.

"My cousin and your sister decided they wanted to walk in the gardens," said Mr. Darcy. Elizabeth followed his gesture with her eyes and noted they had walked to the edge of the gardens and were likely to meander their way back from there. "I would be happy for your company if you are willing. Shall I send for more lemonade?"

Elizabeth acquiesced and took her seat while Mr. Darcy signaled to a footman, passing his instructions to the man. Then he turned back to Elizabeth, though he did not say anything. Engaged as she was in watching her sister and brother, she did not regret the lack of conversation between them. That Jane was happy was evident in her every action. It was all Elizabeth had ever wished for her sister.

"I have been thinking of your father," said Mr. Darcy, drawing Elizabeth's eyes to him. "I believe I understand what he is feeling."

"You do?" asked Elizabeth, curious as to his meaning.

"Yes. In fact, I believe I have experienced much the same only this past summer and autumn." When Elizabeth's look turned questioning, Mr. Darcy said: "When I was at Pemberley, I missed Georgiana dreadfully. Everything was so quiet. While my home has been a solemn sort of place for many years, it was even quieter than usual. I missed her."

"I can understand that sentiment, Mr. Darcy," said Elizabeth. "But I am not certain it is exactly the same. She is your sister, yes, and you are very close to her. But we are my father's children. Those at home have been reduced from five to three within a week's time."

"Have I not been brother *and* father to Georgiana?" asked Mr. Darcy. Elizabeth sensed it was a rhetorical question, and she did not respond. "Even before my father's death, I often assumed that role with her, for my father was often occupied with the estate or mired in his own grief. It is *not* precisely the same, but it is close enough that I can sympathize with Mr. Bennet."

Mr. Darcy's eyes swung to Elizabeth, and she sensed a great warmth within them, warmth which seemed to enter her own breast, making her feel more in response to this man than she ever had before. He held her eyes for a moment before breaking contact, looking out once again over the gardens. At that moment, their lemonade was delivered, and Elizabeth took it upon herself to pour glasses for them both. They sat in silence for several moments before Mr. Darcy was moved to speak again.

"The other part of the matter is, of course, your sister's marriage. You see, I also witnessed my own sister finding her happiness, and while I rejoice that she has, it has been hard letting her go. Mr. Bennet has already been required to make such a sacrifice. I cannot help but think that he expects to be making another in the near future."

"Do you refer to me?" asked Elizabeth, wondering if he was on the verge of a declaration.

"I do," replied Mr. Darcy. "As you have matured, you have, no doubt, traveled further and further from home. A man knows that his daughters will, one day, leave him for the home of another. It is difficult to see that happen, to watch as another man takes the position of prime importance in her life. No man will deny his daughter fulfillment as a wife, a mother, and a woman in her own right—not if he truly loves her. But it *is* hard."

"I have never thought of it that way," replied Elizabeth.

A soft smile was Mr. Darcy's response. "I am not surprised. But a man feels it nonetheless. Your sister has married a man who has an estate in the north, one which is not close to his own home. I think your father suspects you will follow her to her home, and when you eventually marry, you will likely be a similar distance as she."

Elizabeth shook her head. "What you say makes sense. But I have no notion that I shall be married in the near future. I am not exactly surrounded by suitors and admirers."

"You underestimate yourself, Miss Bennet," said Mr. Darcy, though in a quiet voice that Elizabeth could hardly hear.

Nothing further was said, the silence settling between them. Soon Jane and Anthony returned, and the good humor which had existed before was restored. But Elizabeth could not help but wonder if there had been a hidden meaning in Mr. Darcy's words. And she found herself watching him, studying him more than she had previously.

It was not at all a surprise when Lady Catherine requested that Darcy attend her the next day. Darcy wondered that she had not accosted Miss Bennet or lost her temper in the middle of dinner the evening before. The conversation with Miss Bennet had informed Darcy how much he was coming to esteem her, how his life had become empty in the absence of his dear sister. The feeling that he wished to determine whether she would ever consider becoming his companion for the rest of his life began to build in Darcy's breast, demanding release. He had hardly been able to remove his eyes from her the previous evening.

While Lady Catherine did not appear angry or offended or any of the other extremes of emotion he might have attributed to her at such a time, she did seem determined. But Darcy was equally so and had no intention of yielding to her demands concerning Anne. If Miss Bennet was forced to leave Rosings because of this, so be it—she would be better away from Lady Catherine's vindictive anger.

"I am sure you can be at no loss as to why I have asked for your attendance, Darcy."

Darcy nodded, saying: "There is no mystery, Lady Catherine. To be honest, I expected it some time ago."

"That is well," replied the lady with a slow nod. "There is little reason to belabor the issue and speak at length of matters of which you are already well aware. You know of your mother's wishes as well as mine, so no further discussion on the matter is required. Thus, I have one question I must ask of you."

"Lady Catherine—"

"No, Darcy," said his aunt, holding her hand up and demanding silence. "Please do not speak until I have asked my question. And it is this: what are your feelings for Miss Elizabeth Bennet?"

Darcy was nonplused and more than a little alarmed. He gazed at his aunt for some moments, unsure how he should answer, before finally managing to say: "You wish to know about Miss Bennet?"

"Darcy," said her ladyship in a voice calm, yet possessing the firmness of the firmament below their feet, "I know you and Fitzwilliam believe me blind, but I am quite able to see what is happening in my very home. Were you any more open about your admiration for the sister of your cousin's wife, your honor might be engaged. What I wish to know is whether this is some momentary infatuation or your feelings are deeper."

It was inconvenient, the way his aunt seemed to have these moments of perception, though he supposed he should not be surprised. The question now was how to let her down easily, for regardless of what happened with Miss Bennet, Darcy still would not marry Anne. For her part, Darcy suspected that Anne felt much the same way about him, though he had no direct knowledge, given the difficulty of eliciting any response from her regardless of the situation. But he did not wish to offend his aunt.

"At the present, I hardly know," replied Darcy. "You know me well enough to know I am not one for insincere flirtation or unserious wooing."

"Unlike the unfortunate Mr. Baker," said Lady Catherine, and Darcy could only agree.

"But she *is* an estimable woman, and I am only just discovering her true worth. She has not much wealth, and her connections are decidedly unspectacular. But the worth of a woman is not solely in these things. For herself, I know no better woman than Miss Bennet."

"It seems you have given this much thought.

Lady Catherine's tone was a little harsh, but when he looked at her, Darcy did not think her truly displeased. That was a puzzle in itself, considering what he was telling her.

"I have given it some thought. But I stress I have come to no decision yet." Darcy paused and returned his aunt's determined gaze. "As for Anne, I am afraid we do not suit, Aunt."

Though she appeared as if she wanted to respond, Darcy spoke again quickly. "Anne is even more taciturn than I am. Can you imagine Pemberley with the two of us in residence? Can you not see how we each require a more open partner, one to draw us from our quiet and solitude, to live life more fully?"

"But our plans!" said Lady Catherine. It was almost a wail. "Your mother and I had our hearts set on the match. It would be stupendous, the uniting of two great estates, and the joining of our children to each other again. Surely you do not wish to give up such benefits for a young woman of lower birth and little dowry, no matter how pleasant she is!"

"I do not yet know if Miss Bennet and I will suit, Aunt. But the considerations you have mentioned carry little weight with me. I do not think Anne and I would make each other happy. I do not wish to make her *unhappy*."

For a long moment, Lady Catherine looked at him steadily, as if to measure the strength of his will. But then she sighed and settled back into her chair, seeming much diminished.

"I suppose you must be correct, though it is difficult for me to accept it."

His surprise must have shown, for Lady Catherine chuckled at it. "I have suspected for some time that you would not be moved, Darcy. Anne is four and twenty. Had you truly meant to abide by your mother's wishes, you would have done so some time ago."

"You have?" asked Darcy, shocked at the turn in the conversation. "But you have continued to speak on the matter every time we have been in company."

"Yes, well, until you found a woman you wished to marry, I still had hope, did I not?" Darcy stared at his aunt, who seemed to become more amused as they spoke. "My sister tried to tell me you had all the traits of your father and you would not likely fall in line with our plans. But I was stubborn, I will confess. I have kept the dream alive quite long enough, it appears. I suppose I have no choice but to allow it to rest now."

"I do not know what to say, Lady Catherine," said Darcy. And it was the truth—he was quite at a loss for words.

"Then let us not speak of it again. I have only one request for you."

"And that is?"

"Nothing so onerous, I assure you." Lady Catherine shook her head. "If you are not to marry Anne and it becomes known, she will be the target of every fortune hunter in society. I merely wish for your support. Anne will need to marry, and I wish her settled with a good man. I hope you will assist."

"Of course, Aunt Catherine," said Darcy. "That is an easy promise to make. I am sure Fitzwilliam, your brother, and Banbridge will all join in ensuring Anne is well protected."

"Thank you, Darcy," said Lady Catherine, rising to her feet. She placed a hand on Darcy's shoulder. "I believe I shall retire to my room for the evening, for this is more difficult than I might have imagined. I hope you will all excuse me."

"Of course," replied Darcy. "I shall inform Anne to take your position at the table tonight."

Lady Catherine squeezed his shoulder once, and then she was gone.

When Lady Catherine did not appear for dinner that evening, Fitzwilliam knew at once that something had changed. For one, Lady Catherine was a robust sort of woman, rarely suffering from an affliction of any kind, even one so inconsequential as a cold. Furthermore, when he had seen her early that afternoon, Lady Catherine had seemed more contemplative than ill.

They all took their places at the dinner table, Anne sitting in her mother's place with as much disinterest as she normally displayed. Fitzwilliam looked about, trying to learn from the demeanors of the others if anyone knew of what was affecting Lady Catherine. Bingley and Georgiana seemed oblivious; Bingley was his usual cheerful self, and most of Georgiana's attention was fixed on her husband, seeming contented with her life. Elizabeth and Charity were speaking together in low voices, and every so often a giggle would escape one or the other's mouth. And as for Jane . . . Fitzwilliam looked fondly at his wife, knowing that she had not the disposition for such intrigues. That left Darcy.

His cousin was outwardly the same as he ever was. But to one who knew him better than almost any other, Fitzwilliam could see that his cousin was more relaxed than he had ever been at Rosings. He spoke to Anne momentarily, and while Fitzwilliam did not catch the gist of the conversation, it was clear Darcy was completely at ease, though Anne favored him with as much of a response as she ever did. Usually, Darcy stayed strictly away from Anne when in company with her — that suggested a settlement had been reached. Fitzwilliam was eager to know what had occurred.

"I think you know something of Aunt Catherine's absence," said Fitzwilliam to his cousin when he had cornered him later that evening.

"Do you care to share your good information?"

"Actually, I think I shall keep it to myself," replied Darcy.

Fitzwilliam glared at his cousin, annoyed that Darcy had decided at that moment to reply with an unusual bit of teasing. It was clear Darcy had seen it, for he grinned, diverted by Fitzwilliam's pique. Usually, their positions were reversed—rarely had Darcy been in a position to claim the victory in such matters.

"Darcy," said Fitzwilliam, a warning note in his voice.

"You have guessed most of it," replied Darcy. "Suffice it to say that you will not hear Lady Catherine sermonize about my betrothal to Anne any longer, for the matter has been resolved."

"But I must suppose from your lightheartedness it has *not* been resolved in an engagement."

"That is correct. I am not engaged to Anne."

"And you will not share anything further."

"The details are unimportant," said Darcy. "I would not wish to embarrass our aunt. She relinquished her desire when I pointed out that Anne and I did not suit and I had no intention of marrying her. She has retired to her room this evening to compose herself."

Though annoyed, it was clear to Fitzwilliam that his cousin was not about to be more explicit. Thus, Fitzwilliam relinquished his object to learn more. Instead, he nodded and patted Darcy on the back, returning to his usual jovial ways.

"Then I congratulate you, Cousin, though it is deucedly odd to offer felicitations on *not* being engaged, rather than the reverse."

"I suppose it must be so!" declared Darcy with a grin of his own.

Then Darcy turned and made his way to where Charity and Elizabeth were still speaking together, and inserted himself into their conversation. Neither seemed put out by his interruption, though over time Fitzwilliam noted that he and Elizabeth carried the conversation more and more. At length, Charity rose and excused herself, making her way to Fitzwilliam's side, where he sat with Jane.

"Darcy seems to be rather cheerful tonight."

"Aye, that he is," agreed Fitzwilliam.

"That is good." Charity watched them for a moment before she turned to grin at Fitzwilliam. "We should encourage that. I should very much like to have Elizabeth for a cousin. The only concern is we will need to keep the matter from our aunt."

"I think, dear sister, that you may find that Lady Catherine is less of an impediment than you might have thought."

Charity looked at him askance, but Fitzwilliam ignored her look.

For his part, he was seeing the possibility which had sat in the back of his mind bloom like a tulip opening for the sun. And Fitzwilliam decided he was rather pleased himself.

CHAPTER XXXIV

❧❀❧

$\mathcal{T}$here was a subtle change in Lady Catherine when she emerged
from her rooms the following day. She was still the same
woman in many respects, from the tendency to meddle to her
insistence on sharing her opinions when least wanted, to her
unshakable assurance that she knew best about virtually any situation.
But there was a change, and Elizabeth sensed it almost as soon as she
came across her hostess when she arose that day.

"Miss Bennet," said she in a tone which was friendly, yet knowing.
"I see you intend to walk again this morning. I hope you do not intend
to go far."

Suppressing a sigh—for this was the one subject on which no
meeting of minds had been achieved, Elizabeth settled for nodding
and saying: "I do intend to walk this morning. But Charity has agreed
to go out with me, and I do not think we intend to go further than the
pond."

With a look of frank appraisal which bothered Elizabeth ever so
slightly, Lady Catherine nodded. "That is well, then. I shall speak to
you later, for I must meet with my steward this morning."

Though initially alarmed at the lady's stated intention to seek her
out, Elizabeth nodded and left. While she enjoyed her time with

Charity, part of her mind kept returning to Lady Catherine and their short conversation, and she wondered about what the lady could possibly wish to speak with her. In the end, it turned out to be both less than she expected and quite puzzling, indeed.

She might have expected Lady Catherine to search for her after her return. But the lady did not, apparently drawing on some well of patience Elizabeth did not know she possessed. When she emerged from her room some thirty minutes after returning to the house, Elizabeth finally made her way down to the sitting-room where she knew at least some of the company would be gathered.

"Come, sit beside me," said Lady Catherine when Elizabeth entered the room. Elizabeth noted the presence of both Georgiana and Charity, and thought nothing more of the invitation, settling herself in the indicated location without comment. Lady Catherine looked on her with a critical eye. "I can see you returned to your room for a time to repair whatever damage the wind did to your hair. That is well."

"There was little damage done to our hair, Aunt," said Charity. "There is no wind today."

The look Lady Catherine shot her niece was quelling, but Charity seemed undaunted, prompting a scowl. "It appears like the daughters of earls have become more outspoken in the years since I was a young woman."

Charity laughed at Lady Catherine's statement, and for her part, Elizabeth was struck by the absurdity of it, though she managed to restrain herself. "Surely you jest, Aunt! You yourself are the daughter of an earl, and I quite consider you to be among the most outspoken ladies of my acquaintance."

It seemed Lady Catherine was a little embarrassed by this observation, though she responded with a wry grin. "Perhaps I was, Charity. But then again, I have had many years as a wife and mother to hone that outspokenness. Regardless, in my day, a young woman did not interrupt when their elders were speaking."

Though Charity seemed more than a little skeptical of this claim, she subsided and watched, though with evident mirth. Seeing she had managed to silence her niece, Lady Catherine turned her attention back to Elizabeth.

"I do not criticize, Miss Bennet. I will, however, state that as you spend much time out of doors, it would behoove you to ensure your appearance is once again pristine when you return. In Hertfordshire, in the house of your father, much might be forgiven in a young woman who is the daughter of a country squire. But now you will be in the company the son of an earl keeps and will be judged more harshly because of it."

"Vanity, I think, is not one of my failings, Lady Catherine," replied Elizabeth. "But I can see the sense in your words. I am usually careful about maintaining my appearance."

"Good. See that you continue to do so." Lady Catherine paused and looked Elizabeth over, a thoughtful expression coming over her. "I sense you often dispense with your bonnet when you are out walking. Is that true?"

"At times, perhaps," confessed Elizabeth. "There are occasions when I find a bonnet quite constrictive."

Lady Catherine nodded slowly. "You are a little tanned, even though the season is yet early. In the hot summer months it will become more pronounced, the more you are out in the sun. I would recommend that when you are not under the canopies of the trees that you wear your bonnet to avoid excessive tanning."

"Come now, Aunt," said Charity. "Society does not look down on a woman when she is tanned. And besides, summer is the time when most of society have taken residence at their estates."

"That is true," said Lady Catherine with a warning glance at Charity yet again. "But a woman who is excessively tanned can be considered to be coarse.

"Now, Miss Bennet," said Lady Catherine, "let us speak of some other subjects of which we have not spoken before. I have a good notion, for example, of what your accomplishments consist. But I am curious of your ability to manage a gentleman's house and your knowledge of how to behave in a society of which you have not, after all, heretofore been a part."

"Might I ask to what these questions tend?" asked Elizabeth. When Lady Catherine's countenance darkened, she hastened to add: "I have nothing I wish to hide. But I am curious of what you can mean by inquiring after these things."

Lady Catherine's response was too glib by half. "I merely wish to ascertain what assistance I might provide, Miss Bennet. I have been, after all, a member of high society for many years, and a wife and mistress of an estate for longer than you have been alive. Since you are now connected to my nephew, it is reasonable to suppose you will gain some interest from his friends, enough, it is possible, to prompt one of them to make you an offer. You appear to be a capable sort of woman. I merely wish to fill any gaps which might exist in your knowledge."

Something was missing from Lady Catherine's explanation,

something crucial, or so Elizabeth thought. But whatever it was, it was also hidden at present, and as the lady was waiting for her response, Elizabeth decided it was best to push the subject aside and ponder it later. And thus Elizabeth's "education" began.

"What do you make of this?"

Darcy's responding grunt to his cousin conveyed all the sourness he was feeling at the moment. The previous evening had been heady, almost carefree in the knowledge he was now free of Lady Catherine's constant attempts to induce him to propose to Anne. Now, however, he found that he was annoyed with her all over again.

"She has always found the dispensing of advice to be to her taste," continued Fitzwilliam. Darcy noted his conversational tone, knowing he believed himself clever. At the very least, he suspected more than Darcy had revealed concerning what had happened between Darcy and Lady Catherine. "But at present, it seems to me like she is beyond simple advice. Had I not known better, I might have thought she expects Elizabeth to make a match and has determined she should be prepared to be the mistress of an estate."

"Whatever her intentions," said Darcy, his tone a trifle short, he was prepared to confess, "she has fallen into her old habits of officiousness."

"It does not seem to be much of a concern to me," replied Fitzwilliam. "Elizabeth does not appear to be offended. In fact, I suspect she is even enjoying herself to a certain extent."

It was the truth, Darcy decided, though that observation annoyed him all that much more. She was a woman of strong opinions and excessive confidence. Should she not be offended by Lady Catherine's meddling? Just then the three ladies laughed together, further souring Darcy's mood. Miss Bennet was capable the way she was—why could Lady Catherine not simply leave well enough alone?

"Who do you think she suspects?"

The seeming non-sequitur caught Darcy's attention, and he turned to his cousin. "Suspects?"

"Of having caught our Elizabeth's eye?" asked Fitzwilliam as if it were the most reasonable thing in the world. "Baker, perhaps? He is the only one of the neighborhood that *I* have noticed paying her attention."

The reminder of Baker and the necessity of controlling his reaction to the man snapped Darcy's temper, and he made to rise. "I think it is about time I had a word with Lady Catherine."

"Sit down, Darcy," said Fitzwilliam, grasping Darcy's shoulder and preventing him from leaving. "I doubt very much your interference would be welcome by any of them."

Though he was tensed to move again, something stayed Darcy's purpose. Miss Bennet did not, it appeared, need assistance. His sudden movement garnered her attention, and she looked across at him, a question in her countenance. Darcy felt his lips forming into a smile at the sight, which she returned, before turning her attention back to Lady Catherine.

A chuckle by his side caught Darcy's notice, and he turned to his cousin. If he thought Fitzwilliam would be sobered by his raised eyebrow, he was destined to be disappointed. His cousin's amusement turned to a pointed look.

"You are quite transparent, Cousin," said he. "Though you choose not to speak of it, I suspect our aunt approached you concerning Anne because she saw what we all do.

"Keep your secrets if you must," continued Fitzwilliam when Darcy might have said something, though he did not quite know exactly what. "But as I said, your motives are well understood by those of us who know you best."

Then Fitzwilliam rose. Before he departed, he could not resist a parting shot.

"I would not interfere with Elizabeth. Not only is she not offended by Lady Catherine's manners, but she is also quite independent, and will not thank you for inserting your opinion in a matter which is, after all, none of your concern."

Having said this much, Fitzwilliam left the room. Lady Catherine looked up as he left, and then she turned her gaze on Darcy himself. It could not have been more of a challenge had she risen and thrown a gauntlet down before him.

When Darcy shook his head, she smiled in satisfaction before turning back to Miss Bennet. And while Darcy continued to wonder if Miss Bennet was simply enduring her meddling to maintain good relations, soon he was so caught up in watching her, glorying in her smiles, witnessing the intelligence in her dark eyes, or climbing the heights along with her laughter, to consider Lady Catherine. It did not occur to him that he was exhibiting all the signs of a man in love.

Two days later, it was proposed that the company visit Margate, on the eastern coast near the entrance of the River Thames estuary to the North Sea. In the intervening days, Lady Catherine had been so full of advice, suggestions, and, at times outright commands, that Elizabeth was becoming quite desperate to be away. She had long determined that the lady was essentially harmless—except when she thought her advice was not being followed—but a little distance would do her good.

"Margate, you say," said Lady Catherine when the proposal was shared with them all.

"Yes," replied Anthony, who had made the announcement. "A short journey—we shall only stay a day or two. But I think it would be desirable to show some of those who are not familiar with the country some of the local sights."

"Did you not tour Kent after you left Brighton?" asked Lady Catherine, apparently knowing he had referred to Jane and Elizabeth.

"We did," confirmed Anthony. "But Margate is very fine too. The Bakers and the Norlands will also be joining us." Anthony paused and smiled at Lady Catherine and Anne. "You are both invited to go, of course."

The way Lady Catherine regarded Elizabeth suggested she was a young girl, whose governess was not certain she was ready to be unleashed upon society. After a moment, Lady Catherine seemed to come to a conclusion, after which she nodded and looked to her daughter.

"What say you, Anne? Do you wish to go to Margate?"

Though Elizabeth expected the young woman to refuse the invitation, Miss de Bourgh responded, stating she had no disliking for the scheme. Lady Catherine nodded once again and turned back to Anthony.

"Then it seems it is settled. Please be certain to inform me of the length of your stay, so I know when to expect your return."

"You will not join us, Aunt?" asked Mr. Darcy.

Lady Catherine waved her hand and shook her head. "No, I have no interest in Margate. Unless I am very much mistaken, this is a scheme the young people have concocted, and I would only be in the way in such a case. Furthermore, I have much to do on the estate which I have not been diligent in doing of late." Her minute glance at Elizabeth suggested her reasons for not seeing to her tasks, but Elizabeth decided she had best be more amused than offended. "I shall await your return."

So it was that the next morning they gathered together on the front drive of Rosings and after their possessions were loaded onto the carriages, they were off. While Elizabeth had been enjoying her time at

Rosings, she was beset by a feeling of utter freedom from restraint, which made her playful.

"To whom should we give thanks for our deliverance from Rosings? I promise a kiss to whoever accepts the responsibility for it."

Anthony and Mr. Darcy looked at each other and laughed. "Do you not fear to make my wife jealous, Elizabeth?"

A grin was Elizabeth's response. "Only a kiss was promised, Anthony. The identity of the person dispensing the reward was not mentioned, as I recall."

Laughter rang out through the carriage. "And if Darcy is the one to whom you owe your thanks?"

Elizabeth directed a saucy grin at the gentleman. "Again, the manner of bestowing a kiss has not been decided upon. I may simply blow him one."

"In my opinion," said Mr. Darcy, "I wonder if we should be offended on Lady Catherine's behalf. Your words suggest you consider yourself reprieved from the hangman's noose, Miss Bennet."

"Nothing so grave, I assure you. But I must own that your aunt's continual attempts to instruct me have made me weary of it. A day away from the estate, free to explore as I wish sounds heavenly."

"As usual, your command of hyperbole is as strong as ever," said Jane. "I suspect you enjoy Lady Catherine's company, Lizzy."

Elizabeth smiled at Jane and turned an arch look on the gentlemen. "As ever, my sister is correct. Indeed, I believe I must wonder if I can trust you both. Most of what we heard of Lady Catherine was from Anthony, it is true, but I believe I also overheard Mr. Darcy saying some rather choice words about her. She *is* a little forceful, but she is not overbearing, I should say. How do you account for it?"

The gentlemen shared a look, and Elizabeth did not miss the questioning glance from Anthony, or the minute shrug from Mr. Darcy. Diverted by the sight of it, she found it difficult to maintain her disapproving countenance.

"It is astonishing to us, too," said Mr. Darcy.

"Perhaps it is your manner with others, Elizabeth," said Anthony. "Rarely have I seen Lady Catherine warm to new acquaintances as she has to you and Jane."

"It merely shows her discerning tastes and shrewd judge of character," said Elizabeth, effecting a haughty superiority.

Once again they burst out laughing. In this manner, they continued until they had reached Cloverwood, the Norland estate, which had been designated as the gathering point due to its position as the easternmost of the three estates. There the two carriages from Rosings entered the driveway—Charity and Miss de Bourgh having joined the Bingleys in the second carriage—to the sight of the Bakers already present, standing outside the house with the three Norland siblings. A carriage had been made ready nearby.

Upon their arrival, those from Rosings disembarked from the carriages long enough to greet the rest of the party. Before they departed, Mr. and Mrs. Norland emerged from the house to wish them a safe journey and a wonderful time. It was then that Elizabeth found herself to once again be the focus of Mr. Baker.

"Miss Bennet," said he, bowing low, "how very well you look today. I dare say the sun and the open spaces suit you very well, for I could not imagine your appearance improving from the day of the picnic. And yet, here you are."

It seemed the charming Mr. Baker had made an appearance today, and Elizabeth suppressed a sigh of exasperation. On some level, Elizabeth knew he was serious in his praise and in his attraction for her. But when he behaved in this manner, she always felt the urge to count her fingers, fearing he had stolen one in his attempts at flattery and misdirection.

"Thank you, sir," was Elizabeth's reply. "I assume you have traveled to Margate in the past?"

"Many times," replied he. "I have traveled a certain amount around England and beyond, but I love Kent the best. I should be happy to share my knowledge and show you the best Margate has to offer." He leaned forward and in a tone more than usually flirtatious, said: "Norland may have as much knowledge as I, but he will be focused on my sister, and his sisters are too young and inexperienced. As for anyone else of the company . . . Well, it would be best to hear of the place we are going from one who is . . . *intimately* familiar with it. Is it not?"

"We will all rely on your knowledge, I am sure," said Elizabeth, with more politeness than she felt. His emphasis on the word "intimate" had succeeded in nothing more than putting her on her guard.

"Then I would be happy—"

"Miss Bennet," said another voice, speaking over Mr. Baker's. Mr. Darcy had approached, and his interruption caused Mr. Baker to frown and fall silent. "We are ready to depart. May I escort you back to the carriage?"

"Of course, Mr. Darcy," said Elizabeth.

The sour expression which came over Mr. Baker's face suggested to Elizabeth that he had been about to offer her a seat in his own carriage. He opened his mouth to reply, but Elizabeth's hand was already on Mr. Darcy's arm, and he was leading her away. Before they were gone, however, Elizabeth happened to notice a smug grin from Mr. Darcy, followed by a glare of annoyance from Mr. Baker.

For a moment, Elizabeth wondered if she should protest. All along, she had been eager to avoid the possibility of being the prize between two eager men, and yet it appeared the first gauntlet had been thrown down. Even Mr. Darcy's actions at the picnic, where he had allowed Mr. Baker to make his case without argument, faded into the background at that moment.

But another thought struck Elizabeth and stopped her annoyance before it could take root. The fact was that she preferred Mr. Darcy's company to Mr. Baker's. Some women would have considered her daft when separating the question of eligibility, for, despite Mr. Baker's uneven attempts at wooing her, he was, in essence, a congenial man. Mr. Darcy, by contrast, was more severe than genial, more serious than friendly.

And yet Elizabeth felt something when she spoke with Mr. Darcy. He was well-informed and intelligent, possessed a liberal mind, and used his gifts to great effect, speaking in an interesting manner which she found intriguing. Mr. Baker, by contrast, rarely strayed beyond light and flirtatious banter, sometimes giving the impression of being rather frivolous. She did not know if that was the truth about him, for she had rarely spoken with him when he was not behaving in such a manner. But the difference between the two gentlemen was striking, and Elizabeth found herself preferring substance to easiness.

The question was what this meant, now, and in the future. And that question she was not certain she could answer—not with any accuracy. Mr. Darcy was a man of society, the nephew of a peer, and a wealthy man, much sought after in society. He could likely have his pick of brides. Would he, then, settle for a country girl of no consequence, unknown to all who frequented such high society?

Elizabeth could not be certain. But as she stepped into the carriage with Mr. Darcy's assistance, noting absently as the carriage lurched into motion, she realized she wished to know. What was Mr. Darcy's purpose? More importantly, what did she wish it to be?

CHAPTER XXXV

*M*argate was all Elizabeth had ever hoped for. It was a small community, situated on the north coast of the peninsula, boasted an inn, several shops, which she noted Charity and Georgiana eying with some interest, and a clear, beautiful view out over the sea. At times, the profiles of distant ships could be seen, both sailing to and from London down the estuary. It was a charming town, and Elizabeth immediately found herself warming to it.

The line of carriages stopped in front of the inn, where the gentlemen entered and secured rooms for the evening while the ladies stretched their legs, enjoying the freedom from the confined spaces they had endured for the morning and part of the afternoon. There was still some time before the dinner hour would come, and the party set out in search of amusement. And they were not the only ones, for it seemed to Elizabeth that there were many other parties engaged in the same pursuits.

The shops were visited in an almost perfunctory manner, though Charity protested in good-natured annoyance. They clearly catered to visiting gentry, offering trinkets made of sparkling shells, or other items specific to the area. Elizabeth was able to spend some little time in a quaint bookshop, accompanied by Mr. Darcy, and even purchase a small book of poetry. But they were pulled from the shop by their laughing companions, insistent upon seeing more of the small town.

"Wherever there are books, there will also be Lizzy," said Jane with a laugh, pushing Elizabeth before her. "We wish to visit the beach, Lizzy."

Elizabeth assured her sister she was quite eager to join them and allowed herself to be led away. They walked the streets toward the ocean, noting the general cleanliness of the town. The streets were gravel, rather than the grimier dirt roads seen in many communities. It greatly cut down the amount of dust in the air, making the walk much more pleasurable for all involved.

When they neared the shore, Elizabeth saw, laid out before her, a beautiful white sand beach. "How lovely!" she could not help but exclaim.

"Yes, it is lovely, indeed," said Mr. Baker who was hovering nearby. "It is one of Margate's claims to fame, and I dare say would be a match for any of Brighton's famed beaches."

"Perhaps for any one of them," agreed Elizabeth. "But there are several at Brighton, which must give it the edge. But this is very agreeable too. Is there any sea bathing to be had in Margate?"

Elizabeth looked about with interest, but she was destined to be disappointed. "I am afraid not, Miss Bennet. That appears to be a Brighton affectation. Here in Margate, we are limited to simply looking on and enjoying the scene before us."

"I suppose it was too early in the season for sea bathing when you were in Brighton," said Mr. Darcy. "That is a pity, as it is quite an experience."

"You have done it?" asked Elizabeth curiously.

"I have," replied Mr. Darcy. "In fact, Fitzwilliam and I were there together about two years ago, and we took the opportunity to experience it. It is quite fine, I believe, to swim in the ocean, even if is in the small area covered by the bathing machine's awning."

"Come, Miss Bennet," said Mr. Baker, once again asserting himself. "Let us walk on the beach closer to the shore, for I dare say you will find it most interesting."

Elizabeth assented, and she allowed him to guide her out onto the sand. It was a calm day, and the waves washed up on the shore with a gentle rumble, rather than the roaring crash she had seen on occasion. The ladies of the party gathered together and were engaged for some few moments searching the dunes for the glittering little shells washed up on the shore. Finding a matched pair, Elizabeth decided she would take them back to Hertfordshire with her and give them to Kitty and Lydia as souvenirs of her time in Margate.

They continued on, walking down the length of the flowing sands, looking this way and that, taking in the vistas spread out before their eyes. The call of a seabird caught Elizabeth's attention, and she looked up, shielding her eyes against the sun, to see a white gull flying overhead. The call was soon taken up by its fellows, and for a few moments, hundreds were flying about, calling to each other in their harsh voices.

On another occasion, a ship sailed quite near to the shore, its masts filled with billowing sails. The ship sped toward the east, turning toward the south as it passed by the peninsula on which they stood.

"Have you ever been to sea, Mr. Darcy?" asked Elizabeth. The man was standing nearby and watching the scene alongside Elizabeth and the ever-present Mr. Baker.

"I have," replied Mr. Darcy, "when I left for my abbreviated grand tour after graduating from Cambridge. But I have not sailed on such a ship as that."

Elizabeth turned to him askance. Mr. Darcy was more than willing to explain. "That is a frigate, Miss Bennet. "You can tell by the line of square openings along the sides, where the cannons make their appearance in battle."

There were such openings, Elizabeth noted, though they were currently covered by square doors made of heavy wood. "I see them," said she absently.

"Ah, look," said Mr. Baker, pointing back toward the estuary. "There is a passenger ship. Perhaps you would like to sail on one someday, Miss Bennet."

"That would be fine, indeed," replied Elizabeth. She turned to regard him, wondering at his tone. He seemed to think speaking of military vessels with a woman was improper. "There are many exotic places in the world one may visit. I should like to visit them all."

"The world, Miss Bennet, is far too large for such an endeavor." Elizabeth frowned at him, immediately annoyed by his condescending tone. He mistook her look and continued on, saying: "Even if you have one hundred lifetimes and could travel to far off lands in an instant, you could never visit them all."

Mr. Darcy coughed as Elizabeth was working up a retort. "I believe Miss Bennet is well aware of the size of the world and was speaking in hyperbole."

"Yes, well," replied Mr. Baker, apparently not embarrassed in the slightest. "There are many exotic places which are also savage. However, the continent is a place of magnificent locations of culture and history. Perhaps Athens, Paris, or Rome would be to your taste."

"Those are interesting places, of which I have heard much, indeed," replied Elizabeth. "And I would like to go there someday. But I should also like to see the West Indies, fabled Alexandria, and perhaps even far off China."

"That is very unlikely, Miss Bennet."

"I am aware of that, sir," replied Elizabeth. "But that does not prevent me from wishing it might be so."

"I think a lady should be content with her lot in life and not wish for things which cannot be."

"Look at this, Miss Bennet," said Mr. Darcy, interrupting the increasingly tense exchange. Elizabeth, who had been on the verge of castigating the oblivious man, allowed herself to be diverted. "Is this not a lovely shell?"

"It is, indeed," said Elizabeth, looking admiringly on the bit of glowing mother of pearl he had stooped to retrieve. It was small, fitting in the center of his palm, made of a base, fanning out in a wavy semicircle.

"Then you must have it," said he, holding it out and depositing it into her hand. "I dare say its beauty does not do you justice. But perhaps it will enhance what is already there."

"Thank you, sir," whispered Elizabeth, touched by his compliment.

"Come, Miss Bennet," said Mr. Baker, motioning her forward. "Our party appears to be leaving us behind."

Elizabeth darted a look at Mr. Darcy and was almost set to laughter by his rolled eyes. For herself, she agreed. But though Elizabeth allowed herself to be led away, she steadfastly refused to take Mr. Baker's arm which was extended toward her. He was not happy with her refusal, but he said nothing, continuing to walk at her side, pointing out items he thought would be of interest to her. But it was a curious thing that Elizabeth kept returning her attention to Mr. Darcy. For one thing, he was not overly attentive to the point of being overbearing. For another, she appreciated how he spoke to her, without condescension. He had returned to the Mr. Darcy of the picnic, showering her with attention when the opportunity presented itself, but seemingly determined to avoid taking away from her enjoyment.

All in all, it was a good day, even considering the continued presence of Mr. Baker, with which Elizabeth could have easily dispensed. After some time spent in this manner, it began to grow late, and they repaired back to the inn where they partook of dinner. The establishment's ability to cater to gentlefolk was proven again, as the innkeeper kept a cook in his employ who appeared to know something of his craft. It was plainer fare than Lady Catherine would serve at her table, but it was flavorsome and filling. The company stayed in the common room until quite late, speaking in an animated fashion amongst themselves.

When Elizabeth retired to her room to sleep, she was not destined to be allowed that state as soon as she might have wished, for there was a light tapping on her door not long after she had entered therein. Uncertain who could be there late at night, Elizabeth opened the door just a crack, peering out at those in the hallway.

Even so, she was unprepared for the three ladies who pushed forward to enter, the youngest—Georgiana—ensuring the door was closed behind them. Elizabeth, nonplused at their sudden actions, could only gape at them as they crowded around her. It was unsurprising when Charity, the most voluble of them, spoke first.

"Elizabeth," said she, "it appears you have become a great favorite, at least between *two* of the gentlemen present. I dare say neither Darcy nor Mr. Baker left your side all day long. How can you account for such devotion?"

"I am afraid I cannot account for it at all," replied Elizabeth. "I neither asked for nor wished for, their continued presence."

"Methinks the lady doth protest too much," said Jane *sotto voce*. "At least on the subject of *one* of them."

"Aye, I agree," replied Charity. "The question is, which one?"

"Do you like Mr. Baker?" asked Georgiana into the short silence which followed. Elizabeth turned her attention toward Georgiana, noting her diffidence was perhaps more pronounced than usual.

"Given what you three are saying," said Elizabeth, feeling a little cross," should you not also be asking if I like Mr. Darcy?"

"We will get to that," replied Charity. "For now, I am interested to know the answer to Georgiana's question."

Charity regarded her, expectance alive in her posture, her manner of regarding Elizabeth, and in her knowing air. Elizabeth decided there was no reason to become defensive or angry—this was her friend's way, as she had seen many times already. A part of her did not wish to lay her private feelings bare for her friends to see. But in the end, she decided it would do no harm to inform them.

"The answer to your question, Georgiana, is that I have no special regard for Mr. Baker."

"And why is that?" demanded Charity. "He is passably handsome, is possessed of an estate which rivals Rosings, and can provide you with a good home. In fact, I have no doubt he *would*, if you were to give him any hint of encouragement.

"Perhaps there is someone else who has caught your eye?"

"I am sure he is all these things," said Elizabeth, ignoring Charity's final statement. "But there are also times when I find him condescending, arrogant, and almost rude. I suspect he thinks very well of himself. He, no doubt, believes I should simply swoon at his feet for no other reason than that he has deigned to honor me with his notice."

The other women looked at one other and laughed. "He is not all *that* bad!" exclaimed Charity.

"Would *you* wish for him to focus on you?" asked Elizabeth. She kept her tone deliberately mild, and Charity seemed to catch her point, for she shook her head in distaste.

"No, I have no such desire at all. I suspect he would prefer to marry a woman who believes he is the center of all creation, to hang off his every word as if it was spoken from on high."

"Precisely," said Elizabeth. "I am not such a woman. I neither require nor wish for a husband to form my opinions to spare me the trouble of using my own rationality to discover them for myself. Besides, I am convinced I am nothing more than a passing fancy. He is, I think, a man who enjoys the company of women. I would not wish to marry a man who flatters every woman he comes across."

"Very well," said Charity. "Now, what about the other player in today's drama?"

When Elizabeth did not immediately respond, Charity regarded her with exasperation, saying: "Just as Mr. Baker did not leave your side, so too did Darcy stay nearby. You have already stated your opinion of Mr. Baker—it should not be difficult to follow suit on the subject of Darcy."

"I do not wish to speak on the subject," said Elizabeth.

"That in itself is telling, Lizzy," said Jane.

Elizabeth glared at her sister. Jane only returned it, an expectant expression driving Elizabeth to throw her hands up and stalk away. "To be honest," cried Elizabeth in frustration, "I do not know what to think of Mr. Darcy at times. I suspect he possesses some partiality for me, but I cannot be certain. I can tell you, however, that my opinion of him has improved from what it was. But to what extent, I cannot say."

"I think Mr. Darcy is a good man," came Jane's quiet voice.

"He *is* a good man," said Georgiana.

Elizabeth turned back to Georgiana and went to the girl, her hands extended to catch Georgiana's and squeeze them tightly. "I know he is, Georgiana. I do not dispute that. At this moment, however, I cannot be certain of my own feelings, nor can I be certain of the purpose of his actions. I believe he did not think highly of me in Hertfordshire. His transformation is unexpected, and I have not yet had time to sort through my feelings."

"Darcy is not a perfect man," said Charity. "In Hertfordshire, he was struggling with some events which were still fresh in his mind." Elizabeth noted the look which passed between Georgiana and Charity, but she did not comment on it. "Once he was able to work through them, his mood has become much better."

"I think he merely needs a good wife to help him overcome his tendency to dwell on the past." Elizabeth turned to Jane, noting her sister's smile. "What better woman than one whose motto is 'think of the past as it gives you pleasure?'"

"I believe you are putting the cart before the horse, Jane."

"Not by much, she is not," said Charity. "You have not known Darcy long, Elizabeth. If you had seen him in company in previous years, you would know that Darcy keeps himself aloof from any young woman."

"He has been hunted since his coming into society," said Georgiana.

"And it has made him wary," said Charity with a nod. "His actions toward you are so different from how he normally conducts himself that it might be ardent lovemaking in any other man."

Elizabeth was skeptical. It seemed Charity saw it, for she growled in frustration. "Why do you think Lady Catherine has suddenly taken an interest in you? Indeed, you should believe us, Elizabeth, for we know Darcy's ways as well as he knows them himself."

"Lady Catherine suspects?" said Elizabeth.

"Come, Lizzy, you must have suspected yourself," said Jane.

"I wondered," replied Elizabeth. "But I would have thought she would react quite another way to Mr. Darcy's interest in a woman other than her daughter."

"We were no less surprised than you," said Charity. "I do not know what has passed between them, but I am sure that is why Lady Catherine has taken to seeing to your 'education.'" Charity grinned at the term. "Having approved of Jane, she could hardly disapprove of Jane's sister, unless it is because she wishes her daughter to marry him."

"Anthony is convinced Lady Catherine was induced to abandon her hopes," said Jane. "Mr. Darcy will not say as much, but Anthony believes it is so."

"I agree with him," said Charity. "I never would have expected Lady Catherine to forsake her dream with so little inducement, but it seems to be so."

"Perhaps she has," said Elizabeth. "But I shall not marry Mr. Darcy simply because Lady Catherine wishes it."

"And why do you think Lady Catherine wishes it?" demanded Charity. "I am sorry, Elizabeth, but you do not appear to be thinking clearly. I do not think *Lady Catherine* wishes it. I think she knows *Darcy* wishes it and has bowed to his wishes."

There was nothing Elizabeth could say to that, and she did not even make an attempt. She suspected that Charity was completely correct.

"I know you did not have the best beginning with my brother," said Georgiana. "But I am glad you are giving him a chance. I hope you continue to do so, for I know you will love him like I do if you only allow yourself."

Georgiana's cheeks pinked, but she pushed whatever had embarrassed her to the side long enough to make one more statement. "I hope very much you allow him to prove himself. For I would love to have you as a sister, Elizabeth."

Then, having made her statement, Georgiana fled the room, leaving Elizabeth looking after her in shock. For a moment, none of those left said anything.

"I hope you will not claim surprise, Lizzy," said Jane. "Of course, Georgiana wishes you for a sister. You have become as close to her as I have, and as you know, *I* will never be closer than a cousin."

After a moment's thought, Elizabeth nodded slowly. "I suppose when you put it that way, I must agree."

"In fact," continued Jane, "I think you and Mr. Darcy would suit quite well, indeed."

Charity laughed and poked Elizabeth on her shoulder. "Jane is correct. We all know that Darcy is uptight and rigid, but if there is any woman alive who would be able to tame him, I declare you to be that woman."

"Again, let us not be too hasty," said Elizabeth. "You may be correct about Mr. Darcy. But he has made no overtures as of yet. For all I know, he may never."

"Perhaps," was Charity's noncommittal response. "But knowing

Darcy as I do, I suspect he *has* made a decision. He may not know it himself yet. But when he *does* decide, he is as immovable as a mountain."

"And now that you are more informed as to his possible intentions," said Jane, "it would behoove you to understand your own heart and know your answer before the choice is before you."

"Think on it, Elizabeth," urged Charity.

With those final words of admonition, the two ladies took their leave. As the door closed behind them, Elizabeth looked at it with exasperation. They had given her much on which to think, and she knew she would find sleep difficult tonight. Of greater concern was Mr. Darcy. She had asked herself what she wished from him and not come to a satisfactory answer. Now the question was more pressing than it had been before.

The next morning, the company gathered again to break their fast and spend some few more hours exploring the town before they were to return to their homes. The night had been spent in largely a sleepless fashion by one Elizabeth Bennet, though she was not as tired as she might have thought the next morning. One thing her relations and friends had forced her into the previous evening was an acknowledgment that whatever Mr. Baker intended, she was not interested in being the recipient. Of Mr. Darcy, she had no more clarity but reached a resolve to examine their interactions carefully, so she may come to a conclusion.

They spent the morning in much the same fashion as the previous afternoon, though at Charity's insistence, they paid a little more attention to the shops. Elizabeth purchased some small trinkets for her mother and sisters and went along without complaint when they entered shops in which she had little interest. They finished their morning with a light luncheon at the inn, which would satisfy them until they reached their homes, and treated themselves to some ices at a local confectioner.

As the carriages were being made ready, Elizabeth thought to take one last look at the idyllic little town. She indicated this to her sister, who warned her against wandering far, which Elizabeth laughingly promised and set out on foot. The sun was shining that day, and Elizabeth gloried in the light and warmth on her face. And then she saw him.

"Mr. Chandler?" said she with a gasp.

Down the street a short distance, Elizabeth had seen the man emerge from an alley, and his glance down the street in Elizabeth's direction had betrayed his identity to her. He turned and began to walk away from her, his long legs eating the distance. But Elizabeth, who, though she had not thought of him in some time, was curious as to his appearance here, gave chase calling out for him to stop.

For a few moments, as she hurried after him, she thought he would ignore her and leave. She would not screech out like her sisters did, calling for officers in the middle of the street in defiance of all that was proper. But she did call in a low voice, which seemed to catch his attention at last.

"Ah, Miss Bennet, as I recall," said he as he stopped and regarded her. He fixed her with a devastating smile. "It is fortunate to meet you here, though I had no notion you were in the neighborhood."

"Nor I you," replied Elizabeth. "Have you been here long? I had expected to see you again in Brighton, but you did not come."

"You have my apologies, Miss Bennet," said he, though a slow smile spread over his countenance. "Unfortunately, I had business which prevented my coming. Otherwise, I cannot imagine I would have been impervious to your charms."

Elizabeth felt her cheeks heat in response to his words, and she noted his frank appraisal of her person. To be the focus of such a handsome man's attention was a little disconcerting, though she would not allow herself to be intimidated.

"Are you visiting with friends?"

"No, Miss Bennet," said he. He sidled closer to her, looking down with intense interest. "But now I am happy for it. Acquaintances would only be in the way, you see, with such a vision as you before me. Dare I hope you are to be in Margate much longer?"

"We are to depart shortly," said Elizabeth, feeling the effects of his presence on her sensibilities.

"A great pity," said Mr. Chandler.

A frown settled over Elizabeth's face. She could sense some irony in his words, some hidden meaning she could not quite make out. There was no indication of what he felt, but at that moment a sense of disquiet settled over her. She had, after all, met the man only once, and he was now overly flirtatious with her in the middle of a road. Of course, she had attempted to gain his attention. Perhaps that had been a mistake.

"May I ask where you are bound?" said he. "Should you permit it, I would like very much to call upon you. I believe we have many things to discuss."

Before Elizabeth could muster a response to his query, a loud voice assaulted her senses, and she stepped back, looking back down the street. Mr. Darcy was approaching, a thunderous expression etched upon his brow. He strode up to them, his eyes shifting from Elizabeth to Mr. Chandler, and if Elizabeth thought he was angry with her, when his eyes alighted on the form of the other gentleman, they became icy cold, his jaw chiseled from stone.

From his lips issued one word: "Wickham."

Chapter XXXVI

$\mathcal{T}$he sight of the libertine made Darcy's blood boil. The sight of him standing in the middle of the street, bold as brass, using his wiles on Miss Bennet, filled him with a murderous fury. The thought that she might know him, might sympathize with him . . . .

"Miss Bennet," said Darcy when he reached them, noting in the back of his mind how she recoiled at the sound of his voice. "Why are you speaking with *him*, of all people? How long have you been acquainted? How could you possibly have met him?"

"I do not know that it is any of your concern—" she began, but Darcy could not tolerate her prevarication.

"It is most definitely my concern," snapped Darcy. "This man is a bounder and a libertine. I thought more of you than to suspect you would cavort with such men as he."

"I have no notion of what you are saying, sir," was Miss Bennet's frosty reply. "I was doing nothing more than speaking on a public street."

"Last I heard, it was not a crime to speak with a lady," said Wickham. Unfortunately, a glare did not silence the author of Georgiana's distress. "I had not thought you were so interested in Miss Bennet, Darcy, though I will own that your taste is excellent.

Considering it is much the same as my own, I suppose I must congratulate myself as well."

"Silence, cur!" spat Darcy. "Or I will see you in prison.

"What do you know of him?" demanded Darcy, whirling again on Miss Bennet. "For all your profession of affection for Georgiana, it seems to me you are highly untruthful, considering I found you with Wickham."

"Wickham?" asked Miss Bennet. "I know this man as Mr. Chandler."

"And so I am," supplied Wickham. "But it seems I must leave." Wickham bowed to Miss Bennet, saying: "I hope to see you again, Miss Bennet, for you are utterly enchanting."

"You will go nowhere!" snarled Darcy.

By this time, Miss Bennet's anger had finally appeared. "I do not know of what you accuse me, sir. I met this man — whatever his name — once while we were in Brighton. I know nothing of him other than that he owns an estate in Kent."

"Wickham?" sneered Darcy. "Own an estate? He would bleed it dry, no matter how large, in less than a twelvemonth."

"As I said, I know only what he informed me of himself, and certainly nothing of Georgiana."

"I hardly find that likely."

Miss Bennet's eyes burned with a cold fire. "I care not what you believe, sir."

Then she whirled and stalked away, head held high, back straight, her gait stiff. Had Darcy not been so angry, he would have admired her spirit and courage. As it was, there was still a libertine with which to dispense.

"I must hand it to you, Darcy," said Wickham with a dark chuckle. "You always did have a way with the ladies. Is there a woman in all of England you have *not* offended yet?"

Darcy turned his malevolent gaze back to his erstwhile friend, and he noted with some satisfaction that Wickham, though he endeavored to be unmoved, was beset by a sudden pallor which showed his unrelenting cowardice. Nodding with some satisfaction, Darcy turned the full weight of his attention on the libertine who had been the bane of his existence.

"What are you doing here, Wickham? Why have you chosen to ply your trade with Miss Bennet?"

"My concerns are my own," said Wickham. "If Miss Bennet should like me better than you, one must only applaud her good taste."

"One must question her judgment," hissed Darcy, stepping close to his former friend.

"It is not difficult to determine which of us the ladies prefer. You have never met one you did not intimidate by the force of your stare."

"I will ask you one more time, Wickham—what is your game?"

"May a man not live in peace without being accosted? I did nothing improper with Miss Bennet, and your sister is forever beyond my reach if the rumors are true. Why should you care what becomes of me?"

"Because your path keeps crossing mine, and I do not trust you." Darcy's gaze raked over Wickham in disdain. "I suggest you run far from here, Wickham. I hold more power over you than you think, and I will use it if you provoke me."

"I am free to do as I wish," said Wickham. "You may have Miss Bennet, for I care not. But I will go where I please."

With those final words, Wickham turned on his heel and marched away. Darcy watched him for a moment, noting his nonchalant saunter, betrayed as nothing more than a show by the stiffness in his gait. For a moment, Darcy thought to go after him, to beat the answers from Wickham's hide. But he held himself in check, knowing it was too great a risk in such a place as this. Georgiana's near disgrace was not so distant from the tongues of society that such a scene would not revive the talk.

The rest of the party were milling about the courtyard of the inn, some still inside, when Darcy returned. Miss Bennet was nowhere in sight, and given Darcy's state of mind, it was just as well. But Fitzwilliam had noted his return, and given the concern with which he regarded Darcy, it seemed he had some knowledge of Wickham's appearance

"Darcy," said he, "what has happened? Elizabeth returned only a moment ago, obviously angry, and though she did not say much, it was clear she was upset with you."

"What has happened?" demanded Darcy. "I shall tell you, Cousin. I found her speaking with Wickham, of all people!"

"Wickham is here?" asked Fitzwilliam. His stance immediately became that of a seasoned campaigner, and Darcy could see the sudden rage well up in his cousin. "Where is he? I have wished to get my hands on him since last summer."

"Perhaps you should ask your wife's *sister* about Wickham," said Darcy.

Fitzwilliam's rage melted away, and he stared at Darcy,

uncomprehending. "Of what are you speaking? Elizabeth and Wickham?"

"I found them speaking together, as I told you," growled Darcy. "I know not of what their connection consists, for neither was explicit. But she mentioned something about meeting him in Brighton. I have no doubt he wove some story for her, likely of his mistreatment at my hands. How far he has brought her into his schemes I cannot say, but there seemed some familiarity between them."

"That cannot be," said Fitzwilliam, shaking his head. "Elizabeth is a good girl. She would have come to me if Wickham started feeding her stories of you. This talk of her being in league with him is nothing but nonsense."

"I know not what it is," said Darcy. He knew he was being unreasonable, but his ire was flowing through his veins like fire, and the thought that Miss Bennet would betray the family in such a manner made him angry. "Perhaps you should question her further."

The look Fitzwilliam directed at him suggested censure. "Then shall we?"

Darcy nodded curtly and followed his cousin toward the inn. In the back of Darcy's mind, he considered what she had said of Wickham. But the suspicion was strong and the anger overpowering. If she was innocent, let her prove it. Where Wickham was concerned, Darcy would not relent until given incontrovertible proof.

"What is it, Lizzy?"

Though possessing little desire to speak of what had just occurred, Elizabeth could not very well ignore her sister. Having turned her back on Mr. Darcy and Mr. Chandler—or Wickham, or whatever his name was—Elizabeth had returned to the inn, exasperating herself concerning the obtuse Mr. Darcy and the insults and accusations he had leveled in her direction. She had little notion she could be civil with anyone. But Jane had spied her and Charity was nearby, and they had seen her pique. There was little to be done.

"Your cousin, Charity," growled Elizabeth through clenched teeth, "is the most exasperating man I have ever had the misfortune to meet!"

Far from objecting to Elizabeth's characterization of her cousin, Charity only grinned at her. "That much is evident. Will you share the details of what particularly has made you angry? Or are you content to spit and snarl like an angry dog?"

"I do not appreciate the comparison, Charity," replied Elizabeth in a chilly tone.

"Oh, Elizabeth," said Charity, suddenly solicitous. "Darcy must be behaving poorly, indeed, if it has managed to pierce your good humor." Charity escorted Elizabeth to a nearby bench and sat down next to her in a show of solidarity, while Jane sat nearby, clearly curious. "Shall you not inform us of what has happened?"

Though not certain she wished to speak of it, Elizabeth related meeting Mr. Wickham, her sense of indignation rising again at the words Mr. Darcy had flung at her. To think she would conspire against someone as sweet as dear Georgiana in such a manner! Especially when she was connected to Georgiana, albeit in a distant manner. Elizabeth could not fathom such thinking as had induced Mr. Darcy to say such hurtful things.

"But I do not understand," said Jane. "Who is Mr. Chandler, and who is this Mr. Wickham of whom Mr. Darcy speaks?"

"I know something of Mr. Wickham," said Charity, her tone slightly grim. "There is not much good to be said of him, from what I have heard. He is a rake and a gambler, a debtor and a seducer. If you know him, Elizabeth, you should stay clear of him."

"But that is just it," complained Elizabeth. "I *do not* know Mr. Wickham. That is what Mr. Darcy calls him, but he introduced himself as Mr. Chandler. I met him in a shop while we were in Brighton, and he informed me he owned an estate nearby. Other than this, I know nothing of the man. I certainly have not behaved inappropriately with him."

"No one is accusing you of it," soothed Charity.

"Mr. Darcy saw fit to do exactly that," snapped Elizabeth.

"That is because no one has been hurt as Darcy has. And Georgiana, for that matter."

"What of Georgiana?" asked Elizabeth. "I do not understand any of this."

For perhaps the first time since Elizabeth had made Charity's acquaintance, she seemed more than a little reticent. "If you do not know what happened last summer, I should remain silent, for it is not my story to tell." When Elizabeth attempted to protest, Charity put her hand up and said: "It is not a secret, for in some parts of society the story was well known. Or, at least the story that Darcy put out was well known. I doubt anyone but the family and Wickham himself know the truth of the matter."

"Will you not share it, Charity?"

Charity shook her head. "Please ask Darcy if you wish to understand more. No doubt he and Anthony will more clearly inform you of Mr. Wickham's character. But please trust me, Elizabeth—Mr. Wickham is not a good man, and whatever falsehoods he told you about himself should not be believed. You would do well to stay away from him."

"So you would," said a new voice.

Elizabeth looked up and saw that Anthony and Mr. Darcy had entered the room. While Anthony had approached, Mr. Darcy was standing some distance behind, his stony gaze fixed on her, angry and unfriendly. There was nothing to say to the man, so Elizabeth ignored him, instead fixing her attention on her sister's husband.

While Elizabeth expected him to speak immediately, instead he looked about the inn's common room, seeming to notice they were not alone. "This is a matter of which we should not speak so openly."

The request for a private room was submitted to the innkeeper and soon granted. The five entered the room, and Anthony closed the door firmly after them before turning to Elizabeth, who had already seated herself at the table with Jane and Charity and had turned her mutinous gaze on Mr. Darcy, daring him to accuse her again. But Mr. Darcy stayed silent, waiting for his cousin to speak and looking anywhere but Elizabeth.

"Now, what is this I hear of you and Wickham?" asked Anthony.

"I do not *know* this Mr. Wickham," said Elizabeth, feeling the last vestiges of her patience ebbing away. "I met him in Brighton, in the bookstore near the house in which we stayed. He retrieved a book I had dropped and introduced himself as Mr. Chandler."

Anthony appeared thoughtful and then shook his head. "I see the connection, though it is a poor one."

"What do you mean?" asked Mr. Darcy.

"Chandler? Candlemaker? Wick? He is trying to be clever."

Mr. Darcy shook his head but did not say anything. Anthony turned back to Elizabeth.

"What else?"

"Nothing, until today," replied Elizabeth. "Mr. Chandler—or Mr. Wickham, if that is his true name—said he possessed an estate near Brighton and that he often attended events there. But until today, I never saw him again."

"The fact that he attempted to pass himself off as a gentleman is not a surprise. He often does so, though he has not the means to actually live like one. Much to his chagrin."

Anthony and Mr. Darcy shared a significant look, one which included Charity. Elizabeth could not understand it and was beginning to feel cross again when Anthony continued to speak.

"But the rest of it does not make much sense. I might have expected Wickham to continue to try to curry your favor when out of my company, though I suppose the presence of the footman assigned to accompany you might have made him cautious. He was instructed to report anything untoward to me, and Wickham might have known how I would act."

"Your footman was spying on me?" demanded Elizabeth.

"No," replied Anthony. He sat near Elizabeth and grasped one of her hands. "You are far too independent, Elizabeth. My purpose was nothing other than to ensure your safety, as your father had entrusted me with it. The footman did not report the minutia of your outings— he was only to inform me if something unusual occurred, and Wickham's constant appearance would have attracted his attention. As Wickham only approached you once, it must have escaped his notice."

"But what could he have been doing?" asked Charity. "He could not have known who Elizabeth was or known of her connection to you."

"Perhaps it was nothing more than his usual devilry. Unless he happened to see us together previously." Anthony turned to Elizabeth. "Are you certain you did not see him any other time?"

"He may have seen Elizabeth with you without either of you seeing him," said Charity.

Elizabeth was about to shake her head in denial when a sudden thought crossed her mind and she gasped. The others' attention was on her, bearing down on her, and for a moment Elizabeth felt almost suffocated.

"Have you remembered something?" pressed Anthony.

"It may be nothing," said Elizabeth, hesitant to speak. "At the assembly we attended, I remember a man standing on the far side of the room watching us. If you recall, I mentioned it to you. I cannot be absolutely certain, but I think it might have been him."

"The question, then, is why he approached you once and not again," said Charity.

"What did he say to you?" asked Anthony.

"Nothing notable," replied a flustered Elizabeth, trying to remember. "I believe he asked how long I would be in Brighton, and whether I attended society of the city. I told him I was not certain how long we would be there. In the end, though I did look for him on occasion, I never saw him. There is nothing more I can tell you."

Once again Anthony looked to Mr. Darcy, who shrugged. "Though his habits are long known to me, I cannot say I understand how he thinks. As you say, it may be more of his devilry, or it may be he had some purpose in mind. What that may have been, I cannot say."

"It is doubtful his presence in Margate is a coincidence," replied Anthony. "He has likely already fled, but it may be best if we attempt to locate him."

"Perhaps."

Anthony did not appear pleased at all with Mr. Darcy's response. "Your disinclination for speaking of him is well known, Darcy. But I still maintain you should have dealt with him long ago. You have enough of his debt receipts that seeing him in Marshalsea or packed off to Botany Bay would not be difficult at all."

"Then perhaps it is time." Elizabeth did not miss the look Mr. Darcy directed at her, though she could not quite understand its meaning. Anthony, it seemed, had no such difficulty, for he grinned.

"It is, indeed. For the present, let us simply see if we can discover his lair."

With a nod, Mr. Darcy left the room, though not without another quick glance at Elizabeth. Anthony watched him go and then turned back to the ladies.

"We shall not be gone long. If you would like to sit comfortably, this room will be available for you."

"On the contrary," said Elizabeth. "Since we have hours in a carriage to anticipate, I think I will stretch my legs."

Charity giggled and Jane shook her head, but Anthony smiled. "Very well. Please do not stray far from the inn. We do not know if Wickham has some other deviousness in mind, and we shall depart before long."

When Elizabeth gave her assurances, Anthony patted her hand and departed, leaving her with the other two women. Charity grinned at her.

"It seems you do attract trouble, Elizabeth. I would not have expected a short stay in Brighton to have allowed for such intrigue."

"Nothing happened," stressed Elizabeth.

"No, it did not," replied Jane. "But trouble still seems to have found you."

As it turned out, Mr. Baker was waiting for them, hovering about the entrance to the inn as if in ambush. Charity and Jane shook their heads at his approach, likely amused by his dullness. Elizabeth, for her part, was only exasperated. But she could not refuse his escort politely, and thus she allowed herself to be led away for a short walk about the property.

It was no more than thirty minutes later when Mr. Darcy and Anthony returned, and while Elizabeth continued to ignore the former, the latter's minutely shaken head revealed their lack of success in apprehending Mr. Wickham. Elizabeth had not expected them to find him. Given what they had informed her of his character, she had been certain he would immediately decamp from the area to ensure he was not forced to meet with Mr. Darcy again. He was a coward at heart, she decided, given what she had witnessed of his response to Mr. Darcy's presence earlier.

Soon, the carriages had been loaded with their few belongings, and the company made ready to depart. Elizabeth had managed to escape from Mr. Baker's leech-like presence and spend some few moments with the Norland sisters. When it became clear that they were about to leave, Elizabeth noted Mr. Baker approaching her once again, his expression determined.

"Miss Bennet," said he, "do you not think it would be pleasant to exchange traveling companions for our journey home? Variety is, as they say, the spice of life."

"It may be," replied Elizabeth. "I was quite comfortable on the way to Margate."

"But such companionships become stale, do you not agree? I should be happy to take you in my carriage."

Elizabeth was about to respond when Mr. Darcy strode up to them. A curt nod was all he directed at Mr. Baker before he turned his attention on Elizabeth.

"The carriage is about to depart, Miss Bennet. Come, I will escort you."

"I believe Miss Bennet has just agreed to travel in *my* carriage, Darcy," said Mr. Baker. "You may return to your carriage, for Miss Bennet has no need of you."

Mr. Darcy snorted. "I hardly believe she actually wishes to put up with your company the entire distance to Rosings."

"Better me than one silent and aloof as you."

"Gentlemen," said Elizabeth, her patience exhausted. "I would appreciate it if you would not fight over me like a pair of schoolboys. I am not a prize to be won, nor do I appreciate your behavior."

"I have nothing but your comfort in mind, Miss Bennet," said Mr. Baker. He appeared contrite, but Elizabeth was certain it was nothing more than the appearance, rather than the actuality.

"Come, Miss Bennet," said Mr. Darcy. "We may discuss this matter at a later date. At present, it is time to depart, if we are to make Rosings while there is still light."

The heavy-handedness of the man's actions finally broke Elizabeth's temper. She glared at him for a moment, ignoring the arm he extended in her direction, and turned to Mr. Baker.

"It seems you are correct, sir. Making the return journey with new companions would be pleasant. I accept your invitation to ride in your coach."

Elizabeth regretted her impetuous decision the moment it was made. But there was no help for it, for she had already declared her intention—to renege now would be rude in the extreme. Mr. Darcy looked at her, his expression searching, and he bowed once and turned away, striding back toward his cousin. Elizabeth watched him go, a feeling akin to regret welling up in her breast.

"Finally!" said Mr. Baker, his tone full of arrogant assurance. "I thought he would never leave us be."

"Why should you wish it?" asked Elizabeth, unwilling to endure the man any more than necessary. "Mr. Darcy is cousin to my sister's husband, and I respect him a great deal. My decision to accompany you was nothing more and nothing less than I stated."

"Of course, my dear Miss Bennet," said Mr. Baker, his demeanor changing not a whit. "But I cannot help but relish this opportunity to speak with you without Darcy's interference. His presence and behavior of late have been nothing less than insufferable. We are well rid of him."

Then Mr. Baker escorted her toward his carriage, paying no attention to the grinding of Elizabeth's teeth if he even noticed at all. There were a few tasks left to accomplish, and Elizabeth stood next to Mr. Baker, listening to his ubiquitous words, wishing she had been intelligent enough to make a different decision.

When it was almost time to depart, Charity approached them, having linked arms with the eldest Miss Norland, though to Elizabeth's eyes she appeared to be dragging the poor girl with her. She fixed Elizabeth with a smirk, then rolled her eyes and addressed Mr. Baker.

"Sir, your thought of exchanging traveling companions was inspired. Perhaps Miss Norland and I might ride with you."

"Of course, Lady Charity," said the man. "I am vastly pleased to have three such lovely young ladies travel with me."

The carriage was ready and Mr. Baker indicated to the waiting conveyance, handing Miss Norland up first. While he was thus engaged, Charity leaned toward Elizabeth and hissed in her ear.

"You have an interesting way of avoiding gentlemen you do not like, Elizabeth. Or perhaps it is simply that you have a talent for acting without thinking of the consequences."

There was nothing Elizabeth could say, for, in this instance, it was nothing more than the truth. Charity was handed into the carriage next, and she took her seat next to Miss Norland, leaving the opposite bench empty. Elizabeth glared at her friend, her eyes accusing her of treachery. But Charity only nodded to indicate the other seat. Sitting next to Mr. Baker was her punishment for acting with a lack of forethought.

At least Charity did not leave her to suffer Mr. Baker's conversation for the entirety of the journey, though for the first half hour Elizabeth thought she meant to do exactly that. When she did finally speak up, she acted to not only engage Elizabeth and Miss Norland but also endeavored to distract Mr. Baker as much as she could. Elizabeth was grateful for her assistance, for she did not think she could have endured Mr. Baker's forward attentions all the way to Rosings.

Chapter XXXVII

The return journey to Rosings in Mr. Baker's company was insufferable. Elizabeth knew not how she endured it, even with Charity's assistance. She thought she might have some respite from him through changed seating arrangements after their rest stops along the way, but Mr. Baker continued to hand Charity and Miss Norland into the carriage first, and Charity continued to sit by the other girl, leaving Elizabeth to Mr. Baker.

The sensation of being released from his company at the end of the journey was akin to a condemned man receiving a pardon. Even the simple goodbye she hurriedly made as the Rosings party separated from the rest and continued on themselves suggested that the man, in his smug self-assurance, considered the journey a success. Elizabeth could not consider it anything less than a disaster. And to be reunited with Mr. Darcy was no less a punishment. He said nothing and rode in the other carriage, and those who did not know what happened looked on them askance. Elizabeth had not the heart nor the will to respond to any of their veiled questions.

By the next morning, Elizabeth was feeling quite subdued and far from her usual self, so much so that she attracted the attention of the whole party. Most were content to leave her to her own devices. But there was one in the house who was not known for her discretion.

"You are very dull, Miss Bennet," said Lady Catherine when they sat down to luncheon the day of their return. "I had expected you, of all people, to be full of witty observations and interesting anecdotes concerning your experiences."

Though feeling little inclined to reply, Elizabeth attempted an answer: "Our time in Margate *was* pleasant. I simply find myself fatigued from the journey."

If she had heard the explanation from another, Elizabeth could not have imagined herself being taken in by it. Lady Catherine, however, seemed to accept it without question, though, of course, not without comment.

"I am not surprised, Miss Bennet. To travel so far for a single day of amusement is sheer silliness. You ought to have stayed several days, or even a week."

"Perhaps that is what we should have done," said Anthony. "There was certainly little time to see as much as we might have wished."

"That is exactly it," said Lady Catherine. "Had you heeded my advice before you left, you would have stayed longer."

Elizabeth could not miss the grin which passed between Charity and Anthony, and several of the other members of the party. Lady Catherine had made no such statement in Elizabeth's hearing. But a good memory had never been one of Lady Catherine's strengths.

"Next time," said Anthony to his aunt, "we shall take care to listen to your advice, Aunt."

And thus Lady Catherine was diverted, and Elizabeth removed from the focus of her attention. For that, she was grateful, for she had no desire to verbally fence with Lady Catherine. It was not much longer before she was mercifully released from the table and went her own way.

Fortunate it was that Elizabeth was not left to wallow in her dull spirits, for of that much Lady Catherine had been correct. While she spent much of her time that afternoon in her own company, separated from the others by her own choice, her rumination wandered down paths which served only to further depress her. And by the time her sister found her, Elizabeth was quite disheartened.

"I searched for you for some time this morning, Lizzy," said Jane when she stepped into the library. "It is not like you to secrete yourself away from everyone and sit in solitude."

A hint of her humor returned at that moment, and Elizabeth smiled at her sister, saying: "Surely you should have known I could be found in the library. The written word has long been my refuge—you must know this."

Jane's severe look suggested she was not at all misled. "Yes, I do know of it. But I am certain you have not turned a page of that book in the last thirty minutes at least. You are in the same attitude you were in thirty minutes gone."

Elizabeth frowned at her sister's insinuation. "You saw me thirty minutes ago?"

"It was how I found you," said Jane. "And you never noticed more, nor did you see Mr. Darcy."

"Mr. Darcy was here?" asked Elizabeth, the thought of the man observing her prompting a frown.

"As I said—that was how I found you. Mr. Darcy saw you as he opened the door to enter the library, and as I was in a position to see him stop without entering, I also looked in to see you sitting here.

"Now, Lizzy," said Jane, her tone brooking no opposition, "what has led you to this state?"

"I do not wish to speak of it, Jane."

"There is no need to do so in specific terms," replied Jane. "Anthony has already informed me of yesterday's events."

Elizabeth huffed in annoyance. "Then you already know."

"I know you have a right to be angry with Mr. Darcy for how he accused you," replied Jane. "What I do not know is why it has affected you this much. The Lizzy I know would have brushed his comments off, given him a piece of her mind, and then regained her good cheer."

Elizabeth had not thought of it in such terms, and she knew that Jane was completely correct. What she could not account for was why it was so. With Mr. Collins, she had not been affected in this way, and even in Hertfordshire, when she thought Mr. Darcy was not behaving as he ought, she had not wallowed in her self-pity. What was different now?

"Your confusion is evident," said Jane, drawing Elizabeth's attention once again. "Have you no explanation for why you have been so affected?"

Through narrowed eyes, Elizabeth gazed at her sister, wondering at her insinuation. "Do you mean to suggest that Mr. Darcy is different somehow? That he is at the root of my confusion?"

"It was not *I* who said it, Lizzy," was Jane's dry reply. "And it is not I who must decipher my own feelings." Jane paused, and her gaze seemed to go right through Elizabeth, making her quite uncomfortable. "Now that the subject has been raised, however, it seems to me that Mr. Darcy has been rather charming since coming to Rosings. Were I not already happily married to my beloved Anthony, I might have found myself affected by him."

In spite of herself, Elizabeth laughed. "Do not allow Anthony to hear you speak in such a way. You might provoke a duel between cousins."

Jane shook her head and said: "Anthony knows of my devotion. He would laugh and claim that he had the foresight to snap me up first and tease me that I would simply need to learn to live with the superior man."

With a laugh, Elizabeth could only agree. It was exactly what Anthony would have said. But Jane was not finished.

"Well, Lizzy? Do you not think Mr. Darcy has been quite the gentleman since coming? Have you not been affected by it?"

"Except when he is accusing me of conspiring with a man I do not know," muttered Elizabeth."

'It was very wrong of him," agreed Jane. "But I think, if you search within yourself, you will obtain an answer to the question of why you are so moved by this. And I think you will also understand that this is not a matter which should be allowed to come between you. Not when there could be so much more between you and Mr. Darcy."

With those final words, Jane rose and departed, leaving Elizabeth to her thoughts. Perhaps Jane was correct. She had long known or suspected Mr. Darcy's feelings for her, his continued attentions seeming to prove her suppositions. She had never had much luck in understanding how her own feelings were changing in response. Perhaps it was time to discover it.

"Shall I beat him about the head?" asked Anthony when she rejoined his and Jane's company a little later. "I am no more pleased that he would accuse you of such things than you are."

"I beg you do nothing," said Elizabeth, shaking her head vigorously. "There is no reason to say anything."

"There is every reason, as far as I am concerned," grumbled Anthony. "Darcy is so blind when it comes to Wickham that he cannot distinguish friend from foe. And yet he refuses to do anything concerning the libertine."

"What is his connection with Mr. Wickham?" asked Elizabeth, curious of the reason for the virulent response from a normally collected man.

"Wickham is the son of Darcy's father's steward," said Anthony. "I do not wish to say much more of the matter than that he is not a good man. Darcy covered for him for years—paid for his debts, kept him from trouble, paid him far more in lieu of a family living than he deserved. That money soon was lost to Wickham's habits, and the fact that Darcy severed all acquaintance with him did not prevent him from returning with outstretched hand. And even worse."

"Then it must have seemed like I was known to him," said Elizabeth, thinking of the scene on the street and how it must have appeared.

"It does not signify," said Anthony. "Rather than immediately jumping to the conclusion of being in league with him, Darcy's first thought should have been your protection from a man who has no morals."

Elizabeth knew this to be true, and she suspected that Mr. Darcy knew it too. The question was whether he would ever confess to it. Now that she had a clearer picture of her own feelings, Elizabeth hoped he would. But she would not be ruled by it, would not pine for the good opinion of a man when she had done nothing to lose it.

"For a time, I thought to return to Longbourn," said Elizabeth.

Jane gazed at her with such concern that Elizabeth was moved to reassure her. "I *had* considered it, but I do not wish to leave at present. I do enjoy my time here with you, Jane. I do not wish to leave."

"I am happy to hear it," murmured Jane.

"And as for Mr. Darcy," said Elizabeth, "I believe I shall leave him to act in whatever way he sees fit. Should he wish to reconcile and explain his actions, I shall listen. If he wishes to maintain whatever grudge has arisen in his mind, then he is entitled to it. I hope he comes to his senses. But it is his decision to make."

There was nothing to say to Elizabeth's declaration, no dispute to be made, and she was happy when neither of her companions attempted it. The warmth she felt toward Mr. Darcy was cooled somewhat, though the underlying sentiment remained. It was for Mr. Darcy to act to restore their former closeness. And Elizabeth decided he had best do it, for she had little notion to wait.

Just as Elizabeth was feeling down-hearted, so too was Darcy. The afternoon following luncheon was spent in one fruitless activity after another, considering the scene from the previous day over and over again. And Darcy was forced to confess, to himself if no one else, that he may have been wrong.

The thought of Wickham and what he had attempted to do with Darcy's dearest sister was still enough to make him wish to jump on his horse and ride off to find Wickham and administer a richly deserved retribution. The sight of the man the previous day had driven all rational thought from Darcy's head, much to his detriment. Now that he could look back on the matter rationally, it was clear Miss Bennet could have had nothing to do with whatever scheme in which Wickham was now engaged. But he had spoken without thinking, and the damage had been done. The longer he thought on the matter, the more Darcy hoped it was not irreparable.

So he drifted aimlessly throughout the house, nothing holding his attention, nothing stimulating his interest. Had he been Hurst, he might simply have found the nearest bottle of brandy and drowned his sorrows. But that had never been his way. Darcy was happy it was not, for he had never appreciated the sensation of the morning after.

When his sister found him, Darcy was perhaps in the deepest pit of his own making, drowning in his own sorrows. In previous years she may simply have let him be. She was the much younger sister, almost akin to a daughter. She had never presumed to impose her opinions upon him. Perhaps it might have been better if she had. But she was changed. She was a married woman now, and her confidence had grown by leaps and bounds.

"I am confused, Brother," said she, speaking without preamble. "I know something happened yesterday before we left Margate, but I do not know what. But I *do* know it has left you out of sorts. I also know Elizabeth is not right."

That much was true, mused Darcy. Miss Bennet, when he had spied her as he attempted to enter the library, appeared pensive and sad, very unlike her usual cheerful demeanor. The fact that it was *he* who had reduced her to such a state caused a little stab of remorse to pierce his heart.

"Will you not share your troubles with me?"

There were few things of which he wished to speak of less with his sister than Wickham. Thus, Darcy attempted to prevaricate.

"It is nothing, Georgiana. I know nothing of Miss Bennet's troubles."

Georgiana's eyes narrowed. "I have never known you to be untruthful with me, Brother. I beg you do not start now."

"I do not wish to speak of it."

"Because you do not trust me?"

"Because I do not wish to hurt you."

Georgiana gazed at him for a long moment and then proceeded to prove her newfound maturity. "I know you still consider me to be a girl, Brother. But I am not any longer. I am a married woman. There may be nothing I can do to assist you. But would the benefits of sharing your burden with another not also provide assistance?"

"It is not that, Sister," said Darcy.

"Then what is it?" demanded she. "It is almost as if Wickham suddenly appeared in our lives again."

Darcy's countenance must have given away the truth of the matter, for her face fell. Then she gathered her courage and peered at him.

"What does Mr. Wickham have to do with your ennui?"

Clearly, he was not to be successful in diverting her. Thus, Darcy could only sigh and look away in moody resignation.

"Wickham appeared in Margate yesterday. I found Miss Bennet speaking to him in the middle of the street and . . . I reacted badly."

A frown settled over her face. "I do not understand. What could Miss Bennet have to do with Mr. Wickham?"

Darcy released a mirthless chuckle and shook his head. "What, indeed? I am afraid I am asking myself that very question now, though yesterday it all seemed clear."

"Tell me."

And so Darcy did. It was mortifying, in a way, confessing such matters to his sister, who had always looked up to him almost as a father. But it was also cathartic. When he finished his explanation, he felt Georgiana's indignation, and he was forced to own that it was warranted, though he was not above attempting to defend himself.

"I think I am justified in being suspicious of anything connected to Wickham," said Darcy.

"And I do not begrudge you that," replied Georgiana. Her tone was fierce and her cause righteous. "But you can hardly suspect Elizabeth of such nefarious purposes with so little evidence."

Darcy shrugged. "Perhaps I cannot. But at the time it all seemed so clear."

"It was poorly done, William," said Georgiana. "You have offended Elizabeth. I can hardly understand how you could come to such a conclusion."

The heat in Darcy's cheeks did not go unnoticed by his suddenly perceptive sister. Georgiana regarded him for a moment before her lips suddenly curved upwards in a smile.

"Or perhaps I can."

There was no reason to deny it, and Darcy did not even make the attempt.

"The question, then, is what are you to do about it?"

Again, Darcy was reticent about speaking of such matters with her and tried to deflect her. "I am surprised you are taking this matter with such a measure of calm."

With a shrug, Georgiana said: "I have matured, as I said."

"Yes, that much is evident. But you hardly seem like the girl you were a year ago."

"Do not attempt to change the subject, Brother."

"I believe I already have, dear heart," said Darcy, affection filling him with pride. "Are you unaffected by the mention of Wickham?"

The glare she directed at him did not affect Darcy in the slightest. In the end, she seemed to realize he would not answer her question until she answered his.

"Yes, the mention of Mr. Wickham *does* make me uncomfortable. But he now has no power to harm me, for I am married to a good man. And, Brother," said she, her tone as serious as he had ever heard from her, "I am quite happy with Charles. There is no need to concern yourself for me any longer. Nor need you feel guilty. Though we did not come together in terms I might have wished, I cannot imagine marrying anyone else."

"So a little good has come of Wickham's actions after all," said Darcy, bemusement welling up within him.

Georgiana grinned, a gesture which was fierce, like the growl of a wolf. "I would not go so far as to suggest that. Perhaps we should simply say that much good has come *in spite* of his actions.

"Now, will you not answer *my* question?"

"What am I to do on the matter of Miss Bennet?" queried Darcy. When Georgiana nodded, he sighed. "I suppose I owe her an apology, at the very least."

"That is an understatement," said Georgiana, the irony rich in her voice.

"I suppose it is."

"In that case, I suggest you go to it." Georgiana paused and smiled. "You know Elizabeth is not the sort of woman to allow such characterizations of her. I suggest, when you do apologize, that you make it very convincing and sincere."

"That, I had already determined," said Darcy.

Georgiana rose to go, but before she departed, she turned to Darcy and eyed him, a questioning look falling on him. "What do you mean to do about Mr. Wickham? I do not know what his game was with Miss Bennet, but I cannot imagine it was anything good."

What *did* he mean to do? Darcy was not certain, and he had no notion why Wickham had focused on Miss Bennet. But Georgiana was completely correct, and for the first time in his life, Darcy was able to think of the man he had once called a friend, his thoughts untainted by his father's favor, his erstwhile friendship, or even his considerable distaste and wish to disassociate himself from any influence Wickham might exert. The fact of the matter was that Wickham was a scourge on all society, his actions having made himself nigh unredeemable. It would behoove Darcy to ensure he was no longer in a position to prey on society, could not work his vile charms on young ladies such as Georgiana and Miss Bennet.

"At present," said Darcy once these thoughts had passed through his mind, "I do not know what there is to be done. Though he was in Margate only yesterday, I have no doubt he has decamped. If I know Wickham, he has hidden in the deepest hole he can find until my attention is focused elsewhere."

"I am certain you could find him if you wished."

Darcy chuckled. "Perhaps that is so. Allow me a little time to determine what is to be done. Fitzwilliam may have something to say on the matter as well."

"Good," said Georgiana. "I should not like to consider the possibility of George Wickham preying on other young ladies."

With those words, Georgiana left the room, while Darcy stared at the door through which she had departed. She truly had matured and changed. The sister he had all but raised himself had become a woman in her own right. Darcy could not have been prouder.

Chapter XXXVIII

*I*t was too much to hope that Lady Catherine would remain ignorant of the well of unhappiness which existed in her home. It was equally unfathomable that she would ignore it. She was not the kind of woman who allowed matters to rest when she could insert her own opinion. Indeed, Elizabeth might have thought her meddling—*had* thought her meddling—until she had proven she possessed *some* discretion.

Lady Catherine's comments about Elizabeth's dullness the day after their return to Rosings, and Elizabeth's response brought her some reprieve. But though Elizabeth was cheered by her conversations with Anthony and Jane, there still existed some residual gloom. Unfortunately, Lady Catherine proved quite equal to the task of recognizing it.

"I see you remain a little out of spirits," observed Lady Catherine the next morning, the second after their return.

Elizabeth looked to Charity for support, but her friend, it seemed, was not inclined to assist her in this matter. In fact, Charity grinned and motioned toward the lady with her head, a clear invitation to respond to the lady's question. But Elizabeth was not given an opportunity to do so.

"Charity," said Lady Catherine, "I require a few moments to speak to Miss Bennet in private."

"Of course, Aunt," replied Charity, ignoring Elizabeth's accusing glare. "A walk in the garden would do me good, I believe."

Then she rose and departed without another word, leaving Elizabeth alone with the older woman. Lady Catherine stood and went to the door, and after a brief instruction to the footman stationed there, she returned to her chair and regarded Elizabeth.

"It appears, Miss Bennet, that your journey to Margate was far more eventful than I might have expected. Do you care to share what happened with me?"

There were few things Elizabeth wished to share less than the scene between Mr. Wickham, Mr. Darcy, and herself. But it appeared she was not to be given the chance to demur.

"I have divined something of it, enough to know my nephew's former playmate was involved." Lady Catherine sniffed with disdain. "In some respects, his fall was to be expected. Nothing good can come of a servant being raised in such a manner."

Elizabeth frowned. "Are you suggesting a man cannot strive to be more than he is?"

"No, Miss Bennet, I am not." Lady Catherine held Elizabeth's gaze evenly. "You will find that I am quite traditional in my thinking, and I make no apologies for that fact. I will not bore you with a recitation of my feelings on the subject of the classes. In this particular instance, however, Mr. Wickham was treated as a second son by Robert Darcy, and as such, he learned to expect that which he would never be given. He was educated as a gentleman, but as he possessed not the means to live like one, it turned him bitter and grasping. It is unfortunate, indeed, for had he also been taught that hard work can raise a man from his circumstances, much might have been different."

Mollified, Elizabeth wondered at Lady Catherine's turn of phrase. But she was absolutely correct, given what Elizabeth knew of Mr. Wickham, and Elizabeth could not gainsay her. She did not know enough of the situation to properly judge further, so she endeavored to keep silent.

"I see you agree with me," said Lady Catherine. "That is good. But that is not what I wish to speak of. Mr. Wickham is what he is, and nothing can change that. Given the nuisance he has made of himself, I suspect Darcy is nearing the end of his patience." Lady Catherine huffed with disdain. "Had he been *my* responsibility, he would have been shipped off to Botany Bay many moons ago.

"Now, I understand he had something to do with your quarrel with Darcy. Shall you not share it with me?"

Knowing she had little choice in the matter, Elizabeth obliged, sharing the account as briefly as she could. Lady Catherine listened intently, and when Elizabeth had finished speaking, she sat back in her chair and shook her head.

"Well, Darcy, it seems you have stepped in it this time. I cannot imagine why he might have thought you to be in league with Wickham. He has begun to see phantasms around every corner when it concerns that young man."

Then with a glance at Elizabeth, she continued: "And he has hurt his own cause and offended you. I cannot say you are not affronted without reason."

All at once, Elizabeth knew, and she gasped. Lady Catherine kept her gaze steady on Elizabeth, but after a moment her eyebrow rose in a challenging gesture.

"You know of Mr. Darcy's interest in me?"

For a moment she thought the lady would not respond. Then she nodded slowly. "I do."

"Then why have you not spoken to me of it? I know of your wishes with respect to your daughter."

Lady Catherine's lips curled up in amusement. "Of course you do. I did not precisely hide them, and you must remember my words from the day of Darcy's arrival."

"Yes," said Elizabeth, not certain what to say.

"Darcy, Miss Bennet, is my dear sister's son. He is a good man—one of the very best. Any woman would wish for her daughter to have such a good man as her husband. And contrary to what you might hear from Charity or Anthony, my sister and I *did* speak of an engagement."

"That is why I would have expected you to speak to me on the subject at the very least," said Elizabeth.

Her amusement once again shining through, Lady Catherine said: "Yes, I suppose you might have. However, seeing you and Darcy together, I know it was not *you* to whom I must make my appeal. While you have accepted Darcy's overtures, it was clear to me you have not sought them out. What good would speaking to you have done?"

What good, indeed. This was all turning out so different from what Elizabeth might have expected. She felt lost at sea. That Lady Catherine had reacted in such a rational manner was something Elizabeth would not have expected, given all she had heard of the lady in advance.

"So you do not wish for your daughter and your sister's son to marry?"

Had Elizabeth not witnessed it, she might not have believed it. But Lady Catherine colored at her question, and her demeanor turned apologetic.

"I may have been a little . . . zealous on the matter. I confess it without hesitation. It seems neither Darcy nor Anne ever meant to abide by our wishes. My own wishes must be superseded by those at the center of the matter. I am disappointed, but I have decided to accept it, for the good of our children."

"Then that must be why you took an interest in me," said Elizabeth.

Again, Lady Catherine regarded her evenly. "I did. I do not mean any offense, Miss Bennet. You have never inhabited the world my nephews do, even with the elevation of your sister."

"No, but I *do* know how to behave."

"I never claimed you did not. You must acknowledge, however, that Miss Elizabeth Bennet of Longbourn and Mrs. Elizabeth Darcy of Pemberley, with connections to the Fitzwilliam family and several other noble families, are two completely different people."

There was no sense in disagreeing with the lady. Thus, she simply nodded and allowed Lady Catherine's statement to pass without further comment.

"It appears, however, that my nephew has managed to offend you. And if what I suspect of his feelings is true, he has made it more difficult to obtain his happiness." Lady Catherine paused, apparently considering the matter. "I could speak to him if you like. The manner in which he accused you would have embarrassed his mother, I am certain. I could ensure he understands this."

"I beg you, do not speak to him at all!" exclaimed Elizabeth.

Lady Catherine actually laughed at her mortification. "Perhaps you are better for my nephew than I ever thought, Miss Bennet. If you wish him to impress you on his own merits, I can only applaud your courage. I shall say nothing.

"But I wish you to know . . . ."

Lady Catherine paused as if some emotion came over her, and she looked away. Surprised, Elizabeth looked on—she had never thought to see Lady Catherine appearing vulnerable.

"If I cannot have my daughter married to Darcy," said Lady Catherine after mastering herself, "I think I might be tolerably happy to have you as a future niece."

"Thank you, Lady Catherine," said Elizabeth. She rose and kissed the lady's cheek, sharing a smile with her. "I appreciate your confidence in me. Having you as an aunt will be no hardship either. I cannot say what will happen, but I will keep an open mind should Mr. Darcy choose to explain his actions."

With a smile, Lady Catherine shooed her from the room, and Elizabeth, taking it as the lady's desire to be alone, obliged. Though she had given Elizabeth far more of an endorsement than she had ever thought to receive in such circumstances, Elizabeth could sense what the admission had cost her. No doubt she would return to herself, and her meddling would continue once she was composed. Until then, giving her the time she needed to accustom herself to the end of her dream was the least Elizabeth could do.

"So, how did my aunt comport herself?" demanded Charity, accosting Elizabeth as soon as she left the room. "Are you to be returned to your family in disgrace? Or has her ladyship, in great condescension, decreed you shall be married to a tenant to protect her daughter's interests?"

"Charity," said Elizabeth, her tone dripping with exasperation.

But Charity grasped her hand and pulled her down the hall toward a small parlor which was much less used than the main sitting-room. Once they were inside, Charity turned to regard her yet again.

"It seems I shall have no peace until I share the particulars with you."

"I should hope not," replied Charity.

"Then I shall do so." And she did, explaining their conversation, including Lady Catherine's words concerning Elizabeth's suitability to be Mr. Darcy's wife. Charity listened with seeming astonishment. But she thankfully did not interrupt until the end.

"It is true that Lady Catherine's demeanor has changed, much though I would have thought it impossible. For her to say such words to you is beyond anything I might have invented in my wildest fantasies."

"She surprised me too," said Elizabeth. "She is not the dragon you and Anthony described to me."

"Then the dragon's fangs have been blunted," jested Charity. "She was quite fearsome when I was a child. And her insistence on Darcy and Anne's engagement has not abated over the years."

Elizabeth shrugged. There was little else she could do. Lady Catherine could be a trial at times, but she was not intolerable.

"You should take this as a sign, Elizabeth."

"To what do you refer?" asked Elizabeth, certain Charity was teasing her again.

"Why, you should snap Darcy up while you can! You can never know if Lady Catherine will not suddenly change her mind again."

"I am not certain if he is a good catch," muttered Elizabeth.

Charity fixed her with a delighted grin. "Perhaps not. But he *is* very wealthy. Great riches will hide many character defects."

Bursting into laughter, Elizabeth exclaimed: "Or allow one to ignore them. I am not certain it would do anything to hide them!"

Their mirth might have continued unabated, but the door behind them opened, quelling their laughter. It was the subject of their discussion, watching them with all the seriousness Elizabeth had ever seen the man display. She hoped he had not overheard their irreverent jesting.

Georgiana's words stayed with Darcy throughout the day and into the next, giving Darcy much on which to think. The matter of Wickham was the easiest. Darcy had declined to act on several occasions before because of the memory of his father's affection for Wickham. The one time he might have acted, he had been too concerned for Georgiana and too surprised with what he found.

But now his path was clear. Wickham was a menace, and Darcy had dithered too long, allowing him to continue to prey upon others. It was time that stopped, time for the man to pay the price for his actions. And as such, Darcy spoke with the one he knew could be of great assistance in finding him.

"You have finally decided not to protect him any longer," observed Fitzwilliam when Darcy informed him of his intentions.

"He has had enough charity from me," said Darcy shortly. "He can do nothing more to hurt Georgiana, but he continues to be a threat to other young ladies. It is time to call in his debts and have him transported."

Fitzwilliam nodded, the fire in his eyes burning hotly. "Then I shall contact some men of my acquaintance. It may take some time, but we shall run him to ground."

With the matter of Wickham decided, Darcy turned his attention to the other matter of which he had spoken with his sister. It was clear that Darcy had acted badly. The shock of seeing the woman with whom he was falling in love speaking with the libertine had led him to cast aspersions, to accuse where there was no reason to suspect wrongdoing. That needed to be corrected, an apology offered. Perhaps the explanation of Wickham's actions toward Georgiana might help her understand, though it would not excuse his behavior.

It had been pure chance which had allowed Darcy to witness Charity pulling Miss Bennet toward the small parlor. They had some matter to discuss, he supposed, so he waited a few minutes to see if they would emerge again. When his impatience grew too much—and Darcy knew he had begun with little patience at all—he opened the door and stepped in.

"My apologies, Charity," said he, noting the cessation of their humor, "but I wish to have a word with Miss Bennet. Will you oblige me?"

Darcy's request was directed at both young ladies, and he was gratified they had taken it as such. The glance they shared was teeming with some meaning he could not decipher. In the end, Miss Bennet's minute shrug indicated her willingness, and Charity accepted it. But outspoken as she was, she did not depart without making a witty comment.

"I shall leave the door open to protect your reputations." She approached Darcy, but before she left, she hesitated and leaned toward him. "Perhaps it would be most effective if you show humility, Cousin."

Then, her silvery laughter tinkling after her, she quit the room, leaving the door ajar as she had promised. With a shake of his head, Darcy turned to Miss Bennet, noting her slightly rigid stance, the way her arms were wrapped around her, as if in defense. Darcy had no desire to begin a difficult conversation such as this promised to be under such circumstances, and he moved to put her at ease.

"Will you not sit? This will be easier if we are comfortable."

Though her eyes searched his for a moment, Miss Bennet acquiesced and perched herself on the edge of a nearby chair. Darcy chose the sofa sitting perpendicular to it, settling himself in much the same attitude.

"Thank you for agreeing to speak with me, Miss Bennet," said he. "I wished to make some explanation of what happened in Margate. But before I do so, I want you to understand that I do not suspect you of ulterior motives concerning my sister or my family. I accused you without foundation in the emotion of the moment, and I apologize most sincerely. It was poorly done of me."

"It is gratifying to hear it, sir," replied Miss Bennet. "I accept your apology and bear you no ill will."

"Thank you," repeated Darcy, pleased she was a forgiving woman.

"It seems to me that you have no knowledge of the events of last summer, and as they connect to this incident, I thought you should know. If nothing else, it will inform you of the manner of man who, I believe, intended to importune you."

Miss Bennet tilted her head to the side, a curious affectation which Darcy found utterly charming. He forced his thoughts back to the matter at hand—now was not the time to allow his admiration to get the better of him.

"He has some background with you," said she. "Your aunt has alluded to it, as have Charity and Anthony."

"Yes, he has. Wickham is the son of my father's steward, who was a good and upright man, one who fulfilled his duties with distinction. Unfortunately, Wickham has never possessed the same qualities, resembling his mother in character, who was a spendthrift, a grasping woman, envious of my family and jealous of my mother. My father saw only Wickham's charm and garrulous character. But by the time we were at Eton, I knew Wickham was of a base nature.

"I shall not bore you with the details of our past together. Wickham believes I cheated him when he was given more than he ever deserved. Suffice to say, he resents me for it and would do anything to hurt me."

"May I assume he has acted to do so?" asked Miss Bennet.

"Yes," replied Darcy. "Last summer, when Georgiana was at Ramsgate with her companion, he came to her with the connivance of her companion and persuaded her to elope with him."

Miss Bennet gasped, her hand going to her mouth. "Poor Georgiana!" exclaimed she, proving her affection for Darcy's sister. "And yet the elopement obviously did not take place."

"No," said Darcy. "Bingley and I were at a house party in East Sussex when I received a letter from her. I perceived that something was amiss, and as we were not enjoying ourselves, we decided to join her in Ramsgate. There we found Wickham in the act of persuading her to leave.

"Bingley suggested that he marry her to preserve her reputation, and as the matter had become known in the town and would make its way to London as gossip, we both agreed."

"I had not heard even a whisper of it," murmured Miss Bennet.

"The story lost its sting quickly," said Darcy. "We put out that Georgiana and Bingley had been near engaged and that Georgiana had managed to protect herself from a fortune hunter. While marrying a man so closely connected to trade was spoken of for a time, it did not last long. By the time the season started, it was largely forgotten."

"How she must have suffered," said Miss Bennet. She paused and then looked at him, her gaze piercing him to his core. "Tell me, Mr. Darcy—is she happy now with Mr. Bingley?"

"They both assure me they are. In fact, Bingley says he was given a great blessing, one he never would have thought to attempt to seek out for himself."

"Then at least something good has come of it," said Miss Bennet. "Often those in such circumstances are not nearly so happy with the resolution."

"I well know it," replied Darcy. "I am grateful beyond measure. Bingley is such a good friend. That they would be so happy together eases my conscience and lessens my fear for them both."

Miss Bennet regarded him, compassion filling her gaze. "You have taken great care of them, Mr. Darcy. I suspect you have assisted Mr. Bingley greatly over the years, and your sister's character is obviously in large part because of your efforts."

"I thank you for your approbation, Miss Bennet. But I have done little."

"You have done more than you will own, I think." Miss Bennet paused. "I was not of a mind to listen to your explanation until I thought on the matter. It is understandable you would react with anger when seeing a man who has done you so much harm. But I do not appreciate being accused of such things on so little evidence."

Darcy smiled at her. "Nor would anyone in your position. Normally I am very deliberate about every action, Miss Bennet. It is only Wickham who brings out such a side of me. And I cannot think it would have been as severe had it been anyone else of my acquaintance I witnessed speaking with him."

Clearly, she understood his meaning, for she colored and looked away. But again, he was impressed with her prepossession, for her embarrassment did not last long. She turned to him, and with a searching look, said:

"Then I have not been mistaken? You have some interest in me?"

Normally it was not done. A young lady did not ask after a man's intentions—if anyone did so, it would be her father. But Miss Bennet was anything but a typical young lady. And Darcy could not find her confidence anything but charming.

"I do, Miss Bennet. More than I have ever had in any young lady. May I hope there is some possibility of my feelings being returned?"

For a long and terrible moment Miss Bennet did not reply. But when she did, Darcy felt as if a great weight had been removed from his heart.

"You may."

It was a wonderful feeling, indeed, to have an ardent suitor. Elizabeth had not been a stranger to the attentions of men, for she had always been a popular partner at assemblies, had had her share of attention during any events of Meryton society. But their interest had always been tempered by her lack of dowry, her status as naught but the second daughter of a country squire.

This feeling was something completely different. Mr. Darcy that evening was attentive to her like he had never been before. He escorted her to dinner, sat at her side and reserved all his attention for her. And for the first time, Elizabeth realized she had an extraordinary measure of power over this young man. It was a heady feeling that left her wondering how much power *he* had over *her*. She did not know, but she felt the answer was coming into focus.

Mr. Darcy's explanation had been unexpected, the actions of the detestable Wickham beyond anything she could have imagined. And even then Elizabeth was certain she did not know the whole truth. She took care to speak to Georgiana that evening and apologize for whatever pain she had caused, though unknowingly.

"William informed you of what happened?" asked she.

"He did," replied Elizabeth. "I cannot imagine the ache which lodged in your heart because of that man's actions. But I want you to know that I admire you for recovering so quickly. Should I ever meet Mr. Wickham again, I shall kick him in the shin and call him out for being a worthless man."

Georgiana laughed and caught Elizabeth up in an embrace. "I was assisted by my brother and my dearest Charles. I am happy now, Elizabeth. You should not fear for me."

"I do not. But I shall ever be your ardent friend and supporter."

Those words seemed to mean more to Georgiana than anything else Elizabeth had said, for tears leaked from the corners of her eyes. In later years, Elizabeth would point to that moment when they became the closest of friends, a feeling which would last for the rest of their lives.

The observations of the others at the dinner table Elizabeth cheerfully ignored, including Anthony and Charity, who seemed intent upon making a jest of her détente with Mr. Darcy. Even when Anthony made a comment about Mr. Darcy's groveling being effective, she fixed him with an unpleasant glare, and he subsided, though his grin never faded. Lady Catherine seemed smug, Jane happy, and the Bingleys excited. Only Miss de Bourgh showed no particular interest, though Elizabeth thought she detected a hint of contempt on occasion.

Where it would lead them, Elizabeth could not know just yet. But she thought she would enjoy the journey. She thought she would enjoy it very much, indeed.

CHAPTER XXXIX

While it was true that Elizabeth and Mr. Darcy interacted with much more care in the ensuing days, it did not follow their blossoming connection suffered because of it. In fact, it could be argued that they grew in understanding of each other, which would assist them should their relationship grow and mature.

Elizabeth learned that Mr. Darcy, though he always showed a serious demeanor to all, was well able to converse regarding subjects of interest. It seemed he was not skilled when it came to small talk—his true abilities shone through when the discussion turned to matters of more substance. For his part, Mr. Darcy seemed to understand that Elizabeth was an intelligent woman and wished to be treated as such. Thus, he listened to her opinions and offered his own, but he never attempted to condescend to her, and he was always respectful, even when he did not agree.

"It seems you have come to your senses, Darcy," observed Lady Catherine the morning after their reconciliation. "I had thought I might have to box your ears to bring about such understanding."

There were several snickers at the thought of a woman, though she was tall, boxing the ears of a man such as Mr. Darcy. But he turned a smile on his aunt, saying: "It seems I have, Lady Catherine. I assure you that such measures are not required."

"Good. Do not make a mess of it this time."

Mr. Darcy wisely chose to refrain from responding to that statement. Their reconciliation, however, did not prevent others from inserting themselves on Elizabeth's notice when least wanted. She willingly kept up her friendship with Elia Baker and the Norland sisters, but James Baker was another matter entirely. He continued to impose his attentions upon her, ignoring or not understanding all her attempts to inform him of her lack of interest.

With no other choice, Elizabeth endured it as best she could. She was grateful that Mr. Darcy said nothing. Retreat was his usual option when Mr. Baker was present, though he rarely let them out of his sight. Mr. Baker seemed to revel in his perceived victory, never understanding that he could only be in Elizabeth's company for half an hour, whereas she was in the same house as Mr. Darcy every day. In some ways, Elizabeth wished Mr. Baker would simply come to the point, eerily similar to how she had felt when it had been Mr. Collins in Mr. Baker's shoes. If he did, she could refuse him and be free of his presence.

In those days, the Collinses once again intruded on Elizabeth's notice. While Mrs. Collins could be ignored, Mr. Collins was nigh unendurable, and he seemed to blame Elizabeth for his falling out of favor with Lady Catherine. A few days after the party's return from Margate, Elizabeth learned the Collinses were to be invited for dinner yet again.

"Mr. Collins has dined at Rosings at least twice a month since becoming rector of Hunsford," explained Lady Catherine with a hint of apology in her tone. "Since your arrival, they have only come once, though Mr. Collins attends me daily. I know his society is irksome, but I am attentive to those in my employ."

"You need not fear for me, Lady Catherine," said Elizabeth. "Rosings is your home, and you may invite whomever you like. I suspect Mr. Collins will not wish to engage with me, so it is of little matter."

"Thank you, Miss Bennet," said Lady Catherine.

"Perhaps Jane, Elizabeth, and I could deliver the invitation to Mr. and Mrs. Collins," said Charity. "We may observe his behavior and address anything wanting. And we have not attended them at the parsonage yet, which is another oversight which should be remedied."

Lady Catherine eyed Charity for a moment and nodded slowly. "Perhaps that would be wise. Please give Mrs. Collins my regards and inform me of your observations."

And so it was that Elizabeth found herself at the door to the parsonage in company with Jane and Charity. It was a modest building, though Elizabeth thought it comfortable and more than suitable for a man of Mr. Collins's situation in life. The walls were whitewashed, the wooden trim painted, and it stood in a pretty grove, a hint of a garden appearing around the side of the house. They were led into the presence of the master and the mistress of the house, and Elizabeth was treated to the exact kind of behavior she had expected from both.

"Lady Charity!" fawned Mr. Collins. "Welcome to my humble abode! I am certain the parsonage has never been honored by such an esteemed visitor as yourself. I possess not the words to convey my gratitude and the reverence I feel on the occasion of your visit."

Elizabeth was contemplating Mr. Collins's silliness, for she was certain Lady Catherine had visited on several occasions. Elizabeth suspected Mr. Collins had rarely been at a loss for any words, a sad state, indeed. It seemed Charity was in similar straits, considering her bemused smile. But Mr. Collins had already turned to Jane.

"And Mrs. Fitzwilliam," said he, politely but with considerably less enthusiasm. "You are also very welcome."

If any of them thought he would greet or even acknowledge Elizabeth in any way, they would have been sadly mistaken. Mr. Collins did no such thing; he turned, instead, and motioning to his wife. He introduced her again, quite unnecessarily. By this time Charity was watching him, a frown reserved for the silly man. She cleared her throat and glanced at Elizabeth. But Mr. Collins mistook her meaning.

"Come, Lady Charity. Let us have tea. It sounds like you are catching a cold."

"I am quite well, Mr. Collins. But it seems you have neglected to greet your *other* cousin."

For the first time, Mr. Collins looked at Elizabeth, his distaste evident for all to see. He sniffed once and said: "Cousin Elizabeth. I see you have come too."

He did not say anything further to Elizabeth, instead inviting them to sit with the same exaggerated deference for Charity. It took no power of insight to see that Charity was working up a head of anger when Elizabeth reached out and grasped her hand, shaking her head. For a moment, Elizabeth thought she might insist on making an issue of Mr. Collins's behavior. But in the end, she sat where indicated. Mr.

Collins, for his part, glared at Elizabeth, but he mercifully said nothing.

Until the tea service was delivered, they conversed about banal subjects. Or at least it seemed like nothing more than a usual morning visit. In fact, Mr. Collins dominated the conversation, with his wife supporting everything he said while adding more than a few inanities of her own. Charity, at whom their toadying was directed, said nothing, the response mostly carried by Jane, though she rarely said anything more than a monosyllable. For Elizabeth's part, it was readily apparent that she was not welcome and was only tolerated because of Charity's presence. Thus, she kept her silence, which seemed to suit Mr. Collins quite well, indeed.

Once the tea service arrived, and Mr. Collins was distracted by the servant, Charity took the opportunity to offer the invitation. "Mr. and Mrs. Collins, my aunt has asked that I invite you to dinner at Rosings tomorrow evening. She will expect you at the usual time."

Elizabeth fought to hold her countenance at the imperious nature of Charity's invitation. Mr. Collins, however, seemed caught up in such ecstasy at the opportunity to once again dine in his patroness's presence.

"Mrs. Collins and I thank you, most gratefully, for the condescension of your kind invitation. I have felt keenly the lack of Lady Catherine's company of late and am grateful she has once again seen fit to admit us to her company. Of course, had matters been different, I know we would have enjoyed her company more often than has been the case. But I am delighted nonetheless."

His significant glance in Elizabeth's direction was not misunderstood by any of them. For her part, Elizabeth was ready to laugh in the man's face. Charity, however, was at the end of her patience for his absurdity.

"Yes, Mr. Collins, it has been some time since you were last invited to Rosings. When you come this time, I suggest you offer your deference to the entire company and not allow your pride to disapprove of Lady Catherine's guests."

"I am sure I could never do such a thing," said Mr. Collins, this time resisting the impulse to glance at Elizabeth.

"See that you do not," was Charity's stern reply.

Mr. Collins waxed poetic in his determination to do that, which took some moments. In the meantime, the three ladies consumed their tea as quickly as they dared, for none wished to stay any longer than necessary. When Mr. Collins finally exhausted his words of devotion for Lady Catherine, he turned to Elizabeth, his smile obviously false, belied by the hardness in his eyes.

"You have been here for some time, Cousin Elizabeth. I am sure you have benefited greatly from the example of Lady Catherine and her fair daughter. For who could not be uplifted by the very image of gentility and delicacy in their midst? I *hope* it will do you some good."

"I am indebted to Lady Catherine," said Elizabeth simply, knowing that to say anything else would invite his poor behavior.

"Indeed, you are." He paused and then said: "I am certain your father will wish you home soon. You *are* his favorite, are you not?"

"Elizabeth will stay as long as she wishes," said Charity, interrupting before Elizabeth could reply for herself. "As you must know, she travels with my brother and Jane on their honeymoon."

"Of course, of course," was Mr. Collins's hasty reply. "I merely wished to express my certainty of Mr. Bennet's wish for his daughter's return. She has been from home for some time, after all."

"I know exactly to what you referred, Mr. Collins," said Charity, a distasteful frown fixed on the man. For Mr. Collins's part, it was evident he did not understand the hidden meaning in her words, for he simpered and smirked and groveled before her.

"Now, I believe it is time to depart," said Charity, rising from her seat. "Be sure to be punctual, Mr. Collins, for you know my aunt's feelings concerning punctuality."

"We do, Lady Charity," said Mrs. Collins. "We should never dream of arriving even a second late."

"Good," said Charity.

Then with the barest hint of a curtsey—one which Jane mirrored more deeply, and Elizabeth almost not at all—she led them from the room. As soon as they were out of the house, the three ladies exhaled as one. Then they exchanged a glance and laughter welled up between them. It was good to be able to release such a feeling of glee, thought Elizabeth, for where there was absurdity aplenty, one had best laugh.

"The nerve of that man!" exclaimed Charity before they had even passed Hunsford's gate. "To ignore you and then suggest you have stayed too long! I was strongly considering the merits of berating him and his equally useless wife! But I doubt he would have understood one word in three had I done so!"

"Mr. Collins's behavior is not the best," said Jane in her usual tactful fashion.

"He certainly understands how to carry a grudge," said Elizabeth, much more diplomatically than she felt.

"It is difficult to fathom how he could have thought you eager to marry him," said Charity.

"If you find it difficult to fathom, how do you think I felt?" demanded Elizabeth.

Charity once again laughed and threw her arm about Elizabeth's shoulders. "That is what I love about you, Elizabeth. You are able to see the humor in such a ridiculous specimen's behavior, even when the worst of his offenses are directed at you."

"That is the best way to go about it, Charity," said Elizabeth. "Laughter is much more cathartic than anger."

"Aye, it is," replied Charity. "It is, indeed."

One circumstance for which Darcy was grateful was the restoration of his close camaraderie with Fitzwilliam. Disagreeing with his cousin concerning his choice of a wife had been difficult, and learning he was wrong had been even more so. Those months spent alone at Pemberley had been hard, not only because of the silence of the place and the absence of his sister but also because he had missed his cousin's ready humor and jovial disposition.

Now Darcy could readily confess his error. As they stood in the sitting-room waiting for the Collinses to arrive for dinner, he watched the ladies as they sat in a group, laughing amongst themselves. As always, Darcy's eyes were drawn to Miss Bennet. There was much for any man to like, from her light figure to her beautiful dark eyes to her ready wit and laughter.

But the other ladies were not difficult to esteem either. Charity was as vivacious and vocal as usual, and Darcy noted that she appeared as pretty as she ever had. It seemed Miss Elizabeth's friendship agreed with her. Then there was Georgiana, who was as animated as he had ever seen her. Darcy would readily own to bias toward his sister, but he thought her to be especially lovely that day, dressed in a gown of light pink, which highlighted her glowing countenance exceedingly. And then, perhaps outshining them all, sat Mrs. Fitzwilliam. One of the most beautiful women on whom Darcy had ever laid eyes, she was not as vocal as the others, but it was easy to see that she felt deeply, even if she did not always possess the words to expound on those feeling. Darcy wondered that he had not seen it before.

"They make a lovely picture, do they not?"

Darcy turned to regard Bingley, who was watching the ladies, and perhaps more particularly his own wife. Bingley had been a Godsend, a true champion to save his sister from ignominy and give her everything she had ever wished in marriage. They were fortunate, indeed, that he was such a good friend.

"Aye, that they are," said Fitzwilliam, sipping from the drink he held casually in his hand. "A veritable picture of felicity and charm that mortal men are rarely fortunate enough to witness."

"It seems you have turned into a bit of a poet, Fitzwilliam," said Bingley with a grin. "Such a grasp of hyperbole might even do the likes of Shakespeare proud."

"Fitzwilliam has always had such a gift," said Darcy. "It relieves him from taking the trouble to say anything of a serious nature."

A chuckle was Fitzwilliam's response, as Darcy had known it would be. "I shall not bandy words with you, Darcy. I am far too busy enjoying the scene in front of our eyes."

"I shall not disagree," said Darcy, turning his attention back to the ladies. Or, more particularly, one of the ladies. Darcy had just slipped into the contemplation of a pair of very fine eyes in the face of a pretty woman when Fitzwilliam spoke again.

"It seems the sight has grown on you, Darcy."

"How can any man not be affected? I have never disputed the beauty of these ladies." "No, I suppose not."

Though silence settled between them, Darcy felt it incumbent on himself to say something further. Though he knew Fitzwilliam would be insufferably smug, he did not shirk.

"It seems to me you have made a wise choice in a wife, Fitzwilliam." His cousin's eyebrow rose, and his grin widened. "Not only does she appear to be the very essence of gentility, but she possesses patience enough to withstand you."

This time Fitzwilliam guffawed, drawing the ladies' eyes to them. Bingley shook his head at Georgiana, who shrugged, and they began speaking once again. Left to their own devices once again, Fitzwilliam turned to Darcy.

"I thank you for that, Darcy. Your approval means much to me."

Darcy nodded but did not speak. The evening was perfect, the company was nearly so, and Darcy was content.

And then the Collinses arrived.

"Lady Catherine!" were the first enthusiastic words to proceed from the senseless parson's lips. "How truly grateful Mrs. Collins and I are to once again be in your august company, and that of your honorable family, of course."

"Thank you, Lady Catherine, for inviting us," echoed Mrs. Collins.

For once, she seemed to have the sense to say less than she perhaps wished. It was unfortunate that Mr. Collins did not possess the same sagacity. The man spoke on at length, his ability to praise indefatigable, and his pronouncements become sillier the longer he spoke. Lady Catherine bore it all with a tolerance unlike her. No doubt she was regretting the decision to give such a twitter-pated man such a position in her sphere.

All through dinner Mr. Collins continued to speak, at times echoed by his wife, until Lady Catherine finally took the expedient of instructing him on some matter or another, likely to silence him, Darcy thought. Even then she was not entirely successful, as Mr. Collins continued to give praise whenever the opportunity presented itself, which meant whenever Lady Catherine paused to draw breath or eat a forkful of her food.

They retired to the sitting-room after dinner, and Darcy was fortunate enough to find himself next to Miss Bennet. He ignored the reproachful looks Mr. Collins was shooting her, and they had a pleasant time conversing, Darcy speaking of his grand tour and some of the sights he had seen. For her part, Elizabeth seemed interested, even expressing the desire to see them someday. If it was in his power to show them to her, Darcy promised himself that he would.

After a time of this, Lady Catherine spoke up, inserting herself into their various conversations. "Charity, Georgiana, Miss Bennet—I would like some music tonight if I might persuade you."

Darcy cast a long look at his aunt, noting her fatigue. It seemed she had tired of Mr. Collins and his wife and longed for the distraction a bit of music would provide. But even in this, Mr. Collins was unable to keep his own counsel.

"Of course! The company would be vastly pleased to hear Lady Charity and Mrs. Fitzwilliam delight us with their talents." Then he turned to his cousin. "Perhaps my cousin does not possess so much ability, but I am sure she will do her duty as you commanded."

"It was not a command, Mr. Collins," replied Lady Catherine. "I asked the ladies if they would oblige us."

"Of course, Aunt," said Charity, rising to her feet. "If you do not mind, Elizabeth, shall I go first?"

"You only wish to make your playing appear superior by comparison," said Miss Bennet with a laugh. When Charity made to protest, Miss Bennet shook her head. "Be my guest, my dear Charity. It shall be thus no matter how we order our performances."

"Had I any doubt of your prowess, I might demur," said Charity, smiling and shaking her head. "As it is, I have no doubt that you will acquit yourself very well."

Within a few moments, Charity was seated at the instrument, and the sounds of her playing wafted over them all. Darcy turned to Miss Bennet again when he noticed that Mr. Collins was glaring at her. She took no notice, though Darcy returned the parson's glare with one of his own, which caused him to look away when he noticed. But his eyes returned to Miss Bennet frequently, and whatever the man's thoughts were, they were not friendly to Miss Bennet.

In due time, Georgiana and Miss Bennet followed Charity to the instrument and also acquitted themselves well. It was true that Georgiana was the most proficient of the three and Miss Bennet, the least. But she chose songs which fit her level of skill and performed them with such joy and love of the music that Darcy found it as pleasing as anything he had ever heard. It seemed the rest of the company was likewise impressed.

Except for Mr. Collins, of course. When Miss Bennet took her seat, he listened to her for a short time, his eyes narrowed, before he turned to his wife. "I think my cousin would put her time to better use if she practiced, rather than traipsing about the countryside at all hours."

Then, before Mrs. Collins, or anyone else, could respond, he turned to Lady Catherine. "If you recall, Lady Catherine, Mrs. Collins is also able to play."

"Yes, I do recollect you making that claim." Lady Catherine turned her attention to Mrs. Collins. "Though I do not know your family well, I cannot recall instances when you have played for the company."

"Oh, I do not publish my talents, Lady Catherine," said Mrs. Collins, modestly.

"Perhaps you might have judged better," said the lady. "A woman who possesses such talents should display them when the appropriate opportunity presents itself."

"Your ladyship is correct, as always," said Mr. Collins. "At present, there is no pianoforte at the parsonage which would allow Mrs. Collins to practice as she ought."

"No, and there is no call for you to purchase one," said Lady Catherine. "It is an extravagance for a man in your position."

"I am sure you are correct."

"But Mrs. Collins may come to Rosings and practice at any time she likes." Lady Catherine turned her attention to the young woman. "There are several pianofortes in the house. The one in Mrs. Jenkinson's room might be the best, for you will be able to practice without interruption from others in the house."

The woman smiled and nodded, indicating her agreement to the proposal. Mr. Collins, of course, responded as if the lady had just given her entire fortune over to him. In the end, Lady Catherine raised her hand to force his silence.

"In light of your recent lack of practice, we shall not require you to play for us tonight, Mrs. Collins."

"I am certain my wife could acquit herself well," protested Mr. Collins. "Surely it would be the equal of my cousin's playing."

Lady Catherine's eyes found the parson, and he had the understanding to know he should be silent, which was a change for the better. Then she turned her attention back to Mrs. Collins.

"Do you feel equal to it? There is no shame if you do not."

"I am quite equal to it, your ladyship," said Mrs. Collins, not the slightest hesitation in her response. "If you should like me to, I would be happy to play for the company."

"Very well," said Lady Catherine.

When Miss Bennet finished her piece, Lady Catherine motioned her to return to the company, and Mrs. Collins took her place. Curious as to the scene playing out before her eyes, Miss Bennet turned to Darcy, a question in her eyes.

"Mrs. Collins claims her ability to play," said Darcy by way of explanation. "Lady Catherine has granted her leave to delight us."

Hearing the irony in his voice, Miss Bennet shook her head and laughed under her breath. "And what do you expect, sir?"

"I hardly know," said Darcy. "I suspect we shall be treated to a spectacle."

They turned their attention back to the pianoforte where Mrs. Collins had sat. She did not look at the music which was situated on a shelf near the instrument, but instead sat for some few moments, eyes closed and completely unmoving. Then she extended her hands to the keyboard and began to play.

The piece was immediately recognizable as the French folk song *Ah! vous dirai-je Maman*, the first section as Mozart had arranged it in his twelve variations piece. This first section was quite simple, and Darcy knew it well, as Georgiana had first begun learning to play it when she was only ten. The further into the work the pianist progressed, the more difficult the variations, and Darcy wondered if Mrs. Collins meant to play through them all.

But it was soon clear that she was not precisely the proficient she had proclaimed herself to be. Darcy was no expert, but it was soon clear how the woman slurred certain passages. More than once he heard the discordant plunk of two keys next to each other being pressed at the same time producing more than one wince, and this did not even mention the lack of the trills which appeared periodically in the music with which he was familiar.

The company around him watched on with amusement, as it was clear the woman was no great talent. All except for Mr. Collins, of course—he smiled and bobbed his head in time with the music as if his wife was playing the very best and most difficult of Herr Mozart's works.

When she came to the end of the initial piece, she pulled her fingers away from the keyboard, the sustain peddle depressed, allowing the final notes to fade gradually away. Darcy waited with the others, wondering if she would proceed to the first variation. But the woman soon turned and rose from the bench, at which point Mr. Collins leaped from his seat and began to clap enthusiastically, prompting her to blush with pleasure. Having no other choice, the rest of the company clapped as well, though with much greater restraint.

"Thank you, Mrs. Collins," said Lady Catherine, though how she kept a straight face Darcy could not understand. "That was quite . . . interesting, indeed. My offer to you to practice when you like is still open. But do not neglect the parish, for that must be your primary concern."

"Of course not, Lady Catherine," said Mr. Collins, bowing low, his wife mimicking his actions in her deep curtsey. "We shall always strive to uphold the highest standards of care concerning the people within reach of our influence."

He continued on in this manner for some moments, when it was clear Lady Catherine only wished for him to leave. In the end, her intervention became necessary.

"Thank you, Mr. Collins," said she, cutting him off mid praise. "Now, I believe the night is getting late. It would behoove you to return to the parsonage. I shall call the carriage."

It was, of course, necessary for Mr. Collins to genuflect for some more moments on the generosity of his patroness. When at length they finally departed, the company heaved a sigh of relief and separated to return to their rooms. Darcy found himself escorting Miss Bennet up the stairs. They had almost reached their destination when she was finally unable to hold her hilarity.

"Have you ever seen such a spectacle?" exclaimed she with a laugh.

"I consider the matter entirely serious, Miss Bennet," was Darcy, keeping a gravity in his tone. "It is as Mr. Collins has said: if you practice continually, perhaps you shall eventually obtain the level of proficiency his wife possesses."

Miss Bennet laughed again, and Darcy was unable to hold his own mirth. "I dare say I have not the talent, Mr. Darcy. But I shall not be cast down. Not everyone can be as exceptional as Mr. Collins and his silly wife!"

CHAPTER XL

*I*n the gray light of the early morning following dinner with the Collinses, Elizabeth opened her eyes. Instantly awake, she felt refreshed, though it was still early, and though she rolled over, thinking to sleep again, she found that state to be far distant. Instead, her mind was filled with images from the past weeks, more particularly since they had arrived at Rosings. And to her active mind, the whispering of her heart suddenly began to make sense.

Elizabeth rose and looked out the window. It was later than she had initially thought, the sun just short of rising, its rays flying across the morning sky, creating a medley of pinks, blues, and everything in between. It was a lovely and mesmerizing sight. Elizabeth waited until the edge of the great disk of the sun showed over the horizon. Then, suddenly eager to be out in the newly awakening world, she dressed and hurried down the stairs.

Lady Catherine had only accepted Elizabeth's penchant for walking because of her insistence for it, but she still objected to her long absence without any word. Thus, Elizabeth found the housekeeper and informed her that she was walking out, accepting a warm roll from the kitchens wrapped in a handkerchief before she made her way out the back of the house and onto the grounds.

It was not long before Elizabeth's mind was immersed in her thoughts again, even as she gloried in the life surrounding her. And all through that long walk she turned her feelings over and over, analyzed her every feeling, and before long she came to an inescapable conclusion: she was falling in love with Mr. Darcy. She thought it was a little strange, considering how she had been at odds with him recently due to the events at Margate. But she could not deny it. Her feelings were not of the deep kind she had always thought necessary to induce her to accept a man's offer, but they were deepening by the day.

And how could she not love him? He was not perfect—of this, she was well aware. But his imperfections only made him that more irresistible, for what woman would wish to love a man whose perfection only made her feel inadequate? His serious outlook on life, his intelligence, his honor and goodness—she could not imagine a better man to love than he. She also felt he was working his way to a proposal, and it would behoove her to consider the matter and know her own mind before he did so.

How long Elizabeth contemplated the matter, she did not quite know. The sun was high in the sky by the time she took any notice of her surroundings again, and she began to feel like the others would worry if she did not return soon. Thus, she began to take some thought to doing just that.

And that was when she saw it. In the distance, Miss de Bourgh's phaeton rolled along a dirt path, which was not unusual, though perhaps it was earlier than she usually left the house. Situated as she was near a crossroads in the path and knowing Miss de Bourgh was approaching, Elizabeth decided she did not wish to endure the other woman—especially given the thoughts she had been contemplating that morning. Thus, she stepped to the side of the road and hid among the trees, hoping she would drive past without seeing her.

This action proved to be curiously fortuitous, for it gave Elizabeth a clear view down the road which Miss de Bourgh was traveling. Thus, she saw clearly when the woman pulled the horse to a halt and descended from the phaeton. While her presence was not out of the ordinary, her feet touching the ground most certainly was. And what was more curious was the sight of a man stepping out from the trees by the side of the road, grasping her hand, and pulling her with him back into the woods. And as he did so, he peered down both directions, and when his face turned in her direction, Elizabeth gasped with the shock of recognition.

It was Mr. Wickham! She was near enough to make out his features, though apparently hidden enough that he did not see her. Soon they passed from sight, entering the woods where she could not see them on the opposite side of the road from where she stood. Elizabeth was beset by a dilemma — what should she do?

"Speak with Anthony and Mr. Darcy, of course," muttered Elizabeth, scolding herself for not considering it at once. "Mr. Wickham must be up to no good, meeting Miss de Bourgh like this in secret." Then her eyes widened. "He must be attempting with her what he did not accomplish with Georgiana!"

The thought prodded Elizabeth to action, and she turned and took the shorter route back toward Rosings, which loomed in the distance. Elizabeth walked quickly, determined to report this as soon as possible. Why, Mr. Wickham might be spiriting her off even now! A delay of even a few moments might be disastrous!

She was thus hurrying toward Rosings when she caught sight of a man approaching her from the opposite direction. Elizabeth released a startled gasp, thinking Mr. Wickham had managed to get ahead of her and prevent her from reaching her goal. But the man who confronted her was *not* Mr. Wickham, nor could anyone mistake him for such a handsome man upon a second glance. In fact, it was Mr. Collins.

"Cousin Elizabeth," said Mr. Collins, his voice colored with distaste as it usually was when he spoke to her. "I have been walking the grounds for some time, hoping to meet you." He paused and sneered at her. "It is unfortunate that Lady Catherine has not been successful in taming your wild ways, but I suppose even she cannot work miracles with those who do not wish for improvement. Be that as it may, I have been called upon by my position as a clergyman, and more particularly the spiritual advisor to Lady Catherine de Bourgh, to speak with you concerning your recent behavior."

"Mr. Collins," interrupted Elizabeth, already exasperated with the man. "I have no notion of what you speak and even less interest. At present, I am returning to Rosings and must beg leave to defer this conversation for another time."

"You will stay and listen to what I have to say!" said Mr. Collins, though his command was weaker and more ineffectual than he would have wished. "I am your nearest male relation in residence in this county, and I will have your attention."

"My father is my guardian," said Elizabeth from between clenched teeth. "And while I am here, I am in the care of Colonel Fitzwilliam.

You have no authority over me."

Elizabeth attempted to go around him, but Mr. Collins moved to put himself squarely in her path, denying her retreat. Incensed with his stupidity, Elizabeth scowled at the silly man. But she received nothing more than a glare in response.

"I might have expected such behavior as this," snarled the parson. "But I will not be thwarted in my intention. Stand where you are and listen."

There was little she could do to get past him. Though he was not an imposing man, he was large, whereas Elizabeth herself was rather dainty. She had no notion if he would actually descend to placing his hands upon her, but she did not wish to test the theory. As such, she crossed her arms and stood glaring at him, tapping her foot in her impatience. Mr. Collins did not like her demeanor, but Elizabeth did not care for his opinion.

"I am contemplating the benefits of writing to your father," intoned Mr. Collins. "Given your poor behavior, I believe you should be returned to Longbourn, to be relegated to the nursery again until you are able to behave properly."

"Is this all you have to say?" rejoined Elizabeth dismissively. "Because if it is, I should be returning to Rosings."

"Yes," said Mr. Collins as if he had not heard her. "I think I shall write to him."

"If that is what you wish, then go to it," said Elizabeth. "But I will inform you now that my father, if he reads it at all, will be amused at your expense."

Mr. Collins was angry at her interruption, and then he seemed pensive. "I suppose you are correct," he allowed, though grudgingly. "You are his favorite, and he will no doubt hear nothing against you. Then I suppose the task must fall to me.

"Therefore, I will inform you that I will not stand for this behavior, Cousin," said he, turning his displeased frown on Elizabeth. "You speak to Lady Charity as if she was a bosom companion, you pay no respect or attention to your betters, and you insist upon imposing your presence upon Mr. Darcy, in defiance of all that is decent and good. For your own good, you must cease this objectionable behavior!"

Elizabeth's response was a cold laugh, which angered the man even more. "Charity *is* a close friend, Mr. Collins, and she has asked me herself to use her Christian name. As for your other claims, I suggest you focus your attention on your duties."

"Did you not hear me take upon myself this task?" demanded Mr.

Collins. "I have the responsibility of your behavior here, as your senior male relation, and I shall not shirk it. I believe it would be best for you to pack your trunks and remove to the parsonage. There I may attend to your betterment and prevent you from imposing yourself on Lady Catherine and her family."

Throwing her hands up in the air, Elizabeth stalked to the side, feeling a scream of frustration welling up in her breast. She kept control of herself by clenching her fists and stalking about. Then she whirled on Mr. Collins, who actually stepped back, no doubt due to the shock of her abrupt motion.

"You are without a doubt the stupidest, vilest specimen I have ever been forced to endure, Mr. Collins," hissed she. "There is nothing you can do to compel me to abide by your silly decrees, and I will not speak of them any longer. Step aside and allow me to pass!"

Though initially astonished, Mr. Collins's surprise soon gave way to fury. But as he opened his mouth to deliver a stinging retort, they were interrupted by the arrival of another.

"Here, what is the meaning of this?"

Though Elizabeth was angry enough to face down the little tyrant himself, she felt a wave of relief flow through her at the sight of Mr. Darcy striding toward them. He glanced at Elizabeth, seemingly noting her fury, and then rounded on Mr. Collins.

"What do you mean by accosting Miss Bennet in this manner? Have you no sense at all?"

"Mr. Darcy," said Mr. Collins, bowing low and repeatedly. "You have no need to concern yourself, sir. The difficulty you are having with my headstrong cousin is well understood. There is no more reason to concern yourself, for I shall remove her to the parsonage and take her in hand."

"Are you witless?" demanded Mr. Darcy. Mr. Collins gawped at him, clearly not expecting to be contradicted. "Miss Bennet is a guest of Lady Catherine and is traveling with my cousin. How can you imagine you would be allowed to spirit her away?"

"She is in every way unsuitable to be in such company!" cried Mr. Collins. "I have seen her! I have not misunderstood her attempts to entrap you, a man already engaged to that beautiful flower, Miss de Bourgh! How you must wish for her absence!"

"Once again, Mr. Collins, you have it completely wrong." The man's mouth was wide open, but he did not say anything as he stared at Mr. Darcy with astonishment. "In fact, Miss Bennet is very welcome among us. Fitzwilliam would call you out before he would allow you to remove her from his care.

"And for the record," continued Mr. Darcy, "I am *not* engaged to Anne. I believe I told you this once before when we were in Hertfordshire."

"But Mr. Darcy!" cried Mr. Collins.

"No, Mr. Collins," growled Mr. Darcy, sounding like he was grinding his teeth in frustration. "There is no need for me to explain myself to you. It is time for you to leave, for what I do—or, indeed, what Miss Bennet does—is none of your concern."

While it appeared Mr. Collins had more to say, the utter ferocity of Mr. Darcy's scowl induced him to think better of it. He directed one final poisonous glare at Elizabeth before he turned and stalked away in the direction of Rosings. At long last, Elizabeth was mercifully free of her cousin.

"What a loathsome, bacon-brained twit of a man!" exclaimed Elizabeth, not caring that Mr. Collins was still near enough to hear her. His gait stiffened, but he continued to march away in high dudgeon. Elizabeth might almost have welcomed a continuation of the hostilities, for it would have given her a chance to inform Mr. Collins exactly what she thought of him—her first words had been nothing more than an appetizer.

"Calm yourself, Miss Bennet," said Mr. Darcy. He stepped in front of her and dared capture one of her hands in his, stroking it in a soothing motion. "I dare say the likes of Mr. Collins is not worth your fury.

"Perhaps he is not," said Elizabeth, her anger fading in the face of Mr. Darcy's calming actions. "But he has it nonetheless."

"I assume his words to you were similar to what he just told me?"

Elizabeth nodded. "You assume correctly. Apparently, I am fit only to be returned to my father's home, to be confined to the nursery until I have learned enough to be allowed in society again."

"Those were his words?" asked Mr. Darcy, his glare following Mr. Collins's retreat toward the house.

"Some of them," replied Elizabeth with annoyance. "I know I should not be upset with him. He is nothing more than a small-minded man who resents my rejection of his proposal if you can dignify his words with so illustrious a term."

"And do you regret it?"

Elizabeth gazed up at Mr. Darcy like a second head had sprouted up beside the first. A retort was on the tip of her tongue when she noticed the slight upturn at the corner of his mouth. She was far too annoyed with the parson to tease Mr. Darcy on the subject. Even the thought of accepting such a ridiculous man filled her with revulsion!

"I would have to be mad to regret refusing the proposal of such a man. Should I end an old maid, it would be much better than living a life of degradation beside such a foolish specimen as Mr. William Collins!"

A nod was followed by Mr. Darcy's softly spoken: "Then let us return to the house. Mr. Collins is, no doubt, intent upon blackening your name to Lady Catherine, and though she has shown an ability to withstand his inanities, we should be on hand to refute his words."

"Of course," said Elizabeth. She turned and stalked toward the house, catching Mr. Darcy by surprise. He soon caught her and walked by her side. And while they did not exchange a word between them, Elizabeth was comforted by the solidity of his presence.

There was no respite to be had for Miss Bennet—or at least it seemed that way. She was still clearly fuming over her confrontation with the idiot Collins, for she said little on their return to the house. As they walked down the drive, however, they had the misfortune to arrive at the precise moment when Baker and his sister alighted from the carriage.

"Miss Bennet!" exclaimed he with evident satisfaction. "How fortunate it is that we have arrived at the same time. How do you do?"

It was clear to Darcy that Miss Bennet swallowed a retort, for she took a moment to compose herself. "Very well, Mr. Baker," said she. It seemed to be the limit of the civility she was able to summon at the moment.

Baker beamed as if she had just declared her undying devotion to him. There was nothing to do but shake his head, a motion which Darcy noticed was mirrored by Miss Baker. He turned to her and noted her wry look and rolled eyes. Baker captured Miss Bennet's arm and coerced her into allowing him to escort her into the house. Offering his arm to Miss Baker, Darcy followed behind, wondering if she would say something.

"I assume you are as annoyed by my brother's behavior as Elizabeth is?" said Miss Baker.

Darcy turned to regard her with some surprise. She laughed, a bell-like sound which he was forced to own was quite pleasant.

"Come, Mr. Darcy," said she, "you must not suspect me of blindness. It is quite clear that Elizabeth is not as enamored of my brother as he wishes she was." She shook her head at the man in front of them as he leaned down toward Miss Bennet, prompting her to retreat. "It is unfortunate that James does not see it himself."

"Does not see it, or does not wish to see it?" asked Darcy.

Miss Baker nodded to acknowledge his point. "I suspect the latter. James has spent his adult life making himself agreeable to young ladies. While he would never behave *too* inappropriately, he possesses the image of himself as a man who is desirable to young ladies. He cannot imagine Miss Bennet being unmoved."

"I suggest he learn soon," said Darcy, not caring for the dark undertones in his voice.

"I cannot agree more." Darcy turned to regard her, wondering as to her meaning.

"James wishes to elicit some response from Miss Bennet, Mr. Darcy. He is quite desperate for it. If we . . . goad them a little, we might be successful in provoking her in a manner which will put the matter to rest forever. James cannot imagine that it would not be favorable. But once he is confronted by the reality, he will have no choice but to accept it."

Darcy considered it and then nodded. "I agree. What do you think the best approach would be?"

"Challenge him," said Miss Baker. "Make her choose between you."

"Why are you conspiring with me? Do you not wish your brother to be happy?"

"If I thought he would be happy with her — or she with him, for that matter — I might think differently. But she is my friend, and I have seen which way the wind blows. James must release this hopeless infatuation with her."

With a distracted nod, Darcy guided her into the sitting-room. Lady Catherine was absent, no doubt ensconced with the idiot Collins at present, listening to him whine concerning Miss Bennet's behavior. Thus it fell to Miss Bennet to act as hostess, which she did, summoning a maid and ordering a tray of tea and cakes. Then they sat down, and when they did so, Darcy took the opportunity to sit close to Miss Bennet, denying Baker the opportunity of doing the same.

The response from each could not have been different. Mr. Baker glared at Darcy, while Miss Bennet looked at him with some surprise and concern. Miss Baker was amused, nodding at him where her brother could not see. With ill grace, Baker took a seat on a nearby chair, leaning forward to give the illusion of intimacy.

"It seems an age since I last had the pleasure of your company."

"It is naught but a matter of two days," said Miss Bennet.

"Exactly!" exclaimed Baker. "Even such a short time without your company seems like an age."

"I think you exaggerate, sir."

"Is not exaggeration the very soul of courtship?" Baker leaned forward even further. "And it is not overt hyperbole at all, Miss Bennet, for I do long to be in your company when I am out of it."

Miss Bennet regarded him, the pensive half frown seeming to cause Baker some measure of discomfort. While Darcy was curious to hear what she would say, he decided now might be an appropriate time to begin to take Miss Baker's advice.

"I would suggest that if a man truly wishes to impress a woman, he would show her, by word and deed, the depth of his devotion through thoughtful acts of kindness and regard."

The contemplative look Miss Bennet was bestowing on Mr. Baker was suddenly turned on Darcy himself. But Baker was not about to be bested with so little effort.

"Of course, you would think that, Darcy." Baker threw him a contemptuous sneer. "To you, everything must be a business transaction. Matters of the heart cannot be likened to such subjects, for there is often little logic in them."

"I did not say they were merely matters of business," replied Darcy. "But it seems to me that a woman who receives the serious regard of a man, rather than fancy words and gestures, is much more likely to respond in an equally serious manner. There is a time and place for hyperbole, and I do not suggest lively conversation, banter, and the like should not be used when courting. But a true and thoughtful meeting of the minds is more important than simple empty flirting."

Miss Baker coughed at that moment, pulling them all from this confrontation. The tea service arrived and Miss Bennet served them. And when they were served, the conversation continued much as it had before, though Darcy was content to observe, noting that Miss Bennet was becoming more frustrated with Baker's empty flattery and lack of substance. Baker took no notice, and at times he laid it on more than a little brown. But more alarming to the young woman was when he leaned forward, ostensibly to increase their intimacy. All he accomplished at such times was to induce her to pull back, on one occasion, almost pressing against Darcy's arm in her attempt to escape him.

"I wonder, Miss Bennet," said Baker at length, setting his cup to the side and leaning toward her once again. "Might we perhaps walk in the garden? I should like to speak alone with you, for it seems like privacy has been in short supply of late."

The caustic look he directed at Darcy spoke volumes as to his meaning. But Darcy decided he was not about to allow this to proceed any further, especially as Miss Bennet appeared to be searching for some means to refuse his request. The absurdity of the situation prompted Darcy to chuckle.

"You are laughing!" cried Baker in apparent amazement. "It was not clear you were even capable of it."

"Oh, it is well within my capabilities, Baker." Darcy shook his head and focused on the overly amorous and blind man. "It is only that I am always diverted when others make fools of themselves."

"Perhaps you should clarify your comments, Darcy," said Baker.

"Only that you seem intent upon forcing your presence on Miss Bennet when she does not wish to receive you."

"I see no reluctance in her manners."

"That is because you are not looking. It may be best to return to Stauneton. Nothing other than humiliation awaits you here."

Once again Miss Baker coughed, but the two men paid her no heed. Baker was glaring at Darcy, apparently offended at his comments. "Perhaps we should allow Miss Bennet to decide."

"By all means," said Darcy, gesturing toward the young woman. "I am certain she would appreciate the opportunity to clear this matter and divest herself of you."

For a long moment, Baker watched him before turning to Miss Bennet. He favored her with a brilliant smile and said: "What is it to be, Miss Bennet? Shall we walk in the gardens, or do you prefer dull and uninteresting men."

That, it seemed, was Baker's fatal error. Miss Bennet had been watching them with more than a little disbelief, likely wondering what had brought the argument about. Darcy knew she did not appreciate Baker's actions, but she was a woman who would not willfully act to hurt a man unless provoked. His unkindness proved to be that provocation.

"If you will pardon me, Mr. Baker, I have no desire to walk in the garden with you."

For a moment, Baker gaped at her, clearly not understanding her meaning. Then an ugly scowl came over his face. "So, am I to understand you prefer dullness then?"

"It seems you understand nothing," was Miss Bennet's cool reply. "I have given you every indication that I am not interested in you, and yet you have seen fit to continue to impose upon me. My preferences are none of your concern, sir. I ask only to be left alone."

With a huff, Baker rose. "Come, Elia. It seems we are not welcome here."

Then he strode from the room. Elia Baker rose and embraced Miss Bennet, who stood with her. "Might I hope to see you at my wedding?"

"I do not know if I will still be in Kent," replied Miss Bennet. "But perhaps I might return."

"I hope you do. Now that you are free of my brother, I expect you will be more comfortable."

Then she turned to Darcy. "That was a trifle blunter than I might have advised, but effective nonetheless. Thank you, sir."

With a final curtsey and a fond farewell for Miss Bennet, Miss Baker departed, leaving Darcy alone with her. It was clear she wished for an explanation, for she turned to him, her eyebrow raised and her eyes flashing.

CHAPTER XLI

*L*ady Catherine was not a woman who appreciated being kept waiting. This was true, not only in the sense of anticipating a desired event, but also when keeping to a schedule. Though many of her family did not truly understand her, in fact, she was rather set in her ways, preferring order to the chaos she had often seen in the estates run by others. In this particular, she was much like her nephew, who had inherited it from both his Darcy and Fitzwilliam family lines.

Further to the situation at hand, Mr. Collins was a man who required constant supervision. It was not Lady Catherine's desire to meet with him on a daily basis—it was an unfortunate necessity. Left to himself, Mr. Collins was more apt to run amok, taking actions which he imagined would please her, but which invariably caused her much time and effort to repair. Though she had known he was not the brightest specimen when she interviewed him, she had not realized how deep his stupidity ran. Now there was little choice in the matter, for not only was he ensconced in a position where she could not dismiss him, but she knew that sooner or later he would have children to support. Thus, it behooved her to manage him with great care so the work of the parish could continue without interruption.

On the morning in question, the time she had set aside for her daily meeting with the man arrived and departed without his attendance. That was most decidedly odd, for usually Mr. Collins was early. Her instructions were always carried out to the letter, with little deviation. Which was why, after her repeated statements emphasizing the importance of punctuality, it was odd that he should be late that day, as he never had been before.

Muttering imprecations against the stupidity of her parson, Lady Catherine sat and sipped tea while she waited for him to finally appear. She had almost resolved to dispatch a footman to the parsonage to discover what had become of the man when she heard the slapping of rapid footsteps approaching the small parlor she used to meet him. The door swung open, revealing a wild-eyed Mr. Collins. Then the verbal assault began.

"Lady Catherine!" exclaimed he, though it came out more like a squeak. "I have come with the most distressing tidings, of the utmost importance!"

What followed was a rambling diatribe, of most of which Lady Catherine was not even able to make sense. Most of his words seemed to focus on "an egregious betrayal," "behavior too awful to fathom," or other such nonsense. When she finally heard the words "Cousin Elizabeth" on his tongue, she had enough.

"Mr. Collins!"

Instantly the complaints ceased, as she had known they would. The parson stood stock still staring at her, his mouth still gaping open, his eyes utterly vacant.

"That is better," said Lady Catherine. "Now, Mr. Collins—come into the room, close the door behind you, and sit down like a civilized man."

He did so in silence, which was much better than the behavior he had shown before. He sat where indicated, and while he appeared attentive, she could see he was almost bursting with whatever news he deemed important enough to disrupt the calm of her home. But she was not about to allow him to escape her displeasure so easily.

"Now, Mr. Collins, have I not informed you of the importance of punctuality?"

"It was all my cousin's fault!" Lady Catherine winced, for it was almost a scream. "She is a temptress, a veritable succubus—"

"Mr. Collins!" snapped Lady Catherine, once again silencing him. "Have I not made myself clear on the subject of punctuality?

"Answer the question, Mr. Collins," said Lady Catherine when she saw him draw in breath for another diatribe. "Are you or are you not aware of my requirement of punctuality?"

"I am," muttered Mr. Collins.

"Good. Then I do not understand why you would allow yourself to be distracted by your cousin when you are aware that the time for our meeting approaches." Sternness was required, and Lady Catherine fixed it on the silly man, inducing him to mop at his brow with his ever-present handkerchief. "In the future, *nothing* is to distract you from our meeting *at the time I set.* Have I made myself clear?"

"You have," replied he.

"Very well. Now, I do not care for your brand of exaggeration, sir. I highly doubt your cousin is an angel from hell. Furthermore, Miss Bennet is not only your cousin, but she is also a guest in my house."

Mr. Collins's expression darkened as she spoke, but at least he had the sense to remain silent. "You *are* aware, are you not, that my nephew Fitzwilliam would call you out if he heard you speaking in such a manner concerning his wife's sister?" Mr. Collins paled, as well he ought. "And I have it on good authority that my *other* nephew, Darcy, would mop up whatever was left once Fitzwilliam was finished with you."

"But, Lady Catherine—" said Mr. Collins, unable to restrain himself any longer. "My cousin's behavior has been truly reprehensible. That is what I wished to tell you."

"You may state whatever you feel necessary," said Lady Catherine. "But remove the excessive language from the equation, sir, for I would not wish to be forced to restrain my nephews."

"My concern *is* for Mr. Darcy," insisted Mr. Collins. "When you have heard what I have to say, I am sure you will agree that she must be sent back to Longbourn in disgrace!"

"That remains to be seen. Miss Bennet has impressed me as an intelligent, lively sort of girl. She has never misbehaved in my presence."

The mutinous glint in Mr. Collins's eye was such as Lady Catherine had never seen before. In fact, she was certain she knew what Mr. Collins had against his cousin. But it was also clear the silly man was determined to air his grievance. As such, it was the quickest way to silence him.

"Very well, Mr. Collins. You may relate the particulars of the situation to me. But I remind you—keep your language acceptable."

As she might have predicted in advance, what followed was a long and rambling harangue against Miss Bennet's behavior, which more particularly focused on Darcy's duty to Anne. The irony was not lost on the lady—had she been more temperate in speaking of her expectations, Mr. Collins would never have taken the matter so far. Now that she had accepted the inevitability that her wishes would go unanswered, he was still zealously guarding her interests.

"You may be silent now, Mr. Collins," said Lady Catherine, interrupting him, knowing he might have spoken for another hour if she let him. He had already repeated himself several times as it was. "First, let us address your actions in this matter."

The man gazed at her as if bereft of wit. "I appreciate your attempts on my behalf. But let me ask you this, Mr. Collins: do you think me incapable of managing my own affairs?"

An expression of utter consternation came over his silly face. "Of course not! You are the most capable, the noblest woman in all the land! There is nothing beyond your capabilities!"

Lady Catherine gazed at the man with amusement. "I believe Queen Charlotte might dispute your assertion regarding my nobility. But be that as it may, I thank you for your confidence. In light of your statements, however, it follows that you should allow me to act when I see fit. To the point, Mr. Collins—it is not your place to act in my stead."

It was clear Mr. Collins did not understand. Lady Catherine sighed, wishing she had chosen a more intelligent specimen as a parson.

"What I mean, Mr. Collins, is that you must allow me to act in matters which concern me. Your sphere encompasses your own home and the parish over which you preside. As my parson, you are invested with a certain amount of responsibility to protect my interests. With respect to my family and those who are currently guests at Rosings, I do not require your assistance. Should I feel the need to act, you may be certain that I shall."

"You cannot act if you are not aware of it." Mr. Collins's voice was petulant as if he already suspected what she meant to tell him.

"In fact, I am quite aware of Darcy's interest in Miss Bennet. I am also aware that it is returned, though I do not believe her ardency has reached his level yet."

"But, Lady Catherine!" wailed the parson. "What of your fair daughter? What of Miss de Bourgh, who has pined for Mr. Darcy all these years? Is she to be shunted to the side in favor of a temptress such as my cousin? Surely you do not wish to be connected to a family such as the Bennets!"

"What I wish is none of your concern," said Lady Catherine coldly. "Yet again, I will remind you of my nephew, who is eager to protect the honor of his sister by marriage."

Mr. Collins subsided yet again, but that mutinous glare was still present. Had Lady Catherine thought it was directed at her, she would have sent him away, but not before she boxed his ears.

"The fact of the matter is that my opinion carries very little weight in this instance." Mr. Collins made to protest, but she held up a hand, silencing him. "Darcy is his own man, capable of managing his own affairs. I cannot command him, nor do I wish to do so. He has decided he does not wish to marry my daughter, and my daughter has no intention of it either.

"Miss Bennet has lived here this last month, and to be honest, I have been impressed with her. Her lineage is, perhaps, not what I would have wished. But she *is* a gentleman's daughter, and that is all my nephew requires. *If* they decide they wish to unite, there is nothing you or I or anyone may say against them. Should Darcy wish her for a wife, I can do nothing but support them."

For a few moments, Mr. Collins was silent. He had been so convinced she would agree with him that he did not seem to know what to say now. Lady Catherine was forced to own that if it had been several months earlier, she might have agreed with him. But he was meddling in matters which did not concern him, and she knew there was no choice but to take him in hand.

"Surely your nephew may do better than my *cousin*," said Mr. Collins, his voice as petulant as a child of five. "She has nothing to offer him."

"Is that for you to judge?" Mr. Collins had nothing to say to that, though his mouth tightened. "Let us be honest, Mr. Collins. I suspect there is more to your disapproval than a desire to see my nephew marry well. Do you care to explain what, exactly, it is you have against your cousin?"

Mr. Collins became even tighter lipped, and initially, he refused to speak. In time, Lady Catherine was able to draw from him the matter of his proposal to his cousin—if it could be called such. Lady Catherine, of course, already knew of the matter, having heard it from Miss Bennet, and a smattering of comments from her nephew, and as such, she knew much more than Mr. Collins was willing to relate. Having confirmed the grudge he still carried for the young woman, she was not happy at all with him.

"First, Mr. Collins," said she, "let me state that your tale does you no credit. To harbor bitterness for a young woman in such a fashion is not only an insult to your wife, but it is also the action of a schoolboy, rather than a grown man."

Mr. Collins was clearly unhappy, but Lady Catherine did not relent. "Furthermore, it shows a lack of humility which is astonishing in a parson. It is incumbent upon a man to woo a woman in such a way as to make her love him. Only then may he propose. It seems to me that you went about your wooing in a manner which was not sufficient to impress a woman worthy of being impressed, and I suspect your proposal, following so quickly on the heels of my nephew's to her sister, was not well done.

"Humility, Mr. Collins, is a virtue, as is charity and forgiveness. It seems to me that you have forgotten these things in your bitterness against your cousin. A parson installed at Hunsford must rise above such things. Therefore, your sermon next Sunday shall be a dissertation on the subject of humility and forgiveness. Have I made myself understood?"

There existed little possibility that he was happy with her decree. But in the end, Mr. Collins chose the correct path, when he nodded his head, albeit tightly. As such, Lady Catherine decided she had had enough of the man that day.

"Very well. You may go. Please keep your opinions on the subject of your cousin strictly to yourself, Mr. Collins. I suspect it highly likely she will eventually become Darcy's wife. You do not wish to make an enemy of my nephew."

With an abruptness which she had never before seen from the man, he stood and bowed, and then departed. Lady Catherine sat back heavily against her chair. Meeting with Mr. Collins was never less than draining. But she had chosen it herself, and she would not shirk. But she was not required to do so without fortification. So she ordered another pot of tea and sat back to consider the possibility of Miss Elizabeth Bennet as a niece. And Lady Catherine was once again surprised that the thought was actually pleasant.

"I am confused, Mr. Darcy," said Elizabeth when Miss Baker had left the room. "It seems you and Miss Baker were confederates in what just occurred."

"To say we were confederates is overstating the matter," said Mr. Darcy. "Miss Baker was concerned, for she thought you had no interest in her brother and wished to spare you his attentions."

"And what was your part in it?" asked Elizabeth.

"I merely challenged him. Miss Baker was certain he would withdraw if it became clear you did not favor him."

Elizabeth was not certain if she should be angry or relieved. While Miss Baker had been completely correct of her disinterest, Elizabeth almost felt as if she had been manipulated. It was clear Mr. Baker had been. The relief of being free of Mr. Baker's constant attention was welcome, but Elizabeth had never wished to hurt the man or otherwise make him uncomfortable.

Before she was able to think on it further or respond, Miss de Bourgh entered the room. And suddenly the scene Elizabeth had witnessed flooded back to her mind, and she was required to stifle a gasp. While she was dealing with Mr. Collins and Mr. Baker, Mr. Wickham might have been spiriting Miss de Bourgh off to Gretna Green! And it would have been Elizabeth's fault!

"I see you are once again with Miss Bennet," said Miss de Bourgh with a sneer at Elizabeth.

"We had guests who just departed," replied Mr. Darcy.

"I saw them." Miss de Bourgh paused, looking down her nose at them, and Elizabeth noted, with some amusement, that she was as practiced at it as Miss Bingley had been. "I shall leave you to it, then. It seems like something momentous is occurring."

Then with a sarcastic smirk, she turned and departed from the room. Elizabeth lost no time in speaking of what she had seen.

"Mr. Darcy, can you summon Anthony? I have something I must relate to you both which is of some importance."

The look with which Mr. Darcy favored her was searching, but in the end, he did what she asked, seeing she was too agitated for questions. Elizabeth paced while he went to the door, and when he returned he continued to regard her, concern etching his countenance. But again, he eschewed questioning her.

"It seems this matter is giving you some anxiety, Miss Bennet. Perhaps a pot of tea would help calm you?"

"Please," said Elizabeth.

A new pot was ordered and arrived about the same time Anthony stepped into the room with Jane by his side. He was his usual jovial self, but when he saw Elizabeth's tension, his expression turned to concern.

"What is the matter?"

"I saw Mr. Wickham this morning," said Elizabeth with more urgency than tact.

"Wickham?" demanded Mr. Darcy. "Where is he?"

"I know not," said Elizabeth with a shaken head. "But I am certain he is lingering about. In fact, I suspect I know his object."

With as much brevity as she could, Elizabeth explained what she saw in concise terms. She did not speculate, for she knew that Anthony and Mr. Darcy would comprehend the meaning of Mr. Wickham's actions toward Miss de Bourgh as well as she did herself. When she had completed her explanation, silence reigned for several minutes before Anthony turned to his cousin.

"It seems Wickham has decided to try his luck with another of our relations, as he was not successful with Georgiana."

"And Anne has much with which to tempt him," replied Darcy, though his words were little more than a snarl. "More so than Georgiana, actually. Anne's dowry is Rosings itself, which would provide Wickham with an income to squander, rather than a set amount."

Anthony snorted in disdain. "Until he managed to run the estate into the ground." Anthony paused and then turned back to Elizabeth. "This grove you saw them enter—is it the same one where you saw Anne meet a man not long after we arrived?"

"I do not remember," replied Elizabeth with a frown. "I do not think so. And on that occasion, she did not go into the woods."

"That may have been when he first began to pay her attention," said Mr. Darcy. "The question is, what are we to do on the matter?"

"We find Wickham, and we make him pay for what he has done."

For perhaps the first time, Elizabeth saw the savage man in Anthony, the man who had survived a decade in the army, who knew what it took to ensure the enemy was never allowed to triumph. He was civilized, to be certain, but there existed a hint of danger in him at that moment which Elizabeth had never thought to see. She almost pitied Mr. Wickham . . . .

"Follow Anne?" suggested Mr. Darcy. "We may be able to apprehend Wickham when he is meeting with her."

"We will need assistance to ensure he does not escape." Anthony's eyes bored into Mr. Darcy's. "I do not mean to allow him to slip away again, Darcy. This time he pays for his crimes."

"I cannot agree more. We have Bingley, and we have an entire estate full of men who can assist—footmen, stable hands, and tenants. They would not wish to see the estate in the possession of a man like Wickham any more than we would."

The two men shared a feral grin. "Excellent suggestion, old man."

"Should Lady Catherine not be told?" asked Jane, a little diffidently.

Anthony turned and regarded his wife, but it was Mr. Darcy who spoke. "I think that would be for the best. And Bingley should be made aware as soon as possible too. I suspect he would be eager to take a little retribution out on Wickham's hide."

Jane's brow furrowed at this statement, but Elizabeth understood it all too well. It would be best if she were told at some time or another, Elizabeth thought, but that time was not now. Lady Catherine and Mr. Bingley were sent for, as was Georgiana, and when they arrived, Charity was with them, appearing curious as to the impromptu family meeting.

When the matter was explained, Mr. Bingley appeared as eager as Mr. Darcy had suggested. It was Lady Catherine who posed the most threat to their plans.

"I cannot imagine what she is thinking!" exclaimed the lady. "I must speak with her. She cannot possibly think of throwing Rosings away on such a man as Mr. Wickham!"

"Patience, Lady Catherine," said Mr. Darcy. "We shall apprehend Mr. Wickham tomorrow. Then you may speak with your daughter."

"What if they mean to steal away in the night?"

Mr. Darcy glanced at Anthony, who shrugged. "We will post guards who will watch over Anne's room, both from the hall and the window. If she attempts anything, we will have advance warning."

Though it was clear Lady Catherine did not like it, she acquiesced. "Then I will rely on you to ensure nothing untoward happens." She paused, as if considering something, before steeling herself and speaking again. "It is not commonly known, but my husband's will is such that I am granted full control of the disposition of Rosings. Anne is the heir at present, but I may change that if I believe it is warranted. I shall not allow this Wickham to gain control over my husband's legacy. If it should be necessary, I shall disinherit Anne to prevent him from ever setting foot in this house."

"That will not be necessary, Lady Catherine," said Mr. Darcy. He stepped to her and grasped her hand. "We will not allow anything to happen."

Lady Catherine searched his eyes for a moment and nodded. "Thank you, Darcy. You all have my thanks," said Lady Catherine, bestowing her gaze on them all. "Had this happened when no one else was present, I am not certain what I would have done."

"That may have been Wickham's purpose," said Anthony, stroking his chin. He turned to Elizabeth. "You say you saw him at an assembly in Brighton, and then again not long after. I have wondered what his purpose was, given his questions concerning how long you meant to stay. It is possible he was attempting to determine how long he might have to woo Anne."

"That was months ago," protested Elizabeth.

"But Anne's walls are notoriously difficult to pierce," said Charity. "I apologize, Aunt, but it is the truth."

"There is no need to apologize," said Lady Catherine.

"It may have taken him this long to bring her to this point," said Mr. Darcy. "He may not have counted on it. In fact, that may be the reason he risked meeting us in Margate—he must have tried to continue his approaches."

"This is all speculation," said Anthony. "When we apprehend him, we shall beat the information from his hide, if necessary. For this evening we must act as if nothing is amiss before Anne. Otherwise, he may try to escape."

It turned out that it was not that difficult. Though the rest of the company watched Miss de Bourgh carefully that evening, she was, as always, aloof and cold to every member of the company. Her mother was the sole exception, and even then their relationship was not one of open warmth. If Lady Catherine watched her daughter as warily as the rest of the company, Miss de Bourgh seemed not to notice.

As the evening wore on, it seemed they all relaxed, when it appeared she was not about to disappear from under their collective noses. Soon they lapsed into their usual routines at dinner and after, and the party enjoyed one another's company. There was only one small event which marred the evening to any great extent, and even that was minor. Seeing that Elizabeth and Darcy had been sitting together and speaking for some time, Miss de Bourgh made her opinion on the subject known to any who could hear.

"I believe I must question your taste, Darcy," said she, sneering at Elizabeth. "I have known for some time that we were not to marry. But if we are to go our separate ways, you might have attempted to find a woman who has more to offer than a country miss. Is *she* better than the daughter of an earl? Surely you could manage that, for your father did."

It was readily apparent that Mr. Darcy was offended on Elizabeth's behalf. For her own part, Elizabeth was rather amused by Miss de Bourgh's conceit. She was the granddaughter of an earl, to be sure, but she rather behaved like a duchess.

"I have no pretensions toward such lofty standing, Miss de Bourgh. But as Mr. Darcy is a gentleman and I am the daughter of one, I cannot say we are mismatched."

Miss de Bourgh sniffed and turned away. When Elizabeth turned back to Mr. Darcy, she noted he was regarding her, an expression akin to astonishment etched on his brow. And that was when Elizabeth realized what she had essentially declared in fending off Miss de Bourgh's contempt. She felt her face heating, but Mr. Darcy regarded her with a tender smile.

"Well stated, Miss Bennet. Well stated, indeed."

CHAPTER XLII

*P*erhaps it might be considered foolhardy. Elizabeth did not know or care. She knew it was likely better she stayed clear of the matter of Miss de Bourgh and Mr. Wickham. But something in her did not allow her to maintain her distance, would not accept waiting in ignorance while the men attempted to apprehend the libertine.

Elizabeth was uncertain why this was so. It was possibly the fact that the man had duped her, though without any true consequences, filled her with a desire to witness his downfall. Or it may be that she wished to be certain herself that he did not slip away. Whatever it was, Elizabeth was on hand when Miss de Bourgh ordered her phaeton the following morning, noted the looks the gentlemen shared, the pensive gaze of Lady Catherine on her only daughter. And she knew she would not be content waiting.

Excusing herself, Elizabeth departed from the house on her daily walk, and the rest of those at the house were so busy that her actions, indicative of nothing more than a typical daily activity, went unnoticed. Elizabeth had no notion that Miss de Bourgh would meet Mr. Wickham in the same grove where she had seen them the previous day. But it seemed as likely as any, and it was there to which Elizabeth directed her steps.

It seemed an auspicious day for an endeavor of this sort. Overhead, the clouds roiled and seethed, though she did not think there was any threat of rain. On the ground, the wind blew, not a gale, but a steady, constant stream which whipped at her dress and stained her cheeks pink. It was cooler than it had been for most of her residence in Kent, a reminder that spring was still a time of indifferent weather and sudden dips into cooler temperatures.

On one occasion, Elizabeth saw a figure in the distance, walking along the edge of Rosings Park. She stopped and hid, wondering who it could possibly be. But as it drew closer, she could see that it was only Mrs. Collins. Elizabeth chewed her lip in thought. She had no desire to speak to the silly woman, and even less to potentially come in contact with the woman's husband. But walking where she was, Elizabeth was afraid she might venture where she ought not and make Mr. Wickham wary.

Thus, she stepped out of her place of concealment and walked out into full view. Mrs. Collins was not far distant and was startled when she saw Elizabeth. Then she frowned, though she did not attempt to draw away.

"Mrs. Collins," said Elizabeth by way of greeting. "I see you are enjoying the woods of Rosings as I do."

For a moment, Elizabeth thought the woman might turn away without saying a word. But she seemed to remember Lady Catherine's admonishment about rude behavior, for she nodded regally and said:

"It is very pretty, is it not? But, of course, I prefer my father's estate."

"I think it safe to say we all prefer the location where we are raised," said Elizabeth. Then she regarded Mrs. Collins. "Is your father's estate as large as Rosings?"

"No," replied Mrs. Collins. "It is on a small plot of land, but there is a brook running through and several strands of trees which are delightful."

"And is it nearby?" asked Elizabeth, never having heard of her family in the neighborhood.

"It is about fifteen miles to the south."

All conversation topics appeared to be exhausted, and Elizabeth was contemplating how to warn Mrs. Collins away from Rosings that morning. They stood in uncomfortable silence for several moments. It was finally Mrs. Collins who broke the impasse."

"I suppose I must thank you, Miss Bennet," said she, though she did not sound at all grateful.

"For what?"

"For refusing my husband's proposal." Mrs. Collins paused and peered at her. "I know not why Lady Catherine sent him to Hertfordshire to propose to you, but I had met him months before, and we had formed a connection. I understood his desire to obey his patroness, but it was very hard to see him go, knowing he would return engaged."

"There is little I can say on the matter," said Elizabeth, feeling something other than contempt for this woman. "But I had no desire to marry him, especially on so short an acquaintance."

The other woman frowned as if disbelieving Elizabeth's assertion. "You do not pine after him now? Is that not why you came to Kent, to attempt to correct your mistake?"

Elizabeth resisted the urge to burst out laughing. The reason for Mrs. Collins's dislike was now revealed.

"I did not come to steal your husband, Mrs. Collins."

The way Mrs. Collins held up her hands suggested impatience. "Of course, you did not. You could not have known he was already married."

"On the contrary," said Elizabeth. "Mr. Collins wrote my father, informing him of his approaching marriage. I knew of it before I left Hertfordshire."

"Oh!" said the woman, eyes wide. "I had thought you came for an entirely different reason."

"Mrs. Collins," said Elizabeth, stepping forward and grasping her hands. "There is no other purpose for my presence here than that which we stated. I am traveling with my newly married sister and her husband. Refusing Mr. Collins was not an act of which I take any pride, but it *was* necessary, as I am convinced we could not make each other happy."

"Then you do not have designs on him?"

"How could you have thought I did?" asked Elizabeth. "Have I put myself in his path? Have I attempted to brazenly attract his attention? Have you witnessed my longing looks in his direction?"

"No," replied she, seemingly thoughtful.

"Of course not. Even if I did possess a tender regard for your husband, the fact remains that he is *your husband*. I would never attempt to steal another woman's husband or insinuate myself between you. That would be reprehensible behavior, to be sure.

"You have nothing to fear from me, Mrs. Collins. Though my

acquaintance with Mr. Collins ended in acrimony, I can assure you, from the bottom of my heart, that I wish for nothing but happiness for you both. I cannot understand where you have gained such an impression of me, but it is entirely false."

Mrs. Collins processed Elizabeth's words for a moment, and then she broke out into a shy smile. Elizabeth was glad—she had no great opinion of Mrs. Collins, but she did not like to have anyone as an enemy. Then her smile turned into a frown, and she became pensive, and Elizabeth was certain she knew exactly where Mrs. Collins had heard such tales of her.

"Then I must apologize for my behavior," said she. "It is clear I should have trusted my own observations rather than what I heard. I hope you do not think the worst of me because of it."

"Of course not," replied Elizabeth with a bright smile. "It is all forgotten. I hope we can be friends for the remainder of my stay and after. You *are* the future mistress of my beloved home, you know. I care about the fate of Longbourn, I assure you, for it is where I was raised."

"I believe we can." Mrs. Collins smiled again. "Thank you for clarifying matters for me. But I believe I must now return to my home."

They exchanged a few final words, in which Mrs. Collins asked her to visit the parsonage more often than she had previously, and she then took her leave. Elizabeth was of two minds about the invitation, for though she had come to a meeting of the minds with Mrs. Collins, she still did not think she would become a bosom friend. And going thither meant a likelihood of meeting Mr. Collins.

But it was easy enough to promise, and she thought Mrs. Collins might almost be tolerable if she ignored her husband's sibilant whispering in her ear. As she departed, Elizabeth watched her, noting she was carrying herself erect, her walk more a determined march. Clearly, there would be some explanation demanded when she returned to her home. Mr. Collins, as ineffectual a man as Elizabeth had ever met, was about to receive a tongue lashing from his wife. Elizabeth giggled at the thought.

It appeared her departure was just in time as well. For in the distance, Elizabeth could hear the telltale rumbling of the wheels of Miss de Bourgh's phaeton.

Though Anne was unaware, Fitzwilliam had sent instructions to the stables to prepare several horses when the request for Anne's phaeton was given. Thus they were prepared to follow her when she clucked the horse into motion.

"Carefully, Darcy," warned Fitzwilliam when they began to ride after her. "We do not wish Wickham to see us and flee the area. Unless we can apprehend him, he will remain a threat to our cousin."

Darcy turned a cross look on his cousin. "I am aware of this, Fitzwilliam."

"But you have never experienced it," replied Fitzwilliam. "I have. Our men in the forest will prevent him from going far. We need only wait until Wickham is speaking with Anne, and then we may move in for the kill."

"You may be more accurate than you know, Fitzwilliam," said Bingley, a decidedly un-Bingley-ish scowl on his face, a hard note in his voice. "I believe I wish to speak with our dear George myself, for there are his offenses against my wife to discuss." Bingley glanced at Darcy. "That facer you planted on him in Ramsgate was not nearly punishment enough."

"It seems I am surrounded by bloodthirsty men this morning," said Fitzwilliam with a grin of delight. "Good. I am afraid our friend Georgie is about to have a very bad morning."

Choosing not to say anything in response, Darcy turned his attention to the road. Anne was following a track which led through the heart of the woods of Rosings, and which would pass by the grove where Miss Bennet had reported seeing Wickham. It seemed their guess as to the location of their planned tryst was accurate. It heartened him, knowing they had men stationed nearby to prevent any attempt by Wickham to escape.

"She does not appear to be afraid of any pursuit," observed Bingley.

"It is possible she is not meeting him today," replied Fitzwilliam.

Something told Darcy differently. "If Wickham has been lurking about for weeks without attracting attention, he likely fears discovery. I suspect he has been meeting with her as often as he can, trying to persuade her to elope."

"Why do you suppose he did not just throw her over his horse and ride away?" asked Bingley.

"Because our Georgie is a coward, at heart," replied Fitzwilliam. "And he also knows we would never stand for it if he attempted to marry her without her consent. He would quickly find himself in a wooden box if he did so."

"Furthermore," said Darcy, "Anne is difficult and taciturn, even to the members of her own family. I suspect he has had quite the task in persuading her to open up to him, even a little, to allow him to worm his way into her heart."

"Elizabeth said they shared an affectionate greeting," said Bingley.

"That is why he would wish to meet with her every day despite the danger," said Fitzwilliam. "He feels he almost has her."

At that moment, Darcy was not paying attention to their conversation. The thought that both Fitzwilliam and Bingley were afforded the pleasure of calling Miss Bennet by her first name struck him with a longing to do the same. But would she accept a proposal from him at this time? Darcy was not certain, though he knew they had made strides together.

"I believe we have our quarry," said Fitzwilliam, reining in his horse and interrupting Darcy's thoughts.

In the distance, they could see that the phaeton had stopped. Anne climbed down from the box and tied the reins to a nearby tree before she stepped into the grove and disappeared from their sight.

"Now is the time, gentlemen," said Fitzwilliam, kicking his horse into motion.

They approached cautiously, not wishing to spook their quarry, but not wishing to allow his escape either. There was no sign of another mount anywhere in the vicinity, nor could they see anyone through the trees when they reined their mounts beside the phaeton. The horse harnessed to the conveyance whickered in greeting before it returned its attention to the soft grass at its feet. Soon their horses were tied similarly, and the men pushed their way in between the trees, looking for a hint of Anne and her paramour.

"Come, Anne dearest," a voice carried through the trees to where they were walking, provoking them all to stop suddenly in their tracks. "I love you more than I can say. You know your cousins will never allow us to be married in the traditional way. This is the only way—to present them and your mother with a fait accompli. When we return as husband and wife, they will have no choice but to accept it."

"Not likely," growled Fitzwilliam.

Darcy turned a stern eye on his cousin, wishing to know how far Anne had been persuaded. Fitzwilliam only grimaced and fell silent.

"I do not know, George. I want my mother in attendance at our wedding. I am not to marry Darcy now. Surely she will allow me my choice."

"Perhaps she will. But do you wish to take that chance? I burn for you, my love. If I am forced to leave without you, I am sure it will be the end of me. Please, for the sake of our love, let us act with ourselves first in our thoughts. The others will accept us in time!"

"I will not wait a moment longer!" growled Fitzwilliam.

He surged forward, moving through the trees with a grace and agility Darcy had never seen from his large and burly cousin. To Darcy's surprise, Bingley followed him, as if he had been shot from a cannon. With nothing else to do, Darcy chased after them both. It seemed like some signal had been given, for soon the woods were alive with the men they had set to watch the area. And then they were before the couple.

"Well, well," said Fitzwilliam, stalking toward Wickham. "If it is not our good friend Georgie."

Though startled by the sudden activity about them, it was the sight of Fitzwilliam which caused the pallor in Wickham's countenance. He had always been more than a little afraid of Fitzwilliam. For her part, Anne looked confused at the sudden appearance of so many men

"Well, Wickham? What have you to say for yourself?"

"Do you not see, Anne dearest?" said Wickham, turning to his companion, showing her a mournful frown. "I knew how it would be. Darcy hates me and always thinks the worst of me, and his confederates will believe whatever he tells them."

Whatever Wickham expected, Darcy did not think it was laughter from the three gentlemen. It appeared he did not miss the sardonic edge of their amusement, for his stance stiffened, though he kept his pleading directed toward Anne.

"We should have left yesterday," said he, ignoring Darcy and the others. "Now we will be forced to fight for our love in the face of such odds." Anne looked him askance, and Wickham fixed her with a tender smile. "Do not worry, dear heart. I will fight the very demons of hell for you."

"Bravo, Wickham," said Fitzwilliam, sardonic clapping accompanying his words. "Bravo. I might almost have believed you, did I not already know what manner of man you are."

"You see?" hissed Wickham. "Did I not tell you how it would be?"

"That is enough!" cried Bingley.

He stepped forward, pushed Wickham away from Anne, and planted a facer on him, much like Darcy had the year before. Wickham went down in a heap, moaning with his hand pressed against his jaw, though his murderous eyes glinted when he glared at Bingley. Anne screamed at the violence and flung herself at Wickham's feet. Then she turned and with fists clenched, confronted Bingley.

"How dare you?" screamed she. "He has never done anything to you."

"Perhaps you did not know, Miss de Bourgh," snarled Bingley, prompting Anne to take a step back in alarm, "but this cur attempted the same with your cousin Georgiana last year."

"Of course, Anne would not know," said Fitzwilliam. "She does not go to town and would not have heard the rumors."

"I have done no such thing!" exclaimed Wickham in a panic.

"Quiet, cur!" spat Bingley. "Or I will give you another."

To Darcy's surprise, Wickham did subside, though his gaze still spoke of loathing and fear. Darcy stepped forward and stood over Wickham, motioning to a pair of footmen standing close to lift him onto his feet. When he was standing again, Darcy put his face inches from Wickham's. His former playmate shrank away in fear.

"I suggest you be silent, Wickham. You will only make matters worse for yourself."

"It seems that since he was not successful with your cousin," said Bingley to Anne, "he decided to attempt the greater prize of Rosings." Bingley glared at Wickham with almost living contempt. "You are the worst sort of bounder I have ever met, Wickham. That bruise on your face is the least you deserve for my wife's tears."

"Anne, dearest," pleaded Wickham. "You know what they say is not true. I love you and only you! Let us go away from those who would separate us!"

"You must be daft if you think we will simply allow you to walk away from here," growled Fitzwilliam.

Wickham glared at him and turned back to Anne. "Please, dearest. I am innocent of their charges."

It was entirely possible that Anne might have pleaded for him. But at that moment a young woman stepped out from among the trees into plain sight. Miss Bennet, her own indignation for Wickham etched on her countenance, stepped forward and stood next to Anne.

"In fact, everything they have told you is the truth. I have heard the entire account, not only from Mr. Darcy, but also from Georgiana. And then there are my own experiences with this man."

"I know not of what this woman speaks. I have never seen her before in my life."

"When I first met Mr. Wickham, he called himself Chandler. He also claimed to own an estate near Brighton."

"Lies! All lies!"

It seemed Miss Bennet also heard the desperation making itself heard in Wickham's voice for she sneered at him. "Do you also not remember something of a disagreement between myself and your cousin when we left Margate?"

"I do," said Anne slowly. "It seemed you were arguing about something."

"That *something* was actually *someone*," replied Miss Bennet. "I saw Mr. Wickham there and approached him. Mr. Darcy was, of course, concerned at seeing me speaking with a man who is not to be trusted."

"I swear to you, Anne, dearest, that I do not know who this woman is!"

This time even Anne noted the desperation in his tone. She frowned, directing a questioning look at him. Miss Bennet, however, smiled at Wickham, a gesture which suggested she had him right where she wished him to be.

She sneered again and looked critically at him. "He is not even very handsome, after all. A woman with your benefits in life, of your situation, must be desirable to many men, to say nothing of your personal charms. You can do much better than the likes of Mr. Wickham."

Something in Wickham snapped. He snarled at Miss Bennet and moved suddenly to lunge at her. But the footmen were too quick, wrenching his arms behind his back and holding him in place. His murderous glare never slipped, however, and he could not keep quiet as he ought.

"I could have had you, Miss Bennet, had I wished it." He glared at her with utter contempt. "But a man needs more than the sharp tongue of a bluestocking to support him."

Miss Bennet smiled at Wickham as if she had managed to elicit exactly what she wished. Anne, who had stood forgotten during the exchange, gasped and stared at Wickham through wide eyes. Upon hearing her, Wickham started and stared at her, as if he had never seen her before.

But before he began to protest, Anne stepped forward and slapped him, hard across his cheek. Wickham's head snapped to the side at the force of the blow, and for a moment, tears of pain seemed to stream into his eyes. Then he looked back at her, his face filled with rage and contempt.

"I should have known you would listen to these people. Perhaps it is for the best—no one in his right might would wish to bed a thin, waif of a woman. Be happy you have this estate, for that is the *only* thing which will ever attract a man."

"Better a thin waif of a woman than a greedy, immoral shell of a man." Anne stepped forward and hissed: "I suspect your future life will not be pleasant, Mr. Wickham. Do your best to enjoy it."

Then she spun on her heel and marched away toward her phaeton. Miss Bennet threw a glance at Darcy and Fitzwilliam and then went after her, which Darcy thought was likely for the best.

"You certainly do have the gift with women, Wickham," said Fitzwilliam, chuckling.

"I have much more of a way with them than you," snarled Wickham.

Fitzwilliam shook his head and motioned to the footmen to drag him forward. "If you call seduction 'a way with women' then perhaps you are correct. But you never did know when to hold your tongue. Miss Bennet played you admirably."

"Let us get him to Westerham," said Darcy, eager to be done with everything to do with Wickham. "I am certain we will discover enough debts to keep him incarcerated. When the debt receipts arrive from Pemberley, we will have enough to bury him forever."

Wickham paled. "L-let us not be h-hasty!" stammered he. "You would not wish to dishonor your father's memory in such a way. I was his favorite!"

"Favor you have squandered with your profligate ways!" spat Darcy. "You may as well cease wasting your breath, Wickham. You will get no more clemency from me."

The footmen dragged him away, Wickham still howling his protestations at his treatment. Darcy watched him go, knowing it had been too long—he should have dealt with the man many years ago and prevented all that had happened.

"Well, that was a bit of excitement, was it not?" said Fitzwilliam, his usual jesting tone once again firmly in place. "There is one thing I must confess—I did not expect Elizabeth to take such a role. She knew exactly how to stoke his anger and provoke his vanity. She is marvelous, is she not?"

"That she is," said Darcy, not even caring for Bingley's grin and Fitzwilliam's smugness. "As fine a woman as any I have ever met."

CHAPTER XLIII

"*You* must believe I am naught but a silly girl."

Startled from her thoughts, Elizabeth looked over at her companion, noting the long face, the general sense of malaise which hung over Miss de Bourgh. "Indeed, I do not."

With a huff, Miss de Bourgh turned and stared away, moodily gazing out over the landscape, though Elizabeth was certain she saw little of it. She would not be so harsh as to blame Miss de Bourgh—Elizabeth suspected she had not much experience in the world to protect her.

When Elizabeth had followed Miss de Bourgh from the grove in which she had learned the truth of Mr. Wickham, she had found the woman standing beside her phaeton, looking down at the ground. Without saying a word, she had climbed up onto the seat, leaving Elizabeth to take the reins. It was fortunate Elizabeth had driven the wagon on her father's estate in the past, as she found driving the phaeton was not much different from that, though undoubtedly a finer, faster vehicle. Now, seated as she was, beside Miss de Bourgh, driving the carriage, she thought to add something more to her words. But she thought it might be best to simply wait for her to speak again.

"Surely you must now consider yourself superior to me," said Miss de Bourgh, her accusing eyes finding Elizabeth again. "After all, I am the granddaughter of an earl, yet I have allowed myself to be taken in."

"Taken in by a practiced deceiver," noted Elizabeth.

The anger Miss de Bourgh was displaying turned to curiosity. "You do not blame me?"

"I do not believe I am in a position to apportion blame or absolution," said Elizabeth. "If you wish for my opinion, I will give it. But it is not correct that I think you witless or unlearned."

Miss de Bourgh regarded her for a moment, and then she nodded. "Please share your opinion. I would like to hear it."

With a shrug, Elizabeth said: "It is my understanding that Mr. Wickham is a practiced deceiver. I suspect you are not the first he has deceived, and I suspect you will not be the last. As you are well aware, he also deceived me when he misrepresented himself to me as a gentleman."

"But you only met him once or twice."

"That is true. But that does not change the fact that he did so. In your situation, I do not know what he said to convince you or how ready you were to believe him. It seems he told you a little more of the truth than he did me, but I still do not have enough information to form an honest opinion.

"What I can tell you is this: you inhabit a position in life which is to be envied. It is clear you understand the proper way to behave, and yet, in this case, it is undeniable that you contravened it. You must take greater care in the future, for there are many of Mr. Wickham's ilk on the search for a way to grasp hold of another's wealth."

While she appeared thoughtful, Miss de Bourgh again turned away. "I thank you, Miss Bennet," said she. "You have been kinder toward me than I deserve."

"You are welcome."

The rest of the short journey to Rosings was accomplished in silence, Miss de Bourgh staring moodily at the passing scenery, while Elizabeth was lost in her own thoughts. They were not far from the house, however, and soon the phaeton was rolling up the drive. There, on the front steps, Lady Catherine, Jane, Charity, and Georgiana waited for their arrival.

As the phaeton rolled to a stop, Elizabeth noted that Lady Catherine was looking pensive, while the other three ladies simply looked relieved. Miss de Bourgh seemed reluctant to descend and face her mother, but she eventually did so. It might be expected that the lady would launch into a diatribe of the foolishness of her daughter, but when she was confronted with the reality of the young woman standing before her, she seemed to realize it would do more harm than good.

"Come, Anne," said the lady simply, grasping the younger woman's arm and shepherding her away. "I suspect you could use a soothing hot bath."

They climbed the stairs, and while Elizabeth could no longer hear what Lady Catherine said, she noted her leaning close to her daughter, coupled with Anne's periodic nods in response. Soon they had entered the house, leaving the other four ladies behind.

"If it had been our family," said Jane, clearly troubled, "I might have expected us all to gather around the prodigal returned."

"But Anne has no siblings," said Charity. "And her behavior to the family has never been that which would inspire closeness." Elizabeth could see Georgiana nodding in agreement. "Georgiana and I might have gone to her, had we thought she would welcome us."

"She has had a trying time of it," said Elizabeth. Turning, she began to climb the stairs, eager to be out of the wind, which had grown even stronger since her solitary walk in the woods. The other three ladies followed her. "Allow me to refresh myself, and I shall relate the morning's events to you in full."

By the time Lady Catherine descended the stairs with Miss de Bourgh in tow, the matter had been explained to the others. While the comments had been varied and, at times, pointed, the most common sentiment being expressed was relief. It was strange, Elizabeth thought—while her younger sisters were headstrong and difficult, she loved them and would not wish harm to befall them. But the relationship shared by the three cousins was much different from that of close sisters. Perhaps this event would bring a closer future accord between them.

Upon entering the room, Lady Catherine approached Elizabeth directly, showing an expression of utmost determination. "Miss Bennet," said she, "I wish to tender my thanks for the assistance you rendered to my daughter in the face of that rascal. It is a debt I do not think we shall ever be able to repay."

"You are very welcome," replied Elizabeth, smiling at Miss de Bourgh, who held back, more subdued than she had ever been before. "There was no danger to me from Mr. Wickham, as the gentlemen were already at hand. I was happy to do whatever I could."

Lady Catherine pursed her lips. "I suppose that is true. Yet, you were the one who alerted the family as to the situation. Furthermore, from what Anne has told me, you goaded Mr. Wickham into revealing his true colors."

"If I had not heard it from his own mouth, I might not have believed you," added Miss de Bourgh in a quiet voice.

"And that may have led to resentment and strife in the family," said Lady Catherine.

"We are determined to thank you, Elizabeth," said Charity with a grin. "It would be best if you would simply accept our praise with whatever grace you can muster."

Elizabeth threw a wry grin, tinged with exasperation, at Charity. "As I said, you are very welcome for whatever part I played. I am only happy that everything has ended well."

"We share a common bond now, Anne," said Georgiana, going to her cousin and giving her an affectionate embrace. "I do not know if you are aware, but I have also been the victim of Mr. Wickham's schemes."

Miss de Bourgh glanced at her mother, who nodded slightly. "The matter has been made known to me. Please accept my apologies if this matter has dredged up unpleasant memories for you."

"Oh, Anne," said Georgiana. "I am quite recovered from my experience. This has not affected me in the slightest. The more pertinent question, in my opinion, is to what extent it has distressed you."

The look Miss de Bourgh bestowed on them all was searching as if disbelieving that they were concerned about her. The conclusion must have been that they were in earnest, for she hung her head. Elizabeth thought she might even have some mistiness in her eyes.

"There is nothing the matter with me. I . . . The effects of Mr. Wickham's attentions will not be long-lasting, for I am convinced that I was not in love with him."

"That is probable," said Charity. "Though I have never met the man, everything I have heard suggests that he is adept at inducing a woman to *believe* she is in love with him, without provoking the necessary depth of regard."

"I can well believe it," said Elizabeth. "Had Mr. Wickham turned his charm on me, I suspect I would not have remained unmoved."

"Is it wrong to wish to be loved?" asked Miss de Bourgh, a plaintive tone in her voice. "I saw Fitzwilliam with Mrs. Fitzwilliam, and the way Mr. Bingley dotes on Georgiana, and I wanted that for myself." Miss de Bourgh's eyes found Elizabeth. "It is also clear how Darcy feels about you, Miss Bennet. I only wished for the same for myself."

"First," said Jane, speaking for the first time, "we are cousins. Shall you not call me Jane?"

With a shy smile, almost the first Elizabeth had ever seen from the woman, Miss de Bourgh nodded. "No, it is not wrong, Anne," continued Jane. "But a woman in your position must be certain that the man on whom she bestows her affections is worthy of them. There is no doubt you can find what Anthony and I share. But you must go about it properly."

"We are all willing to assist," said Georgiana.

Charity nodded and added: "It has been difficult at times coming to know you, Anne, as you have seemed content to keep us all at arm's length."

Miss de Bourgh frowned. "I . . . I have never thought of it that way."

"It is likely my fault more than any other," said Lady Catherine. "This business with Darcy and my insistence on your marrying has kept us at Rosings. Your health has not helped matters."

"But I am not unhealthy, Mother," said Anne with more than a hint of exasperation. "I am not robust, it is true, but I am not nearly so unwell as I was when I was a child."

A slow nod from the lady was followed by: "Then perhaps we should re-enter society. Since you are not to marry Darcy, we should see about introducing you to potential husbands. The house in town has been let out for many years, but I am certain my brother would allow us to stay in his house."

"Without a doubt," said Charity. "We would love to have you." She paused and pursed her lips. "It is a little late to be attending the season, now that May is upon us. Perhaps we should take the next months to prepare and introduce Anne during the little season. The events are not so well attended, which means less of a crush and more time to prepare yourself."

"That would be agreeable," said Miss de Bourgh. "It would be less intimidating."

"But, Anne," said Charity, "we are your family. It is not in your nature to be open—this we all know. But you must try to do better. We cannot help you if you do not allow us to do so."

"I know," replied a still subdued Miss de Bourgh. "I will try."

By the time the gentlemen returned, the ladies had spent some pleasant hours discussing their plans for the summer, and autumn months to follow. Anne—as she had requested Elizabeth call her—was struggling to be more open to her family, and while it was still early,

Elizabeth thought she saw some measure of success in her endeavor. She would never be as open as Charity—or Elizabeth herself—but Elizabeth thought she could eventually be similar to Jane in company.

"What of Wickham?" asked Lady Catherine bluntly as soon as she saw them. "May I assume he is decorating the inside of a cell in Westerham prison?"

"Yes," replied Anthony. He directed a sidelong glance at Mr. Darcy and then turned back to Lady Catherine. "Even Darcy has been convinced that it is finally time to hold Wickham to account for his misdeeds."

"It is well past time," said Lady Catherine, directing an imperious glare at Mr. Darcy. "This should have been managed long ago, Darcy. That man has been a millstone about the family's neck for much too long."

"Do not blame Darcy, Mother," said Anne. "It is my own fault. It was wrong of me to allow myself to be charmed."

"Your mother is correct," interjected Mr. Darcy. "I should not have allowed Wickham to continue unchecked this long."

"That much is evident," said Anthony. "But I am curious, Anne, as to the sequence of events which led to today. Can you illuminate us?"

It was clear that Anne was not quite ready to be so open or perhaps to speak so much. As a result, Charity took pity on her and responded to her brother's question.

"It seems Mr. Wickham first made an appearance not long before you came to Rosings, Brother. According to Anne, she met him by seeming accident one day as she was driving her phaeton."

"How long, Anne?" asked Anthony, leaning forward and regarding her with intense interest.

"P-Perhaps a week," replied Anne.

Anthony's gaze turned to Elizabeth, a raised eyebrow acting as a question. Elizabeth nodded.

"Yes, that is about right, Anthony. I met him about two weeks before we departed. It seems he proceeded to Rosings not long after."

A grim nod met her declaration. "He must have had the idea to pursue Anne from seeing us."

"And he specifically asked how long we were to be in Brighton," said Elizabeth. She blushed a little but composed herself and said: "At the time, I thought his questions indicated some interest in me."

"A reasonable assumption," said Lady Catherine.

Anthony nodded but turned back to Anne. "Can you tell me anything else?"

Though she swallowed a little in discomfort, Anne nodded. "I recognized him immediately, though I had not seen him in many years. He informed me he had studied the law and was staying with a friend at an estate some distance from here. At first, I did not think much of him. But then . . ."

"Yes?" asked Anthony, when she fell silent.

Anne directed an apologetic smile at them all. "When you and Jane arrived, and then Darcy soon after, I could see his interest in Miss Bennet. I wished for the same thing for myself and found myself responding to Mr. Wickham's overtures."

"Which led to further meetings."

Red stained her cheeks, but she nodded. "There seemed to be little harm in it, and he made me feel good with his interest."

"Oh, Anne," said Lady Catherine, shaking her head. "There is no harm in meeting with a man in secret, in a grove no less? Many reputations have been ruined for much less."

"They have," said Anne, "but I was careful to ensure we were never seen."

"I did see you one morning not long after we arrived," said Elizabeth. Anne turned to her askance. "It was from a distance, but I saw you stop and talk to a man. It was the morning you drove by and I asked you about him."

The confusion on Anne's face turned to understanding. "That was before Darcy arrived; before I started allowing him to charm me." Then Anne turned and looked at the rest of them, her challenging expression evident. "To the best of my knowledge, no one else saw us or suspected anything amiss."

There were several murmurs of agreement. Even Elizabeth owned that she had not seen Anne with Wickham again until the day before.

"Nothing more needs be said," said Lady Catherine. "But I would like to make one thing clear: you did not allow Mr. Wickham any . . . liberties with your person?"

It was almost a plea, and one for which Anne had the correct answer. "Of course not," said she with an echo of her mother's haughty sniff. "If given the opportunity, I have no doubt he would have pressed it. But he did not."

Lady Catherine shuddered and sighed in relief. Clearly, her concern that her daughter had been ruined, or even worse, might be with child, had been assuaged. The lady favored her daughter with a tremulous smile, but she did not speak again.

"The question of what happened after can be readily understood by us all," said Anthony, "especially those who have experienced Wickham's brand of charm." His glances at both Elizabeth and, more significantly, Georgiana, were readily understood by everyone present. "There is little to be gained from requiring Anne to speak further.

"Of greater pertinence is the situation as it stands now. Wickham, as you all know, is incarcerated in the jail at Westerham, and his residence there shall be of some duration, at least until all the evidence against him may be assembled."

"After Miss Bennet's report of seeing him in the area yesterday," said Mr. Darcy, "I sent to Pemberley for the packet of debt receipts I own from Wickham's time in Cambridge, Lambton, and a few sundry other items. They should arrive in the next week."

"Given the sum of what he owes," said Anthony, "of which the debts we discovered in Westerham and its environs only make his situation more damning, I have written to my father to be of assistance in his case. Putting Wickham in debtors' prison is not ideal, as there is no way he would ever have the means to leave it, and there is always the possibility of escape. Instead, I have asked my father to assist in having him transported. Not only will it put Wickham on the far side of the world with little chance of ever returning, but it will also give him an opportunity to make something of his life, should he ever choose to take advantage of it."

"Van Diemen's Land is not precisely what I would call an opportunity," said Lady Catherine. When Anthony made to respond, she only waved him off. "Yes, yes, Fitzwilliam—I know. It is better than any prospect he would ever find in prison. And I agree. It is the best place for him."

Anthony nodded. "It is. In all honesty, a part of me would prefer to simply call him out and be done with the matter forever."

"That I will not allow," said Mr. Darcy, speaking firmly. "We both know Wickham has not maintained whatever skills he once had with either blade or pistol, and I will not allow my cousin to become a murderer."

"Besides," said Mr. Bingley, "Wickham does not possess the honor necessary to participate in such an activity."

"*A part of me* wishes it," said Anthony airily. "I am well aware of his lack of honor."

"There is another matter which must be addressed," said Mr. Darcy.

He approached Anne and kneeled next to her, catching her hand up in his. The shock of seeing him in such a position shook Elizabeth's sensibilities, for he appeared like he was about to make her an offer. The wave of pain which swept through her at such a thought surprised Elizabeth as if he had become something necessary for her continued survival.

"It appears I have not done my own duty as a cousin, Anne. There have been few occasions in which I treated you as a dear cousin, rather than as a potential wife to be avoided."

"Part of that was *my* fault, as you recall," said Lady Catherine, amusement coloring her voice.

"Perhaps it was," replied Mr. Darcy. "But that does not remove my guilt. The unfortunate fact is that I never thought we suited as a couple, and I suspect you agree."

Anne looked at Mr. Darcy for a long moment, as if attempting to divine his purposes. Elizabeth felt a little relief pass through her, though it appeared as if Mr. Darcy intended to allow his cousin to make the decision. In the end, her concern was for naught.

"I do agree," said Anne, her voice soft yet firm. "It may be that was a part of my vulnerability with Mr. Wickham. You and I do not suit, and I knew this instinctively, even while I wished to be treated as you treat Miss Bennet."

Mr. Darcy's smoldering gaze caught Elizabeth's for a moment, taking her breath away. Then he looked back at Anne, releasing her from the power of his scrutiny. Feeling a warmth flow through her at the thought of what this man did to her, Elizabeth wondered if her effect on him was as profound.

"Then we are agreed," said Mr. Darcy.

Before anything else could be said, the door was opened, and Mr. Collins was escorted into the room. He bowed as was his wont and opened his mouth to speak, when his attention was caught by Mr. Darcy's position next to Anne's chair. A slow smile spread across his ugly face, and he turned a haughty sneer on Elizabeth.

"Well, Cousin, it seems your pretensions have all come to naught. Clearly, Mr. Darcy, as I knew he would, has done his duty. Now, what have you to say?"

It is a commonly understood truth that a man of scarce wit and holding a grudge will come to the wrong conclusion, especially when the surface evidence supports it. Elizabeth, knowing this of Mr. Collins, did the only thing she could, under the circumstances—she laughed. It began as a titter under her breath, grew to a giggle, in which many unladylike snorts escaped her efforts to hold it in. Then it grew to an open laughter, by which time most of the rest of those in the room had joined her.

Not accustomed to being made to look ridiculous—the man was eminently capable of managing that feat on his own—Mr. Collins's dander rose in response. His color obtained the hue of a ripe tomato in an instant, and he stalked to Elizabeth's side, loudly berating her, saying: "Enough of this unseemly laughter, Cousin! It has never been clearer to me that you are fit for nothing more than to languish at Longbourn until you are forced to leave when I inherit, and that is where you shall go. Rise at once! I insist upon your removal from this house!"

"You have forgotten one thing, Collins," said Anthony, rising to his feet and standing over Mr. Collins like an angry titan. "Elizabeth is under *my* protection and authority while she is at Rosings."

"Of course, you have my apologies," replied Mr. Collins, his voice containing a distinct lack of any such timbre, "but my duty is clear in this matter. *I* am the ranking member of Miss Bennet's family. Your lady aunt must not be burdened with her presence any longer."

"Oh, leave off, Mr. Collins!" said Lady Catherine. Even Mr. Collins could not miss the irritation in her voice. "There is nothing you can do, for you have no authority over Miss Bennet, as I have informed you before. It would be best if you simply return to the parsonage, for your opinion is not wanted here."

"Yes, Mr. Collins," said Mr. Darcy, rising to his feet. He loomed over the parson, who was himself no small man, his gaze unfriendly and intimidating. "Once again, you do not understand. It is unfortunate for you, but I have no desire to explain it to you. Begone!"

In perhaps the only sensible action Mr. Collins ever took, he turned and marched from the room, muttering under his breath. When the door closed behind him, Mr. Darcy turned to Lady Catherine.

"If you will pardon me for saying it, I cannot fathom what possessed you to offer the living to Mr. Collins."

"At times, I wonder myself, Darcy."

CHAPTER XLIV

To everyone's relief, Mr. Collins avoided Rosings for the rest of their stay. It seemed he considered them all interlopers, taking his rightful place of favor by Lady Catherine's side. How he could have thought such things, as those in residence were mostly Lady Catherine's family, Elizabeth could not say. But she was grateful for his absence nonetheless.

As for Mrs. Collins, matters changed with her in a startling fashion. Informed of the woman's request and their exchange the day of Mr. Wickham's capture, Charity had been intrigued and had agreed to visit her with Elizabeth. And there, they received a cordial welcome, far more than Elizabeth had received the last time she had gone to the parsonage. And it was clear that the master of the house was not happy about it.

"Thank you for visiting me, Miss Bennet," said Mrs. Collins when they entered, greeting the other four ladies as brightly as she had Elizabeth. "I am grateful you have kept your word and forgiven me for my previous behavior."

"What cause could my cousin have to forgive you?" asked Mr. Collins, who was, unfortunately, on hand. Mr. Collins looked down his nose on Elizabeth, sniffing in disdain. "It should be *she* who apologizes for imposing upon *us*."

"Perhaps you should go to the church and prepare your sermon," said Mrs. Collins. Though her words were phrased as a question, there was no mistaking the command inherent in tone. "I am hosting my *friends* at the moment and have no doubt you would not find our conversation interesting."

As Elizabeth might have expected, Mr. Collins puffed himself up, apparently ready to assert himself as the master in his own home. Whether it was the sight of six ladies peering at him, unfriendly first to last, she could not say. But in the end, Mr. Collins wilted and turned to depart, muttering and shaking his head.

The ladies sat down to converse for some minutes, their tones lively and gay, and while Elizabeth partook in the discussion, she found herself bemused by the way Mrs. Collins had handled her husband. During a lull in the conversation, when the others were all occupied, Elizabeth caught her hostess's attention.

"Thank you, Mrs. Collins, but you have no need to act in my defense."

"Think nothing of it, Miss Bennet," replied Mrs. Collins. "It is unfortunate, but my husband has not yet accepted that I will befriend whom I please. Should he prove difficult, I shall have Lady Catherine speak with him."

While she could not be certain, Elizabeth thought this boded well for Mrs. Collins's future. She would not always have Lady Catherine at hand to browbeat her husband into compliance, but if the habit was established now, it should be possible for her to manage him herself one day. Now that she could acknowledge that Mrs. Collins was not quite the dullard her husband was, Elizabeth hoped she was happy in her marriage. Whatever respectability she could preserve would be achieved by preventing his making a fool of himself.

Their visit continued apace after that, and Elizabeth left that first meeting at the parsonage with a warmer feeling toward its mistress than she had before. Mrs. Collins was, she decided, a good sort of woman. Her doubt about their becoming close friends remained, but Elizabeth thought she could now tolerate Mrs. Collins with a friendlier attitude than she had thought.

In the waning days of their visit to Rosings, the patterns established previously continued to prevail, though with a few additions which had not been there before. Elizabeth continued to walk out every day, but there were other outings, rides in Anne's phaeton, and much congress between the young ladies. They saw the other friends to whom they had become close often, and Elizabeth thought she had succeeded in making friendships which would last for a lifetime.

Around them, the world continued to revolve, time to flow, and the events beyond their little corner proceeded apace. The old campaigner in Anthony drew Mr. Darcy and Mr. Bingley into conversations concerning the state of the Peninsular War, while Mr. Darcy was much more concerned about the spreading Luddite rebellions which had begun to grip the kingdom. The shocking news of the assassination of Prime Minister Spencer Perceval reached them, and many an hour was spent discussing it, even among the ladies.

But in the back of Elizabeth's mind, the most important event in her life was the continuing dance with Mr. Darcy. The gentleman continued his attentions, his focus often fixed on her, even when she thought he might be distracted by his conversations with the other gentlemen. And more than once Elizabeth saw the indulgent smiles of those who watched their courtship, some with happiness, whereas others—such as Anthony—were filled with self-satisfied amusement.

On a day late in May, Elizabeth sat in the garden, a letter in her lap, forgotten as she gazed out on the blooms which had begun to show their summer colors to the world. There had been many events during her stay at Rosings, and while there had been exasperations aplenty, she reflected on how happy she had been staying at such a beautiful estate. And while she had not thought it possible only a few months earlier, those in residence were becoming as dear to her as any in her family—even Lady Catherine, in her own irascible way, had found a place in Elizabeth's heart. She knew, however, that it was coming to an end.

The snapping of a twig caught Elizabeth's attention, and she looked up to see Mr. Darcy approaching. The gentleman's presence had been a constant these past weeks. Elizabeth found it comforting, for he was solid and dependable, a steady presence in a group of characters who were prone to high spirits.

"Miss Bennet," said he when he strode up, his gaze descending on her like the caress of a sun's ray. "It should not be a surprise to find you here, I suppose." Mr. Darcy paused and looked about. "This has become a favorite place at Rosings, has it not?"

"It has," replied Elizabeth, glancing about herself. "Lady Catherine's gardeners have done wonders. But I find myself wondering what it might have looked like when your mother was still alive. The rose garden at Longbourn is naught but a few low bushes in a patch Jane loved to tend. This one must have been a true sight to see."

"I remember it well," said Mr. Darcy, his eyes unfocused. "Behind this bench were the pink roses my mother loved so well, and the red ones framed the outer edges. The combination of their scents, according to her, was heavenly. As one proceeded along the avenue, the colors varied, seeming like every hue of the rainbow was represented."

"Lady Catherine may be persuaded to restore them eventually."

Mr. Darcy shook his head. "I would not even make the request. I understand her reason for wishing them gone."

"But now she seems to have more energy and zest for life. Perhaps they will not be so painful for her in the future."

It was true, Elizabeth reflected. The reclamation of her daughter, the cessation of the lady's attempts to marry Anne to Mr. Darcy, and their coming plans to show Anne to best advantage in the little season had all worked on Lady Catherine, seeming to give her a new purpose. She had become too complacent, too removed from life about her in the years since her sister's death. Moving among society again would be good for the lady, Elizabeth reflected.

"It is possible," said Mr. Darcy. He gestured to the bench. "May I sit?"

"Of course," replied Elizabeth.

Perching himself on the bench at a respectable distance, Mr. Darcy immediately turned to Elizabeth, regarding her as if attempting to divine some mystery. His eyes flicked to the letter in her lap, and at that moment a slight gust of wind lifted a corner of the paper off her dress. Elizabeth put a hand down on it, preventing it from being carried off, and then folded it and held it in one hand.

"I heard you had received a letter. Might I inquire if the news you received is good?"

"It is not news at all," replied Elizabeth with a laugh.

"There does not seem much to it. Georgiana usually writes long letters to me, and that does not seem to be more than a single page."

"It is the truth. My father has ever been a negligent correspondent. Even when he demands my return, there is a brevity in his words which defies description."

Mr. Darcy eyed her closely. "So it has finally happened. Your father has commanded your return."

"'Commanded' is a strong word, Mr. Darcy," replied Elizabeth. "Rarely has my father commanded me in anything. But his request has been worded rather strongly—with far more insistence than I have ever seen before."

"Fitzwilliam mentioned that he suspected he would have to return you soon. Have you taken thought to when you wish to go?"

"I have not," replied Elizabeth. "Your cousin is still my protector and guardian. The decision about when to depart is his. However, I suspect we will not stay in Kent much longer."

"Do you wish to leave?"

It was a far blunter question than Elizabeth had thought to hear from the gentleman. It took no measure of insight to understand that Mr. Darcy did not wish her to go. But then again, nothing was holding him to this place either.

"It matters not what I wish, Mr. Darcy. At some time or another, I shall be required to return home. Rosings has been a haven for me, and I have not been unhappy here. I must return at some time or another, nevertheless."

"And your plans for the future?" asked he. "Do you return to Longbourn forever, or do you mean to go elsewhere after you have visited for a time? Your sister, for example, wishes your presence in her house."

"I cannot return to Longbourn forever," chided Elizabeth gently. "It will someday be the property of Mr. Collins, after all. Only a simpleton would think I would be welcome there for even a single minute after the gentleman comes to claim it."

An exchanged look caused them both to burst out laughing. Mr. Collins had been a matter of some amusement for the entire party these past days.

"In answer to your other question," continued Elizabeth, "if Jane will have me, I would be happy to live with her. The future, however, is not set. There is no telling what might happen."

"Miss Bennet, I must assume you have seen and understood my actions toward you these past weeks." It seemed he had had enough of this dancing about the subject and had decided to be direct.

"Your intentions have not precisely been hidden," Elizabeth remarked.

"And might I know if you have welcomed my presence?" asked Mr. Darcy, a slow smile lighting up his face.

"Had I been unwelcoming, you would not have been in any doubt of it, sir."

A laugh escaped his lips. Whatever tension had existed before now melting away in favor of his pleasure. Elizabeth grinned along with him, happily thinking this was how it should be. A couple who committed their lives to each other must be friends first—it would make what would follow so much easier. And she did think of him as a friend, for his unsociable behavior from the previous year had been washed away by his actions in Kent, the misunderstanding in Margate notwithstanding.

"It is foolish of me to have thought anything else," said Mr. Darcy at length. "I know of your forthright character, after all."

"I am certain you do."

"Then, it follows that should I wish for a closer connection between us, I have only to ask. Some women might play with a man's affections to keep him in her thrall. You would never descend to such paltry devices."

"There is little to be gained by behaving in such a manner, Mr. Darcy," said Elizabeth, playing along with his teasing. "If a woman means to accept the man's suit, she would jeopardize her happiness. If she did not, why would she wish to leave him in any doubt? I have been accused of such devices before, sir. Now, as then, I have no intention of increasing anyone's love by suspense."

"It seems to me impossible that any amount of suspense would increase my love," said Mr. Darcy. "But I have it in abundance, I assure you. I have not a poetic turn of mind, Miss Bennet. I am a forthright man. There is little I can say except that I love and respect you and wish you for my wife. Will you do me the honor?"

Some perverse part of Elizabeth's mind considered continuing their previously playful banter, to express a sentiment she did not feel for the sake of acting in a manner contrary to what she had just stated. But such actions in this instance were, as she had stated, nothing more than a threat to her future happiness, though she thought Mr. Darcy was made of sterner stuff than that. Still, it was better not to take the chance.

"If you believe you can withstand my impertinence," said Elizabeth, giving the lie to her thoughts, "then I would be happy to accept."

Before Elizabeth could react, Mr. Darcy had closed the space between them, taking her near hand between his, and pressing a kiss against her palm. "Believe me, Miss Bennet, your impertinence is what drew me in. You must promise me you will keep that impertinence, for I would not change you for the world."

"Then it is easy to promise," said Elizabeth, feeling a little overwhelmed by the nearness of his person. "I shall promise to vex and torment you for the rest of our lives."

"Teasing woman!" growled Mr. Darcy. "There is a limit to what I will tolerate from you. I must administer your punishment."

Before Elizabeth could further respond or even think, Mr. Darcy's head descended to hers, and he kissed her. It was soft and sweet and spoke to further delights, ones which she could not, as a modest young lady, understand at present. But she thought she would very much enjoy discovering them with this man.

They were pleasantly engaged for some time, their delighted sighs and caresses speaking to the intimacy of their situation.

It was hardly surprising that they returned to a company who seemed to know what had happened between them. Whether they had been seen through the windows of the house overlooking the gardens or there was something in their manners which gave them away, Elizabeth could not be certain. But the knowing glances, the grinning, the impatience of both Charity and Georgiana were evidence enough of their good information.

Perhaps it was a perverse desire to tease which led Elizabeth to ignore the expectant gazes with which she and Mr. Darcy were regarded. Upon entering the room, Elizabeth ignored them and approached her sister and the woman who would be her cousin and sat between them.

"How has your planning for London proceeded? Are we to return soon?"

Charity looked at Elizabeth through narrowed eyes, a slight tick in her brow attesting to her displeasure. Jane, however, readily responded.

"Early next week, perhaps. I still have not seen my home, and Anthony wishes to take me there for the summer."

"We will do some shopping and have Anne measured for new dresses," added Lady Catherine, "I have little desire to subject her to summer in London."

"My aunt often complains of it," said Elizabeth, nodding with a knowing smile. "Shall you then return to Rosings?"

"I believe we shall visit my uncle's estate instead," said Miss de Bourgh. In the days since the events with Mr. Wickham, she had grown more accustomed to speaking to them all, but she almost always spoke in a quiet, diffident sort of tone, as if she were still gaining her confidence.

"My brother will come here to escort us to town," said Lady Catherine. "I also understand that he will take the final actions against Mr. Wickham." The lady's lip curled with distaste. "It is to Botany Bay for him, and it is none too soon."

Mr. Darcy nodded in agreement while Anthony only crossed his arms, looking for all the world like he would cheerfully take ship with Wickham if only to throw him over the side once they were at sea. In all this, Charity glared about her, though focusing more on Elizabeth, and as the conversation continued, she was certain her friend would soon be able to stand it no longer. That moment came earlier than Elizabeth could have guessed.

"Yes, yes, Wickham and London and shopping," snapped Charity. "I want to know of *you*, Elizabeth!"

"I suppose I shall return to Longbourn," said Elizabeth. "But at some time or another, I believe I am for the north." Elizabeth turned and smiled at Jane. "If my sister will have me. And there is my aunt and uncle's proposed visit to the Lake Country."

A growl issued forth from Charity's breast. "Will you not be bound for Pemberley? What has happened between you? I saw you through the upstairs window, and it appeared to me you were quite cozy with Darcy, indeed."

"Oh that," said Elizabeth, keeping her tone bored. "Yes, I suppose I shall go to Pemberley at some time or another. It is to be my new home, after all."

With a squeal of delight, Georgiana threw herself into Elizabeth's arms, laughing as she did so. The other ladies all crowded around them, though Charity still glared in annoyance at Elizabeth's teasing. On the other side of the room, the gentlemen were congratulating Mr. Darcy and slapping him on the back. Elizabeth caught her fiancé's eye and grinned at him, to which he replied with a genuine smile of pleasure.

"It is such a wonderful thing!" exclaimed Georgiana. "I had thought you would be good for my brother, but for a time I wondered if it would never come about. You are both far too stubborn for your own good."

"So we should have simply listened to you?" asked Elizabeth?"

"Of course," was the other woman's airy reply. "It was obvious to me and to everyone else in this house."

"It was," added Anne quietly. "It was clear not long after Darcy arrived."

"Yes, of course, it was," said Lady Catherine. "But there were other matters which needed to be settled. I, for one, do not countenance these hasty engagements which young people sometimes enter into. It is better to be rational and consider one's wishes and desires carefully, without rushing into marriage."

"Oh, Aunt!" exclaimed Georgiana. "Charles and I are very happy, you know. I do not consider our courtship and marriage hasty."

While one might have expected Lady Catherine to continue to promote her opinion, she declined to do so. Instead, she shook her head at Georgiana and smiled. It was clear to a vigilant observer that she was still uncomfortable speaking of Darcy's potential marriage to anyone other than Anne. Elizabeth's heart went out to the lady.

"Thank you for your support, Lady Catherine," said she, emotion coloring her voice. "It means the world to me to know you approve."

"Yes, well," said Lady Catherine, the pink in her cheeks standing out against the paleness of her skin. "I should not be nearly so sanguine if I was not convinced of your suitability."

"You know, Darcy," said Anthony, "Bingley and I shall never let you live this down. It was evident to us both that Elizabeth would be good for you, long before the notion managed to penetrate through your thick head."

"As long as I have Elizabeth in my life," said Mr. Darcy, "I shall be happy to bear it. I am too happy to be cross with you at present."

"Just wait until we tease you ten years after your marriage," said Bingley. "Then we shall see if you still tolerate it with equanimity."

The party laughed, and they continued to banter in a similar manner. The love and affection of these people was a physical entity, and Elizabeth found that she was as at home among them as she was in the comfort of Longbourn itself. It was strange, she decided, that it should be so. Not because she could not imagine loving these people with whom she was surrounded, but because her definition of home had changed these last months. She was now an engaged woman, one who would leave her childhood home for that of a good man, a man who would care for her all the days of her life.

Her eyes caught Mr. Darcy's, and he smiled a secret, special smile of his, one which was for her alone. And Elizabeth's heart whispered to her that she would be home wherever he was. It told her that all would be well, that she would be happy.

EPILOGUE

*H*appiness was a state with which Mrs. Elizabeth Darcy had plenty of experience. As the completion of that happiness slept in the cradle by her side, Elizabeth looked down on the tiny figure, humming a lullaby as the young master of Pemberley squirmed in his sleep. Master Bennet Andrew Darcy was a matter of a month old and the apple of his father's eye. Elizabeth knew that he would be put upon a horse and taught to follow in his father's footsteps almost as soon as he could walk. As his father was the best man she had ever known, Elizabeth wholeheartedly supported his future education.

When it appeared he was completely asleep and would not wake for some time, Elizabeth rose and, smiling at the nurse, made her way from the nursery. The halls of Pemberley were as quiet as they usually were, but to Elizabeth, who had never seen the estate in the years after its last master and mistress had passed away, they had never been solemn. There was a respectful sense of awe which hung over those venerable halls, one which spoke to history and accomplishment, but also to the future, embodied in the young master who now slept within.

But now there was also laughter and joy, and while Elizabeth might not have seen the man with whom she shared her life as ebullient, there were times at present when he could be referred to in such a manner. Though never one to allow his happiness to overflow in mirth, Mr. Darcy—or William as Elizabeth now called him—was shedding the reputation of a dour man. Their first season in town, Elizabeth had witnessed many an astonished look from more than one lady who had pursued him or gentleman who had thought him unapproachably proud. It had been all over town in a trice that theirs was a love match, for the change in Mr. Darcy alone was enough to prove to even the most skeptical that she had not married him for his money alone.

As Elizabeth walked through the halls of the venerable mansion which was now her home, she considered those who had played some small part in her current happiness. The despicable Mr. Wickham was the first to leave her life forever, for the earl had used his influence to send the bane of the Darcy family's existence to the other side of the world. Elizabeth had it on good authority—that of her beloved husband, who had gone to the docks to see his former companion off himself—that Mr. Wickham had gone to his fate in the manner he had lived his life. Bitter recriminations filled his speech as he had gone, and he had been forced to board the ship, as he would not meet his fate under his own power.

The agent they had contracted to ensure his arrival in Van Diemen's Land had sent word that Mr. Wickham had, indeed, disembarked there in the penal colony and had been set to work. Whether he would ever again be a free man, Elizabeth could not say, nor did she concern herself with such matters. The chances of his ever being in a position to pay for passage back to England were so remote as to be non-existent, and for that Elizabeth was satisfied.

Thoughts of Mr. Wickham almost always brought thoughts of the two women who had been cruelly used by him. Georgiana Bingley had settled with her husband, as had been their design, but their estate was a little further than they had wished. However, the price had been good, the estate extensive, and both felt that the added distance was more than made up for by the perfect situation in which they had found themselves. Though almost fifty miles away in Nottinghamshire, the Bingleys were often to be found at Pemberley, the ancestral home of Mrs. Bingley. And the Bingley dynasty was well and truly begun, as Georgiana had delivered a healthy girl three months before Master Bennet's birth.

As for Anne de Bourgh, while she had not suffered as much as Georgiana had, the changes in her were nearly as profound. As had been observed more than once, Miss de Bourgh was of a taciturn disposition, one which was not at all comfortable being open with others. But she had endeavored to make herself more open and had become friends of them all, though she remained ever a little aloof. She had even managed to procure a gentleman caller, one who seemed intent upon making her his. Whether he would ultimately be successful, Elizabeth could not say. But he was deemed a good man by both Anthony and William, which cleared his path for his eventual union if he chose to make that final step.

Even Lady Catherine had warmed to him, though Elizabeth could tell the lady was still wistful at times about the lost opportunity to unite Rosings and Pemberley. But her inner thoughts were never stated out loud, and the lady was outwardly as supportive of Elizabeth and William as any of the family. Indeed, it was in large part due to her efforts that Elizabeth's debut had been so successful. Lady Catherine and Anne were to join them later in January, and after visiting some time in Derbyshire, they were all to return to London for the upcoming season. Now with a young child, Elizabeth was not certain she wished to spend all her time attending balls and parties, but she supposed the Darcy reputation must be maintained.

Of course, Elizabeth could not think of Lady Catherine and Anne de Bourgh without her thoughts once again settling on that odious creature installed at the nearby parsonage. Mr. Collins, though happy to see the entire party leave, was dismayed, if Lady Catherine's report was to be believed, that he did not enjoy the favor he had previously, in his own mind, possessed. Lady Catherine still directed him in everything he did, but she was more wont to hold him at arms' length than she had before. Mr. Bennet reported that his gloating letter to the silly man, announcing Elizabeth's engagement to Mr. Darcy, had gone unanswered. Though the Bennet patriarch regretted the loss of the amusement Mr. Collins provided, Elizabeth thought his dismay had been rather fleeting.

The study door, which had been her destination, loomed before Elizabeth, and she paused in her thoughts in order to knock, entering the room when the command was given. Seated behind the desk was her husband of nearly a year and a half. He looked up and smiled at her, though it was one which was tinged with exasperation.

"You know you do not need to knock when you enter," chided he, rising from his desk and moving around it to greet her.

Elizabeth reveled in the kiss on the top of her head he bestowed on her, responded with one of her own on his cheek. "At Longbourn, no one was allowed in my father's study unless *she* knocked first."

A chuckle escaped William's lips. This conversation had played out more times than Elizabeth could count, as she could never quite put the habit of knocking first aside.

"At Pemberley, that stricture does not apply to you, my dearest wife."

"Perhaps one day I might even become accustomed to it," replied Elizabeth. "But for now, I believe you will simply be required to endure my knocking."

William shook his head and guided her to the nearby pair of chairs which stood in front of a roaring fireplace. "I suppose Bennet is enjoying his nap now?"

"That he is," replied Elizabeth. "He appears content as can be. I wonder, however, if taking him to London in February is the proper course of action."

"You know I would forego London if we could," replied William.

"But the Darcy position in society must be maintained," said Elizabeth, a dry echo of those words her husband often spoke but regretted more than anyone knew.

"Exactly," replied William. "And then there is Charity's wedding to anticipate. At least that will allow us to leave early."

"That is true," said Elizabeth. "But it does not ease my worries when I consider the dangers of traveling with an infant in the dead of winter."

"He will be warmly wrapped and protected. I, myself, traveled with my parents to London when just a babe, or so my aunt says. He will be well."

"When do we expect Anthony and Jane?" asked Elizabeth, changing the subject.

"In fact, I have had a letter from my cousin this morning," said William. "They will come to Pemberley on Friday."

"I would not be in Jane's position for all the world," said Elizabeth. "Being with child was difficult enough without having to travel to London to partake in the season and then leave in time for the lying in."

"It is understandable for you to think like that," said William. "But I think my cousin and your sister are simply happy to finally have the expectation of having an heir."

It was true, Elizabeth decided. While Jane had been married to Anthony for more than half a year longer than Elizabeth had been married to William, there had been no hint of a child. It had only been in the last month that Jane had written to Elizabeth, excited to inform her that she was certain she was now with child. Not only were they anticipating their own addition arriving in about six months, but Mrs. Bennet's paroxysms on the subject might now finally come to a close.

"There will be some impact upon us," replied Elizabeth, looking to her husband for his reaction. "Now Kitty and Lydia will both come to us after the season, rather than Lydia going to Thorndell."

While he affected nonchalance, Elizabeth could easily see her husband's grimace at the thought. Elizabeth knew he found her sisters a challenge to endure at the best of times. Now, he would be taking the responsibility of seeing to their improvement. The initial plan was to separate them and improve them separately, and thereby avoid each feeding off the other's poor behavior. But with Jane now expecting, that plan would be changed, at least for the first few months of their residence in the north.

"I know Fitzwilliam made an impression on your youngest sister in particular," said William, speaking of his actions at the ball at Netherfield and the few times they had been in company since. "But they will find me no less stern when necessary. My uncle has decreed that their comportment must be improved before they can be acknowledged as connected to him, and you know he does not instruct such things lightly."

Well did Elizabeth know it, she thought with a grimace. The one time the earl and countess had been in company with her youngest sisters had been a disaster. Elizabeth had been surprised when he had not simply severed all congress with them, rather than demanding their improvement.

"The sooner we induce them to behave better, the sooner they will be off our hands," said Elizabeth.

"I hope Lady Susan knows what she is taking on in agreeing to host them," muttered William.

"I am certain she does," said Elizabeth, amused. While the countess had Charity's wedding to see to, she informed Elizabeth privately that she was well able to control even so unruly a pair of girls as Catherine and Lydia Bennet. But she wished to see some improvement in them first, which was why they would come to Pemberley.

"You have my apologies, William," said Elizabeth. "This task should rightly belong to my father. He, unfortunately, does not possess the fortitude to withstand their complaints."

William only grunted at her words, and the subject was dropped. This was another conversation which had played out many times, and while Elizabeth thought William appreciated his father-in-law for his good points, the matter of the man's youngest daughters was one he did not. But there was nothing to be done, and good man that he was, William agreed to assist in her sisters' improvement himself. Elizabeth loved him for it.

They stayed in the study for some time, talking in quiet voices, delighted in their communion with each other. Theirs had been a union which had been long in the making, rocky at times. It had, however, emerged the stronger because of it. They relished these few moments they had together, moments which were destined to become more difficult to find, given the first arrival of their family. But neither would change it for the world, happy as they had become.

The End

For Readers Who Liked *Whispers of the Heart*

A Tale of Two Courtships
Two sisters, both in danger of losing their hearts. One experiences a courtship which ends quickly in an engagement, the other must struggle against the machinations of others. And one who will do anything to ensure her beloved sister achieves her heart's desire.

Out of Obscurity
Amid the miraculous events of a lost soul returning home, dark forces conspire against a young woman, for her loss was not an accident. A man is moved to action by a boon long denied, determined to avoid being cheated by Miss Elizabeth Bennet again.

Murder at Netherfield
After the ball at Netherfield, a fault in their carriage results in the Bennet family being forced to stay at the Bingley estate, and when a blizzard blows in overnight, the Bennets find themselves stranded there. When a body is found, leading to a string of murders which threaten the lives of those present, Elizabeth and Darcy form an alliance to discover the identity of the murderer and save those they care about most. But the depraved actions of a killer, striking from the shadows, threatens their newly found admiration for each other.

Netherfield's Secret
Elizabeth soon determines that her brother's friend, Fitzwilliam Darcy, suffers from an excess of pride, and it comes as a shock when the man reveals himself to be in love with her. But even that revelation is not as surprising as the secret Netherfield has borne witness to. Netherfield's secret shatters Elizabeth's perception of herself and the world around her, and Mr. Darcy is the only one capable of picking up the pieces.

The Companion
A sudden tragedy during Elizabeth's visit to Kent leaves her directly in Lady Catherine de Bourgh's sights. With Elizabeth's help, a woman long-oppressed has begun to spread her wings. What comes after is a whirlwind of events in which Elizabeth discovers that her carefully held opinions are not infallible. Furthermore, a certain gentleman of her acquaintance might be the key to Elizabeth's happiness.

What Comes Between Cousins
A rivalry springs up between Mr. Darcy and Colonel Fitzwilliam, each determined to win the fair Elizabeth Bennet. As the situation between cousins deteriorates, clarity begins to come for Elizabeth, and she sees Mr. Darcy as the man who will fill all her desires in a husband. But the rivalry between cousins is not the only trouble brewing for Elizabeth.

For more details, visit
http://www.onegoodsonnet.com/genres/pride-and-prejudice-variations

Also by One Good Sonnet Publishing

The Smothered Rose Trilogy

Book 1: Thorny

In this retelling of "Beauty and the Beast," a spoiled boy who is forced to watch over a flock of sheep finds himself more interested in catching the eye of a girl with lovely ground-trailing tresses than he is in protecting his charges. But when he cries "wolf" twice, a determined fairy decides to teach him a lesson once and for all.

Book 2: Unsoiled

When Elle finds herself practically enslaved by her stepmother, she scarcely has time to even clean the soot off her hands before she collapses in exhaustion. So when Thorny tries to convince her to go on a quest and leave her identity as Cinderbella behind her, she consents. Little does she know that she will face challenges such as a determined huntsman, hungry dwarves, and powerful curses . . . .

Book 3: Roseblood

Both Elle and Thorny are unhappy with the way their lives are going, and the revelations they have had about each other have only served to drive them apart. What is a mother to do? Reunite them, of course. Unfortunately, things are not quite so simple when a magical lettuce called "rapunzel" is involved.

If you're a fan of thieves with a heart of gold, then you don't want to Miss . . .

THE PRINCES AND THE PEAS
A TALE OF ROBIN HOOD

A NOVEL OF THIEVES, ROYALTY, AND IRREPRESSIBLE LEGUMES

BY LELIA EYE

An infamous thief faces his greatest challenge yet when he is pitted against forty-nine princes and the queen of a kingdom with an unnatural obsession with legumes. Sleeping on top of a pea hidden beneath a pile of mattresses? Easy. Faking a singing contest? He could do that in his sleep. But stealing something precious out from under "Old Maid" Marian's nose . . . now that is a challenge that even the great Robin Hood might not be able to surmount.

When Robin Hood comes up with a scheme that involves disguising himself as a prince and participating in a series of contests for a queen's hand, his Merry Men provide him their support. Unfortunately, however, Prince John attends the contests with the Sheriff of Nottingham in tow, and as all of the Merry Men know, Robin Hood's pride will never let him remain inconspicuous. From sneaking peas onto his neighbors' plates to tweaking the noses of prideful men like the queen's chamberlain, Robin Hood is certain to make an impression on everyone attending the contests. But whether he can escape from the kingdom of Clorinda with his prize in hand before his true identity comes to light is another matter entirely.

About the Author

Jann Rowland is a Canadian, born and bred. Other than a two-year span in which he lived in Japan, he has been a resident of the Great White North his entire life, though he professes to still hate the winters.

Though Jann did not start writing until his mid-twenties, writing has grown from a hobby to an all-consuming passion. His interests as a child were almost exclusively centered on the exotic fantasy worlds of Tolkien and Eddings, among a host of others. As an adult, his interests have grown to include historical fiction and romance, with a particular focus on the works of Jane Austen.

When Jann is not writing, he enjoys rooting for his favorite sports teams. He is also a master musician (in his own mind) who enjoys playing piano and singing as well as moonlighting as the choir director in his church's congregation.

Jann lives in Alberta with his wife of more than twenty years, two grown sons, and one young daughter. He is convinced that whatever hair he has left will be entirely gone by the time his little girl hits her teenage years. Sadly, though he has told his daughter repeatedly that she is not allowed to grow up, she continues to ignore him.

Website: http://onegoodsonnet.com/
Facebook: https://facebook.com/OneGoodSonnetPublishing/
Twitter: @OneGoodSonnet
Mailing List: http://eepurl.com/bol2p9

Made in United States
North Haven, CT
09 March 2023

33846241R00264